D0961915

# 100
# Hilarious
# Little
# Howlers

# 100
# Hilarious
# Little
# Howlers

### Edited by
### Stefan Dziemianowicz,
### Robert Weinberg,
### & Martin H. Greenberg

BARNES
&NOBLE
BOOKS
NEW YORK

The acknowledgments appearing on pages 479–83 constitute an
extension of this copyright page.

This edition published by Barnes & Noble, Inc.,
by arrangement with Tekno-Books.

1999 Barnes & Noble Books

ISBN 0-7607-1385-5

Printed and bound in the United States of America

99 00 01 02 03 MC 9 8 7 6 5 4 3 2 1

BVG

# CONTENTS

# Introduction

Everybody likes a funny story, but not everybody can tell one. Maybe that's why books of so-called serious fiction greatly outnumber books of comic writing. The relative scarcity of funny fiction and the high esteem in which we hold humorists are testaments to the unique character of comic storytelling. You know that old saying: tragedy is easy, comedy is hard.

The funny thing about funny stories is that their raw materials are not much different from those used to create their more sober counterparts. Cut through the corn, dissect the delirium, and you find many of the same themes and concerns around which dramatic writing is built: the home, the family, the workplace, the battle of the sexes, differences of opinion, clashes of values, miscommunication. The difference between the two types of stories is the perspective. Our best writers know that humor is just a way of looking at life cockeyed so that the contour of the commonplace is distorted or the absurd is made to look fairly rational. Like alchemists, they transmute the basic into the rarefied, filtering the seriousness out of a slice of life and refracting the blandly universal through the prism of their antic imaginations.

*100 Hilarious Little Howlers* is a book of alchemy, the product of almost two centuries of experimentation. In pursuit of that cherished philosopher's stone, a good laugh, its contributors take the profane materials of ordinary experience—romantic relationships, holiday celebrations, sports, popular entertainment—and reconstitute them as the sacred stuff of the slightly silly. Their efforts are a reference guide to the tricks of the humorist's trade. Some apply the technique of the jokester, detonating a solidly straight story with an expertly planted punch line. Others take the satirist's approach, working a giddy variation on a familiar theme or style. Many of the selections have a fantasy element, but why should that be surprising? The abnormal and the absurd have a relationship as well established as—well, Abbott and Costello's.

Plenty of chuckles are to be found here, and a few genuine surprises as well. Who would have thought a writer as dark and dour as Edgar Allan Poe capable of lighter fare such as "Diddling"? Or what about Sir Arthur Conan Doyle—creator of that paragon of reason, Sherlock Holmes—indulging eagerly in the comic irrationality of "His First Operation"? Ambrose Bierce, best known as a writer of horror and of the horrors of the U.S. Civil War, is also on hand with a masterpiece of mordant merriment with the unlikely title "Oil of Dog." Such unexpected delights express the essence of the comic: moments of uncharacteristic whimsy that offer a pleasant break from the expected.

Whatever your preference—the discreet snicker or the boisterous belly laugh—you'll find a generous helping of humor in *100 Hilarious Little Howlers*. The only thing serious here is the fun that awaits you.

—Stefan Dziemianowicz
New York, 1999

# Absent-Mindedness in a Parish Choir

## Thomas Hardy

It happened on Sunday after Christmas—the last Sunday ever they played in Longpuddle church gallery, as it turned out, though they didn't know it then. As you may know, sir, the players formed a very good band—almost as good as the Mellstock parish players that were led by the Dewys; and that's saying a great deal. There was Nicholas Puddingcome, the leader, with the first fiddle; there was Timothy Thomas, the bass-viol man; John Biles, the tenor fiddler; Dan'l Hornhead, with the serpent; Robert Dowdle, with the clarionet; and Mr Nicks, with the oboe—all sound and powerful musicians, and strong-winded men—they that blowed. For that reason they were very much in demand Christmas week for little reels and dancing parties: for they could turn a jig or a hornpipe out of hand as well as ever they could turn out a psalm, and perhaps better, not to speak irreverent. In short, one half-hour they could be playing a Christmas carol in the Squire's hall to the ladies and gentlemen, and drinking tay and coffee with 'em as modest as saints; and the next, at The Tinker's Arms, blazing away like wild horses with the "Dashing White Sergeant" to nine couple of dancers and more, and swallowing rum-and-cider hot as flame.

'Well, this Christmas they'd been out to one rattling randy after another every night, and had got next to no sleep at all. Then came the Sunday after Christmas, their fatal day. 'Twas so mortal cold that year that they could hardly sit in the gallery; for though the congregation down in the body of the church had a stove to keep off the frost, the players in the gallery had nothing at all. So Nicholas said at morning service, when 'twas freezing an inch an hour, "Please the Lord I won't stand this numbing weather no longer: this afternoon we'll have something in our insides to make us warm, if it cost a king's ransom."

'So he brought a gallon of hot brandy and beer, ready mixed, to church with him in the afternoon, and by keeping the jar well wrapped up in Timothy Thomas's bass-viol bag it kept drinkably warm till they wanted it, which was just a thimbleful in the Absolution, and another after the Creed, and the remainder at the beginning o' the sermon. When they'd had the last pull they felt quite comfortable and warm, and as the sermon went on—most unfortunately for 'em it was a long one that afternoon—they fell asleep, every man jack of 'em; and there they slept on as sound as rocks.

' 'Twas a very dark afternoon, and by the end of the sermon all you could see of the inside of the church were the pa'son's two candles alongside of him in the pulpit, and his spaking face behind 'em. The sermon being ended at last, the pa'son gie'd out the Evening Hymn. But no quire set about sounding up the tune, and the people began to turn their heads to learn the reason why, and then Levi Limpet, a boy who sat in the gallery, nudged Timothy and Nicholas, and said, "Begin! begin!"

' "Hey? what?" says Nicholas, starting up; and the church being so dark and his head so muddled he thought he was at the party they had played at all the night before, and away he went, bow and fiddle, at "The Devil among the Tailors," the favourite jig of our neighbourhood at that time. The rest of the band, being in the same state of mind and nothing doubting, followed their leader with all their strength, according to custom. They poured out that there tune till the lower bass notes of "The Devil among the Tailors" made the cobwebs in the roof shiver like ghosts; then Nicholas, seeing nobody moved, shouted out as he scraped (in his usual commanding way at dances when the folk didn't know the figures), "Top couples cross hands! And when I make the fiddle squeak at the end, every man kiss his pardner under the mistletoe!"

'The boy Levi was so frightened that he bolted down the gallery stairs and out homeward like lightning. The pa'son's hair fairly stood on end when he heard the evil tune raging through the church, and thinking the quire had gone crazy he held up his hand and said: "Stop, stop, stop! Stop, stop! What's this?" But they didn't hear'n for the noise of their own playing, and the more he called the louder they played.

'Then the folks came out of their pews, wondering down to the ground, and saying: "What do they mean by such wickedness! We shall be consumed like Sodom and Gomorrah!"

'And the Squire, too, came out of his pew lined wi' green baize, where lots of lords and ladies visiting at the house were worshipping along with him, and went and stood in front of the gallery, and shook his fist in the musicians' faces, saying, "What! In this reverent edifice! What!"

'And at last they heard'n through their playing, and stopped.

' "Never such an insulting, disgraceful thing—never!" says the Squire, who couldn't rule his passion.

' "Never!" says the pa'son, who had come down and stood beside him.

' "Not if the Angels of Heaven," says the Squire (he was a wicked-ish man, the Squire was, though now for once he happened to be on the Lord's side)—"not if the Angels of Heaven come down," he says, "shall one of you villainous players ever sound a note in this church again; for the insult to me, and my family, and my visitors, and the pa'son, and God Almighty, that you've a-perpetrated this afternoon!"

'Then the unfortunate church band came to their senses, and remembered where they were; and 'twas a sight to see Nicholas Puddingcome and Timothy Thomas and John Biles creep down the gallery stairs with their fiddles under their arms, and poor Dan'l Hornhead with his serpent, and Robert Dowdle with his clarionet, all looking as little as ninepins; and out they went. The pa'son might have forgi'ed 'em when he learned the truth o't, but the Squire would not. That very week he sent for a barrel-organ that would play two-and-twenty new psalm-tunes, so exact and particular that, however sinful inclined you was, you could play nothing but psalm-tunes whatsomever. He had a really respectable man to turn the winch, as I said, and the old players played no more.'

# The Advent on Channel Twelve

## C. M. Kornbluth

It came to pass in the third quarter of the fiscal year that the Federal Reserve Board did raise the rediscount rate and money was tight in the land. And certain bankers which sate in New York sent to Ben Graffis in Hollywood a writing which said, Money is tight in the land so let Poopy Panda up periscope and fire all bow tubes.

Whereupon Ben Graffis made to them this moan:

3

O ye bankers, Poopy Panda is like unto the child of my flesh and you have made of him a devouring dragon. Once was I content with my studio and my animators when we did make twelve Poopy Pandas a year; cursed be the day when I floated a New York loan. You have commanded me to make feature-length cartoon epics and I did obey, and they do open at the Paramount to sensational grosses, and we do re-release them to the nabes year on year, without end. You have commanded me to film live adventure shorts and I did obey, and in the cutting room we do devilishly splice and pull frames and flop negatives so that I and my cameras are become bearers of false witness and men look upon my live adventure shorts and say lo! these beasts and birds are like unto us in their laughter, wooing, pranks, and contention. You have commanded that I become a mountebank for that I did build Poopy Pandaland, whereinto men enter with their children, their silver, and their wits, and wherefrom they go out with their children only, sandbagged by a thousand catch-penny engines; even this did I obey. You have commanded that Poopy Panda shill every weekday night on television between five and six for the Poopy Panda Pals, and even this did I obey, though Poopy Panda is like unto the child of my flesh.

But O ye bankers, this last command will I never obey.

Whereupon the bankers which sate in New York sent to him another writing that said, Even so, let Poopy Panda up periscope and fire all bow tubes, and they said, Remember, boy, we hold thy paper.

And Ben Graffis did obey.

He called unto him his animators and directors and cameramen and writers, and his heart was sore but he dissembled and said:

In jest you call one another brainwashers, forasmuch as you addle the heads of children five hours a week that they shall buy our sponsors' wares. You have fulfilled the prophecies, for is it not written in the Book of the Space Merchants that there shall be spherical trusts? And the Poopy Panda Pals plug the Poopy Panda Magazine, and the Poopy Panda Magazine plugs Poopy Pandaland, and Poopy Pandaland plugs the Poopy Panda Pals. You have asked of the Motivational Research boys how we shall hook the little bastards and they have told ye, and ye have done it. You identify the untalented kid viewers with the talented kid performers, you provide in Otto Clodd a bumbling father image to be derided, you furnish in Jackie Whipple an idealized big brother for the boys and a sex-fantasy for the more precocious girls. You flatter the cans off the viewers by ever saying to them that they shall rule the twenty-first century, nor mind that those who shall in good sooth come to power are doing their homework and not watching television programs. You have created a liturgy of opening hymn and closing benediction, and over all hovers the spirit of Poopy Panda urging and coaxing the viewers to buy our sponsors' wares.

And Ben Graffis breathed a great breath and looked them not in the eye and said to them, Were it not a better thing for Poopy Panda to coax and urge no more, but to command as he were a god?

And the animators and directors and cameramen and writers were sore amazed and they said one to the other, This is the bleeding end, and the bankers which sit in New York have flipped their wigs. And one which was an old animator said to Ben Graffis, trembling, O chief, never would I have stolen for thee Poopy Panda from the Winnie the Pooh illustrations back in twenty-nine had I known this was in the cards, and Ben Graffis fired him.

Whereupon another which was a director said to Ben Graffis, O chief, the thing can be done with a two-week buildup, and Ben Graffis put his hands over his face and said, Let it be so.

And it came to pass that on the Friday after the two-week buildup, in the closing quarter-hour of the Poopy Panda Pals, there was a special film combining live and animated action as they were one.

And in the special film did Poopy Panda appear enhaloed, and the talented kid performers did do him worship, and Otto Clodd did trip over his feet whilst kneeling, and Jackie Whipple did urge in manly and sincere wise that all the Poopy Panda Pals out there in televisionland do likewise, and the enhaloed Poopy Panda did say in his lovable growly voice, Poop-poop-poopy.

And adoration ascended from thirty-seven million souls.

And it came to pass that Ben Graffis went into his office with his animators and cameramen and directors and writers after the show and said to them, It was definitely a TV first, and he did go to the bar.

Whereupon one which was a director looked at Who sate behind the desk that was the desk of Ben Graffis and he said to Ben Graffis, O chief, it is a great gag but how did the special effects boys manage the halo?

And Ben Graffis was sore amazed at Who sate behind his desk

and he and they all did crowd about and make as if to poke Him, whereupon He in His lovable growly voice did say, Poop-poop-poopy, and they were not.

And certain unclean ones which had gone before turned unbelieving from their monitors and said, Holy Gee, this is awful. And one which was an operator of marionettes turned to his manager and said, Pal, if Graffis gets this off the ground we're dead. Whereat a great and far-off voice was heard, saying, Poop-poop-poopy, and it was even so; and the days of Poopy Panda were long in the land.

Filtered for error,
Jan. 18th 36 P.P.
Synod on Filtration & Infiltration
O. Clodd, P.P.P.
J. Whipple, P.P.P.

# The Adventures of Shamrock Jolnes

O. Henry

I am so fortunate as to count Shamrock Jolnes, the great New York detective, among my muster of friends. Jolnes is what is called the "inside man" of the city detective force. He is an expert in the use of the typewriter, and it is his duty, whenever there is a "murder mystery" to be solved, to sit at a desk telephone at Headquarters and take down the message of "cranks" who 'phone in their confessions to having committed the crime.

But on certain "off" days when confessions are coming in slowly and three or four newspapers have run to earth as many different guilty persons, Jolnes will knock about the town with me, exhibiting, to my great delight and instruction, his marvellous powers of observation and deduction.

The other day I dropped in at Headquarters and found the great detective gazing thoughtfully at a string that was tied tightly around his little finger.

"Good morning, Whatsup," he said, without turning his head. "I'm glad to notice that you've had your house fitted up with electric lights at last."

"Will you please tell me," I said, in surprise, "how you knew that? I am sure that I never mentioned the fact to any one, and the wiring was a rush order not completed until this morning."

"Nothing easier," said Jolnes, genially. "As you came in I caught the odor of the cigar you are smoking. I know an expensive cigar; and I know that not more than three men in New York can afford to smoke cigars and pay gas bills too at the present time. That was an easy one. But I am working just now on a little problem of my own."

"Why have you that string on your finger?" I asked.

"That's the problem," said Jolnes. "My wife tied that on this morning to remind me of something I was to send up to the house. Sit down, Whatsup, and excuse me for a few moments."

The distinguished detective went to a wall telephone, and stood with the receiver to his ear for probably ten minutes.

"Were you listening to a confession?" I asked, when he had returned to his chair.

"Perhaps," said Jolnes, with a smile, "it might be called something of the sort. To be frank with you, Whatsup, I've cut out the dope. I've been increasing the quantity for so long that morphine doesn't have much effect on me any more. I've got to have something more powerful. That telephone I just went to is connected with a room in the Waldorf where there's an author's reading in progress. Now, to get at the solution of this string."

After five minutes of silent pondering, Jolnes looked at me, with a smile, and nodded his head.

"Wonderful man!" I exclaimed; "already?"

"It is quite simple," he said, holding up his finger. "You see that knot? That is to prevent my forgetting. It is, therefore, a forget-me-knot. A forget-me-not is a flower. It was a sack of flour that I was to send home!"

"Beautiful!" I could not help crying out in admiration.

"Suppose we go out for a ramble," suggested Jolnes.

"There is only one case of importance on hand now. Old man McCarty, one hundred and four years old, died from eating too many bananas. The evidence points so strongly to the Mafia that the police have surrounded the Second Avenue Katzenjammer Gambrinus Club No. 2, and the capture of the assassin is only the matter of a few hours. The detective force has not yet been called on for assistance."

Jolnes and I went out and up the street toward the corner, where we were to catch a surface car.

Halfway up the block we met Rheingelder, an acquaintance of ours, who held a City Hall position.

"Good morning, Rheingelder," said Jolnes, halting.

"Nice breakfast that was you had this morning."

Always on the lookout for the detective's remarkable feats of deduction, I saw Jolnes's eyes flash for an instant upon a long yellow splash on the shirt bosom and a smaller one upon the chin of Rheingelder—both undoubtedly made by the yolk of an egg.

"Oh, dot is some of your detectiveness," said Rheingelder, shaking all over with a smile. "Vell, I bet you trinks and cigars all around dot you cannot tell vot I haf eaten for breakfast."

"Done," said Jolnes. "Sausage, pumpernickel, and coffee."

Rheingelder admitted the correctness of the surmise and paid the bet. When we had proceeded on our way I said to Jolnes:

"I thought you looked at the egg spilled on his chin and shirt front."

"I did," said Jolnes. "That is where I began my deduction. Rheingelder is a very economical, saving man. Yesterday eggs dropped in the market to twenty-eight cents per dozen. To-day they are quoted at forty-two. Rheingelder ate eggs yesterday, and to-day he went back to his usual fare. A little thing like this isn't anything, Whatsup; it belongs to the primary arithmetic class."

When we boarded the street car we found the seats all occupied—principally by ladies. Jolnes and I stood on the rear platform.

About the middle of the car there sat an elderly man with a short, gray beard, who looked to be the typical, well-dressed New Yorker. At successive corners other ladies climbed aboard, and soon three or four of them were standing over the man, clinging to straps and glaring meaningly at the man who occupied the coveted seat. But he resolutely retained his place.

"We New Yorkers," I remarked to Jolnes, "have about lost our manners, as far as the exercise of them in public goes."

"Perhaps so," said Jolnes, lightly; "but the man you evidently refer to happens to be a very chivalrous and courteous gentleman from Old Virginia. He is spending a few days in New York with his wife and two daughters, and he leaves for the South to-night."

"You know him, then?" I said, in amazement.

"I never saw him before we stepped on the car," declared the detective, smilingly.

"By the gold tooth of the Witch of Endor!" I cried, "if you can construe all that from his appearance you are dealing in nothing else than black art."

"The habit of observation—nothing more," said Jolnes. "If the old gentleman gets off the car before we do, I think I can demonstrate to you the accuracy of my deduction."

Three blocks farther along the gentleman rose to leave the car. Jolnes addressed him at the door:

"Pardon me, sir, but are you not Colonel Hunter, of Norfolk, Virginia?"

"No, suh," was the extremely courteous answer. "My name, suh, is Ellison—Major Winfield R. Ellison, from Fairfax County, in the same state. I know a good many people, suh, in Norfolk—the Goodriches, the Tollivers, and the Crabtrees, suh, but I never had the pleasure of meeting yo' friend, Colonel Hunter. I am happy to say, suh, that I am going back to Virginia to-night, after having spent a week in yo' city with my wife and three daughters. I shall be in Norfolk in about ten days, and if you will give me yo' name, suh, I will take pleasure in looking up Colonel Hunter and telling him that you inquired after him, suh."

"Thank you," said Jolnes; "tell him that Reynolds sent his regards, if you will be so kind."

I glanced at the great New York detective and saw that a look of intense chagrin had come upon his clear-cut features. Failure in the slightest point always galled Shamrock Jolnes.

"Did you say your *three* daughters?" he asked of the Virginia gentleman.

"Yes, suh, my three daughters, all as fine girls as there are in Fairfax County," was the answer.

With that Major Ellison stopped the car and began to descend the step.

Shamrock Jolnes clutched his arm.

"One moment, sir," he begged, in an urbane voice in which I alone detected the anxiety—"am I not right in believing that one of the young ladies is an *adopted* daughter?"

"You are, suh," admitted the major, from the ground, "but how the devil you knew it, suh, is mo' than I can tell."

9

"And mo' than I can tell, too," I said, as the car went on.

Jolnes was restored to his calm, observant serenity by having wrested victory from his apparent failure; so after we got off the car he invited me into a café promising to reveal the process of his latest wonderful feat.

"In the first place," he began after we were comfortably seated, "I knew the gentleman was no New Yorker because he was flushed and uneasy and restless on account of the ladies that were standing, although he did not rise and give them his seat. I decided from his appearance that he was a Southerner rather than a Westerner.

"Next I began to figure out his reason for not relinquishing his seat to a lady when he evidently felt strongly, but not overpoweringly, impelled to do so. I very quickly decided upon that. I noticed that one of his eyes had received a severe jab in one corner, which was red and inflamed, and that all over his face were tiny round marks about the size of the end of an uncut lead pencil. Also upon both of his patent-leather shoes were a number of deep imprints shaped like ovals cut off square at one end.

"Now, there is only one district in New York City where a man is bound to receive scars and wounds and indentations of that sort— and that is along the sidewalks of Twenty-third Street and a portion of Sixth Avenue south of there. I knew from the imprints of trampling French heels on his feet and the marks of countless jabs in the face from umbrellas and parasols carried by women in the shopping district that he had been in conflict with the amazonian troops. And as he was a man of intelligent appearance, I knew he would not have braved such dangers unless he had been dragged thither by his own women folk. Therefore, when he got on the car his anger at the treatment he had received was sufficient to make him keep his seat in spite of his traditions of Southern chivalry."

"That is all very well," I said, "but why did you insist upon daughters—and especially two daughters? Why couldn't a wife alone have taken him shopping?"

"There had to be daughters," said Jolnes, calmly. "If he had only a wife, and she near his own age, he could have bluffed her into going alone. If he had a young wife she would prefer to go alone. So there you are."

"I'll admit that," I said; "but, now, why two daughters? And how, in the name of all the prophets, did you guess that one was adopted when he told you he had three?"

"Don't say guess," said Jolnes, with a touch of pride in his air;

"there is no such word in the lexicon of ratiocination. In Major Ellison's button-hole there was a carnation and a rosebud backed by a geranium leaf. No woman ever combined a carnation and a rose-bud into a boutonnière. Close your eyes, Whatsup, and give the logic of your imagination a chance. Cannot you see the lovely Adele fastening the carnation to the lapel so that papa may be gay upon the street? And then the romping Edith May dancing up with sis-terly jealousy to add her rosebud to the adornment?"

"And then," I cried, beginning to feel enthusiasm, "when he declared that he had three daughters—"

"I could see," said Jolnes, "one in the background who added no flower; and I knew that she must be—"

"Adopted!" I broke in. "I give you every credit; but how did you know he was leaving for the South to-night?"

"In his breast pocket," said the great detective, "something large and oval made a protuberance. Good liquor is scarce on trains, and it is a long journey from New York to Fairfax County."

"Again, I must bow to you," I said. "And tell me this, so that my last shred of doubt will be cleared away; why did you decide that he was from Virginia?"

"It was very faint, I admit," answered Shamrock Jolnes, "but no trained observer could have failed to detect the odor of mint in the car."


# After You, Montagu*
(and after getting the hell out of certain eating places)

Howard Wandrei


This salesman named Harold Swampfellow pulled off U.S. 61 on the dirtiest and thickest night in nine years. You couldn't see whether trees had been planted on the road, whether you were roaming through the woods and ponds, nor determine whether it was the dankness which had awakened you at home on your settee

* John, 4th Earl of Sandwich.

where you had napped too late into the darkness to keep an engagement, or whether something had happened and this wasn't the same world any more.

Swampfellow rolled in on crushed granite beyond the gas pumps, because he could see the fuzzy eyes of lights in the diner through the dense fog. He walked in. There was no more fog inside than there was in London, if the windows are kept closed.

It was a diner. A sort of pair of counters, with leather stools of the swivel kind running along the whole length. Swampfellow knew every type of human being, was a master psychologist and he knew it, because salesmen get to know that and will pity you if you think otherwise. He sized up the counterman, the same sort as all countermen, and looked up at the menu of enamelled letters stuck into the black frame. One of them caught his eye. It read: FRIED BONE S'WICH.

"What in the hell is that?" Harold asked.

"Fried bone sandwich," said the counterman.

"How do you prepare those?" Swampfellow asked.

"Just fry them," said the bored counterman. He had his sleeves rolled up and he had hairy arms. Nice looking lad. "Sometimes," he said, "with cheese. We have them cold, too."

"I'll try one," Swampfellow decided. It was so thick and filthy outside that he expected to try several other items on the menu before he left, for he was one of those stringbeans able to pack away either a section of pie and ice cream or the same size of juicy steak for dessert and never weigh more than a hundred and forty-two pounds. It was his standard weight, never changed.

The counterman complied, turning up the gas. The sandwich was a hot one with cheese.

"Why, it *is* fried bone!" Swampfellow exclaimed in astonishment, after trying his teeth gently on the rigid spread inside the slices of toast. He cast his thoughts about for the calcium content of bone.

"Well, just eat the cheese and bread if you don't like the bone," the counterman suggested. "We really have only one customer for that sandwich. He comes in here all the time, just around now."

He drew coffee and set it down, and placed another sandwich on the counter. Swampfellow hadn't heard anyone come in, but he was aware of company, particularly because he heard snapping and crackling sounds only a foot or two from his right ear. He turned his head slowly to regard the newcomer sitting on the stool next to him. Harold had already left a half-dollar on the black-composition counter. He got up cautiously, involuntarily making a sound of "nnng-nnng," wavering up and down. He circled wide around The Thing on the stool, and it seemed that no sooner had he exploded through the doorway than his car spat its wheels on the crushed granite; Swampfellow jumped from raving low gear into high and went roaring down the highway into the night.

"What's the matter with *him?*" The Thing asked.

"Oh, one of those smart-aleck salesmen," said the counterman. "I guess he didn't believe it was a fried bone sandwich."

"Well, it *is,* isn't it?" asked The Thing that came down from the hills on rotten nights, like this one.

"Are you kidding me?" the counterman demanded, leaning forward. "Of course not! You know damned well we haven't got any saw here for slicing bone that thin. These sandwiches that you've been eating for the last four years are window-glass."

"Hoo-oo!" chortled The Thing; it crunched the sandwich with a sound like clamshells going through an old-fashioned meat-grinder, with relish. "I *thought* it was kinda funny I could see through those slices of bone. Sure was a good joke on *him!*" . . . .


# Agamemnon's Career

## Lucretia P. Hale

There had apparently been some mistake in Agamemnon's education. He had been to a number of colleges, indeed, but he had never completed his course in any one. He had continually fallen into some difficulty with the authorities. It was singular, for he was of an inquiring mind, and had always tried to find out what would be expected of him, but had never hit upon the right thing.

Solomon John thought the trouble might be in what they called the elective system, where you were to choose what study you might take. This had always bewildered Agamemnon a good deal.

"And how was a feller to tell," Solomon John had asked, "whether he wanted to study a thing before he tried it? It might turn out awful hard!"

Agamemnon had always been fond of reading, from his childhood up. He was at his book all day long. Mrs. Peterkin had imagined he would come out a great scholar, because she could never get him away from his books.

And so it was in his colleges; he was always to be found in the library, reading and reading. But they were always the wrong books.

For instance: the class were required to prepare themselves on the Spartan war. This turned Agamemnon's attention to the Fenians, and to study the subject he read up on "Charles O'Malley," and "Harry Lorrequer," and some later novels of that sort, which did not help him on the subject required, yet took up all his time, so that he found himself unfitted for anything else when the examinations came. In consequence he was requested to leave.

Agamemnon always missed in his recitations, for the same reason that Elizabeth Eliza did not get on in school, because he was always asked the questions he did not know. It seemed provoking; if the professors had only asked something else! But they always hit upon the very things he had not studied up.

Mrs. Peterkin felt this was encouraging, for Agamemnon knew the things they did not know in colleges. In colleges they were willing to take for students only those who already knew certain things. She thought Agamemnon might be a professor in a college for those students who didn't know those things.

"I suppose these professors could not have known a great deal," she added, "or they would not have asked you so many questions; they would have told you something."

Agamemnon had left another college on account of a mistake he had made with some of his classmates. They had taken a great deal of trouble to bring some wood from a distant wood-pile to make a bonfire with, under one of the professors' windows. Agamemnon had felt it would be a compliment to the professor.

It was with bonfires that heroes had been greeted on their return from successful wars. In this way beacon-lights had been kindled upon lofty heights, that had inspired mariners seeking their home after distant adventures. As he plodded back and forward he imagined himself some hero of antiquity. He was reading "Plutarch's Lives" with deep interest. This had been recommended at a former college, and he was now taking it up in the midst of his French course. He fancied, even, that some future Plutarch was growing up in Lynn, perhaps, who would write of this night of suffering, and glorify its heroes.

For himself he took a severe cold and suffered from chilblains, in consequence of going back and forward through the snow, carrying the wood.

But the flames of the bonfire caught the blinds of the professor's room, and set fire to the building, and came near burning up the whole institution. Agamemnon regretted the result as much as his predecessor, who gave him his name, must have regretted that other bonfire, on the shores of Aulis, that deprived him of a daughter.

The result for Agamemnon was that he was requested to leave, after having been in the institution but a few months.

He left another college in consequence of a misunderstanding about the hour for morning prayers. He went every day regularly at ten o'clock, but found, afterward, that he should have gone at half-past six. This hour seemed to him and to Mrs. Peterkin unseasonable, at a time of year when the sun was not up, and he would have been obliged to go to the expense of candles.

Agamemnon was always willing to try another college, wherever he could be admitted. He wanted to attain knowledge, however it might be found. But, after going to five, and leaving each before the year was out, he gave it up.

He determined to lay out the money that would have been expended in a collegiate education in buying an Encyclopaedia, the most complete that he could find, and to spend his life studying it systematically. He would not content himself with merely reading it, but he would study into each subject as it came up, and perfect himself in that subject. By the time, then, that he had finished the Encyclopaedia he should have embraced all knowledge, and have experienced much of it.

The family were much interested in this plan of making practice of every subject that came up.

He did not, of course, get on very fast in this way. In the second column of the very first page he met with A as a note in music. This led him to the study of music. He bought a flute, and took some lessons, and attempted to accompany Elizabeth Eliza on the piano. This, of course, distracted him from his work on the Encyclopaedia. But he did not wish to return to A until he felt perfect in music. This required a long time.

Then in this same paragraph a reference was made; in it he was requested to "see Keys." It was necessary, then, to turn to "Keys." This was about the time the family were moving, which we have mentioned, when the difficult subject of keys came up, that suggested to him his own simple invention, and the hope of getting a patent for it. This led him astray, as inventions before have done with master-minds, so that he was drawn aside from his regular study.

The family, however, were perfectly satisfied with the career Agamemnon had chosen. It would help them all, in any path of life, if he should master the Encyclopaedia in a thorough way.

Mr. Peterkin agreed it would in the end be not as expensive as a college course, even if Agamemnon should buy all the different Encyclopaedias that appeared. There would be no "spreads" involved; no expense of receiving friends at entertainments in college; he could live at home, so that it would not be necessary to fit up another room, as at college. At all the times of his leaving he had sold out favorably to other occupants.

Solomon John's destiny was more uncertain. He was looking forward to being a doctor some time, but he had not decided whether to be allopathic or homoeopathic, or whether he could not better invent his own pills. And he could not understand how to obtain his doctor's degree.

For a few weeks he acted as clerk in a druggist's store. But he could serve only in the tooth-brush and soap department, because it was found he was not familiar enough with the Latin language to compound the drugs. He agreed to spend his evenings in studying the Latin grammar; but his course was interrupted by his being dismissed for treating the little boys too frequently to soda.

The little boys were going through the schools regularly. The family had been much exercised with regard to their education. Elizabeth Eliza felt that everything should be expected from them; they ought to take advantage from the family mistakes. Every new method that came up was tried upon the little boys. They had been taught spelling by all the different systems, and were just able to read, when Mr. Peterkin learned that it was now considered best that children should not be taught to read till they were ten years old.

Mrs. Peterkin was in despair. Perhaps, if their books were taken from them even then, they might forget what they had learned. But no, the evil was done; the brain had received certain impressions that could not be blurred over.

This was long ago, however. The little boys had since entered the public schools. They went also to a gymnasium, and a whittling school, and joined a class in music, and another in dancing; they went to some afternoon lectures for children, when there was no other school, and belonged to a walking-club. Still Mr. Peterkin was dissatisfied by the slowness of their progress. He visited the schools himself, and found that they did not lead their classes. It seemed to him a great deal of time was spent in things that were not instructive, such as putting on and taking off their india-rubber boots.

Elizabeth Eliza proposed that they should be taken from school and taught by Agamemnon from the Encyclopaedia. The rest of the family might help in the education at all hours of the day. Solomon John could take up the Latin grammar; and she could give lessons in French.

The little boys were enchanted with the plan, only they did not want to have the study-hours all the time.

Mr. Peterkin, however, had a magnificent idea, that they should make their life one grand Object Lesson. They should begin at breakfast, and study everything put upon the table,—the material of which it was made, and where it came from. In the study of the letter A, Agamemnon had embraced the study of music, and from one meal they might gain instruction enough for a day.

"We shall have the assistance," said Mr. Peterkin, "of Agamemnon, with his Encyclopaedia."

Agamemnon modestly suggested that he had not yet got out of A, and in their first breakfast everything would therefore have to begin with A.

"That would not be impossible," said Mr. Peterkin. "There is Amanda, who will wait on table, to start with"—

"We could have 'am-and-eggs," suggested Solomon John.

Mrs. Peterkin was distressed. It was hard enough to think of anything for breakfast, and impossible if it all had to begin with one letter.

Elizabeth Eliza thought it would not be necessary. All they were to do was to ask questions, as in examination papers, and find their answers as they could. They could still apply to the Encyclopaedia, even if it were not in Agamemnon's alphabetical course.

Mr. Peterkin suggested a great variety. One day they would

study the botany of the breakfast-table; another day, its natural history. The study of butter would include that of the cow. Even that of the butter-dish would bring in geology. The little boys were charmed at the idea of learning pottery from the cream-jug, and they were promised a potter's wheel directly.

"You see, my dear," said Mr. Peterkin to his wife, "before many weeks we shall be drinking our milk from jugs made by our children."

Elizabeth Eliza hoped for a thorough study.

"Yes," said Mr. Peterkin, "we might begin with botany. That would be near to Agamemnon alphabetically. We ought to find out the botany of butter. On what does the cow feed?"

The little boys were eager to go out and see.

"If she eats clover," said Mr. Peterkin, "we shall expect the botany of clover."

The little boys insisted that they were to begin the next day; that very evening they should go out and study the cow.

Mrs. Peterkin sighed, and decided she would order a simple breakfast. The little boys took their note-books and pencils, and clambered upon the fence, where they seated themselves in a row.

For there were three little boys. So it was now supposed. They were always coming in or going out, and it had been difficult to count them, and nobody was very sure how many there were.

There they sat, however, on the fence, looking at the cow. She looked at them with large eyes.

"She won't eat," they cried, "while we are looking at her!"

So they turned about, and pretended to look into the street, and seated themselves that way, turning their heads back, from time to time, to see the cow.

"Now she is nibbling a clover."

"No, that is a bit of sorrel."

"It's a whole handful of grass."

"What kind of grass?" they exclaimed.

It was very hard, sitting with their backs to the cow, and pretending to the cow that they were looking into the street, and yet to be looking at the cow all the time, and finding out what she was eating; and the upper rail of the fence was narrow and a little sharp. It was very high, too, for some additional rails had been put on to prevent the cow from jumping into the garden or street.

Suddenly, looking out into the hazy twilight, Elizabeth Eliza saw six legs and six india-rubber boots in the air, and the little boys disappeared!

"They are tossed by the cow! The little boys are tossed by the cow!"

Mrs. Peterkin rushed for the window, but fainted on the way. Solomon John and Elizabeth Eliza were hurrying to the door, but stopped, not knowing what to do next. Mrs. Peterkin recovered herself with a supreme effort, and sent them out to the rescue.

But what could they do? The fence had been made so high, to keep the cow out, that nobody could get in. The boy that did the milking had gone off with the key of the outer gate, and perhaps with the key of the shed door. Even if that were not locked, before Agamemnon could get round by the wood-shed and cow-shed, the little boys might be gored through and through!

Elizabeth Eliza ran to the neighbors, Solomon John to the druggist's for plasters, while Agamemnon made his way through the dining-room to the wood-shed and outer-shed door. Mr. Peterkin mounted the outside of the fence, while Mrs. Peterkin begged him not to put himself in danger. He climbed high enough to view the scene. He held to the corner post and reported what he saw.

They were not gored. The cow was at the other end of the lot. One of the little boys was lying in a bunch of dark leaves. He was moving.

The cow glared, but did not stir. Another little boy was pulling his india-rubber boots out of the mud. The cow still looked at him.

Another was feeling the top of his head. The cow began to crop the grass, still looking at him.

Agamemnon had reached and opened the shed-door. The little boys were next seen running toward it.

A crowd of neighbors, with pitchforks, had returned meanwhile with Elizabeth Eliza. Solomon John had brought four druggists. But, by the time they had reached the house, the three little boys were safe in the arms of their mother!

"This is too dangerous a form of education," she cried; "I had rather they went to school."

"No!" they bravely cried. They were still willing to try the other way.

# All Moon-Beasts Amorphous and Mephitic

## Peter Cannon

Ah, James," cried Siegfried as I came down to the consulting room, "a messenger has just arrived for you from one of your most exalted clients—King Kuranes. His moon-beast is in need of your services." Siegfried was grinning like a gug as he spoke.

I gave my partner a "ghastly" smile in reply. "Oh, swell. You didn't fancy going there yourself, did you?"

"No, no, my boy. Wouldn't dream in the waking world of depriving you of the fun."

I looked at my checkbook. The bill for that last cask of moon-wine I'd bought from the almost-human merchants in Dylath-Leen was overdue. They say in Dylath-Leen that those almost-human merchants have strange and unpleasant ways of dealing with customers whose accounts remain unsettled for too long.

"Remember, James, Kuranes always pays on the nose—in rubies." Siegfried waved cheerfully and climbed onto his yak.

I got my bag and set off on my zebra, relieved to be spared the company of the messenger—a ghoul in the king's employ—who glibbered how he was sorry he couldn't join me on the return trip but he had a further errand to perform at the Celephaïs cemetery. I rode out the eastern gate and across the tract of English countryside—verdant valleys, Norman abbeys, Cornish fishing villages—that had been designed and built for the monarch of the land of dream by the Disney corporation. (It is said that from the sea-cliffs to the foot of the Tanarian Hills King Kuranes had been losing precious gems by the bushel because "Eng-Land" clashed with the local culture. In my view it had been the sheerest folly to ban the sale of wine, even the mild vintages brewed by the zoogs from tree sap.)

Two days later I came to the moat of a grey Gothic manor-house, and when I threw a stone in the water there slithered to admit me a voonith in a "Black Magic Kingdom" tee-shirt who spoke as best it could in the unintelligible tones—at least to a native Glaswegian like me—of far Cornwall. Leaving my zebra in the care of that amphibious terror, I walked up the parched path between trees as near as possible to England's trees (which frankly wasn't all that near), and climbed the terraces among gardens neglected since Queen Anne's time. At the door, flanked by stuffed cats (former pets evidently), I was met by an unshaven butler in a bhole skin, and was presently taken to the library where Kuranes, Lord of Ooth-Nargai and the Sky around Serannian, sat on the floor in a sailor suit playing with his blocks.

"If you've come to scold me because my mother's nearly out of patience waiting in the carriage to go to that hateful lawn-party at the vicar's, I'm not ready."

"I beg your pardon, your Majesty, I—"

"Oh, it's you, Herriot," exclaimed the king looking up. "I thought you were my nurse. My apologies, old boy."

"Not at all, your Majesty—"

"Come, come, Herriot, no need to stand on formality. I'm only a humble dreamland despot, you know. Call me Kuranes."

"As you wish, sir."

King Kuranes had a reputation for being something of an eccentric, but I will credit him for his ability to put commoners like myself at their ease.

"I'm awfully glad you're here, Herriot," he said, staggering to his feet and giving the wooden fort he'd just constructed a good kick. "Matilda has not been her usual slimy self of late."

"Have you noticed any change in her eating habits?"

"No, I can't say that I have. She still consumes her weight in fish and fungi like clockwork every day."

"Fish and fungi?"

"Well, mostly fungi."

"Fried fungi?"

Kuranes nodded as if it were the most natural thing in the dream world. While it probably did no harm, fried fungi was about the last food I would've expected a moon-beast to relish. The king's realm boasted a chain of fish and fungi shops, and I had a strong suspicion Matilda was the chief beneficiary of the leftovers.

"Any symptoms of ill health?"

"I'm afraid she no longer plays her disgustingly carven flute of ivory."

"Oh, dear. We better go have a look at her straight away, then."

As we descended a fathomless spiral of steep and slippery stairs to the dungeon, the king sang the praises of moon-beasts, in particular of his prize. Matilda was clearly in a class by herself. Not only was she a champion racer but she excelled at dressage as well as at zoog hunting. Personally I've never been fond of those polypous and amorphous monsters, but thought it politic not to mention the fact to my royal client.

At the bottom we followed a passage lined with torch-bearing slaves until we came to a mephitic pit. Below lay the moon-beast, a great greyish-white toad-like thing, expanding and contracting in its sleep. By the light of a brace of torch-bearing slaves I dropped into the pit, praying to the tame gods atop Kadath that the patient wouldn't suddenly wake up.

Since Matilda's hindquarters were pointed in my direction, I decided to begin my examination there. I rolled up my sleeve and gingerly stuck my arm as far as it would reach up her nether orifice. One has to be careful handling these jellyish entities, which can easily burst with results highly offensive to the sight and smell. All seemed normal, normal that is for a carnivorous creature on a diet of fish and fungi—and so primitive that it has only one organ system for both sexual reproduction and waste elimination.

Next I tiptoed around toward the mouth, the beast's business end and by far the most dangerous. I was in luck. I could spot the problem from a safe distance. The curiously vibrating mass of tentacles on the tip of the blunt, vague snout instead of being a healthy pink was a sickly green. It was little wonder flute playing was out. The formless abomination had a cold.

"I think I know what's ailing Matilda, sir," I said as I clambered up a pyramid of torch-bearers to the top of the pit. "I'll have to give you some antibiotic ointment and you must rub some onto her tentacles three times a day. You'll be able to do that, won't you?"

"Actually, I believe I'll have the butler take charge of a gang of slaves to perform that chore, thank you."

"Good, good." As I rummaged in my bag for the ointment I had the old feeling of fraud, but there was nothing for it. I pocketed my fee—a couple of low-grade rubies—and skedaddled back to Skeldale House, wondering if my esteemed client's cash-flow problem was as dire as my own.

One morning a week or two later King Kuranes showed up at our consulting room, with the eyeless abnormality in tow. Matilda was no better; in fact, she was worse. Her tentacles and snout were now encrusted with great gobs of greenish-brown mucus.

"You said you'd cure her, Herriot," the monarch of dream sniffled, doing his best to fight back the tears.

"There, there, your Highness. Bring her into the surgery why don't you, and we'll see what we can do. It's only a little discharge."

"Discharge! I don't like the sound of that." The king began to sob.

"Oh, it's nothing to worry about. It'll be child's play to remove it and she'll be right as a bog-wraith afterwards."

I spoke lightly because these procedures were routine. A massive injection of local anesthetic and some judicious pruning with a pair of hedge clippers would do the trick, but as I looked at the moon-beast I felt a twinge of unutterable loathing. Things might not be so easy with Matilda.

There was, for instance, the trifling matter of one of us grasping that noxious head while the other inserted the needle into that repulsive snout. Matilda made it very clear that we would share the fate of the black men of Parg if we dared take any liberties with her. Being on unfamiliar ground and feeling hungry, she came waddling, open-mouthed, at Siegfried and me as soon as we tried to enter the room. We retreated hastily and barred the door.

"Looks like one for the nembutal," murmured Siegfried.

"With zoog," I added.

For unapproachable cases we kept a supply of the succulent small brown burrowers in a pen in the garden. Live zoog was a delicacy no moon-beast could resist. It was a simple matter to grab one, force a few capsules of nembutal down its throat, and heave it through the half-open surgery window that faced the garden. It always worked.

When we came back twenty minutes later we expected to find Matilda beyond the Gate of Deeper Slumber, but when we peered in she lumbered against the window, shifting shape like an accordion. On the floor the comatose zoog lay untouched.

"By Azathoth, look at that!" I cried. "No moon-beast's ever refused one of those weird-eyed flutterers before!"

Siegfried scratched his armpit. "What a damned nuisance! Do you think she can smell the nembutal on the zoog's breath? Better try her with a larger creature."

Fortunately, there was a turbaned almost-human in the waiting room who was only too glad to accept the flagon of nembutal-laced moon-wine we were shortly to offer him. As we guided that evil wide-mouthed merchant out to the garden, he muttered something about the wine's bouquet which reminded him that he hadn't come to avail himself of our veterinary services but to collect— He was down the seventy steps to lighter slumber by the time we shoved him through the surgery window.

When we peeked in fifteen minutes later the picture hadn't changed. The almost-human was sprawled on the floor next to the zoog—untasted.

"What in the Cold Waste are we going to do?" Siegfried exploded. "We can't afford to upset the king any more than he already is."

Inside we could hear Kuranes complaining that it was time for his lunch. He wanted something English, like his favorite food, fish and—

"Just hang on for a minute," I said. "I think I know the answer."

I rushed in the door past Kuranes, who was squirming in his chair, and up to our living quarters where even then my wife was fixing a mixed fungi salad for our own mid-day meal. It was the work of a moment to seize the bowl she was preparing and dump the contents into a skillet coated with nembutal-saturated oil. The fragrance of frying fungi must have wafted down to the offices below, for the house soon started to shake with the sounds of some heavy body repeatedly launching itself against an interior wall. It was the work of another moment to run downstairs with a glowing platter of the phosphorescent treat and toss it through the surgery window. Matilda was on the stuff like a shantak and swallowed it whole without hesitation.

As we watched the flabby moon-beast roll over, we knew we had won. When we finally unbarred the door and entered the room, Matilda was dozing, her expression as goofy as a night-gaunt's. We administered the anesthetic and applied the shears; the operation was over within five minutes.

Matilda was still dopey as a Doel when her master had finished his luncheon—some extra drug-free fungi that my wife had managed to scrape up (or off)—and was ready to go home.

"We've removed that little discharge, your Worship," I said. "Her tentacles will be fine now, but I'm prescribing a course of Lindane tablets to stop any further infection."

As I reached for my 1906 Waterman to write the instructions, I glanced at some of the other labels I had written. "Pepto-bismol for ghoul. To be given in a pint of offal." "Vitamin C for web-footed wamp. To be given in a pint of human blood."

I poised my pen for a moment, then, for the first time in my dream life, I wrote, "Tablets for moon-beast. One to be given three times daily inserted in fried fungi."

"I'm much obliged to you, Herriot. Matilda seems her old slimy self again," the king said as we exchanged papers. "Say, I'm a bit short of rubies at the moment. I trust, my dear fellow, you won't mind accepting this certificate for a hundred shares of Kuranes Enterprises Limited instead."

"Ah, James," said Siegfried as we watched our august client ride off on his filthy mount, "our almost-human visitor should be waking up directly. Let's hope he'll be as delighted as you were to be paid in Kuranes Enterprises stock."

# At Arms with Morpheus

## O. Henry

I never could quite understand how Tom Hopkins came to make that blunder, for he had been through a whole term at a medical college—before he inherited his aunt's fortune—and had been considered strong in therapeutics.

We had been making a call together that evening, and afterward Tom ran up to my rooms for a pipe and a chat before going on to his own luxurious apartments. I had stepped into the other room for a moment when I heard Tom sing out:

"Oh, Billy, I'm going to take about four grains of quinine, if you don't mind—I'm feeling all blue and shivery. Guess I'm taking cold."

"All right," I called back. "The bottle is on the second shelf. Take it in a spoonful of that elixir of eucalyptus. It knocks the bitter out."

After I came back we sat by the fire and got our briars going. In about eight minutes Tom sank back into a gentle collapse.

I went straight to the medicine cabinet and looked.

"You unmitigated hayseed!" I growled. "See what money will do for a man's brains!"

There stood the morphine bottle with the stopple out, just as Tom had left it.

I routed out another young M.D., who roomed on the floor above, and sent him for old Doctor Gales, two squares away. Tom Hopkins has too much money to be attended by rising young practitioners alone.

When Gales came we put Tom through as expensive a course of treatment as the resources of the profession permit. After the more drastic remedies we gave him citrate of caffeine in frequent doses and strong coffee, and walked him up and down the floor between two of us. Old Gales pinched him and slapped his face and worked hard for the big check he could see in the distance. The young M.D. from the next floor gave Tom a most hearty, rousing kick, and then apologized to me.

"Couldn't help it," he said. "I never kicked a millionaire before in my life. I may never have another opportunity."

"Now," said Doctor Gales, after a couple of hours, "he'll do. But keep him awake for another hour. You can do that by talking to him and shaking him up occasionally. When his pulse and respiration are normal then let him sleep. I'll leave him with you now."

I was left alone with Tom, whom we had laid on a couch. He lay very still, and his eyes were half closed. I began my work of keeping him awake.

"Well, old man," I said, "you've had a narrow squeak, but we've pulled you through. When you were attending lectures, Tom, didn't any of the professors ever casually remark that m-o-r-p-h-i-a never spells 'quinia,' especially in four-grain doses? But I won't pile it up on you until you get on your feet. But you ought to have been a druggist, Tom; you're splendidly qualified to fill prescriptions."

Tom looked at me with a faint and foolish smile.

"B'ly," he murmured, "I feel jus' like a hum'n bird flyin' around a jolly lot of most 'shpensive roses. Don' bozzer me. Goin' sleep now."

And he went to sleep in two seconds. I shook him by the shoulder.

"Now, Tom," I said, severely, "this won't do. The big doctor said you must stay awake for at least an hour. Open your eyes. You're not entirely safe yet, you know. Wake up."

Tom Hopkins weighs one hundred and ninety-eight. He gave me

another somnolent grin, and fell into deeper slumber. I would have made him move about, but I might as well have tried to make Cleopatra's needle waltz around the room with me. Tom's breathing became stertorous, and that, in connection with morphia poisoning, means danger.

Then I began to think. I could not rouse his body; I must strive to excite his mind. "Make him angry," was an idea that suggested itself. "Good!" I thought; but how? There was not a joint in Tom's armor. Dear old fellow! He was good nature itself, and a gallant gentleman, fine and true and clean as sunlight. He came from somewhere down South, where they still have ideals and a code. New York had charmed but had not spoiled him. He had that old-fashioned, chivalrous reverence for women, that—Eureka!—there was my idea! I worked the thing up for a minute or two in my imagination. I chuckled to myself at the thought of springing a thing like that on old Tom Hopkins. Then I took him by the shoulder and shook him till his ears flopped. He opened his eyes lazily. I assumed an expression of scorn and contempt, and pointed my finger within two inches of his nose.

"Listen to me, Hopkins," I said, in cutting and distinct tones, "you and I have been good friends, but I want you to understand that in the future my doors are closed against any man who acts as much like a scoundrel as you have."

Tom looked the least bit interested.

"What's the matter, Billy?" he muttered, composedly. "Don't your clothes fit you?"

"If I were in your place," I went on, "which, thank God, I am not, I think I would be afraid to close my eyes. How about that girl you left waiting for you down among those lonesome Southern pines—the girl that you've forgotten since you came into your confounded money? Oh, I know what I'm talking about. While you were a poor medical student she was good enough for you. But now, since you are a millionaire, it's different. I wonder what she thinks of the performances of that peculiar class of people which she has been taught to worship—the Southern gentlemen? I'm sorry, Hopkins, that I was forced to speak about these matters, but you've covered it up so well and played your part so nicely that I would have sworn you were above such unmanly tricks."

Poor Tom. I could scarcely keep from laughing outright to see him struggling against the effects of the opiate. He was distinctly angry, and I didn't blame him. Tom had a Southern temper. His eyes were open now, and they showed a gleam or two of fire. But the drug still clouded his mind and bound his tongue.

"C-c-confound you," he stammered, "I'll s-smash you."

He tried to rise from the couch. With all his size he was very weak now. I thrust him back with one arm. He lay there glaring like a lion in a trap.

"That will hold you for a while, you old loony," I said to myself. I got up and lit my pipe, for I was needing a smoke. I walked around a bit, congratulating myself on my brilliant idea.

I heard a snore. I looked around. Tom was asleep again. I walked over and punched him on the jaw. He looked at me as pleasant and ungrudging as an idiot. I chewed my pipe and gave it to him hard.

"I want you to recover yourself and get out of my rooms as soon as you can," I said, insultingly. "I've told you what I think of you. If you have any honor or honesty left you will think twice before you attempt again to associate with gentlemen. She's a poor girl, isn't she?" I sneered. "Somewhat too plain and unfashionable for us since we got our money. Be ashamed to walk on Fifth Avenue with her, wouldn't you? Hopkins, you're forty-seven times worse than a cad. Who cares for your money? I don't. I'll bet that girl don't. Perhaps if you didn't have it you'd be more of a man. As it is you've made a cur of yourself, and"—I thought that quite dramatic—"perhaps broken a faithful heart." (Old Tom Hopkins breaking a faithful heart!) "Let me be rid of you as soon as possible."

I turned my back on Tom, and winked at myself in a mirror. I heard him moving, and I turned again quickly. I didn't want a hundred and ninety-eight pounds falling on me from the rear. But Tom had only turned partly over, and laid one arm across his face. He spoke a few words rather more distinctly than before.

"I couldn't have—talked this way—to you, Billy, even if I'd heard people—lyin' 'bout you. But jus' soon's I can s-stand up—I'll break your neck—don't f'get it."

I did feel a little ashamed then. But it was to save Tom. In the morning, when I explained it, we would have a good laugh over it together.

In about twenty minutes Tom dropped into a sound, easy slumber. I felt his pulse, listened to his respiration, and let him sleep. Everything was normal, and Tom was safe. I went into the other room and tumbled into bed.

I found Tom up and dressed when I awoke the next morning.

He was entirely himself again with the exception of shaky nerves and a tongue like a white-oak chip.

"What an idiot I was," he said, thoughtfully. "I remember thinking that quinine bottle looked queer while I was taking the dose. Have much trouble in bringing me 'round?"

I told him no. His memory seemed bad about the entire affair. I concluded that he had no recollection of my efforts to keep him awake, and decided not to enlighten him. Some other time, I thought, when he was feeling better, we would have some fun over it.

When Tom was ready to go he stopped, with the door open, and shook my hand.

"Much obliged, old fellow," he said, quietly, "for taking so much trouble with me—and for what you said. I'm going down to telegraph to the little girl."

# Believing in the Twentieth Century

## Darrell Schweitzer

About the time they reached the Twentieth Century, Egon wondered what had ever caused him to marry Draxilla. Maybe she had her redeeming features. Maybe he'd even loved her once. But now there were only her crazy obsessions, which ran her life, and his.

Twentieth Century clubs. Twentieth Century fashions, tableaus, re-enactments, rituals, research, facsimiles, holoresurrections. And when that wasn't enough—

He felt increasingly queasy as the last few decades slipped by.

She kept on arguing.

"It's all true," she said. *"Now* you're going to find out—"

He sighed. "You're endlessly credulous. Such things were *never* possible—"

"Closed-minded skeptic!"

The time-bubble burst. Pop. Thud. The two of them tumbled

into a deserted field. He lurched to his feet, gingerly brushing strange particulate matter from his bare skin.

"We're *here*," she said. "Welcome to the Twentieth Century."

"I loathe it already."

He found that he could not cleanse himself. He rubbed his arms and sides hard, and realized he was shivering from . . . what was the word? The auxiliary data-brain embedded in his skull behind his ear kicked in and supplied the answer, silently, inside his head: *cold*. The atmosphere was uncontrolled. Appalling. The thought of gases drifting randomly made him vaguely nauseous.

"In the Twentieth Century," Draxilla said, the patronizing tone in her voice terribly unsubtle, "people would wear body-coverings called clothes." She touched the subcutaneous implant beneath her chin and ludicrous coverings materialized over most of her body, doubtless the properly researched costume for the period. "It's part of the experience. Learn to enjoy it."

"I don't think I can." Already he longed for the rational, sanitary world they'd left behind—or ahead—thirty thousand years in the future, when things made sense, the laws of nature were understood, and there were no miracles.

They had come here in search of miracles. That was the essence of the Twentieth Century, she insisted, that miracles still happened. It was a time to *believe* rather than to *know*. The data-brain supplied an endless stream of nonsense words: *psychic healing, UFOs, telepathy, astrology*. All of them had been a part of daily life, if the literature of the era was to be taken seriously.

(His data-brain supplied a bibliography: MacLaine, Von Däniken, Dixon, a complete sequence of something called *Weekly World News*.)

"Please," he said. "Let's just go back now—"

She hooked a finger under his chin, and he too was clothed, scraped and clawed from every direction by repulsive vegetable and animal fibers he didn't care to ask the data-brain to catalog.

"Come along," she said, dragging him.

"Yes, Dear."

"What a wonderful Twentieth Century expression! You *have* been doing your homework!"

"Homework?"

"Never mind. Come."

They rose into the air. By moonlight he could see that the field was filled almost to the horizon with gently swaying objects . . .

matter . . . *crops* the data-brain told him. Stationary, living organisms the people of this barbaric epoch ate for food. *Wheat.*

He couldn't bring himself to care that the bursting time-bubble had flattened some of the *wheat* in a broad, circular pattern. The whole thing was too revolting to contemplate.

He alighted beside Draxilla on a pathway of some kind, made of what must have been molded stone. (*Asphalt,* said the data-brain.)

"No more antigravity from now on," she said. "We can't attract attention—"

"If we can't use the most rudimentary conveniences, I'm leaving."

"You are *not,* until our argument is settled. Remember. You *promised.*"

"Yes," he said. "I did." He'd made that promise in a moment of weakness, in the vain hope that it would put an end to Draxilla's absurdities.

(*Marital psychology,* said the data-brain. *Data inadequate for full explication.*)

"You and me both," Egon whispered under his breath.

"Did you say something?" Draxilla asked.

"No, no. Nothing."

The asphalt path entered a gloomy stand of larger plants. (*Highway, forest,* the data-brain supplied. *Trees.*) Something ugly and green, uncomfortable to the touch, brushed into Egon's face and broke off in his hand. (*Leaf.*) He threw it after Draxilla, who pressed fearlessly onward. The highway looped and twisted in an erratic manner utterly offensive to civilized aesthetics.

"Can't we just stop?" he gasped, already out of breath. "Let's just pretend we were here. Tell your friends back home anything you want."

She stood still, sucking in the cool, strangely-scented night air.

"No. We've only just begun. We're *fated* to be here. It is our *destiny!*"

"Utterly irrational!"

"Gloriously so. Now stop complaining—Oh!" She held both hands to her temples. "Oh! I'm having a psychic flash! Something is near, an intelligence, non-human. . . . Oh!"

"You're faking."

"I—"

A huge manlike shape, startled, stood up from where it had been crouching by the edge of the highway. All Egon could make out in the darkness was that the creature was easily twice his height and covered with fur. It grunted, bared its fangs, and loped off into the forest on enormous feet.

"I knew it!" she said. "I *told* you so! In the Twentieth Century there *are* such things!"

"An animal," he said. "Yes, they had animals running around loose. A bear, I think." (But his data-brain insisted it had not been a bear.) "How could it have been anything else? There are no gorillas in North America." (The data-brain backed him up on that. It offered one more nonsense word: *Sasquatch*.)

"Never mind," she said. "You'll *see*."

But as they approached a town in the morning twilight, it was far worse than merely *seeing* anything. Massive, uncontrolled vehicles roared past.

Irrelevant, disturbing thoughts touched his mind, as lightly and irritatingly as a feather, tickling him. (The data-brain supplied the imagery.)

Something was clearly wrong. He couldn't concentrate. If either his primary, organic brain or the implanted data-brain malfunctioned, he knew, he would be helpless. He wouldn't be able to make himself understood. He'd have to return home at once. He almost hoped it *was* his brain "on the blink," as the local idiom had it.

"I have a bad feeling about this," he said.

"That's *wonderful!*"

"It is? Why?"

"It's an essential Twentieth Century experience. You're having a *premonition!*"

"I feel sick."

Now the feather-tickling had become iron spikes driven into his head. The Twentieth Century was *bedlam*. (Images, metaphors supplied by the data-brain.) Even among the crowded buildings, vast metal machines hurled perilously through the streets.

The noise. The smells. The thousand voices jabbering in his mind, extraneous thoughts, repulsive imagery, as if all the strangely garbed citizenry shouted their innermost thoughts directly at him.

But Draxilla was ecstatic.

"That *proves* I'm right! We're experiencing telepathy!"

Only after concentrated effort was he able to reply. "The human mind has no such capacity! It is biologically impossible."

"Here in the Twentieth Century, no one cared about that. They believed in telepathy, so they experienced it."

"The next thing you'll be telling me is that they believed the Earth was flat, so it was flat."

"Some of them *did* believe, but not enough. It remained round."

He was in too much discomfort to argue. The sensation of telepathy was wretched. He tried to remember how it had been in the future, floating alone in silent, sanitary light, but he couldn't hold the thought as Draxilla hauled him through the streets for what must have been hours. She touched innumerable minds *deliberately*, sometimes joining hands with passers-by to feel their "energy" (a word she used with decreasing precision). She led him into a shop where, by some medium of exchange he couldn't understand (the data-brain muttered something; he didn't bother to listen), she acquired two fragments of crystalline quartz strung on animal-tissue fibers. She placed one over her own head, so that the crystal hung down her chest, and insisted he do the same with the other.

"It's very powerful," she said. "Don't you feel the vibrations?"

As much as he wanted to deny it, he did indeed feel the vibrations. Whether they had any significance or not, he didn't care to discuss. He tried to reserve what little mental coherence he had left for the formulation of a theory that the chief, and in fact *only*, experience of the Twentieth Century was, by definition, mass insanity.

"Oh!" she shouted aloud, clapping her hands, leaping into the air, dancing and twirling on the (*sidewalk*, said his data-brain), "it's everything I had hoped for, a whole new *world* filled with wonders!"

Twentieth Century people turned to stare.

(*Is she on something?* The thought came to him from somewhere. The data-brain researched the metaphor, but could not define it.)

"It's so different from our own," she continued. "Here each individual is *special*. What they *feel*, that is real. Nothing else. How did we ever give it all up?"

He shrugged wearily. His data-brain launched into a history lecture until he told it to stop.

"Never mind," she said. "Now what I want to know is the *future*."

That snapped him out of his stupor. He grabbed her by the arm and yanked her to a halt.

"We have to return home right *now*. You are obviously dysfunctional. You forget that we're *from* the future!"

She made a face at him, stuck out her tongue (*Twentieth Century mode of communication,* said his data-brain, *meaning uncertain*), and wriggled free of his grasp. "Silly! This is what I mean—"

She snatched a sheaf of (*newspaper,* said his data-brain) from a sidewalk stand, flipped through it, and read aloud: "Taurus. Today marks the beginning of your ultimate quest." She closed the paper. "There you have it. The stars have spoken."

"The stars, you know perfectly well, are masses of fusing hydrogen. They do *not* speak."

"Here in the Twentieth Century, they control our lives. As long as you're here, you're going to have to get used to it."

"We're leaving—*right now!*"

But the future, their future, from which they had journeyed in the time-bubble, seemed unreachably far away just then. Was this another . . . what was it? (*Premonition.*)

"Not so fast," she said, grabbing hold of him as he had grabbed her. She waved her free hand in the air. "Taxi!"

One of the hurtling metal machines screeched to a stop. They climbed inside. Incomprehensible transactions with the device's operator followed. (The very idea of a machine directed by a *living* being seemed too fantastically cruel for words. *Slavery*, the data-brain suggested, searching for a more precise analogy.) His stomach seemed to heave one way, his head the other, as the *taxi* sped through the streets, finally slamming to a halt at a location Draxilla and the operator had somehow agreed upon.

When they got back home, he swore, he was going to pop the module out of *her* data-brain some night while she slept and purge this Twentieth Century rubbish from memory. All of it. He didn't care about the legal consequences.

Draxilla shoved him out of the taxi.

Outside on the sidewalk, he swayed dizzily for several seconds before blearily noting the sign on the building in front of them. The script said (as his data-brain translated): MADAME ESTELLA, PSYCHIC READER.

Draxilla herded him up the walkway to the door and rang the bell. Footsteps approached from within. "This is very special indeed. Think of it as a shrine to the collective faith of the Twentieth Century."

(*Church,* his data-brain said.)

"Not a church," Draxilla said. "Something more important." So now she could read his mind too. It only figured.

The door opened. The old, bent woman standing there was eccentrically dressed, even by Twentieth Century standards. (*Gypsy,* the data-brain supplied, then supplied an ethnological treatise that did not seem immediately relevant.)

"Ah," the Gypsy woman said, "I was expecting you."

(*Yep, another premonition,* Egon's data-brain observed dryly. *Are you surprised, I mean, really?* He felt a moment of helpless terror. He was becoming corrupted. Here in the Twentieth Century, machines allegedly developed personalities. All he needed now to make the nightmare complete was a wise-cracking data-brain.)

Inside, they sat around a table in semi-darkness, in a curtained room filled with the paraphernalia of the Gypsy's profession: crystal ball; astrological charts; a paperback *Necronomicon;* statues of multi-armed, dancing figures; a shrunken head; numerous crystal pyramids, some with razor blades beneath them; and much more the data-brain could not identify. The old woman served them cups of a hot beverage which had, he admitted, a genuinely pleasant odor. For an instant he almost relaxed, but as he went to stir his drink *(tea)* the instrument provided for the purpose *(spoon)* suddenly bent itself into uselessness for no apparent reason. The old Gypsy woman and Draxilla likewise held damaged spoons.

Childish laughter came from an adjoining room.

"Junior!" shouted the Gypsy. "That's enough! Stop it at once!"

"Sorry, Gramma."

They put their spoons aside and drank their tea. Then the old woman took his hand in hers and traced the lines on his palm with her index finger.

Her eyes widened. "This is very strange. You don't seem to have any fingerprints."

"Of course not," he said in his most patronizing voice. ("You ignorant savage," he wanted to add, but restrained himself.) "No one has had individual markings since the middle of the Twenty-Fourth Century at least—"

Draxilla kicked him under the table, hard and painfully. (*Twentieth Century method to tell you to shut up,* her voice announced inside his head, telepathically.)

"Nevertheless," Madame Estella continued, "I see quite clearly that you have come on a long journey, and that very soon your existence will undergo an abrupt transition—"

(*You can hardly deny now,* Draxilla continued inside his head, *that I've won the argument. This is what the Twentieth Century is all about.*)

He yanked his hand away from the startled Madame Estella. "I can't take any more of this! Look! Look! I'm psychic too! I foresee a definite parting of the ways, Dearest." He glared at his wife. "That means I'm *leaving*, right now. You can stay here if you like. I don't care anymore! That's my prediction! I can do it! I can do it! I prophesy a divorce!"

He ran out of the building, down the steps, into the street.

Machine parts squealed. (*Truck,* the data-brain identified the on-coming vehicle as it hit him.)


Egon's organic mind was filled with murmurings, like a gentle tide. (The data-brain, damaged, supplied the imagery, but failed to define.) Draxilla wept over him (whatever weeping was) and held his hand, begging him to let the healing "energy" flow into him. (By now that term seemed to mean anything she wanted it to, or nothing at all.) They were in a room somewhere, surrounded by others, amid burning plant-matter *(herbal incense).* He watched dully as crystals and assorted brightly-colored stones were placed on the injured parts of his body. Fortunately there was no pain. In his own time, in the future, people learned how to shut off pain in earliest childhood.

Once he thought he'd known what the future was. Now he wasn't sure. How could anyone? The very idea involved several logical fallacies.

The people around him were chanting words he couldn't make out. His data-brain failed to translate. Someone asked what his spirit-animal was.

"Oh," Draxilla whispered to him. "How I envy you! You're so lucky!"

"Lucky?"

"This is the core experience of the Twentieth Century. Haven't you learned *anything?*"

"I don't know . . ." he said.

"I wish I could share it with you . . ."

"Didn't you once say that in the Twentieth Century wishes are everything?"

He couldn't hear her answer. Somehow he managed to slip off into sleep, into a dream in which he struggled to climb a glass slope up out of darkness and into light; but he made no progress at all, slipping ever downward despite his desperate efforts. As he slid, his body changed, becoming coarser, bent, covered with hair. Somehow he knew his brain was getting smaller. (*Australopithicus,* the data-brain said before it shut off once and for all, no longer able to fit into his diminishing skull.) Near the very end he seemed to have scales and fins, as he flopped in the muck at the edge of a dark, cold sea, gasping for breath, unable to care about anything anymore.

And then he was in a different place, strangely serene, completely at peace. His beloved Draxilla stood beside him in the moonlight at the edge of the same field where the time-bubble had deposited them. He felt increasingly light-headed.

"At last," he said. "We're going home."

"You are," she said, "in a sense. But to a new home."

He searched his mind for his data-brain, but it wasn't there.

"I don't understand. Aren't you coming with me?"

"This is where we part," she said. He thought he detected genuine regret in her voice.

"But . . . I'm returning to our own time, aren't I? Why can't you come with me?"

"*I* could return to our original time," she said, "if I wanted to. But *you* couldn't exist there."

All his anger had left him. "Please explain," he said softly.

"Look at yourself. Look closely."

He saw that he was naked once more, but somehow his body had become transparent as smoke. It glowed slightly.

She sobbed. "We couldn't save you. There was just too much negative energy. You shut us out by your refusal to believe."

"I—"

Something bright and round moved across the sky. It wasn't the moon, he realized.

"You have to go away now," she said, "the way many people did, in the Twentieth Century."

The flying saucer settled into the field as gently as a cloud. Its hatchway opened in a burst of blinding light. Hesitantly, he made his way toward it, until at last he could make out faces in the light, smiling at him. Voices beckoned. Even without the data-brain he recognized some of the people there . . . JFK, Marilyn, Elvis . . .

He turned back toward the field only once, and waved briefly.

"I guess you win," he said.

# The Belle of Vallejo

## W. L. Alden

Vallejo, California, possesses a young lady of extraordinary beauty. She is, moreover, as intelligent and bold as she is beautiful, and in grappling with a sudden emergency she is probably unequaled by any one of her sex. Naturally, she is the admiration of every young man in the town. In fact, she is beyond the reach of rivalry. The other young ladies of Vallejo are perfectly well aware that it is hopeless for them to enter the lists with her. They never expect to receive calls from marriageable young men except on the off nights of the Vallejo belle, and though they doubtless murmur secretly against this dispensation, they apparently accept it as a law of nature.

For two years the beauty in question, whom we will call Miss Ecks, received the homage of her multitudinous admirers, and took an evident delight in adding to their number. So far from selecting any particular young man for front-gate or back-piazza duty, she preferred to entertain one or two dozen simultaneous admirers in the full blaze of the brilliantly lighted front parlor. It is only fair to add that she was an earnest young woman, who despised coquetry and never dreamed of showing favor to one young man in order to exasperate the rest.

That so brilliant a girl should have finally selected a meek young minister on whom to lavish her affections was certainly a surprise to all who knew her, and when it was first rumored that she had made such a selection, Vallejo refused to believe it. The minister made his regular nightly calls upon the object of his affections, but an average quantity of eleven other young men never failed to be present. Of course, he could not obtain a single moment of private happiness with his eleven rivals sitting all around the room, unless he made his evening call at a preposterously early hour. He did try this expedient once or twice, but the only result was that the eleven admirers at once followed his example. In these circumstances he began to grow thin with suppressed affection, and the young lady, alarmed at his condition, made up her mind that something must be done without delay.

About three weeks ago the young minister presented himself in his beloved's front parlor at 6:50 P.M., and, in the ten minutes that elapsed before the first of his rivals rang the bell, he painted the misery of courting by battalions in the most harrowing terms. Miss Ecks listened to him with deep sympathy, and promised him that if he would stay until nine o'clock, the last of the objectionable young men would be so thoroughly disposed of that for the rest of the evening he would have the field to himself. Full of confidence in the determination and resources of his betrothed, his spirits returned, and he was about to express his gratitude with his lips, as well as his heart, when the first young man was ushered into the room.

Miss Ecks received her unwelcome guest with great cordiality, and invited him to sit on a chair the back of which was placed close to a door. The door in question opened outward, and upon the top of a flight of stairs leading to the cellar. The latch was old and out of order, and the least pressure would cause it to fly open. In pursuance of a deep-laid plan, Miss Ecks so molded her conversation as to place the visitor at his ease. In a very few moments, he ceased to twist his fingers and writhe his legs, and presently tilted back his chair after the manner of a contented and happy man. No sooner did the back of the chair touch the door than the latter flew open, and the unhappy guest disappeared into the cellar with a tremendous crash. Checking the cry that arose from the astonished clergyman, Miss Ecks quietly reclosed the fatal door, placed a fresh chair in its vicinity, and calmly remarked, "That's one of them."

In five minutes more the second young man entered. Like his predecessor, he seated himself on the appointed chair, tipped back upon its hind-legs, and instantly vanished. "That's two of them," remarked the imperturbable beauty, as she closed the door and once more re-set the trap. From this time until nine o'clock a constant succession of young men went down those cellar stairs. Some of them groaned slightly after reaching the bottom, but not one returned. It was an unusually good night for young men, and Miss Ecks caught no less than fourteen between seven and nine o'clock. As the last one disappeared she turned to her horrified clergyman and said, "That's the last of them! Now for business!" but that mild young man had fainted. His nerves were unable to bear the strain, and when the moment of his wished-for monopoly of his betrothed had arrived he was unable to enjoy it.

Later in the evening he revived sufficiently to seek a railway station and fly forever from his remorseless charmer. The inquest that was subsequently held upon the fourteen young men will long be remembered as a most impressive scene. Miss Ecks was present with her back hair loose, and the tears stood in her magnificent eyes as she testified that she could not imagine what induced the young men to go down cellar. The jury without the slightest hesitation found that they had one and all committed suicide, and the coroner personally thanked the young lady for her lucid testimony. She is now more popular than ever, and, with the loss of her own accepted lover, has renewed her former fondness for society, and nightly entertains all the surviving young men of Vallejo.

This shows what the magnificent climate of California can accomplish in the production of girls, when it really tries.

# Boots

## Anton Chekhov

A piano-tuner called Murkin, a close-shaven man with a yellow face, with a nose stained with snuff, and cotton-wool in his ears, came out of his hotel-room into the passage, and in a cracked voice cried: "Semyon! Waiter!"

And looking at his frightened face one might have supposed that the ceiling had fallen in on him or that he had just seen a ghost in his room.

"Upon my word, Semyon!" he cried, seeing the attendant running towards him. "What is the meaning of it? I am a rheumatic, delicate man and you make me go barefoot! Why is it you don't give me my boots all this time? Where are they?"

Semyon went into Murkin's room, looked at the place where he was in the habit of putting the boots he had cleaned, and scratched his head: the boots were not there.

"Where can they be, the damned things?" Semyon brought out. "I fancy I cleaned them in the evening and put them here. . . . H'm! . . . Yesterday, I must own, I had a drop. . . . I must have put them in another room, I suppose. That must be it, Afanasy Yegoritch, they are in another room! There are lots of boots, and how the devil is one to know them apart when one is drunk and does not know what one is doing? . . . I must have taken them in to the lady that's next door . . . the actress. . . ."

"And now, if you please, I am to go in to a lady and disturb her all through you! Here, if you please, through this foolishness I am to wake up a respectable woman."

Sighing and coughing, Murkin went to the door of the next room and cautiously tapped.

"Who's there?" he heard a woman's voice a minute later.

"It's I!" Murkin began in a plaintive voice, standing in the attitude of a cavalier addressing a lady of the highest society. "Pardon my disturbing you, madam, but I am a man in delicate health, rheumatic. . . . The doctors, madam, have ordered me to keep my feet warm, especially as I have to go at once to tune the piano at Madame la Générale Shevelitsyn's. I can't go to her barefoot."

"But what do you want? What piano?"

"Not a piano, madam; it is in reference to boots! Semyon, stupid fellow, cleaned my boots and put them by mistake in your room. Be so extremely kind, madam, as to give me my boots!"

There was a sound of rustling, of jumping off the bed and the flapping of slippers, after which the door opened slightly and a plump feminine hand flung at Murkin's feet a pair of boots. The piano-tuner thanked her and went into his own room.

"Odd . . ." he muttered, putting on the boots, "it seems as though this is not the right boot. Why, here are two left boots! Both are for the left foot! I say, Semyon, these are not my boots! My boots have red tags and no patches on them, and these are in holes and have no tags."

Semyon picked up the boots, turned them over several times before his eyes, and frowned.

"Those are Pavel Alexandritch's boots," he grumbled, squinting at them.

He squinted with the left eye.

"What Pavel Alexandritch?"

"The actor; he comes here every Tuesday. . . . He must have put on yours instead of his own. . . . So I must have put both pairs in her room, his and yours. Here's a go!"

"Then go and change them!"

"That's all right!" sniggered Semyon. "Go and change them.

. . . Where am I to find him now? He went off an hour ago. . . . Go and look for the wind in the fields!"

"Where does he live then?"

"Who can tell? He comes here every Tuesday, and where he lives I don't know. He comes and stays the night, and then you may wait till next Tuesday. . . ."

"There, do you see, you brute, what you have done? Why, what am I to do now? It is time I was at Madame la Générale Shevelitsyn's, you anathema! My feet are frozen!"

"You can change the boots before long. Put on these boots, go about in them till the evening, and in the evening go to the theatre. . . . Ask there for Blistanov, the actor. . . . If you don't care to go to the theatre, you will have to wait till next Tuesday; he only comes here on Tuesdays. . . ."

"But why are there two boots for the left boot?" asked the piano-tuner, picking up the boots with an air of disgust.

"What God has sent him, that he wears. Through poverty . . . where is an actor to get boots? I said to him, 'What boots, Pavel Alexandritch! They are a positive disgrace!' and he said: 'Hold your peace,' says he, 'and turn pale! In those very boots,' says he, 'I have played counts and princes.' A queer lot! Artists, that's the only word for them! If I were the governor or anyone in command, I would get all these actors together and clap them all in prison."

Continually sighing and groaning and knitting his brows, Murkin drew the two left boots on to his feet, and set off, limping, to Madame la Générale Shevelitsyn's. He went about the town all day long tuning pianos, and all day long it seemed to him that everyone was looking at his feet and seeing his patched boots with heels worn down at the sides! Apart from his moral agonies he had to suffer physically also; the boots gave him a corn.

In the evening he was at the theatre. There was a performance of *Bluebeard*. It was only just before the last act, and then only thanks to the good offices of a man he knew who played a flute in the orchestra, that he gained admittance behind the scenes. Going to the men's dressing-room, he found there all the male performers. Some were changing their clothes, others were painting their faces, others were smoking. Bluebeard was standing with King Bobesh, showing him a revolver.

"You had better buy it," said Bluebeard. "I bought it at Kursk, a bargain, for eight roubles, but, there! I will let you have it for six. . . . A wonderfully good one!"

"Steady. . . . It's loaded, you know!"

"Can I see Mr. Blistanov?" the piano-tuner asked as he went in.

"I am he!" said Bluebeard, turning to him. "What do you want?"

"Excuse my troubling you, sir," began the piano-tuner in an imploring voice, "but, believe me, I am a man in delicate health, rheumatic. The doctors have ordered me to keep my feet warm . . ."

"But, speaking plainly, what do you want?"

"You see," said the piano-tuner, addressing Bluebeard. "Er . . . you stayed last night at Buhteyev's furnished apartments . . . No. 64 . . ."

"What's this nonsense?" said King Bobesh with a grin. "My wife is at No. 64."

"Your wife, sir? Delighted. . . ." Murkin smiled. "It was she, your good lady, who gave me this gentleman's boots. . . . After this gentleman"—the piano-tuner indicated Blistanov—"had gone away I missed my boots. . . . I called the waiter, you know, and he said: 'I left your boots in the next room!' By mistake, being in a state of intoxication, he left my boots as well as yours at 64," said Murkin, turning to Blistanov, "and when you left this gentleman's lady you put on mine."

"What are you talking about?" said Blistanov, and he scowled. "Have you come here to libel me?"

"Not at all, sir—God forbid! You misunderstand me. What am I talking about? About boots! You did stay the night at No. 64, didn't you?"

"When?"

"Last night!"

"Why, did you see me there?"

"No, sir, I didn't see you," said Murkin in great confusion, sitting down and taking off the boots. "I did not see you, but this gentleman's lady threw out your boots here to me . . . instead of mine."

"What right have you, sir, to make such assertions? I say nothing about myself, but you are slandering a woman, and in the presence of her husband, too!"

A fearful hubbub arose behind the scenes. King Bobesh, the injured husband, suddenly turned crimson and brought his fist down upon the table with such violence that two actresses in the next dressing-room felt faint.

"And you believe it?" cried Bluebeard. "You believe this worthless rascal? O-oh! Would you like me to kill him like a dog? Would you like it? I will turn him into a beefsteak! I'll blow his brains out!"

And all the persons who were promenading that evening in the town park by the Summer theatre describe to this day how just before the fourth act they saw a man with bare feet, a yellow face, and terror-stricken eyes dart out of the theatre and dash along the principal avenue. He was pursued by a man in the costume of Bluebeard, armed with a revolver. What happened later no one saw. All that is known is that Murkin was confined to his bed for a fortnight after his acquaintance with Blistanov, and that to the words "I am a man in delicate health, rheumatic" he took to adding, "I am a wounded man. . . ."

# Broker's Loan

## Donald Wandrei

The offices of Farnham and Lane, brokers, are furnished with taste. The luxurious chairs and thick rugs hold a quiet dignity. There is nothing lavish, though it is quite evident that money has been lavishly spent in making them attractive.

Even when you first enter the reception room, you are impressed by its reserve. It is like your own living room—a few excellent etchings on the walls, a small bookcase in a corner, a table with several current magazines, some comfortable overstuffed chairs, and a long, inviting lounge.

On this lounge a young woman was seated. She was idly flipping the pages of a weekly and intermittently toying with a cigarette. She awaited the return of the attendant to whom she had just given her name as "Miss Carter, to see Mr. Lane by appointment."

The cigarette was only a third consumed when the attendant reappeared and asked her to accompany him. Miss Carter betrayed a very slight nervousness as she extinguished her cigarette and rose.

The attendant led her down a passage past several doors to an inner private office whose doors bore a brass nameplate: MR. ALFRED B. LANE. From here a confused noise of tickers, voices, and typewriters could be heard; the dignity of the outer rooms became partly lost in these customary sounds of a busy office.

The attendant opened the door, announced, "Miss Carter, by appointment," and withdrew.

The man inside politely inquired, "Won't you be seated?" He seemed not only to have expected, but also to have been well acquainted with her. Yet his manner remained superficially formal.

Mr. Lane may have been forty. He had a cat-like ease of carriage, showing good physical condition, but the thing you noticed most were his eyes. They had a queer trick of focusing inward at times as if he were examining something in his mind. They were the eyes of a man whose plans were laid well, of a man who could arrange coups even while he carried on a conversation.

"I should have preferred the transaction to take place elsewhere." It was a matter of fact statement.

"I am so sorry," murmured Miss Carter. "But it seemed to me the best place for a business . . . exchange." Her voice had hesitated on the last word.

Mr. Lane's eyes reflected inward. "You have the letters with you, then?"

"Yes." She withdrew a thin package from her handbag.

Mr. Lane's eyes rested on it for barely an instant. He unlocked a drawer in his desk, removed a sealed envelope, and handed it to the girl. She opened it—inside was a check, payable to "Cash," for fifty thousand dollars.

"Thank you," she said in a cool voice and surrendered the parcel. Mr. Lane quickly untied it. Eleven letters—yes, they were all there. "I am indebted to you," he stated in the same unemotional voice.

"No more perhaps than I am to you." She arose. The transaction had been made with a speed satisfactory to both. Perhaps she was thinking of the extraordinary value of indiscreet love-letters, for a faintly ironic smile curved her lips. "Mrs. Lane is fortunate in having a husband so successful in business."

Mr. Lane detected the undertone but answered, "You are complimentary."

"Perhaps rightly so."

Mr. Lane himself opened the door.

There was still the slight smile on her lips as she said, "I am, of course, turning the apartment back to you." She handed him a key. "Good-bye, and thank you!"

She did not offer her hand as she departed.

For the next few minutes, Mr. Lane was absorbed in shredding to bits eleven letters for which he had just paid fifty thousand dollars. Immediately that was finished, he made three 'phone calls. The first was to a certain lady, who, though she possessed an apartment, would never possess a line in Mr. Lane's handwriting. The second was his wife, who would be without his company until sometime during the evening—"Rush of business—bull market," etc. The third was the Banker's Bank. "This is Mr. Alfred B. Lane speaking. Check No. C937 to my account, for fifty thousand dollars payable to 'Cash,' was lost this morning. Will you kindly stop payment? Thank you."

He pushed a button. Leaving a few instructions with the secretary who answered, he announced he would be absent the rest of the day.

As he was leaving, his eyes focused inward again. Perhaps he thought of the breach-of-promise suit, the flaming headlines and scandal which he had averted; or perhaps of his most recent action. After all, the price was ridiculous for a temporary infatuation. It really amounted to blackmail.

Mr. Lane was in good humor when he entered the following morning. He even halted at Mr. Farnham's office and greeted him amiably—a pleasantry that he occasionally omitted.

Mr. Farnham glanced up. "Good morning—did you enjoy your afternoon?"

"Very much. A little golf is fine for clearing one's mind. I feel as if I could stand any antics of the market today."

"You may have to," his partner commented, dryly. "The 'rails' have come to life for the first time in months. No telling what may happen."

"Any large blocks turned over?" Mr. Lane asked perfunctorily.

"One of 500 A. & P. at 99⅛."

"Who is so interested in A. & P.?"

"A new client—a Miss Carter. She was in yesterday shortly after you left and bought the stock outright—gave me your check for fifty thousand dollars to cover it."

# The Captain's Story

## Mark Twain

There was a good deal of pleasant gossip about old Captain "Hurricane" Jones, of the Pacific Ocean,—peace to his ashes! Two or three of us present had known him; I, particularly well, for I had made four sea-voyages with him. He was a very remarkable man. He was born on a ship; he picked up what little education he had among his shipmates; he began life in the forecastle, and climbed grade by grade to the captaincy. More than fifty years of his sixty-five were spent at sea. He had sailed all oceans, seen all lands, and borrowed a tint from all climates. When a man has been fifty years at sea, he necessarily knows nothing of men, nothing of the world but its surface, nothing of the world's thought, nothing of the world's learning but its A B C, and that blurred and distorted by the unfocussed lenses of an untrained mind. Such a man is only a gray and bearded child. That is what old Hurricane Jones was,—simply an innocent, lovable old infant. When his spirit was in repose he was as sweet and gentle as a girl; when his wrath was up he was a hurricane that made his nickname seem tamely descriptive. He was formidable in a fight, for he was of powerful build and dauntless courage. He was frescoed from head to heel with pictures and mottoes tattooed in red and blue India ink. I was with him one voyage when he got his last vacant space tattooed; this vacant space was around his left ankle. During three days he stumped about the ship with his ankle bare and swollen, and this legend gleaming red and angry out from a clouding of India ink: "Virtue is its own R'd." (There was a lack of room.) He was deeply and sincerely pious, and swore like a fish-woman. He considered swearing blameless, because sailors would not understand an order unillumined by it. He was a profound Biblical scholar,—that is, he thought he was. He believed everything in the Bible, but he had his own methods of arriving at his beliefs. He was of the "advanced" school of thinkers, and applied natural laws to the interpretation of all miracles, somewhat on the plan of the people who make the six days of creation six geological epochs, and so forth. Without being aware of it, he was a rather severe satire on modern scientific religionists. Such a man as I have been describing is rabidly fond of disquisition and argument; one knows that without being told it.

One trip the captain had a clergyman on board, but did not know he was a clergyman, since the passenger list did not betray the fact. He took a great liking to this Rev. Mr. Peters, and talked with him a great deal: told him yarns, gave him toothsome scraps of personal history, and wove a glittering streak of profanity through his garrulous fabric that was refreshing to a spirit weary of the dull neutralities of undecorated speech. One day the captain said, "Peters, do you ever read the Bible?"

"Well—yes."

"I judge it ain't often, by the way you say it. Now, you tackle it in dead earnest once, and you'll find it'll pay. Don't you get discouraged, but hang right on. First, you won't understand it; but by and by things will begin to clear up, and then you wouldn't lay it down to eat."

"Yes, I have heard that said."

"And it's so, too. There ain't a book that begins with it. It lays over 'em all, Peters. There's some pretty tough things in it,—there ain't any getting around that,—but you stick to them and think them out, and when once you get on the inside everything's plain as day."

"The miracles, too, captain?"

"Yes, sir! the miracles, too. Every one of them. Now, there's that business with the prophets of Baal; like enough that stumped you?"

"Well, I don't know but—"

"Own up, now; it stumped you. Well, I don't wonder. You hadn't had any experience in ravelling such things out, and naturally it was too many for you. Would you like to have me explain that thing to you, and show you how to get at the meat of these matters?"

"Indeed, I would, captain, if you don't mind."

Then the captain proceeded as follows: "I'll do it with pleasure. First, you see, I read and read, and thought and thought, till I got to understand what sort of people they were in the old Bible times, and then after that it was clear and easy. Now, this was the way I put it up, concerning Isaac* and the prophets of Baal. There was some mighty sharp men amongst the public characters of that old ancient

* This is the captain's own mistake.

48

day, and Isaac was one of them. Isaac had his failings,—plenty of them, too; it ain't for me to apologize for Isaac; he played on the prophets of Baal, and like enough he was justifiable, considering the odds that was against him. No, all I say is, 't wa' n't any miracle, and that I'll show you so's 't you can see it yourself.

"Well, times had been getting rougher and rougher for prophets,—that is, prophets of Isaac's denomination. There were four hundred and fifty prophets of Baal in the community, and only one Presbyterian; that is, if Isaac *was* a Presbyterian, which I reckon he was, but it don't say. Naturally, the prophets of Baal took all the trade. Isaac was pretty low-spirited, I reckon, but he was a good deal of a man, and no doubt he went a-prophesying around, letting on to be doing a land-office business, but 't wa' n't any use; he couldn't run any opposition to amount to anything. By and by things got desperate with him; he sets his head to work and thinks it all out, and then what does he do? Why, he begins to throw out hints that the other parties are this and that and t'other,—nothing very definite, may be, but just kind of undermining their reputation in a quiet way. This made talk, of course, and finally got to the king. The king asked Isaac what he meant by his talk. Says Isaac, 'Oh, nothing particular; only, can they pray down fire from heaven on an altar? It ain't much, may be, your majesty, only can they *do* it? That's the idea.' So the king was a good deal disturbed, and he went to the prophets of Baal, and they said, pretty airy, that if he had an altar ready, *they* were ready; and they intimated he better get it insured, too.

"So next morning all the children of Israel and their parents and the other people gathered themselves together. Well, here was that great crowd of prophets of Baal packed together on one side, and Isaac walking up and down all alone on the other, putting up his job. When time was called, Isaac let on to be comfortable and indifferent; told the other team to take the first innings. So they went at it, the whole four hundred and fifty, praying around the altar, very hopeful, and doing their level best. They prayed an hour,—two hours,—three hours,—and so on, plumb till noon. It wa' n't any use; they hadn't took a trick. Of course they felt kind of ashamed before all those people, and well they might. Now, what would a magnanimous man do? Keep still, wouldn't he? Of course. What did Isaac do? He gravelled the prophets of Baal every way he could think of. Says he, 'You don't speak up loud enough; your god's asleep, like enough, or may be he's taking a walk; you want to holler, you know,'—or words to that effect; I don't recollect the exact language. Mind, I don't apologize for Isaac; he had his faults.

"Well, the prophets of Baal prayed along the best they knew how all the afternoon, and never raised a spark. At last, about sundown, they were all tuckered out, and they owned up and quit.

"What does Isaac do now? He steps up and says to some friends of his, there, 'Pour four barrels of water on the altar!' Everybody was astonished; for the other side had prayed at it dry, you know, and got white-washed. They poured it on. Says he, 'Heave on four more barrels.' Then he says, 'Heave on four more.' Twelve barrels, you see, altogether. The water ran all over the altar, and all down the sides, and filled up a trench around it that would hold a couple of hogsheads,—'measures,' it says; I reckon it means about a hogshead. Some of the people were going to put on their things and go, for they allowed he was crazy. They didn't know Isaac. Isaac knelt down and began to pray: he strung along, and strung along, about the heathen in distant lands, and about the sister churches, and about the state and the country at large, and about those that's in authority in the government, and all the usual programme, you know, till everybody had got tired and gone to thinking about something else, and then, all of a sudden, when nobody was noticing, he outs with a match and rakes it on the under side of his leg, and pff! up the whole thing blazes like a house afire! Twelve barrels of *water? Petroleum*, sir, PETROLEUM! that's what it was!"

"Petroleum, captain?"

"Yes, sir; the country was full of it. Isaac knew all about that. You read the Bible. Don't you worry about the tough places. They ain't tough when you come to think them out and throw light on them. There ain't a thing in the Bible but what is true; all you want is to go prayerfully to work and cipher out how 't was done."

# The Case of Jack the Clipper, or A Fimbulwinter's Tale

## David Langford

L ife is filled with bodings and portents. When I encountered my old acquaintance Smythe in the High Street I sensed that my own life was about to take some strange new turning . . . specifically, into the King's Head lounge bar, where with old-fashioned courtesy the renowned specialist in the uncanny reminded me that it was my shout.

"Cheers," I said a minute later, as we sat and sipped our bitter.

*"Ph'nglui mglw'nafh Cthulhu R'lyeh wgah'nagl fhtagn,"* he responded eruditely; these occultists know many unfamiliar toasts. "I have just been picking up my new business cards—here, allow me to present you with one."

I studied the ornately engraved slip of pasteboard. *Dagon Smythe, Psychic Investigator.* "I can only admire the Seal of Solomon hologram . . . but, *Dagon* Smythe?"

"It is often advantageous, in this hazardous line of work, to have been prudent in one's choice of godparents. But stay! As a trained observer, I see that you have torn the sleeve of your jacket, probably on a protruding nail. I am reminded . . ."

"Is *that* the time?" I cried with the spontaneity that comes of long practice. "Well, I really must—"

"I am reminded," said Smythe inexorably, placing a gentle but firm hand on my forearm, "of a certain rather curious investigation in which nails played an interesting role. Nails, and old gods, and the end of the world."

"Why, yes! I remember that case well. One of your finest. The crooked occult-supplies house that used scanning tunnelling microscope technology to dismantle a nail from the True Cross into its individual atoms, enabling them to flood the market with countless billions of genuine if very tiny talismans and . . ."

"A different case, my friend, and a different kind of nail. This was some years ago in the small old town of F—— which lies close to D—— in the county of B——. It was there that I investigated a weird reign of nightly terror. You must imagine the town's twisty streets swirling with late autumn fogs, so that every passer-by appeared as an eerie, phantasmal silhouette. And any one of those shadows in the night might be the creature that had earned the nickname . . . Jack the Clipper."

"Ripper?" I enquired.

"Clipper. For, time and again, the men (never the women) of that accursed town would report dim memories of a particularly strange shape that loomed through icy fog. A shape with a hint of flickering flame about it, no sooner perceived than lost in a mysterious tumble into unconsciousness. Then, seconds or minutes afterwards, the victim would find himself sprawled on the chilly stone of the pavement, his shoes and socks mysteriously removed in that interlude of missing time, and—sinister and eldritch beyond all imagining—*his toenails neatly clipped.*"

At this point, being caught in mid-gulp, I suffered a regrettable accident with my pint of bitter.

"You laugh, do you? You laugh?"

"Some of the beer went the wrong way," I lied, shaking my head determinedly.

"Shallow and innocent person that you are, ignorant of all occult implication, you laughed. It is not so funny when you recollect that nail-clippings—the *exuviae* coveted by witches—play an important part in rituals of binding, of magical domination. And this elusive Jack the Clipper had struck again and again, night after night, amassing these means of sorcerously controlling what might ultimately prove to be the entire male population of the town of F——." He shuddered dramatically. "The hidden hand that wielded such control had the potential for unleashing very great evil indeed, up to and including a by-election victory for the Conservative Party. No . . . this was indeed no laughing matter."

I nodded dutifully. "And, er, this kind of voodoo control with sympathetic magic and waxen dolls and toenails, this was indeed the secret behind what was happening?"

"Oddly enough, it was not." Smythe drained his glass and placed it meaningfully on the table. I did the same, a trifle more meaningfully. There was a short pause.

*   *   *

Abruptly he continued: "You will remember my fervent belief in the value of applying the full range of modern technology to problems of occult investigation. I pioneered the Laser Pentacle, which out-did dear old Carnacki's electric version by vaporizing the more susceptible ab-human manifestations even as they attempted to pass through the wards. It was I who designed what has become the standard electronic probe for registering demonic presences, the Baphometer. Now the town of F—— offered an opportunity to field-test my experimental, computerized zombie spotter."

"Pardon?" Sometimes my friend's uncanny intuitive leaps eluded me.

"This mechanism was inspired by what students of artificial intel-ligence call the Eliza Effect . . . a shorthand for a kind of mental blindness which most human minds share. ELIZA is a rudimentary computer program which tries to imitate a psychotherapist—you type in something like 'WOULD YOU LIKE A DRINK?'—"

"Yes please," I said, quick as a flash; and quick as a flash, Smythe ignored me.

"—and the ELIZA program might come back with 'WHY DO YOU THINK I WOULD LIKE A DRINK?', or throw in some random question like 'WHAT MAKES YOU SAY THAT?' or 'INPUT ERROR $FF0021 REDO FROM START?' All very *mechanical* and uncreative. But such is the power of wishful thinking—the Eliza Effect—that it's incredibly easy to fall into the belief that the program's responses come from some real intelligence."

"From some real intelligence," I repeated intelligently.

"This, of course, is how zombies routinely pass in modern soci-ety: they have no more true conversation than ELIZA, but our natu-ral, human weakness is to give them the benefit of the doubt. My zombie spotter, though, is a pocket computer with a speech-recognition facility. It lacks any power of wishful thinking. It analy-ses conversations with cold logic, and reports when the responses are sufficiently simple, repetitive and content-free—as is the case with zombies, and with minds whose free will has been overlaid by some form of malign poppetry, voodoo, or other sorcerous control. With this device—"

Here Smythe seemed to remember something, and mumbled briefly in what I took to be Gaelic. I felt suddenly impelled to carry the empty beer-glasses to the bar, order two fresh pints of Ticklepenny's Old Ichorous, and bring them to our table.

"With this device in my pocket," Smythe went on after several grateful sips, "I sampled the population of F——, entering into numerous conversations in the local public houses, identifying victims of Jack the Clipper, and surreptitiously assessing the speakers' Zombie Quotient."

"You bought drinks for 'numerous' people!?" I said, aghast. Smythe's parsimony was famous in our little circle of friends.

"Er . . ." The eminent occultist looked momentarily embarrassed. "Actually I used an old Irish charm I'd learned in my travels—a tiny *geas* that compels the hearer to acts of senseless generosity. It's quite harmless, although it does slightly lower the intelligence of the subject."

I didn't quite follow this odd explanation, and after puzzling over it for a few moments I indicated that Smythe should continue his fascinating narrative.

"On the whole, my zombie scan simply drew a blank. Of course there were a few significant ZQ readings from individuals whose higher brain functions had been depressed by excess alcohol, extreme fatigue or compulsive perusal of *The Sun*. But there was just no sign of the widespread occult control which I'd feared."

"Oh, bad luck. One of your rare failures, then."

"Failure? Am I not a scientific investigator? Was I to be discouraged by the slaying of my initial hypothesis by ugly fact? Never! However, I confess that I found myself momentarily at a loss; and so I determined to seek a new line of attack by the traditional means of haruspication."

I pondered that word. "What, cutting out someone's entrails? Did you call for volunteers, or something? 'Intrepid investigator needs men with guts.'"

"Tut, tut. Haruspication is the *examination* of entrails for hints of things to come. The definition says nothing about cutting them out. That was merely an unfortunate necessity imposed on the ancients by lack of appropriate technology. As you say, I called for an amply paunched volunteer, a recent victim of Jack the Clipper. The rest was merely a matter of a little influence and a little bribery at a convenient hospital which possessed . . ." he paused dramatically . . . "an ultrasound scanner."

"Excellent!" I cried.

"Elementary," said he. "Interpreting the convolutions of intestines which are quivering and peristalsing in real time is something of a specialist craft, I must remark, but well worth anyone's study.

Long and hard I gazed into the ultrasound scan display, as one delusive word after another took shape in those loops and coils. And this—" he turned over the business card still lying on the table, and scribbled on its back— "*this* is the word that I finally read there."

I took up the card. "*Naglfar?* . . . You're quite sure it isn't a misprint?"

"That one word, my friend, should have told you the whole story, had you been the ideal reasoner which, in fact, I am."

"It's an anagram of 'flagrant'? Well, nearly."

"It was sufficient, when I had thought things through, to persuade me to make a few unusual purchases: scuba gear, cylinders of oxygen and Halon 1301, the makings of a protective pentacle, and a small pair of toenail clippers.

"Picture me now, that night in my room at the town's one hotel, the Marquis of G——. I stood at the centre of an improvised defence pentacle which, for a particular reason, was picked out in ice cubes. I nervously checked the oxygen flow in the scuba rig, I struck a small flame from my cigarette lighter, and I cast my clipped toenails out across the psychic defences with the trembling words, 'An offering to you, oh Loki!'

"And, as I had hardly dared to hope, the god Loki appeared, emerging somehow from the fiery interior of the central heating pipes. Being a trickster deity, he had adopted the aspect of a used car salesman, but with hot flame flickering in his eyes. His questioning gaze seemed to burn through my skin.

" 'I read the clues,' I said. 'Jack the Clipper preys on men and never on women, and as the world's foremost occult investigator I know my Norse myths. The *Naglfar* is the ship made of men's nails which you are fated to steer through the sea that rises to engulf the land when all Earth is destroyed in the final days of Ragnarok. Of course you chose toenails rather than fingernails, owing to their superior quality as a maritime construction material. But I've no idea why you should collect the wherewithal to build that dread vessel in a dull town like this.'

" 'Trickster gods are allowed to be as silly and capricious as they like,' Loki explained, stepping forward: 'And *of course* I picked an obscure place where Odin wouldn't think to look.' The words emerged in individual gouts of flame, reminiscent of a circus fire-eater with hiccups. 'Ouch. By Niflheim!' Being also a fire god, my visitor did not relish the ice pentacle . . . but nevertheless slowly forced his way through my wards in a cloud of hissing steam. His nostrils literally flared. 'I should add that fire gods have this regrettable habit of slowly incinerating mortals who ask impertinent questions.'

"But I had already clapped the scuba mask to my face and released the valve on that Halon 1301 cylinder. The occult words of banishment which I pronounced—the unknown last line of the Maastricht agreement—were drowned in the hiss of escaping gas and might or might not have been effective. But I think I have successfully ascertained that fire gods particularly detest an atmosphere that's rich in fire-inhibiting Halon. Before he could reach me, Loki fizzled and shrank and went out like, if you'll excuse the cliché, a light.

"And so the mystery was solved. The town of F—— heard no more of Jack the Clipper. Perhaps the fiery prankster's sinister work continues elsewhere in the world. . . ."

"A truly remarkable farrago," I mumbled, my head still spinning slightly.

"All of which explains my new-found interest in cryonics," said Smythe with an air of considerable smugness.

"Of course," I replied weakly, determined not to ask the obvious question. My friend was visibly too pleased with himself to prolong the suspense any further.

"I have a notion, you see, that Loki the trickster was also maliciously sowing trouble for the gods themselves. The whole Norse pantheon is notoriously bound up in chains of unescapable fate. That which is written will be . . . and one of the things clearly written about the *Naglfar* is that it will be made of *dead* men's nails. So, you see, the end of the world, Ragnarok, can't come to pass until all those victims of 'Jack the Clipper'—men whose toenails are built into the fateful ship—are safely dead."

"Oh, wonderful. The world's safe for another—what?—fifty years?"

"Forever, perhaps, if some of those toenail donors are kept cryonically preserved at liquid-nitrogen temperatures. You must know that some people actually *pay* to be frozen in hope of eternity. So I am currently working to make certain lucrative arrangements with sympathetic Scandinavian governments, in hope of financing cryonics projects which could hold off Ragnarok indefinitely. You may be sitting with—and, indeed, about to buy another drink for—the saviour of this world." Smythe gave a little bow.

A single, tiny fragment of Norse myth had meanwhile floated to the surface of my own mind. "Ah . . . Smythe. According to those same legends, one of the fated circumstances that leads up to Ragnarok and the last battle is the Fimbulwinter. A deep, unnatural winter. A long period of intense and artificial cold. Um, are you sure your cryonics scheme isn't already part of what's written?"

For the first time since I'd known him, Smythe looked nonplussed.

# Chalk Talk

Edward Wellen

**M**aybe because it was May. But Professor Rood felt carbonated blood bubble-dance through his veins. It gave such bounce to his morning greeting of his tall leathery colleague and rival, Professor Kriss, when they met in the hallway that he drew a look of surprise.

Maybe because Zoë Albemarle—the chalk broke twice before he got hold of himself and used the proper pressure—sat in class in an even more revealing dress than usual.

Maybe it was feeling the potency of mind over matter and of energy over both.

In any case, he found himself launching into his old lecture on linguistics with new zest.

"Thanks to Noam Chomsky and Transformational Grammar, we learn that—" He chalked on the blackboard:

> John loves Mary.
> Mary is loved by John.

"—which is one sentence, in its active and passive voices, is merely the 'surface structure' of the sentence.

"We may think we see it plain, as *from* a plane—" He waited till laughter had manifested itself, then went on. "—the solid green of a rain forest. But below the surface are the reelings and writhings that make the floor of a Freudian jungle a lively place. Dr. Chomsky calls this underneathness, this grimmer grammar, the 'deep structure.'

"But it is just here where things are getting interesting that Dr. Chomsky fails us. At least, in spite of his computer readouts and world view, he has not made clear to me the nature of this deep structure. He tells us that the foundations of all languages are a finite set of innate universals. But just what are these universals?

"As I hesitate to break in on Dr. Chomsky and his greater concerns to ask him for—to follow the forest metaphor—'clear-cutting,' I've been trying to work it out for myself.

"I began by fantasying the deep structure. I've said it's a Freudian jungle, and I won't describe it except to say I was damn happy to hack my way out. After that bum trip I withdrew to the comparative safety and sanity of surface structure."

Another pause for laughter to manifest itself. It manifested itself delightfully through Zoë Albemarle.

Where was he? Ah, yes.

"I might have vegetated there, forever unable to see the trees for the forest. But luckily surface structure lends itself Proteus-like to variations. Of these the most promising seemed—" He chalked:

> John generates love for Mary.
> Mary attracts love from John.

"This at once suggested an electromagnetic infrastructure, quite in keeping with the make-up of the brain. Hardly a breakthrough, however. Then it struck me. In changing 'love' from verb to noun, I had stumbled across an innate universal!

"Long before the Industrial Revolution, man had the feeling things are taking over, or at least have a will of their own. Picture Neanderthal Man chipping a flint and blaming a skinned knuckle on the perversity of the material or the tool. Love, of course, is not a thing but a process. Still, this *further* formulation of the sentence gives a true sense of the underlying nature of this depersonalized world in which we are all strangers." He chalked:

> Love connects John to Mary.
> Mary is connected to John by love.

There it was, in white and black. And it had finished itself right on time. The classroom began emptying. He stood looking at the writing on the blackboard. Carve *that* on a tree, Noam, he thought with a smile. The smile was as much for Zoë Albemarle lingering in the tail of his eye. His chest swelled, sending the dribbles of chalk on his jacket flying in a cloudy cascade.

"Yes, my dear?" The voice did not sound quite like his own.

Zoë leaned plumply toward him.

"There's this I don't understand, Professor Rood—" She pointed to the blackboard.

He dusted his fingers and reached out to touch her.

Then it happened.

Zoë screeched.

He saw the writing on the blackboard shiver loose.

It slid down the slate, tripped the eraser off the ledge, followed the eraser to the floor, gathered itself, then struck out for the doorway. Zoë had beat it out and vanished. It flowed over floorboards, doorsill, floorboards, slithering along the hallway toward Professor Kriss's classroom.

Professor Rood trailed his handwriting. Stooping and straining to see, he thought it crawled along on tiny rootlike pseudopodia. In the mud at the bottom of the sea a living jelly feeds, grows, and multiplies. It takes carbonate of lime from the brine to make a skeleton for itself. The jelly dies and rots and adds its skeletal corpse's mite to the chalk deposit that has been building since long before the coming of man. This living jelly puts forth rootlike pseudopodia.

Professor Kriss's classroom was empty but for Professor Kriss sitting at her desk over student papers. She did not look up as the chalking climbed baseboard and wall and, an inverted waterfall, streamed up over the ledge and onto the blackboard.

She looked up as Professor Rood's shadow fell across her desk and found him staring at the blackboard. Professor Kriss followed his gaze.

Six times the sentence had written itself:

John loves Mary.

Mary Kriss got up, and up, and nearly swept John Rood off his feet in a hug.

"Why didn't you say so before, John?"

# A Change of Lifestyle

### Joe and Karen Lansdale

Got up this morning and couldn't take it anymore. I'd had all the cutesy words and hugs I could take from the old bag, and I'd also had it with my food. She thought that just because I liked something once, I couldn't wait to have it every day.

Course, it beat hell out of that McWhipple burger I got out of the next-door neighbor's trash can. I saw him toss it out, and as I recall, he was looking mighty green and holding his stomach. Didn't bother me none, though; I'd eaten out of his trash can before. (He even took a shot at me one night on account of it.) But this McWhipple burger would have made a vulture choke! Must've been kangaroo meat or something. Or maybe the burger had just been lying on the assembly line too long. In any case, it sure made me sick, and up until then I could eat anything short of strychnine.

See, that's part of the problem. Suddenly I couldn't stand the way I'd been living. Just came over me, you know? One day I was fine and happy as a tick in an armpit, and the next day things were no longer hokay-by-me. I wanted a change of lifestyle.

It was all so goofy . . . the way I was feeling in the head, I thought maybe I'd got some medical problems, you know? So first thing I thought of was to go see the doc. Figured I ought to do that before I made any drastic changes—changes like getting the old lady out of my life, finding a new place to live, that sort of thing. I just wanted to make sure I wasn't having a spell of some sort, one of them metabolistic shake-ups.

So the doc was the ticket. I mean, he'd always been nice to me. A few pills and needles, but that's to be expected, right?

Next problem was getting out of the house without making a scene. Old gal treated me like some sort of prisoner, and that didn't make it easy.

The window over the sink was open, though, and that's how I plotted my escape. It was hard for me to get my body up and through the opening, but I managed. Made the six-foot drop without so much as a sprained ankle.

I got my thoughts together, charted out the doc's office, and set out. On the way, I noticed something weird: not only was I having this change in attitude, I seemed to be having some physical problems, too. I could feel stuff shifting around inside me, the way you feel the wind when it changes.

When I finally reached the doc's, man, was I bushed. Caught this lady coming out with a white cat under her arm, and she looked at me like I was the strange one. I mean, here she was with a cat under her arm, things hanging off her ears and wrists and wearing as much war paint as an Indian in a TV western, and she looks at me like I'm wearing a propeller beanie or something.

I slid in before she closed the door, and I looked around. People were sitting all over the place, and they had their pets with them. Dogs, cats, even a pet monkey.

I suddenly felt mighty sick, but I figured the best thing to do was to hang tough and not think about my problem. I decided to get a magazine down from the rack, but I couldn't get one down. Couldn't seem to hold on to it.

People were staring.

So were their pets.

I decided the heck with this and went right over to the receptionist. Standing on my hind legs, I leaned against the desk and said, "Listen, sweetheart, I've got to see the doc, and pronto."

"Oh, my God!" she screamed. "A talking Siberian husky!" Then she bounced her appointment book off one of my pointy ears.

Was this any way to run a veterinarian's office?

Man, did that place clear out fast. Nothing but a few hairs—dog, cat, and blue rinse—floating to the floor.

The doc obviously wasn't the ticket. I cleared out of there myself and ran three blocks on my hind legs before I realized it. I felt good, too. Problem was, it tended to stop traffic.

I got down on all fours again, and though it hurt my back, I walked like that until I got to the park. As soon as I reached it, I stood up on my hind legs and stretched my back. I tell you, that felt some better.

There was a bum sitting on a park bench tipping a bottle, and when he lamped me coming toward him, he jumped up, screamed, and ran away, smashing his bottle on a tree as he went.

Sighing, I took his place on the bench, crossed my legs, and noticed that a fleshy pink knee was poking up through a rip in my fur. Man, what next?

There was a newspaper lying beside me, and having nothing better to do, I picked it up. Didn't have a lick of trouble holding it. My toes had lengthened now, and my dew claw could fold and grasp. The hair on the back of my paws had begun to fall off.

The paper was the morning edition. The first article that caught my eye was about this guy over on Winchester—and why not? That was right next door to from where I'd been living with the old hag. It was the fellow who'd tossed out the hamburger.

Seems he went weird. Woke up in the middle of the night and started baying at the moon through his bedroom window. Later on he got to scratching behind his ears with his feet, even though he was still wearing slippers. Next he got out of the house somehow and started chasing cars. Lady finally had to beat him with a newspaper to make him stop—at which point he raised his legs and peed on her, then chased the neighbor's cat up a tree.

That's when the old lady called the nut-box people.

By the time they got there the guy'd gotten a case of hairy knees, a wet nose, and a taste for the family dog's Gravy Train. In fact, the man and the dog got into a fight over it, and the man bit the rat terrier's ear off.

Yeeecccchhh—fighting over Gravy Train! They can have the stuff. Give me steak and 'taters.

Lady said she didn't know what had gone wrong. Said he'd gone to bed with a stomach ache and feeling a bit under the weather. And why not?—he'd got hold of a week-old hamburger from McWhipple's that she'd set on top of the refrigerator and forgotten about. Seems this guy was a real chow hound and went for it. Ate a couple of big bites before his taste buds had time to work and he realized he was chomping sewer fodder.

Ouch and flea bites! That must have been the same green meat I got a bite of.

I tossed the paper aside and patted my chest for a cigarette. No pockets, of course.

Just then, my tail fell off. It went through the slats in the park bench and landed on the ground. I looked down and saw it turn to dust, hair and all, till a little wind came along and whipped it away.

Man, some days the things that happen to you shouldn't happen to a dog.

# Chasing the Ugly Dog

## Tom Piccirilli

They are producing a play and the play is working on their minds, drawing up archetypes from their collective unconsciousness the way Jung first described it. The curtain goes up on a pale half moon and a few cardboard gray cutouts.

"No, no, wrong, all wrong," the director shouts, stamping his foot. The stage manager gives him a tired look, the old, Uy uy auyy, what now? . . . his fists futilely working the air in empty gestures. The two men wave their scripts around for a while and finally throw them into the empty orchestra pit, now yelling back and forth, disgusted.

"Full moon and no clouds!"

"Just how many times do we have to go through this?" Again? . . . no, no way, my pancreas is killing me, the stage manager asserts, but he knows he must give in; he is young, and the rule is to bend until you are old, then break in front of the young so they know what's waiting for them. The director searches his pockets. "Where's my blood pressure pills? Yes, again, of course again, once more. Stop holding your pancreas."

Blackout.

This is how it begins, sometimes, most of the time in fact, in the darkness and comfort of seventh row center. Between eight and eight-twenty in the morning the dream starts, now, heavy in Patterford's mind, on the bus. For weeks there's been only one non-erotic dream he can remember—he tries hard to forget—but it's not a recurring dream, and it no longer dissipates after he wakes up.

It is almost continuous, this dream, always in the same vein, like a series of books being written by a man who types badly, one volume after another, the wods to o bdly mps-spele d to mean anything much after a while. On the bus Patterford rubs his head against the cool window.

"Masher!"

He takes his head off the fat woman's shoulder and rubs his face in his hands, trying to sort out the contents of his thoughts, but the images scamper away. From out of his childhood it has come looking for him, the nightmare, of that much he's certain. As if a pop-up storybook from the past is jumping at his face, he feels that the Gingerbread man that scared him at age four is close by, waiting to take over. Maybe the subtext is hiding his symbols, but the symbols are so faded they are lost on him now (Freud chases after them down an alleyway and is splashed by the bus going through a rain-filled pothole; he spins quickly but is too late, the Id is gone) (he turns once more and is goosed by a prostitute named Cassandra; Freud is so smitten that within three days they have moved into a condo together). But that's not right either.

It feels more real than that, this nightmare. It goes:

Curtain up on a bright full moon, the cloudless sky. The wind is tearing leaves from the top of the highest treetops. The rain has stopped but the ground is muddy, and there's a countryside of rainy summer night before him—shabby elms scattered across a shadowy field, the corn rows in the distance, high grass all around. Patterford's thirteen and dressed in his good Sunday clothes: a jacket, tie, shoes. He's been running for a long time and he's tired, but he could keep going if only he knew in which direction to head. Nervous jitters in his arms and legs are throwing off his step and speed, his breathing is erratic, bordering on hyperventilation.

There is a friendly dog barking behind him. No growls or snarling, just frisky romp barks calling for him to come and play. Patterford, as a kid—(Freud nods and, having found one of the elusive symbols, kneels down to pet the ugly dog. It's a basset hound with wildly drooping eyes that nearly pull its face off its head; Cassandra is lying in bed, her robe gracelessly open [how he wishes she wouldn't use so much lipstick])—falls and hits the ground hard, then lies there in the mud catching his breath. His hair drips into his eyes and he wants to sleep, but he keeps moving. His chest and stomach hurt, and he takes the time to undo the tie, throwing it aside.

The tie hits the stage manager in the face and the director smirks. Patterford (still a kid) (Freud still petting the ugly dog) can feel the shoes rubbing the skin off his ankles, but he knows there's rough terrain ahead and it's best to leave them on.

The bus stops at twenty-fifth and the driver yells at a teenager trying to slip on without paying. Behind the teenager is Patterford's lover from almost fourteen years ago, holding a leash and leading a basset hound up the steps. The teenager can't get out with the lady and the dog in the way, and Patterford's former lover can't get on the bus until the foul-mouthed adolescent stops getting smacked in the chest by the red-faced bus driver. It's one of those bad situations everyone is getting used to in the city. Patterford is about to get up when the driver finally lifts up the little guttersnipe, tosses him over the ugly dog, and shuts the door.

Patterford and the lady had been reckless lovers once, but it was clear she didn't remember him. She'd been getting on his bus for about three months now; at first he thought she had noticed him and was simply too uncomfortable to approach him, so he waited to see if she would stop taking this bus or would come over to him and attempt to start up some feeble conversation.

But he was wrong, she didn't know him. The dog, however, did recognize him, and always became frisky when seeing him. Each morning, between eight and eight-twenty, the floppy-eared basset hound would pull at its leash trying to get to him, tail wagging, playfully barking. Patterford had bought that dog for his lover a long time ago when they were kids, and its eyes, like its age, reminded him of things best left in the past which he didn't want to think about. (Freud makes a notation. Cassandra puts on more lipstick.)

The ugly dog begins to bark again, straining its chain, forcing the lady to chastise the animal, smacking it forcelessly between its batwing ears. Patterford feels sorry for the dog he had bought with the money he'd been saving to get himself a fishing pole. The bus passes a bakery and Patterford smells fresh cookies, and again he thinks of the Gingerbread man; with amazing abruptness the fear enfolds him like Cassandra's robe and the smell of lipstick enfolds Freud, Freud's note pad, and the ugly dog. Heading toward midtown the dog begins to quiet down and Patterford knows his ex-lover will be getting off at fifty-seventh.

The stage manager and the director stop giving each other paranoid glances and sit back to watch the prostitute begin to dance, carefully—without music—around Freud and the stumpy-legged dog, weaving like night.

Patterford (always this kid) is sitting on a pile of rocks, scratching softly at the welts on his ankles, his Sunday shoes killing him. Behind him he hears a girl singing—her voice is coming closer. He scrambles off the boulders in hopes of finding a hiding spot for himself, down there maybe, in what looks to be a cave; his head is pounding, he's not exactly sure what it is that is closing in on him, why this is happening. At thirteen he does not like caves, he likes to fish. The dog saunters off to do what it has to do.

"Augh!" the director screams. "Get somebody to clean that up, and get me a paper towel!" Freud cannot write fast enough to make all the notes he wants, and Cassandra tousles his hair with her fingers, tickling him, twisting beneath the open robe, slithery. The stage manager really likes her. Patterford (the kid), in the cave, covers his ears, shutting his eyes tightly as the haunting song falls on him and kisses his face, tugs at his belt buckle, and he opens his eyes and looks up into the face of his former lover (now only a kid too, a soon-to-be lover, in like five minutes) smiling at him, lovingly, wanting, pushing her mouth against his and nibbling at his tongue—which he cannot fathom—frightening him even worse than before, knowing he will never get his fishing pole now.

Cassandra misses a beat in the rhythm and accidentally steps on the basset hound's paw; the ugly dog yelps and goes after her calf, which somehow also tastes of lipstick; Freud can't handle getting everything that is pertinent, his pencil is crumbling in his hand, the notebook paper shredding beneath the weight of all he has discovered in the Id—too many symbols . . . these representations so distinguished, all so pertinent to his own microcosm—and he is too greedy to call in Jung.

Jung runs in with the director's paper towels. Patterford sees his lover leave the bus at fifty-seventh, alone. Sitting on the seat, watching him closely, remains the ugly dog. The basset hound cocks its head at him and, in its weary eyes, Patterford notices a gleam of forgiveness.

"Get away from me!" Cassandra shrieks, kicking at the mutt. "I can't take this, I can't take any more!" To which Freud responds, "What, what? . . . more paper, dear." She pushes him away but the ugly dog is now chewing on the edge of her robe, so that she's trapped between notebook and slobbering symbol. With a cry of anguish she tears off the robe, yanks open the rear door of the theater trying to escape and goes fluttering out onto the street, leaving the stage manager with his mouth open, leaving the director wiping down his shoes. The proscenium archway is beginning to sink, but no one cares about that now. Jung is grinning.

Freud wants to scream but he cannot find his voice as he stares at his notes in horror—the papers are all covered with pencil scratches he can't decipher—he runs outside, snakes his hand forward trying to stop Cassandra from leaving him. He grabs her by the hair.

"Philistine!"

He lets go of the fat woman's hair as she gets off the bus and reaches again for the love of his life, only to find that he is too late, she has gotten on as the bus pulls away from the curb. The ugly dog licks at the windowpane as the bus goes by—Patterford waves so long.

Freud, wondering where to go now, what to do, throws his arms up. He hails a taxi to follow the bus, hoping to find his love, swearing to never invade another Id, wanting, yes, daring to regain some of the symbols which had once composed his life. Freud lights a cigar, and Jung starts the meter.

"Step on it, Carl," Freud says.

Jung sighs and tells him, "Those things'll kill you."

Blackout.

Curtain.

The standing ovation deafens the Gingerbread man, who sits contentedly in seventh row center.


# Christmas Afternoon

### Robert C. Benchley

*(Done in the Manner, If Not the Spirit, of Dickens)*

What an afternoon! Mr. Gummidge said that, in his estimation, there never had *been* such an afternoon since the world began, a sentiment which was heartily endorsed by Mrs. Gummidge and all the little Gummidges, not to mention the relatives who had come over from Jersey for the day.

In the first place, there was the *ennui*. And such *ennui* as it was! A heavy, overpowering *ennui*, such as results from a participation in eight courses of steaming, gravied food, topping off with salted nuts which the little old spinster Gummidge from Oak Hill said she never knew when to stop eating—and true enough she didn't—a dragging, devitalizing *ennui*, which left its victims strewn about the living-room in various attitudes of prostration suggestive of those of the petrified occupants in a newly unearthed Pompeiian dwelling; an *ennui* which carried with it a retinue of yawns, snarls and thinly veiled insults, and which ended in ruptures in the clan spirit serious enough to last throughout the glad new year.

Then there were the toys! Three and a quarter dozen toys to be divided among seven children. Surely enough, you or I might say, to satisfy the little tots. But that would be because we didn't know the tots. In came Baby Lester Gummidge, Lillian's boy, dragging an electric grain-elevator which happened to be the only toy in the entire collection which appealed to little Norman, five-year-old son of Luther, who lived in Rahway. In came curly-headed Effie in frantic and throaty disputation with Arthur, Jr., over the possession of an articulated zebra. In came Everett, bearing a mechanical ne-gro which would no longer dance, owing to a previous forcible feeding by the baby of a marshmallow into its only available aper-ture. In came Fonlansbee, teeth buried in the hand of little Or-mond, which bore a popular but battered remnant of what had once been the proud false-bosom of a hussar's uniform. In they all came, one after another, some crying, some snapping, some pull-ing, some pushing—all appealing to their respective parents for aid in their intra-mural warfare.

And the cigar smoke! Mrs. Gummidge said that she didn't mind the smoke from a good cigarette, but would they mind if she opened the windows for just a minute in order to clear the room of the heavy aroma of used cigars? Mr. Gummidge stoutly maintained that they were good cigars. His brother, George Gummidge, said that he, likewise, would say that they were. At which colloquial sally both the Gummidge brothers laughed testily, thereby breaking the laughter record for the afternoon.

Aunt Libbie, who lived with George, remarked from the dark corner of the room that it seemed just like Sunday to her. An amendment was offered to this statement by the cousin, who was in the insurance business, stating that it was worse than Sunday. Murmurings indicative of as hearty agreement with this sentiment as their lethargy would allow came from the other members of the family circle, causing Mr. Gummidge to suggest a walk in the air to settle their dinner.

And then arose such a chorus of protestations as has seldom been heard. It was too cloudy to walk. It was too raw. It looked like snow. It looked like rain. Luther Gummidge said that he must be starting along home soon, anyway, bringing forth the acid query from Mrs. Gummidge as to whether or not he was bored. Lillian said that she felt a cold coming on, and added that something they had had for dinner must have been undercooked. And so it went, back and forth, forth and back, up and down, and in and out, until Mr. Gummidge's suggestion of a walk in the air was reduced to a tattered impossibility and the entire company glowed with ill-feeling.

In the meantime, we must not forget the children. No one else could. Aunt Libbie said that she didn't think there was anything like children to make a Christmas; to which Uncle Ray, the one with the Masonic fob, said, "No, thank God!" Although Christmas is supposed to be the season of good cheer, you (or I, for that matter) couldn't have told, from listening to the little ones, but what it was the children's Armageddon season, when Nature had decreed that only the fittest should survive, in order that the race might be carried on by the strongest, the most predatory and those possessing the best protective coloring. Although there were constant admonitions to Fonlansbee to "Let Ormond have that now; it's his," and to Arthur, Jr., not to be selfish, but to "give the kiddie-car to Effie; she's smaller than you are," the net result was always that Fonlansbee kept the whistle and Arthur, Jr., rode in permanent, albeit disputed, possession of the kiddie-car. Oh, that we mortals should set ourselves up against the inscrutable workings of Nature!

Hallo! A great deal of commotion! That was Uncle George stumbling over the electric train, which had early in the afternoon ceased to function and which had been left directly across the threshold. A great deal of crying! That was Arthur, Jr., bewailing the destruction of his already useless train, about which he had forgotten until the present moment. A great deal of recrimination! That was Arthur, Sr., and George fixing it up. And finally a great crashing! That was Baby Lester pulling over the tree on top of himself, necessitating the bringing to bear of all of Uncle Ray's knowledge of forestry to extricate him from the wreckage.

And finally Mrs. Gummidge passed the Christmas candy around. Mr. Gummidge afterward admitted that this was a tactical error on the part of his spouse. I no more believe that Mrs. Gummidge thought they wanted that Christmas candy than I believe that she thought they wanted the cold turkey which she later suggested. My opinion is that she wanted to drive them home. At any rate, that is what she succeeded in doing. Such cries as there were of "Ugh! Don't let me see another thing to eat!" and "Take it away!" Then came hurried scramblings in the coat-closet for overshoes. There were the rasping sounds made by cross parents when putting wraps on children. There were insincere exhortations to "come and see us soon" and to "get together for lunch some time." And, finally, there were slammings of doors and the silence of utter exhaustion, while Mrs. Gummidge went about picking up stray sheets of wrapping paper.

And, as Tiny Tim might say in speaking of Christmas afternoon as an institution, "God help us, every one."

## Christmas Eve in the Blue Chamber

### Jerome K. Jerome

I don't want to make you fellows nervous," began my uncle in a peculiarly impressive, not to say blood-curdling, tone of voice, "and if you would rather that I did not mention it, I won't; but, as a matter of fact, this very house, in which we are now sitting, is haunted."

"You don't say that!" exclaimed Mr. Coombes.

"What's the use of your saying I don't say it when I have just said it?" retorted my uncle somewhat annoyed. "You talk so foolishly. I tell you the house is haunted. Regularly on Christmas Eve the Blue Chamber," (they call the room next to the nursery the "Blue Chamber" at my uncle's) "is haunted by the ghost of a sinful man—a man who once killed a Christmas carol singer with a lump of coal."

"How did he do it?" asked Mr. Coombes, eagerly. "Was it difficult?"

"I do not know how he did it," replied my uncle; "he did not explain the process. The singer had taken up a position just inside the front gate, and was singing a ballad. It is presumed that, when he opened his mouth for B flat, the lump of coal was thrown by the sinful man from one of the windows, and that it went down the singer's throat and choked him."

"You want to be a good shot, but it is certainly worth trying," murmured Mr. Coombes thoughtfully.

"But that was not his only crime, alas!" added my uncle. "Prior to that he had killed a solo cornet player."

"No! Is that really a fact?" exclaimed Mr. Coombes.

"Of course it's a fact," answered my uncle testily. "At all events, as much a fact as you can expect to get in a case of this sort.

"The poor fellow, the cornet player, had been in the neighborhood barely a month. Old Mr. Bishop, who kept the 'Jolly Sand Boys' at the time, and from whom I had the story, said he had never known a more hard-working and energetic solo cornet player. He, the cornet player, only knew two tunes, but Mr. Bishop said the man could not have played with more vigor, or for more hours a day, if he had known forty. The two tunes he did play were 'Annie Laurie' and 'Home, Sweet Home'; and as regarded his performance of the former melody, Mr. Bishop said that a mere child could have told what it was meant for.

"This musician—this poor, friendless artist—used to come regularly and play in this street just opposite for two hours every evening. One evening he was seen, evidently in response to an invitation, going into this very house, *but was never seen coming out of it!*"

"Did the townsfolk try offering any reward for his recovery?" asked Mr. Coombes.

"Not a penny," replied my uncle.

"Another summer," continued my uncle, "a German band visited here, intending—so they announced on their arrival—to stay till the autumn.

"On the second day after their arrival, the whole company, as fine and healthy a body of men as one would wish to see, were invited to dinner by this sinful man, and, after spending the whole of the next twenty-four hours in bed, left the town a broken and dyspeptic crew; the parish doctor, who had attended them, giving it as his opinion that it was doubtful if they would, any of them, be fit to play an air again."

"You—you don't know the recipe, do you?" asked Mr. Coombes.

"Unfortunately I do not," replied my uncle; "but the chief ingredient was said to have been railway dining-room hash.

"I forget the man's other crimes," my uncle went on; "I used to know them all at one time, but my memory is not what it was. I do not, however, believe I am doing his memory an injustice in believing that he was not entirely unconnected with the death, and subsequent burial, of a gentleman who used to play the harp with his toes; and that neither was he altogether unresponsible for the lonely grave of an unknown stranger who had once visited the neighborhood, an Italian peasant lad, a performer upon the barrel-organ.

"Every Christmas Eve," said my uncle, cleaving with low impressive tones the strange awed silence that, like a shadow, seemed to have slowly stolen into and settled down upon the room, "the ghost of this sinful man haunts the Blue Chamber, in this very house. There, from midnight until cock-crow, amid wild muffled shrieks and groans and mocking laughter and the ghostly sound of horrid blows, it does fierce phantom fight with the spirits of the solo cornet player and the murdered carol singer, assisted at intervals by the shades of the German band; while the ghost of the strangled harpist plays mad ghostly melodies with ghostly toes on the ghost of a broken harp."

Uncle said the Blue Chamber was comparatively useless as a sleeping apartment on Christmas Eve.

"Hark!" said my uncle, raising a warning hand toward the ceiling, while we held our breath, and listened: "Hark! I believe they are at it now—in the Blue Chamber!"

I rose up and said that *I* would sleep in the Blue Chamber.

"Never!" cried my uncle, springing up. "You shall not put yourself in this deadly peril. Besides, the bed is not made."

"Never mind the bed," I replied. "I have lived in furnished apartments for gentlemen, and have been accustomed to sleep on beds that have never been made from one year's end to the other. I am young, and have had a clear conscience now for a month. The spirits will not harm me. I may even do them some little good, and induce them to be quiet and go away. Besides, I should like to see the show."

They tried to dissuade me from what they termed my foolhardy enterprise, but I remained firm and claimed my privilege. I was "the guest." "The guest" always sleeps in the haunted chamber on Christmas Eve; it is his right.

They said that if I put it on that footing they had, of course, no answer, and they lighted a candle for me and followed me upstairs in a body.

Whether elevated by the feeling that I was doing a noble action or animated by a mere general consciousness of rectitude is not for me to say, but I went upstairs that night with remarkable buoyancy. It was as much as I could do to stop at the landing when I came to it; I felt I wanted to go on up to the roof. But, with the help of the banisters, I restrained my ambition, wished them all good-night and went in and shut the door.

Things began to go wrong with me from the very first. The candle tumbled out of the candlestick before my hand was off the lock. It kept on tumbling out again; I never saw such a slippery candle. I gave up attempting to use the candlestick at last and carried the candle about in my hand, and even then it would not keep upright. So I got wild and threw it out the window, and undressed and went to bed in the dark.

I did not go to sleep; I did not feel sleepy at all; I lay on my back looking up at the ceiling and thinking of things. I wish I could remember some of the ideas that came to me as I lay there, because they were so amusing.

I had been lying like this for half an hour or so, and had forgotten all about the ghost, when, on casually casting my eyes round the room, I noticed for the first time a singularly contented-looking phantom sitting in the easy-chair by the fire smoking the ghost of a long clay pipe.

I fancied for the moment, as most people would under similar circumstances, that I must be dreaming. I sat up and rubbed my eyes. No! It was a ghost, clear enough. I could see the back of the chair through his body. He looked over toward me, took the shadowy pipe from his lips and nodded.

The most surprising part of the whole thing to me was that I did not feel in the least alarmed. If anything I was rather pleased to see him. It was company.

I said: "Good evening. It's been a cold day!"

He said he had not noticed it himself, but dared say I was right.

We remained silent for a few seconds, and then, wishing to put it pleasantly, I said: "I believe I have the honor of addressing the ghost of the gentleman who had the accident with the carol singer?"

He smiled and said it was very good of me to remember it. One singer was not much to boast of, but still every little helped.

I was somewhat staggered at his answer. I had expected a groan of remorse. The ghost appeared, on the contrary, to be rather conceited over the business. I thought that as he had taken my reference to the singer so quietly perhaps he would not be offended if I questioned him about the organ grinder. I felt curious about that poor boy.

"Is it true," I asked, "that you had a hand in the death of that Italian peasant lad who came to the town with a barrel-organ that played nothing but Scotch airs?"

He quite fired up. "Had a hand in it!" he exclaimed indignantly. "Who has dared to pretend that he assisted me? I murdered the youth myself. Nobody helped me. Alone I did it. Show me the man who says I didn't."

I calmed him. I assured him that I had never, in my own mind, doubted that he was the real and only assassin, and I went on and asked him what he had done with the body of the cornet player he had killed.

He said: "To which one may you be alluding?"

"Oh, were there any more then?" I inquired.

He smiled and gave a little cough. He said he did not like to appear to be boasting, but that, counting trombones, there were seven.

"Dear me!" I replied, "you must have had quite a busy time of it, one way and another."

He said that perhaps he ought not to be the one to say so; but that really, speaking of ordinary middle-class society, he thought there were few ghosts who could look back upon a life of more sustained usefulness.

He puffed away in silence for a few seconds while I sat watching him. I had never seen a ghost smoking a pipe before, that I could remember, and it interested me.

I asked him what tobacco he used, and he replied: "The ghost of cut cavendish as a rule."

He explained that the ghost of all the tobacco that a man smoked in life belongs to him when he became dead. He said he himself had smoked a good deal of cut cavendish when he was alive, so that he was well supplied with the ghost of it now.

I thought I would join him in a pipe, and he said, "Do, old man"; and I reached over and got out the necessary paraphernalia from my coat pocket and lit up.

We grew quite chummy after that, and he told me all his crimes. He said he had lived next door once to a young lady who was learning to play the guitar, while a gentleman who practiced on the bass-viol lived opposite. And he, with fiendish cunning, had intro-

74

duced these two unsuspecting young people to one another, and had persuaded them to elope with each other against their parents' wishes, and take their musical instruments with them; and they had done so, and before the honeymoon was over, *she* had broken his head with the bass-viol, and *he* had tried to cram the guitar down her throat, and had injured her for life.

My friend said he used to lure muffin-men into the passage and then stuff them with their own wares till they burst. He said he had quieted eighteen that way.

Young men and women who recited long and dreary poems at evening parties, and callow youths who walked about the streets late at night, playing concertinas, he used to get together and poison in batches of ten, so as to save expenses; and park orators and temperance lecturers he used to shut up six in a small room with a glass of water and a collection-box apiece, and let them talk each other to death.

It did one good to listen to him.

I asked him when he expected the other ghosts—the ghosts of the singer and the cornet player, and the German band that Uncle John had mentioned. He smiled, and said they would never come again, any of them.

I said, "Why, isn't it true, then, that they meet you here every Christmas Eve for a row?"

He replied that it was true. Every Christmas Eve, for twenty-five years, had he and they fought in that room; but they would never trouble him or anybody else again. One by one had he laid them out, spoiled and made them utterly useless for all haunting purposes. He had finished off the last German band ghost that very evening, just before I came upstairs, and had thrown what was left of it out through the slit between the window sashes. He said it would never be worth calling a ghost again.

"I suppose you will still come yourself, as usual?" I said. "They would be sorry to miss you, I know."

"Oh, I don't know," he replied; "there's nothing much to come for now; unless," he added kindly, "*you* are going to be here. I'll come if you will sleep here next Christmas Eve."

"I have taken a liking to you," he continued; "you don't fly off, screeching, when you see a party, and your hair doesn't stand on end. You've no idea," he said, "how sick I am of seeing people's hair standing on end."

He said it irritated him.

Just then a slight noise reached us from the yard below, and he started and turned deathly black.

"You are ill," I cried, springing toward him; "tell me the best thing to do for you. Shall I drink some brandy, and give you the ghost of it?"

He remained silent, listening intently for a moment, and then he gave a sigh of relief, and the shade came back to his cheek.

"It's all right," he murmured; "I was afraid it was the cock."

"Oh, it's too early for that," I said. "Why, it's only the middle of the night."

"Oh, that doesn't make any difference to those cursed chickens," he replied bitterly. "They would just as soon crow in the middle of the night as at any other time—sooner, if they thought it would spoil a chap's evening out. I believe they do it on purpose."

He said a friend of his, the ghost of a man who had killed a tax collector, used to haunt a house in Long Acre, where they kept fowls in the cellar, and every time a policeman went by and flashed his searchlight down the grating, the old cock there would fancy it was the sun, and start crowing like mad, when, of course, the poor ghost had to dissolve, and it would, in consequence, get back home sometimes as early as one o'clock in the morning, furious because it had only been out for an hour.

I agreed that it seemed very unfair.

"Oh, it's an absurd arrangement altogether," he continued, quite angrily. "I can't imagine what our chief could have been thinking of when he made it. As I have said to him, over and over again, 'Have a fixed time, and let everybody stick to it—say four o'clock in summer, and six in winter. Then, one would know what one was about.' "

"How do you manage when there isn't any clock handy?" I inquired.

He was on the point of replying, when again he started and listened. This time I distinctly heard Mr. Bowles' cock, next door, crow twice.

"There you are," he said, rising and reaching for his hat; "that's the sort of thing we have to put up with. What *is* the time?"

I looked at my watch, and found it was half-past three.

"I thought as much," he muttered. "I'll wring that blessed bird's neck if I get hold of it." And he prepared to go.

"If you can wait half a minute," I said, getting out of bed, "I'll go a bit of the way with you."

"It's very good of you," he replied, pausing, "but it seems unkind to drag you out."

"Not at all," I replied; "I shall like a walk." And I partially dressed myself, and took my umbrella; and he put his arm through mine, and we went out together, the best of friends.

# Cinderella

## Ring Lardner

Once upon a time they was a prominent clubman that killed his wife after a party where she doubled a bid of four diamonds and the other side made four odd, giving them game and a $26.00 rubber. Well, she left him a daughter who was beginning to run absolutely hog wild and he couldn't do nothing with her, so he married again, this time drawing a widow with two gals of her own, Patricia and Micaela.

These two gals was terrible. Pat had a wen, besides which they couldn't nobody tell where her chin started and her neck left off. The other one, Mike, got into a brawl the night she come out and several of her teeth had came out with her. These two gals was impossible.

Well, the guy's own daughter was a pip, so both her stepmother and the two stepsisters hated her and made her sleep in the ashcan. Her name was Zelda, but they called her Cinderella on account of how the ashes and clinkers clang to her when she got up noons.

Well, they was a young fella in the town that to see him throw his money around, you would of thought he was the Red Sox infield trying to make a double play. So everybody called him a Prince. Finally he sent out invitations to a dance for just people that had dress suits. Pat and Mike was invited, but not Cinderella, as her best clothes looked like they worked in a garage. The other two gals made her help them doll up and they kidded her about not going, but she got partly even by garnisheeing their hair with eau de garlic.

Well, Pat and Mike started for Webster Hall in a bonded taxi and they hadn't much sooner than went when a little bit of an old dame stepped out of the kitchen sink and stood in front of Cinderella and says she was her fairy godmother.

"Listen," says Cinderella: "don't mention mother to me! I've tried two different kinds and they've both been a flop!"

"Yes, but listen yourself," says the godmother: "wouldn't you like to go to this here dance?"

"Who and the h—l wouldn't!" says Cinderella.

"Well, then," says the godmother, "go out in the garden and pick me a pumpkin."

"You're pie-eyed," was Cinderella's criticism, but anyway she went out and got a pumpkin and give it to the old dame and the last named touched it with her wand and it turned into a big, black touring car like murderers rides in.

Then the old lady made Cinderella go to the mouse-trap and fetch her six mice and she prodded them with her wand and they each became a cylinder. Next she had her bring a rat from the rat trap and she turned him into a big city chauffeur, which wasn't hardly any trouble.

"Now," says the godmother, "fetch me a couple lizards."

So Cinderella says, "What do you think this is, the zoo?" But she went in the living-room and chose a couple lizards off the lounge and the old lady turned them into footmen.

The next thing the old godmother done was tag Cinderella herself with the wand and all of a sudden the gal's rags had become a silk evening gown and her feet was wrapped up in a pair of plate-glass slippers.

"How do you like them slippers?" asked the old dame.

"Great!" says Cinderella. "I wished you had of made the rest of my garments of the same material."

"Now, listen," says the godmother: "don't stay no later than midnight because just as soon as the clock strikes twelve, your dress will fall off and your chauffeur and so forth will change back into vermin."

Well, Cinderella clumb in the car and they was about to start when the chauffeur got out and went around back of the tonneau.

"What's the matter?" says Cinderella.

"I wanted to be sure my tail-light was on," says the rat.

Finally they come to Webster Hall and when Cinderella entered the ballroom everybody stopped dancing and looked at her pop-eyed. The Prince went nuts and wouldn't dance with nobody else and when it come time for supper he got her two helpings of stewed rhubarb and liver and he also had her laughing herself sick at the different wows he pulled. Like for instance they was one occasion when he looked at her feet and asked her what was her shoes made of.

"Plate glass," says Cinderella.

"Don't you feel no pane?" asked the Prince.

Other guests heard this one and the laughter was general.

But finally it got to be pretty near twelve o'clock and Cinderella went home in her car and pretty soon Pat and Mike blowed in and found her in the ashcan and told her about the ball and how the strange gal had come and stole the show.

"We may see her again to-morrow night," says Pat.

"Oh," says Cinderella, "is they going to be another ball?"

"Why, no, you poor sap!" says Mike. "It's a Marathon."

"I wished I could go," says Cinderella. "I could if you would leave me take your yellow dress."

The two stepsisters both razzed her, little wreaking that it was all as she could do to help from laughing outright.

Anyway they both went back to the dance the next night and Cinderella followed them again, but this time the gin made her drowsy and before she realized it, the clock was striking twelve. So in her hurry to get out she threw a shoe and everybody scrambled for it, but the Prince got it. Meanw'ile on account of it being after midnight, the touring car had disappeared and Cindy had to walk home and her former chauffeur kept nibbling at her exposed foot and annoying her in many other ways.

Well, the Prince run a display ad the next morning that he would marry the gal who could wear the shoe and he sent a trumpeter and a shoe clerk to make a house to house canvass of Greater New York and try the shoe on all the dames they could find and finally they come to the clubman's house and the trumpeter woke up the two stepsisters for a fitting. Well, Pat took one look at the shoe and seen they was no use. Mike was game and tried her best to squeeze into it, but flopped, as her dogs was also mastiffs. She got sore and asked the trumpeter why hadn't he broughten a shoe horn instead of that bugle. He just laughed.

All of a sudden him and the shoe clerk catched a glimpse of Cinderella and seen that she had small feet and sure enough, the slipper fitted her and they run back to the Prince's apartment to tell him the news.

"Listen, Scott," they says, for that was the Prince's name: "we have found the gal!"

So Cinderella and the Prince got married and Cinderella forgive her two stepsisters for how they had treated her and she paid a high-priced dentist to fix Mike up with a removable bridge and staked Pat to a surgeon that advertised a new, safe method of exterminating wens.

That is all of the story, but it strikes me like the plot—with the poor, ragged little gal finally getting all the best of it—could be changed around and fixed up so as it would make a good idear for a play.


# The Cleft

## Gahan Wilson

The monastery was located atop a huge mountain formed of one enormous rock thrusting upward at a slight angle from the surrounding plain. The top of the mountain stood a full hundred feet high. Its tilted upper surface had posed endless problems for the architects and the resulting building was at the same time both oddly beautiful and amusing to see.

If asked why this sacred edifice had been erected in such an unlikely place, a monk would explain that the eleventh Patriarch, passing by on a journey to the north, saw the Holy One in the form of shining gold standing atop the mountain pointing at the stern rock under his sandaled feet and that the Patriarch had heard Him say: "Even here, in this peculiar place, shall the Truth be known."

There was only one mode of access to the monastery from the plain beneath, and this was by way of a shallow cleft which meandered up the side of the mountain from its base to its peak. Because it zigzagged at reasonable angles and because its rough surface provided sufficient traction, the cleft formed a crude but usable natural stairway. It was, however, only wide enough to allow for the passage of a single user at a time; this limitation had led to a meticulous etiquette that had been elaborated on and added to through the centuries until the pilgrims' passage up or down the mountain was not only physically taxing but one which demanded spiritual and ritualistic exercises of extreme complexity, surrounded by a multitude of harsh enforcements.

In the early period a simple instruction by a monk stationed at the foot of the cleft sufficed to give the novice climber enough information to make his way to the top in full confidence he was ascending with complete correctness.

First the aspiring climber was instructed to listen quietly for a moment in order to hear whether a huge gong standing at the cleft's head was ringing. If he did not hear the gong he was to sound one note on an identical gong situated by his side at the cleft's foot. If he then heard the gong above ring once in reply he knew the cleft was clear for ascent, but two ringings gave warning that a personage was about to begin the process of descent and that the cleft was therefore in full use and that he would have to wait.

Once the signals indicated the way was clear, the climber was handed a small, portable gong in order to perform the secondary precaution of ringing it every fifth step along the way up and told to listen carefully for the next five steps just in case there was a reply to be heard from a descending party who was somehow on his way down in spite of the previous business with the two large gongs. If he did hear such a thing he was to turn around immediately and return to the base of the cleft as it was understood that people going down always had priority over people coming up since it was considerably more difficult for the descenders to retrace their steps, particularly if they were aged or otherwise infirm.

This simple procedure worked admirably and it is not unreasonable to speculate that it would have continued to work well up to the present day if it had been left alone, but as the good monks of the monastery found their attention drawn to the process again and again, since it was in constant usage with them, they simply could not resist adding elaborations to it.

For example, when a visiting abbot scoldingly observed that there was not a single image of the Holy One throughout the entire length of the cleft, the monks placed statues of Him at both the cleft's base and head and carved a bas-relief of Him into its middle. Some decades later it occurred to another abbot that incense should be burnt at each one of these points, and yet a third abbot composed three prayers, one to be intoned at what had come to be called the Upper Lord, one for the Middle, and one for the Bottom or Welcoming Lord.

The accumulation of these improvements seemed to cry out for the construction of a temple at each stopping place, so a lovely little one was duly set up at each place of the Three Lords, the middle one being an absolute masterpiece of cantilevering.

Of course once these edifices had been erected it seemed obvious that they called for the devising of more elaborate rituals, but the creation of each new rite only led the way to another of increased subtlety and depth, and as this process continued with the passing of time the necessary proprieties en route became so involved and required so much apparatus that no one but an advanced adept could be expected to work his way through them in a manner which would be pleasing to the increasingly watchful and ever more astoundingly expert authorities.

The answer to this was to create an entire subclass of priests whose sole duty was to see to it that the rituals of the cleft were always scrupulously performed. Anyone wishing to mount or descend it had to be accompanied by at least two of these priests attending, one to read the appropriate prayers and incantations and commit the proper sacrifices, the other to carry the large quantity of scrolls, costumes, gongs, banners, incense burners, and other equipment which was now absolutely vital for the execution of a satisfactory passage.

There were many expansions of cleft ceremonies for special occasions, the most elaborate recorded being the visit of a particularly devout and especially high-ranking dignitary in which the ascent and descent of the cleft took no less than thirteen days, required the services of some 2,438 persons, not counting the said dignitary's own personal staff and choir, and called for the sacrifice of armies of goats, uncounted wicker baskets stuffed with doves, and an elephant. This last sacrifice had to be performed at the foot of the mountain once it was realized the creature could not be fitted into the cleft itself.

A month or so after the possible excesses of this last event, at the first light of a bright morning in the spring of the year, an unlettered monk began pushing an enormous bundle wrapped in ragged fabric from the scullery, where he worked, to the edge of the mountain directly opposite the cleft.

As a growing number of other monks watched in fascination, their brother pounded several huge stakes into cracks in the rock, tied a thick rope extending from the bundle firmly around them, then pulled aside the stitched and tattered covering to reveal an enormously long rope worked into large knots at regular intervals. He kicked the rope off the edge of the mountain and stood watching calmly as it tumbled its full length and its bottom end dangled less than a foot above the ground of the plain beneath.

Saying not a single word, the scullery monk climbed down the rope, going hand over hand from knot to knot, and when he reached the ground he walked away without a backward glance, leaving his brothers above to watch him dwindle to a dot and eventually vanish into a far gully. He never returned.

The monks silently and rather furtively studied their present Patriarch, who had come among them quietly during this strange procedure. They had observed, with growing trepidation, a wide variety of expressions cross his face and were both vastly relieved and somewhat astonished when he finally broke out with a large, beaming smile.

Clasping his hands before him, and bowing in the direction the scullery monk had taken, he declared to the other monks that their brother was a precious example to them and that they must never forget what he had taught them.

Then, in order to begin the long task of commemoration which would continuously accrue over the endless centuries to come, he solemnly ordered that the stakes which held the rope's upper end be thickly coated in the purest gold.

# Deflation 2001

## Bob Shaw

Having to pay ten dollars for a cup of coffee shook Lester Perry. The price had been stabilized at eight dollars for almost a month, and he had begun to entertain an irrational hope that it would stay there. He stared sadly at the vending machine as the dark liquid gurgled into a plastic cup. His expression of gloom became more pronounced when he raised the cup to his lips.

"Ten dollars," he said. "And when you get it, it's cold!"

His pilot, Boyd Dunhill, shrugged, then examined the gold braid of his uniform in case he had marred its splendor with the unaccustomed movement of his shoulders. "What do you expect?" he replied indifferently. "The airport authorities refused the Coffee Machine Maintenance Workers' pay claim last week, so the union told its members to work to rule, and that has forced up the costs."

"But they got 100 per cent four weeks ago! That's when coffee went up to eight dollars."

"The union's original claim was for 200 per cent."

"But how could the airport pay 200 per cent, for God's sake?"

"The Chocolate Machine Workers got it," Dunhill commented.

"Did they?" Perry shook his head in bewilderment. "Was that on television?"

"There hasn't been any television for three months," the pilot reminded him. "The technicians' claim for a basic two million a year is still being disputed."

Perry drained his coffee cup and threw it into a bin. "Is my plane ready? Can we go now?"

"It's been ready for four hours."

"Then why are we hanging around here?"

"The Light Aircraft Engineers' productivity agreement—there's a statutory minimum of eight hours allowed for all maintenance jobs."

"Eight hours to replace a wiper blade!" Perry laughed shakily. "And that's a productivity deal?"

"It has doubled the number of man-hours logged at this field."

"Of course it has, if they're putting down eight hours for half-hour jobs. But that's a completely false . . ." Perry stopped speaking as he saw the growing coldness on his pilot's face. He remembered, just in time, that there was a current pay dispute between the Flying Employers' Association and the Low-wing Twin-engined Private Airplane Pilots' Union. The employers were offering 75 per cent and the pilots were holding out for 150 per cent, plus a mileage bonus. "Can you get a porter to carry my bag?"

Dunhill shook his head. "You'll have to carry it yourself. They're on strike since last Friday."

"Why?"

"Too many people were carrying their own bags."

"Oh!" Perry lifted his case and took it out across the tarmac to the waiting aircraft. He strapped himself into one of the five passenger seats, reached for a magazine to read during the flight to Denver, and then recalled that there had been no newspapers or magazines for over two weeks. The preliminaries of getting airborne took an unusually long time—suggesting that the air traffic controllers were engaged in some kind of collective bargaining—and finally Perry drifted into an uneasy sleep.

He was shocked into wakefulness by a sound of rushing air, which told him that the door of the aircraft had been opened in flight. Physically and mentally chilled, he opened his eyes and saw Dunhill standing at the yawning door. His expensive uniform was pulled into peculiar shapes by the harness of a parachute.

"What . . . what is this?" Perry said. "Are we on fire?"

"No." Dunhill was using his best official voice. "I'm on strike."

"You're kidding!"

"You think so? I just got word on the radio—the employers have turned down the very reasonable demands of the Low-wing Twin-engined Private Airplane Pilots' Union and walked out on the negotiations. We've got the backing of our friends in the Low-wing Single-engined and in the High-wing Twin-engined unions; consequently all our members are withdrawing their labor at midnight, which is about thirty seconds from now."

"But, *Boyd!* I've no 'chute—what'll happen to me?"

A look of sullen determination appeared on the pilot's face. "Why should I worry about you? You weren't very concerned about me when I was trying to get along on a bare three million a year."

"I was selfish. I see that now, and I'm sorry." Perry unstrapped himself and stood up. "Don't jump, Boyd—I'll double your salary."

"That," Dunhill said impatiently, "is less than our union is claiming."

"Oh! Well, I'll triple it then. Three times your present salary, Boyd."

"Sorry. No piecemeal settlements. They weaken union solidarity." He turned away and dived into the roaring blackness beyond the doorway.

Perry stared after him for a moment, then wrestled the door shut and went forward to the cockpit. The aircraft was flying steadily on autopilot. Perry sat down in the left-hand seat and gripped the control column, casting his mind back several decades to his days as a fighter pilot in Vietnam. Landing the aircraft himself would get him in serious trouble with the unions for strike-breaking, but he was not prepared to die just yet. He disengaged the autopilot and began to get in some much-needed flying practice.

Some thousands of feet below the aircraft, Boyd Dunhill pulled the ripcord and waited for his 'chute to open. The jolt, when it came, was less severe than he had expected, and a few seconds later he was falling at the same speed as before. He looked upward and saw—instead of a taut canopy—a fluttering bunch of unconnected nylon segments.

And, too late, he remembered the threat of the Parachute Stitchers and Packers' Union to carry out disruptive action in support of their demand for longer vacations.

"Communists!" he screamed. "You lousy Red anarchist ba . . ."
**CRUNCH!**

# Dentondagon!

## Don Webb

Had I but known that the trip to my ancestral home was fated to end in such horror, fear, loathing and yuckiness—I would not have gone. I had been pursuing my genealogical pursuits, when I discovered that the root of my mother's family sprang from Denton, Texas. As I was (as usual) between jobs, I resolved forthwith to travel to that eldritch burg looking for a distant cousin to sponge off of.

Stopping at a Stuckey's on the way, I inquired of the directions to the accursed village. The counter person was able to answer my queries, albeit whilst making a curious sign with her middle finger to ward off evil and ringing up the price of a pecan log.

My cream-colored Dodge Dart rolled into witch-haunted Denton at 4:30 in the afternoon. I parked in the public square and ventured forth to gain the lay of the land. I had scarce stepped from my vehicle when I was overcome by the strangely alien architecture surrounding the square. What a festering of obscene angles that seemed to hint at other dimensions beyond the known and to colossal bad taste as well. I staggered away from my car into the immense fleshly arms of a Denton matron. For an instant I feared I was being devoured by one of the detestable shoggoths whose existence is hinted at in the detestable *Newark Shards*.

The matron turned out not only not to be a shoggoth but was in fact Mae Bishop, a third cousin once removed. She welcomed me to Denton and said that she would take me to Denny's for a coke and some of the local cuisine.

"Everybody must go to Denny's, afterward," she said; but I was at that time unaware of the cosmic horror in that seemingly innocent remark.

She forced me to eat some of the local dishes, a slimy mucus-like concoction called okra and a hardened rugose patty called a chicken fried steak. I do not know what horrible means they used to force chickens into such servitude!

Cousin Mae suggested that I come to a family get-together tonight at 9:00. Since she looked like she might have a few bucks to spare, I agreed.

The old Bishop house had stood for a hundred years and it might stand for a hundred more.

Everyone sat around awkwardly as though waiting for a signal. They were dressed in greens and blacks, and I fancied that there was a greenish cast to their skin. My cousin Mae said, "Tonight Don becomes one of us."

There was a horrible batrachian cheer at this, and all began to rise from their chairs.

"One of us! One of us! Gabba-gabba! We accept you!"

This warm familial chanting continued as cousin Mae prepared for the ritual. Mae lifted up a section of carpet disclosing a trap-door. She raised the same and the ghoul hungering odor of moldering gym socks filled the room. My relatives began descending into the netherworld, and I was carried along by the press of bodies. Strange fungi lit the vast grotto below, in the center of which stood a ring of stones. In the center of this subterranean Stonehenge was a vast statue—an idol to some god. The god was vaguely manlike save for his beard of tentacles and the webbing of his hands and feet. But what made the most horrible impression was the careful artist's rendering to suggest that this extraterrestrial monstrosity was composed wholly of fried fish fillets. An air of palpable evil mixed with the miasma of fried foods came from this hideous idol. I knew without a doubt that this was the god Dentondagon, spoken of by the mad Arab poet Abdul Alhazred:

> That which is not baked may long lie fried,
> and after strange entrees you may wish you
>> had died!

As I turned to run for the stairs—for that visible square of sanity that was my cousins' parlor—I thought that I saw the thing open its eyes!

I ran to my car and drove like a madman out of Denton.

Now I spend my time trying to blot out that searing vision with drugs and alcohol. I have moved a dozen times (and of course have adopted a diet free of fried foods). Yet still I wonder if I really saw the idol move. I wonder yet more if my tainted blood has somehow pledged me to that horror—if my family is somehow in its oily grip. I have strange dreams—even here in my San Francisco apartment.

Wait! What is that outside my window? Can it be? Yog Sothoth save me! It is a giant hand! I smell fried fish. . . .


## Detection Perfection

### Tim Lebbon

Alex Jordan's mum always said he'd choose to urinate out of spite. On a family trip they'd invariably have to stop the car every hour, on the hour, for Alex to piss over the nettles in a ditch. Failing that he'd be sick, but that was simply because he ate too many wine gums.

The truth was, Alex pissed out of boredom. Some people slept, some turned moody or groggy. With Alex, his bladder became overactive, as if punishing him for not keeping it sufficiently entertained. It was something that *Detection Perfection* (Startup Books, £13.99) completely failed to allow for in their experts' guide to private detection. Still, Chapter Five preached use of initiative, and Alex felt a smug satisfaction as he aimed a comforting stream into a two-litre plastic bottle. His friends in work would be impressed.

The house was as it had been for the past three hours. Unchanged. Innocuous. Front downstairs light a blur in the dark, the intermittent silver flicker of a television set flashing the thin curtains. Car slightly askew in the big driveway. Alex had parked several spaces further along the street, in the shadow between streetlights, on the same side as the house he was observing. He had not opened the car door for three hours. He had let a dusting of rust spread across the bonnet over the last few months. The driver's seat was moved as far back as possible so that he could stretch his legs, preventing his muscles from sleeping or cramping. And he had taken cheese sandwiches in a foil wrapper. Chapter Three of *Detection Perfection* was entitled Stakeout. Alex had read it a dozen times.

When he'd opened his sandwiches, they were as sweaty and pungent as his feet. He had eaten them anyway, to relieve the monotony.

Sometimes, behind his square desk at the local council offices, he wondered just when his hobby-come-new-career would become more interesting. Moonlighting was a phrase he loved to use, because it conjured images of dark side-streets, cars with their lights turned off, midnight trysts with desperate clients. In the depths of boredom, it also allowed Cybil Sheppard to be sitting there with him.

It was true that most of the stories he told about his evening activities were, to say the least, embellished. Willing citizen's arrestees became knife-wielding maniacs who had to be restrained using an obscure, illegal martial art. So far, Alex's imagination had been more interesting than being a private detective. And that was saying something.

The van pulled up while Alex was in mid-flow. He hunkered down in his seat, cursing as he sprayed his hand. He tried to stop but it began to sting, so he carried on and watched.

Surely nothing to do with him. Rob Slater was inside, obviously giving his nineteen-year-old girlfriend a royal screwing, and all Alex had to do was witness, record and report (*Detection Perfection* Chapter One). There were twenty other houses in the cul-de-sac, plenty of targets for shady nocturnal visitors.

In black vans.

With darkened windows and doors that remained shut, even after the engine had been turned off.

. . . still pissing . . .

He'd drunk too much coffee. He didn't like coffee, but private detectives drank it, so he felt obliged. They smoked like power stations too, but Alex hated smoking with a vengeance. So he drank more coffee to make up for this failing.

. . . still pissing . . .

The van doors opened. All of them, simultaneously: two front, one sliding side, two back. Five shapes slid straight into shadows, mere spectres themselves. Alex stopped urinating through shock, then when he realised he had stopped, started again. The shapes converged on the house, steering their way across lawns and through hedges without penetrating any lit area. Still the flicker of the TV, manic in pop-video epilepsy.

The bottle was almost full now, warm and heavy in his hand, but still the flow continued. The men had vanished from his view, blending into the garden of the detached house. If it were not for the van, doors still open, insides blacker than black, Alex would have thought that tiredness was inviting hallucinations.

He'd almost finished pissing. In a way, he wanted to continue. If he finished, he'd have to make a decision, plan a move. At work this was easy; send this letter, withhold that one. Here, now, his mind stuttered and stammered. Here was excitement, but suddenly he'd rather boredom. At least boredom was a blank canvas on which to paint any story he wished. Excitement . . . well, that was danger.

Explosions in the night. Three, in rapid succession, so close that the last two could have been echoes. Warm splash on his hands. Flashes of light illuminating the gardens in stroboscopic snap-shots. The men squatting down below windows, sheltering black-suited bodies from the showering glass. "Christ!" Cool wetness on his legs, the bottle forgotten. Darkness again, and a brief burst of gunfire, unbelievably loud, shattering silence like a scream in a library. Echoing between executive houses, rattling windows, throwing on an occasional light. A car alarm, startled by the sudden excitement, shrilling briefly, lonesome in the distance. Then the shapes again (four?), back across the pavement, into the van, five doors whisper- ing shut. Derisive fart of exhaust fumes, then away, engine a purr even in the shattering silence.

"Shit in a hubcap," Alex muttered. A final dribble of urine spat wanly onto his abused car seat. He had the presence of mind to screw the lid onto his plastic bottle before he let out the breath he had been holding.

Across the street, a curtain twitched. A pale face ghosted a window for a moment then, seeing nothing amiss, returned to suburban dreams.

Alex was reaching for his pencil and pad

(Use a pencil, pens run out)

when his door window shattered and an arm encircled his throat.

He had never, ever believed that he would one day find himself staring into an interrogation lamp. *Ve haff vays* . . . he wanted to say, but the situation was beyond humour.

"Who are you?" a voice said as soon as Alex opened his eyes.

"Wha . . . ?"

"Who are you?" There was a shadow, behind the lamp; these people must have been born shadows. He wondered whether their mothers knew them.

"Alex."

An impatient pause. "Alex who?"

"Jordan."

"Right, Alex Jordan." More silence, this pause stretching on for so long that Alex began to get scared. Maybe they simply wanted his name to put on his toe-tag. Maybe they were filling it out even now.

"Mr Jordan, what is your connection with, or interest in Robert Slater? And please note, you have been injected with a truth drug which causes blinding pain should you lie."

Alex had never heard of this. He guessed it was possible, but nothing he had ever read or seen had suggested its existence. Thinking about it, he realised it was a pretty cool idea. "I have no interest—" he began. Then his kidneys exploded.

Later, as the pain died down, the light seemed to intensify. "Disbelief retracted, Mr Jordan. Now then. Robert Slater. Your reasons for watching him."

"I was paid to watch him," Alex muttered carefully. His insides throbbed, as if the light were slowly microwaving him.

"Paid by whom?"

He hesitated, but only for a moment. "I can't tell you that. Client confidentiality." He'd always wanted to say that, and there was no pain. Obviously omitting to tell something was not deemed as lying, as far as his physiology was concerned. Pleased with his petty victory, Alex did not see the fist come sailing past the light and connect with his nose. He felt it, but he did not see it.

"One more time. Paid by whom?"

"By his wife." He'd never talked with a crushed nose, and the pain was immense. It almost made him want to lie, to have something to take his mind off it.

Mumbled words from beyond the light; there was obviously more than one person in the room with him. "What do you know about Robert Slater's Bad Blood Cult connections?"

"What?"

"What was your involvement with the Gatwick Airport massacre? The Bad Blood attack on the House of Commons last June? Were you Slater's driver? Who is your paymaster? Are you the quartermaster for their British contingent? What do you know of—"

"Nothing! I had nothing to do with any of that. I'm a council worker!" A noise not unlike a giggle, then silence. A long silence. "Look, what's all this about. I'm a private detective—"

"I thought you said you were a council worker," the voice cut in.

"Yes. Well, I am. I mean, during the day. At night I'm a private detective."

"Magnum PI," another, deeper voice came from beyond the light. Two chuckles this time, neither of them particularly friendly.

"What did you do to Slater?" Alex asked, suddenly recalling the gunshots and explosions.

"None of your business." The voice was serious again, full of intent.

Alex's nose was hurting, his insides were still tingling, as if his whole body had pins and needles. "Well," he said, "I have to report to Mrs Slater tomorrow. On my reconnaissance. Give her the results, you know?"

"I'm sure Mrs Slater will not be worried about her unenvious matrimonial circumstances by then, Alex. Now then. We're going to let you go. But let me tell you something." And the voice threatened him, warned against talking about what he had seen and the discussion that had taken place here.

Chapter Six of *Detection Perfection* advises against taking threats seriously. They are never carried out, it says, and intimidation is the criminal's greatest weapon. In this case, however, Alex preferred to refer to Chapter Five.

He used his initiative. And vowed never to say a word.

* * *

"How'd you get your black eye, Alex? Karate fight with some Shogun assassins?"

"Fell over," Alex said. A mild thrill jolted through his body, like an electric shock from a cattle fence. Not painful, but unpleasant. He carried the tepid cup of coffee to his desk. Helen from Personnel dropped off his mail and stared open-mouthed at Alex's smudged-palette bruise.

"Alex, what the hell have you been up to? Arresting drug barons again?"

"Fell over," Alex said, smiling feebly, wincing inwardly as the twinge came again. The drug was fading, though still berating him for the fresh lies he was feeding his work colleagues. Putting the mockers on their sarcasm was a small return on the pain.

The cleaning carriage winched down in front of his window, two men wetting and drying the glass, and Alex wondered what the men in black had looked like.

The morning passed slowly and painfully. Each time he told someone he had fallen down, the flickers of pain retreated to his extremities, then became even more remote. He eventually decided that with each action the drug became more diluted, so he spent teabreak touring the open plan office and consciously telling lies. Each of them involved him falling over, but the peripherals of the story changed with each telling, just to make it less monotonous for him.

"Hear about the murders last night?" someone said as Alex passed a nook in the filing section, but he walked on without answering (murders?), pretended not to hear. It was possible that the office was bugged and the mystery men from last night would hear any discussion of his experiences, however misleading he tried to make them. He knew that bugging was an art form, now. Directional microphones, subject-active transmitters, micro-recorders. He'd read all about them.

By lunchtime, Alex could lie without pain. However, by early afternoon he found that he no longer wished to. He avoided any further queries about his swollen nose and puffy eye, took himself away to town as soon as he could. One o'clock was when he was due to meet up with Mrs Slater, if she showed. However much she had pretended to hate her husband, she had thought enough of him to hire Alex to discover whether she was being two-timed. He recalled their initial meeting: If the bastard is screwing behind my back, I'll have him killed, she had said. Shock you, does it? she had asked.

Now he was dead, she must be feeling pretty guilty. Mustn't she?

He had still not figured out what to tell her. That yes, her husband had been cheating her? Or that he was involved with the Bad Blood Cult, and had been executed by security forces because he was a threat to national security?

Which would be more hurtful?

Chapter Six of *Detection Perfection* gives hints about how to broach difficult subjects with clients. Many a husband or wife may suspect that their partner is being unfaithful, but actually being presented with solid evidence to confirm this is often extremely traumatic. One route, it says, is to present documentary evidence in nicely packaged folders. The professionalism of the job may then detract attention from its results. Something seedy and grim is made worse by being presented as such. Explicit photographs need not be divulged—merely use those sufficient to state the case. Tape or video recordings (illegal though they may be), should be held strictly in reserve, sitting on the detective's shelf at home like murders waiting to happen.

Another approach, the book states, is to go straight for the jugular. Why beat around the metaphorical bush when the truth, is the truth, is the truth? Alex was actually considering the purchase of a follow-up volume called *Documentary Truth, And How To Distort It* (Startup Books, £16.99 + £3.99 p&p), but it was a move he could only make when funds permitted. Besides, Alex was an honest man. If truth needed to be changed, he would do it himself.

The decision as to how to present his case to Mrs Slater, and what exactly to tell her, was snatched from his hands. The door to the Temple Cafe grunted open on grit left by a workman's boots and Mrs Slater marched by grease-smeared tables and teacups stained with a decade's service. "So, was he fucking her, or not?" she said. She was tall and dyed blonde, a fur hanging around her throat like a dead poodle. Each wrist was a rich vein of gold on bottle-tanned arms.

Heads turned. Then, because of the type of place this was, turned back again. The modulus of elasticity of neck skin seemed to alter according to the class of joint one frequented.

"Mrs Slater," Alex said, "may I pour you some coffee."

She shook her head. "No thanks. Champagne at home on ice. I'm just here to settle our account. So," she continued, lighting a cigarette and staring through the smoke, "was he fucking her?"

Was, she had said. Was. She knew Rob Slater was dead. And she did not seem to care.

"Mrs Slater. This has been a very awkward assignment for me. I've seen things, heard things . . . well. My mind has been opened up, I can tell you."

"Glad for you. Keep the tapes and photos, if they're that entertaining."

"I didn't mean—"

"Keep them anyway." Mrs Slater dragged so hard on her cigarette that Alex thought she was going to smoke the filter. Her cheeks puckered in as if trying to kiss each other. She stared at him for a while, her stern expression softening, though her eyes never changed. Scheming eyes, Alex thought. Hard eyes. "I'll recommend you to my friends, you know," she said. "You did a real job for me. Used your initiative."

Alex tried to feel grateful for the praise, but images of last night kept intruding, and he could only feel wretched. The gunfire, the light, drowning in pain after the fist had flattened his nose.

"Put up a bit of a fight, did he?" Mrs Slater said.

"What?"

She nodded, patted his hand. Cigarette ash spotted his skin. "That's alright. Here." She dropped an envelope onto the table. It was brown, for Heaven's sake. And unsealed, so that the uneven crinkle of paper money showed through. "You've saved me a lot of time and money."

She stood to leave. Alex put his hand on the envelope, his eyes closed. "Oh, shit in a hubcap," he said under his breath.

Mrs Slater bent down and whispered into his ear. "Thanks, Mr Jordan. You didn't have to do her as well. But, well . . . thanks." She left, without looking back. Alex noticed that she had cigarette ash smudged across the back of her dress. The tag stuck from her collar, it was Marks and Spencer. Red shoes. He was observant, that was for sure. Be observant at all times, the book said. Chapter One.

He grabbed the envelope and felt its surprising thickness. His bill had been for three hundred pounds, there must be ten times that in here.

You didn't have to do her as well.

Surely they didn't, either.

Alex gulped down his coffee. It tasted bitter, but that was good. He smacked his lips, pocketed the envelope and left the cafe. Heads turned to follow him out. But only briefly.

# Diddling
## Considered as One of the Exact Sciences

### Edgar Allan Poe

> Hey, diddle diddle,
> The cat and the fiddle.

Since the world began there have been two Jeremys. The one wrote a Jeremiad about usury, and was called Jeremy Bentham. He has been much admired by Mr. John Neal, and was a great man in a small way. The other gave name to the most important of the Exact Sciences, and was a great man in a *great* way—I may say, indeed, in the very greatest of ways.

Diddling—or the abstract idea conveyed by the verb to diddle— is sufficiently well understood. Yet the fact, the deed, the thing, *diddling*, is somewhat difficult to define. We may get, however, at a tolerably distinct conception of the matter in hand, by defining— not the thing, diddling, in itself—but man, as an animal that diddles. Had Plato but hit upon this, he would have been spared the affront of the picked chicken.

Very pertinently it was demanded of Plato, why a picked chicken, which was clearly a "biped without feathers," was not, according to his own definition, a man? But I am not to be bothered by any similar query. Man is an animal that diddles, and there is *no* animal that diddles *but* man. It will take an entire hen-coop of picked chickens to get over that.

What constitutes the essence, the nare, the principle of diddling is, in fact, peculiar to the class of creatures that wear coats and pantaloons. A crow thieves; a fox cheats; a weasel outwits; a man diddles. To diddle is his destiny. "Man was made to mourn," says the poet. But not so:—he was made to diddle. This is his aim—his object—his *end*. And for this reason when a man's diddled we say he's "*done*."

Diddling, rightly considered, is a compound, of which the ingredients are minuteness, interest, perseverance, ingenuity, audacity, *nonchalance,* originality, impertinence, and *grin.*

*Minuteness:*—Your diddler is minute. His operations are upon a small scale. His business is retail, for cash, or approved paper at sight. Should he ever be tempted into magnificent speculation, he then, at once, loses his distinctive features, and becomes what we term "financier." This latter word conveys the diddling idea in every respect except that of magnitude. A diddler may thus be regarded as a banker *in petto*—a "financial operation," as a diddle at Brobdignag. The one is to the other, as Homer to "Flaccus"—as a mastodon to a mouse—as the tail of a comet to that of a pig.

*Interest:*—Your diddler is guided by self-interest. He scorns to diddle for the mere *sake* of the diddle. He has an object in view—his pocket—and yours. He regards always the main chance. He looks to Number One. You are Number Two, and must look to yourself.

*Perseverance:*—Your diddler perseveres. He is not readily discouraged. Should even the banks break, he cares nothing about it. He steadily pursues his end, and

> *Ut canis a corio nunquam absterrebitur uncto,*

so he lets go of his game.

*Ingenuity:*—Your diddler is ingenious. He has constructiveness large. He understands plot. He invents and circumvents. Were he not Alexander he would be Diogenes. Were he not a diddler, he would be a maker of patent rat-traps or an angler for trout.

*Audacity:*—Your diddler is audacious.—He is a bold man. He carries the war into Africa. He conquers all by assault. He would not fear the daggers of Frey Herren. With a little more prudence Dick Turpin would have made a good diddler; with a trifle less blarney, Daniel O'Connell; with a pound or two more brains, Charles the Twelfth.

*Nonchalance:*—Your diddler is *nonchalant.* He is not at all nervous. He never *had* any nerves. He is never seduced into a flurry. He is never put out—unless put out of doors. He is cool—cool as a cucumber. He is calm—"calm as a smile from Lady Bury." He is easy—easy as an old glove, or the damsels of ancient Baiæ.

*Originality:*—Your diddler is original—conscientiously so. His thoughts are his own. He would scorn to employ those of another. A stale trick is his aversion. He would return a purse, I am sure, upon discovering that he had obtained it by an unoriginal diddle.

*Impertinence:*—Your diddler is impertinent. He swaggers. He sets his arms a-kimbo. He thrusts his hands in his trowsers' pocket. He sneers in your face. He treads on your corns. He eats your dinner, he drinks your wine, he borrows your money, he pulls your nose, he kicks your poodle, and he kisses your wife.

*Grin:*—Your *true* diddler winds up all with a grin. But this nobody sees but himself. He grins when his daily work is done—when his allotted labors are accomplished—at night in his own closet, and altogether for his own private entertainment. He goes home. He locks his door. He divests himself of his clothes. He puts out his candle. He gets into bed. He places his head upon the pillow. All this done, and your diddler *grins*. This is no hypothesis. It is a matter of course. I reason *a priori,* and a diddle would be *no* diddle without a grin.

The origin of the diddle is referable to the infancy of the Human Race. Perhaps the first diddler was Adam. At all events, we can trace the science back to a very remote period of antiquity. The moderns, however, have brought it to a perfection never dreamed of by our thick-headed progenitors. Without pausing to speak of the "old saws," therefore, I shall content myself with a compendious account of some of the more "modern instances."

A very good diddle is this. A housekeeper in want of a sofa, for instance, is seen to go in and out of several cabinet warehouses. At length she arrives at one offering an excellent variety. She is accosted, and invited to enter, by a polite and voluble individual at the door. She finds a sofa well adapted to her views, and upon inquiring the price, is surprised and delighted to hear a sum named at least twenty per cent lower than her expectations. She hastens to make the purchase, gets a bill and receipt, leaves her address, with a request that the article be sent home as speedily as possible, and retires amid a profusion of bows from the shop-keeper. The night arrives and no sofa. The next day passes, and still none. A servant is sent to make inquiry about the delay. The whole transaction is denied. No sofa has been sold—no money received—except by the diddler, who played shop-keeper for the nonce.

Our cabinet warehouses are left entirely unattended, and thus afford every facility for a trick of this kind. Visitors enter, look at furniture, and depart unheeded and unseen. Should any one wish to purchase, or to inquire the price of an article, a bell is at hand, and this is considered amply sufficient.

Again, quite a respectable diddle is this. A well-dressed individual enters a shop; makes a purchase to the value of a dollar; finds, much to his vexation, that he has left his pocket-book in another coat pocket; and so says to the shop-keeper—

"My dear sir, never mind!—just oblige me, will you, by sending the bundle home? But stay! I really believe that I have nothing less than a five dollar bill, even *there*. However, you can send four dollars in change *with* the bundle, you know."

"Very good, sir," replies the shop-keeper, who entertains, at once, a lofty opinion of the high-mindedness of his customer. "I know fellows," he says to himself, "who would just have put the goods under their arm, and walked off with a promise to call and pay the dollar as they came by in the afternoon."

A boy is sent with the parcel and change. On the route, quite accidentally, he is met by the purchaser, who exclaims:

"Ah! this is my bundle, I see—I thought you had been home with it, long ago. Well, go on! My wife, Mrs. Trotter, will give you the five dollars—I left instructions with her to that effect. The change you might as well give to *me*—I shall want some silver for the Post Office. Very good! One, two, is this a good quarter?—three, four—quite right! Say to Mrs. Trotter that you met me, and be sure now and *do* not loiter on the way."

The boy doesn't loiter at all—but he is a very long time in getting back from his errand—for no lady of the precise name of Mrs. Trotter is to be discovered. He consoles himself, however, that he has not been such a fool as to leave the goods without the money, and re-entering his shop with a self-satisfied air, feels sensibly hurt and indignant when his master asks him what has become of the change.

A very simple diddle, indeed, is this. The captain of a ship which is about to sail, is presented by an official looking person with an unusually moderate bill of city charges. Glad to get off so easily, and confused by a hundred duties pressing upon him all at once, he discharges the claim forthwith. In about fifteen minutes, another and less reasonable bill is handed him by one who soon makes it evident that the first collector was a diddler, and the original collection a diddle.

And here, too, is a somewhat similar thing. A steamboat is casting loose from the wharf. A traveller, portmanteau in hand, is discovered running toward the wharf, at full speed. Suddenly, he makes a dead halt, stoops, and picks up something from the ground in a very agitated manner. It is a pocket-book, and—"Has any gentleman lost a pocket-book?" he cries. No one can say that he has exactly lost a pocket-book; but a great excitement ensues, when the treasure trove is found to be of value. The boat, however, must not be detained.

"Time and tide wait for no man," says the captain.

"For God's sake, stay only a few minutes," says the finder of the book—"the true claimant will presently appear."

"Can't wait!" replies the man in authority; "cast off there, d'ye hear?"

"What *am* I to do?" asks the finder, in great tribulation. "I am about to leave the country for some years, and I cannot conscientiously retain this large amount in my possession. I beg your pardon, sir," [here he addresses a gentleman on shore,] "but you have the air of an honest man. *Will* you confer upon me the favor of taking charge of this pocket-book—I *know* I can trust you—and of advertising it? The notes, you see, amount to a very considerable sum. The owner will, no doubt, insist upon rewarding you for your trouble—"

"*Me!*—no, *you!*—it was *you* who found the book."

"Well, if you *must* have it so—*I* will take a small reward—just to satisfy your scruples. Let me see—why these notes are all hundreds—bless my soul! a hundred is too much to take—fifty would be quite enough, I am sure—"

"Cast off there!" says the captain.

"But then I have no change for a hundred, and upon the whole, *you* had better—"

"Cast off there!" says the captain.

"Never mind!" cries the gentleman on shore, who has been examining his own pocket-book for the last minute or so—"never mind! *I* can fix it—here is a fifty on the Bank of North America—throw me the book."

And the over-conscientious finder takes the fifty with marked reluctance, and throws the gentleman the book, as desired, while the steamboat fumes and fizzes on her way. In about half an hour after her departure, the "large amount" is seen to be a "counterfeit presentment," and the whole thing a capital diddle.

A bold diddle is this. A camp-meeting, or something similar, is to be held at a certain spot which is accessible only by means of a free bridge. A diddle stations himself upon this bridge, respectfully informs all passers by of the new county law, which establishes a toll of one cent for foot passengers, two for horses and donkeys, and so forth, and so forth. Some grumble but all submit, and the diddler goes home a wealthier man by some fifty or sixty dollars well earned. This taking a toll from a great crowd of people is an excessively troublesome thing.

A neat diddle is this. A friend holds one of the diddler's promises to pay, filled up and signed in due form, upon the ordinary blanks printed in red ink. The diddler purchases one or two dozen of these blanks, and every day dips one of them in his soup, makes his dog jump for it, and finally gives it to him as a *bonne bouche*. The note arriving at maturity, the diddler, with the diddler's dog, calls upon the friend, and the promise to pay is made the topic of discussion. The friend produces it from his *escritoire*, and is in the act of reaching it to the diddler, when up jumps the diddler's dog and devours it forthwith. The diddler is not only surprised but vexed and incensed at the absurd behavior of his dog, and expresses his entire readiness to cancel the obligation at any moment when the evidence of the obligation shall be forthcoming.

A very minute diddle is this. A lady is insulted in the street by a diddler's accomplice. The diddler himself flies to her assistance, and, giving his friend a comfortable thrashing, insists upon attending the lady to her own door. He bows, with his hand upon his heart, and most respectfully bids her adieu. She intreats him, as her deliverer, to walk in and be introduced to her big brother and her papa. With a sigh, he declines to do so. "Is there no way, then, sir," she murmurs, "in which I may be permitted to testify my gratitude?"

"Why, yes, madam, there is. Will you be kind enough to lend me a couple of shillings?"

In the first excitement of the moment the lady decides upon fainting outright. Upon second thought, however, she opens her purse-strings and delivers the specie. Now this, I say, is a diddle minute—for one entire moiety of the sum borrowed has to be paid to the gentleman who had the trouble of performing the insult, and who had then to stand still and be thrashed for performing it.

Rather a small, but still a scientific diddle is this. The diddler approaches the bar of a tavern, and demands a couple of twists of tobacco. These are handed to him, when, having slightly examined them, he says:

"I don't much like this tobacco. Here, take it back, and give me a glass of brandy and water in its place."

The brandy and water is furnished and imbibed, and the diddler makes his way to the door. But the voice of the tavern-keeper arrests him.

"I believe, sir, you have forgotten to pay for your brandy and water."

"Pay for my brandy and water!—didn't I give you the tobacco for the brandy and water? What more would you have?"

"But, sir, if you please, I don't remember that you paid me for the tobacco."

"What do you mean by that, you scoundrel?—Didn't I give you back your tobacco? Isn't *that* your tobacco lying *there?* Do you expect me to pay for what I did not take?"

"But, sir," says the publican, now rather at a loss what to say, "but sir—"

"But me no buts, sir," interrupts the diddler, apparently in very high dudgeon, and slamming the door after him, as he makes his escape.—"But me no buts, sir, and none of your tricks upon travellers."

Here again is a very clever diddle, of which the simplicity is not its least recommendation. A purse, or pocket-book, being really lost, the loser inserts in *one* of the daily papers of a large city a fully descriptive advertisement.

Whereupon our diddler copies the *facts* of this advertisement, with a change of heading, of general phraseology, and *address.* The original, for instance, is long, and verbose, is headed "A Pocket-Book Lost!" and requires the treasure, when found, to be left at No. 1 Tom Street. The copy is brief, and being headed with "Lost" only, indicates No. 2 Dick, or No. 3 Harry Street, as the locality in which the owner may be seen. Moreover, it is inserted in at least five or six of the daily papers of the day, while in point of time, it makes its appearance only a few hours after the original. Should it be read by the loser of the purse, he would hardly suspect it to have any reference to his own misfortune. But, of course, the chances are five or six to one, that the finder will repair to the address given by the diddler, rather than to that pointed out by the rightful proprietor. The former pays the reward, pockets the treasure and decamps.

Quite an analogous diddle is this. A lady of *ton* has dropped, somewhere in the street, a diamond ring of very unusual value. For its recovery, she offers some forty or fifty dollars reward—giving, in her advertisement, a very minute description of the gem, and of its settings, and declaring that, on its restoration at No. so and so, in such and such Avenue, the reward will be paid *instanter,* without a single question being asked. During the lady's absence from home, a day or two afterwards, a ring is heard at the door of No. so and so, in such and such Avenue; a servant appears; the lady of the house is asked for and is declared to be out, at which astounding information, the visitor expresses the most poignant regret. His business is of importance and concerns the lady herself. In fact, he had the good fortune to find her diamond ring. But perhaps it would be as well that he should call again. "By no means!" says the servant; and "By no means!" says the lady's sister and the lady's sister-in-law, who are summoned forthwith. The ring is clamorously identified, the reward is paid, and the finder nearly thrust out of doors. The lady returns and expresses some little dissatisfaction with her sister and sister-in-law, because they happen to have paid forty or fifty dollars for a *fac-simile* of her diamond ring—a *fac-simile* made out of real pinchbeck and unquestionable paste.

But as there is really no end to diddling, so there would be none to this essay, were I even to hint at half the variations, or inflections, of which this science is susceptible. I must bring this paper, perforce, to a conclusion, and this I cannot do better than by a summary notice of a very decent, but rather elaborate diddle, of which our own city was made the theatre, not very long ago, and which was subsequently repeated with success, in other still more verdant localities of the Union. A middle-aged gentleman arrives in town from parts unknown. He is remarkably precise, cautious, staid, and deliberate in his demeanor. His dress is scrupulously neat, but plain, unostentatious. He wears a white cravat, an ample waistcoat, made with an eye to comfort alone; thick-soled cosy-looking shoes, and pantaloons without straps. He has the whole air, in fact, of your well-to-do, sober-sided, exact, and respectable "man of business," *par excellence*—one of the stern and outwardly hard, internally soft, sort of people that we see in the crack high comedies—fellows whose words are so many bonds, and who are noted for giving away guineas, in charity, with the one hand, while, in the way of mere bargain, they exact the uttermost fraction of a farthing with the other.

He makes much ado before he can get suited with a boarding-house. He dislikes children. He has been accustomed to quiet. His habits are methodical—and then he would prefer getting into a private and respectable small family, piously inclined. Terms, however, are no object—only he must insist upon settling his bill on the first of every month (it is now the second) and begs his landlady, when he finally obtains one to his mind, *not* on any account to forget his instructions upon this point—but to send in a bill, *and* receipt, precisely at ten o'clock, on the *first* day of every month, and under no circumstances to put it off to the second.

These arrangements made, our man of business rents an office in a reputable rather than a fashionable quarter of the town. There is nothing he more despises than pretence. "Where there is much show," he says, "there is seldom any thing very solid behind"—an observation which so profoundly impresses his landlady's fancy, that she makes a pencil memorandum of it forthwith, in her great family Bible, on the broad margin of the Proverbs of Solomon.

The next step is to advertise, after some such fashion as this, in the principal business sixpennies of the city—the pennies are eschewed as not "respectable"—and as demanding payment for all advertisements in advance. Our man of business holds it as a point of his faith that work should never be paid for until done.

"WANTED.—The advertisers, being about to commence extensive business operations in this city, will require the services of three or four intelligent and competent clerks, to whom a liberal salary will be paid. The very best recommendations, not so much for capacity, as for integrity, will be expected. Indeed, as the duties to be performed, involve high responsibilities, and large amounts of money must necessarily pass through the hands of those engaged, it is deemed advisable to demand a deposit of fifty dollars from each clerk employed. No person need apply, therefore, who is not prepared to leave this sum in the possession of the advertisers, and who cannot furnish the most satisfactory testimonials of morality. Young gentlemen piously inclined will be preferred. Application should be made between the hours of ten and eleven A.M., and four and five P.M., of Messrs.

"BOGS, HOGS, LOGS, FROGS, & CO.,
"No. 110 Dog Street."

By the thirty-first day of the month, this advertisement has brought to the office of Messrs. Bogs, Hogs, Logs, Frogs, and Company, some fifteen or twenty young gentlemen piously inclined. But our man of business is in no hurry to conclude a contract with any—no man of business is *ever* precipitate—and it is not until the most rigid catechism in respect to the piety of each young gentleman's

inclination, that his services are engaged and his fifty dollars re-
ceipted for, *just* by way of proper precaution, on the part of the
respectable firm of Bogs, Hogs, Logs, Frogs, and Company. On the
morning of the first day of the next month, the landlady does *not*
present her bill, according to promise—a piece of neglect for which
the comfortable head of the house ending in *ogs* would no doubt
have chided her severely, could he have been prevailed upon to
remain in town a day or two for that purpose.

As it is, the constables have had a sad time of it, running hither
and thither, and all they can do is to declare the man of business
most emphatically, a "hen knee high"—by which some persons
imagine them to imply that, in fact, he is n. e. i.—by which again the
very classical phrase *non est inventus,* is supposed to be understood.
In the meantime the young gentlemen, one and all, are somewhat
less piously inclined than before, while the landlady purchases a
shilling's worth of the best Indian rubber, and very carefully obliter-
ates the pencil memorandum that some fool has made in her great
family Bible, on the broad margin of the Proverbs of Solomon.

# A Difficult Subject

Jane Rice

**M**r. Greeble lowered his paper. He looked at his wife.
"All right," he said. "Quit it. Cut it out."

Mrs. Greeble permitted one corner of her mouth to quirk into
the semblance of a half smile.

"I thought you didn't believe in it."

"Just because I ask you, as a personal favor, to lay off, doesn't
mean I believe in it or don't believe in it." His lips tightened. "Holy
cats, Hortense, all I'm saying is let me read my paper in peace. For
once. Just for once. That's all."

"If you didn't believe in it subconsciously," Mrs. Greeble replied
equably, "it wouldn't bother you."

"It doesn't bother me," Mr. Greeble said. "*You* do. First it was tea
leaves. Then it was spiritualism. Then astrology. Then that Yogi or

Swami or whatever the devil he called himself. Then something about vibrating properly to numbers. And now, mental telepathy. All I'm asking is—"

"Thought transference," Mrs. Greeble interposed.

"Okay. Thought transference. All I'm asking is that you leave me out of it. If you've got to think at somebody, think at Baldwin Locomotive and see if you can't get them to declare an extra dividend."

"Very funny," Mrs. Greeble said. "Very funny."

"Sure," Mr. Greeble said. "It's funnier than Abbott and Costello."

"It might interest you to know," Mrs. Greeble said, "that it worked."

"What worked?"

"I made you put down your paper."

"You what?"

"I made you put down your paper."

"Oh, God," Mr. Greeble said.

"I must admit you're a difficult subject," Mrs. Greeble said, "but I did get through to you. You might as well own up to it."

"Subject," Mr. Greeble said. "Get through to me." He leaned forward a trifle. "Look, it's me. Your husband. Remember?"

"You put down your paper," Mrs. Greeble reiterated.

"If there's much more of this," Mr. Greeble said, "I'll be cutting it up into paper dolls."

"Scoff if you want, the fact remains you put it down." She gazed at him steadily. Intently.

"*Now* what is it?" the object of her scrutiny inquired caustically. "I guess you want me to bark like a dog. Or maybe, recite 'Horatio at the Bridge.' Look, Hortense—"

"If you'll only *con*centrate," Mrs. Greeble said in a faraway voice.

"What for?" Mr. Greeble asked with heavy sarcasm. "You're so good you can make me put my paper down, you don't need any help. While you're at it, see if you can't get the plumber to put *his* down and come over here to fix the bathroom faucets. That'll be a concrete example. You do that and I'll concentrate like Billy-be-damned."

"You're close," Mrs. Greeble said. "The Billy part is right."

"Billy Mitchell," Mr. Greeble said mockingly. "Where are you going Billy boy, Billy boy. And he sang as he waited, waited while his billy boiled, Come go ta tum ta, Matilda with me. Billy Howard

106

Taft. Billy Shakespeare. Billy Goat Gruff. Billy Whosit who used to go with you. Billings, Montana. Nuts."

"Billy McDonough," Mrs. Greeble said. "You see?"

"Billy McDonough," Mr. Greeble parroted. "What about him?"

"That's who I was thinking about. Billy McDonough, my old flame. I got through to you again, in spite of yourself. You *see?*"

A little silence sifted down between them. It deepened and grew. Finally, Mr. Greeble cleared his throat.

"Oke doke," he said. "*I've* got one. It's your turn. I'm so hot at this without even trying, it ought to be a cinch for you. Go ahead. I'm thinking it at you."

Mrs. Greeble closed her eyes. She clasped her hands loosely in her lap. An expression of peace and serenity slipped over her countenance. She sat very still. Mr. Greeble thought she looked as if she had just died of some mild ailment.

"The storeroom!" she said suddenly. Triumphantly.

"Nope."

"The furnace."

"Nope."

"The hot-water boiler?"

"Nope."

"It's *something* to do with the basement."

"Nope. You're way off."

"It isn't *anything* to do with the basement?"

"You're asking me?"

"No. No, I was just. . . . The bathroom fixtures."

"Nope."

"Is it something I know about?"

"Yep."

"No fair using baseball or anything like that."

"It isn't baseball. Or anything like that."

"I seem to keep getting a B. It starts with a B. Bowling?"

"Nope."

"It does start with a B, though? Let me see . . . B. . . ."

"I didn't say it started with a B."

"It doesn't start with a B? Odd. I seem to . . . golf?"

"It doesn't start with a G, either. There's not a B or a G in it. It starts with a K. There's a hyphen in it. It's—"

"Krafft-Ebing!"

"Nope."

"Kriss-Kringle."

"Kriss-hyphen-Kringle. Ho. Since when?"

Mrs. Greeble threw him a poisonous glance. "K. Hmmmm. Let me see. . . . *Coca-Cola!*" Mrs. Greeble pinkened. "I didn't mean that," she said.

"K-o-k-a hyphen K-o-l-a, Coca-Cola," Mr. Greeble said.

Mrs. Greeble regarded him for a long moment without speaking. "You *do* have such a word in mind?" she queried with chill politeness.

"Yep."

"You're *quite* sure?"

"Yep."

"Oh stop saying nope and yep. You sound like a fox terrier."

"You sound like an ice kold Koka-Kola," Mr. Greeble rejoined. "The word is Kamms-Korners, a small hamlet situated on Highway 60, approximately two miles from here, where your best friend Marge Emmonds lives. Hooray for thought transference."

Mrs. Greeble lifted her chin. "You would tell me," she said. "You'd *rather*, wouldn't you? I don't suppose—" She broke off abruptly.

"Baxter," she exclaimed. "Of course! I *knew* I was getting a B."

"The word was Kamms-Korners."

"Marge Baxter," Mrs. Greeble repeated. "Well, I'll be darned."

She got up and went to the phone. She dialed a number and stood, humming happily under her breath, waiting.

"Hello," she said when the connection was completed. "Is that you, Marge? Listen to this. It will slay you. Simply *slay* you. You know what we were talking about? Well, just now, Wilfred and I. . . ."

Wilfred Greeble carefully folded his paper. He put it under his arm. As if he were seeing her for the first time, or the last, he looked at his wife talking animatedly, her face alight.

Rising, he left the room. Quietly.

# The Dog That Spoke French

### Vincent Starrett

For the origins of the story of Grosse Boule, the dog that spoke French, you must seek in the folklore of Old France, where it is variously—and somewhat more roguishly—told; but as I first heard this hilarious tale its setting was a French-Canadian parish in the province of Quebec. As told in the parish of St. Madeleine this was the way of it:

Old Ozias was wealthy and respectable and illiterate. He was, also, alas, henpecked. With his wife Petronille, who was troubled by rheumatism, and his son, young Ozias, the old man lived quietly in the parish, thinking long thoughts of his vanished youth; and with them lived the big dog, Grosse Boule, whose favorite spot of an evening was a warm place behind the kitchen stove. An occasional visitor, when Mme. Petronille's rheumatism kept her upstairs, was the attractive young housewife, Marie, who came up from the village to help with the work. Once a week, on Saturday nights, it was the duty of young Ozias to read aloud from the weekly news sheet, since neither of his parents could read.

One night, while Mme. Petronille was a prisoner in her bed, and Marie was busy elsewhere, young Ozias found a news article about the remarkable results obtained by a New York dog trainer; and the story was all the more remarkable as read by young Ozias to his father. The young man, who was fond of romancing, embellished the account with fancies of his own. In the racy version of young Ozias, the dog in the newspaper story was taught to read and speak.

Old Ozias was fascinated, for it occurred to him that if Grosse Boule could be taught to read and speak they could make money exhibiting him. He talked it over with his son.

Young Ozias also was fascinated, for an exciting idea now entered his mind. For some time he had been eager to get away from the village and see the world. Playing on his father's credulity, he extracted enough money from the old man for a fling in New York and departed with the dog for the big city, leaving his father to explain that he had gone away on business.

His letters home were filled with enthusiastic reports of progress. These were guardedly expressed, since the letters had to be read to old Ozias by Marie, the young housewife from the village. "Everything is going splendidly," he would write; or, "I am at work all the time on that important business, father. It is wonderful how it is coming on!" And in every letter there was a request for more money for the education of Grosse Boule which money his father privately dispatched.

Young Ozias certainly had a good time in the big city, which was everything he expected it to be; but naturally he often required refinancing.

When some months had passed in this fashion, however, the old man grew tired of sending money, and also he was having increasing difficulty explaining to Mme. Petronille the business their son was about. He had Marie write a letter to young Ozias ordering him home, and young Ozias—in a tight spot—had to obey.

Grosse Boule lay heavy on the young man's conscience as he returned to Quebec. He had sold the dog long since, and it occurred to him that explanations were not going to be easy.

His father was at the wharf when the Montreal boat put in. He had been there most of the day. His first words as young Ozias came down the gangplank were: "Where's Grosse Boule?"

"Hush, father," said his son quickly. "Wait till we are in the charette."

In the charette the old man repeated his question: "Where's Grosse Boule?"

"Now, father," said young Ozias, "I want you to listen quietly till I have done. I'll tell you the whole story. I found that dog trainer like I wrote you, and Grosse Boule was coming along like wonderful. He was learning French, father. I wanted him to be able to talk with you on the long winter evenings when mother is kept upstairs. I didn't want him to say anything you could not understand."

The old man was so pleased that he pinched his son's arm. "Well, father, we worked with Grosse Boule by day and night, and I tell you he learned fast. You should see how he worked! Sometimes when I said to him, 'Come on Grosse Boule, let's go over on the boulevard and flirt with the girls,' he would give me a reproachful look and make answer: 'Ozias, I'm ashamed of you! What would Mme. Petronille say if she heard you talk like that? Go on by yourself. I'm not going to spend your father's money on girls.' And then he would open his book and go at it again."

The old man was delighted. "Grosse Boule could read in a book?" he asked. "He was just beginning to read when you wrote me to come home. But never mind that! It's just as well."

Young Ozias sighed. "Father, we started home together, Grosse Boule and I. In the train he never said a word, but when we got on the boat at Montreal and I brought him his supper I said to him: 'Grosse Boule, I will be glad to get home.' "

" 'Me, too,' he said. 'I'm lonesome for the old man.' That made me glad, father, and I said to him: 'Why are you so lonesome for the old man, Grosse Boule?' And he said: 'The old man makes plenty of good jokes, I can tell you.'

"I was surprised. 'How do you mean, Grosse Boule?' I asked. And then, father, he said—he said—'Ozias, you remember when your mother was laid up with rheumatism before we went away?— and that pretty Marie came up from the village to help? Well, many's the time I've laid there behind the stove, nights, and laughed fit to split my sides to hear that old fool make love nonsense with Marie.' And he laughed, father! My, how he laughed. 'Won't I have something to talk about to the old man now!'

"Father," said young Ozias angrily, "when I heard these lies about you I was so mad I forgot all about the money we spent on that ungrateful dog. I just took him by the throat and threw him in the river."

The old man drew a deep breath. After a moment he gently pressed his son's knee.

"Ozias, my son," he said, "you done right!"

# The Drawing-Room Bureau

E. F. Benson

Mrs Audley had left London the week before the war began, but she lost little time in putting her charming house in Curzon Street in commission again, when it was clear to her that London and not the country was to be the home of civilized people this autumn. She herself was intensely civilized; indeed, she had almost civilized herself away, so to speak, and really only existed in the midst of other people where she could hear what was being said, and say it herself. It was this latter instinct that led her to aspire to the position of Drawing-Room Bureau, and spend her days in retailing news connected with the war, and not officially published.

Decidedly she had gifts which fitted her for her self-created post. Physically, she had height and distinction; materially, she had money, which she liked spending in the entertainment of other people; and psychically she had a delightful manner when talking to anyone, which conveyed the impression that this particular opportunity for conversation with this particular individual was to her the crown and fulfilment of her existence. In her vague violet eyes there dwelt (how it had got there I cannot imagine) a look of earnest and limpid sincerity, and, like all those who have a very clear consciousness of their mission (hers being Drawing-Room Bureau), she was almost completely devoid of humour. And though one did not feel any overpowering confidence in her communiqués, it was impossible not to be slightly flattered when she beckoned with her serious eyes and made a place on the sofa close beside her.

'Perhaps I oughtn't to tell you,' she would say, 'but I know it won't go any further. It is very doubtful if we shall send an Expeditionary Force to France at all. I was in Whitehall this morning, though I mustn't say exactly where, nor who was my informant, though I can't help your guessing. Well, the matter is still under discussion, I can tell you that, and today the discussion was hot. Mind, I don't say there is any serious discussion between, well, between A and B, but what somebody feels is that if we guarantee, as we are doing, the safety of the French coast, that is a good deal. Hush! There's Mr Armine coming; we will talk about something else. But drop in tomorrow—let me see, not at five, but at twenty minutes to five—when we shall be uninterrupted, and I may be able to tell you more, though I can't promise. Good evening, Mr Armine! How unkind you are! You haven't let me have a word with you yet.'

Now it was impossible not to feel, so confidential was the manner in which Mrs Audley distinguished you thus, that you had not been admitted into the secret councils of the War Office or Admiralty (whichever it was that had been visited by her this morning), and that she had taken you, as by some discreet and delicious back-door, into the very presence of A and B. You might have a fleeting scepticism about it all when, subsequently, you found out that on the very evening when she had told you that the Expeditionary Force was not yet finally decided on, it had already arrived in France, or feel less personally flattered when it appeared that she had told Mr Armine exactly what she had told you. But such impressions soon faded, and when next Mrs Audley confided something that must on no account go any further until Tuesday at the earliest, you listened with undiminished avidity, and almost marked off the days as they passed, like a schoolboy with his calendar that records the approach of the holidays. She served her information up so appetizingly, like some consummate chef, and it tasted so good that it was out of the question to consider seriously what it was made of.

All through the autumn her standing as Drawing-Room Bureau grew steadily in importance. Despite occasional lapses, she was very alert to find out what was likely to happen, and the very fact that she never directly told you who her informant was added a piquancy to her secrets. She was Delphically mysterious with regard to the two hundred thousand Cossacks who were supposed to have passed through England on the way to the French battle-line; but her reticence here, you felt, was of the nature of a thin layer of ice over impenetrable depths and boiling springs.

'You will be right,' she said, 'not to believe half you hear about trains passing through Willesden and Swindon with all the blinds drawn down. Mind, I don't say that there were not such trains, but, as far as I know—and my information is, I think, the latest that is authentic—there was no movement of troops through Swindon, anyhow. As to the transports to and from Archangel about which you asked me just now, it is quite true that the *Oceanic* was up there, and that she has gone down. And I can tell you that Archangel is still clear of ice, which is unusual, and that at present it is being kept clear. I was at the Russian—well, perhaps I had better not say exactly where—I was at a certain house last night, and heard some very strange things. Don't you wish I was like the majority of my sex, and didn't mind whether I was pledged to secrecy or not? But at present I can't tell you more. Ah, here is Lady Weyburne; let us make room for her. Dear Claire, come and talk to us. We are longing to know what Italy is going to do.'

Now this, without doubt, was meant to be a disarming remark, but it unhappily failed in its intention, and only made Lady Weyburne buckle on her armour instead of taking it off. She was, in fact, beginning to be a serious rival to Mrs Audley in this Bureau business, and was getting on so well that probably Mrs Audley wanted to amalgamate. But Lady Weyburne had no idea of doing so; when she had rivals she did not want to propitiate them, but to pommel them. She ran her establishment on very different lines from Mrs Audley's discreet and personal methods. She made no quiet confidences, but told stories that she had heard or invented to rooms full of people at the top of her shrill and raucous voice. Already the rivalry had led to tiresome situations, as, for instance, when she announced to the entire dinner table that Sir John French had been in London, at the very moment when Mrs Audley was imparting that fact to the man on her right (in Italian, so that the servants could not understand what she was saying) as the most precious of all secrets that must on no account be known till Wednesday evening.

Tonight it was evident that Lady Weyburne, instead of being disarmed by this request for information, flung it back, so to speak—a gauntlet of challenge.

'Dear Madge,' she said, 'fancy you of all people asking poor me for information. Why, I am told on all sides that the only person who knows anything about the war is you. Indeed, I was on the point of asking you if it is really true that immense quantities of macaroni and Capri wine have been shipped to Marseilles for the consumption of the Italian troops that arrived there on Sunday afternoon?'

Mrs Audley's serious mind scented war.

'No, dear, I have heard nothing about that,' she said, 'but then I hear so little. How interesting it must be to be told these wonderful things! Capri wine and macaroni! Dear me! I remember, darling, how you thrilled me with delicious stories of the Russian troops passing through Swindon, and knocking the snow off their boots. I wonder what has happened to them all. Have you heard anything further?'

Lady Weyburne laughed; she laughed as if she was thoroughly amused.

'My dear, what can you be dreaming of?' she said. 'I never believed in the Russian troops at all, in spite of all you said about them.'

'No?' said Mrs Audley dreamily.

'Of course not. There never were any. I can't think why your friends at the Embassy made such a mystery of it, if you really understood them correctly. No, I won't sit down; I am just off to the Foreign Office. Ah, perhaps I had better not have said that! Forget it, won't you?'

Now here was a declaration of war, a challenge as to Drawing-Room Bureau, as direct as words could possibly make it, for the last sentences were a pure parody of Mrs Audley's unmistakable style, and from that moment the Bureau war may be said to have definitely begun. Instantly both sides, already completely mobilized, violently attacked and counter-attacked. It was enough for Lady Weyburne to learn that Mrs Audley had made the faintest suggestion about the attitude of Romania, to cause her to quote her cousin at the Foreign Office, with or without his authority, in support of her contradiction of whatever Mrs Audley had said. This was a real, genuine cousin (though whether he was strictly responsible for all the war-news which Lady Weyburne fathered on him is another question), and all the information which Mrs Audley hinted that she had received in letters from her husband who undoubtedly was at the front could not quite hold their own against these cousinly pronouncements, especially since everybody knew that letters from the front were heavily censored and probably did not contain so much direct news as Mrs Audley hinted at. On the other hand, the latter had a really magnificent innings about Christmas when Major Audley got four days' leave; after his departure the town rang with stories of remarkable strategy, which Mrs Audley told everybody, with strict injunctions that they must never be repeated at all, not even after next Tuesday.

On the whole, then, the honours of the campaign were for many weeks about equally divided, and neither side could claim an unchallenged supremacy, nor completely round the other up. In point of industry and imagination the two were very equally matched, though in different styles, and while Mrs Audley was content to confide to you that a wonderful new type of gun, about which the utmost secrecy must be observed, had been landed (though she mustn't say where) in France, Lady Weyburne boldly announced its calibre and range, confusing inches with millimetres and miles with kilometres, without the smallest embarrassment or hesitation. Though this wealth of amazing detail carried you off your feet for the moment, Lady Weyburne lacked the impressiveness of Mrs Audley and her subtly dropped hints that the Ambassadors of the Allied Powers were in the habit of dropping in to tea and pouring out their hopes and fears. Mrs Audley, in fact, produced atmosphere; her Turneresque mists and gleams were full of suggestion, while Lady Weyburne reminded you more of some Dutch painter in whose landscape you could count the leaves of the trees and the number of hairs on the cow's tail. Some minds preferred one, some the other, but all alike waited with breathless interest to see the outcome of this brave rivalry. It came early in March, when Lady Weyburne won all down the line by a stroke so Machiavellian that she almost ought to have forfeited all claims to be considered a civilized being. It certainly was war, but morally it could not be called magnificent. The fiendish manner of it was in this wise.

In spite of the deadliness of the struggle the two were otherwise on perfectly friendly terms. The area of conflict in which neither gave nor asked for quarter was strictly circumscribed to the question of supremacy in the dissemination of Admiralty and War Office news not officially promulgated. Where that was concerned there was no act of hostility which they would not cheerfully perpetrate on each other, but apart from that their relations were completely amicable. In the ordinary course of life, then, Mrs Audley, by appointment, went to tea one afternoon with Claire Weyburne, and on arrival was told that she had been unexpectedly detained, but would be in presently, and hoped that Mrs Audley would wait.

Mrs Audley did so, and, as was natural, wandered round her friend's newly decorated room, appraising and approving. A Chippendale bureau stood open, with some charming examples of Copenhagen china on the top, and on the flap a few papers and a blotting-book. Having admired the china, her eye fell (it was no more than that) on the papers, and she found it impossible not to observe that one had the insignia of the Foreign Office stamped on it. It followed that she could hardly help seeing what was written on it. It ran thus:

DEAR CLAIRE,

I send you a communication which will interest you. The message was taken from a German wireless. Keep it to yourself, won't you, as there are reasons why it should not be made public at present, if indeed ever.

Your affectionate cousin,
S. BURGIN.

Mrs Audley was not probably much more dishonourable than most of us. But she was at this moment transplanted to the dire field

116

of battle, and her ordinary human scruples gave but one thin, sad cry and expired. She saw that a further sheet was attached to this covering letter, and she took the two up, not observing that a pin that lightly held them together slipped out, and, turning the covering letter back, she read:

German wireless reports that one of the enemy's cruisers in the Pacific has taken Ipecacuanha. The Admiralty admits this, but doubts the ability of the enemy to retain it. The internal disturbances that will almost certainly result—

She broke off suddenly, hearing a step on the stairs, and hastily replacing the papers moved swiftly away from the bureau. When Lady Weyburne entered she was absorbed in the Japanese silk curtains which hung at quite the other end of the room.

'Darling, so sorry not to have been in,' said Lady Weyburne, not looking anywhere near the Chippendale bureau, 'but I simply couldn't help it. Have you been here long?'

'Just a couple of minutes.'

Lady Weyburne, still with eyes averted, rang the bell for tea.

'And we meet again this evening,' she said, 'for Daisy Johnston told me you were dining with her. But that shan't prevent us having a good talk now. Tell me what you think of my room. You have such taste.'

This was not in the least ironical, and during the course of a chattering hour Mrs Audley made several excellent suggestions. She even had nerve enough to look closely at the Chippendale bureau, just as if she had not seen it at all before her hostess arrived. And she did not glance even for a fraction of a second at the letters and papers that lay there. . . .

But when she had gone Lady Weyburne looked rather closely at them. She observed that a pin which held two papers lightly together had fallen out. Then, after sudden and unexplained laughter, she sat down quietly to think, with a broad grin on her acute and pleasant face.

That evening, accordingly, they met at dinner, and it might have been noticed that Lady Weyburne did not, as was her usual custom, sit down to play Bridge afterwards, but engaged in trifling conversation near the fireplace. Mrs Audley never played, and, as was usual with her, sat and talked in a low voice to a man for whom she made room on the sofa. Her voice was quite inaudible to Lady

Weyburne, but that she expected. The man in question was Dick Ransom, who was keenly interested in the fortunes of the Drawing-Room Bureau war.

'I am afraid that things are not going very well in the Pacific,' said Mrs Audley to him. 'Do you remember that German cruiser which escaped and made its way up some river in East Africa? We thought we had prevented her getting out again, but I know that I was never quite easy about it. I'm afraid she must have escaped, for I have heard a disquieting item of news. If you will promise not to let it go further, I can tell you. She has taken Ipecacuanha—indeed, the Admiralty admits it—though they say that owing to the internal disturbances that will probably result, the enemy will not be able to retain it. Very likely you will never see the taking of it officially announced—'

Suddenly Dick Ransom gave a great shout of laughter, and on the moment Lady Weyburne rose, interrupting her trivial conversation, and came towards them. Without a shadow of doubt she had been waiting just for that, for Dick's uproarious laugh.

'Ah, do tell me what the joke is,' she said. 'I long to hear something amusing in these dull days. Madge, darling, what have you been telling Mr Ransom?'

Dick laughed again, slapping his great thigh.

'Best thing out,' he said. 'A German cruiser has taken Ipecacuanha, and the Admiralty think they mayn't be able to retain it. Ha! You'll never beat that, Mrs Audley!'

Lady Weyburne looked enquiringly at her rival, who rose suddenly, with a certain hunted and dismayed expression in her violet eyes.

'Ah, that silly joke of my cousin's,' she said. She paused a moment, and her laughter shrilled high above Dick's.

'But you told it Dick as serious war-news?' she asked. 'Dear Madge, you should get somebody to censor your war-news for you, in case it happens to be a joke. And who could have told you this, I wonder?'

But she was very busy for the next day or two in telling absolutely everybody exactly what she wondered.

# The Egg

## Sherwood Anderson

My father was, I am sure, intended by nature to be a cheerful, kindly man. Until he was thirty-four years old he worked as a farm-hand for a man named Thomas Butterworth whose place lay near the town of Bidwell, Ohio. He had then a horse of his own and on Saturday evenings drove into town to spend a few hours in social intercourse with other farm-hands. In town he drank several glasses of beer and stood about in Ben Head's saloon—crowded on Saturday evenings with visiting farm-hands. Songs were sung and glasses thumped on the bar. At ten o'clock father drove home along a lonely country road, made his horse comfortable for the night and himself went to bed, quite happy in his position in life. He had at that time no notion of trying to rise in the world.

It was in the spring of his thirty-fifth year that father married my mother, then a country school-teacher, and in the following spring I came wriggling and crying into the world. Something happened to the two people. They became ambitious. The American passion for getting up in the world took possession of them.

It may have been that mother was responsible. Being a school-teacher she had no doubt read books and magazines. She had, I presume, read of how Garfield, Lincoln, and other Americans rose from poverty to fame and greatness and as I lay beside her—in the days of her lying-in—she may have dreamed that I would some day rule men and cities. At any rate she induced father to give up his place as a farm-hand, sell his horse and embark on an independent enterprise of his own. She was a tall silent woman with a long nose and troubled grey eyes. For herself she wanted nothing. For father and myself she was incurably ambitious.

The first venture into which the two people went turned out badly. They rented ten acres of poor stony land on Griggs's Road, eight miles from Bidwell, and launched into chicken raising. I grew into boyhood on the place and got my first impressions of life there. From the beginning they were impressions of disaster and if, in my turn, I am a gloomy man inclined to see the darker side of life, I attribute it to the fact that what should have been for me the happy joyous days of childhood were spent on a chicken farm.

One unversed in such matters can have no notion of the many and tragic things that can happen to a chicken. It is born out of an egg, lives for a few weeks as a tiny fluffy thing such as you will see pictured on Easter cards, then becomes hideously naked, eats quantities of corn and meal bought by the sweat of your father's brow, gets diseases called pip, cholera, and other names, stands looking with stupid eyes at the sun, becomes sick and dies. A few hens and now and then a rooster, intended to serve God's mysterious ends, struggle through to maturity. The hens lay eggs out of which come other chickens and the dreadful cycle is thus made complete. It is all unbelievably complex. Most philosophers must have been raised on chicken farms. One hopes for so much from a chicken and is so dreadfully disillusioned. Small chickens, just setting out on the journey of life, look so bright and alert and they are in fact so dreadfully stupid. They are so much like people they mix one up in one's judgments of life. If disease does not kill them they wait until your expectations are thoroughly aroused and then walk under the wheels of a wagon—to go squashed and dead back to their maker. Vermin infest their youth, and fortunes must be spent for curative powders. In later life I have seen how a literature has been built up on the subject of fortunes to be made out of the raising of chickens. It is intended to be read by the gods who have just eaten of the tree of the knowledge of good and evil. It is a hopeful literature and declares that much may be done by simple ambitious people who own a few hens. Do not be led astray by it. It was not written for you. Go hunt for gold on the frozen hills of Alaska, put your faith in the honesty of a politician, believe if you will that the world is daily growing better and that good will triumph over evil, but do not read and believe the literature that is written concerning the hen. It was not written for you.

I, however, digress. My tale does not primarily concern itself with the hen. If correctly told it will centre on the egg. For ten years my father and mother struggled to make our chicken farm pay and then they gave up that struggle and began another. They moved into the town of Bidwell, Ohio and embarked in the restaurant business. After ten years of worry with incubators that did not hatch, and with tiny—and in their own way lovely—balls of fluff that passed on into semi-naked pullethood and from that into dead henhood, we threw all aside and packing our belongings on a wagon drove down Griggs's Road toward Bidwell, a tiny caravan of hope looking for a new place from which to start on our upward journey through life.

We must have been a sad looking lot, not, I fancy, unlike refugees fleeing from a battlefield. Mother and I walked in the road. The wagon that contained our goods had been borrowed for the day from Mr Albert Griggs, a neighbor. Out of its sides stuck the legs of cheap chairs and at the back of the pile of beds, tables, and boxes filled with kitchen utensils was a crate of live chickens, and on top of that the baby carriage in which I had been wheeled about in my infancy. Why we stuck to the baby carriage I don't know. It was unlikely other children would be born and the wheels were broken. People who have few possessions cling tightly to those they have. That is one of the facts that make life so discouraging.

Father rode on top of the wagon. He was then a bald-headed man of forty-five, a little fat and from long association with mother and the chickens he had become habitually silent and discouraged. All during our ten years on the chicken farm he had worked as a laborer on neighboring farms and most of the money he had earned had been spent for remedies to cure chicken diseases, on Wilmer's White Wonder Cholera Cure or Professor Bidlow's Egg Producer or some other preparations that mother found advertised in the poultry papers. There were two little patches of hair on father's head just above his ears. I remember that as a child I used to sit looking at him when he had gone to sleep in a chair before the stove on Sunday afternoons in the winter. I had at that time already begun to read books and have notions of my own and the bald path that led over the top of his head was, I fancied, something like a broad road, such a road as Caesar might have made on which to lead his legions out of Rome and into the wonders of an unknown world. The tufts of hair that grew above father's ears were, I thought, like forests. I fell into a half-sleeping, half-waking state and dreamed I was a tiny thing going along the road into a far beautiful place where there were no chicken farms and where life was a happy eggless affair.

One might write a book concerning our flight from the chicken farm into town. Mother and I walked the entire eight miles—she to be sure that nothing fell from the wagon and I to see the wonders of the world. On the seat of the wagon beside father was his greatest treasure. I will tell you of that.

121

On a chicken farm where hundreds and even thousands of chickens come out of eggs surprising things sometimes happen. Grotesques are born out of eggs as out of people. The accident does not often occur—perhaps once in a thousand births. A chicken is, you see, born that has four legs, two pairs of wings, two heads or what not. The things do not live. They go quickly back to the hand of their maker that has for a moment trembled. The fact that the poor little things could not live was one of the tragedies of life to father. He had some sort of notion that if he could but bring into henhood or roosterhood a five-legged hen or a two-headed rooster his fortune would be made. He dreamed of taking the wonder about to county fairs and of growing rich by exhibiting it to other farmhands.

At any rate he saved all the little monstrous things that had been born on our chicken farm. They were preserved in alcohol and put each in its own glass bottle. These he had carefully put into a box and on our journey into town it was carried on the wagon seat beside him. He drove the horses with one hand and with the other clung to the box. When we got to our destination the box was taken down at once and the bottles removed. All during our days as keepers of a restaurant in the town of Bidwell, Ohio, the grotesques in their little glass bottles sat on a shelf back of the counter. Mother sometimes protested but father was a rock on the subject of his treasure. The grotesques were, he declared, valuable. People, he said, liked to look at strange and wonderful things.

Did I say that we embarked in the restaurant business in the town of Bidwell, Ohio? I exaggerated a little. The town itself lay at the foot of a low hill and on the shore of a small river. The railroad did not run through the town and the station was a mile away to the north at a place called Pickleville. There had been a cider mill and pickle factory at the station, but before the time of our coming they had both gone out of business. In the morning and in the evening busses came down to the station along a road called Turner's Pike from the hotel on the main street of Bidwell. Our going to the out of the way place to embark in the restaurant business was mother's idea. She talked of it for a year and then one day went off and rented an empty store building opposite the railroad station. It was her idea that the restaurant would be profitable. Travelling men, she said, would be always waiting around to take trains out of town and town people would come to the station to await incoming trains. They would come to the restaurant to buy pieces of pie and drink coffee. Now that I am older I know that she had another motive in going. She was ambitious for me. She wanted me to rise in the world, to get into a town school and become a man of the towns.

At Pickleville father and mother worked hard as they always had done. At first there was the necessity of putting our place into shape to be a restaurant. That took a month. Father built a shelf on which he put tins of vegetables. He painted a sign on which he put his name in large red letters. Below his name was the sharp command—"EAT HERE"—that was so seldom obeyed. A show case was bought and filled with cigars and tobacco. Mother scrubbed the floor and the walls of the room. I went to school in the town and was glad to be away from the farm and from the presence of the discouraged, sad-looking chickens. Still I was not very joyous. In the evening I walked home from school along Turner's Pike and remembered the children I had seen playing in the town school yard. A troop of little girls had gone hopping about and singing. I tried that. Down along the frozen road I went hopping solemnly on one leg. "Hippity Hop To The Barber Shop," I sang shrilly. Then I stopped and looked doubtfully about. I was afraid of being seen in my gay mood. It must have seemed to me that I was doing a thing that should not be done by one who, like myself, had been raised on a chicken farm where death was a daily visitor.

Mother decided that our restaurant should remain open at night. At ten in the evening a passenger train went north past our door followed by a local freight. The freight crew had switching to do in Pickleville and when the work was done they came to our restaurant for hot coffee and food. Sometimes one of them ordered a fried egg. In the morning at four they returned north-bound and again visited us. A little trade began to grow up. Mother slept at night and during the day tended the restaurant and fed our boarders while father slept. He slept in the same bed mother had occupied during the night and I went off to the town of Bidwell and to school. During the long nights, while mother and I slept, father cooked meats that were to go into sandwiches for the lunch baskets of our boarders. Then an idea in regard to getting up in the world came into his head. The American spirit took hold of him. He also became ambitious.

In the long nights when there was little to do father had time to think. That was his undoing. He decided that he had in the past been an unsuccessful man because he had not been cheerful enough and that in the future he would adopt a cheerful outlook on life. In the early morning he came upstairs and got into bed with mother. She woke and the two talked. From my bed in the corner I listened.

It was my father's idea that both he and mother should try to entertain the people who came to eat at our restaurant. I cannot now remember his words, but he gave the impression of one about to become in some obscure way a kind of public entertainer. When people, particularly young people from the town of Bidwell, came into our place, as on very rare occasions they did, bright entertaining conversation was to be made. From father's words I gathered that something of the jolly inn-keeper effect was to be sought. Mother must have been doubtful from the first, but she said nothing discouraging. It was father's notion that a passion for the company of himself and mother would spring up in the breasts of the younger people of the town of Bidwell. In the evening bright happy groups would come singing down Turner's Pike. They would troop shouting with joy and laughter into our place. There would be song and festivity. I do not mean to give the impression that father spoke so elaborately of the matter. He was as I have said an uncommunicative man. "They want some place to go. I tell you they want some place to go," he said over and over. That was as far as he got. My own imagination has filled in the blanks.

For two or three weeks this notion of father's invaded our house. We did not talk much, but in our daily lives tried earnestly to make smiles take the place of glum looks. Mother smiled at the boarders and I, catching the infection, smiled at our cat. Father became a little feverish in his anxiety to please. There was no doubt, lurking somewhere in him, a touch of the spirit of the showman. He did not waste much of his ammunition on the railroad men he served at night but seemed to be waiting for a young man or woman from Bidwell to come in to show what he could do. On the counter in the restaurant there was a wire basket kept always filled with eggs, and it must have been before his eyes when the idea of being entertaining was born in his brain. There was something pre-natal about the way eggs kept themselves connected with the development of his idea. At any rate an egg ruined his new impulse in life. Late one night I was awakened by a roar of anger coming from father's throat. Both mother and I sat upright in our beds. With trembling hands she lighted a lamp that stood on a table by her head. Downstairs the front door of our restaurant went shut with a bang and in a few minutes father tramped up the stairs. He held an egg in his hand and his hand trembled as though he were having a chill. There was a half insane light in his eyes. As he stood glaring at us I was sure he intended throwing the egg at either mother or me. Then he laid it gently on the table beside the lamp and dropped on his knees beside mother's bed. He began to cry like a boy and I, carried away by his grief, cried with him. The two of us filled the little upstairs room with our wailing voices. It is ridiculous, but of the picture we made I can remember only the fact that mother's hand continually stroked the bald path that ran across the top of his head. I have forgotten what mother said to him and how she induced him to tell her of what had happened downstairs. His explanation also has gone out of my mind. I remember only my own grief and fright and the shiny path over father's head glowing in the lamp light as he knelt by the bed.

As to what happened downstairs. For some unexplainable reason I know the story as well as though I had been a witness to my father's discomfiture. One in time gets to know many unexplainable things. On that evening young Joe Kane, son of a merchant of Bidwell, came to Pickleville to meet his father, who was expected on the ten o'clock evening train from the South. The train was three hours late and Joe came into our place to loaf about and to wait for its arrival. The local freight train came in and the freight crew were fed. Joe was left alone in the restaurant with father.

From the moment he came into our place the Bidwell young man must have been puzzled by my father's actions. It was his notion that father was angry at him for hanging around. He noticed that the restaurant keeper was apparently disturbed by his presence and he thought of going out. However, it began to rain and he did not fancy the long walk to town and back. He bought a five-cent cigar and ordered a cup of coffee. He had a newspaper in his pocket and took it out and began to read. "I'm waiting for the evening train. It's late," he said apologetically.

For a long time father, whom Joe Kane had never seen before, remained silently gazing at his visitor. He was no doubt suffering from an attack of stage fright. As so often happens in life he had thought so much and so often of the situation that now confronted him that he was somewhat nervous in its presence.

For one thing, he did not know what to do with his hands. He thrust one of them nervously over the counter and shook hands with Joe Kane. "How-de-do," he said. Joe Kane put his newspaper down and stared at him. Father's eye lighted on the basket of eggs

125

that sat on the counter and he began to talk. "Well," he began hesitatingly, "well, you have heard of Christopher Columbus, eh?" He seemed to be angry. "That Christopher Columbus was a cheat," he declared emphatically. "He talked of making an egg stand on its end. He talked, he did, and then he went and broke the end of the egg."

My father seemed to his visitor to be beside himself at the duplicity of Christopher Columbus. He muttered and swore. He declared it was wrong to teach children that Christopher Columbus was a great man when, after all, he cheated at the critical moment. He had declared he would make an egg stand on end and then when his bluff had been called he had done a trick. Still grumbling at Columbus, father took an egg from the basket on the counter and began to walk up and down. He rolled the egg between the palms of his hands. He smiled genially. He began to mumble words regarding the effect to be produced on an egg by the electricity that comes out of the human body. He declared that without breaking its shell and by virtue of rolling it back and forth in his hands he could stand the egg on its end. He explained that the warmth of his hands and the gentle rolling movement he gave the egg created a new centre of gravity, and Joe Kane was mildly interested. "I have handled thousands of eggs," father said. "No one knows more about eggs than I do."

He stood the egg on the counter and it fell on its side. He tried the trick again and again, each time rolling the egg between the palms of his hands and saying the words regarding the wonders of electricity and the laws of gravity. When after a half hour's effort he did succeed in making the egg stand for a moment he looked up to find that his visitor was no longer watching. By the time he had succeeded in calling Joe Kane's attention to the success of his effort the egg had again rolled over and lay on its side.

Afire with the showman's passion and at the same time a good deal disconcerted by the failure of his first effort, father now took the bottles containing the poultry monstrosities down from their place on the shelf and began to show them to his visitor. "How would you like to have seven legs and two heads like this fellow?" he asked, exhibiting the most remarkable of his treasures. A cheerful smile played over his face. He reached over the counter and tried to slap Joe Kane on the shoulder as he had seen men do in Ben Head's saloon when he was a young farm-hand and drove to town on Saturday evenings. His visitor was made a little ill by the sight of the body of the terribly deformed bird floating in the alcohol in the bottle and got up to go. Coming from behind the counter father took hold of the young man's arm and led him back to his seat. He grew a little angry and for a moment had to turn his face away and force himself to smile. Then he put the bottles back on the shelf. In an outburst of generosity he fairly compelled Joe Kane to have a fresh cup of coffee and another cigar at his expense. Then he took a pan and filling it with vinegar, taken from a jug that sat beneath the counter, he declared himself about to do a new trick. "I will heat this egg in this pan of vinegar," he said. "Then I will put it through the neck of a bottle without breaking the shell. When the egg is inside the bottle it will resume its normal shape and the shell will become hard again. Then I will give the bottle with the egg in it to you. You can take it about with you wherever you go. People will want to know how you got the egg in the bottle. Don't tell them. Keep them guessing. That is the way to have fun with this trick."

Father grinned and winked at his visitor. Joe Kane decided that the man who confronted him was mildly insane but harmless. He drank the cup of coffee that had been given him and began to read his paper again. When the egg had been heated in vinegar father carried it on a spoon to the counter and going into a back room got an empty bottle. He was angry because his visitor did not watch him as he began to do his trick, but nevertheless went cheerfully to work. For a long time he struggled, trying to get the egg to go through the neck of the bottle. He put the pan of vinegar back on the stove, intending to reheat the egg, then picked it up and burned his fingers. After a second bath in the hot vinegar the shell of the egg had been softened a little but not enough for his purpose. He worked and worked and a spirit of desperate determination took possession of him. When he thought that at last the trick was about to be consummated the delayed train came in at the station and Joe Kane started to go nonchalantly out at the door. Father made a last desperate effort to conquer the egg and make it do the thing that would establish his reputation as one who knew how to entertain guests who came into his restaurant. He worried the egg. He attempted to be somewhat rough with it. He swore and the sweat stood out on his forehead. The egg broke under his hand. When the contents spurted over his clothes, Joe Kane, who had stopped at the door, turned and laughed.

A roar of anger rose from my father's throat. He danced and shouted a string of inarticulate words. Grabbing another egg from the basket on the counter, he threw it, just missing the head of the young man as he dodged through the door and escaped.

Father came upstairs to mother and me with an egg in his hand. I do not know what he intended to do. I imagine he had some idea of destroying it, of destroying all eggs, and that he intended to let mother and me see him begin. When, however, he got into the presence of mother something happened to him. He laid the egg gently on the table and dropped on his knees by the bed as I have already explained. He later decided to close the restaurant for the night and to come upstairs and get into bed. When he did so he blew out the light and after much muttered conversation both he and mother went to sleep. I suppose I went to sleep also, but my sleep was troubled. I awoke at dawn and for a long time looked at the egg that lay on the table. I wondered why eggs had to be and why from the egg came the hen who again laid the egg. The question got into my blood. It has stayed there, I imagine, because I am the son of my father. At any rate, the problem remains unsolved in my mind. And that, I conclude, is but another evidence of the complete and final triumph of the egg—at least as far as my family is concerned.

# The Errors of Santa Claus

## Stephen Leacock

It was Christmas Eve.

The Browns, who lived in the adjoining house, had been dining with the Joneses.

Brown and Jones were sitting over wine and walnuts at the table. The others had gone upstairs.

"What are you giving to your boy for Christmas?" asked Brown.

"A train," said Jones, "new kind of thing—automatic."

"Let's have a look at it," said Brown.

Jones fetched a parcel from the sideboard and began unwrapping it.

"Ingenious thing, isn't it?" he said, "goes on its own rails. Queer how kids love to play with trains, isn't it?"

"Yes," assented Brown, "how are the rails fixed?"

"Wait, I'll show you," said Jones, "just help me to shove these dinner things aside and roll back the cloth. There! See! You lay the rails like that and fasten them at the ends, so—"

"Oh, yes, I catch on, makes a grade, doesn't it? Just the thing to amuse a child, isn't it? I got Willie a toy aeroplane."

"I know, they're great. I got Edwin one on his birthday. But I thought I'd get him a train this time. I told him Santa Claus was going to bring him something altogether new this time. Edwin, of course, believes in Santa Claus absolutely. Say, look at this locomotive, would you? It has a spring coiled up inside the fire box."

"Wind her up," said Brown with great interest, "let's see her go."

"All right," said Jones, "just pile up two or three plates or something to lean the end of the rails on. There, notice the way it buzzes before it starts. Isn't that a great thing for a kid, eh?"

"Yes," said Brown, "and say! see this little string to pull the whistle. By Gad, it toots, eh? Just like real?"

"Now then, Brown," Jones went on, "you hitch on those cars and I'll start her. I'll be engineer, eh!"

Half an hour later Brown and Jones were still playing trains on the dining-room table.

But their wives upstairs in the drawing room hardly noticed their absence. They were too much interested.

"Oh, I think it's perfectly sweet," said Mrs. Brown, "just the loveliest doll I've seen in years. I must get one like it for Ulvina. Won't Clarisse be perfectly enchanted?"

"Yes," answered Mrs. Jones, "and then she'll have all the fun of arranging the dresses. Children love that so much. Look! there are three little dresses with the doll, aren't they cute? All cut out and ready to stitch together."

"Oh, how perfectly lovely," exclaimed Mrs. Brown, "I think the mauve one would suit the doll best—don't you?—with such golden hair—only don't you think it would make it much nicer to turn back the collar, so, and to put a little band—so?"

"*What* a good idea!" said Mrs. Jones, "do let's try it. Just wait, I'll get a needle in a minute. I'll tell Clarisse that Santa Claus sewed it himself. The child believes in Santa Claus absolutely."

*　*　*

And half an hour later Mrs. Jones and Mrs. Brown were so busy stitching dolls' clothes that they could not hear the roaring of the little train up and down the dining table, and had no idea what the four children were doing.

Nor did the children miss their mothers.

"Dandy, aren't they?" Edwin Jones was saying to little Willie Brown, as they sat in Edwin's bedroom. "A hundred in a box, with cork tips, and see, an amber mouthpiece that fits into a little case at the side. Good present for dad, eh?"

"Fine!" said Willie, appreciatively. "I'm giving father cigars."

"I know, I thought of cigars too. Men always like cigars and cigarettes. You can't go wrong on them. Say, would you like to try one or two of these cigarettes? We can take them from the bottom. You'll like them, they're Russian—away ahead of Egyptian."

"Thanks," answered Willie. "I'd like one immensely. I only started smoking last spring—on my twelfth birthday. I think a feller's a fool to begin smoking cigarettes too soon, don't you? It stunts him. I waited till I was twelve."

"Me too," said Edwin, as they lighted their cigarettes. "In fact, I wouldn't buy them now if it weren't for dad. I simply *had* to give him something from Santa Claus. He believes in Santa Claus absolutely, you know."

And while this was going on, Clarisse was showing little Ulvina the absolutely lovely little bridge set that she got for her mother. "Aren't these markers perfectly charming?" said Ulvina, "and don't you love this little Dutch design—or is it Flemish, darling?"

"Dutch," said Clarisse, "isn't it quaint? And aren't these the dearest little things—for putting the money in when you play. I needn't have got them with it—they'd have sold the rest separately—but I think it's too utterly slow playing without money, don't you?"

"Oh, abominable," shuddered Ulvina, "but your mamma never plays for money, does she?"

"Mamma! Oh, gracious, no. Mamma's far too slow for that. But I shall tell her that Santa Claus insisted on putting in the little money boxes."

"I suppose she believes in Santa Claus, just as my mamma does."

"Oh, absolutely," said Clarisse, and added, "What if we play a little game! With a double dummy, the French way, or Norwegian Skat, if you like. That only needs two."

"All right," agreed Ulvina, and in a few minutes they were deep in a game of cards with a little pile of pocket money beside them.

About half an hour later, all the members of the two families were down again in the drawing room. But of course nobody said anything about the presents. In any case they were all too busy looking at the beautiful big Bible, with maps in it, that the Joneses had bought to give to Grandfather. They all agreed that with the help of it, Grandfather could hunt up any place in Palestine in a moment, day or night.

But upstairs, away upstairs in a sitting room of his own, Grandfather Jones was looking with an affectionate eye at the presents that stood beside him. There was a beautiful whisky decanter, with silver filigree outside (and whisky inside) for Jones, and for the little boy a big nickel-plated Jew's harp.

Later on, far in the night, the person, or the influence, or whatever it is called Santa Claus, took all the presents and placed them in the people's stockings.

And, being blind as he always has been, he gave the wrong things to the wrong people—in fact, he gave them just as indicated above.

But the next day, in the course of Christmas morning, the situation straightened itself out, just as it always does.

Indeed, by ten o'clock, Brown and Jones were playing with the train, and Mrs. Brown and Mrs. Jones were making dolls' clothes, and the boys were smoking cigarettes, and Clarisse and Ulvina were playing cards for their pocket money.

And upstairs—away up—Grandfather was drinking whisky and playing the Jew's harp.

And so Christmas, just as it always does, turned out all right after all.

# The Final Apprentice

## Steve Rasnic Tem

The tiny creature struggled mightily between the narrow arms of Andrew's forceps. With a slight tremble in his pudgy hand Andrew held the magnifying glass for his apprentice to see (again his final apprentice was reminded of the great age of this, the last wizard of the world, semi-retired). "There boy—identify that one for me."

Apprentice (still wearing "the horns of befuddlement" Andrew had awarded him the week before) sidled slowly over and bobbed his head dumbly like a reluctant steer at a Texas barbecue. He draped one bloodshot eye over the glass. "Ummm . . . ummm."

"I'm waiting, Apprentice."

"Well . . . he's approximately two inches high, I'd say. His coat is covered with several dozen patches of bright colors. His face is withered, wrinkled, a lost, panicked look to the eyes . . ." He straightened suddenly. "I swear, Master Andrew, Lord of the Pierced Earrings, Enchanter of the Fifteen Speedy Laundrettes, Vizier to the Sweaty But . . ."

"Apprentice, *please* . . ."

"Oh . . . well, he appears to resemble the former president."

Andrew shook his head. "All presidents look like that once they're out of office. It's all the acrobatics, I hear. But his identity, Apprentice? Of what species is this particular elf?"

Again Apprentice leaned over the glass. By now his breath had quite fogged it, but he did not dare tell Andrew this. He absently stroked his horns. "Massariol?"

"Apprentice! Massariol come a foot high with red knee socks!"

"Ummm . . . ummm. Salvanel? Bwbach?"

"Apprentice!" Andrew's great beard unfurled in anger. He took a sudden step toward him in his baggy green overalls.

"Barabao? Giane? Follet?"

"Apprentice!" Andrew's beard curled and uncurled like a party horn.

"Kobolde? Pixie? Rutabaga? Republican?" Andrew started swinging his arms in rage, the magnifying glass in one hand, the elf-between-forceps in the other. "Castanet? Calliope? Kristofferson?" Andrew started chasing Apprentice around the room, the horns of befuddlement catching on beaker stands and distillation tubes and pulling it all crashing down. "Diehard? Veg-o-Matic? Energizer?" Andrew threw up his arms and the magnifying glass wedged into one eye socket like a monocle. "Brassier? Brisket? Bluebird? Brownie?" The elf-between-forceps flew end over end and landed with a tiny but fruitful thud. "Magpie? Mistress? Misogyny?" Apprentice had no opportunity to avoid it. "Diaphra . . ." *SPLAGG!* And suddenly Apprentice's feet had left him and were flying south for the winter.

Andrew attempted to follow them but couldn't quite attain departure speed, his own feet snared by the horns of befuddlement which, for the first time, he regretted having given his apprentice. Suddenly he was draping Apprentice like a rug woven by Persian opium addicts.

Avoiding eye contact with his all-powerful mentor, Apprentice poked a finger into the sticky mess in his right palm and stirred it. "Of course!" he cried. "It's a Portune! And here I thought they were extinct!"

Apprentice mopped the specimen room wearing the long, tattered "ears of the hopeless" (the horns of befuddlement were currently keeping his boss the last wizard Andrew entertained—even now he could hear from down the corridor the hatchet ringing off those noble branches of bone, punctuated by his master's shouts of glee). An open copy of *The Field Guide to Elves, Dwarves, and Others of Abbreviated Stature* hung suspended from a stiff wire that curved over his head and attached to the back of his collar. He had to turn the pages with his tongue. He observed that the colored illustrations tasted not unlike his mother's home-baked matzo. So Apprentice mopped and read and toiled with tears in his eyes, now and again pausing to wipe his nose with one ragged, hopeless ear.

"Hey, burro-head, got a match?"

Apprentice looked warily at the row of cages lining the far wall. Leprechauns, Goat People, Fountain Women . . . all the bigger types were quartered there. Then he noticed the one who had spoken to him: fiery red eyes and eagle-taloned fingers, protruding teeth and that unmistakable red cap. Like one of Santa's elves the day after the Christmas Eve keg party.

He wasn't supposed to speak to the Red Caps. Ever. "Fairy-punks," Andrew called them. They lived only in places with a history of violence, like fortified castles or discount stores. They dropped great stones on the salesmen who came to their doors and dyed their caps with the blood. And on top of that they wouldn't even return their victims' sample cases. Their filthy chambers were littered with desk calendars and ballpoint pens. They also could foretell disasters by making a loud noise like three cats Scotch-taped to the vanes of a ceiling fan (as part of his home-study course in wizardry Apprentice had tried this out just so that he might recognize the sound—now and then his pets still thanked him for this experience with small aromatic gifts left in his sock drawer).

The Red Caps were a sturdy, gray, and exceedingly cranky breed of elf.

"Come on, kid. Bloody hell. I'm dyin' in here."

Apprentice could see that the nasty-looking creature had at least seven or eight cigarettes shoved into his wide, tooth-studded maw. "Don't you know that besides being bad for you, smoking is terribly out of fashion now?"

"Bloody hell. We Red Caps are from the British Isles. Scottish, mostly." The Red Cap wiggled his heavy eyebrows. The cigarettes bobbed up and down like albino porcupine quills piercing his lips.

"*Oh* . . ." Comprehension dawned so unfamiliarly across Apprentice's face he had an urge to run and wash it off. Then he frowned. "No. I'm not supposed to talk to you. I'm in enough trouble already."

"Is this the way you treat a guest? No towels, no little soaps, no mints on the pillow?"

Apprentice patted his pockets. "I've got a little piece of Baby Ruth here somewhere . . . it's a little linty . . . er . . . the lint is probably green . . ." He wrestled not to look confused and lost the match. "But you're a prisoner."

"Iron bars do not a prison . . . oh, forget it. What's your name, kid?"

"Apprentice."

"I didn't ask you what you did for a living."

"No . . . Apprentice."

"Funny name to give a kid, even one with long ears."

"My mother had very definite vocational plans for me."

"Mothers are like that. Unrealistic. It can be pretty traumatic for a kid. Mine wanted me to be a Boston Celtic."

"Is that like a Druid?"

"Forget it, kid. Don't strain your ears. What's that book you got?"

"An identification manual, for you little people."

"That's very politically correct of you. I bet in private you refer to us as *shrimpy bastards* or *elven scum,* right?" Apprentice did his best to look indignant. "What's the matter? Stomachache?" Apprentice buried his face in his guidebook, stroking the pages with his tongue (and wincing at another paper cut), pretending to read. "You should try that with some ketchup."

"We're collecting you, I suppose you know that." Apprentice peered around the edge of the book, looking for the Red Cap's reaction.

"Yeah, I figured. I used to collect you big guys, but I had a problem finding large enough jars."

Apprentice leaned forward on his mop, then struggled to remove the handle from one nostril. "Thish ismot . . . *ah* . . . this isn't something to joke about, you know. Master Andrew, Keeper of the Jerusalem Stringball, Protector of the Westminster Pail, Litigant in the Superior Court of the State of New York, Finder of Lost Loves, er, and many other things too numerous to mention in this particular bit of dialogue, is the world's last remaining wizard and I am his final apprentice and it is our task now that magic grows old-fashioned and passé to capture every last remaining sprite and elf of whatever stripe . . . er, *some* of you are striped, I'm sure of it . . ." He fumbled uselessly with his guidebook. ". . . after which time there will be no more magic or fantasy to . . . well, to confuse the issue."

"He, this Andrew-of-the-tortured-explanation, *he* taught you this?"

"Er . . . yes."

"And what, pray tell, is to replace magic and elves in this new world order?"

"Well, *science,* of course, and domestic services. That sort of thing. Of course, we already *have* science—rockets and electricity and gravity and all that stuff—but so many people still believe in magic and fairies and other superstitious things. Master Andrew says science doesn't work as well as it ought to and so now it's time to get rid of all that other stuff and as the world's last wizard the responsibility has fallen to him and it's a lousy job but the benefits aren't so bad."

"Bloody hell, I'm a *superstition?*"

"Well, you have to admit you *do* look like one."

The Red Cap nodded as if in grudging agreement. He wiggled his cigarettes again. Apprentice was amazed at the elf's talent. *He* could never have talked so clearly around that many cigarettes and protruding teeth. "Your Master Andrew wears green overalls."

"He's preparing for a life after magic. He's been taking a correspondence course in Electronics and Small Appliance Repair. He says green overalls are a more fitting uniform for the new age."

"His green overalls are baggy. They're not 'fitting' at all."

"Master Andrew says comfort in the seat area helps him to think."

"He *must* be in control of a powerful magic, if he hasn't broken down and turned you into a doorstop yet."

Andrew thought this might be the famous Red Cap sarcasm he'd heard so much about, but wanted to see the elf's face to make sure. He moved his head to the side quickly, hoping to get a better look at the Red Cap, but the book sprang immediately to partially block his view. He jerked his head back and forth several times in this manner, until finally the book shot back violently and slapped him in the face. "I'mb sborry," he mumbled through his bleeding nose. "That bwas siblly."

"Your Master Andrew doesn't look like much of a wizard to me."

Apprentice was seriously offended, a difficult feat to manage with a bloody nose. "How can you say that?"

"He's, well, a bit on the chubby side for a wizard, isn't he?"

"He likes chocolates. He says they help him focus."

"Well, Mr. Accessory . . ."

"Apprentice."

"Everybody knows you should never trust a fat wizard. It shows he's been spending more time with the cakes and custards than with his studies. They say the more rib that shows, the wiser the wizard." By logical progression, of course, this meant that the wisest wizards were the dead ones, but Apprentice said nothing. After all, the Red Cap's teeth *were* sharp. "*You,* at least, study hard, I hope."

Apprentice casually reached up and rubbed from his chin the white sugar left over from his late morning snack. "Hard as a Poltersprite."

"Ah, they just like to make noise. A wizard has to be more than that. A wizard is a self-starter like, well, like a pig on hot asphalt."

Apprentice blushed. His master had told him this very thing many times. Apprentice himself was not so enterprising. Sometimes it was necessary to light a fire under his feet, and in fact oftentimes Master Andrew had cheerfully obliged. But the blisters felt much better now. "Master Andrew always says mosquitoes would make great wizards—that is, if they weren't so small and if they weren't insects and if they didn't die so quickly and all . . ."

"A wizard has to be forceful, determined," the Red Cap continued, "and bondable. To the talented wizard, nothing can ever be totally unexpected, except perhaps finding a chicken with decent athletic ability."

Here, the evil imp had hit a sore point. Many had been the hours Master Andrew had laughed out loud while perusing this very same volume, and yet he selfishly refused to underline the good parts for Apprentice.

Apprentice raised his hand, dropping the mop handle. "Wizards know how to *transubstantiate!* Oh, they're *big* on that. You know, base metal into gold, water into wine, vast forests into knickknack shelves, that sort of thing . . ."

"A wizard understands everything about spirits and their doings. He knows their abilities, their tricks, their secret savings accounts. A good wizard can play a spirit like Eric Clapton plays guitar, although perhaps with a little more bass."

"Oh, and don't forget their knack for finding magical objects: amulets, lamps, swords, crotchless panties, potions . . ."

"They tend to be loners. Now, occasionally they might attend an office party, but they always leave before those funny games with the photocopier begin . . ." The Red Cap stopped. "You know, I *like* you, kid."

Apprentice looked down, embarrassed. Not only because unsolicited expressions of endearment made him shy, but because he had just discovered he had one foot wedged inside his mop bucket. "Well . . . maybe you Red Caps aren't so bad, either." He tittered softly.

"How about that match, then? You know me . . . I'm not going to *bite.*" The Red Cap laughed, too vigorously it seemed. But Apprentice made himself laugh too.

"Sh-sh-sure. Why not?" Apprentice walked over to the cage, lit a lint-encrusted match that had been resting in his pocket for years it seemed, and lit each of the Red Cap's cigarettes in turn.

"Apprentice?"

"Yes, Mr. Red Cap, sir?"

"You just lit three of my teeth."

"Oh, sorry . . ."

The Red Cap leaned back against his cell wall, sighing, blowing smoke, and wincing from the pain, although not necessarily in that order. "By the way . . . did your Master Andrew explain to you how, after he collects us all, he's going to get rid of the various members of fairydom?"

"Well, not exactly."

"Guns or poison, probably."

"Oh! Of course not!"

"Bloody hell. Sounds like a little fairycide to me, leprechaun-lynching, dwarf-butchery, coup de gnome. Many names, but the results are always the same."

"Never! Never!"

"Well, enough of *my* problems. You have your studies to complete, right? Read me a little from your guidebook. After all, I *can't* know *everybody*."

Apprentice ventured to formulate a studious expression, but as in most of his attempts to strike a particular pose, he looked to be in the throes of indigestion. "Well, let's see, there's the Giane from Sardinia. Wood spirits with long breasts who occupy themselves with spinning and memorizing soup can labels. Despite their talents they have difficulty finding dates on the weekends."

"Maybe if they memorized the sports page . . ."

"It says here they sing sweet lullabies in their caves to men who fall in love with legumes and are brokenhearted when these haughty legumes refuse to wear the lingerie the men have ordered specially for them from mail-order houses in California."

The Red Cap nodded sagely. "The Giane have lost all interest in normal sexual relations, I hear, nine of ten greatly preferring animal husbandry."

"Then you know them?"

"Not intimately. I assume you've captured these creatures?"

"They're in the back playing poker with the goat people."

"Then I hope it isn't too friendly a game. What's in it for you, anyway, 'Prentice?"

"I get to become the next wizard, after."

"After what?"

"After all the magic is gone."

"Isn't that a little like being made captain of the ship after it's been left permanently in dry dock?"

"It's not all magic, being a wizard, you know."

"Enlighten me."

"Wizards get to know things. I like knowing things. Master Andrew, Grand Dragon of Small Appliance Maintenance and Repair, is learning all about televisions, radios, microwaves, that sort of thing. I'd like to know things like that. I'd like to know anything, Mr. Red Cap."

The elf looked at the guidebook in Apprentice's hand. "You know your elf and fairy families, or at least you're *working* on it."

"But what good is that going to do?" Apprentice blushed. "I'm sorry, Mr. Red Cap, but all you folks are going to be gone soon. Remember science? Maintenance and repair?"

The Red Cap smiled, his countless huge teeth practically exploding up out of his gums. "Bloody hell, Apprentice. I have an idea."

"Apprentice! Apprentice, where are you?" Master Andrew splashed across the wet floor. He had been unable to find his assistant anywhere. And worse, all their specimens were gone, every last variety of dwarf, fairy, elf had vanished. "Oh, damn!"

He didn't really care all that much, actually. It was a new world out there. There was no place for a fairy kingdom anymore. They had lost their ecological niche. He and Apprentice had been feeding and sheltering most of them for years. They wouldn't be able to last more than a few days on their own.

He stopped and stared at the counter that ran across the back of the room. All the cages for the smaller sprites had been removed and the space had been filled with a variety of electronic gear instead. Upon closer examination he discovered they were some of the televisions, stereos, home computers, CD players, and VCRs from his shop upstairs, the ones he hadn't yet been able to figure out how to repair. They were all plugged in to the strip of outlets above the counter.

He walked up to a stereo and turned it on. Beautiful, almost unearthly music flooded the chamber.

He flipped on a TV. Cowboys rode across an endless range of variegated browns, a sunset of reds, blues, and greens sweeping the background.

He pushed a button and the computer beeped into life. He poked and stroked VCR and CD player controls. Lights blinked. Motors whirred smoothly.

"They're all in perfect working order, sir," Apprentice said behind him.

Master Andrew turned to his apprentice, who wore identical green overalls to his own. "Very impressive, Apprentice," he said. "I didn't even know you were studying such things."

"I . . . I seem to have a natural affinity for the work."

"Yes . . ." Master Andrew gazed about at the happily humming machinery, filling the air with the warm aroma of electrified chips, diodes, and resistors. "Very impressive. There are more upstairs . . . I'll bring them down to you straightaway." He started toward the staircase, then turned. "The fairies, Apprentice? The elves? What did you do with them all?"

Apprentice smiled and laughed softly. "Never-never land, boss. Never-never land." Then he winked.

Master Andrew laughed with him. "Ah, yes, never-never land. I didn't think you had it in you, Apprentice." Then he climbed the stairs.

Apprentice went over to the stereo and peered closely at the speaker cloth. The voice inside was unearthly. With his eye up to the loose weave he could just barely make out the tiny siren within, its head thrown back, mouth open to expose a throat that plunged deep into the heart of fairyland.

He moved to the television and lowered his head as close as he dared to the screen (he knew he would never be able to quite trust the radiation given off by such things). The tiny cowboys inside turned on their horses and waved to him, the artificial sun in the distance reflecting off their elven smiles.

Finally he stood by the desktop computer. A toothy grin filled the screen. "What did I tell you?" The Red Cap's voice was static-filled, but recognizable just the same on the cheap speaker. Tiny puffs of cigarette smoke exploded rhythmically from the disk drive door. "A little cramped, but still . . . I don't mind calling it home. Certainly better than the alternative."

"There's some dirt on your little window thingie," Apprentice said with concern. He raised the mop that had been leaning against the wall. "Let me get it for you."

"Apprentice . . ."

Too late the mop slopped over the screen, water sloshing into the ventilation grille. The screen made a popping noise, and there was a soft scraping from somewhere deep inside the computer and the straining sound of something winding down.

"Bloody hell," the speaker said softly. "Bloody hell."

# Forgetful Charlie

## Hugh B. Cave

Charles Collingham was only six years old when his mother called him the untidiest boy in America. "Just look at this room!" Mrs. Collingham said. "Clothes every which way. Crayons under the bed. Waste-basket full of scrunched-up paper. Chubby, I swear I'll be old before my time if you don't stop it!"

Charles could see that his mother was upset, and solemnly promised to reform. But he didn't reform, and Mrs. Collingham tearfully begged her husband to do something about it.

"Chubby," Mr. Collingham said sternly, "we'll have no more of this. From now on you'll be neat." His heart wasn't in it, though; Charles could tell. Later Charles overheard his father saying to his mother, "Now be reasonable, Florence. All little boys are thoughtless at that age. He'll grow out of it."

Charles was nine when he decided one Saturday morning to build a wagon. He worked all day at it. That night it rained, and after church on Sunday Mr. Collingham grasped Charles by an arm and marched him out to the driveway.

"Look!" Mr. Collingham shouted. "My best saw, left out overnight and now ruined with rust! My hammer! My new set of screwdrivers! Even my miter box!" He said some forbidden words under his breath—on Sunday, too—and made Charles clean all the tools with kerosene and return them to their proper places in the cabinet over the workbench.

Charles promised never to do it again.

By the time he was sixteen and in high school, Charles had become a genuine problem. "You just watch him," Mrs. Collingham said to a visiting neighbor when Charles came whistling up the walk one December afternoon on his way from school. "You watch what he does now, and tell me if I don't have a right to be losing my mind."

Charles threw open the front door, kicked his rubbers off, dropped an armful of books on the hall table and called, "Hi!" The books fell off the table and papers spilled out of them, but Charles paid no attention. Slouching into the living room, he tossed his jacket onto the divan, his hat onto a chair, remarked with a grin that he had flunked an English test, and thumped up to his room to listen to his favorite disk jockey.

Mrs. Collingham waved her hands helplessly at her neighbor. "You see?"

"I know what I would do," the neighbor said. "I would get a large box, and anything of his that I found lying around I would drop into it. He would soon get tired of rummaging through it every time he wanted something."

Mrs. Collingham discussed this with Mr. Collingham and he thought it an excellent idea. They placed a large cardboard carton in their son's room, behind the door, and Mrs. Collingham dropped things into it.

This seemed to work very well. "Hey," Charles would say, "where did my trombone music get to?"

"In the box," Mrs. Collingham would inform him triumphantly.

"Oh yeah, the box." And Charles would go to the box and grumble while pawing through its contents.

But one day after Mrs. Collingham had told Charles that a misplaced school book was in the box, Charles said, "Oh yeah, the box," and added brightly, "You know, Mom, that box was a neat idea. Now I know where things are."

Mrs. Collingham talked it over with her husband and they removed the box.

Charles became more and more set in his ways. He would take a piece of cake and leave the kitchen counter covered with crumbs. He would finish a bowl of leftover macaroni and return the empty bowl unwashed to the refrigerator. He would do his homework and half an hour later be unable to find it.

Mr. and Mrs. Collingham tried every persuasion they could think of, then gave up in despair.

"You are hopeless," Mr. Collingham said.

"All I can say is, heaven help the girl who marries you," Mrs. Collingham sobbed.

"But, good grief," Charles protested. "I try to be neat, don't I?"

When Charles was nineteen and attending a small local college—the better colleges had all turned him down because of his grades, though he was certainly not stupid—the Japanese attacked Pearl Harbor. Charles enlisted in the Marines.

The Marines, as everyone knows, are orderly people: a place for everything and everything in its place. But they could not reform Charles. If the Japanese had not been doing so well in the South Pacific, Charles would certainly have been sent home.

Instead, he was sent to the island of New Georgia, and presently found himself encamped in a clearing deep in the jungle, engaged in searching for tenacious Japanese who had been left behind when their companions retreated. It was considered important to round up these phantom foes lest they reorganize behind the American advance.

One day the chaplain said to Charles severely, "I have received a letter from your mother, begging me to find out why you have not written. Why haven't you written?"

"I have," Charles protested. "I guess the letters got mislaid before I could mail them."

"Write tonight," the chaplain ordered. "And be careful to shade the light in your tent, because the jungle is full of foes who are hungry and impoverished, and your tent is on the edge of camp."

Dutifully, Charles sat down that evening to compose a letter. There was no chance of his being interrupted by ribald companions seeking to play cards or tell stories; he had been given a small tent all to himself because no one could be found who would put up with his untidiness. He wrote sitting on his cot with the paper on a board across his knees.

Halfway through the letter he heard a stealthy footstep outside and shot to his feet. *Japs!* he thought, and looked wildly around for his rifle.

For the life of him he could not remember where he had put it. His tent was so cluttered that the rifle might be anywhere.

Charles was frantically pawing through his possessions when a grinning enemy soldier appeared in the doorway and pointed a pistol at him. Charles could only stare, with his mouth open.

The Japanese looked back at Charles and squeezed the trigger. The pistol went *Click*.

Leaping forward, Charles threw the surprised man to the ground and thoroughly clobbered him.

When the Japanese was delivered to headquarters he was found to be carrying a frayed shoelace, some cartridges for his pistol, a bit of raw taro root and a water-stained letter. The letter was handed to an intelligence officer named Brady who spoke Japanese, and everyone waited with held breath while Brady studied it.

"Amounts to nothing," Brady said with a shrug. "It's from his mother in Yokohama. 'Your father and I are so glad to hear that you are in good health and rapidly winning the war. No doubt you will soon be home again. All we hope, dear Hodashi, is that the army will have taught you to be more careful and less untidy, or as far as we are concerned, this war will have been a waste of time!'"

Hodashi, covering his face with his hands, began to weep.

"What are you crying for?" Brady asked him.

Hodashi pointed to the gun which, when aimed at Charles, had gone *Click*. Brady examined it. "Well, whaddaya know," he said, "it's empty. The dope forgot to load it!"

The prisoner sobbed uncontrollably in his grief, and the sound pursued Charles all the way back to his tent. A shaken man, Charles paused in his doorway to survey the clutter.

Let this be a lesson to me, Charles thought. Never again will I be untidy.

Before retiring, he picked up his belongings, folded his clothes, swept the floor and made his bed properly. There wasn't a neater tent—no doubt of it—in the entire Southwest Pacific.

The imp inside him did not give up without a struggle, though. In the morning Charles was run up before the Old Man for going to sleep with his light on.

# Gandhi at the Bat

## Chet Williamson

History books and available newspaper files hold no record of the visit to America in 1933 made by Mohandas K. Gandhi. For reasons of a sensitive political nature that have not yet come to light, all contemporary accounts of the visit were suppressed at the request of President Roosevelt. Although Gandhi repeatedly appeared in public during his three-month stay, the cloak of journalistic silence was seamless, and all that remains of the great man's celebrated tour is this long-secreted glimpse of one of the Mahatma's unexpected nonpolitical appearances, written by an anonymous press-box denizen of the day.

Yankee Stadium is used to roaring crowds. But never did a crowd roar louder than on yesterday afternoon, when a little brown man in a loincloth and wire-rimmed specs put some wood on a Lefty Grove fastball and completely bamboozled Connie Mack's A's.

It all started when Mayor John P. O'Brien invited M. K. ("Mahatma") Gandhi to see the Yanks play Philadelphia up at "The House That Ruth Built." Gandhi, whose ballplaying experience was limited to a few wallops with a cricket bat, jumped at the chance, and 12 noon saw the Mayor's party in the Yankee locker room, where the Mahatma met the Bronx Bombers. A zippy exchange occurred when the Mayor introduced the Lord of the Loincloth to the Bambino. "Mr. Gandhi," Hizzoner said, "I want you to meet Babe Ruth, the Sultan of Swat."

Gandhi's eyes sparkled behind his Moxie-bottle lenses, and he chuckled. "Swat," quoth he, "is a sultanate of which I am not aware. Is it by any chance near Maharashtra?"

"Say," laughed the Babe, laying a meaty hand on the frail brown shoulder, "you're all right, kiddo. I'll hit one out of the park for you today."

"No hitting, please," the Mahatma quipped.

In the Mayor's front-row private box, the little Indian turned down the offer of a hot dog and requested a box of Cracker Jack instead. The prize inside was a tin whistle, which he blew gleefully whenever the Bambino waddled up to bat.

The grinning guru enjoyed the game immensely—far more than the A's, who were down 3–1 by the fifth. Ruth, as promised, did smash a homer in the seventh, to Gandhi's delight. "Hey, Gunga Din!" Ruth cried jovially on his way to the Yankee dugout. "Know why my battin' reminds folks of India? 'Cause I can really Bangalore!"

"That is a very good one, Mr. Ruth!" cried the economy-size Asian.

By the top of the ninth, the Yanks had scored two more runs. After Mickey Cochrane whiffed on a Red Ruffing fastball, Gandhi remarked how difficult it must be to hit such a swiftly thrown missile and said, "I should like to try it very much."

"Are you serious?" Mayor O'Brien asked.

"If it would not be too much trouble. Perhaps after the exhibition is over," his visitor suggested.

There was no time to lose. O'Brien, displaying a panache that would have done credit to his predecessor, Jimmy Walker, leaped up and shouted to the umpire, who called a time-out. Managers McCarthy and Mack were beckoned to the Mayor's side, along with Bill Dinneen, the home-plate umpire, and soon all of Yankee Stadium heard an unprecedented announcement: "Ladies and gentlemen, regardless of the score, the Yankees will come to bat to finish the ninth inning."

The excited crowd soon learned that the reason for such a breach of tradition was a little brown pinch hitter shorter than his bat. When the pinstriped Bronx Bombers returned to their dugout after the last Philadelphia batter had been retired in the ninth, the Nabob of Nonviolence received a hasty batting lesson from Babe Ruth under the stands.

Lazzeri led off the bottom of the stanza, hitting a short chop to Bishop, who rifled to Foxx for the out. Then, after Crosetti fouled out to Cochrane, the stadium became hushed as the announcer intoned, "Pinch-hitting for Ruffing, Mohandas K. Gandhi."

The crowd erupted as the white-robed holy man, a fungo bat propped jauntily on his shoulder, strode to the plate, where he remarked to the crouching Mickey Cochrane, "It is a very big field, and a very small ball."

"C'mon, Moe!" Ruth called loudly to the dead-game bantam batter. "Show 'em the old pepper!"

"I will try, Mr. Baby!" Gandhi called back, and went into a batting stance unique in the annals of the great game—his sheet-draped posterior facing the catcher, and his bat held high over his head, as if to clobber the ball into submission. While Joe McCarthy called time, the Babe trotted out and politely corrected the little Indian's position in the box.

The time-out over, Grove threw a screaming fastball right over the plate. The bat stayed on Gandhi's shoulder. "Oh, my," he said as he turned and observed the ball firmly ensconced in Cochrane's glove. "That *was* speedy."

The second pitch was another dead-center fastball. The Mahatma swung, but found that the ball had been in the Mick's glove for a good three seconds before his swipe was completed. "Steerike two!" Dinneen barked.

The next pitch was high and outside, and the ump called it a ball before the petite pundit made a tentative swing at it. "Must I sit down now?" he asked.

"Nah, it's a ball," Dinneen replied. "I called it before you took your cut."

"Yes. I *know* that is a ball, and I did swing at it and did miss."

"No, no, a ball. Like a free pitch."

"Oh, I see."

"Wasn't in the strike zone."

"Yes, I see."

"So you get another swing."

"Yes."

"And if you miss you sit down."

"I just *did* miss."

"Play ball, Mister."

The next pitch was in the dirt. Gandhi did not swing. "Ball," Dinneen called.

"Yes, it is," the Mahatma agreed.

"Two and two."

"That is four."

"Two balls, two strikes."

"Is there not but one ball?"

"Two balls."

"Yes, I see."

"And two strikes."

"And if I miss I sit down."

Ruth's voice came booming from the Yankee dugout: "Swing early, Gandy baby!"

"When is early?"

"When I tell ya! I'll shout 'Now!'"

Grove started his windup. Just as his leg kicked up, the Bambino's cry of "Now!" filled the park.

The timing was perfect. Gandhi's molasses-in-January swing met the Grove fastball right over the plate. The ball shot downward, hit the turf, and arced gracefully into the air toward Grove. "Run, Peewee, run!" yelled Ruth, as the crowd went wild.

"Yes, yes!" cried Gandhi, who started down the first-base line in what can only be described as a dancing skip, using his bat as a walking stick. An astonished Grove booted the high bouncer, then scooped up the ball and flung it to Jimmie Foxx at first.

But Foxx, mesmerized by the sight of a sixty-three-year-old Indian in white robes advancing merrily before him and blowing mightily on a tin whistle, failed to descry the stitched orb, which struck the bill of his cap, knocking it off his head, and, slowed by its deed of déshabillé, rolled to a stop by the fence.

Gandhi paused only long enough to touch first and to pick up Jimmy's cap and return it to him. By the time the still gawking Foxx had perched it once more on his head, the vital vegetarian was halfway to second.

Right-fielder Coleman retrieved Foxx's missed ball and now relayed it to Max Bishop at second, but too late. The instant Bishop tossed the ball back to the embarrassed Grove, Gandhi was off again. Grove, panicking, overthrew third base, and by the time left-fielder Bob Johnson picked up the ball, deep in foul territory, the Tiny Terror of Tealand had rounded the hot corner and was scooting for home. Johnson hurled the ball on a true course to a stunned Cochrane. The ball hit the pocket of Cochrane's mitt and popped out like a muffin from a toaster.

Gandhi jumped on home plate with both sandaled feet, and the crowd exploded as Joe McCarthy, the entire Yankee squad, and even a beaming Connie Mack surged onto the field.

"I ran home," giggled Gandhi. "Does that mean that I hit a run home?"

"A home run, Gandy," said Ruth. "Ya sure did."

"Well, technically," said Umpire Dinneen, "it was a single and an overthrow and then—"

"*Shaddup*," growled a dozen voices at once.

"Looked like a homer to me, too," the ump corrected, but few heard him, for by that time the crowd was on the field, lifting to their shoulders a joyous Gandhi, whose tin whistle provided a thrilling trilling over the mob's acclaim.

Inside the locker room, Manager McCarthy offered Gandhi a permanent position on the team, but the Mahatma graciously refused, stating that he could only consider a diamond career with a different junior-circuit club.

"Which club would that be, kid?" said the puzzled Bambino.

"The Cleveland Indians, of course," twinkled the Mahatma.

An offer from the Cleveland front office arrived the next day, but India's top pinch hitter was already on a train headed for points west—and the history books.

# Getting Enough

### Chet Williamson

I need life, Marty. I need *life*." Frank Ames looked over the rim of his third gin and tonic at his friend Marty Green. "Christ, I'm forty and not getting any younger, I've been married to the same woman for seventeen years; I got three kids. . . ."

"I have somebody for you."

"Huh?"

"A girl. When you going up to the city again?"

"Two weeks."

"Good." Marty pulled from his pocket the stubby pencil he'd used to score their match, smoothed out his cocktail napkin on the bar and scribbled on it. "Here." It read, SHARON——815-8872.

"This on the level?"

"I kid you? She's the best I ever found. You want *life*, this is the lady."

Frank didn't wait two weeks to go to the city. Monday morning, he told his wife he had agency meetings both that afternoon and the following day. She drove him to the station, smiled and kissed him

149

good-bye, not realizing that along with his clothes, he had packed the unopened bottle of cologne his daughter had given him last Father's Day.

When Frank checked into his hotel, he brushed his teeth, then dialed the number.

"Hello, Sharon Allison speaking. . . ." The voice reminded Frank of a Black Velvet billboard.

"Uh, hello, Sharon. My name is Frank. Marty Green gave me your number."

"Oh, yes, he told me you'd be calling. He thought that maybe you and I could . . . do some business together."

God, this is easy, Frank thought.

"Would you like to come over here?" Her voice *dripped* with lust, with the promise of clandestine acts of indescribable whoopee.

He was about to ask for the address when, amid thoughts of silky flesh, came creeping other thoughts of hidden cameras, blackmail, divorce settlements, lawyers. "Well, maybe it would be better here. I'm expecting some calls."

"And when would be convenient?"

"Um . . . any time."

"Say in an hour?"

"Ah . . . sure."

"So tell me a little about yourself."

"Why?"

"Well, I have to know what you want."

Frank thought for a moment. "The usual, I guess."

"The usual?" She laughed, a clear, bell-like sound that made the base of Frank's spine sweat. "There are so many ways to go, Mr. . . ."

"Ames." He bit his tongue. He'd been planning to tell her his name was Smith, but the truth had jumped out of his mouth faster than a bad clam.

"Mr. *Ames.* . . ." He had always thought his name was short, but her voice made it delightfully polysyllabic. "And I *do* want to work up something very special for you, since you're a friend of Marty's. Now. How old are you?"

How *old* was he? Was she worried about his heart, or what? "Thirty-seven," he lied.

"Are you married?"

"Uh. . . ." Why should I lie? Maybe there's a discount. "Yes."

"Children?"

Children? "Three. But. . . ."

"You like to . . . travel?"

A leading question if ever there was one. "Oh, yeah."

"Yes?"

What the hell; he'd said sillier things. "Around the world . . . you know?"

"Hmm," she mused breathily. "That could be a little extra."

"No problem."

"Now, how about any illnesses?"

Although it was an intrusive question, it made him feel relaxed. If she was so concerned, the chances of picking up anything from her would be very small. And Marty, as Frank knew, was a very cautious man. "Oh, no, I'm clean."

"Oh!" She laughed again, and his toes curled. "It's so *good* to be clean. Just one more thing—do you smoke?"

"Smoke . . . what?"

"Cigarettes."

"No."

"Good. That'll make things much nicer. And less expensive, too."

Frank wondered if she were associated with the American Cancer Society or if she simply detested smoker's breath. Either way, he was glad he had quit.

"So," she went on, "I'll be there at six. Where are you?"

He gave her the name of his hotel and the room number.

"I assume you have everything we need?"

Another leading question. "Well, I . . . should hope so."

"Fine. Then you'll be all ready for me when I arrive."

He frowned. "You mean . . . be ready to start as soon as you get here?" He realized she was a professional, but there were, after all, amenities.

"Sure."

"Well, do you want anything to drink first?"

"Oh, no, I really don't like to drink on the job."

"Ah. I'll just be ready to go, then."

"Yes. Have everything out when I get there."

"Everything *out?*"

"Mmm-hmm. *You* know."

"Everything out."

"Right."

"Right."

"See you."

"Right."

There was a click, and she was gone. Frank sat thinking for a minute, then went into the bathroom, showered, shaved and splashed the Father's Day cologne into all his cracks and crevices. There was no telling what she might do, and if she was so concerned about smoker's breath, he wanted to make sure he didn't offend in any other way.

Cleansed and anointed, he stood before the full-length mirror in the bathroom door and looked at his pink and naked body. Not bad for 40. He thought the two miles a day on the stationary bike had helped. He brushed his teeth again, sat on the bed and waited.

At six o'clock, there was a knock on his door. He thought of getting up to open it, but romance and bravado overcame him, and he lay back on the bed, arranged himself to his best advantage and called, "Come in, Sharon!"

The door opened and she walked in, wearing a black dress that clung to her tall and slender body. Her face and form were so lovely that he didn't notice the briefcase in her hand until she slowly moved it in front of her like a shield.

He looked at her, she looked at him, neither saying a word. They remained like that for several minutes, giving Frank plenty of time to wonder what bizarre devices she might have in her case.

At last he spoke. "Well," he said, "aren't you going to say anything?"

She swallowed heavily, and he became suddenly and horribly aware that the red flush in her cheeks was not merely healthy color.

"I *was* going to ask," she whispered huskily, her voice trembling, "if you wanted term, whole life or endowment. . . ."

Sharon left ten minutes later. In her briefcase, along with the print-outs she had brought for Frank Ames, was a check for $900, the first of four quarterly payments he would send to her company every year for the next two decades to pay for his $250,000 Flexible-Premium Policy.

At least, he thought that evening on the train home, she had complimented him on his cologne.

# Great-Aunt Ella and the Stanley Steamer

## Jane Rice

When great-aunt Ella died, my seven-year-old mind simply refused to digest, in one lump, such an improbability. Dead? Great-aunt Ella? Forever and ever? Unthinkable! I was taken to "pay my respects" and I remember, quite clearly, wondering if there wasn't some mistake as I stood on tiptoe to peer into the red velvet-lined casket at the strange, peaceful, great-aunt Ella therein. It was not until the funeral that I finally realized she *must* be dead and, as the coffin was placed in the black-draped, horse-drawn hearse, a startled, blinking thought sent tingles up my spine: "Wouldn't she be *furious!*"

There is no doubt about it. She would have been. Great-aunt Ella's temperamental outbursts were legion. In her day, she had *almost* been an opera singer, and she was convinced that one of the requisites of a true *artiste*—even an almost one—was temperament. She had it by the bucketful. It was, in a way, rather majestic, since she had bosom for it. This physiological masterpiece developed a regular ground swell that was fascinating to watch when she got it going. By its rise and fall, one could gauge fairly accurately whether or not she would leave the room, slowly and impressively, or suddenly "go to pieces" and have to be restored with smelling salts, and eau de cologne patted on the wrists and temples.

Occasionally she remained, unmoving, where she was and let her boiling ire be perfectly apparent, while maintaining a deceivingly unemotional expression. When this happened, everyone took to the nearest refuge as speedily as the bounds of politeness allowed, because then it was anybody's guess what she would do. My father always said, dryly, that if there were such a thing as reincarnation, great-aunt Ella would turn up as Niagara Falls in the Fourth of July fireworks display at the fairgrounds.

Great-uncle Will's married life must have been, at best, a sort of connubial hairshirt, but he never complained. It wouldn't have done any good. Instead, he developed a sort of wispy, protective

153

coloration that melted into his surroundings. No chameleon ever did a better job of self-effacement than great-aunt Ella's husband, Will. It was hard to believe the legend that, in his salad days, he had gone in for checked suits and a sporty buggy with yellow wheels, and had been a bit of a rake.

I feel reasonably sure that great-aunt Ella's death affected him much the same as it did me. It was impossible. Period. For the first time in thirty-five years, he was a free agent. That he automatically rejected this status as untenable is a reflection on great-aunt Ella's character rather than on his—although perhaps he *was* merely lonely for her, as my mother blindly insisted. Also, habits have a habit of becoming a way of life, and I suppose if you've lived in a cave of winds for well over a quarter of a century it becomes difficult to differentiate between echo and reality. Too, as great-uncle Will was a churchly man, there may have been the sobering thought that he would again meet great-aunt Ella face to face on the Day of Judgment, which might have accounted for his subsequent peculiar behavior.

On the other hand, maybe great-aunt Ella *did* "come back." I wouldn't have put it past her.

At any rate, and whatever the explanation, great-uncle Will slipped easily and gently—as if he were shrugging on an old famil-iar coat—into the belief that great-aunt Ella was *not* dead.

"Ella won't be here," he would inform mother when he came for Sunday dinner. "She has one of her headaches."

Or, "As Ella was saying only last night—"

And, "Ella said to tell you—"

When we called on great-uncle Will, there was, inevitably, the spooky, scalp-prickling moment when he departed stairward to im-part the news of our arrival to great-aunt Ella. He would disappear up the stairway, in the eerie purple light that seeped through the stained glass windowpane on the landing, to descend presently bearing tidings from great-aunt Ella to the effect that she would be down shortly and for us to make ourselves comfortable.

This, of course, was a physical impossibility for anyone with an ounce of imagination. The slightest squeak, the faintest rustle of a portiere, was enough to curdle your blood and make it run back-wards. A commonplace jaunt to the bathroom became a terrifying ordeal to be avoided at all costs. I have a cousin who claims that his current kidney ailment stems from his childhood aversion to the trek upstairs and down the long dim hall, *past great-aunt Ella's closed bedroom door,* to the john.

In the initial stages of great-uncle Will's "quirk," the family had attempted to "reason him out of it." This had culminated in an unsuccessful trip to the cemetery where he was confronted with the undeniable evidence of his wife's grave. His reaction baffled diagnosis. With no trouble whatsoever, he mated Reason with Fancy, and the issue from this highly incompatible union chased the family up a tree and kept them there.

"My goodness," he had exclaimed, staring at the grassy mound and the chiseled tombstone, "I hope Ella doesn't find out about this." He had sucked in his breath sharply. "Not a word to her. Understand."

After that fiasco, it had been decided at a family conclave that there was nothing for it but to carry it off with a high hand, a solid family front having many of the properties ascribed to pigiron.

Since great-uncle Will steadfastly refused to live anywhere but in his own house, something had to be done about that, also. Every family can, in a pinch, dig up a sacrificial offering.

There were two likely possibilities: Miss Margaret and Miss Emily, both of whom were approaching thirty. It long had been conceded that as far as "prospects" (a term used loosely to denote any marriageable male) were concerned, their collective fate Was Sealed. The subject of martyrdom was broached, tactfully, and Miss Margaret—who had red hair and a small private income—at once eliminated herself as a candidate by refusing, with some asperity, to run for the office. That left Miss Emily.

Miss Emily had a sturdy build, and a sturdy mind, and a sturdy soul that was just right for shouldering a cross. Furthermore, she recognized a responsibility when it was pointed out to her. She quit her job at Ludlow's bookstore, marched herself over to great-uncle Will's, moved in, and began turning mattresses and whittling at the grocery bill—a totally unnecessary procedure, as great-uncle Will, though not rich, had what used to be known as "means." Nevertheless, maiden ladies who assumed the role of housekeeper were expected to "cut corners" wherever possible, and Miss Emily hewed sturdily to the line.

As for great-uncle Will, he apparently labored under the delusion that she was there to minister unto great-aunt Ella; which, come to think of it, I guess maybe she was. Anyway, week followed week, and he came and went: a quiet, spare figure in conservative blue serge and a string tie. Gradually, as month succeeded month, his "quirk" came to rest in the same category as Cousin Charley's "inventions" and Aunt Isabelle's "premonitions." And Cousin Robin's bride, Estelle, usurped first place as topic of the day.

Estelle was an Easterner and had highfaluting ideas. Highfaluting for us, anyway. She had us whopperjawed from the moment she stepped off the train trailed by Cousin Robin, who was toting what looked like an outsize lunch box with holes punched in it, but which proved to contain a disgruntled Pekinese instead of ham sandwiches. From then on it was—as father would say, shaking his head—"one fool thing after another."

Their acquisition of a Stanley Steamer, however, easily took the cake. We could hardly believe our ears when Aunt Isabelle brought the news from Aix to Ghent. A *Stanley Steamer! Holy cow!*

The motor car, having emerged from its mechanical womb, was just beginning to take its first erratic steps towards the bright and distant future undeterred by blowouts, internal disturbances of a volcanic nature, and raucous cries of "Git a horse!"

The Stanley Steamer was top-flight stuff. It had *everything* from a double-action engine and a flue-welded boiler to a coal-oil vaporizer and a pump-drive gear. It operated on six hundred pounds of steam pressure and its water capacity of twenty gallons was, by gosh, sufficient for a whole day's run. It required only fifteen minutes to "steam" it from a cold start, and this included filling the tanks and boiler as well as raising the pressure. Hot ziggety!

"I knew they had been discussing it," my mother said to Aunt Isabelle, wiping up the Easter-egg dye I had spilled in my excitement, "but I didn't *dream*—"

"Such goings-on," Aunt Isabelle said. "I never heard the like. They ought to have their heads examined." She pursed her lips. "As sure as you're born, something is going to happen to those two. Mark my words. I have a *feeling*."

For once, one of her premonitions came to pass. We're still saying, "Remember the Easter Robin and Estelle drove to church in the Stanley Steamer?" For something *did* happen. That it didn't happen to the two she had specified is neither here nor there.

It was a perfect Easter Sunday. Mild, and warm, and filled with daffodils, and church bells, and new hats. Everyone had heard about the Stanley Steamer, and we walked in reflected glory down Catalpa Street to church. In fact, I was pretty insufferable about it, as Cousin Robin had taken us for a spin in it late Saturday afternoon and had "gotten her up" to twenty-five miles an hour. He would have gotten her up higher than that if mother hadn't become a borderline hysteria case.

Where Catalpa crossed Republic, we caught up to and fell in step with great-uncle Will and Miss Emily.

"What's this nonsense I hear about Robin buying a motor car?" great-uncle Will asked father, after we had dispensed with the amenities and had received with kind negative smiles the information that "Ella would be along in a minute."

"It's true," father said. "He has. And it's really all they say it is. Has an automatic water valve and a power pump. He got her up to twenty-five in nothing flat."

Mother laughed, indulgently. "Harvey," she said to father, "you're as bad as Jen," meaning me. She straightened my bonnet. "Walk ahead, dear, so we don't crowd the pavement. And pick up your heels. Here they come."

This last was in reference to Robin and Estelle, who glided smoothly and splendidly into view. The Steamer was a silent number, and it tooled along in all its majesty with the powerful ease of a Juggernaut that had been dipped in butter. As they swept by, they waved and we waved, with the exception of great-uncle Will, who stared after them with a puzzled expression. They drew up before the church with a flourish, and Robin alighted and gallantly helped Estelle to alight. She made a very charming picture, indeed, in her violets and veiling, but the Steamer walked off with the honors. The violets and veiling couldn't hold a candle to a steam-expansion piston drive. And when it came to *valves*—well!

I think it was those valves that did it. No mortal man can resist the lure of valves. Not even on Easter Sunday. And what man in the center of an admiring knot of other men, all of whom are interested in "her valves," isn't going to show them off? There was a steam-controlled valve, two hand valves, and a release valve in the fuel plan alone, plus an automatic valve and two check valves in the water system. On the steering apparatus was a valve for turning gasoline into the main burner, another for shutting off fuel, and—oh, well—

Father joined the happy valvular throng, while mother, Miss Emily and I (my protests having been stifled by one of mother's See-here-young-lady glances) ascended the wide steep steps to chat a moment with Estelle, and Aunt Isabelle, and Miss Margaret, and a few other ladies, in the cool shadow of the pillars. Great-uncle Will was forgotten in the shuffle.

The first inkling we had of anything wrong was in the sudden respectful widening of the circle around Cousin Robin and the Steamer. Robin, red-faced and perspiring, was in the driver's seat obviously trying to "get her percolating." The Steamer stayed right where it was—its attitude phlegmatic—but from its innards issued a persistent, ominous sssssssss that steadily increased. Slowly and impressively it moved forward—two inches. And stopped again. It began to tremble, and the hissing grew positively malevolent.

Somebody called warningly, "Watch her pressure gauge, Rob!"

Whereupon somebody else immediately yelled, *She's a-going to explode!"*

There was a babble of masculine voices (all shouting advice, as I recall), a sprinkling of feminine shrieks, and, at that instant, and as if on cue, the church bell began to ring, thus adding what seemed to be an authentic note of impending Doom straight from God. The circle scattered abruptly and Robin—quite sensibly—united himself with it.

Only one person remained. Great-uncle Will. His gaze was glued fixedly on the Steamer and his countenance wore a queer, unfathomable expression. For a second or two he stood where he was; then, his eyes narrow, his jaw firm, he advanced purposefully on the Steamer and, before we could recover our wits, had climbed in and was manipulating the various levers and pedals. The Steamer shuddered and began to move backwards. Loud and clear in the still hush that held us in thrall came his voice:

"Dammit, you *behave!"*

The Steamer gave a little hiccupy lurch and, miraculously, obeyed. Before it could pick up speed, Robin leaped in and switched off the fuel valve. The vehicle rolled to a defeated stop.

"Will, such *language*," mother said, in a low shocked tone as the congregation, having pulled itself together, filed into church. "What would Ella say!"

"Not one dadblame thing," great-uncle Will answered equably. "Being as how she's been dead since last February a year ago."

That was the end of great-uncle Will's "quirk." It was, likewise, the end of the string tie, and the blue serge suits, and Lord knows what all.

The day he and Miss Emily left on a Great Lakes cruise, he was wearing a checked suit and he smelled of whiskey and cigars. While on the cruise, Miss Emily became engaged to a well-to-do widower "of family" who lived in New Orleans. Great-uncle Will staked her to a big wedding with all the trimmings, and gave the happy couple a block of motor stock for a wedding present. They went to Bermuda on their honeymoon, and I still have a blurred snapshot, somewhere, of Miss Emily riding a bicycle!

Miss Margaret was sore as hell about the whole deal.

# Gremlin

## Karl Edward Wagner

Once upon a time in a village not unlike your own, there lived a kindly old author, who, although he worked very hard, was always poor . . .

Blaine Adams was a writer of good intentions but minimal abilities, and he liked his gin. That he ever managed to publish at all was primarily due to his prolific output and to his persistence. Given skin thick enough and time, he could usually find some second-rate publisher who would accept his third-rate novels for bottom-list rates. He wrote equally well in all categories—gothics, mysteries, westerns, science fiction, swords-and-sorcery, bodice rippers, horror, whatever markets were receptive at the moment. It's just that he never wrote very well. Once Edmond Hamilton, a venerable pulp writer, had told him, "No writer is a hack if he enjoys what he's doing." Within these parameters, Blaine Adams was not a hack.

When his wife left him for an androgynous artist with an attitude and good coke connections, Blaine Adams' world caved in upon him.

Blaine Adams lived in a small cottage in the deep, deep woods. It was a small frame house, actually, and it was on the edge of a state forest preserve. He enjoyed walks in the woods with his dog, a shaggy mutt named Buford, as exercise after hours of abusing his typewriter. Karen, his wife, was a potter, and she plied her wares from a mall shoppe in the nearby university town. Buford died not long after she left him, and he couldn't decide which emptiness was the more painful.

His had been a simple life. Hours at his typewriter—he planned to purchase a word processor whenever he got a really big advance. Boring lines at the post office waiting to mail manuscripts and collect rejected ones sent out weeks before—he really hoped to find a good agent soon. Chores about the house and unkempt yard while his wife was in town, plying her trade, and then start dinner. Adams was as good a cook as writer—enthusiastic, undaunted, and incompetent. At night, some cable and a cold cuddle; he suggested that she see a doctor about her headaches. Anyway, there was the gin to keep him company.

Blaine Adams was really only thirty-something, but he appeared older due to a receding hairline and a bookish nature that peered out from behind bifocals. Given that, he was tall, had once been rangy, but was now showing an incipient double chin from beneath his craggly black beard where grey hairs were beginning to show through.

The walks in the woods kept him fit, despite his sedentary occupation. When the state had purchased the sweep of ridges, they had enclosed a number of old farming settlements—abandoned since the Depression or earlier, and now little more than tree-grown foundations, forest-claimed fields, and collapsed barns. Here and there yellow daffodils, orange day-lillies, and purple cemetery vine still bloomed beside old homesites and forgotten stones of weed-covered family cemeteries. Buford used to hunt here in vain for slow-moving squirrels.

Blaine Adams had published thirty-something books—almost half of them under his own name—but none were ever reprinted.

For weeks he waited for Karen to return, numb from shock and disbelief. After some months, he stayed numb from gin, still hoping against his blurred reality. He tried to force himself to write, but even he saw the hopeless mediocrity of his efforts. Bills began to accumulate, and Tanqueray became Gordon's generic gin. Enough royalties trickled in to keep him afloat—his lifestyle was a modest one—and he might have made it had not his companion of sixteen years died one horrible night.

He buried Buford in the yard.

And he could no longer bear to walk in the woods.

Loneliness and depression set in with killing certainty. Blaine Adams stumbled through his gin-fogged days in utter isolation, staring dumbly at his typewriter without inspiration, feeding himself without thought.

It is difficult enough to cook for one person, harder still when there is little appetite. Adams left barely tasted pots of chili, overdone meatloaves, half-eaten hamburgers, meal after wretched meal—all to moulder in his refrigerator. Somehow Adams always thought he would get around to finishing his leftovers, but, of course, these held even less appeal to his appetite than they did when freshly cooked. But Blaine Adams was a frugal man, and he hated to let anything go to waste.

A manuscript entitled *Wire Edge* awaited Adams the next morning. The opening chapters of the novel bore some minimal resemblance to *House of the Hungry Dead*. The manuscript for the latter had been neatly torn into quarters—all 372 pages at once—and dumped into the wastebasket. There were stains of barbecue sauce on the torn pages. Adams sniffed cautiously. There was also the faint odor of dirt and ancient decay. Of mildew and mould.

Of a neglected graveyard.

Blaine Adams remembered his walks through the forest preserve, with its tumbled-down farmhouses and forgotten family cemeteries. His mind refused to accept it, but his writer's imagination whispered mad thoughts that he could not flee from.

Adams drank gin-laced coffee all afternoon. That evening he filled Buford's bowl with rancid collard greens, a stone-hard chunk of pound cake, the scrapings of a container of jalapeno and bean dip, half a bag of stale corn chips, and the smouldering last of another ill-fated pot of chili. Then he waited quietly.

The wind began to stir about the midnight. Adams kept the television blasting as usual, and pretended to sleep through the Val Lewton flick on AMC. He could see the screen door from his chair, and, despite the wind and the television, he could hear the sound of the crockery food dish being pushed about on the porch. He remembered how Buford used to push the bowl across the floor in a feeding frenzy, rasping his teeth to chew the last crumbs from the edges.

Silence, then the lapping of water. Adams thought he heard a soft belch.

The screen was securely latched, but the hook flipped open as a small hand reached through the torn screen. The hand that touched the door was about the size of a child's hand, but thick-fingered and with spadelike stubby claws.

It entered the kitchen confidently, gazing briefly at Adams in his chair. Adams had kept his eyes lowered, and now he clamped them shut.

It was somewhere between a toad and a dwarf. As a writer, Adams had read too much about elves and fairies and trolls and goblins. His guest was a hobbit from Hell. It was just over four feet in height, and it was almost human in shape, but the coarse scales interspersed with tufts of grey fur that covered its body were proof it wasn't human—even without looking at its face. Large, toad-like eyes, yellow and slit-pupiled, peered from about flattened nostrils and a wide, wide mouth with thin lips and very many pointed yellow teeth. Pointed ears poked through the long tufts of fur that hung down from its scaly scalp, and a short pair of crooked horns grew out of the top of its skull. Its arms were too long, its legs were too short, and its feet were narrow and taloned. A pronounced potbelly hung out over a dirty pair of cut-off houndstooth check slacks—these last missing from Adams' clothesline many weeks back.

It's a gremlin—that was all Adams could think. My God, I've got a gremlin. He cracked open his eyelids.

The gremlin had opened his refrigerator. Pleased, it nodded and ran a long black tongue over its thin lips. Then, moving almost noiselessly, it quickly entered Adams' study and sat down at his desk. For a moment it shuffled papers about, then it stretched its stubby fingers, cracked its knuckles. Leaning forward, it began to type.

The clawed fingers seemed to rush across the keyboard too fast to follow as page after page spun out like magic. The gremlin was composing final copy faster than a word processor could print out. And the only noise from the typewriter was a soft strumming sound. Adams was right: it was magic.

After about an hour, the gremlin stopped typing. It read through the new chapters of *Wire Edge*, nodded and placed them in a neat stack—then stretched languidly and got up. Rubbing its belly happily, it beamed a horrible smile at Adams in his chair, and let itself out by the kitchen door.

Adams did not fall asleep until dawn.

He remembered the fairy tale about the elves and the shoe-maker. And in his fumbling efforts at research, he had read about the little people in the myths of many cultures. Sometimes friendly, sometimes mischievous, sometimes inimical. In days gone by, peasants would leave out bowls of milk or meal as offerings to win their favor. Sometimes the little people would repay them with acts of kindness. Sometimes it just held them at bay.

Blaine Adams had no illusions as to his culinary skills. Only a gremlin could love the dismal messes he left out. And he'd been adopted by a gremlin.

Where had it come from? There were miles of forest, the ruins of old settlements, the forgotten graveyards. Had some immigrant brought the creature here, or was it native to these woods? Useless to attempt to explain magic. Gin and exhaustion called a halt to Adams' speculations.

Go with the flow, Adams decided, and the next night he lavished half a bottle of Tabasco sauce on the dreadful failure of short ribs and dumplings he had seen the gremlin eyeing in his refrigerator.

*Wire Edge* came in at about 200,000 words a few weeks later. The contract had called for only 75,000 words, but Adams' editor was basking in the praise for having brought in a potential year's best seller for a mere $5,000 advance. She generously sent him a small bonus check and another three-book contract, but a hungry agent had got wind of her new discovery, and he tracked Blaine Adams down.

Negotiations. Contracts. Mega bucks. Mega hype. Hardcovers. Film options. Cover blurbs from the genre's finest.

*The Calling* was rushed into print amidst a flurry of extravagant reviews and enthusiastic reader reception. The publisher promised more Blaine Adams shock classics in the near future, and the public grabbed up copies of *Stalker* as fast as the news-stands could stock them.

It was all happening very fast.

By nature shy and reclusive, Blaine Adams left everything to his new agent. He was content to bank his checks, and he refused to appear on talk shows or to do a signing tour.

The elves had abandoned the shoemaker after they realized he had discovered them. Adams did not stray from his routine. Each night he set out leftovers. As the contracts for new books came in, he foraged through his boxes of rejected manuscripts and hopeless starts—leaving them on his desk when required.

Life was good. For both of them.

And then a local bookstore insisted on having a meet-the-author signing party.

Adams should have refused, but the proprietor was an old friend.

He was seated at a table laden with hot-off-the-press copies of *Wire Edge,* when the screaming started.

Fans lined up before his table suddenly bolted for exits. Wine glasses shattered on the floor; a buffet table went crashing. Some, suspecting a publicity stunt, crouched behind shelves of books. Adams stumbled to his feet, staring in horror.

The gremlin moved complacently through the scene of panic, pausing briefly to swallow a handful of chicken wings. It wiped its fingers on the remains of the tattered and mouldering antique tuxedo it wore, then hurried over to where Adams stood frozen.

"Sorry I'm late," the gremlin apologized, "but it took me a while to dig up this tux for the occasion."

Adams guessed where it had dug up the tux, but he was past shuddering.

The gremlin climbed into his vacated chair and beamed over the stacks of books at what remained of its fans. It slung a long arm affectionately around the slumping Blaine Adams.

"Hey, I love this guy!" the gremlin proclaimed. "And just wait till you read his cookbook!"

# The Grilling of Loren Ellery

## Jack London

The bon Dieu, in His inscrutable wisdom, had seen fit to place two women's souls within two fairly beautiful bodies, and to cause them to love each other dearly. He had likewise deemed it discretionary to create them sister and sister, that this affection might bloom rich and full, nor fall a prey to the deadly germs ordinarily sown in the course of feminine existence. Having done these things, it is evident He rested from His labours, leaving these two creatures to the whirl of chance.

Chance behaved sanely for a long while; but, having permitted them to gain womanhood in each other's companionship, it flung them apart by half the girth of a Western State, and caused them to dwell in separate places, one in a smoky metropolis by the seaboard, and one in a great valley where meridians were as common as pebbles in a gravel bank. Chance also brought many strange things into their lives, and last of all, a man. And this man came well recommended, with moral probity, business integrity, healthy bank books, unqualified letters of credit and introduction, and good looks. He became great friends with Ernestine, who lived in the city by the sea, and thought he thought much of her. After they had come to know each other well, Lute, whom an imbecile ancestor had classified as Luella, and who lived in the valley, came on a visit to her sister Ernestine. And the man, who may be known as Loren Ellery, came to know her likewise.

"And what do you think of Lute?" Ernestine, who was the elder, asked one day, after her sister's visit had terminated in a climacteric of sisterly love, kisses, admonitions, and promises.

"Now, Erna," Ellery answered—he had long since taken unto himself this prerogative of address; "it's this way: Lute's a fine girl. There's no mistaking it. She is bright, good looking, with vim and go about her, and a glorious colour. But her brightness is of a different order from yours, as are her looks, her vivacity, her complexion. You understand. She's a pretty little witch and all that, but—" Here he threw the proper expression into his eyes and gazed upon his interlocutor just the correct number of instants to be thoroughly effective, and resumed: "But she could never be to me what you are. I like her, but in a different way from you. I admire her, but not as I admire you. I can respect her, and I might have loved her had you and I never met. As it is—"

Ernestine said "Oh!" afterward, and they both felt a high satisfaction with themselves, each other, and things in general and particular.

After some time Chance, with his accustomed arch manipulation of his human dice, tossed a man with a mine across Loren Ellery's path. And according to the affinity which exists between men possessing natural capital and men possessing industrial capital, these two foregathered for cooperative exploitation and mutual benefit.

In the course of the deal Loren Ellery, not desiring to be mulcted by the Western Gentile, hired a mining expert and went to investigate the pretensions of the hole in the ground. It so happened that the mine lay among the outjutting spurs of the mountains which fringed the rim of the valley where Lute lived and moved.

Naturally, society being limited, and travellers rare, she and Ellery met, and they saw much of each other. So pleasurable did he find her company that he dallied, day by day, and postponed the date of his return. And as he took liberties with time, so did his tongue with him, till he said to Lute things which he should not have said, and which he had said before.

"It's something like this, Lute," he said one day, as they drank iced tea on her long, shaded piazza and thus strove to adapt themselves more comfortably to their torrid environment. "It's something like this, you see, now that sister of yours is a jolly nice girl, clever and all that. Not the slightest doubt in the world of it. She's got looks and health, and complexion, and all that sort of stuff. You understand. She's just the kind of a girl to carry most fellows away, fall in love with her on the jump, but—" and here he expressed that "but" in a mild pantomime, rendered more effective by long practice, and went on: "But she never could be to me what you are. She is pretty, but so are you, and in a different way. She may appeal to most men, but not to me as you can. In short, I like your sister, but there is no similarity between that and my affection for you. I can admire her and respect her, and it might have been I could have loved her had I not met you. As it is—tell me, Lute, dear, tell me you understand."

As this repetition of stereotyped niceties is an infirmity from which all masculines suffer to greater or less extent, and which, in like measure, gives pleasure to all feminines, it can be considered no great evil; and evil things would not have resulted from it had not the bon Dieu made Lute's a very confiding nature and Chance sent her down on another visit to the seaboard city.

In the meantime Ellery was prevented from changing the trend of events by catching the mining fever and going off to the outjutting spurs to explore more holes in the ground.

No matter how slightly and carefully some women lift the lids of their hearts in confidence, like the box of Pandora, the contents thereof are likely to fly out to the last little particle. Lute happened to be such a creature, and it also happened that Ernestine had acquired a certain knack necessary to draw from her her maiden secrets.

The night they remained awake, and talked so long, Lute's intentions were to divulge, oh, such a little bit of the case; but gradually, insensibly, she drifted on, giving notice to more and more, till suddenly Ernestine's ears caught the concatenation of familiar phrases, and her "What's that?" precipitated affairs. Then a reciprocal relation attached itself to their confidences, and they weighed and balanced their respective merits and demerits as interpreted by the protean-tongued Loren Ellery. After that, and the immediate pangs of chagrin and personal affront had passed, they laughed and fell asleep in each other's arms, as sisters should.

Loren Ellery unconcernedly staged and trailed it through the mountains, descending deep shafts and winding through deviously constructed man burrows, learning the ways of the Western man and his habitat, and adding to his vocabulary the nomenclature of the mines and the idiom of the frontier. And he had become quite Western himself, don't you know, and quite proud of his attainments and his mineral properties by the time of the fall of the year, when he returned to the city and betook himself to a certain residence and sent up his card. He had asked for Ernestine, but incidentally it so happened that Lute aided her sister in receiving him.

Conversation picked its sinuous thread through the unctuous nothings and polite inanities of impersonal small talk; Ellery contriving, in his subtle way, to convey to each that his interest had not dwindled, and all went well. Words flowed easily, naturally, without jar or premonition of coming discord.

"Ah, what a striking young man," Ellery murmured, in a lull, gazing admiringly upon a portrait suspended from the wall opposite him. "And may I ask whose it is?"

"My cousin George," Ernestine informed him; "the one in the navy I think I told you about."

"And is he not a handsome chap?" he continued.

"Indeed he is," authenticated Ernestine.

"Ah?"

"But not like his brother Herman," Lute chimed in.

"An extremely nice young man," Ernestine continued, "with a vim and go about him, and energy and manliness."

"Yes, I dare say," Ellery put in, absently, puzzling over the vague familiarity of the phrases.

"And yet so different from his brother," came back from Lute's side of the duet.

"Isn't it funny," from Ernestine; "he's just the kind of a man girls lose their hearts to, yet—"

"I could not love him as I would Herman," Lute interpolated, taking up her portion of the measure.

"How strange!" Ellery was beginning to fall a victim to decidedly definite suspicions.

"An estimable young man—"

"Whom I could like—"

"But not as I could his brother—"

"Whom I could admire—"

"But not as Herman—"

Ellery knew they were grilling him and smiled vacuously.

"Whom I can respect—"

"And might have loved—"

"Had I not met—"

"His brother Herman—"

"And who—why, Mr. Ellery," Ernestine broke off, as innocently as she did abruptly; "you are not going? And so soon?"

"Most charming time, I assure you." Ellery had glanced at his watch and risen to his feet, a barely discernible colour in his cheeks, but managing to hold himself in hand. "So nice to see you girls again, don't you know; but I must be moving on."

"But won't you stay just a moment and have some tea?" Ernestine made a half move to strike the bell.

"Really, I would like to, ever so much." He was methodically edging to the door the while he spoke. "Had no idea it was so late, time flew so; but I must meet a man with a prospectus—this mining, you know, is so deucedly distracting."

"Then good-bye, Mr. Ellery." Ernestine's larynx was delicately vibrant with disappointment as she finally extended her hand. "You must come again—"

"And see our cousin George—"

"And his brother Herman—"

"He's just as he is in his picture, and I know you will like him—"

"But different from the way you will like his brother Herm—"

But Loren Ellery, fearing an attack of primordial passion, fled incontinently down the stairs.

# The Hand That Feeds

## John Maclay

**H**erb was a vampire, and we all knew it. A tall, dark, often cadaverous man of thirty-five, he worked for the biological company where I was personnel manager. We made blood agar culture plates, and he was night manager of the farm where our own herd of sheep was kept. The 150 sheep were bled periodically, not enough to kill them, and their blood was mixed with the agar to fill the plates. The result, which was used to grow bacterial cultures, was a three-inch plastic disc filled with a red, jelly-like matter.

We found out that Herb was a vampire when the sheep started to get a bit anemic. Records showed that they hadn't been bled any more than usual, at least officially, and our consulting veterinarian was puzzled. But then one night he surprised Herb sucking blood from one of them through a sterile needle and tube, and after overcoming his initial shock he reported it. I was there when our president, a tolerant man, called Herb into his paneled office one evening and confronted him.

"It's true," Herb said, looking shamefaced. "I did it because I'm one of the Immortals."

"Hmmm," our president replied, scanning the night manager's file. "It says here you were formerly employed as a blood bank technologist."

Herb nodded sadly. "Yes. But they caught me drinking the goods, so to speak, and besides there wasn't much human blood to spare. So I thought if I came to work for you, there'd be plenty, and it wouldn't be missed."

"Well, it wasn't, not really," the president said. "You just should have told us about your special needs, and we'd have made some minor adjustments. After all, we are an Equal Opportunity Employer, M-F . . . V, and such things do happen. You're doing a good job otherwise."

"Then you're not going to fire me?" Herb asked, his spirits rising.

"No," came the reply. "Just give us an estimate of your monthly intake, and we'll take it out of your salary, at a discount. Maybe we'll get a few more sheep, or bleed the ones we have a little more efficiently for the plates."

"Oh, thank you," Herb gushed. "You're a very understanding man."

As if to prove it, our president went on. "Then you don't mind sheep blood, as opposed to human?"

"Not at all," the night manager replied. "We keep the herd so well, the blood's rich and tasty, and besides it's drawn under sterile conditions. That was one of the attractions in the first place."

"Good. And do you need anything like a coffin, to sleep in during the daytime?"

"Thanks, but no. I found a nice old one at a country antique shop. You know, the one out road by . . ."

But the president, being a man of business too, cut him off. "Good. We try to take care of our employees." Then he thought for a moment. "Uh, along those lines, can we be sure you won't try to make . . . others like yourself? We have some pretty attractive female workers."

Herb put up his hand. "Oh, no. I've become more settled over the years. All I want to do now is to work hard, relax . . . and, of course, drink."

"Well, that's fine," said our president, getting up from behind his desk, signaling the end of the interview. "At least it isn't alcohol." He put his arm around Herb and escorted him to the office door, with me following.

Yet at the last minute, the night manager looked uneasy again. "You've treated me so fairly, I have to confess one more thing. I . . . I shaved a few years off my age on my job application."

"No problem," was the ever-tolerant reply. "How many?"

"Uh . . . four hundred?"

"Fine. We'll simply make the correction in your file."

So Herb went on working for the company, and a model employee he was. It did my personnel manager's heart good to see the way in which a minority person adjusted to the business, given the chance. A few years later he was even promoted to manager—night shift—of the blood agar culture plate department, though of course he retained his blood-sucking privileges at the sheep farm. Our president was fond of saying that, being a vampire, Herb was indeed a rare find, ideally suited to his line of work.

But as human—or other—nature would have it, there eventually came a downfall. Maybe it's an element of greed in our society, maybe an innate flaw, but too often when someone is treated well, he goes on to bite the hand that feeds him.

This time the president called me into his office alone. "The auditors have found a shortage in the blood plate department," he told me, looking sad and disappointed. "More product is coming off the line at night than ends up in the warehouse."

"It must be Herb again," I said, so that the kind man wouldn't have to. "He runs his shift so tightly, it can only be him."

"Yes," was the reluctant response. "I was going to ask him, but I don't understand why he'd do it. The records show that he's still drawing all he can drink at the farm."

"Maybe he's selling it," I suggested. "Or at least sharing it with others of his kind."

"Yes. And I wouldn't feel so betrayed if it was going to charity. But it isn't the blood that's missing, it's the finished plates. What on earth could he be doing with those?"

I was stumped too. So, out of a proprietary interest in the situation, and a sense of responsibility to our beloved president, I volunteered to find the answer.

The next morning I got to the plant early, while it was still dark outside, toward the end of Herb's shift. Undetected, I watched him wind things up, marveling at his efficiency. After all, he had several hundred years of experience. But then, with a sinking heart, I saw him tuck a carton of blood plates under his arm, as if to carry it to the warehouse, and instead take it out the back door to his car.

I followed in my car as he drove into the city, into a section where some of the odder people lived. He parked, got out with his package, and walked to a small store which, unlike its neighbors, was open, or still open, in the pre-dawn. And when I looked in the window, I couldn't believe, yet maybe half-expected, what I saw.

There were children, of all ages and sizes, lined up at the counter, eagerly awaiting what Herb had brought. They were dressed normally, yet the one thing they had in common, as they handed over their quarters and walked away, each hungrily clutching one of the jellied blood plates, was a certain cadaverous look. Soon, I knew, that look would be gone, and they would sleep peacefully until the next . . . night.

Herb was stealing, ingeniously lining his own pockets, but . . .

It was a vampire candy store. And as I drove away, I was damned if I knew what our ever-tolerant president would do now!

# The Hapless Bachelors

### E. F. Benson

It had been a shattering blow to those two middle-aged bachelors when Mrs Nicholson announced her miserably selfish intention of getting married.

For ten years she had managed their house for them with economy and sublime efficiency, cooking and serving for them their punctual and delicious meals, calling them in the morning, and bringing in their bedroom candles to their sitting-room at night when she thought it was time for them to go to bed, valeting them, telling them to order new clothes when necessary, reminding them when it was seemly to have their hair cut, ordering coal and wine when required, checking their bills and thwarting unscrupulous trades-people, counting the very heads of asparagus in the bed and the strawberries under their nets, and, in a word, taking off their hands the whole burden of those interminable domestic details in which, like midges on a summer evening, life is so annoyingly enveloped.

There was a gardener, whom she controlled (for the rolling of the croquet-lawn, the production of abundant vegetables, the glowing evidence of flower-beds were outside her immediate management), and there was a girl who came in at break of dawn and worked under Mrs Nicholson's sweet supervision till she staggered home at sunset, exhausted in body but wonderfully enlightened in methodic industry. But before she came Mrs Nicholson would have lit the kitchen fire, and laid the grate in the dining-room and sitting-room, if she thought the weather sufficiently inclement to justify such a proceeding, and after the girl had gone she would serve dinner and do some sewing. There was not such a word as 'fatigue' in Mrs Nicholson's dictionary; if there had been she would not have comprehended it.

Six months of intolerable discomfort succeeded for her two unhappy masters, Mr Beaumont and Mr Bradley, and though they were of normal and kindly dispositions, they became frankly misogynistic under the blast of the incompetent females who now witheringly blighted their household.

Instead of one benignant and all-pervasive personality who allowed them to lead smooth and untroubled lives and devote the whole of their leisure to their own hobbies, they were harassed and rendered miserable by three inadequate females—a cook, a parlour-maid, and a housemaid—who between them did with notable inefficiency what Mrs Nicholson had done with the speed and precision of a planet moving in its splendid orbit.

The cook could not get on without a charwoman, the parlour-maid without two evenings out a week, and the housemaid without breaking Beaumont's choicest pieces of Salopian china and knocking down Bradley's setting-boards on which were impaled his latest captures of butterflies and moths. The machinery of life creaked and groaned under these nincompoops, and however often they were replaced, the change never produced any better results.

Neither Beaumont nor Bradley had a moment's leisure. The cook's melancholy face would succeed her mournful rap on the door, and she would announce that the fish had not come, or, having come, had gone bad; the parlour-maid would rustle in to ask what wine she was to open for dinner; the housemaid would want some new dusters.

Buttons came off their coats and were not replaced, lamps smoked, things went wrong with the supply of hot water, letters were not posted, devitalized syphons refused to give up their contents, keys were lost, books were put upside-down into their shelves, and a gramophone wheezed nightly in the kitchen.

The general disintegration, too, was not confined to the house, for, with the departure of Mrs Nicholson, a similar deterioration set in in the garden.

The croquet-lawn, that smooth sheet of green velvet, began to grow bumpy; the asparagus-bed provided only a week's refreshment; the early potatoes were a complete failure, and the roses had blight. None of these things had been in Mrs Nicholson's direct province, but her effulgent example had shone on the garden no less than the house, her supreme efficiency had infected that once productive acre.

Worst of all, most ruinous to content and leisure, were endless minute complaints. 'It's not what I've been accustomed to, sir,' was the burden of them, delivered in various cold and acid voices. As for the household bills, they rose like snow-drifts in some bitterly inclement winter.

Toothache had taken Beaumont to London one bright June morning (no tooth of his had ever ached in the reign of Mrs Nicholson), and while waiting to enter the torture-chamber, his attention was attracted by an advertisement in a magazine which was headed, 'No more Blood or Cinders for Dinner'.

This extolled the merits of an electric oven, which roasted or grilled or fried whatever was submitted to its ministrations. No trained cook—here Beaumont quite forgot about his tooth—was necessary: the householder merely ascertained by consultation of a small hand-book supplied gratis with the oven, how long a sole or a mackerel or a chop required for its perfect presentation at table, turned the dial on the oven for the required number of minutes, and could rest assured that a delicious dish awaited him.

Should he desire a joint prepared with the same perfection, he had but to weigh his joint and allow for its cooking its weight in pounds multiplied with the number of minutes required for each pound.

Milk, water, and vegetables could be boiled by the application of a simple formula; in fact, there was no act of cooking which the 'Ichabod-oven' did not accomplish with invariable nicety.

At the expiration of the minutes indicated on the dial (brass with enamelled face), the heat was automatically cut off.

There was no more stoking of the kitchen fire, no more waste of coal; the 'Ichabod-oven' had but to be connected by a cord to a plug in the wall, it cooked, and it cut off its own current. Should the cooking be done and the current cut off before the viands were needed, there was nothing easier, when the last guest had arrived, than to switch on the Ichabod again, and heat up in a couple of minutes the cooling delicacies.

A picture of a smiling hostess welcoming a guest who was half an hour late for dinner, owing to a breakdown on the Tube, endorsed and crowned the merits of the Ichabod. 'That makes no inconvenience in our house,' she benignantly observed. 'George will turn on the current to the Ichabod-oven, and in two minutes you will have your dinner as hot as hot.'

Beaumont always propitiated his dentist with pleasant conversation when his mouth was not full of wads, and he selected this subject for his spasmodic remarks. Between whirlings of the electric wheel and manual jabs and stabs, his torturer upheld from personal experience all that the advertisement had claimed for the Ichabod-oven, and told Beaumont of a dozen labour-saving apparatuses of the same kind, which could be seen at Messrs Milliken's furnishing establishment in Bond Street.

'Electricity,' he observed, as he applied the whizzing wheel to Beaumont's tooth, 'takes the place of manual energy. One moment: a little wider, please! There!'

Beaumont had no time that day to test the merits of these admirable contrivances, and arrived home to find Bradley in the most morose spirits. The housemaid in a fervour of dusting had whisked her napkin over one of his collecting-boxes, plucking the wings and antennae off two Purple Emperors and six Clouded Yellows. Even as he recounted his irremediable disaster, Beaumont, who had opened a cabinet containing his choicest pieces of Salopian china, gave a shrill squeal of dismay.

'Who has broken my toy Salopian milk-jug?' he asked.

'Oh, Jane,' said Bradley. 'It flew out of her hand, she told me, as she was dusting it.'

'But she had no business to dust it,' cried Beaumont.

'I know she hadn't, nor my Purple Emperors. We must give her notice. It's your turn.'

'I can hunt for ten years without finding another toy Salopian milk-jug,' moaned Beaumont. 'Yet even the worst servants are getting scarce.'

At dinner the two carved in turn, week by week about. As Bradley plunged a blunt knife into the leg of lamb, a torrent of blood poured out, as if he had beheaded a vampire.

'Totally uneatable,' he said. 'We must cut some slices and have them grilled.'

The slices were cut and sent back to the kitchen. After a long delay there returned some thin crackling cinders.

'First blood, then cinders,' observed Beaumont, and into his mind there came the remembrance of the advertisement he had seen. The loss of his toy Salopian milk-jug had put it and his tooth out of his head. Now as he crashed into a cinder they both returned to him.

Though Beaumont had been to town that day, an hour's discussion with his friend decided them! He and Bradley went up again next morning, and after a succulent lunch prepared exclusively by the Ichabod, spent the entire afternoon at Messrs Milliken's.

Long before tea-time—with hot buttered scones from the Ichabod—they had completely made up their minds, and having ascertained that every labour-saving device in stock could be installed in their house in three weeks, they dismissed the entire household with a month's wages instead of a month's warning, and moved across to the admirable hotel, where, in comfort, they could superintend the refitting of their home.

Electricity, that stern but obedient force, was to take the place of a staff of greedy, incompetent females; in the garden alone was male labour to be retained, since weeding and the care of vegetables were not yet within the scope of electrical energy, but within doors the two intended to take on themselves the entire labour—a matter, it appeared, of some half-hour a day—of the house.

A crippled soldier with the resounding name of Fotheringay would make beds and empty slops, which was sordid employment; but when once these were done, there was nothing which could not be effected swiftly and without loss of dignity.

It was positively exhilarating to hold a muddy shoe to the bright, whirling electric brush; five seconds sufficed for the complete removal of mud, five more for its superb polishing.

In the kitchen stood the resplendent Ichabod, which cooked dinner for ten—should that be necessary. On the kitchen-table, over which no longer querulous females stuffed themselves four times a day with expensive food, was the Universal Washer-up. Into its convenient racks you placed the sullied plates and dishes and teacups and knives and forks, filled it with hot water from the Ichabod, and connected it with a plug in the wall. The Universal Washer-up then took on a majestic rocking movement, and in five minutes the implements of feeding were spotlessly clean and the hot water incredibly dirty. A tap let out the foul fluid, and a little more exercise on the part of the Universal Washer-up sufficed to dry its contents.

Where the kitchen-range had been, there was now a stove which heated the boiler to such an extent that oceans of scalding water rumbled in the bath-room and squirted from the hot-water taps that steamed in every bedroom.

Central heating had been installed all over the house, and the same supply of water rushed madly through miles of radiators. There was a machine like a small grass-cutter so light that it could be taken up in one hand, which had only to be connected with a plug in the wall to cause it to give forth thirsty, sucking sounds. When pushed over a carpet, it absorbed into a small chamber every particle of dust that had lurked there. This provender was invaluable for garden-beds.

A whirling brush of soft feathers dusted everything that the thirsty grass-cutter could not reach and pleasantly ventilated the rooms. Then, as there would be no permanent resident in the kitchen, it was undesirable that tradesmen should enter, and so in the middle of the kitchen-door was inserted a commodious safe. The tradesman—butcher or baker or grocer—had but to press a conspicuous button, and the door of the safe flew open. He then inserted in it such goods as had been ordered by telephone, together with the bill, closed the door of the safe again, and went away, conscious that if he had not placed there what was ordered and what was detailed on his invoice, detection would inevitably await him.

A complicated sewing-machine undertook all hemming and stitching, and by a special adjustment put on buttons. Clothes, after the ministration of the grass-cutter, were pressed by the turn of a screw; and all cotton, woollen, or linen garments were washed by the Universal Washer-up in its off-moments. But the starching-machine was not yet quite perfect, and the Messrs Milliken did not recommend it.

For a couple of days after this inclusive instalment an intelligent young man remained on the premises and cooked dinners and supplied hot water, and washed plates and pressed clothes, and dusted with a perfection that Mrs Nicholson might have envied.

One morning Bradley tore his trousers quite badly over barbed wire in the pursuit of a Humming-bird Hawk moth, and the young man in two minutes, with the aid of the sewing-machine, repaired the rent in a perfectly amazing manner. The entire housework seemed to occupy him but a couple of hours in the day, and he said that he could run half a dozen houses single-handed without turning a hair.

With a final injunction not to employ the full current for the lift which conveyed the hot fruits of the Ichabod to the dining-room, he got on to his motor-bicycle and disappeared with the speed of the Vanishing Lady.

Beaumont had the first day of housework (for they had settled not to share these duties, but each of them to perform all of them on alternate days) and produced an excellent supply of hot water for the morning baths. Owing to some oversight with regard to the Ichabod, the eggs for breakfast were boiled as if for canaries, but the bacon was crisp and good.

Fotheringay's notion of making beds was sketchy, for he merely replaced the bed-clothes, and he emptied the slops into the bath, but promised to do better in future.

About the middle of the morning loud and agonized yells from outside the house caused Beaumont to conclude that something was wrong somewhere, but he did not think it worthwhile to interrupt his dusting to investigate the matter, for these screams probably came from the house of a noisy Irish family a few doors off, where the children were always quarrelling.

An hour or so later, having occasion to visit the kitchen, he was astonished to observe the lower part of a human arm in the safe inserted into the back door, and found that it had slammed to with incredible violence as the grocer was in the act of putting a pound of sugar into it. The poor man was faint with pain when he was released, and Beaumont, lucidly explaining the mechanism of it, had the end of his nose severely slapped as the door unexpectedly flew back again.

The grocer, humbly but firmly, announced his intention of, for the future, leaving his parcels outside that deadly trap. This rank cowardice had something in its favour, for he pointed out that fresh butter, if left as long as his arm had been left in the safe, would not be materially improved by contact with raw meat, whiting, candles, and possibly onions.

The rest of the day passed in a blaze of efficient mechanism. No gramophone had interrupted the studious quiet, no servants had protested against things they were not accustomed to, while the financial gain seemed to Beaumont, as he added up the bills for goods supplied, to be most encouraging.

'Electricity doesn't spend the day in guzzling in the kitchen,' he finally observed. 'Electricity doesn't interrupt one every minute with complaints. What peace to know that there isn't a woman in the house!'

Bradley breathed a sign of sympathetic relief.

'I entirely agree,' he said, 'as far as female servants are concerned. Women may be, in fact, they are, ornamental little things; they have a brightness, a charm about them. For the purposes of the propagation of the species, they seem to be essential.'

'Doubtless; but you and I do not propose to propagate the species. And I was talking about their domestic efficiency.'

'There was Mrs Nicholson,' began Bradley.

'But did you ever, even in Mrs Nicholson's reign, spend a more tranquil day than to-day?' asked Beaumont.

'No, I can't say I did. The eggs at breakfast—"

'Which you ate with considerable relish in the salad at dinner,' interrupted his friend.

'Quite true. I withdraw the eggs. The imprisoned grocer, however. I think, perhaps, we should be wise not to continue using that safe. It would, by the way, make a magnificent breeding-box for my caterpillars.'

A faint humming sound had been audible during this conversation, and Beaumont visited the kitchen to see whether any electric energy had been left running. He found that he had forgotten to turn off the apparatus that cleaned boots, and a pair of his own which he had left in contact with the revolving brushes were almost on fire with the friction. The post had just come in, and he opened a letter from his widowed sister, Mrs Glover, who usually spent the month of August with them, proposing her annual visit. She would bring down with her, if convenient, her new French maid, Hortense, who ran her house for her with exquisite finish, and was really more of a friend and companion than a servant. A most superior woman, and pretty enough, as she observed, to capture even Mr Bradley's hitherto impregnable heart. This last sentence made her brother frown; Mabel had set her becoming cap at Bradley for years.

'Mabel suggests herself for early in August,' he said on his return. 'She proposes to bring a marvellous maid, a sort of Mrs Nicholson. We'll teach these women a lesson as to how to run a house!'

'And no message for me?' asked Bradley.

'Some silly joke about the good-looks of her maid. Mabel is rather vulgar sometimes. Bless me! it's nearly eleven. How quickly time goes when one is peaceful and tranquil! I'll put the burglar-alarm shutters up.'

He got one rather severe shock from making the electric connection before he let go of the bell.

Bradley's day began inauspiciously. He must have made some mistake in the taps that controlled the hot and cold water, for every drop of water in the house speedily rose to boiling-point. It was impossible to shave or to wash or to have a bath, for scalding fluid poured out of both taps alike, wherever situated. Boiling water thrummed and chuckled everywhere, the whole central-heating apparatus was in full operation, and this, added to the heat of the morning, made the house absolutely untenable, and unwashed and unshaved and streaming with perspiration, they breakfasted in the garden.

The Ichabod, on the other hand, however much Bradley turned taps and adjusted dials, developed no heat whatever; and though they could have plenty of tea by filling the teapot at any tap in the house, nothing could be cooked. Eggs, however, could be boiled in the bath, and before long the slight initial error about the cold-water supply was remedied.

Bradley had another smart shock when he took the burglar-alarm shutter off the pantry window, but consolation for his tingling arm was administered by the discovery that he had merely forgotten to connect the Ichabod up with the supply of electricity.

Beaumont offered to help with the dusting, and unfortunately brought the whisking feather-brush too near a shelf of Salopian china. Plates and teapots rose in the air like a covey of partridges. Meantime, Bradley, by a too-energetic application of the grass-cutter machine, caused it to suck up not only the dust from a valuable Persian rug, but a strip of nap. A lane was cut in it like the path of a tornado.

He then transferred his caterpillars into the discarded safe in the back-door, but as he forgot to close the door, they crawled all over the kitchen. He recaptured most of them, and began work on the Ichabod for lunch.

There is no need to dwell on the horrors of the next three weeks. From native inefficiency combined with steadily accelerating nervousness, if one of two taps had to be turned, Beaumont and Bradley alike turned the wrong one. The Universal Washer-up was altogether forgotten one night after dinner, and continued to rock backwards and forwards till all the plates and glasses and dishes came out of their racks and formed a heap at the bottom. A soup-ladle which should never have been put there at all dealt stunning blows at the defenceless crockery and speedily reduced it all to shards.

In the night the burglar-alarm continued to ring at intervals until dawn. But with the pathetic obstinacy of men they continued unbroken in their determination to show Mrs Glover and the fascinating Hortense how vastly more efficient was the male sex in all domestic matters, and, the weather continuing very hot, they laid in, at staggering expense, quantities of cold delicacies which did not require cooking.

Hortense, on arrival, modestly established herself in the kitchen, and professed a delightful willingness to help in the housework; so Beaumont explained to her at considerable length the merits of the Ichabod and left the preparation of dinner in her hands.

She appeared to be most intelligent, and promised to do her best. It was only for tonight, so Beaumont assured her, that they would trouble her, but he had not seen his sister for so long, and he had many things to talk over with her. He had not, however, any immediate opportunity of doing so, since Mabel and Bradley had already gone for a walk, and did not return till close on dinner-time.

Hortense sent them up, serving it herself, a most delicious repast, and four perfect courses inspired a spirit of boastful insincerity on the part of Beaumont.

'You see, my dear Mabel,' he said, 'what can be done by two bachelors. You have dined, as you know, not badly—'

'Perfectly, exquisitely!' said Mabel. 'Too good for words!'

'Well, cooking is child's play if you have an Ichabod. That's the sort of dinner Bradley and I get every night. All the wages and bother of a cook are saved. I can cook just such a dinner in half an hour. No knowledge of anything is required. Bradley will cook for us tomorrow.'

'Ah, but how clever of you, Mr Bradley,' said she. 'And you will be housemaid too? Men are wonderful! I always said so.'

Hortense, one way and another during the next week, seemed to have taken charge of the house. When Bradley's day came he explained to her the virtues of the whirling feather-brush and the dust-sucker, and warned her against the employment of the Universal Washer-up unless strict supervision was given it. While Beaumont merely endorsed all his friend had said.

As a matter of fact, they were both revelling in the smoothness and perfection which recalled, and indeed exceeded, the reign of Mrs Nicholson; both looked forward with something remarkably resembling dread to the fatal day when Mabel Glover would depart and take her Hortense with her. Dire misgivings, never communicated and internally suppressed, occasionally seized them when they came into a room and found Hortense sweeping a carpet without the aid of the grass-cutter, or dusting shelves without the whirling circle of feathers, but as a rule all housemaid's work was over before they came downstairs, and Fotheringay somehow had melted away, and was no more seen.

All this was observed and forgotten, and Beaumont, with slightly more difficulty, managed to forget the fact that on visiting the kitchen one day when the Ichabod should have been at the height of its activities, he found that his culinary expert stood cold and with open doors. Hortense explained that just for tonight she had not used it.

The smooth, delicious days slipped by; neither Beaumont nor Bradley now made the smallest pretence of going into the kitchen at all, and week by week, though they were all pampered with toothsome viands, the house-books showed a splendid economy.

Bradley, who, on the whole, was the greedier and the more luxuriously-minded of the two bachelors, viewed with the greater despair the resumption of their usual bachelor establishment. The prospect of that appeared to him increasingly insupportable, and increasingly pleasant seemed the companionship of Mabel Glover, who helped him to set his moths with wonderful delicacy of touch, and was never tired of procuring fodder for his imprisoned caterpillars.

Essentially, he was hooked already; practically, two days before Mabel's proposed departure, he proposed to her and was instantly landed. But what, so thought the impassioned swain, would happen if Beaumont, goaded by ignoble revenge, proposed to Hortense?

No such heart-breaking calamity occurred. The only thing that Hortense insisted on was that electricity should only be used for bells and illuminations, and that she should have no cage for caterpillars in the door of *her* kitchen.

# Hearing Aid

## David Langford

It was one of those parties where the decor was very expensive and very sparse, and the drinks likewise. Anderson studied his thimbleful of terrifyingly high-class sherry, and had a wistful vision of a large tumbler of Algerian plonk—a large tumbler of practically anything, for that matter. Of course one should not be dwelling on the alcohol famine, one should be making witty conversation: only Anderson found himself cut off from conversation by the probably musical noises coming from speakers in each corner of the room. He'd heard of the 'cocktail party effect' whereby you could unerringly pick a single voice from amid twenty-seven others (he'd counted, three times), but for him it never seemed to work. Perhaps it was something you hired people to teach you when you had the necessary style, flair or connections to be invited to parties like this more often than a token once a year.

The host was doing things at an intricate console which seemed wasted on a mere hi-fi system; it was so obviously capable of running vast automated factories, with possibly a sideline in tax avoidance. A different and louder sound of probable music drifted over the chattering crowd. Anderson made a face, knocked back his homeopathic dose of sherry, and realized this had been a tactical error since there would be nowhere to put down the glass until another tray of drinks came by—if one ever did. Worse, Nigel had abandoned the console and was moving towards him with the manner of a snake converging on a rabbit.

"Hel-lo, Colin . . . what do you think of the music?"

Anderson didn't think anything at all of the music. Music was simply music, a kind of sonic fog which made conversation difficult or even dangerous. Audibility now down to eighteen inches . . . speak only along the central lane of the motorway and make lots of hand signals. Music, bloody music.

"Technically interesting," he said cautiously.

Nigel Winter moved a little closer and twinkled at Anderson with

183

the confidence of one whose shirt would never become limp and vaguely humid like that of his audience. "So *tuneful*, isn't it," he said with a smile.

"Oh yes. It makes me want to take all my clothes off and do the rhumba," said Anderson without conviction.

"Ah, but seriously, don't you think there's a Mozartian flavour there?"

"Pretty damn Mozartian, yes . . ." He knew it was a mistake before he'd finished saying it.

"Caught you there! You weren't *listening*—hear it now? It's what they call stochastic music, random notes . . . very experimental. The composer simply conceptualizes his starting figures for the random-number generators. Intellectually it's all tremendously absorbing; but I'm afraid I was pulling your leg a teensy bit about Mozart. You just weren't trying to *listen*, were you?"

Anderson thought fleetingly of his days at Oxford, when people like Nigel could with a certain legitimacy be divested of their trousers and placed in some convenient river. "Ha ha," he said. "Music's not really my thing," he said. "Why, before I met you I used to think pianissimo was a rude word in Italian."

Nigel pulled the unfair trick of becoming suddenly and offensively serious. "I do think that's a terrible thing to say," he said quietly.

A fume from the sherry—there hadn't been enough to make it fumes in the plural—coiled about Anderson's brain and lovingly urged him to say *Go to hell, you loathsome little person*. "You must remember I'm tone-deaf," he said, falling back on his final line of defence. "Unless the pitch is different enough, I mean really different, I can't tell one note from another."

(He could remember a time when this fact had seemed a rock-solid defence. "Come sir, why do you not appreciate da Vinci's great masterpiece?" "Well, actually, I'm blind." "Oh my God, I didn't know, I'm so sorry, please do forgive me—" Somehow the revelation of tone-deafness never produced quite this reaction. Instead—)

"Oh, that's just an excuse," said Nigel. "I'm sure you really aren't . . . I've read how true tone-deafness is *extremely* rare, and most people who say they've got it are simply musically illiterate. You're not *trying*, that's all. You really should make an effort."

"How much effort do I have to put in before I appreciate a team of monkeys playing pianos, or whatever you said *this* godawful noise is?"

Nigel sniffed. "Really, Colin, one has to master traditional music before one can expect to follow conceptual works which reject its conventions. Now do promise me you'll *try*."

Rather to his horror, Anderson heard himself mumble something that sounded hideously like acquiescence. Then Nigel was gone, off to adjust the noise machine further, and Anderson was left peering suspiciously at his tiny, empty glass. As a small measure of revenge, and because there was still nowhere to deposit it, he put the glass in his pocket before leaving.

"What brought you to us?" asked the white-coated man, suddenly and treacherously forcing quantities of ice-cold goo into Anderson's left ear.

"I saw the small ad in the *Times*," he said. "Ouch."

"There, it doesn't hurt a bit, does it?" said the man from Computer Audio Services, kneading the stuff with his fingertips until Anderson felt his eardrum was pressing alarmingly against his brain. "Ouch," he agreed.

"Just a moment while it hardens," the man said chattily. "I'm so glad when people aren't ashamed of coming to CAS. After all, the world's so complicated today that busy men like yourself just can't take time out to learn little things like musical appreciation . . . That's what I always say," he added with the epigrammatic air of a man who always said it.

"I'm tone-deaf," Anderson said.

"Oh quite. There's no need for excuses with us, Mr Anderson. *We* understand."

"But I *am* tone-deaf."

"Of course . . . Now this isn't going to hurt a bit." For the next several seconds Anderson enjoyed the sensation of having his ear cleared of blockages with a rubber suction-plunger. Blockages such as eardrums, he thought. At last the mould was out, and the CAS technician summoned a flunky to carry it away.

"There. It'll be cured, machined, drilled, tapped and ready in fifteen minutes. Now I think you'd decided to try our Analyzer aid . . . our cheapest model," he said reproachfully.

"The cheapest model," Anderson said with rather more enthusiasm.

"But I expect that in no time at all you'll want to trade it in for our Scholar, with fifty times the memory storage at less than twice the price. You could be ready to cope with *fifty* composers and not just one—"

"The Analyzer," Anderson said inexorably.

"Well, of course it's your decision. Now which composer dataset would you prefer? With the Analyzer, of course, you can only have one."

Anderson contemplated the bandaged finger which he'd cut on some broken glass in his pocket. He massaged it gently and said, "Mozart."

"Oh, a very good choice, sir. What was the name again?"

Anderson told him again, and wonders of technology were duly set into motion. The result was a transparent ear-mould with the thumbnail-sized bulge of the Analyzer protruding; there was also a discreet invoice which made his credit card seem ready to wilt Dali-fashion as he passed it over.

"The battery is extra, sir. Would you be wanting a battery?"

"On the whole, yes."

"Then if you'll sign *here* . . . Thank you so much. I'm sure you'll find your computer aid a real social help, and something which a busy person like you needn't be in the slightest ashamed of using."

"A tone-deaf person like me."

"Of course."

After playing for an afternoon with his new toy Anderson felt himself rather well up on music and Mozart, rather as his first day with a pocket calculator had given him the air of an expert on the theory of numbers. In the evening he paid a call.

"Hello—just thought I'd drop in to say thanks for the party."

"Why, how charmingly old-fashioned of you, Colin. Do come in and have a quick one. I really don't know *why* I throw these parties; one loses so much glassware. I'll only be a second, now." And Nigel vanished, presumably to manipulate the combination lock on his secret drinks cupboard.

The room's trendy bareness seemed to shout at Anderson now it was emphasized by the lack of crowd. He wandered to the intricate hi-fi console and allowed himself to be discovered peering at it.

"Oh! Did you want to hear some *music?*"

"I was just thinking I'd probably . . . appreciate it more without all those people shouting their heads off."

"Well, well." Nigel looked at him with eyes slightly narrowed, and then turned to the smart brushed-aluminum console. Anderson noted that the drinks provided for single callers weren't any bigger than those at vast parties—but was he imagining it, or did this sherry taste slightly more, as it were, British than last Saturday's offering? He longed to sniff Nigel's glass and compare; but already the sound of what might very well have been music was spilling from each corner of the room.

"Now what d'you think of this delightful tune," said Nigel with a false smile.

Anderson cupped his ear at the nearest speaker with the gesture he'd been practising, and flipped a fingernail at the Analyzer nestling there. The noise was like a small gunshot; he suppressed the resulting wince before it reached the outside world. "Interesting," he said with what he hoped was an air of deep concentration. Nigel watched him, faintly smiling. Then after a moment, a mechanical version of the still small voice of conscience whispered in Anderson's ear, saying: *"Random notes, 87% probability . . . random notes, 92% probability . . . random notes, 95% probability . . ."*

"Oh, this is more of your stochastic music," Anderson murmured. "Now I can listen to it properly I can see it's just random notes. I mean, I can hear it's random."

Nigel's smile became at once more visible and less convincing. "Of course that was rather obvious, after our little chat on Saturday," he said, and fiddled again with the controls. "Let's have something of the real thing." The speaker noises changed to something quite definitely though indefinably different, and Nigel turned again towards his guest like a restaurant waiter offering a selection of red herrings. "What d'you think of that?"

Anderson consulted the Analyzer, and after a short pause came back with, "Come on, Nigel, pull the other one. It's random again, isn't it? Only this time it's the change in pitch between successive notes that gets randomized over a certain interval, so it sounds that little bit more musical than just random notes."

"Can't fool you," said Nigel, hardly smiling at all. "Anything *you'd* like to hear?"

"I've been listening to a few things by the chap you recommended—Mozart. Not bad."

"My God. I recommended him? I must have been really pissed. Still, there should be something of his in the databank—" He turned back towards the console keyboard.

A minute or two later Anderson was able to say with quiet confidence, "Ah yes, that's the K.169 string quartet, isn't it?" Following an irresistible urge, he breathed gently over his fingernails and polished them on the lapel of his jacket. Half-heartedly his host caused the equipment to play further noises which the Analyzer rapidly identified as the Serenade in D Major, adding the useful information that it had been composed in Salzburg. Nigel seemed a little shaken by this onslaught, and was breathing more heavily as he returned to the console.

*"Not recognized,"* said the small voice. *"Transition probability analysis suggests Mozart work, 82% probability . . ."*

"That's Mozart all right," said Anderson, thinking fast. "But hardly one of his best pieces . . . in fact I must admit I don't recognize it at all."

"Er, yes, just an obscure oboe quartet I thought might amuse you. H'm." A thought appeared to have struck Nigel, and he punched another sequence on the keyboard—savagely, as though squashing small insects.

*"Not recognized. Transition probability analysis suggests not Mozart work, 79% probability . . ."*

"You've got the wrong composer, old chap."

"It's so easy to make mistakes with equipment as sophisticated as this," Nigel said viciously. "I'll have to throw you out soon—I'm meeting someone tonight—but first, what d'you think of this one?"

The lights on the hi-fi console flickered alarmingly for nearly a minute; Anderson fantasized that Nigel's expensive gadgetry, like Nigel, was baffled and irritated. Then more musical noises seeped through the room. Anderson cupped his ear attentively, and clicked his fingernail again at what was hidden inside. There was a pause.

*"Not recognized. Transition probability analysis suggests Mozart work, 94% probability."*

The transition probability jargon was something to do with sequences of notes favoured by given composers. In the long run they left their fingerprints all over their work so obviously that even a machine could catch them red-handed.

"Ah, you can't mistake Mozart," Anderson sighed, wondering if he was overdoing it a trifle. "Even in a minor work like this—no, I don't actually recognize it—the towering genius of the man comes across so clearly." He definitely was overdoing it, he decided.

Nigel seemed to have brightened surprisingly. "This really is a *very* sophisticated system, you know. I'm rather proud of it. One thing you can do with it, if you know how, is to have the processor run through a selection of someone's works and cobble up a sort of cheap and nasty imitation—something to do with transition probabilities, it says in the manual. Of course you couldn't expect it to fool anyone who knew anything about music. . . . But I'll have to say goodbye now. Do come round again whenever you like. It's nice to see you making an effort, musically, but you really will have to try much harder yet. Old chap."

Anderson looked down into his empty glass and thought of thrusting it into his pocket quickly, or perhaps up Nigel's nostril, slowly.

"It's very kind of you," he said with a titanic effort.

The CAS salesman studied him wisely. "Now if you cared to exchange it for the Scholar model we could in fact allow quite a generous trade-in price, Mr Anderson."

"And then I suppose I'd have a wonderful machine that could fail to spot imitations of fifty composers rather than just one?"

"Our clients usually find the Scholar very satisfactory," the other said severely.

"So will I—if it can tell inspired music from cobbled-together computer rubbish, the way this one doesn't."

The salesman sighed. "To handle that would need a full-scale Artificial Intelligence. CAS isn't in that business . . . yet. Now if you come back next year, when we hope to have chased out the last bugs, then perhaps we can sell you our Mark III model—the Audio-Brain."

Anderson reflected for a moment, and then leant forward with what he considered to be an expression of great shrewdness. He'd practised it in the mirror for use on Nigel. "If you're likely to market it next year there must be prototypes around the place right now. In fact you must be market-researching the thing already. It wouldn't hurt to let me try one out a little for you."

Licking his lips, the CAS man murmured that it would be, well, rather irregular, but . . . Anderson reached for his wallet.

\* \* \*

"How am I doing, Nigel?" he asked confidently, back in the bare, expensively-carpeted room.

"Not bad," Nigel muttered. "You must be trying a bit harder than you were—I told you understanding music was mainly a matter of *trying*. How does this sound to you?"

One of Anderson's ears took in the new meaningless noises that were tinkling from all four corners of the pastel room. In his other ear, the AudioBrain prototype whispered to him: *"Sounds like Bach, I should say . . . but that's just the TP analysis. As a whole it's hardly an inspired piece, and the long-term melodic structure is absolutely shot to hell. No, it has to be another faked-up computer piece . . ."*

"Synthetic Bach," Anderson said casually. "Come on, Nigel, no need to keep on pulling my leg like that."

Nigel looked thoroughly annoyed. Possibly to conceal this and reduce Anderson's satisfaction temporarily, he took the tiny glasses away for replenishment from the hundred-gallon plastic tank of British sherry which Anderson was now convinced existed somewhere towards the rear of the flat.

Despite having defeated Nigel in umpteen straight sets of hard-fought musical appreciation, Anderson still didn't feel wildly happy. It might have been that he was tiring of the game; it might have been the artificial-intelligence program built into this new hearing aid, which was now saying: *"You should be able to tell this for yourself, dumbo. Only a real musical illiterate could miss spotting that one . . . you're not trying, that's all. You really should make an effort."*

"But I'm tone-deaf," Anderson said aloud.

*"That's what they all say,"* said the AudioBrain. *"Come off it!"*

Thus it was that as Nigel returned, Anderson was addressing the empty air and saying, "Go to hell, you loathsome little person."

It was another of those parties whose expensive minimalism extended to the furniture, the pictures on the walls and (inevitably) the drinks.

"Hello Nigel, long time no see," said Anderson.

"Um. How's the culture, then? Still working to better yourself on the musical front?"

"Pardon?"

"I said, are you still slogging away at the musical appreciation?"

"Pardon?—Oh, that. No, I find I can't handle music any more. I'm going deaf—and not just tone-deaf." He pushed back his hair and tapped the thing plugged into his ear.

"Oh my God, I didn't know, I'm so sorry . . ."

Anderson decided again that he liked the AudioBrain a good deal more with its battery removed.

# The Helping Hand

### Robert Sheckley

Travis had been fired from his job that morning. Boring and low-paying though it had been, it had given him something to live for. Now he had nothing at all, and in his hand he held the means of cutting short a futile and humiliating existence. The bottle contained pellis annabula, a quick, sure, and painless poison. He had stolen it from his former employer, Carlyle Industrial Chemicals. PA was a catalyst used to fix hydrocarbons. Travis was going to fix himself with it, once and for all.

His few remaining friends thought Travis was a neurotic attention-seeker because of his previous suicide attempts. Well, he would show them this time, and they'd be sorry. Perhaps even his wife would shed a tear or two.

The thought of his wife steeled Travis's resolution. Leota's love had changed into an indifferent tolerance, and finally into hate—the sharp, domineering, acidic sort against which he was helpless. And the damnable thing was that he still loved her.

Do it now, he thought. He closed his eyes and raised the bottle.

Before he could drink, the bottle was knocked out of his hand. He heard Leota's sharp voice: "What do you think you're doing?"

"It should be obvious," Travis said.

She studied his face with interest. Leota was a large, hard-faced woman with a gift for never-ending beastliness. But now her face had softened.

"You were really going to do it this time, weren't you?"

"I'm still going to," Travis said. "Tomorrow or next week will do as well."

"I never believed you had it in you," she said. "Some of our friends thought you had guts, but I never did. Well, I guess I've really put you through hell all these years. But *someone* had to run things."

"You stopped caring for me a long time ago," Travis said. "Why did you stop me now?"

Leota didn't answer immediately. Could she be having a change of heart? Travis had never seen her like this before.

"I've misjudged you," she said at last. "I always figured you were bluffing, just to annoy me. Remember when you threatened to jump from the window? You leaned out—like this."

Leota leaned from the window, her body poised over the street twenty stories below. "Don't do that!" Travis said sharply.

She moved back in, smiling. "That's funny, coming from you. Don't tell me you still care?"

"I could," Travis said. "I know I could—if only you and I—"

"Perhaps," Leota said, and Travis felt a flash of hope, though he barely dared acknowledge it. Women were so strange! There she was, smiling. She put her hands firmly on his shoulders, saying, "I *couldn't* let you kill yourself. You have no idea how strongly I feel about you."

Travis found it impossible to answer. He was moved. His wife's strong, caring hands on his shoulders had moved him inexpressibly—straight through the open window.

As his fingers missed the sill and he fell toward the street, Travis heard his wife calling, "I feel enough, darling, to want this done *my* way."

# The Hexer

## Howard Wandrei

**O**xboro *Enquirer*, June 2.—at the departmental hearing on the Kramer case, Patrolman Brian Daugherty insisted stubbornly on his original version of the odd affair. Off duty and in plain clothes, he was walking home. He was nearing the deserted intersection of Dale Avenue and Fourth Street shortly after ten o'clock last Monday evening when a man "come helling around the corner." Asked what he meant by "helling," Daugherty explained, "Like mad, like a banshee. He was traveling like a bat out of—I mean he was really traveling."

Commissioner Hopkins asked: "Are you familiar with banshees, Daugherty?"

Without cracking a smile, Daugherty said: "My old lady told me about a couple of them she saw in Ireland, but I never saw one myself."

Mayor Anderson said impatiently: "Let's get ahead."

Daugherty recited, "Another man busts around the corner almost as fast as the first one who I was shagging."

"Got eyes in the back of your head?"

"I heard him. The first guy was running light; the second guy was running heavy."

"The second guy. That would be Heinrich Kramer?"

"Yessir; only I didn't know who he was then, though. He come boiling around the corner hanging on to his head. Like this." Daugherty demonstrated, grabbing his head like a basketball and making a face. "He looked nuts, with his eyes glaring that way. I had my gun out, and when he saw it he stopped. I asked him what was his hurry, and he said his head. 'My head,' he says, just like that. The guy he was chasing was gone already, so I went for Kramer, just walking easy toward him. Right away he ducked back around the corner, and when I got there, he was halfway down the block already and picking up speed all the time."

Jan Kupra, representing the *Enquirer,* asked: "Aren't you pretty handy with your gun, Daugherty?"

"I'm a good shot," Daugherty admitted modestly. "I got him when he was over a block away."

"You just took aim and shot him. If you'd killed him, it would have been murder."

Daugherty got red in the face, and said: "He'll tell you so himself. First I yelled him to halt and he—"

"You yelled him to halt?" Kupra mimicked.

"Get along with this," the mayor ordered.

"I yelled him to halt, and he kept on going. Then I fired over his head, and he still kept on going, so I brung the aim down a little bit."

"And you got him," said Kupra. "And he skinned his nose and his knees, and might have cracked his skull and died, and it would still be murder. Do you like to shoot men in the back, Daugherty?"

"Shut up!" Mayor Anderson shouted, "or I'll throw you right out of here myself!"

"I was shooting for his legs," Daugherty said, "but the way he was running, I had to aim higher. He ain't hurt much, except he ain't comfortable sitting down. What the hell, I thought he was trying to hold up that other guy, and I had to stop him.

"When I got to him, chief, he was cussing around like I'd have to throw him in the klink if there was anybody listening to him but me. He was calling me names that—"

"Never mind. Mr. Kramer is noted for his vocabulary outside of Oxboro."

"Yessir. Then he started talking wild about his head again. He said that guy he was chasing done something to his head. I asked him what, and he clammed up. I took him to the hospital on account of that little puncture, and that's all, sir."

Heinrich Kramer, of course, is the bard of Oxboro. He is as well known for his several great novels as for his own almighty opinion of them, classing himself with Hardy, Maugham and others. He has long been considered the leader of Oxboro's café society. It was ascertained by police that on Monday evening Kramer the Great was drinking in the exclusive Number 400 and holding forth to companions, when he was annoyed by a stranger staring at him and chuckling. Kramer made a comment to his friends about the stranger, abruptly clapped his hands to his head and knocked over a table on his way to reach the man who was staring at him. The man got up hurriedly and left, with Kramer in chase.

Mr. Kramer has confined himself to his home, refusing to be interviewed, refusing in fact to bring charges against Patrolman Daugherty.

"There's no sense in it; it's whacky," Kupra said. "What's all this business about his head? There was nothing wrong with his head except for its size. You can't go around shooting prominent citizens indiscriminately, Daugherty."

Mayor Anderson said: "I warned you, Kupra; you're only here to listen. Now GET OUT!"

The mayor screamed the way he does whenever he gets the chance, and everybody in Oxboro knows how he gets grapefruit-purple in the face and sticks his hammy ears out, and hikes his shoulders up so that it looks as though he hasn't got any neck.

The mayor then told Daugherty, "You, too, patrolman. Get out, and take your banshees along with you. Get back to your post, and next time don't be too handy with your gun."

Why the famous Heinrich Kramer acted as he did, is a mystery. But he chose to run when arrested, and he didn't stop when Daugherty fired a warning shot.

The only description of the man whom Kramer was chasing is that he was slight, elderly but athletic, and well-dressed in a dark suit, black topcoat, hat and shoes. As yet no clue to this individual's identity has been found—

A few days later in his column, *The Banana Stem,* Jan Kupra wrote:

There is something funny going on in Oxboro. The secret won't last long, because the mortality among secrets shaves one hundred percent pretty close. For the time being, certain people are acting with suspicious furtiveness; they jump up and beat it out of restaurants while you're talking to them, snub old friends on the street, and some of them stick inside their houses as though there's a plague on the loose. Maybe it's a secret society, and maybe it's political, huh? If you don't think strange habits and unnatural actions and secret plots are dangerous, remember what happened to Heinrich Kramer. According to the way they're behaving, we could name a few names who belong in the bughouse down the river. Names you've seen in print before, too—

The streetcars in Oxboro are way longer and wider and more powerful than the trolleys in New York. They are painted bright canary-yellow, and the seating accommodations consist of lengthwise seats in front and rear, crosswise seats in the middle. In the crosswise seats passengers look at the backs of heads and study dandruff, coiffures, and types of ears. In the lengthwise seats passengers sneak looks at pretty legs, succumb to the hypnotic interest of blemishes and deformities, and shorten the ride with successive mental sneers at all those hopeless, idiotic specimens of humanity lined up across the aisle.

Kupra owned an expensive sedan which he used for pleasure; he took the streetcar to the shop and elsewhere during the day, because it looked democratic; besides, being a born snoop, he never tired of studying faces, strange or familiar. He liked to analyze, to sift all the fascinating details which make up a countenance, to take a face apart and put it back together again like God. An old hand at the game, he was able to say, "That man has the eyes of a murderer"; or "Well-dressed as he is, the man's ears are more animal than human." On the 7th of June, Kupra was riding in the rear section of a streetcar on the Hill Park line, and practicing industriously his refined, private brand of cannibalism.

The sky was all blue, and the sun was shining particularly on Oxboro. Some of the green lawns and boulevards were splashed with dandelions in beds, like microspores of pollen each expanded to giant size. Having finished his covert inspection of Passengers Number 1 and 2, Kupra went to work with his eyes and mind on the third individual from the left. Kupra read from left to right.

This person was an old man of perhaps seventy winters. Whatever his stature was in its prime, he had diminished to gnomelike proportions. Height: five-feet-four; weight: a hundred to a hundred and ten pounds; white hair, fashionably barbered. He was a neat person, and sat with his knees close together, his spine straight, his slim, girlish hands folded asleep composedly in his lap. His necktie was correct with his shirt, whose collar encircled his slender throat with accurate, soft dimensions. He wore a dark-gray hat, a suit of hard gray worsted that was immaculately pressed and tailored, sheer socks that were snug around his ankles, shapely shoes which were narrow and short and pointed, painstakingly carved out of solid ebony and polished with oil. His lips were compressed to a thin line, and he was so smoothly shaven that his face was a girlishly fresh cameo. His ears were Puckish, close to his head. Kupra observed the observant stillness of the stranger's eyes, and afterward he could never remember what color they were. All told, the dear little old man who was riding on the seat across the aisle was a diminutive aristocrat whose lips smiled subtly about something.

Kupra looked along his nose with great dubiety, then slowly raised his face to the varnished, hooded architecture of the ceiling, just to make sure; his nose was a yard long, or longer. He sighted along it, in the manner of a hunter centering on a deer with a .351 rifle.

None of the other passengers observed the casual lifting of his eyebrows.

Kupra brought his attention down again and the attenuated schnozzle wabbled elastically. When he turned his head too suddenly, his newly acquired deformity wagged obscenely, like the tail

196

of a hairless dog. He lifted his hand to his face with a careless gesture, and made sure that the long, nude proboscis was there. It was there, all right, equal in length to four or five frankfurters joined end to end, about a pound in weight since it was boneless. It was his own secret, obviously invisible to all the other passengers. Save perhaps one. He stared hard at the beautifully tailored old pixie across the aisle.

He was shaking with some private mirth. When Kupra's eyes returned to him, he rang the bell abruptly and reached the back platform as the car arrived at an intersection. The back gates opened and he got off, and was gone at a brisk, catfooting walk after a glance through the windows at the stricken Kupra.

The broomstick of a nose was the old man's doing. It was he who had escaped from Heinrich Kramer, chasing him because he had made the Oxboro bard's big head a private actuality. And now he had hexed Kupra, hanging a pole of a snout on his face, giving the keyhole-peeper a branch of anatomy which he could really snoop with.

Appalled by the indecency of the fate that had overtaken him, Kupra turned his head to look out the window at the green lawns riding by and get rid of the whole idea. There was a man sitting beside him, and the gun barrel of Kupra's nose batted him across the Adam's apple.

"Glob!" exclaimed the man, and took hold of his throat. He glared suspiciously at the columnist, who sat with hands folded, staring innocently across the way. Frowning with puzzlement and worry, the man kept swallowing experimentally and gently massaging his gozzle.

As for Kupra, he refrained from stroking the pain out of the marvelous beak where its architecture had bent across his fellow-passenger's neck.

For the duration of the ride he kept the phantom schnozzle gently clamped between his knees, anchoring it out of harm's way and pondering the immaculately dressed old Hexer's malicious talent.

He got off at Ashland, his street. Big elms were spaced along the boulevard, and the warm shadow under their canopy of foliage was conducive to thought and experimentation. With no citizens in sight, he explored the ghostly sniffer from end to end as though playing a dirge on a flute, and there was not the least doubt about its authenticity. It was a hell of a quandary to be in.

A housewife interrupted the chore of sweeping off her porch to watch the rapt, sleepwalking exercises which Kupra was doing with his arms.

"Hello, Mr. Kupra," she called, in the tone of a person addressing a drunk. "Is something the matter?"

"Just exercising, Mrs. Jefferson," he lied resignedly. "You know how your arms get stiff."

He continued on his way with his hands in his pockets, shaking his head slowly with dull disbelief. His nose wagged; it had the same flexibility as its length in garden hose. He was the proprietor of a phenomenon which would baffle surgery. No wonder Kramer had run from Daugherty; if he had divulged what the Hexer had done to his head, the authorities might have consigned him to the nuthouse down the river. On Kupra it was a terrible punishment to visit for his crimes of reporting. With a stroke of his eye the old man had done it, the mischievous devil.

When he reached his number, he observed two cars parked at the curb, empty. He had guests as usual. He had loaned his keys a couple of times, and the girls had had duplicates made; he hadn't gotten around to having the locks changed; the girls were sources of information as to who was having babies, when, what guy or gal was breaking up whose home, and so on.

There were five people sitting in his living room, drinking Collinses made out of his fancy gin. Morosely he looked around at Johnny Pollet, Jeannette Shires, Dave Martinson, Anne Pryor and Betty Turner.

"Want a drink?" Anne asked.

"Yeah, will you mix me one?" he asked. "I'll be taking a shower; I'm all sticky."

Perspiring and shaken because of what the Hexer had done to him, he closed his bedroom door, stripped and stepped under the shower for a quick one. He forgot about the nose until the last, soaped it then and wagged it under the spray to rinse it. The magnitude of the unmerciful disaster which had overtaken him numbed his wits; he moved like an automaton, stepping out of the tub and toweling himself. He made a complete change of clothing even to shoes. As he selected a new shirt from a bureau drawer and got into it, he hung a new necktie temporarily on his bugaboo of nose, about midway along. In the mirror, the necktie looked as though it were suspended in midair. In spite of its stick-out reality, the nose didn't reflect.

He closed the drawer, fortunately not hard because his nose got caught in the crack. He clawed the drawer open. Pain streamed up the schnozzle into his skull and nearly blew off the top of his head. Shuddering, he screwed his eyes up; tears trickled, tickling, down his olfactory extension.

Dabbing at his eyes, he gained control of himself and joined the chattering party in the living room. A drink had been made for him.

When Anne tendered the glass she performed in a most peculiar manner. Instead of turning around and going back to her chair in a normal way, she backed warily with a very odd smile, passing a hand behind her and making a gesture as though catching something up. Kupra, who had held his head aside with an absent-minded expression to keep his nose out of the way, stared speculatively at her while she smoothed her dress with singular extravagance and drew her legs up onto a window seat. Anne was a brunette, choicely rounded and graceful; she had the right height and heft and resiliency of anatomy, and cultivated a pronounced ability to pose. She was feline in her exact graduations of movement, and her voluptuousness was contained this afternoon in a handkerchief-linen dress opaqued with a satin slip. The wrinkling across the hips and in the skirt behind did not diminish her attractiveness, and she didn't need to worry about showing an amount of knee and a moon-gleam of thigh, because she was among friends.

Wondering why she acted as though she thought he would give her a kick if she turned her back on him, Kupra went to a chair and sat on its arm, keeping the lengthy quiver of his nose away from his drink so that he wouldn't knock it out of his hand himself.

"Well, what's the important word?" he asked at large.

Around the room he got serial answers, "Nothing happens," "Mh-mh. Hm-m-m," "I don't know a thing," "What have *you* got?" and "There's nobody in town but us."

"Oh, you just dropped in," Kupra commented. He tried his drink, and it was pretty good for a girl's work. No taste of gin. He arrived at the conclusion that there was no gin in the drink, and repaired to the kitchen, returning to hear a lot of conversation about nothing going on. Anne was highly decorative and posey, and was strolling about for effect as usual. Kupra observed that now and then she gave her hips an inexplicable galvanic twist as though she were muscling an appendage, like a cat. A cat she was, of course,

and eventually someone stepped on her tail. She let out an agonized caterwaul, grabbed behind her and snatched to her breast the
injured member, which, of course, was just as invisible as Kupra's
nose.

Everyone jumped and Kupra asked: "What was that for?"

"Why, nothing," she said breathlessly. She forced a laugh. "I just
wanted to see you all jump."

"A fine sense of humor you've got," Kupra remarked. "Don't do
that again; it's too hot to jump."

He let the party go on as it would, just listening. Being host was
never any exertion to him, because if anyone wanted a drink the
person made it himself. He kept an eye on Anne, remembering the
torment in the screech she had let out. When he had a chance he
told her: "I want to talk to you."

She agreed, and they drifted unobserved into the bedroom of
the bungalow. When he had closed the door he asked: "What's on
your mind, Anne? Come on, what's the matter?"

"I don't know what you mean. Honestly, I haven't got anything
for you. Please." She was out of breath.

He stared at her, and there was fright in her eyes. "Maybe nothing I can print," he suggested, "but something else?"

"Always the snoop," she bantered. "It might be something very
personal, none of your business at all, you know."

"I can almost guess what it is," he hinted.

"You couldn't possibly."

"Listen, Anne," he urged. "Haven't I always been a mommie and
poppie to you? Have I ever done you dirty? Gimme."

"All right; it's just this. Well," she groped, "I . . . I think I'm
going crazy. Really bughouse, I mean."

"What makes you think you're going bughouse?"

"I've got a tail," she said shakily.

"What kind of a tail?"

"A cat's tail. I mean I really have," she said in a rush of words. "It
was trailing on the rug, and Dave Martinson sank his heel into it."

"Well, I'll be a son of a gun," Kupra mused. Anne looked as
though she were going to cry. He saw her wet eyes and said hastily:
"Don't worry, Anne; you're no battier than I am. Just a minute,
though. If you've got a tail, how do you get a dress on over it?"

"I don't know," she said, with a shrug of despair. "It just works
that way."

"Line of cleavage," he muttered.

She turned, and he made a pass at the supposedly empty air. She said: "There. Oh, damn it!"

Rooted to the base of her spine was indubitably the tail of a cat, its proportions proper for her size. It was covered with fur, and flexible, and she could twitch it, having full muscular control over it. He let it slip through his fingers to the end, ascertaining that it was a generous five feet long. Experimentally he tugged, and she was compelled to back up protestingly.

"It's there beyond a doubt," he said. "Now guess what I've got. A nose." He had her stand just so, and gave her a gentle bat across the side of the head.

With awe, after feeling along its length, Anne said: "For heaven's sake." She laughed uncertainly.

"I guess," he said sardonically, "that he wanted to bring home the idea that I was sticking my nose into other people's business, like the feline streak in your case."

"I'm not feline."

"You've given me some pretty catty gossip."

"But how can such a thing happen? It's utterly wild!"

"Very utterly. When did this tail grow on you?"

"Just a couple of days ago. I was having cocktails with a couple of the girls down at the Casino, and we were chatting—"

"Cutting each other's throats, and snickering at your friends, maybe telling a nasty story about some Hollywood actress because you're not in Hollywood."

"Gee, you've got a mean tongue," she said. "Anyhow, all at once it happened. Umph. As quick as that. I left right away, of course, as soon as I was sure. I'm positive the girls didn't suspect anything, because they had engagements and were in a hurry, too."

"I wonder what he did to them."

"What did who do?"

"Hoodoo is right," Kupra cracked. "Did you happen to notice a pink-faced shrimp of an old man anywhere in the Casino? A skinny old geezer all barbered and manicured and tailored up."

"Oh! He was all alone at the next table, and he bought all our drinks for us. He looked charming, but I wondered if he wasn't senile and thinking he was going to get something out of it."

"Rest your mind. That old monkey is the one responsible for this. He got me on the streetcar only a little while ago on the way uptown."

"Oh, no!"

"Oh, yes!"

"Why, that devilish little mummy!"

"Sure. He gave Henny Kramer a head the size of a beer barrel; Kramer was quick on the trigger and chased the buzzard who hexed him up like that. Damn that cop Daugherty. Henny was just about grabbing the old guy's coat tails."

"Kramer was a fool to run."

"Sure he was. But are you going to go around advertising the fur job he did on you?"

"You won't tell on me, will you?" she begged. "It's so devastatingly ridiculous."

"As long as you don't give me away about my nozzle."

They regarded each other strickenly, and with the baffled compassion of companions in misery.

"I wonder if the condition is permanent," she hazarded. There was a wail in her inflection. "People are beginning to think I'm queer. I have to positively sprint into a room so that I don't get a door closed on my tail. And I get tired of keeping it curled in the air all the time so that it doesn't get stepped on. Besides, it's nervous; it's got a tic in it that's driving me out of my mind. And it gets matted the way fur does and feels terrifically uncomfortable. I'm combing it all the time. And even with an electric dryer, after I give it a bath, it's ages before it's all fluffy again."

"I just closed a drawer on my beak when I changed my shirt," Kupra chimed in somberly. "When I go to bed tonight I guess I'll have to lie on my back and do a juggling act. And I never was able to sleep on my back."

"You know," said Anne, "I think there's something wrong with Jeannette and Betty, too. They've been acting as though they've eaten a goblin apiece."

"There's something screwy about Martinson, too."

After kissing Anne, just to see whether it could be done with the handicap of his nasal equipment, Kupra eased open the latch of the bedroom door and looked through the crack. They rejoined the party which had formed through the usual happenstance. People who had nothing important to do in hot weather, collecting in comfortable surroundings in which someone had snitched a key—Betty or Anne or both.

The drinking went on through the afternoon past twilight. Kupra found things out. Across the room, Dave Martinson was getting himself soused. He was a lawyer, somber in appearance, dark and devious in the ways of his mind. His forehead was smooth, white, as unblemished as a boy's. Absently, he was tracing with a forefinger an invisible mark, a certain letter which the Hexer had branded there above his eyes. The habit of tracing the letter revealed it in pinkish outline. Martinson caught Kupra staring, and the lanky lawyer jerked his hat on, sat staring morosely at the rug, inevitably to raise his finger to his forehead again.

Jeannette Shires spent a couple of hours a day on her marvelous complexion; she had gardenia-petal skin, its purity accented by magnificent black hair in a carved coiffure of gleaming curls. During the evening she got Kupra aside and asked to borrow his razor. She had a whim to shave her legs, she said. Kupra told her they didn't look as though they needed it.

"What do you know about it?" she retorted.

"The more you shave your legs, the hairier they'll get," he warned.

"That's all right with me," she retorted. "All I've got to do is keep them shaved."

The Hexer had got her. He had given her a heavy black beard, and she had to shave twice a day.

That made it five out of six. If this group was representative of the town, the Hexer had already distributed his wares among five-sixths of the citizens of Oxboro.

Keeping his eyes skinned for the next few days, Kupra found plenty of evidence that such was the case, that the Hexer had spared very few in squeegeeing the town. Some of the deeds were good; most appeared to have been committed with the most greedy malice.

There was a certain loud-mouthed cop, notorious for his insolence of manner in writing out tickets, who had mule's ears. From the length of the stroke, for he was continually feeling them to see if they were still there, it could be determined that they were a full eighteen inches of botheration. A certain blind beggar, who had salted away something like sixty thousand dollars at his profession, really went blind and got run down by a truck. That was how the money turned up.

The best-dressed man in town started growing flowers back of his ears. The narcissus scent was unmistakable. A listener could detect the snap of stems when he picked them daily. He got round-shouldered and ceased wearing a gardenia in his lapel.

The meanest man in town had a face like a saint. Overnight a caprice of paralysis struck his benign countenance into an iron mask of virulent detestation of the whole human race.

And so on down the line.

Mostly, the Hexer avoided repetition in his works, indicating interest in his profession, or hobby. Not everyone was affected by the potent gleam of that gray eye, but his goal was not necessarily a hundred percent. Too, it was presumable that only he could take back his gifts; widely as he plied his mischief, however, none of his victims saw him more than once; he returned no more, deaf in his mad glee to prayers in whatever humility or rage pronounced. What he did he would not undo.

All Kupra found to do was hope futilely that his particular curse would wear off; while the phantom schnozzle might yield to surgery, he had the dark conviction that another one would spontaneously sprout. At the typewriter, when he knocked off his daily column for the *Enquirer,* he kept on printing capital letters, quotation marks and the like on his beak. Sometimes he wondered whether mass insanity had hit town. Otherwise he wondered where the little old man had come from, and where the little old man had gone.

He certainly did his cussedest in Oxboro.

Oxboro *Enquirer,* June 25; Public Notices. WANTED: Works on black magic, secret doctrines, hypnotism, Tibetan mysteries, ancient lore, occult and mystic sciences, and the evil eye, with emphasis on lifting spells. Premium prices paid. Phone Jan Kupra, *Enquirer,* or Oxboro 2748.

# His First Day at Editing

Eugene Field

Yesterday morning, Mr. Horace A. Hurlbut took formal possession of *The Chicago Times,* in compliance with the mandate of justice making him receiver of that institution. Bright and early he was at his post in *The Times* building; and the expression that coursed over his mobile features, as he lolled back in the editorial chair and abandoned himself to pleasing reflections, was an expression of conscious pride and ineffable satisfaction.

"I have now attained the summit and the goal of earthly ambition," quoth Mr. Hurlbut to himself. "Embarking in the drug-business at an early age, I have progressed through the intermediate spheres of real estate, brokerage and money-lending, until finally I have reached the top round of the ladder of fame, and am now the head of the greatest daily newspaper on the American continent. I expect and intend to prove myself equal to the demands which will be made upon me in this new capacity. I have my own notions about journalism—they differ somewhat from the conventional notions that prevail, but that is neither here nor there; for, as the dictator of this great newspaper, I shall have no difficulty in putting my theories into practice."

"Here's the mornin' mail, major," said the office-boy, laying innumerable packages of letters and circulars on the table before Mr. Hurlbut.

"Why do you call me major?" inquired Mr. Hurlbut, with an amused twinkle in his eyes.

"Oh! we always call the editors majors," replied the office-boy. "Major Dennett made that rule a long time ago."

"It is not a bad idea," said Major Hurlbut, "for it gives one a dignity and prestige which can never maintain among untitled civilians. So this is the morning mail, is it?"

Major Hurlbut picked up one of the letters, scrutinized the superscription, heaved a deep sigh, picked up several other letters, blushed, frowned, and appeared much embarrassed.

"Can you tell me," he asked, "whether there are any reporters about this office by the names, or aliases, or nom de plume, or pseudonym of 'M 33,' and 'X 14,' or 'S 5,' or 'G 38'? I find numerous letters directed in this wise, and I mistrust that some unseemly work is being done under cover of these bogus appellations. I will make bold to examine one of these letters."

So Major Hurlbut tore open one of the envelopes, and read as follows:

"G 38, *Times* Office: I have a nice, quiet, furnished room. Call after eight o'clock P.M., at No. 1143 Elston Road."

"As I suspected," cried Major Hurlbut, with a profound groan. "Under these strange pseudonyms, the reporters of this paper are engaging in a carnival of vice! But the saturnalia must end at once. From this moment *The Times* becomes a moral institution. I shall ascertain the names of these reporters, and have them peremptorily discharged!"

"H'yar's a package for you, sah," said the dusky porter, Martin Lewis, entering, and placing a small bundle before Major Hurlbut.

"Ah, yes! I see," quoth the major, "they are the new cards I ordered last Saturday. We editors have to have cards, so as to let people know we are editors."

With this philosophic observation, the major opened the bundle, and disclosed several hundred neat pasteboard cards, printed in red and black as follows:

---

HORACE A. HURLBUT,

Receiver and Editor, "Chicago Times."

*Real Estate A Specialty.*
*Drug Orders Promptly Filled.*

Loans Negotiated without Publicity.

---

"They are very handsome," said Major Hurlbut, "but I am sorry I did not have the title of Major prefixed to my name. However, I will take that precaution with the next lot I have printed."

"Majah Dennett would like to speak with you, sah," said Martin, the porter.

"Although I am very busy with this mail, you may show him in," remarked Major Hurlbut.

Major Dennett pigeon-toed his way into the new editor's presence, and was loftily waved to a chair, in which he dropped, and sat with his toes turned in. Major Hurlbut heaved a weary sigh, ran his fingers through his hair, and regarded his visitor with a condescending stare.

"This is a busy hour with us editors," said Major Hurlbut, "therefore I hope you will state your business as succinctly as possible."

"I merely called to receive orders," explained Major Dennett, with an astonished look.

"Orders for what?" cried Major Hurlbut. "Perhaps you forget, sir, that I am out of the drug business, and am an editor. Permit me, sir, to hand you one of my professional cards."

"You mistake me, sir," replied Major Dennett; "I am connected with this paper, and have been managing editor for years."

Major Hurlbut's manner changed instantly. His cold reserve melted at once, and he became docile as a sucking-dove.

"My dear Major," he exclaimed cordially, "I am overjoyed to meet you. Draw your chair closer, and let us converse together upon matters which concern us both. Each of us has the interests of this great paper at heart; but I, as the head of the institution, have a fearful responsibility resting upon my shoulders. It behooves you to assist me; and, as the first and most important step, I must beg of you to inform me what is expected of me as an editor. I am willing and anxious to edit, but how can I?"

Major Dennett undertook to explain a few of the duties which would fall upon the editor's shoulders, and would have continued talking all day, had not the venerable Major Andre Matteson been ushered into the room, thereby interrupting the conversation. Upon being formally introduced to the new editor, Major Matteson inquired what the policy of *The Times* would be henceforward touching the tariff, the civil service, the war in the Soudan, and the doctrine of the transmigration of souls.

"I have not decided fully what the policy of the paper will be in these minor matters," quoth Major Hurlbut, "except that we shall favor the abolition of the tariff on quinine, cochineal, and other drugs and dyestuffs. I have made up my mind, however, to advocate the opening of a boulevard in Fleabottom subdivision; and, as you are one of the editorial writers, Major Matteson, I would like to have you compose a piece about the folly of extending the Thirtieth Street sewer through the Bosbyshell subdivision. And you may give the firm of Brown, Jones & Co. a raking over, for they have seriously interfered with the sale of my lots out in that part of the city."

Major George McConnell and Major Guy Magee filed into the room at this juncture, and were formally presented to editor Hurlbut, who looked impressive, and received them with a dignity that would have done credit to a pagan court.

"I had hoped to be in a position to boom the city department of the paper," said Major Magee, "but I find that three of the reporters are sick with headache to-day."

"Sick? What appears to be the matter?" asked the editor.

"I didn't ask them," replied Major Magee; "but they said they had headaches."

"They should try bromide of potassium, tincture of valerian, and aromatic spirits of ammonia," observed Major Hurlbut. "By the way, whenever any of our editors or reporters get sick, they should come to me; for I can give them prescriptions that will fix them up in less than no time."

"I presume the policy of the paper touching the theatres will remain unchanged?" inquired Major McConnell.

"That reminds me," said Major Hurlbut: "who gets the show-tickets?"

"Well, I have attended to that detail heretofore," replied Major McConnell.

"We get as many as we want, don't we?" asked Major Hurlbut.

"Certainly," said Major McConnell.

"Well, then, we must give the shows good notices," said the editor; "and, by the way, I would like to have you leave six tickets with me every morning; they will come in mighty handy, you know, among friends. Do we get railroad-passes too?

"Yes, all we want," said Major Dennett.

"I am glad I am an editor," said Major Hurlbut, softly but feelingly.

The foreman came in.

"Shall we set it in nonpareil to-night?" he asked.

"Eh?" ejaculated Editor Hurlbut.

"Does nonpareil go?" repeated the foreman.

"What has he been doing?" inquired Editor Hurlbut.

"The minion is so bad that we ought to put the paper in nonpareil," exclaimed the foreman.

"It must be understood," thundered Major Hurlbut, "that no bad minions will be tolerated on the premises. If there is any minion here who is dissatisfied, let him quit at once."

"Then I am to fire the minion?" asked the foreman.

"No," said Major Hurlbut, "do not fire him, for that would constitute arson; discharge him, but use no violence."

We deeply regret that this astute mandate was followed by an interchange of sundry smiles, nods and winks between the foreman and the members of the editorial staff, which, however, Major Hurlbut did not see, or he most assuredly would have reproved this unseemly and *mal-apropos* levity.

And so they talked and talked. And each moment Major Hurlbut became more and more impressed with the importance and solemnity of the new dignity he had attained, and each moment he became more and more impressive in his mien and conversation. And each moment, too, he silently and devoutly thanked High Heaven that in its goodness and mercy it had called him to the ennobling profession of journalism.

# His First Operation

### Sir Arthur Conan Doyle

It was the first day of a winter session, and the third year's man was walking with the first year's man. Twelve o'clock was just booming out from the Tron Church.

"Let me see," said the third year's man, "you have never seen an operation?"

"Never."

"Then this way, please. This is Rutherford's historic bar. A glass of sherry, please, for this gentleman. You are rather sensitive, are you not?"

"My nerves are not very strong, I am afraid."

"Hum! Another glass of sherry for this gentleman. We are going to an operation now, you know."

The novice squared his shoulders and made a gallant attempt to look unconcerned.

"Nothing very bad—eh?"

"Well, yes—pretty bad."

"An—an amputation?"

"No, it's a bigger affair than that."

"I think—I think they must be expecting me at home."

"There's no sense in funking. If you don't go to-day you must to-morrow. Better get it over at once. Feel pretty fit?"

"Oh, yes, all right."

The smile was not a success.

"One more glass of sherry, then. Now come on or we shall be late. I want you to be well in front."

"Surely that is not necessary."

"Oh, it is far better. What a drove of students! There are plenty of new men among them. You can tell them easily enough, can't you? If they were going down to be operated upon themselves they could not look whiter."

"I don't think I should look as white."

"Well, I was just the same myself. But the feeling soon wears off. You see a fellow with a face like plaster, and before the week is out he is eating his lunch in the dissecting rooms. I'll tell you all about the case when we get to the theatre."

The students were pouring down the sloping street which led to the infirmary—each with his little sheaf of note-books in his hand. There were pale, frightened lads, fresh from the High Schools, and callous old chronics, whose generation had passed on and left them. They swept in an unbroken, tumultuous stream from the University gate to the hospital. The figures and gait of the men were young, but there was little youth in most of their faces. Some looked as if they ate too little—a few as if they drank too much. Tall and short, tweed coated and black, round-shouldered, bespectacled and slim, they crowded with clatter of feet and rattle of sticks through the hospital gate. Now and again they thickened into two lines as the carriage of a surgeon of the staff rolled over the cobblestones between.

"There's going to be a crowd at Archer's," whispered the senior man with suppressed excitement. "It is grand to see him at work. I've seen him jab all round the aorta until it made me jumpy to watch him. This way, and mind the whitewash."

They passed under an archway and down a long, stone-flagged corridor with drab-coloured doors on either side, each marked with a number. Some of them were ajar, and the novice glanced into them with tingling nerves. He was reassured to catch a glimpse of cheery fires, lines of white-counterpaned beds and a profusion of coloured texts upon the wall. The corridor opened upon a small hall with a fringe of poorly clad people seated all round upon benches. A young man with a pair of scissors stuck, like a flower, in his button-hole, and a note-book in his hand, was passing from one to the other, whispering and writing.

"Anything good?" asked the third year's man.

"You should have been here yesterday," said the out-patient clerk, glancing up. "We had a regular field day. A popliteal aneurism, a Colles' fracture, a spina bifida, a tropical abscess, and an elephantiasis. How's that for a single haul?"

"I'm sorry I missed it. But they'll come again, I suppose. What's up with the old gentleman?"

A broken workman was sitting in the shadow, rocking himself slowly to and fro and groaning. A woman beside him was trying to console him, patting his shoulder with a hand which was spotted over with curious little white blisters.

"It's a fine carbuncle," said the clerk, with the air of a connoisseur who describes his orchids to one who can appreciate them. "It's on his back, and the passage is draughty, so we must not look at it, must we, daddy? Pemphigus," he added carelessly, pointing to the woman's disfigured hands. "Would you care to stop and take out a metacarpal?"

"No, thank you, we are due at Archer's. Come on"; and they rejoined the throng, which was hurrying to the theatre of the famous surgeon.

The tiers of horse-shoe benches, rising from the floor to the ceiling, were already packed, and the novice as he entered saw vague, curving lines of faces in front of him, and heard the deep buzz of a hundred voices and sounds of laughter from somewhere up above him. His companion spied an opening on the second bench, and they both squeezed into it.

"This is grand," the senior man whispered; "you'll have a rare view of it all."

Only a single row of heads intervened between them and the operating table. It was of unpainted deal, plain, strong and scrupulously clean. A sheet of brown waterproofing covered half of it, and beneath stood a large tin tray full of sawdust. On the farther side, in front of the window, there was a board which was strewed with glittering instruments, forceps, tenacula, saws, cannulas, and trocars. A line of knives, with long, thin, delicate blades, lay at one side. Two young men lounged in front of this; one threading needles, the other doing something to a brass coffee-pot-like thing which hissed out puffs of steam.

"That's Peterson," whispered the senior. "The big, bald man in the front row. He's the skin-grafting man, you know. And that's Anthony Browne, who took a larynx out successfully last winter. And there's Murphy the pathologist, and Stoddart the eye man. You'll come to know them all soon."

"Who are the two men at the table?"

"Nobody—dressers. One has charge of the instruments and the other of the puffing Billy. It's Lister's antiseptic spray, you know, and Archer's one of the carbolic acid men. Hayes is the leader of the cleanliness-and-cold-water school, and they all hate each other like poison."

A flutter of interest passed through the closely packed benches as a woman in petticoat and bodice was led in by two nurses. A red, woollen shawl was draped over her head and round her neck. The face which looked out from it was that of a woman in the prime of her years, but drawn with suffering and of a peculiar bees-wax tint. Her head drooped as she walked, and one of the nurses, with her arm round her waist, was whispering consolation in her ear. She gave a quick side glance at the instrument table as she passed, but the nurses turned her away from it.

"What ails her?" asked the novice.

"Cancer of the parotid. It's the devil of a case, extends right away back behind the carotids. There's hardly a man but Archer would dare to follow it. Ah, here he is himself."

As he spoke, a small, brisk, iron-grey man came striding into the room, rubbing his hands together as he walked. He had a clean-shaven face of the Naval officer type, with large, bright eyes, and a firm, straight mouth. Behind him came his big house surgeon with his gleaming pince-nez and a trail of dressers, who grouped themselves into the corners of the room.

"Gentlemen," cried the surgeon in a voice as hard and brisk as his manner. "We have here an interesting case of tumour of the parotid, originally cartilaginous but now assuming malignant characteristics, and therefore requiring excision. On to the table, nurse! Thank you! Chloroform, clerk! Thank you! You can take the shawl off, nurse."

The woman lay back upon the waterproofed pillow and her murderous tumour lay revealed. In itself it was a pretty thing, ivory white with a mesh of blue veins, and curving gently from jaw to chest. But the lean, yellow face, and the stringy throat were in horrible contrast with the plumpness and sleekness of this monstrous growth. The surgeon placed a hand on each side of it and pressed it slowly backwards and forwards.

"Adherent at one place, gentlemen," he cried. "The growth involves the carotids and jugulars, and passes behind the ramus of the jaw, whither we must be prepared to follow it. It is impossible to say how deep our dissection may carry us. Carbolic tray, thank you! Dressings of carbolic gauze, if you please! Push the chloroform, Mr. Johnson. Have the small saw ready in case it is necessary to remove the jaw."

The patient was moaning gently under the towel which had been placed over her face. She tried to raise her arms and to draw up her knees, but two dressers restrained her. The heavy air was full of the penetrating smells of carbolic acid and of chloroform. A muffled cry came from under the towel and then a snatch of a song, sung in a high, quavering, monotonous voice.

> "He says, says he,
>   If you fly with me
>   You'll be mistress of the ice-cream van;
>   You'll be mistress of the—"

It mumbled off into a drone and stopped. The surgeon came across, still rubbing his hands, and spoke to an elderly man in front of the novice.

"Narrow squeak for the Government," he said.

"Oh, ten is enough."

"They won't have ten long. They'd do better to resign before they are driven to it."

"Oh, I should fight it out."

"What's the use. They can't get past the committee, even if they get a vote in the House. I was talking to—"

"Patient's ready, sir," said the dresser.

"Talking to McDonald—but I'll tell you about it presently." He walked back to the patient, who was breathing in long, heavy gasps. "I propose," said he, passing his hand over the tumour in an almost caressing fashion, "to make a free incision over the posterior border and to take another forward at right angles to the lower end of it. Might I trouble you for a medium knife, Mr. Johnson?"

The novice, with eyes which were dilating with horror, saw the surgeon pick up the long, gleaming knife, dip it into a tin basin and balance it in his fingers as an artist might his brush. Then he saw him pinch up the skin above the tumour with his left hand. At the sight, his nerves, which had already been tried once or twice that day, gave way utterly. His head swam round and he felt that in another instant he might faint. He dared not look at the patient. He dug his thumbs into his ears lest some scream should come to haunt him, and he fixed his eyes rigidly upon the wooden ledge in front of him. One glance, one cry, would, he knew, break down the shred of self-possession which he still retained. He tried to think of cricket, of green fields and rippling water, of his sisters at home—of anything rather than of what was going on so near him.

And yet, somehow, even with his ears stopped up, sounds seemed to penetrate to him and to carry their own tale. He heard, or thought that he heard, the long hissing of the carbolic engine. Then he was conscious of some movement among the dressers. Were there groans, too, breaking in upon him, and some other sound, some fluid sound, which was more dreadfully suggestive still? His mind would keep building up every step of the operation, and fancy made it more ghastly than fact could have been. His nerves tingled and quivered. Minute by minute the giddiness grew more marked, the numb, sickly feeling at his heart more distressing. And then suddenly, with a groan, his head pitching forward and his brow cracking sharply upon the narrow, wooden shelf in front of him, he lay in a dead faint.

When he came to himself he was lying in the empty theatre with his collar and shirt undone. The third year's man was dabbing a wet sponge over his face, and a couple of grinning dressers were looking on.

"All right," cried the novice, sitting up and rubbing his eyes; "I'm sorry to have made an ass of myself."

"Well, so I should think," said his companion. "What on earth did you faint about?"

"I couldn't help it. It was that operation."

"What operation?"

"Why, that cancer."

There was a pause, and then the three students burst out laughing.

"Why, you juggins," cried the senior man, "there never was an operation at all. They found the patient didn't stand the chloroform well, and so the whole thing was off. Archer has been giving us one of his racy lectures, and you fainted just in the middle of his favourite story."

# If at First You Don't Succeed, to Hell with It!

Charles E. Fritch

Editor,
MAGAZINE OF FANTASY
Dear Sir,
Enclosed is a short story, PACT WITH THE DEVIL, for your consideration. A fact which may not surprise you is that it concerns a man who sells his soul to the devil. A fact which *may* surprise you is that, unlike the stories in your magazine, this one is based on personal experience.

Sincerely,
Peter Piper

MAGAZINE OF FANTASY INTEROFFICE MEMO:
Ed—
Here's one via the slush pile. Writing's not bad, but the theme may be too familiar.

Frank

MAGAZINE OF FANTASY INTEROFFICE MEMO:
Frank—
I don't intend running another pact-with-the-devil story for at least ninety-nine years.

Ed

From MAGAZINE OF FANTASY:
Dear Mr. Piper,
Thanks for letting us see your short story, PACT WITH THE DEVIL. Unfortunately, this theme is overworked and would have to be far different in its approach to have us seriously consider it.

The Editors

Editor,
MAGAZINE OF FANTASY
Dear Sir,
I have revised my previously submitted story according to your instructions. Enclosed is PACT WITH A DEVIL'S FOOD BAKERY.

Sincerely,
Peter Piper

MAGAZINE OF FANTASY INTEROFFICE MEMO:
Ed—
This is a kind of interesting twist on the old theme. Thought you'd like to look at it.

Frank

MAGAZINE OF FANTASY INTEROFFICE MEMO:
Frank—
You thought wrong. The notion that devil's food is actually made by devils in competition with angels who bake angel food cake hasn't to my knowledge been used. However, it's *still* a pact-with-the-devil story. You KNOW how I feel about pact-with-the-devil stories!

Ed

From MAGAZINE OF FANTASY:
Dear Mr. Piper,
Thanks for letting us see your latest story. Unfortunately, it does not meet our needs at the moment.

The Editors

Editor,
MAGAZINE OF FANTASY
Dear Sir,
Enclosed is a short story in which a packing plant worker inadvertently gets trapped in a seafood container. I call it PACKED WITH THE DEVILFISH.

Sincerely,
Peter Piper

MAGAZINE OF FANTASY INTEROFFICE MEMO:
Ed—
Here's another Piper story. Do you think he's putting us on?

Frank

216

MAGAZINE OF FANTASY INTEROFFICE MEMO:
Frank—
I am not, *not,* NOT publishing any more pact-with-the-devil stories, not even if they're disguised. Send it back!

Ed

From MAGAZINE OF FANTASY:
Dear Mr. Piper,
Thanks for letting us see the enclosed story. We felt this one was too far out for us.

The Editors

Editor,
MAGAZINE OF FANTASY
Dear Sir,
Here's one you might like. It's entitled SO ROUND, SO FIRM, SO FULLY PACKED (WITH THE DEVIL).

Sincerely,<br>Peter Piper

MAGAZINE OF FANTASY INTEROFFICE MEMO:
Ed—
Persistent, isn't he? What'll I tell him on this one?

Frank

MAGAZINE OF FANTASY INTEROFFICE MEMO:
Frank—
You might try telling him to go to hell.

Ed

From MAGAZINE OF FANTASY:
Dear Mr. Piper,
Sorry we can't use the enclosed story. The writing is readable, but once again the problem is the theme. Is there some reason you *insist* on writing pact-with-the-devil stories?

The Editors

Editor,
MAGAZINE OF FANTASY
Dear Sir,
Funny you should ask. The answer is yes. I have tried to explain it

in the enclosed short story, PETER PIPER WAS PICKED IN THE PARK FOR A PACT WITH THE DEVIL. As you may suspect, it is autobiographical.

Sincerely,
Peter Piper

MAGAZINE OF FANTASY INTEROFFICE MEMO:
Ed—
I wasn't even going to show you this one. But then I got to thinking. I know it's crazy, and he's probably some kind of a nut . . . but suppose the devil is actually forcing him to write pact-with-the-devil stories and he has to have one published within a time limit or his soul is snatched off to Hades?

Frank

MAGAZINE OF FANTASY INTEROFFICE MEMO:
Frank—
I never told you this before, but I have a pact with the devil myself—not to buy any more pact-with-the-devil stories!
You're the last person I expected to be taken in by a ruse like this. Under the circumstances, my previous suggestion to you seems more valid than ever. Tell him to go to hell.

Ed

From MAGAZINE OF FANTASY:
Dear Mr. Piper,
I've enclosed an interoffice memo spelling out our senior editor's feelings about the theme you seem to have chosen for your life's work. Sorry.

The Editors

Editor,
MAGAZINE OF FANTASY
Dear Sir,
Your suggestion that I go to Hell is superfluous. My time is up, and I haven't sold any of the stories. I imagine I'll be seeing you there in person one of these days.

Till then,
Peter Piper

MAGAZINE OF FANTASY INTEROFFICE MEMO:
Ed—
No story this time. Just the enclosed letter. I have an uncanny feeling we won't be hearing from him again.

Frank

MAGAZINE OF FANTASY INTEROFFICE MEMO:
Frank—
I hope you're right about that. Would you believe I was beginning to have nightmares about pact-with-the-devil stories? There was PARKED WITH THE DEVIL—about this cab driver whose passenger has horns and a forked tail. Then there was PARCHED WITH THE DEVIL, about two thirsty men who meet in a bar, and one of them is guess who? And PUCK WITH THE DEVIL, in which a hockey player doesn't go to Hades until Hell freezes over. And so forth.
Anyway, I feel much relieved. Maybe we should tell more writers where to go!

Ed

To Lucifer Satan
EARTH STORIES MAGAZINE
Hades
Dear Sir,
Enclosed is a story which might be of interest to you for your magazine.

Sincerely,
Peter Piper

From EARTH STORIES MAGAZINE:
Dear Mr. Piper,
While we encourage the submission of stories from our newer tenants, we cannot use the enclosed. We have decided that unless they are sufficiently different, we are not going to run any more pact-with-the-editor stories.

Lucifer Satan

# An Imperfect Conflagration

## Ambrose Bierce

Early one June morning in 1872 I murdered my father—an act which made a deep impression on me at the time. This was before my marriage, while I was living with my parents in Wisconsin. My father and I were in the library of our home, dividing the proceeds of a burglary which we had committed that night. These consisted of household goods mostly, and the task of equitable division was difficult. We got on very well with the napkins, towels and such things, and the silverware was parted pretty nearly equally, but you can see for yourself that when you try to divide a single music-box by two without a remainder you will have trouble. It was that music-box which brought disaster and disgrace upon our family. If we had left it my poor father might now be alive.

It was a most exquisite and beautiful piece of workmanship—inlaid with costly woods and carven very curiously. It would not only play a great variety of tunes, but would whistle like a quail, bark like a dog, crow every morning at daylight whether it was wound up or not, and break the Ten Commandments. It was this last mentioned accomplishment that won my father's heart and caused him to commit the only dishonorable act of his life, though possibly he would have committed more if he had been spared: he tried to conceal that music-box from me, and declared upon his honor that he had not taken it, though I knew very well that, so far as he was concerned, the burglary had been undertaken chiefly for the purpose of obtaining it.

My father had the music-box hidden under his cloak; we had worn cloaks by way of disguise. He had solemnly assured me that he did not take it. I knew that he did, and knew something of which he was evidently ignorant; namely, that the box would crow at daylight and betray him if I could prolong the division of profits till that time. All occurred as I wished: as the gaslight began to pale in the library and the shape of the windows was seen dimly behind the curtains, a long cock-a-doodle-doo came from beneath the old gentleman's cloak, followed by a few bars of an aria from *Tannhauser,* ending with a loud click. A small hand-axe, which we had used to break into the unlucky house, lay between us on the table; I picked it up. The old man seeing that further concealment was useless took the box from under his cloak and set it on the table. "Cut it in two if you prefer that plan," said he; "I tried to save it from destruction."

He was a passionate lover of music and could himself play the concertina with expression and feeling.

I said: "I do not question the purity of your motive: it would be presumptuous in me to sit in judgment on my father. But business is business, and with this axe I am going to effect a dissolution of our partnership unless you will consent in all future burglaries to wear a bell-punch."

"No," he said, after some reflection, "no, I could not do that; it would look like a confession of dishonesty. People would say that you distrusted me."

I could not help admiring his spirit and sensitiveness; for a moment I was proud of him and disposed to overlook his fault, but a glance at the richly jeweled music-box decided me, and, as I said, I removed the old man from this vale of tears. Having done so, I was a trifle uneasy. Not only was he my father—the author of my being—but the body would be certainly discovered. It was now broad daylight and my mother was likely to enter the library at any moment. Under the circumstances, I thought it expedient to remove her also, which I did. Then I paid off all the servants and discharged them.

That afternoon I went to the chief of police, told him what I had done and asked his advice. It would be very painful to me if the facts became publicly known. My conduct would be generally condemned; the newspapers would bring it up against me if ever I should run for office. The chief saw the force of these considerations; he was himself an assassin of wide experience. After consulting with the presiding judge of the Court of Variable Jurisdiction he advised me to conceal the bodies in one of the book-cases, get a heavy insurance on the house and burn it down. This I proceeded to do.

In the library was a book-case which my father had recently purchased of some cranky inventor and had not filled. It was in shape and size something like the old-fashioned "wardrobes" which one sees in bed-rooms without closets, but opened all the way down, like a woman's night-dress. It had glass doors. I had recently laid out my parents and they were now rigid enough to stand erect; so I stood them in this book-case, from which I had removed the shelves. I locked them in and tacked some curtains over the glass doors. The inspector from the insurance office passed a half-dozen times before the case without suspicion.

That night, after getting my policy, I set fire to the house and started through the woods to town, two miles away, where I managed to be found about the time the excitement was at its height. With cries of apprehension for the fate of my parents, I joined the rush and arrived at the fire some two hours after I had kindled it. The whole town was there as I dashed up. The house was entirely consumed, but in one end of the level bed of glowing embers, bolt upright and uninjured, was that book-case! The curtains had burned away, exposing the glass doors, through which the fierce, red light illuminated the interior. There stood my dear father "in his habit as he lived," and at his side the partner of his joys and sorrows. Not a hair of them was singed, their clothing was intact. On their heads and throats the injuries which in the accomplishment of my designs I had been compelled to inflict were conspicuous. As in the presence of a miracle, the people were silent; awe and terror had stilled every tongue. I was myself greatly affected.

Some three years later, when the events herein related had nearly faded from my memory, I went to New York to assist in passing some counterfeit United States bonds. Carelessly looking into a furniture store one day, I saw the exact counterpart of that book-case. "I bought it for a trifle from a reformed inventor," the dealer explained. "He said it was fireproof, the pores of the wood being filled with alum under hydraulic pressure and the glass made of asbestos. I don't suppose it is really fireproof—you can have it at the price of an ordinary book-case."

"No," I said, "if you cannot warrant it fireproof I won't take it"—and I bade him good morning.

I would not have had it at any price: it revived memories that were exceedingly disagreeable.

# In Mid-Atlantic

## W. W. Jacobs

No, sir," said the night-watchman, as he took a seat on a post at the end of the jetty, and stowed a huge piece of tobacco in his cheek. "No, man an' boy, I was at sea forty years afore I took on this job, but I can't say as ever I saw a real, downright ghost."

This was disappointing, and I said so. Previous experience of the power of Bill's vision had led me to expect something very different.

"Not but what I've known some queer things happen," said Bill, fixing his eyes on the Surrey side, and going off into a kind of trance. "Queer things."

I waited patiently; Bill's eyes, after resting for some time on Surrey, began to slowly cross the river, paused midway in reasonable hopes of a collision between a tug with its flotilla of barges and a penny steamer, and then came back to me.

"You heard that yarn old Cap'n Harris was telling the other day about the skipper he knew having a warning one night to alter his course, an' doing so, picked up five live men and three dead skeletons in a open boat?" he inquired.

I nodded.

"The yarn in various forms is an old one," said I.

"It's all founded on something I told him once," said Bill. "I don't wish to accuse Cap'n Harris of taking another man's true story an' spoiling it; he's got a bad memory, that's all. Fust of all, he forgets he ever heard the yarn; secondly, he goes and spoils it."

I gave a sympathetic murmur. Harris was as truthful an old man as ever breathed, but his tales were terribly restricted by this circumstance, whereas Bill's were limited by nothing but his own imagination.

"It was about fifteen years ago now," began Bill, getting the quid into a bye-way of his cheek, where it would not impede his utterance. "I was A.B. on the *Swallow,* a barque, trading wherever we could pick up stuff. On this v'y'ge we was bound from London to Jamaica with a general cargo.

"The start of that v'y'ge was excellent. We was towed out of the St. Katherine's Docks here, to the Nore, an' the tug left us to a stiff breeze, which fairly raced us down Channel and out into the Atlantic. Everybody was saying what a fine v'y'ge we was having, an' what quick time we should make, an' the fust mate was in such a lovely temper that you might do anything with him a'most.

"We was about ten days out, an' still slipping along in this spanking way, when all of a sudden things changed. I was at the wheel with the second mate one night, when the skipper, whose name was Brown, came up from below in a uneasy sort o' fashion, and stood looking at us for some time without speaking. Then at last he sort o' makes up his mind, and ses he—

" 'Mr McMillan, I've just had a most remarkable experience, an' I don't know what to do about it.'

" 'Yes, sir?' ses Mr McMillan.

" 'Three times I've been woke up this night by something shouting in my ear, "Steer nor'-nor'-west!" ' ses the cap'n very solemnly, ' "Steer nor'-nor'-west!" that's all it says. The first time I thought it was somebody got into my cabin skylarking, and I laid for 'em with a stick; but I've heard it three times, an' there's nothing there.'

" 'It's a supernatural warning,' ses the second mate, who had a great uncle once who had the second sight, and was the most unpopular man of his family, because he always knew what to expect, and laid his plans according.

" 'That's what I think,' ses the cap'n. 'There's some poor shipwrecked fellow creatures in distress.'

" 'It's a verra grave responsebeelity,' ses Mr McMillan. 'I should just ca' up the fairst mate.'

" 'Bill,' ses the cap'n, 'just go down below, and tell Mr Salmon I'd like a few words with him partikler.'

"Well, I went down below, and called up the first mate, and as soon as I'd explained to him what he was wanted for, he went right off into a fit of outrageous bad language, an' hit me. He came right up on deck in his pants an' socks. A most disrespekful way to come to the cap'n, but he was that hot and excited he didn't care what he did.

" 'Mr Salmon,' ses the cap'n gravely, 'I've just had a most solemn warning, and I want to—'

" 'I know,' says the mate gruffly.

" 'What! have you heard it too?' ses the cap'n, in surprise. 'Three times?'

" 'I heard it from him,' ses the mate, pointing to me. 'Nightmare, sir, nightmare.'

" 'It was no nightmare, sir,' ses the cap'n, very huffy, 'an' if I hear it again, I'm going to alter this ship's course.'

"Well, the fust mate was in a hole. He wanted to call the skipper something which he knew wasn't discipline. I knew what it was, an' I knew if the mate didn't do something he'd be ill, he was that sort of man, everything flew to his head. He walked away, and put his head over the side for a bit, an' at last, when he came back, he was, comparatively speaking, calm.

" 'You mustn't hear them words again, sir,' ses he; 'don't go to sleep again to-night. Stay up, an' we'll have a hand o' cards, and in the morning you take a good stiff dose o' rhoobarb. Don't spoil one o' the best trips we've ever had for the sake of a pennyworth of rhoobarb,' ses he, pleading-like.

" 'Mr Salmon,' ses the cap'n, very angry, 'I shall not fly in the face o' Providence in any such way. I shall sleep as usual, an' as for your rhoobarb,' ses the cap'n, working hisself up into a passion—'damme, sir, I'll—I'll dose the whole crew with it, from first mate to cabin-boy, if I have any impertinence.'

"Well, Mr Salmon, who was getting very mad, stalks down below, followed by the cap'n, an' Mr McMillan was that excited that he even started talking to me about it. Half-an-hour arterwards the cap'n comes running up on deck again.

" 'Mr McMillan,' ses he excitedly, 'steer nor'-nor'-west until further orders. I've heard it again, an' this time it nearly split the drum of my ear.'

"The ship's course was altered, an' after the old man was satisfied he went back to bed again, an' almost directly arter eight bells went, an' I was relieved. I wasn't on deck when the fust mate come up, but those that were said he took it very calm. He didn't say a word. He just sat down on the poop, and blew his cheeks out.

"As soon as ever it was daylight the skipper was on deck with his glasses. He sent men up to the masthead to keep a good look-out, an' he was dancing about like a cat on hot bricks all the morning.

" 'How long are we to go on this course, sir?' asks Mr Salmon, about ten o'clock in the morning.

" 'I've not made up my mind, sir,' ses the cap'n, very stately; but I could see he was looking a trifle foolish.

"At twelve o'clock in the day, the fust mate got a cough, and every time he coughed it seemed to act upon the skipper, and make him madder and madder. Now that it was broad daylight, Mr Mc-Millan didn't seem to be so creepy as the night before, an' I could see the cap'n was only waiting for the slightest excuse to get into our proper course again.

" 'That's a nasty, bad cough o' yours, Mr Salmon,' ses he, eyeing the mate very hard.

" 'Yes, a nasty, irritating sort o' cough, sir,' ses the other; 'it worries me a great deal. It's this going up nor'ards what's sticking in my throat,' ses he.

"The cap'n give a gulp, and walked off, but he comes back in a minute, and ses he—

" 'Mr Salmon, I should think it a great pity to lose a valuable officer like yourself, even to do good to others. There's a hard ring about that cough I don't like, an' if you really think it's going up this bit north, why, I don't mind putting the ship in her course again.'

"Well, the mate thanked him kindly, and he was just about to give the orders when one o' the men who was at the masthead suddenly shouts out—

" 'Ahoy! Small boat on the port bow!'

"The cap'n started as if he'd been shot, and ran up the rigging with his glasses. He came down again almost direckly, and his face was all in a glow with pleasure and excitement.

" 'Mr Salmon,' ses he, 'here's a small boat with a lug sail in the middle o' the Atlantic, with one pore man lying in the bottom of her. What do you think o' my warning now?'

"The mate didn't say anything at first, but he took the glasses and had a look, an' when he came back anyone could see his opinion of the skipper had gone up miles and miles.

" 'It's a wonderful thing, sir,' ses he, 'and one I'll remember all my life. It's evident that you've been picked out as a instrument to do this good work.'

"I'd never heard the fust mate talk like that afore, 'cept once when he fell overboard, when he was full, and stuck in the Thames mud. He said it was Providence; though, as it was low water, according to the tide-table, I couldn't see what Providence had to do with it myself. He was as excited as anybody, and took the wheel himself, and put the ship's head for the boat, and as she came closer, our boat was slung out, and me and the second mate and three other men dropped into her, an' pulled so as to meet the other.

" 'Never mind the boat; we don't want to be bothered with her,' shouts out the cap'n as we pulled away—'Save the man!'

"I'll say this for Mr McMillan, he steered that boat beautifully, and we ran alongside o' the other as clever as possible. Two of us shipped our oars, and gripped her tight, and then we saw that she was just an ordinary boat, partly decked in, with the head and shoulders of a man showing in the opening, fast asleep, and snoring like thunder.

" 'Puir chap,' ses Mr McMillan, standing up. 'Look how wasted he is.'

"He laid hold o' the man by the neck of his coat an' his belt, an', being a very powerful man, dragged him up and swung him into our boat, which was bobbing up and down, and grating against the side of the other. We let go then, an' the man we'd rescued opened his eyes as Mr McMillan tumbled over one of the thwarts with him, and, letting off a roar like a bull, tried to jump back into his boat.

" 'Hold him!' shouted the second mate. 'Hold him tight! He's mad, puir feller.'

"By the way that man fought and yelled, we thought the mate was right, too. He was a short, stiff chap, hard as iron, and he bit and kicked and swore for all he was worth, until at last we tripped him up and tumbled him into the bottom of the boat, and held him there with his head hanging back over a thwart.

" 'It's all right, my puir feller,' ses the second mate; 'ye're in good hands—ye're saved.'

" 'Damme!' ses the man; 'what's your little game? Where's my boat—eh? Where's my boat?'

"He wriggled a bit, and got his head up, and, when he saw it bowling along two or three hundred yards away, his temper got the better of him, and he swore that if Mr McMillan didn't row after it he'd knife him.

" 'We can't bother about the boat,' ses the mate; 'we've had enough bother to rescue you.'

" 'Who the devil wanted you to rescue me?' bellowed the man. 'I'll make you pay for this, you miserable swabs. If there's any law in Amurrica, you shall have it!'

"By this time we had got to the ship, which had shortened sail, and the cap'n was standing by the side, looking down upon the stranger with a big, kind smile which nearly sent him crazy.

" 'Welcome aboard, my pore feller,' ses he, holding out his hand as the chap got up the side.

" 'Are you the author of this outrage?' ses the man fiercely.

" 'I don't understand you,' ses the cap'n, very dignified, and drawing himself up.

" 'Did you send your chaps to sneak me out o' my boat while I was having forty winks?' roars the other. 'Damme! that's English, ain't it?'

" 'Surely,' ses the cap'n, 'surely you didn't wish to be left to perish in that little craft. I had a supernatural warning to steer this course on purpose to pick you up, and this is your gratitude.'

" 'Look here!' ses the other. 'My name's Cap'n Naskett, and I'm doing a record trip from New York to Liverpool in the smallest boat that has ever crossed the Atlantic, an' you go an' bust everything with your cussed officiousness. If you think I'm going to be kidnapped just to fulfil your beastly warnings, you've made a mistake. I'll have the law on you, that's what I'll do. Kidnapping's a punishable offence.'

" 'What did you come here for, then?' ses the cap'n.

" 'Come!' howls Cap'n Naskett. 'Come! A feller sneaks up alongside o' me with a boat-load of street-sweepings dressed as sailors, and snaps me up while I'm asleep, and you ask me what I come for. Look here. You clap on all sail and catch that boat o' mine, and put me back, and I'll call it quits. If you don't, I'll bring a lawsuit agin you, and make you the laughingstock of two continents into the bargain.'

"Well, to make the best of a bad bargain, the cap'n sailed after the cussed little boat, and Mr Salmon, who thought more than enough time had been lost already, fell foul o' Cap'n Naskett. They was both pretty talkers, and the way they went on was a education for every sailorman afloat. Every man aboard got as near as they durst to listen to them; but I must say Cap'n Naskett had the best of it. He was a sarkastik man, and pretended to think the ship was fitted out just to pick up shipwrecked people, an' he also pretended to think we was castaways what had been saved by it. He said o' course anybody could see at a glance we wasn't sailormen, an' he supposed Mr Salmon was a butcher what had been carried out to sea while paddling at Margate to strengthen his ankles. He said a lot more of this sort of thing, and all this time we was chasing his miserable little boat, an' he was admiring the way she sailed, while the fust mate was answering his reflexshuns, an' I'm sure that not even our skipper was more pleased than Mr Salmon when we caught it at last, and shoved him back. He was ungrateful up to the last, an', just before leaving the ship, actually went up to Cap'n Brown, and advised him to shut his eyes an' turn round three times and catch what he could.

"I never saw the skipper so upset afore, but I heard him tell Mr McMillan that night that if he ever went out of his way again after a craft, it would only be to run it down. Most people keep pretty quiet about supernatural things that happen to them, but he was about the quietest I ever heard of, an', what's more, he made everyone else keep quiet about it, too. Even when he had to steer nor'-nor'-west arter that in the way o' business he didn't like it, an' he was about the most cruelly disappointed man you ever saw when he heard afterwards that Cap'n Naskett got safe to Liverpool."

# The Independent Fiend

### Gordon Linzner

Kirby MacElroy wedged his package under one arm to tug his sports jacket free of the subway door that had closed on its tail. The opening of the Japan Cultural Exhibit at the World Trade Center had been a formal affair, or he wouldn't have worn the coat over his turtleneck and jeans. He disliked feeling overdressed, especially during a New York heat wave. Five minutes earlier, however, the weather had broken in a rousing thunderstorm, cancelling his planned walk from the reception to his Chelsea apartment.

He started to remove the jacket, but changed his mind. The train's air-conditioning, set for a rush-hour crowd, was more than adequate at one in the morning. Broad-shouldered Kirby was alone on the car, except for a teen-age boy at the other end who'd discovered new graffiti territory: the floor.

Kirby settled into a corner seat for the next five stops. The train did not move. Of course not, he fumed, now that he'd almost broken his neck racing aboard. It would sit with doors closed, waiting for someone else to rush up before it pulled out. To soothe himself, the big man shut his eyes and recalled some of the intricately patterned swordhilts he'd seen displayed this evening. Many were for sale, but most far beyond his financial reach. Even the contents of the long flat package now resting in his lap, unquestionably a bargain, had cost more than he could really afford.

His thick fingers smudged the brown wrapping paper. A gloomy man with a fierce temper, Kirby could not hold down any job that promised a steady paycheck. His rent money came haphazardly from odd tasks, an occasional bartending stint . . . and, of course, assisting the mysterious Evelyn Slade on some of her bizarre investigations. Kirby sometimes suspected that the silvery-haired Slade, an ageless woman who could appear to be sixteen and sixty at the same moment if she chose, enlisted his aid less because she needed him than because he needed the money; but he could not be sure. Slade paid him fairly for his time but not generously, and she claimed that the very qualities that made him unemployable in the nine-to-five world were definite assets in dealing with the occult. And the work was undeniably interesting: few people had a chance to spar with a zombie or joke with a djinn, and get paid for it, too.

Kirby grunted. Now that he thought of it, Evie was really responsible for the thinness of the wallet in his hip pocket. Not only had the invitation to tonight's exhibition opening been addressed to her, and passed on to him because she had other plans, but the woman was always harping on how good his instincts were and how he should give in to his impulses more often. He crinkled the paper covering his recent impulse. He hoped Evelyn Slade had some work for him soon. She owed it to him now.

Kirby's musings were interrupted when his fellow passenger began to sing a flat, tuneless ditty, the artifact of some top forty radio station, he presumed. Kirby stoically fixed his gaze on an advertisement for cold capsules and tried to will the train to move. At least the soloist did not carry a tape-deck; the volume was limited to human range.

Then the over-achieving ventilation brought to his nostrils the bitter stench of a fresh-struck match. Kirby leapt to his feet and stalked down the aisle. Sadly, it often took someone of Kirby's bulk and quick temper to explain to the average offender why smoking was forbidden on mass transportation.

Halfway along the car's twenty-three meter length, Kirby saw that the match had been applied to neither tobacco nor marijuana, but to the wicks of five stubby black candles standing in a pattern on the grimy floor. Kirby scowled. Hot wax was an unlikely substitute for spray paint. He drew closer, and saw that the lad stood in the center of a white chalk pentagram, each corner marked by a candle. His song was a chant.

Kirby MacElroy inhaled sharply. His association with Evelyn Slade primarily involved cleaning up after amateurs who'd dabbled in the Black Arts. It took more years of study than this boy had lived to do what he was doing safely.

"You'd better cut that out, kid."

The youth seemed not to hear. Kirby growled, balling a fist. Evie could terminate a spell in an eyeblink. Although Kirby held his own slugging it out with a werewolf, the mental disciplines largely eluded him. The best he could do was grab the chanter's shoulders and try shaking some sense into him, if it wasn't too late. Kirby reached forward.

An acrid indigo cloud enveloped him. He staggered back, coughing, wiping watery eyes. When he could see again, the demon stood before him.

He was a head shorter than Kirby, given to a paunch, bald with a fringe of gray that matched his moustache. His clothing was the height of late 1930's fashion. Not very impressive, as demons went.

"You look familiar," Kirby said at last.

The demon spoke with a rumbling bass. "The first time the ritual is performed on a subway car, and it has to be a lousy R-46! No matter how many of these I sabotage, they keep buying more! No wonder the city's broke!"

"What?"

"Oh, sorry. I was side-tracked, if you'll excuse the pun. Not that I care whether you do or not, since I see you've been stupid enough to invoke me without even rudimentary protections. I'll just destroy you and be on my way . . ."

Kirby raised his left hand in protest. "*I* didn't summon you! *He* did!"

The demon looked at the teen-ager who stood, gawking and speechless, within his pentagram.

"A punk kid. That explains the R-46. No feeling for tradition. If you had any class, kid, you'd have snuck into the Subway Museum and used an IRT Low V. *There* was a subway car!"

"I saw one last winter," Kirby commented. "It had been converted into a snowplow."

The demon spun about, glaring at the dark-haired man. "Don't mock me. You're still fair game!"

"I didn't say it was an improvement!"

The demon accepted this with a nod. "Ah, it's better than seeing them scrapped completely. Back in the mid-sixties I helped hide a whole train of Low Vs the city wanted to scrap."

The youth finally found his voice. "Hey, I didn't get you here to jaw all night with this turkey!"

The demon glowered at his summoner. "Kid's got no manners."

"Could be he's just scared."

"You keep out of this, mister!"

"Told you," the demon said to Kirby.

"Knock it off, baldy. You're supposed to do my bidding."

The demon examined the pentagram. It was carefully drawn, without even a hair-thin breach. He was stuck. "So bid."

The teen-ager rubbed his chin, looked down at his sneakers. "You don't look like a demon."

"What do you want, fangs?" Canines extended past his lower lip. "A tail?" The appendage curled discreetly from beneath the pin-striped suit jacket and over his shoulder.

"All right! That's more like it!"

"Is that it? Hardly seems worth the risk you're taking."

"Don't rush me. There's plenty I want, but I got to say it right. I hear you guys are always looking for loopholes."

"Those aren't very big candles. You've got maybe twenty minutes. You should have had your requests ready."

"I didn't know it would really work!"

The demon sighed, turned back to Kirby. "How often I've heard that one!"

Kirby sympathized. After an awkward silence, he said, "I've suspected there were gremlins in New York's subways, but never demons."

"We've got to live someplace. There were some wonderfully spooky valleys we used to chase the Indians from. Then your kind flattened almost the whole island. I was down to a single underground stream when my home was invaded by the City Hall loop in 1902. Since then, every new line has extended my range. Do you think they'll ever finish the Second Avenue subway?"

Kirby shook his head glumly. "Damned political games," he muttered. He suddenly snapped his fingers, looking up. "That's who you remind me of: Orson Welles."

The demon grinned slyly. "Almost."

"Right. An aging Orson Welles, but not the real one. Welles as the dying Charles Foster Kane!"

The demon clapped his hands in glee, raising a small blue cloud. "You're a movie buff, too! This *is* a treat! When I think of some of the boors I've dealt with . . . Call me Kane, if you like."

The teen-ager stamped his foot. "Shut up, you two. It's my time you're wasting. I'm trying to think."

Kane snarled, eyes flashing, tongue extending like a serpent's. "If you had thought, punk, we wouldn't be waiting for you now. Until you give an order, I'm on my own time."

The youth looked at Kirby. "Who asked you to butt in, anyway?"

"Who gave you permission to deface city property?" Kirby pointed to the melting candles.

"Crap. You want an order, demon? Get rid of this clown."

Kane stroked his tail. "Now, is that a reasonable request? I thought you were going to choose your words carefully."

"After you've spread motor mouth all over this car."

Kane looked at Kirby and spread his arms in a gesture of helplessness. The fingers lengthened into razor-sharp talons. He sprang at Kirby's throat.

The big man somersaulted backwards, landing on his feet, hand extended to brace himself on a stanchion against the train's movement. Then he realized the train still hadn't moved. Yet when he glanced out the window where the Hudson Terminal station had been was pitch black. Talk about smooth rides!

"Why don't I just get off at the next stop?"

"That's no tunnel out there, friend. See, not even a signal light. We're not between stops; we're between planes of existence." A claw raked the air where Kirby had stood a second before. The burly man vaulted over a pair of seats.

"We're outside reality?"

"Outside of *your* reality." Another lunge. Kirby's jacket lost a side pocket.

Kirby's shoulders slammed the door at the end of the car. His sweating fingers jiggled its handle. Locked, as cars of this type always were, a safety measure necessitated by poor exterior design. Although, if the Kane creature spoke truth, there was no place to go.

"If we're not real, you can't hurt me. Can you?"

"Stand still and we'll find out."

Kirby didn't like that idea. As Kane dove for his midriff, the man leapfrogged over his back. Nor did he pause when his feet slapped the tile floor. There was but one sanctuary available: the pentagram.

The youth read Kirby's intention in his blazing eyes.

"There's not enough room for both of us!"

Kirby growled. "It's probably too small for me alone, but I'd as soon find out for myself."

"Wait! Demon! Listen! I changed my mind! The big guy's my buddy! Don't kill him! I was joking!"

Kane loped forward. "You can't joke in this business, punk, and you can't cancel orders that easily."

"Suppose I order you to return to your . . . wherever?"

"Gladly. Once I've fulfilled your task. Until then I'm bound."

"They have a strict union," Kirby said. His left hand gripped the youth's T-shirt, lifting his feet off the ground preparatory to exchanging places.

Tears streamed down the boy's face as it came even with Kirby's. "Please, mister, I didn't mean anything bad to happen to you. I got pissed, is all. You can't let me die for that!"

"Damn." Kirby let go of the shirt; the youngster dropped back inside the pentagram. "No wonder Evie calls me soft." He stared past the trembling boy as his doom approached. "Kane, has it occurred to you that you're better off not killing me, since the kid can't give you another order until you do?"

Kane shook his head sadly. "He can't release me until I slay you. I don't want this; it's what has to be. If you co-operate, I can make it less painful."

Kirby tore the brown paper from his package. A curving blade three-quarters as long as his forearm glinted in the artificial light. According to Evelyn Slade, most demons feared the touch of steel. He hoped Kane was one of them.

"This katana was fashioned five hundred years ago by one of Japan's finest swordsmiths."

Kane stopped just beyond the weapon's reach. "Toshiro Mifune, you're not."

"At this range, I don't have to be."

"Ah, but you'll have to strike a vital spot, and my vital spots are not the same as yours. Nor as numerous."

"Still, I notice your enthusiasm has waned. I'd prefer to work this out some other way. You're pretty decent for a hellspawn."

Kane glowered at the youth. "I can think of other humans I'd rather sink my claws into." He worried his lower lip with his fangs. "Look, I shouldn't tell you this, but if you speak my name—my real name—you'll automatically banish me."

234

"Sounds good. What is it?"

Kane sighed. "I can't tell you that! Anyway, you've had more than enough clues."

Tugging his ear, Kirby turned to the youngster. The boy shook his head. He pulled a wrinkled magazine from his back pocket and held it out.

"I don't know who he is, either. I got the spell from this comic book."

Kirby did not even reach for the magazine. He saw from Kane's expression that it was worthless.

"One guess. Then we mix." Kane raised his right hand. The claws doubled in length. It did nothing for Kirby's peace of mind to be reminded that the demon could change shape at will, though for the moment he basically retained the old, fat, balding form he'd started with . . .

Kirby suddenly laughed out loud. "Of course! Sometimes I wonder why Evie puts up with me!" He lowered the point of the katana to the floor of the car. "If this isn't it, pal, I deserve to be shredded."

Talons clacked together. "Say it."

"Rosebud."

The train's lurching threw Kirby off-balance. He grasped a stanchion and recovered. The teen-ager was seated in the center of his pentagram, shaking and sobbing, face buried in his hands. Otherwise, the car was empty.

Kirby rewrapped the short sword and snatched up the comic book and now-extinguished candles. His rubber soles erased the chalk marks.

"Kid?"

The boy looked up reluctantly.

"Don't do this again. Understand?"

A nod. He'd lost his voice again.

The train pulled into the 34th Street station, to Kirby's irritation. He'd passed his stop. He left the train and stood on the platform, looking back at the unmoving youngster, until the doors closed and it continued uptown.

Then he exhaled a shaky breath and let the shiver run through his massive body.

Now. To go back, he'd have to take the passage under the express tracks and probably wait half an hour. Nuts. His apartment was only ten blocks away. The storm must have ended by now. A walk would do him good.

He tossed the candles and magazine into an orange trashcan, pushed through the revolving exit door, and climbed slowly to street level.

# Interlude in a Laboratory

Steve Rasnic Tem

"Hey, what's that?"

"Talking goose."

"No kidding? That's really amazing!"

"Oh, not really; only speaks three languages—Russian, English, and Spanish. Can't get him to tackle French or German at all."

"But still, must have been quite a breakthrough."

"Oh, that's nothing. We have a muskrat here who plays jazz trumpet, a zebra who can sing the parts to all known operas, and a porcupine who can handle any of your standard household appliances."

"You must be rather proud."

"It's a job."

"Hey, what's that wolf doing?"

"Probably a rhumba."

"No, not *that* one. The one dressed in a white smock."

"Bow tie?"

"Yeah!"

"Oh, you mean Bartholemew? He works as a lab assistant here now."

"Why . . . why that's astounding! That's the most miraculous thing I've ever seen!"

"Oh, I don't know. Actually I thought old B. was a bit of a disappointment myself. Didn't quite live up to his potential."

"But the things he's doing! Blowing glass, running tests, operating that centrifuge, and mopping the floor all at the same time! I hadn't realized you genetic engineers had gotten so far!"

"I'm no genetic engineer, buddy. I'm a camel."

# Kitty Answers

## William Dean Howells

It was dimmest twilight when Kitty entered Mrs. Ellison's room, and sank down on the first chair in silence.

"The Colonel met a friend at the St. Louis, and forgot about the expedition, Kitty," said Fanny, "and he only came in half-an-hour ago. But it's just as well; I know you've had a splendid time. Where's Mr. Arbuton?"

Kitty burst into tears.

"Why, has anything happened to him?" cried Mrs. Ellison, springing towards her.

"To him? No! What should happen to *him?*" Kitty demanded, with an indignant accent.

"Well, then, has anything happened to *you?*"

"I don't know if you can call it *happening*. But I suppose you'll be satisfied now, Fanny. He's offered himself to me."

Kitty uttered the last words with a sort of violence, as if, since the fact must be stated, she wished it to appear in the sharpest relief.

"Oh, dear!" said Mrs. Ellison, not so well satisfied as the successful match-maker ought to be. So long as it was a marriage in the abstract, she had never ceased to desire it; but as the actual union of Kitty and this Mr. Arbuton, of whom, really, they knew so little, and of whom, if she searched her heart, she had as little liking as knowledge, it was another affair. Mrs. Ellison trembled at her triumph, and began to think that failure would have been easier to bear. Were they in the least suited to each other? Would she like to see poor Kitty chained for life to that impassive egotist, whose very merits were repellent, and whose modesty even seemed to convict and snub you? Mrs. Ellison was not able to put the matter to herself with moderation, either way; doubtless she did Mr. Arbuton injustice now.

"Did you accept him?" she whispered feebly.

"Accept him?" repeated Kitty. "No!"

"Oh, dear!" again sighed Mrs. Ellison, feeling that this was scarcely better, and not daring to ask further.

"I'm dreadfully perplexed, Fanny," said Kitty, after waiting for the questions which did not come, "and I wish you'd help me think."

"I will, darling. But I don't know that I'll be of much use. I begin to think I'm not very good at thinking."

Kitty, who longed chiefly to get the situation more distinctly before herself, gave no heed to this confession, but went on to rehearse the whole affair. The twilight lent her its veil; and in the kindly obscurity she gathered courage to face all the facts, and even to find what was droll in them.

"It was very solemn, of course, and I was frightened; but I tried to keep my wits about me, and *not* to say yes, simply because that was the easiest thing. I told him that I didn't know,—and I don't; and that I must have time to think,—and I must. He was very ungenerous, and said he had hoped I had already had time to think; and he couldn't seem to understand, or else I couldn't very well explain, how it had been with me all along."

"He might certainly say you had encouraged him," Mrs. Ellison remarked, thoughtfully.

"Encouraged him, Fanny? How can you accuse me of such indelicacy?"

"Encouraging isn't indelicacy. The gentlemen *have* to be encouraged, or of course they'd never have any courage. They're so timid, naturally."

"I don't think Mr. Arbuton is very timid. He seemed to think that he had only to ask as a matter of form, and I had no business to say anything. What has he ever done for me? And hasn't he often been intensely disagreeable? He oughtn't to have spoken just after overhearing what he did. It was horrid to do so. He was very obtuse, too, not to see that girls can't always be so certain of themselves as men, or, if they are, don't know they are as soon as they're asked."

"Yes," interrupted Mrs. Ellison, "that's the way with girls. I do believe that most of them—when they're young like you, Kitty—never think of marriage as the end of their flirtations. They'd just like the attentions and the romance to go on for ever, and never turn into anything more serious; and they're not to blame for that, though they *do* get blamed for it."

"Certainly," assented Kitty eagerly, "that's it; that's just what I was saying; that's the very reason why girls must have time to make up their minds. *You* had, I suppose."

"Yes, two minutes. Poor Dick was going back to his regiment, and stood with his watch in his hand. I said no, and called after him to correct myself. But, Kitty, if the romance had happened to stop without his saying anything, you wouldn't have liked that either, would you?"

"No," faltered Kitty; "I suppose not."

"Well, then, don't you see? That's a great point in his favour. How much time did you want, or did he give you?"

"I said I should answer before we left Quebec," answered Kitty, with a heavy sigh.

"Don't you know what to say now?"

"I can't tell. That's what I want you to help me think out."

Mrs. Ellison was silent for a moment before she said, "Well, then, I suppose we shall have to go back to the very beginning."

"Yes," assented Kitty, faintly.

"You did have a sort of fancy for him the first time you saw him, didn't you?" asked Mrs. Ellison coaxingly, while forcing herself to be systematic and coherent, by a mental strain of which no idea can be given.

"Yes," said Kitty, yet more faintly, adding, "but I can't tell just what sort of a fancy it was. I suppose I admired him for being handsome and stylish, and for having such exquisite manners."

"Go on," said Mrs. Ellison; "and after you got acquainted with him?"

"Why, you know we've talked that over once already, Fanny."

"Yes, but we oughtn't to skip anything now," replied Mrs. Ellison, in a tone of judicial accuracy, which made Kitty smile.

But she quickly became serious again, and said, "Afterwards I couldn't tell whether to like him or not, or whether he wanted me to. I think he acted very strangely for a person in—love. I used to feel so troubled and oppressed when I was with him. He seemed always to be making himself agreeable under protest."

"Perhaps that was just your imagination, Kitty."

"Perhaps it was; but it troubled me just the same."

"Well, and then?"

"Well, and then after that day of the Montgomery expedition he seemed to change altogether, and to try always to be pleasant, and to do everything he could to make me like him. I don't know how to account for it. Ever since then he's been extremely careful of me, and behaved—of course without knowing it—as if I belonged to him already. Or maybe I've imagined that too. It's very hard to tell what has really happened the last two weeks."

Kitty was silent, and Mrs. Ellison did not speak at once. Presently she asked, "Was his acting as if you belonged to him disagreeable?"

"I can't tell. I think it was rather presuming. I don't know why he did it."

"Do you respect him?" demanded Mrs. Ellison.

"Why, Fanny, I've always told you that I did respect some things in him."

Mrs. Ellison had the facts before her, and it rested upon her to sum them up, and do something with them. She rose to a sitting posture, and confronted her task.

"Well, Kitty, I'll tell you. I don't really know what to think. But I can say this: if you liked him at first, and then didn't like him, and afterwards he made himself more agreeable, and you didn't mind his behaving as if you belonged to him, and you respected him, but after all didn't think him fascinating—"

"He *is* fascinating—in a kind of way. He was, from the beginning. In a story his cold, snubbing, putting-down ways would have been perfectly fascinating."

"Then why didn't you take him?"

"Because," answered Kitty, between laughing and crying, "it isn't a story, and I don't know whether I like him."

"But do you think you might get to like him?"

"I don't know. His asking brings all the doubts I ever had of him, and that I've been forgetting the past two weeks. I can't tell whether I like him or not. If I did, shouldn't I trust him more?"

"Well, whether you are in love or not, I'll tell you what you *are*, Kitty," cried Mrs. Ellison, provoked with her indecision, and yet relieved that the worst, whatever it was, was postponed thereby for a day or two.

"What?"

"You're—"

But at this important juncture the colonel came lounging in, and Kitty glided out of the room.

"Richard," said Mrs. Ellison, seriously, and in a tone implying that it was the colonel's fault, as usual, "you know what has happened, I suppose?"

"No, my dear, I don't; but no matter: I will presently, I daresay."

"Oh, I wish for once you wouldn't be so flippant. Mr. Arbuton has offered himself to Kitty."

Colonel Ellison gave a quick, sharp whistle of amazement, but trusted himself to nothing more articulate.

"Yes," said his wife, responding to the whistle, "and it makes me perfectly wretched."

"Why, I thought you liked him."

"I didn't *like* him; but I thought it would be an excellent thing for Kitty."

"And won't it?"

"She doesn't know."

"Doesn't know?"

"No."

The colonel was silent, while Mrs. Ellison stated the case in full, and its pending uncertainty. Then he exclaimed vehemently as if his amazement had been growing upon him. "This is the most astonishing thing in the world! Who would ever have dreamt of that young iceberg being in love?"

"Haven't I *told* you all along he was?"

"Oh yes, certainly! but that might be taken either way, you know. You would discover the tender passion in the eye of a potato."

"Colonel Ellison," said Fanny, with sternness, "why do you suppose he's been hanging about us for the last four weeks? Why should he have stayed in Quebec? Do you think he pitied *me*, or found *you* so very agreeable?"

"Well, I thought he found us just tolerable, and was interested in the place."

Mrs. Ellison made no direct reply to this pitiable speech, but looked a scorn which, happily for the colonel, the darkness hid. Presently she said that bats did not express the blindness of men, for any bat could have seen what was going on.

"Why," remarked the colonel, "I did have a momentary suspicion that day of the Montgomery business; they both looked very confused when I saw them at the end of that street, and neither of them had anything to say; but that was accounted for by what you told me afterwards about his adventure. At the time I didn't pay much attention to the matter. The idea of his being in love seemed too ridiculous."

"Was it ridiculous for you to be in love with me?"

"No; and yet I can't praise my condition for its wisdom, Fanny."

"Yes! that's *like* men. As soon as one of them is safely married, he thinks all the love-making in the world has been done for ever, and he can't conceive of two young people taking a fancy to each other."

"That's something so, Fanny. But granting—for the sake of argument merely—that Boston has been asking Kitty to marry him, and she doesn't know whether she wants him, what are we to do about it? *I* don't like him well enough to plead his cause; do you? When does Kitty think she'll be able to make up her mind?"

"She's to let him know before we leave."

The colonel laughed. "And so he's to hang about here on uncertainties for two whole days! That *is* rather rough on him. Fanny, what made you so eager for this business?"

"Eager? I *wasn't* eager."

"Well, then,—reluctantly acquiescent?"

"Why, she's so literary and that."

"And what?"

"How insulting! Intellectual, and so on; and I thought she would be just fit to live in a place where everybody is literary and intellectual. That is, I thought that, if I thought anything."

"Well," said the colonel, "you may have been right on the whole, but I don't think Kitty is showing any particular force of mind, just now, that would fit her to live in Boston. My opinion is, that it's ridiculous for her to keep him in suspense. She might as well answer him first as last. She's putting herself under a kind of obligation by her delay. I'll talk to her—"

"If you do, you'll kill her. You don't know how she's wrought up about it."

"Oh, well, I'll be careful of her sensibilities. It's my duty to speak with her. I'm here in the place of a parent. Besides, don't I know Kitty? I've almost brought her up."

"Maybe you're right. You're all so queer that perhaps you're right. Only do be careful, Richard. You must approach the matter very delicately, indirectly, you know. Girls are different, remember, from young men, and you mustn't be blunt. Do manœuvre a little, for once in your life."

"All right, Fanny; you needn't be afraid of my doing anything awkward or sudden. I'll go to her room pretty soon, after she is quieted down, and have a good, calm, old, fatherly conversation with her."

The colonel was spared this errand; for Kitty had left some of her things on Fanny's table, and now came back for them with a lamp in her hand. Her averted face showed the marks of weeping; the corners of her firm-set lips were downward bent, as if some resolutions which she had taken were very painful. This the anxious Fanny saw; and she made a gesture to the colonel which any woman would have understood to enjoin silence, or, at least, the utmost caution and tenderness of speech. The colonel summoned his *finesse* and said, cheerily, "Well, Kitty, what's Boston been saying to you?"

Mrs. Ellison fell back upon her sofa as if shot, and placed her hands over her face.

Kitty seemed not to hear her cousin. Having gathered up her things, she bent an unmoved face and an unseeing gaze full upon him, and glided from the room without a word.

"Well, upon my soul," cried the colonel, "this is a pleasant, nightmarish, sleep-walking, Lady-Macbethish, little transaction. Confound it, Fanny! this comes of your wanting me to manœuvre. If you'd let me come straight *at* the subject, like a *man*—"

"*Please*, Richard, don't say anything more now," pleaded Mrs. Ellison in a broken voice. "You can't help it, I know; and I must do the best I can, under the circumstances. Do go away for a little while, darling! Oh dear!"

# The Legend of Scotland

## Lewis Carroll

Being a true and terrible report touching the rooms of Auckland Castell, called Scotland, and of the things there endured by Matthew Dixon, Chaffer, and of a certain Ladye, called Gaunless of some, there apparent, and how that none durst in these days sleep therein (belike through fear,) all which things fell out in ye days of Bishop Bec, of chearfull memorie, and were writ down by mee in the Yeere One Thousand Three Hundred and Twenty Five, in the Month February, on a certayn Tuesday and other days.

*Edgar Cuthwellis*

Now the said Matthew Dixon, having fetched wares unto that place, my Loords commended the same, and bade that hee should be entertained for that night, (which in sooth hee was, supping with a grete Appetite,) and sleep in a certayn roome of that apartment now called Scotland—From whence at Midnight hee rushed forth with so grete a Screem, as awaked all men, and hastily running into those Passages, and meeting him so screeming, hee presentlie faynted away.

Whereon they hadde hym into my Loorde's parlour, and with much ado set hym on a Chaire, wherefrom hee three several times split even to the grounde, to the grete admiration of all men.

But being stayed with divers Strong Liquors, (and, chifest, wyth Gin,) he after a whyle gave foorth in a lamentable tone these following particulars, all which were presentlie sworn to by nine painful and stout farmers, who lived hard by, which witness I will heare orderlie set downe.

Witness of Matthew Dixon, Chaffer, being in my right minde, and more than Fortie Yeeres of Age, though sore affrighted by reason of Sightes and Sounds in This Castell endured by mee, as touching the Vision of Scotland, and the Ghosts, all two of them, therein contayned, and of A certayn straunge Ladye, and of the lamentable thyngs by her uttered, with other sad tunes and songs, by her and by other Ghosts devised, and of the coldness and shakyng of my Bones (through sore grete feer,) and of other things very pleasant to knowe, cheefly of a Picture hereafter suddenlie to bee taken, and of what shall befall thereon, (as trulie foreshowne by Ghosts,) and of Darkness, with other things more terrible than Woordes and of that which Men call Chimera.

Matthew Dixon, Chaffer, deposeth: "that hee, having supped well over Night on a Green Goose, a Pasty, and other Condiments of the Bishop's grete bountie provided, (looking, as he spake, at my Loorde, and essaying toe pull offe hys hatte untoe hym, but missed soe doing, for that hee hadde yt not on hys hedde,) soe went untoe hys bedde, where of a long tyme hee was exercysed with sharp and horrible Dreems. That hee saw yn hys Dreem a young Ladye, habited, not (as yt seemed) yn a Gaun, but yn a certayn sorte of Wrapper, perchance a Wrap-Rascal." (Hereon a Mayde of the House affirmed that noe Ladye woold weare such a thing, and hee answered, "I stand corrected," and indeed rose from hys chaire, yet fayled to stand.)

Witness continued: "that ye sayde Ladye waved toe and froe a Grete Torche, whereat a thin Voyce shreeked Gaunless! Gaunless!' and Shee standyng yn the midst of the floor, a grete Chaunge befell her, her Countenance waxing ever more and more Aged, and her Hayr grayer, shee all that tyme saying yn a most sad Voyce, 'Gaunless, now, as Ladyes bee: yet yn yeeres toe come they shall not lacke for Gauns.' At whych her Wrapper seemed slowlie toe melte, chaunging into a gaun of sylk, which puckered up and down, yea, and flounced itself out not a lyttle": (at thys mye Loorde, waxing impatient, smote hym roundlie onne the hedde, bydding hym finish hys tale anon.)

Witness continued: "that the sayd Gaun thenne chaunged ytself into divers fashyons whych shall hereafter bee, loopyng ytself uppe yn thys place and yn that, soe gyving toe View ane pettycote of a most fiery hue, even Crimson toe looke upon, at whych dismal and blodethirstie sight he both groned and wepte. That at the laste the skyrt swelled unto a Vastness beyond Man's power toe tell ayded, (as hee judged,) bye Hoops, Cartwheels, Balloons, and the lyke, bearing yt uppe within. That yt fylled alle that Chamber, crushing hym flat untoe hys bedde, tylle such as she appeared toe depart, fryzzling hys Hayre with her Torche as she went.

"That hee, awakyng from such Dreems, herd thereon a Rush, and saw a Light." (Hereon a Mayde interrupted hym, crying out that there was yndeed a Rush-Light burning yn that same room, and woulde have sayde more, but that my Loorde checkt her, and sharplie bade her stow that, meening thereby, that she shoulde holde her peece.)

Witness continued: "that being muche affrited thereat, whereby hys Bones were, (as hee sayde,) all of a dramble, hee essayed to leep from hys bedde, and soe quit. Yet tarried hee some whyle, not, as might bee thought from being stout of Harte, but rather of Bodye; whych tyme she caunted snatches of old lays, as Maister Wil Shakespeare hath yt."

Hereon my Loorde questioned what lays, bydding hym syng the same, and saying hee knew but of two lays: " 'Twas yn Trafalgar's bay wee saw the Frenchmen lay," and "There wee lay all that day yn the Bay of Biscay-O," whych hee forthwyth hummed aloud, yet out of tune, at whych somme smyled.

Witness continued: "that hee perchaunce coulde chaunt the sayde lays wyth Music, but unaccompanied hee durst not." On thys they hadde hym to the Schoolroom, where was a Musical Instrument, called a Paean-o-Forty, (meaning that yt hadde forty Notes, and was a Paean or Triumph or Art,) whereon two young ladyes, Nieces of my Loorde, that abode there, (lerning, as they deemed, Lessons; but, I wot, idlynge not a lyttle,) did wyth much thumpyng playe certyn Music wyth hys synging, as best they mighte, seeing that the Tunes were such as noe Man had herde before.

Lorenzo dwelt at Heighington,
  (Hys cote was made of Dimity,)
Least-ways yf not exactly there,
  Yet yn yts close proximity.
Hee called on mee—hee stayed to tee—
  Yet not a word he ut-tered,
Untyl I sayd, "D'ye lyke your bread
  Dry?" and hee answered "But-tered."

(Chorus whereyn all present joyned with fervour.)

    Noodle dumb
    Has a noodle-head,
  I hate such noodles, *I* do.

Witness continued: "that shee then appeared unto hym habited yn the same loose Wrapper, whereyn hee first saw her yn hys Dreem, and yn a stayd and piercing tone gave forth her History as followeth."

## The Ladye's History

On a dewie autumn evening, mighte have been seen, pacing yn the grounds harde by Auckland Castell, a yong Ladye of a stiff and perky manner, yet not ill to look on, nay, one mighte saye, faire to a degree save that haply that hadde been untrue.

"That yong Ladye, O miserable Man, was I" (whereon I demanded on what score shee held mee miserable, and shee replied, yt mattered not). "I plumed myself yn those tymes on my exceeding not soe much beauty as loftiness of Figure, and gretely desired that some Painter might paint my picture; but they ever were too high, not yn skyll I trow, but yn charges." (At thys I most humbly enquired at what charge the then Painters wrought, but shee loftily affirmed that money-matters were vulgar and that she knew not, no, nor cared.)

"Now yt chaunced that a certyn Artist, hight Lorenzo, came toe that Quarter, having wyth hym a merveillous machine called by men a Chimera (that ys, a fabulous and wholy incredible thing;) where wyth hee took manie pictures, each yn a single stroke of

Tyme, whiles that a Man might name 'John, the son of Robin' (I asked her, what might a stroke of Tyme bee, but shee, frowning, answered not).

"He yt was that undertook my Picture: yn which I mainly required one thyng, that yt shoulde bee at full-length, for yn none other way mighte my Loftiness bee trulie set forth. Nevertheless, though hee took manie Pictures, yet all fayled yn thys: for some, beginning at the Hedde reeched not toe the Feet; others, takyng yn the Feet, yet left out the Hedde; whereof the former were a grief unto myself, and the latter a Laughing-Stocke unto others.

"At these thyngs I justly fumed, having at the first been frendly unto hym (though yn sooth hee was dull), and oft smote hym gretely on the Eares, rending from hys Hedde certyn Locks, whereat crying out hee was wont toe saye that I made hys lyfe a burden untoe hym, whych thyng I not so much doubted as highlie rejoyced yn.

"At the last hee counselled thys, that a Picture shoulde bee made, showing so much skyrt as mighte reasonably bee gotte yn, and a Notice set below toe thys effect: 'Item, two yards and a Half Ditto, and then the Feet.' Byt thys no Whit contented mee, and thereon I shut hym ynto the Cellar, where hee remaned three Weeks, growing dayly thinner and thinner, till at the last hee floted up and downe like a Feather.

"Now yt fell at thys tyme, as I questioned hym on a certyn Day, yf hee woulde nowe take mee at full-length, and hee replying untoe mee, yn a little moning Voyce, lyke a Gnat, one chaunced to open the Door: whereat the Draft bore hym uppe ynto a Cracke of the Cieling, and I remaned awaytyng hym, holding uppe my Torche, until such time as I also faded ynto a Ghost, yet stickyng untoe the Wall."

Then did my Loorde and the Companie haste down ynto the Cellar, for to see thys straunge sight, to whych place when they came, my Loorde bravely drew hys sword, loudly crying "Death!" (though to whom or what he explained not); then some went yn, but the more part hung back, urging on those yn front, not soe largely bye example, as Words of cheer; yet at last all entered, my Loorde last.

Then they removed from the wall the Casks and other stuff, and founde the sayd Ghost, dredful toe relate, yet extant on the Wall, at which horrid sight such screems were raysed as yn these days are seldom or never herde; some faynted, others bye large drafts of

Beer saved themselves from that Extremity, yet were they scarcely alive for Feer.

Then dyd the Ladye speak unto them yn suchwise:

> "Here I bee, and here I byde,
> Till such tyme as yt betyde
> That a Ladye of thys place,
> Lyke to mee yn name and face,
> (Though my name bee never known,
> My initials shall bee shown,)
> Shall be fotograffed aright—
> Hedde and Feet bee both yn sight—
> Then my face shall disappear,
> Nor agayn affrite you heer."

Then sayd Matthew Dixon unto her, "Wherefore holdest thou uppe that Torche?" to whych shee answered, "Candles Gyve Light": but none understood her.

After thys a thyn Voyce sayd from overhedde:

> "Yn the Auckland Castell cellar,
>     Long, long ago,
> I was shut—a brisk young feller—
>     Woe, woe, ah woe!
>     To take her at full-lengthe
>     I never hadde the strengthe
> Tempore (and soe I tell her)
>     Practerito!"

(Yn thys Chorus they durst none joyn, seeing that Latyn was untoe them a Tongue unknown.)

> "She was hard—oh, she was cruel—
>     Long, long ago,
> Starved mee here—not even gruel—
>     No, believe mee, no!—
>     Frae Scotland could I flee,
>     I'd gie my last bawbee,—
> Arrah, bhoys, fair play's a jhewel,
>     Lave me, darlints, goe!"

248

Then my Loorde, putting bye hys Sworde, (whych was layd up thereafter, yn memory of soe grete Bravery,) bade hys Butler fetch hym presentlie a Vessel of Beer, whych when yt was brought at hys nod, (nor, as hee merrily sayd, hys "nod, and Bec, and wreathed smyle,") hee drank hugelie thereof: "for why?" quoth hee, "surely a Bec ys no longer a Bec, when yt ys Dry."

## The Life of Anybody

### Robert Sheckley

Last night, as I lay on the couch watching "The Late Show," a camera and sound crew came to my apartment to film a segment of a TV series called "The Life of Anybody." I can't say I was completely surprised, although I had not anticipated this. I knew the rules; I went on with my life exactly as if they were not there. After a few minutes, the camera and recording crew seemed to fade into the wallpaper. They are specially trained for that.

My TV was on, of course; I usually have it on. I could almost hear the groans of the critics: "Another goddamned segment of a guy watching the tube. Doesn't anybody in this country do anything but watch the tube?" That upset me, but there was nothing I could do about it. That's the way it goes.

So the cameras whizzed along, and I lay on the couch like a dummy and watched two cowboys play the macho game. After a while my wife came out of the bathroom, looked at the crew, and groaned, "Oh, Christ, not *tonight*." She was wearing my CCNY sweatshirt on top, nothing on the bottom. She'd just washed her hair and she had a towel tied around her head. She had no makeup on. She looked like hell. Of all nights, they had to pick this one. She was probably imagining the reviews: "The wife in last night's turgid farce . . ."

I could see that she wanted badly to do something—to inject a little humor into our segment, to make it into a domestic farce. But she didn't. She knew as well as I did that anyone caught acting, fabricating, exaggerating, diminishing, or otherwise distorting his

249

life, would be instantly cut off the air. She didn't want that. A bad appearance was better than no appearance at all. She sat down on a chair and picked up her crocheting hook. I picked up my magazine. Our movie went on.

You can't believe it when it happens to you. Even though you watch the show every evening and see it happen, you can't believe it's happening to you. I mean, it's suddenly *you* there, lying on the couch doing your nothing number, and there they are, filming it and implying that the segment represents *you*.

I prayed for something to happen. Air raid—sneak Commie attack—us a typical American family caught in the onrush of great events. Or a burglar breaks in, only he's not just a burglar, he's something else, and a whole fascinating sequence begins. Or a beautiful woman knocks at the door, claiming that only I can help her. Hell, I would have settled for a phone call.

But nothing happened. I actually started to get interested in that movie on TV, and I put down my magazine and actually watched it. I thought they might be interested in that.

The next day my wife and I waited hopefully, even though we knew we had bombed out. Still, you can never tell. Sometimes the public wants to see more of a person's life. Sometimes a face strikes their fancy and you get signed for a series. I didn't really expect that anyone would want to see a series about my wife and me, but you can never tell. Stranger things have happened.

Nowadays my wife and I spend our evenings in very interesting ways. Our sexual escapades are the talk of the neighborhood, my crazy cousin Zoe has come to stay with us, and regularly an undead thing crawls upstairs from the cellar.

Practically speaking, you never get another chance. But you can never tell. If they do decide to do a follow-up segment, we're ready.

# A Little Joke

## Sir Anthony Hope Hawkins

A day or two before Easter, I was sitting in my office, finishing up some scraps of work, and ever and anon casting happy glances at my portmanteau, which stood in the corner. I was just off to spend a fortnight with my old friend Colonel Gunton, in Norfolk, and I was looking forward to seeing him again with great pleasure. We had not met for ten years, and I had never been to his place or seen any of his family. It would be delightful.

The telephone bell rang.

"Oh, confound it! I hope that's nothing to keep me!" I exclaimed; and I rose to see to it.

"Mr. Miller? Are you there?"

"Yes."

"All right. I'll come round."

A few minutes passed, and then my clerk announced, "A lady to see you, sir."

A remarkably pretty girl of about eighteen was ushered in. She stood still some way from me till the door was closed. Then she suddenly rushed toward me, fell at my feet, and exclaimed, "You will protect me, won't you?"

"My dear young lady, what in the world—"

"You're the famous Mr. Miller, aren't you? Mr. Joseph Miller, the philanthropist?"

"My name is Joseph Miller certainly."

"Ah! Then I am safe;" and she sat down in an armchair, and smiled confidingly at me.

"Madam," said I sternly, "will you have the goodness to explain to what I owe the pleasure of this visit?"

"They told me to come to you."

"Who?"

"Why, the people at the police station."

"The police station?"

"Yes, when they let me go—because it was a first offense, you know. They said you always took up cases like mine, and that if I stuck to you I should be well looked after."

It was quite true that I have taken an interest in rescuing young persons from becoming habitual criminals; but I was hardly prepared for this.

"What have you been doing?"

"Oh, nothing this time—only a bracelet."

"This time?"

"They didn't know me up here," she explained smilingly. "I've always practiced in the country. Wasn't it lucky? But really, Mr. Miller, I'm tired of it; I am indeed. The life is too exciting: the doctors say so; so I've come to you."

The case was a strange one, but I had no time to investigate it now. It wanted only half an hour to the time my train left Liverpool Street.

"What is your name?" I asked.

"Sarah Jones."

"Well, I will have your case looked into. Come and see me again; or, if you are in distress, you may write to me—at Colonel Gunton's, Beech Hill, Norfolk. I shall be staying there—"

"Going now?"

"I start in a few minutes."

"Oh, I'll come with you."

"Madam," I answered, with emphasis, "I will see you—out of the office first."

"But what am I to do? Oh, it's nonsense! I shall come. I shall say I belong to you."

I rang the bell. "Show this lady out, Thomas, at once."

She laughed, bowed, and went. Evidently a most impudent hussy. I finished my business, drove to Liverpool Street, and established myself in a first-class smoking carriage. I was alone, and settled myself for a comfortable cigar. I was rudely interrupted. Just as the train was starting, the door opened—and that odious young woman jumped in.

"There! I nearly missed you!" she said.

"I can hold no communication with you," said I severely; "you are a disgrace to your—er—sex."

"It's all right. I've wired to the colonel."

"You've wired to my friend Colonel Gunton?"

"Yes, I didn't want to surprise them. I said you would bring a friend with you. It's all right, Mr. Miller."

"I don't know who you are or what you are; but the Guntons are respectable people, and I am a respectable man, and—"

"That's no reason why you should promenade up and down, Mr. Miller. It's very uncomfortable for me."

"What is the meaning of this insolent behavior?"

"Why not be friendly? We're off now, and I must go on."

"I shall give you in charge at the next station."

"What for?"

On reflection, I supposed she had committed no criminal offense; and with a dignified air I opened my paper.

"I don't mind you smoking," she said, and took out a box of chocolates.

I was at my wits' end. Either this girl was mad or she was a dangerous and unscrupulous person. She was quite capable of making a most unpleasant and discreditable commotion on the platform at Beech Hill Station. What in the world was I to do?

"Shall we stay long at the Guntons'?" she asked.

"You, madam, will never go there."

"Oh, yes, I shall."

"Indeed you won't. I'll take care of that. The police will see to that."

"I don't care a fig for the police. I shall go and stay as long as you do. They told me to stick to you."

I became angry. Any man would have. But nothing was to be gained by losing my temper. I took out a sovereign.

"If you'll get out at the next station, I'll give you this."

She laughed merrily. "I thought you went in for personal supervision, not mere pecuniary doles," she said; "I read that in your speech at the Charity Organization meeting. No; I'm not to be bribed. I'm going to the Guntons'."

"It's absurd. It's preposterous. What will—what will Mrs. Gunton say?"

"Oh, *she* won't mind," answered my companion, with a confident nod. "She's used to girls like me."

"You surprise me," I retorted sarcastically; but she only laughed again. I returned to my paper.

An hour passed in silence. The train began to slacken speed as we neared the station next before Beech Hill. She looked up and said:

"Would you really rather I didn't come with you?"

I had passed a wretched hour. This girl was evidently bent on blasting my character.

"Madam," I said, "if you'll get out at this station, I'll give you a five-pound note."

"What? I heard you never gave away a farthing! They said no one could get a penny out of you."

"It is true that I disapprove of indiscriminate charity; but, under the circumstances, I—"

"Think I am a deserving object? Well, I'll take it."

With a sigh of relief, I took a note from my pocket-book, and gave it her.

"I'll pay it back soon," she said.

"Never let me see your face again."

"Apologize for me to the Guntons. Good-by."

She jumped out lightly, and I sank back, murmuring, "Thank Heaven!"

After I got rid of her my journey was peaceful and happy, and I forgot my troubles in the warm greeting my old friend Bob Gunton and his wife gave me. The girl must have lied about the telegram; at least, Bob made no reference to it. He had a fine family of boys and girls, and presented them to me with natural pride.

"That's my lot—except Addie. She's gone to see some friends; but we expect her back every minute. They keep me alive, I can tell you, Miller."

After tea, my host and hostess insisted on taking me for a stroll on the terrace. It was a beautiful evening, and I did not mind the cold. As we were talking together, I heard the rumble of wheels. An omnibus stopped at the gate.

"Ah, the 'bus," said Gunton; "it runs between here and our market-town."

I hardly heard him; for, to my horror, I saw, descending from the 'bus and opening the gate, that girl!

"Send her away!" I cried; "send her away! On my honor, Bob, as a gentleman, I know nothing about her."

"Why, what's the matter?"

"I solemnly assure Mrs. Gunton and yourself that—"

"What's the matter with the man? What's he talking about?"

"Why, Bob, that girl—that barefaced girl!"

"That girl! Why, that's my daughter Addie!"

"Your daughter?"

The little minx walked up to me with a smile, dropped a little courtesy, and said: "I knew, Mr. Miller, that it wasn't true that you would refuse to help a really deserving case. The others said you would; but I thought better of you."

And she had the effrontery, then and there, to tell her parents all about it!

I think parents are the most infatuated class of persons in the community. They laughed, and Mrs. Gunton said, "How clever of you, Addie! You must forgive her, Mr. Miller. My dear girls are so playful!"

*Playful!* And she never returned the five-pound note!


# Little Red in the Hood

### Linda Addison

L ay another one on me, Goosie," she said, flicking the ashes from her cigarette across the bar into the ash tray next to the cash register. The scratched mirror over the bar reflected a perfect little girl, with curly hair, wearing a red velvet dress. Most of the usual crowd was missing, no doubt resting up for the evening ahead. It was Saturday, one of the busiest nights of the week.

"You really oughta slow down—" The bartender pushed her wire frame glasses up on her nose and poured two fingers of vodka into Red's glass.

"Easy to say when it ain't you that's gotta go skipping through the same dark woods day after day only to end up in a wolf's belly," Red replied.

"Hey, kid," the wolf croaked from a small table in the corner, where he nursed a bottle of rum. "I've eaten better before I got stuck with this gig. At least you don't have to go through a c-section every night."

"Yeah, so am I supposed to feel better about getting dragged out of you?" She threw the cold, clear liquid to the back of her throat and shuddered. Smooth warmth filled her for a brief moment before the dusty, dank air of the bar cut back through her body.

"The Three Pigs tell me our hours might get cut back now that the Power Rangers are taking over," the wolf said.

"Yeah, yeah, I heard that same talk when that purple people eater was the in thing, but nothing changed. I'm not holding my breath waiting for those pastel freaks to change things."

"Things did slow down when Big Bird was topping the charts," Old MacDonald said two seats to her right.

"Those were good days," Red said softly, taking a drag on her cigarette. "We had time to hang out with Dorothy in the Green City, live a little. Now—"

A screeching siren filled the air. A red light in the ceiling pulsed brightly. The siren stopped when two hulks dressed in green fatigues walked in. One jerked his finger at the girl and tossed her a bright red hooded cape. The other one gave the wolf the thumbs up. The wolf stood and limped towards the door.

"We've got a reading alert, bedtime stories starting on Grant street. Let's go, and no trouble this time, girlie," the first one said.

"Come, my hairy one," she said, draping the cape over her shoulders and letting the wolf lean on her as they walked out the door. "Time to live happily ever after."

# The Lot's Wife Caper

## Edward D. Hoch

I'd had a busy morning with the animals, and with a number of small errands around the city. I'd hauled feed for the antelope and a bucket of fish for the seals, and on the way back from the last trip I'd run into Norm O'Brian, the councilman, down near the Shady Dell Motel and stopped the truck to chat with him for a while.

That was why, when Mayor Smith phoned me at one that afternoon, I was still only half finished cleaning out the hippopotamus cage. "Did I take you away from anything?" he asked, and I knew right away he was not his usual cheerful self.

"I'm up to my neck in work, but I'm never too busy to talk with you, Mayor."

I call him Mayor because it only seems right, although everyone else in town calls him Lot. His first name is actually Lothar; he was named after some comicstrip character who appealed to his father. But he shortened the name to Lot when he entered politics, and of course the newspapers loved it.

Even his everyday activities are good for front-page photographs with trick captions like (the Mayor leaving his car) *Parking Lot,* or (the Mayor showing off his bulging middle-aged waistline) *Lots of Lot.* Everyone thinks they are awfully funny, and everyone likes Lot Smith. They didn't mind when his campaign slogan became: *Vote for Smith—It Means a Lot to You!* And of course they've taken to calling his beautiful young wife Yolanda Lot's wife, though some say *she* doesn't see the humor in it.

"I need your help," Mayor Smith told me on the phone. "Can you come over now, Sidney? You know where I live."

"Certainly, sir. But could you tell me what it's about? Murder? Robbery? Arson?"

Mayor Smith sighed into the telephone. "Worse than any of those, I'm afraid, Sidney. My wife has been turned into a pillar of salt."

My name is Sidney Sparrow, and as you might have gathered I'm the zookeeper here in our little town. Since we only have about 25 animals that isn't much of a job, and it leaves me plenty of time to pursue my first love—detection. I specialize in crimes that baffle the police. The police have called on me several times in the past, in cases as diverse as the Greasy Fingers Caper and the Scentless Skunk Caper. I liked working with them when I could, even though they sometimes called me a sparrow cop because of my name. I realized it's a derogatory term for a policeman who is out of favor with his superiors, but I didn't mind because they were a fine bunch of fellows. It's just that the Chief finally objected to Arnold and Rudy always being with me, and pretty soon he wouldn't let me into the station house any more.

Mayor Lot Smith lives on top of a hill, in one of our best neighborhoods. He was in the driveway when I pulled up in my truck, and he hurried over to greet me. "Sidney—I appreciate your coming right over! I'm beside myself—I don't know whether to call the police or a doctor or what!"

"A pillar of salt, you said on the phone."

"That's right! It's horrible, horrible! . . ."

Then I guess he must have noticed Arnold and Rudy because he let out a gasp. "That . . . creature! You still have it with you! And the bird!"

"Of course, Mayor. Arnold and Rudy are my mascots. Rudy the Raven has a wing span of 25 inches, and he talks. The creature, as you call him, is Arnold. He's an armadillo. He's a nine-banded armadillo, and he can roll himself into a ball inside his bony outer plates."

Unfortunately, as we were entering the side door of the house and I was holding the screen door for the always slow Arnold, Rudy took off from my shoulder on a flight across the kitchen. His long wings brushed a few dishes and a tray on top of the refrigerator, and before I knew it the whole thing had toppled to the floor.

"Blast it, Sidney," the Mayor said, "how can you collect clues with these animals around all the time?"

"Oh, I don't go in much for clues, sir. My methods are psychological."

"I see," the Mayor murmured. He hurried on into the living room, and I followed. "There she is," he said.

I hadn't known exactly what to expect, but even his warning had not prepared me for what I saw. There, in an overstuffed chair facing the television set, rested a hundred-pound sack of rock salt.

"It's not exactly a pillar," I pointed out. "More like a sack."

"What difference does that make? She's been changed into a pillar of salt, just like Lot's wife in the Bible."

I bent closer to the sack. "You're sure it's Mrs. Smith?"

"Of course I'm sure! That's her pin."

And it was—a large diamond-and-pearl pin with the pearls spelling out the initials YES, puncturing the sack at about chest level. Yolanda Elizabeth Smith had never been without that pin while she was alive. Some cynics even went so far as to imply that her main reason for marrying the Mayor was to acquire those initials. She had YES lettered on everything, from the familiar expensive pin to the little white sports car she drove.

"What was she watching on television?" I asked.

258

"The national political convention in St. Louis. A lot of our friends are there. She wanted to go, but I couldn't get away."

I grunted and glanced up at Rudy, who was perched on top of a bookcase. "Nevermore," he said.

"What was that?" the Mayor asked.

"Just Rudy saying *nevermore*. Ravens always say *nevermore*." I didn't explain that after trying to teach Rudy to talk for six months I'd finally given up and taken a course in simple ventriloquism instead. People expected the bird to say it, and I didn't feel it was really cheating if I helped him along.

"What about my wife? What about Yolanda?"

"Perhaps it's not really her," I ventured. "Perhaps someone kidnaped her and left the sack of salt in her place."

"But who? The Organization?"

The city had experienced a number of Mob-type killings in recent months, and Mayor Smith had been demanding police action. It was just possible that the Mob was behind this.

"Don't you worry, Mayor. Whoever did this, I'll get to the bottom of it."

Mayor Smith stared uncertainly at the sack of rock salt. "Do you think we should—bury it?"

"Perhaps we should just move it out to the garage. Here, I'll give you a hand."

We each grabbed an end, and tugged the thing off the chair. "Careful, careful now," the Mayor cautioned. "We mustn't jar her!"

"Keep your end up, sir."

We deposited the sack gently on the garage floor. Mayor Smith was out of breath. "I hope you'll be able to do something, Sidney," he told me.

I was eyeing the diamond-and-pearl pin with the YES on it. Yolanda Smith's trademark. "May I borrow that pin for a few days, Mayor? And could you give me a list of your friends?"

"Certainly," he said. "But almost everyone's out of town at the convention. That's why I think it must be the Organization."

"Then I'll get right to work on it," I promised. Since I never bother to search for clues, there was nothing more to be gained at the Mayor's house. I put the pin in my pocket, gathered up Arnold and Rudy, and went back to the truck.

The Mob's headquarters is located in a shopping center near the airport. I parked my truck out front and went in to see the big boss.

The character at the front desk eyed me with distaste and finally spoke into an intercom.

"That bird Sparrow is here to see you, Boss."

"Send him up," came the reply.

The head of the Mob in our town is Bill Adams, a middle-aged businessman who has risen fast in the ranks. He was brought into the Organization a few years ago when someone decided it wasn't good public relations for the Mob to limit its membership—not in the liberal atmosphere of today. Bill was a good man for them, a witty talker and a fast man with a gun.

"Well," he said, taking off his sunglasses to examine me. "It's my old friend and archrival, Sidney Sparrow! What can I do for you, Sidney?"

"The Mayor's wife got changed into a pillar of salt," I said, getting right to the point. "What do you know about it?"

Adams eyed Rudy suspiciously as the raven banked and glided about the room. Finally he answered, "Not a thing, Sidney. Should I know anything?"

"The Mayor thinks she's dead. He thinks the Organization did it."

"My hands are clean," he said, holding them up. "Pillars of salt aren't in our line."

I showed him the YES pin she'd been wearing. "Recognize this?"

"Sure. Everyone knows that pin. It's worth a few thousand. We'd have taken it along if we did anything to her."

Arnold was next to the chair, gnawing at my feet. I slapped him on the shell and said, "What about those other recent killings, Adams? They were Organization jobs, and the Mayor was investigating them."

"Sometimes our business gets competitive," Adams answered with a shrug.

Rudy settled on the desk and croaked, "Nevermore."

"What'd he say?"

"Nothing. Just raven talk."

But Adams was eyeing the bird with open suspicion now. "Is he one of those birds who repeats what he hears?"

I shook my head. "Those are stool pigeons, not ravens."

"Still . . ." And before I knew what was happening, his hand had dropped to the desk drawer and come up fast holding a small automatic. "The only good raven is a dead raven."

I was terrified, helpless. I had no weapon, nothing with which to stop him. Rudy took flight again, but Adams followed him with the gun.

I had only an instant to act.

I rolled Arnold into a ball and hurled him with all my strength straight at the Mob chief's head.

"What happened?" he asked when he came to ten minutes later and saw me standing over him with the gun. "What in hell did you hit me with?"

"Arnold. He's a very effective weapon at close range. You're lucky he didn't fracture your skull."

Adams glared at Arnold and Rudy. "Call these damn things off me! I don't know anything about Lot's wife and any pillar of salt."

"Somehow I believe you," I told him. "You never would have pulled that gun if you were lying low. I'll be going now. But watch your step."

"Yeah," Adams answered, rising from the floor. "I'll do just that."

I drove back to the zoo for the afternoon feeding and sat for a long time thinking about the case. It certainly was not without interest, but the problem was, I lacked suspects. Everybody was out of town. I didn't think Bill Adams was involved, but that left no one but the Mayor himself. Might he have killed his wife, and buried her in the garage or the garden? Somehow I couldn't quite believe it.

I went out to the elephant cage and sprayed Toby with the hose. He likes that, especially on hot days. Then I tossed a few fish to the seals, and all of a sudden everything fell into place. I remembered going for the fish that morning, and suddenly it all began to make sense.

I drove the truck back over to the Shady Dell Motel and asked the room clerk if there was anyone named Jones registered.

"Yes, sir. Room 7-B."

"Thanks."

"You can't take those animals up!" he yelled after me, but I ignored him.

I rapped on the door of 7-B, and after a time the door was opened by Norm O'Brian, the councilman. "Well, it's Sidney again! How are you, anyway?"

"I'm fine, Norm. Where is she?"

"Where's who?"

"The Mayor's wife. I know she's here with you."

Yolanda Smith came out of the bathroom then, wearing a robe that must have belonged to Norm O'Brian. She saw me looking at the embroidered NO on the chest. "I decided it was time to change my image," she explained.

"I figured that," I said, "when you left your YES pin on the sack of salt. You were starting a new life, and all I had to do was figure out where. I remembered meeting Norm over near here this morning. He was one of the few politicians left in town this week, and of course he had the right initials for a change of image."

"But how did you know we registered under the name Jones?" Norm asked.

I ran my hand over Rudy's feathers to keep him under control. "You could hardly register as Smith, because that's her name."

"I'm not going back," she said.

"Sure you are. You scared the wits out of Lot with that sack of salt. You owe him something." I had another thought. "Besides, Norm, the Mayor is pretty friendly with the Organization these days. When I tell him where she is, he'll probably send a few of the gang over to collect her."

Norm O'Brian was not a fighter. At the mention of the Organization he seemed to collapse. "There's no defense against them."

"Not unless you've got a hard shell," I agreed.

The councilman was silent.

"All right," Yolanda said finally, "I'll go."

"Good. Get dressed."

I drove her back home in the truck, and we never told the Mayor where she'd been. He had me take the sack of rock salt back to the zoo with me, but I haven't decided what I'm going to do with it yet.

Maybe I'll just keep it as a memento of my triumph in the Lot's Wife Caper.

# Luck*

## Mark Twain

It was at a banquet in London in honor of one of the two or three conspicuously illustrious English military names of this generation. For reasons which will presently appear, I will withhold his real name and titles, and call him Lieutenant-General Lord Arthur Scoresby, Y.C., K.C.B., etc., etc., etc. What a fascination there is in a renowned name! There sat the man, in actual flesh, whom I had heard of so many thousands of times since that day, thirty years before, when his name shot suddenly to the zenith from a Crimean battle-field, to remain forever celebrated. It was food and drink to me to look, and look, and look at that demigod; scanning, searching, noting: the quietness, the reserve, the noble gravity of his countenance; the simple honesty that expressed itself all over him; the sweet unconsciousness of his greatness—unconsciousness of the hundreds of admiring eyes fastened upon him, unconsciousness of the deep, loving, sincere worship welling out of the breasts of those people and flowing toward him.

The clergyman at my left was an old acquaintance of mine—clergyman now, but had spent the first half of his life in the camp and field, and as an instructor in the military school at Woolwich. Just at the moment I have been talking about, a veiled and singular light glimmered in his eyes, and he leaned down and muttered confidentially to me—indicating the hero of the banquet with a gesture,—

"Privately—he's an absolute fool."

This verdict was a great surprise to me. If its subject had been Napoleon, or Socrates, or Solomon, my astonishment could not have been greater. Two things I was well aware of: that the Reverend was a man of strict veracity, and that his judgment of men was

---

* NOTE.—This is not a fancy sketch. I got it from a clergyman who was an instructor at Woolwich forty years ago, and who vouched for its truth. —M. T.

good. Therefore I knew, beyond doubt or question, that the world was mistaken about this hero: he *was* a fool. So I meant to find out, at a convenient moment, how the Reverend, all solitary and alone, had discovered the secret.

Some days later the opportunity came, and this is what the Reverend told me:

About forty years ago I was an instructor in the military academy at Woolwich. I was present in one of the sections when young Scoresby underwent his preliminary examination. I was touched to the quick with pity; for the rest of the class answered up brightly and handsomely, while he—why, dear me, he didn't know *anything*, so to speak. He was evidently good, and sweet, and lovable, and guileless; and so it was exceedingly painful to see him stand there, as serene as a graven image, and deliver himself of answers which were veritably miraculous for stupidity and ignorance. All the compassion in me was aroused in his behalf. I said to myself, when he comes to be examined again, he will be flung over, of course; so it will be simply a harmless act of charity to ease his fall as much as I can. I took him aside, and found that he knew a little of Cæsar's history; and as he didn't know anything else, I went to work and drilled him like a galley-slave on a certain line of stock questions concerning Cæsar which I knew would be used. If you'll believe me, he went through with flying colors on examination day! He went through on that purely superficial "cram," and got compliments too, while others, who knew a thousand times more than he, got plucked. By some strangely lucky accident—an accident not likely to happen twice in a century—he was asked no question outside of the narrow limits of his drill.

It was stupefying. Well, all through his course I stood by him, with something of the sentiment which a mother feels for a crippled child; and he always saved himself—just by miracle, apparently.

Now of course the thing that would expose him and kill him at last was mathematics. I resolved to make his death as easy as I could; so I drilled him and crammed him, and crammed him and drilled him, just on the line of questions which the examiners would be most likely to use, and then launched him on his fate. Well, sir, try to conceive of the result: to my consternation, he took the first prize! And with it he got a perfect ovation in the way of compliments.

Sleep? There was no more sleep for me for a week. My conscience tortured me day and night. What I had done I had done purely through charity, and only to ease the poor youth's fall—I never had dreamed of any such preposterous result as the thing that had happened. I felt as guilty and miserable as the creator of Frankenstein. Here was a wooden-head whom I had put in the way of glittering promotions and prodigious responsibilities, and but one thing could happen: he and his responsibilities would all go to ruin together at the first opportunity.

The Crimean war had just broken out. Of course there had to be a war, I said to myself: we couldn't have peace and give this donkey a chance to die before he is found out. I waited for the earthquake. It came. And it made me reel when it did come. He was actually gazetted to a captaincy in a marching regiment! Better men grow old and gray in the service before they climb to a sublimity like that. And who could ever have foreseen that they would go and put such a load of responsibility on such green and inadequate shoulders? I could just barely have stood it if they had made him a cornet; but a captain—think of it! I thought my hair would turn white.

Consider what I did—I who so loved repose and inaction. I said to myself, I am responsible to the country for this, and I must go along with him and protect the country against him as far as I can. So I took my poor little capital that I had saved up through years of work and grinding economy, and went with a sigh and bought a cornetcy in his regiment, and away we went to the field.

And there—oh dear, it was awful. Blunders?—why, he never did anything *but* blunder. But, you see, nobody was in the fellow's secret—everybody had him focussed wrong, and necessarily misinterpreted his performance every time—consequently they took his idiotic blunders for inspirations of genius; they did, honestly! His mildest blunders were enough to make a man in his right mind cry; and they did make me cry—and rage and rave too, privately. And the thing that kept me always in a sweat of apprehension was the fact that every fresh blunder he made increased the lustre of his reputation! I kept saying to myself, he'll get so high, that when discovery does finally come, it will be like the sun falling out of the sky.

He went right along up, from grade to grade, over the dead bodies of his superiors, until at last, in the hottest moment of the battle of * * * * down went our colonel, and my heart jumped into my mouth, for Scoresby was next in rank! Now for it, said I; we'll all land in Sheol in ten minutes, sure.

The battle was awfully hot; the allies were steadily giving way all over the field. Our regiment occupied a position that was vital; a blunder now must be destruction. At this crucial moment, what does this immortal fool do but detach the regiment from its place and order a charge over a neighboring hill where there wasn't a suggestion of an enemy! "There you go!" I said to myself; "this *is* the end at last."

And away we did go, and were over the shoulder of the hill before the insane movement could be discovered and stopped. And what did we find? An entire and unsuspected Russian army in reserve! And what happened? We were eaten up? That is necessarily what would have happened in ninety-nine cases out of a hundred. But no; those Russians argued that no single regiment would come browsing around there at such a time. It must be the entire English army, and that the sly Russian game was detected and blocked; so they turned tail, and away they went, pell-mell, over the hill and down into the field, in wild confusion, and we after them; they themselves broke the solid Russian centre in the field, and tore through, and in no time there was the most tremendous rout you ever saw, and the defeat of the allies was turned into a sweeping and splendid victory! Marshal Canrobert looked on, dizzy with astonishment, admiration, and delight; and sent right off for Scoresby, and hugged him, and decorated him on the field, in presence of all the armies!

And what was Scoresby's blunder that time? Merely the mistaking his right hand for his left—that was all. An order had come to him to fall back and support our right; and instead, he fell *forward* and went over the hill to the left. But the name he won that day as a marvellous military genius filled the world with his glory, and that glory will never fade while history books last.

He is just as good and sweet and lovable and unpretending as a man can be, but he doesn't know enough to come in when it rains. Now that is absolutely true. He is the supremest ass in the universe; and until half an hour ago nobody knew it but himself and me. He has been pursued, day by day and year by year, by a most phenomenal and astonishing luckiness. He has been a shining soldier in all our wars for a generation; he has littered his whole military life with blunders, and yet has never committed one that didn't make him a knight or a baronet or a lord or something. Look at his breast; why, he is just clothed in domestic and foreign decorations. Well, sir, every one of them is the record of some shouting stupidity or other;

and taken together, they are proof that the very best thing in all this world that can befall a man is to be born lucky. I say again, as I said at the banquet, Scoresby's an absolute fool.

# Lynx-Hunting

## Stephen Crane

Jimmie lounged about the dining-room and watched his mother with large, serious eyes. Suddenly he said, "Ma—now—can I borrow pa's gun?"

She was overcome with the feminine horror which is able to mistake preliminary words for the full accomplishment of the dread thing. "Why, Jimmie!" she cried. "Of al-l wonders! Your father's gun! No indeed you can't!"

He was fairly well crushed, but he managed to mutter, sullenly, "Well, Willie Dalzel, he's got a gun." In reality his heart had previously been beating with such tumult—he had himself been so impressed with the daring and sin of his request—that he was glad that all was over now, and his mother could do very little further harm to his sensibilities. He had been influenced into the venture by the larger boys.

"Huh!" the Dalzel urchin had said; "your father's got a gun, hasn't he? Well, why don't you bring that?"

Puffing himself, Jimmie had replied, "Well, I can, if I want to." It was a black lie, but really the Dalzel boy was too outrageous with his eternal bill-posting about the gun which a beaming uncle had entrusted to him. Its possession made him superior in manfulness to most boys in the neighbourhood—or at least they enviously conceded him such position—but he was so overbearing, and stuffed the fact of his treasure so relentlessly down their throats, that on this occasion the miserable Jimmie had lied as naturally as most animals swim.

Willie Dalzel had not been checkmated, for he had instantly retorted, "Why don't you get it, then?"

"Well, I can, if I want to."

"Well, get it, then!"

"Well, I can, if I want to."

Thereupon Jimmie had paced away with great airs of surety as far as the door of his home, where his manner changed to one of tremulous misgiving as it came upon him to address his mother in the dining-room. There had happened that which had happened.

When Jimmie returned to his two distinguished companions he was blown out with a singular pomposity. He spoke these noble words: "Oh, well, I guess I don't want to take the gun out to-day."

They had been watching him with gleaming ferret eyes, and they detected his falsity at once. They challenged him with shouted gibes, but it was not in the rules for the conduct of boys that one should admit anything whatsoever, and so Jimmie, backed into an ethical corner, lied as stupidly, as desperately, as hopelessly as ever lone savage fights when surrounded at last in his jungle.

Such accusations were never known to come to any point, for the reason that the number and kind of denials always equalled or exceeded the number of accusations, and no boy was ever brought really to book for these misdeeds.

In the end they went off together, Willie Dalzel with his gun being a trifle in advance and discoursing upon his various works. They passed along a maple-lined avenue, a highway common to boys bound for that free land of hills and woods in which they lived in some part their romance of the moment, whether it was of Indians, miners, smugglers, soldiers, or outlaws. The paths were their paths, and much was known to them of the secrets of the dark green hemlock thickets, the wastes of sweetfern and huckleberry, the cliffs of gaunt bluestone with the sumach burning red at their feet. Each boy had, I am sure, a conviction that some day the wilderness was to give forth to him a marvellous secret. They felt that the hills and the forest knew much, and they heard a voice of it in the silence. It was vague, thrilling, fearful, and altogether fabulous. The grown folk seemed to regard these wastes merely as so much distance between one place and another place, or as a rabbit-cover, or as a district to be judged according to the value of the timber; but to the boys it spoke some great inspiring word, which they knew even as those who pace the shore know the enigmatic speech of the surf. In the meantime they lived there, in season, lives of ringing adventure—by dint of imagination.

The boys left the avenue, skirted hastily through some private grounds, climbed a fence, and entered the thickets. It happened that at school the previous day Willie Dalzel had been forced to read and acquire in some part a solemn description of a lynx. The meagre information thrust upon him had caused him grimaces of suffering, but now he said, suddenly, "I'm goin' to shoot a lynx."

The other boys admired this statement, but they were silent for a time. Finally Jimmie said, meekly, "What's a lynx?" He had endured his ignorance as long as he was able.

The Dalzel boy mocked him. "Why, don't you know what a lynx is? A lynx? Why, a lynx is a animal somethin' like a cat, an' it's got great big green eyes, and it sits on the limb of a tree an' jus' glares at you. It's a pretty bad animal, I tell you. Why, when I—"

"Huh!" said the third boy. "Where'd you ever see a lynx?"

"Oh, I've seen 'em—plenty of 'em. I bet you'd be scared if you seen one once."

Jimmie and the other boy each demanded, "How do you know I would?"

They penetrated deeper into the wood. They climbed a rocky zigzag path which led them at times where with their hands they could almost touch the tops of giant pines. The grey cliffs sprang sheer toward the sky. Willie Dalzel babbled about his impossible lynx, and they stalked the mountainside like chamois-hunters, although no noise of bird or beast broke the stillness of the hills. Below them Whilomville was spread out somewhat like the cheap green-and-black lithograph of the time—"A Bird's-eye View of Whilomville, N.Y."

In the end the boys reached the top of the mountain and scouted off among wild and desolate ridges. They were burning with the desire to slay large animals. They thought continually of elephants, lions, tigers, crocodiles. They discoursed upon their immaculate conduct in case such monsters confronted them, and they all lied carefully about their courage.

The breeze was heavy with the smell of sweetfern. The pines and hemlocks sighed as they waved their branches. In the hollows the leaves of the laurels were lacquered where the sunlight found them. No matter the weather, it would be impossible to long continue an expedition of this kind without a fire, and presently they built one, snapping down for fuel the brittle under branches of the pines. About this fire they were willed to conduct a sort of play, the Dalzel boy taking the part of a bandit chief, and the other boys being his trusty lieutenants. They stalked to and fro, long-strided, stern yet devil-may-care, three terrible little figures.

Jimmie had an uncle who made game of him whenever he caught him in this kind of play, and often this uncle quoted derisively the following classic: "Once aboard the lugger, Bill, and the girl is mine. Now to burn the château and destroy all evidence of our crime. But, hark 'e, Bill, no violence." Wheeling abruptly, he addressed these dramatic words to his comrades. They were impressed; they decided at once to be smugglers, and in the most ribald fashion they talked about carrying off young women.

At last they continued their march through the woods. The smuggling *motif* was now grafted fantastically upon the original lynx idea, which Willie Dalzel refused to abandon at any price.

Once they came upon an innocent bird which happened to be looking another way at the time. After a great deal of manœuvring and big words, Willie Dalzel reared his fowling piece and blew this poor thing into a mere rag of wet feathers, of which he was proud.

Afterward the other big boy had a turn at another bird. Then it was plainly Jimmie's chance. The two others had, of course, some thought of cheating him out of this chance, but of a truth he was timid to explode such a thunderous weapon, and as soon as they detected this fear they simply overbore him, and made it clearly understood that if he refused to shoot he would lose his caste, his scalp-lock, his girdle, his honour.

They had reached the old death-coloured snake-fence which marked the limits of the upper pasture of the Fleming farm. Under some hickory trees the path ran parallel to the fence. Behold! a small priestly chipmunk came to a rail and, folding his hands on his abdomen, addressed them in his own tongue. It was Jimmie's shot. Adjured by the others, he took the gun. His face was stiff with apprehension. The Dalzel boy was giving forth fine words. "Go ahead. Aw, don't be afraid. It's nothin' to do. Why, I've done it a million times. Don't shut both your eyes, now. Jus' keep one open and shut the other one. He'll get away if you don't watch out. Now you're all right. Why don't you let 'er go? Go ahead."

Jimmie, with his legs braced apart, was in the centre of the path. His back was greatly bent, owing to the mechanics of supporting the heavy gun. His companions were screeching in the rear. There was a wait.

Then he pulled trigger. To him there was a frightful roar, his cheek and his shoulder took a stunning blow, his face felt a hot flush of fire, and, opening his two eyes, he found that he was still alive.

He was not too dazed to instantly adopt a becoming egotism. It had been the first shot of his life.

But directly after the well-mannered celebration of this victory a certain cow, which had been grazing in the line of fire, was seen to break wildly across the pasture, bellowing and bucking. The three smugglers and lynx-hunters looked at each other out of blanched faces. Jimmie had hit the cow. The first evidence of his comprehension of this fact was in the celerity with which he returned the discharged gun to Willie Dalzel.

They turned to flee. The land was black, as if it had been overshadowed suddenly with thick storm-clouds, and even as they fled in their horror a gigantic Swedish farm-hand came from the heavens and fell upon them, shrieking in eerie triumph. In a twinkle they were clouted prostrate. The Swede was elate and ferocious in a foreign and fulsome way. He continued to beat them and yell.

From the ground they raised their dismal appeal. "Oh, please, mister, we didn't do it! He did it! I didn't do it! We didn't do it! We didn't mean to do it! Oh, please, mister!"

In these moments of childish terror little lads go half blind, and it is possible that few moments of their after life made them suffer as they did when the Swede flung them over the fence and marched them toward the farmhouse. They begged like cowards on the scaffold, and each one was for himself. "Oh, please let me go, mister! I didn't do it, mister! He did it! Oh, p-l-ease let me go, mister!"

The boyish view belongs to boys alone, and if this tall and knotted labourer was needlessly without charity, none of the three lads questioned it. Usually when they were punished they decided that they deserved it, and the more they were punished the more they were convinced that they were criminals of a most subterranean type. As to the hitting of the cow being a pure accident, and therefore not of necessity a criminal matter, such reading never entered their heads. When things happened and they were caught, they commonly paid dire consequences, and they were accustomed to measure the probabilities of woe utterly by the damage done, and not in any way by the culpability. The shooting of the cow was plainly heinous, and undoubtedly their dungeons would be knee-deep in water.

"He did it, mister!" This was a general outcry. Jimmie used it as often as did the others. As for them, it is certain that they had no direct thought of betraying their comrade for their own salvation.

They thought themselves guilty because they were caught; when boys were not caught they might possibly be innocent. But captured boys were guilty. When they cried out that Jimmie was the culprit, it was principally a simple expression of terror.

Old Henry Fleming, the owner of the farm, strode across the pasture toward them. He had in his hand a most cruel whip. This whip he flourished. At his approach the boys suffered the agonies of the fire regions. And yet anybody with half an eye could see that the whip in his hand was a mere accident, and that he was a kind old man—when he cared.

When he had come near he spoke crisply. "What you boys ben doin' to my cow?" The tone had deep threat in it. They all answered by saying that none of them had shot the cow. Their denials were tearful and clamorous, and they crawled knee by knee. The vision of it was like three martyrs being dragged toward the stake. Old Fleming stood there, grim, tight-lipped. After a time he said, "Which boy done it?"

There was some confusion, and then Jimmie spake. "I done it, mister."

Fleming looked at him. Then he asked, "Well, what did you shoot 'er fer?"

Jimmie thought, hesitated, decided, faltered, and then formulated this: "I thought she was a lynx."

Old Fleming and his Swede at once lay down in the grass and laughed themselves helpless.

# Malice Aforethought

## Donald A. Wollheim

It was bad enough that people always mistook Allen San Sebastian for the writer, Marvin Dane. It was worse how the society of the literary world kept shoving the two together until, having met at so many parties and people's homes, they were regarded by the outside world as being friends.

Actually neither liked the other very much—that is always the curse of similarity in competitors—they would have avoided each other if they could, but they couldn't, not without snubbing too many valuable intermediaries. Both wrote stories for the same magazine, both did their best to toady up to the impossible boor who was its editor.

LeClair B. Smith, who was owner and editor of *Grimoire*, "The Magazine of Spectral Fiction," was a sharp-dealing, coarse-tongued, self-educated businessman who knew nothing about real literature, had a Sunday supplement taste in art, but knew just about everything when it came to squeezing the pennies from the newsdealers and the trusting public. That *Grimoire* was such a success was due to that grim jest of fate that made Smith capable of enjoying a good horror tale when he read one. Possibly it was a subconscious reflection of the sadism that makes so many successful men scornful of the feelings of others. Certainly his handling of his authors instilled horror in those who had perforce to deal with him.

For it was good business to stay in his favor, as San Sebastian well knew, and when you had to depend on Smith's checks for your living, it became a matter of life and death.

San Sebastian had left his parental farm, somewhere in the Middle West, after selling several stories, and had made himself to live in the intellectual slums of the big city. It was good business, besides he could concentrate better where there were no infernal roosters to rouse him from bed at half-past four, and he could stay up as late as he pleased with decent conversations and a half-gallon of thick, sweet muscatel to sip from. The fly in his ointment was Marvin Dane.

They looked alike, both tall, gaunt, dark-haired. Both had a tendency to squint, both had the same dry sense of humor. But there, insisted San Sebastian, the resemblance ended. He could write and Dane couldn't. Smith, their god and judge, didn't share San Sebastian's opinion. He thought they could both write—and also happened to think that San Sebastian was slipping and Dane coming up.

San Sebastian had begun to realize the horrible truth himself when three stories in a row were rejected as being too similar to material bought just previously. He didn't know what this material was until two months later when he saw a story of Dane's in the latest *Grimoire* that shook him to the core. It was quite identical, plot, writing and all, to his story—the one that had been the first to be rejected.

Dane a plagiarist? Hard to see how. San Sebastian, after over-coming his first fit of fury and black anger, found himself lost in a reflex of puzzlement. Nobody, but nobody, saw San Sebastian's sto-ries until he'd written them out, rewritten them, pecked out a copy painfully on his typewriter and then, after waiting a week or so to reread again, made his further corrections, and brought the pages in for LeClair Smith's cold eyes to read.

Dane couldn't possibly have seen the stories before; he couldn't possibly have sneaked into San Sebastian's rooms to copy his tales; that was impossible and besides, San Sebastian never discussed plots with any of his friends. Yet there it was. They were almost identical stories.

By the time the third similar story of Dane's had appeared in print and two other tales of San Sebastian's had been rejected by Smith with the cutting insinuation that he, San Sebastian, must have peeked at Dane's red-hot typewriter, Allen San Sebastian was in a state bordering on madness. He could, of course, try and sell his rejected tales to a competitor magazine. But besides the fact that he didn't go over as well with the other editors, they might holler bloody murder when Dane's duplicates hit the stands first.

San Sebastian finally took a friend into his confidence. A rather older man, more steady in his ways, with a bent for the psychologi-cal and the occult. He discussed the matter, showed this friend Dane's published stories and his own originals. It was, he insisted, not possible for either writer to have seen the other's work in pro-duction. He didn't even know exactly where Dane lived, and he doubted if Dane knew precisely where he lived. But they had seen lots of each other in past few months at the homes of mutual friends.

San Sebastian's friend, a man of considerable experience, after giving the matter much thought, pointed out that the coincidence of ideas was not precisely new in history. It happened before, it happened often in fact with creative minds that two persons would think of the same thing at the same time. It seems, his friend said, that the universe moved at a certain pace, and then when condi-tions were ready for certain ideas, they developed spontaneously to the first minds that bothered to look for them.

For instance, when the science of mathematics had reached an impasse in the old arithmetics, Newton and Leibnitz, separated by two different nations, without knowledge of each other, individually invented and worked out the system of calculus. Again the planet Neptune had been seen by two different astronomers almost simultaneously. Again and again, inventions were duplicated, sometimes at half a world's distance, by minds of similar caliber and training, hitting upon the same problem.

It was as if there was an invisible telegraphic network linking all the minds of the world. So that when a Frenchman named Ader made a wild short flight in a crazy apparatus of canvas and propellers in 1898, two young mechanics in Ohio should conceive a mad inspiration for a miracle that would mature at Kitty Hawk a few years later.

Now, reasoned San Sebastian's learned friend, was it not logical that when two minds as similar as Dane's and San Sebastian's were living within a few blocks of each other, were simultaneously trying to determine the demands of the same mind, LeClair B. Smith's, in the same specialized style of writing, *Grimoire*'s, that one should telegraph his ideas to the other, just as a powerful sending station transmits instantly to the receivers of a waiting set. Who is to say which of the two originated the ideas of these stories? It may be San Sebastian glimpsing them from Dane's mind, or vice versa. No personal guilt could be placed.

The reason, the only reason, why Dane was winning was that he was the faster writer. Dane wrote by typewriter the first time and never rewrote. Once he tore his first draft from the keys of his machine, it went within hours to Smith's desk. And it would not be for two weeks before San Sebastian's tortoise-paced prose would reach that same destination. By which time, of course, Dane would long ago have eaten into the proceeds of *Grimoire*'s check of acceptance.

Marvin Dane was clever enough, beyond doubt. He had often irked San Sebastian by his boasting that he never cluttered up his imagination with the stories of others. He never read other writers' efforts and he never relied on the classics and anthologies for inspiration. His mind was very probably wide open for stray plots coming over the telepathic ether.

This answer satisfied San Sebastian's curiosity, but left him in an even grimmer plight than before. Was he doomed always to lose out in this ghastly race? Did this spell his end as a writer—this constant, hopeless race with a nemesis hidden at a machine out of his sight sucking the very thoughts from his head?

For several days Allen San Sebastian wandered the streets of the big city lost in wonder and despair. There must be an answer, but what, but how? This was to be a struggle to the death—for it was clear that the only obvious course that would clear his future would be Dane's death, or at least incapacitation.

He could, for instance, break into Dane's apartment and smash his typewriter with an axe. By the time Dane could borrow or buy another machine, he, San Sebastian, would have at least one new story on Smith's desk first. But this was obviously an impractical solution. He could pay someone to beat up Dane and put him in a hospital. This too did not exactly appeal to him. Besides, it invited a host of trouble; who would he get to do it and how could he keep himself from being blackmailed thereafter? As for murder, the idea didn't appeal to him at all.

Then, one afternoon, the idea came to him. Almost in a fever flush, San Sebastian made his way home, closed and locked the door behind him and dashed to his bookcase. Pulling out a volume therein, he seated himself at his desk, took pen in hand and began transcribing the pages of the book that he had opened. Carefully he bent himself to his task, concentrating heavily on each word and line.

In two hours he had completed the first writing. Setting the manuscript aside, he waited. Next day he again repeated the process, laboriously copying out the printed pages for a second time. Yet a third day he worked on it, then set up his typewriter and began typing out the pages slowly in his usual faltering and painstaking manner. He drew out the work as long as possible.

On the fourth day, upon typing finis to the last page, he clipped all the completed pages together, read through them very carefully once more, and then, taking the various manuscripts into his little kitchenette, burned them each and every one over a jet of his gas stove.

Then he took a rest from literary work for two months, two months during which he found a job running an elevator. He had to wait.

Now LeClair B. Smith was, as has been said, pretty much of a nonliterary businessman, self-educated and self-opinionated. He knew a good horror story when he saw one and when Marvin Dane submitted a humdinger to him, he bought it on that same day and fitted it into his magazine's schedule. Dane, we must digress, had the not unadmirable quality of keeping his mind clear of other horror writer's works; in this case, the price of this attitude came high.

It was very embarrassing when a host of discerning readers and fans flooded the magazine with angry letters for publishing H.P. Lovecraft's "The Rats in the Walls" under the title of "The Mumbling Vermin of Oxham Priory" by Marvin Dane—"A gripping tale of ancestral doom, written specially for *Grimoire* by a modern de Maupassant." It was disastrous for Marvin and when Smith not only threw him out of the office but sued him for the return of his money and damages.

And it didn't do Allen San Sebastian any harm when Dane's new stories were constantly returned to him by the office boy unopened, as per editorial orders. You could be sure to find San Sebastian's name in any table of contents in any new issue of *Grimoire*. As for Dane, after that ruinous climax to his literary career, for which he was quite unable to blame anyone but himself and his sizzling typewriter, he became a moderate sort of success as the clerk in a small but select bookstore catering to modernist and other obscurantist prosody.

# Mirror, Mirror

## Tina and Tony Rath

When Nievis Bianca was seventeen her old man married again, for the fourth, or maybe it was the fifth time, as he certainly hadn't bothered to keep count and no-one else had either. And the lady he married was a real Queen of the Witches. Well, she was heavily into the occult anyway, and she certainly looked the part. She had long, long, night black hair, that Nievis thought must be a dye job because she never would go in swimming, even on the hottest day, and a pale skin that owed a whole lot to heavy foundation and light green face powder. Now this may have been the cause of the trouble between them, because Nievis was by nature exactly what her step-mother aspired to be by art. She had a skin like white rose petals, because she knew all about the bad effects of sunbathing and never went out without her broad-brimmed hat. And she too had long, long hair like black satin, but she got that from her own mama, who had been Spanish as you might guess from the name she gave her baby daughter. She had also been Old Man Bianca's One True Love as he was apt to tell everyone when he'd been drinking, which was most days, and this did not help things between Nievis and her step-mother either.

Now, the day after the wedding the new Mrs Bianca took a long look at her step-daughter, as if she was measuring her for a shroud, and then she enrolled herself at a gym which offered aerobics and beauty therapy and all the aids a rich man's wife could ever ask to get her into top condition. And they gave her a diet sheet and an exercise programme, and they massaged her and depilated her and exfoliated her and gave her mud baths and vapour baths, and they brushed herbal jells into her long black hair, and when they had finished they started in and did it over again. Well, at last she decided she was ready for the final test. So she went into her bedroom and closed the shutters and locked the door. Then she lit three black candles and opened a locked drawer in her dressing table, and she took out a little tarnished square of glass. And holding it in her palm she intoned:

> "Mirror, mirror in my hand
> Who's the fairest in the land?"

And the mirror wrinkled as if it was shrugging its shoulders and replied: "Well, you're not bad for your age, baby, but let's face it, you'll never be eighteen again."

"You mean, like Nievis?" she gritted.

"You said it, snookums, not me," said the mirror.

She swung back her arm as if to throw the glass against the wall, but it only sniggered and said: "OK, go ahead honey, get yourself seven years bad luck, but remember it's the real double whammy if you break a magic mirror." So the new Mrs Bianca, who was naturally rather superstitious, dared not take out her bad temper on the mirror, but turned it on Nievis instead. Unfortunately Nievis was as good as she was beautiful. She responded to her step-mother's jealous rages by saying that she understood that she (Mrs Bianca) was going through a difficult time of life, and suggesting holistic remedies, or psychotherapy, which, for some reason, made her step-mother angrier than ever.

One evening, after a conversation with Nievis about the marvellous effects of the oil of evening primrose on the health and temper of the menopausal woman, the new Mrs Bianca locked herself in her bedroom again. But this time she consulted the telephone directory instead of her magic mirror. Now, in the course of his business, Mr Bianca had made a wide range of acquaintances, and some (well, practically all, really) were from the criminal classes. One of them in particular was a hitman who happened to admire Mrs Bianca very much, so much indeed that he had once rashly told her that if she ever wanted anyone removed from her circle of friends in a perfectly private and genteel style, she had only to ask. That evening she did ask; and the person scheduled for removal was, of course, the beautiful Nievis.

The hitman was very sorry to hear such a request from Mrs Bianca but he had given his word, and he felt honour-bound to do as she asked. So he waited outside Nievis's high school and prepared to do what he had promised. But when he saw her tripping blithely down the steps, swinging her school-books in her hand, she reminded him so sharply of his own baby sister that instead of shooting her he took her to a drug store, and over a chocolate soda he told her just what her step-mother had asked him to do.

"But," he said, "now I have seen you, I know I cannot do any such thing. I will go back and tell your step-mother that I have reformed my life and I will never shoot people for money again."

Now Nievis was good and beautiful, but she was by no means a bimbo. So she said to the hitman, "Don't do that, because she will only find someone else, who has fewer scruples, or no baby sister, who will shoot me instead. Go and tell her you have done the dreadful deed, and take my locket as proof. But first please drive me to somewhere where I will be safe from her."

So, following her directions he drove her over seven rivers, through seven forests, and over seven mountains until—very late at night—they came to a little ranch-style house in the middle of nowhere. And Nievis pushed open the door and went in. The hitman went back to her step-mother and showed her the locket. He was so convincing that as soon as he had gone Mrs Bianca went to her room, lit her candles, picked up her mirror, and demanded:

>"Mirror, mirror in my hand
>Who's *now* the fairest in the land?"

But the mirror said: "Like I said, sugar, you're OK for your age, but your step-daughter, Nievis, currently living in a ranch-style bungalow with the seven dwarves, is still better-looking."

"She's doing what!" shrieked the Witch Queen.

"You heard, angel-pie. So what do you expect? You get into the occult, find yourself a magic mirror, and marry a man called Bianca, who has a daughter named Nievis, which makes her Snow White in plain American English, and you don't expect the seven dwarves to turn up somewhere? Now you have to disguise yourself as an Avon lady and make with the poisoned apples."

But the Witch Queen said: "No way!"

"What do you mean 'No way,'" the mirror demanded shrilly. "You can't fly in the face of tradition."

"Just watch me," said Mrs Bianca, who was beginning to remember the rest of the story. "You really think I'm schlepping across seven mountains, to say nothing of the forests and the rivers just to poison some ungrateful girl who'll only be revived by a handsome prince, and marry him, while I get to dance at her reception in centrally heated shoes? If she wants to play house with seven short persons, let her! If her poor father ever finds out it will kill him, that's all."

And she flounced off to tell him.

However, Mr Bianca accepted the news philosophically. After all, Nievis would have been leaving home to go to college quite soon and, all things considered, there was probably less to worry about if she was living in the middle of nowhere chaperoned by seven dwarves than if she was at a college, however respectable, exposed to the triple evils of Drugs, Feminism, and College Athletes. So he was not unhappy. But others were.

To begin with, there were the dwarves. They had accepted custody of Nievis in the belief that she would shortly succumb to her step-mother's poisoned apple and spend the rest of her stay in a trance, until her prince arrived to take her away. They certainly had not expected an open-ended contract, with no prospect of release from the regimen of low-fat, whole-food vegetarian meals she inflicted on them, to say nothing of the music that blared from her little radio cassette player morning, noon, and night. They began to picket the Bianca residence, and it was not long before other interested groups joined them. A number of Writers' Guilds and Groups objected to Snow White's story being deprived of its traditional happy ending. Romantic novelists were especially concerned, as they said it undermined all they stood for. When the lady novelists and the dwarves were joined by a delegation of English actors representing the pantomime interest, the Biancas' front lawn began to resemble a three-ring circus. The dispute escalated. Questions were asked in Congress, and all the participants appeared on most of the major chat shows.

Mrs Bianca had some supporters. An anonymous but encouraging note arrived from a Big Bad Wolf trying to start a new life as a vegetarian chef in San Francisco, and a group calling itself Woman In Total Charge of Herself (Eastern Section) mounted a counter-picket. But even if the whole world had been against her, she announced, she still had no intention of relenting and poisoning her step-daughter.

The deadlock was broken by someone that almost everyone else had forgotten about. One day the reformed hitman got in his car and travelled over seven mountains, across seven rivers, and through seven forests until he found Nievis sitting by the fake wishing well that the dwarves had set up on their front lawn. He went down on one knee and said: "Snow White, you should marry the handsomest prince in the world. But he could not love you more than I do. I was a hitman and to tell you the truth, not much of a one at that: it was mostly talk with me. Now I am only a poor salesman. But if you will marry me I promise we will live happily ever after."

And Nievis smiled and got into his car, and they drove off into the sunset. They were married very quietly, and all that danced at their wedding were their hearts.

The years passed. The ex-hitman never did make a lot of money, but he and Nievis had many beautiful children, and they were very happy. And Mrs Bianca? Well, she was very happy too. She watched as Nievis—as women with low incomes and large families will—grew fat. Nievis cut off her long black hair because it was just too much trouble, and she forgot to wear her broad-brimmed hat, and her skin coarsened. To her husband she was always the beautiful Snow White he had first married; but often, after her step-daughter and her family had visited with her father at Christmas or Thanksgiv-

ing, Mrs Bianca would go to her bedroom and look into the little
tarnished mirror with the gold frame she now kept on her bedroom
wall, and she would say:

> "Mirror, mirror on the wall
> Cosmetic surgery beats them all."

And the mirror would chuckle and reply:

> "You said it, honey-pie, you said it."

# Miss Crump's Song

### Augustus Baldwin Longstreet

Miss Crump was inexorable. She declared that she was entirely
out of practice. "She scarcely ever touched the piano;"
"Mamma was always scolding her for giving so much of her time to
French and Italian, and neglecting her music and painting; but she
told mamma the other day that it really was so irksome to her to
quit Racine and Dante, and go to thrumming upon the piano, that,
but for the obligations of filial obedience, she did not think she
should ever touch it again."

Here Mrs. Crump was kind enough, by the merest accident in
the world, to interpose, and to relieve the company from farther
anxiety.

"Augusta, my dear," said she, "go and play a tune or two; the
company will excuse your hoarseness."

Miss Crump rose immediately at her mother's bidding, and
moved to the piano, accompanied by a large group of smiling faces.

"Poor child," said Mrs. Crump, as she went forward, "she is
frightened to death. I wish Augusta could overcome her diffi-
dence."

Miss Crump was educated in Philadelphia; she had been taught
to sing by Madame Piggisqueaki, who was a pupil of Ma'm'selle
Crokifroggietta, who had sung with Madame Catalani; and she had

taken lessons on the piano from Seignor Buzzifussi, who had played with Paganini.

She seated herself at the piano, rocked to the right, then to the left, leaned forward, then backward, and began. She placed her right hand about midway the keys, and her left about two octaves below it. She now puts off to the right in a brisk canter up the treble notes, and the left after it. The left then led the way back, and the right pursued it in like manner. The right turned, and repeated its first movement; but the left outran it this time, hopped over it, and flung it entirely off the track. It came in again, however, behind the left on its return, and passed it in the same style. They now became highly incensed at each other, and met furiously on the middle ground. Here a most awful conflict ensued for about the space of ten seconds, when the right whipped off all of a sudden, as I thought, fairly vanquished. But I was in the error against which Jack Randolph cautions us; "it had only fallen back to a stronger position." It mounted upon two black keys, and commenced the note of a rattlesnake. This had a wonderful effect upon the left, and placed the doctrine of "snake charming" beyond dispute. The left rushed furiously towards it repeatedly, but seemed invariably panic-struck when it came within six keys of it, and as invariably retired with a tremendous roaring down the bass keys.

It continued its assaults, sometimes by the way of the naturals, sometimes by the way of the sharps, and sometimes by a zigzag through both; but all its attempts to dislodge the right from its stronghold proving ineffectual, it came close up to its adversary, and expired.

Any one, or rather no one, can imagine what kind of noises the piano gave forth during the conflict. Certain it is, no one can describe them, and, therefore, I shall not attempt it. The battle ended, Miss Augusta moved as though she would have arisen, but this was protested against by a number of voices at once.

"One song, my dear Aurelia," said Miss Small; "you must sing that sweet little French air you used to sing in Philadelphia, and which Madame Piggisqueaki was so fond of."

Miss Augusta looked pitifully at her mamma, and her mamma looked "sing" at Miss Augusta; accordingly, she squared herself for a song.

She brought her hands to the campus this time in fine style, and they seemed now to be perfectly reconciled to each other. They commenced a kind of colloquy; the right whispering treble very softly, and the left responding bass very loudly. The conference had been kept up until I began to desire a change of the subject, when my ear caught, indistinctly, some very curious sounds, which appeared to proceed from the lips of Miss Augusta; they seemed to be compounded of a dry cough, a grunt, a hiccough, and a whisper; and they were introduced, it appeared to me, as interpreters between the right and the left.

Things progressed in this way for about the space of fifteen seconds, when I happened to direct my attention to Mr. Jenkins, from Philadelphia. His eyes were closed, his head rolled gracefully from side to side; a beam of heavenly complacency rested upon his countenance; and his whole man gave irresistible demonstration that Miss Crump's music made him feel good all over. I had just turned from the contemplation of Mr. Jenkins' transports, to see whether I could extract from the performance anything intelligible, when Miss Crump made a fly-catching grab at half-a-dozen keys in a row and at the same instant she fetched a long, dunghill-cock crow, at the conclusion of which she grabbed as many keys with her left. This came over Jenkins like a warm bath, and over me like a rake of bamboo briers.

My nerves had not recovered from this shock before Miss Augusta repeated the movement, and accompanied it with a squall of a pinched cat. This threw me into an ague fit; but, from respect to the performer, I maintained my position.

She now made a third grasp with the right, boxed the faces of six keys in a row with the left, and at the same time raised one of the most unearthly howls that ever issued from the throat of a human being. This seemed the signal for universal uproar and destruction. She now threw away all her reserve, and charged the piano with her whole force. She boxed it, she clawed it, she raked it, she scraped it. Her neck-vein swelled, her chin flew up, her face flushed, her eye glared, her bosom heaved; she screamed, she howled, she yelled, cackled, and was in the act of dwelling upon the note of a screech-owl, when I took the St. Vitus's dance, and rushed out of the room. "Good Lord," said a bystander, "if this be her *singing*, what must her *crying be!*" As I reached the door I heard a voice exclaim, "By heavens! she's the most enchanting performer I ever heard in my life!" I turned to see who was the author of this ill-timed compliment, and who should it be but Nick Truck, from Lincoln, who seven years before was dancing "Possum up the Gumtree" in the chimney-corner of his father's kitchen. Nick had entered the counting-room of a merchant in Charleston some five or six years before, had been sent out as supercargo of a vessel to Bordeaux, and while the vessel was delivering one cargo and taking in another, had contracted a wonderful relish for French music.

As for myself, I went home in convulsions; took sixty drops of laudanum, and fell asleep. I dreamed that I was in a beautiful city, the streets of which intersected each other at right angles; that the birds of the air and the beasts of the forest had gathered there for battle, the former led on by a Frenchman, the latter by an Italian; that I was looking on their movements towards each other, when I heard the cry of "Hecate is coming!" I turned my eye to the northeast, and saw a female flying through the air toward the city, and distinctly recognised in her the features of Miss Crump. I took the alarm, and was making my escape, when she gave command for the beasts and birds to fall on me. They did so, and, with all the noises of the animal world, were in the act of tearing me to pieces, when I was waked by the stepping of Hall, my room-mate, into bed.

"Oh, my dear sir," exclaimed I, "you have waked me from a horrible dream. What o'clock is it?"

"Ten minutes after twelve," said he.

"And where have you been to this late hour?"

"I have just returned from the party."

"And what kept you so late?"

"Why, I disliked to retire while Miss Crump was playing."

"In mercy's name!" said I, "is she playing yet?"

"Yes," said he; "I had to leave her playing at last."

"And where was Jenkins?"

"He was there, still in ecstasies, and urging her to play on."

"And where was Truck?"

"He was asleep."

"And what was she playing?"

"An Italian—"

Here I swooned, and heard no more.

# Miss Rennsdale Accepts

## Booth Tarkington

"One-two-three; one-two-three—glide!" said Professor Bartet, emphasizing his instructions by a brisk collision of his palms at "glide." "One-two-three; one-two-three—glide!"

The school week was over, at last, but Penrod's troubles were not.

Round and round the ballroom went the seventeen struggling little couples of the Friday Afternoon Dancing Class. Round and round went their reflections with them, swimming rhythmically in the polished, dark floor—white and blue and pink for the girls; black, with dabs of white, for the white-collared, white-gloved boys; and sparks and slivers of high light everywhere as the glistening pumps flickered along the surface like a school of flying fish. Every small pink face—with one exception—was painstaking and set for duty. It was a conscientious little merry-go-round.

"One-two-three; one-two-three—glide! One-two-three; one-two-three—glide! One-two-th——Ha! Mister Penrod Schofield, you lose the step. Your left foot! No, no! This is the left! See—like me! Now again! One-two-three; one-two-three—glide! Better! Much better! Again! One-two-three; one-two-three—gl——Stop! Mr. Penrod Schofield, this dancing class is provided by the kind parents of the pupilses as much to learn the mannerss of good societies as to dance. You think you shall ever see a gentleman in good societies to tickle his partner in the dance till she say Ouch? Never! I assure you it is not done. Again! Now then! Piano, please! One-two-three; one-two-three—glide! Mr. Penrod Schofield, your right foot—your right foot! No, no! Stop!"

The merry-go-round came to a standstill.

"Mr. Penrod Schofield and partner"—Professor Bartet wiped his brow—"will you kindly observe me? One-two-three—glide! So! Now then—no; you will please keep your places, ladies and gentlemen. Mr. Penrod Schofield, I would puttickly like your attention; this is for you!"

"Pickin' on me again!" murmured the smouldering Penrod to his small, unsympathetic partner. "Can't let me alone a minute!"

"Mister Georgie Bassett, please step to the centre," said the professor.

Mr. Bassett complied with modest alacrity.

"Teacher's pet!" whispered Penrod hoarsely. He had nothing but contempt for Georgie Bassett. The parents, guardians, aunts, uncles, cousins, governesses, housemaids, cooks, chauffeurs and coachmen, appertaining to the members of the dancing class, all dwelt in the same part of town and shared certain communal theories; and among the most firmly established was that which maintained Georgie Bassett to be the Best Boy in Town. Contrariwise, the unfortunate Penrod, largely because of his recent dazzling but disastrous attempts to control forces far beyond him, had been given a clear title as the Worst Boy in Town. (Population, 135,000.) To precisely what degree his reputation was the product of his own energies cannot be calculated. It was Marjorie Jones who first applied the description, in its definite simplicity, the day after the "pageant," and, possibly, her frequent and effusive repetitions of it, even upon wholly irrelevant occasions, had something to do with its prompt and quite perfect acceptance by the community.

"Miss Rennsdale will please do me the fafer to be Mr. Georgie Bassett's partner for one moment," said Professor Bartet. "Mr. Penrod Schofield will please give his attention. Miss Rennsdale and Mister Bassett, obliche me, if you please. Others please watch. Piano, please! Now then!"

Miss Rennsdale, aged eight—the youngest lady in the class—and Mr. Georgie Bassett one-two-three-glided with consummate technique for the better education of Penrod Schofield. It is possible that amber-curled, beautiful Marjorie felt that she, rather than Miss Rennsdale, might have been selected as the example of perfection— or perhaps her remark was only woman.

"Stopping everybody for that boy!" said Marjorie.

Penrod, across the circle from her, heard distinctly—nay, he was obviously intended to hear; but over a scorched heart he preserved a stoic front. Whereupon Marjorie whispered derisively in the ear of her partner, Maurice Levy, who wore a pearl pin in his tie.

"Again, please, everybody—ladies and gentlemen!" cried Professor Bartet. "Mister Penrod Schofield, if you please, pay puttickly attention! Piano, please! Now then!"

The lesson proceeded. At the close of the hour Professor Bartet stepped to the centre of the room and clapped his hands for attention.

"Ladies and gentlemen, if you please to seat yourselves quietly," he said; "I speak to you now about to-morrow. As you all know—— Mister Penrod Schofield, I am not sticking up in a tree outside that window! If you do me the fafer to examine I am here, insides of the room. Now then! Piano, pl——no, I do not wish the piano! As you all know, this is the last lesson of the season until next October. To-morrow is our special afternoon; beginning three o'clock, we dance the cotillon. But this afternoon comes the test of mannerss. You must see if each know how to make a little formal call like a grown-up people in good societies. You have had good, perfect instruction; let us see if we know how to perform like societies ladies and gentlemen twenty-six years of age.

"Now, when you are dismissed each lady will go to her home and prepare to receive a call. The gentlemen will allow the ladies time to reach their houses and to prepare to receive callers; then each gentleman will call upon a lady and beg the pleasure to engage her for a partner in the cotillon to-morrow. You all know the correct, proper form for these calls, because didn't I work teaching you last lesson till I thought I would drop dead? Yes! Now each gentleman, if he reach a lady's house behind some other gentleman, then he must go somewhere else to a lady's house, and keep calling until he secures a partner; so, as there are the same number of both, everybody shall have a partner.

"Now please all remember that if in case—— Mister Penrod Schofield, when you make your call on a lady I beg you please remember that gentlemen in good societies do not scratch the back in societies as you appear to attempt; so please allow the hands to rest carelessly in the lap. Now please all remember that if in case—— Mister Penrod Schofield, if you please! Gentlemen in societies do not scratch the back by causing frictions between it and the back of your chair, either! Nobody else is itching here! *I* do not itch! I cannot talk if you must itch! In the name of Heaven, why must you always itch? What was I saying? Where—ah! the cotillon—yes! For the cotillon it is important nobody shall fail to be here to-morrow; but if any one should be so very ill he cannot possible come he must write a very polite note of regrets in the form of good societies to his engaged partner to excuse himself—and he must give the reason.

"I do not think anybody is going to be that sick to-morrow—no;

and I will find out and report to parents if anybody would try it and not be. But it is important for the cotillon that we have an even number of so many couples, and if it should happen that some one comes and her partner has sent her a polite note that he has genuine reasons why he cannot come, the note must be handed at once to me, so that I arrange some other partner. Is all understood? Yes. The gentlemen will remember now to allow the ladies plenty of time to reach their houses and prepare to receive calls. Ladies and gentlemen, I thank you for your polite attention."

It was nine blocks to the house of Marjorie Jones; but Penrod did it in less than seven minutes from a flying start—such was his haste to lay himself and his hand for the cotillon at the feet of one who had so recently spoken unamiably of him in public. He had not yet learned that the only safe male rebuke to a scornful female is to stay away from her—especially if that is what she desires. However, he did not wish to rebuke her; simply and ardently he wished to dance the cotillon with her. Resentment was swallowed up in hope.

The fact that Miss Jones' feeling for him bore a striking resemblance to that of Simon Legree for Uncle Tom, deterred him not at all. Naturally, he was not wholly unconscious that when he should lay his hand for the cotillon at her feet it would be her inward desire to step on it; but he believed that if he were first in the field Marjorie would have to accept. These things are governed by law.

It was his fond intention to reach her house even in advance of herself, and with grave misgiving he beheld a large automobile at rest before the sainted gate. Forthwith, a sinking feeling became a portent inside him as little Maurice Levy emerged from the front door of the house.

" 'Lo, Penrod!" said Maurice airily.

"What you doin' in there?" inquired Penrod.

"In where?"

"In Marjorie's."

"Well, what shouldn't I be doin' in Marjorie's?" Mr. Levy returned indignantly. "I was inviting her for my partner in the cotillon—what you s'pose?"

"You haven't got any right to!" Penrod protested hotly. "You can't do it yet."

"I did do it yet!" said Maurice.

"You can't!" insisted Penrod. "You got to allow them time first." He said the ladies had to be allowed time to prepare."

"Well, ain't she had time to prepare?"

"When?" Penrod demanded, stepping close to his rival threatening. "I'd like to know when——"

"When?" echoed the other with shrill triumph. "When? Why, in mamma's sixty-horse powder limousine automobile, what Marjorie came home with me in! I guess that's when!"

An impulse in the direction of violence became visible upon the countenance of Penrod.

"I expect you need some wiping down," he began dangerously. "I'll give you sumpthing to remem——"

"Oh, you will!" Maurice cried with astonishing truculence, contorting himself into what he may have considered a posture of defense. "Let's see you try it, you—you itcher!"

For the moment, defiance from such a source was dumfounding. Then, luckily, Penrod recollected something and glanced at the automobile.

Perceiving therein not only the alert chauffeur but the magnificent outlines of Mrs. Levy, his enemy's mother, he manœuvred his lifted hand so that it seemed he had but meant to scratch his ear.

"Well, I guess I better be goin'," he said casually. "See you t'-morrow!"

Maurice mounted to the lap of luxury, and Penrod strolled away with an assumption of careless ease which was put to a severe strain when, from the rear window of the car, a sudden protuberance in the nature of a small, dark, curly head shrieked scornfully:

"Go on—you big stiff!"

The cotillon loomed dismally before Penrod now; but it was his duty to secure a partner and he set about it with a dreary heart. The delay occasioned by his fruitless attempt on Marjorie and the altercation with his enemy at her gate had allowed other ladies ample time to prepare for callers—and to receive them. Sadly he went from house to house, finding that he had been preceded in one after the other. Altogether his hand for the cotillon was declined eleven times that afternoon on the legitimate ground of previous engagement. This with Marjorie, scored off all except five of the seventeen possible partners; and four of the five were also sealed away from him, as he learned in chance encounters with other boys upon the street.

One lady alone remained; he bowed to the inevitable and entered this lorn damsel's gate at twilight with an air of great discouragement. The lorn damsel was Miss Rennsdale, aged eight.

We are apt to forget that there are actually times of life when too much youth is a handicap. Miss Rennsdale was beautiful; she danced like a première; she had every charm but age. On that account alone had she been allowed so much time to prepare to receive callers that it was only by the most manful efforts she could keep her lip from trembling.

A decorous maid conducted the long-belated applicant to her where she sat upon a sofa beside a nursery governess. The decorous maid announced him composedly as he made his entrance.

"Mr. Penrod Schofield!"

Miss Rennsdale suddenly burst into loud sobs.

"Oh!" she wailed. "I just knew it would be him!"

The decorous maid's composure vanished at once—likewise her decorum. She clapped her hand over her mouth and fled, uttering sounds. The governess, however, set herself to comfort her heartbroken charge, and presently succeeded in restoring Miss Rennsdale to a semblance of that poise with which a lady receives callers and accepts invitations to dance cotillons. But she continued to sob at intervals.

Feeling himself at perhaps a disadvantage, Penrod made offer of his hand for the morrow with a little embarrassment. Following the form prescribed by Professor Bartet, he advanced several paces toward the stricken lady and bowed formally.

"I hope," he said by rote, "you're well, and your parents also in good health. May I have the pleasure of dancing the cotillon as your partner t'-morrow afternoon?"

The wet eyes of Miss Rennsdale searched his countenance without pleasure, and a shudder wrung her small shoulders; but the governess whispered to her instructively, and she made a great effort.

"I thu-thank you fu-for your polite invu-invu-invutation; and I ac——" Thus far she progressed when emotion overcame her again. She beat frantically upon the sofa with fists and heels. "Oh, I *did* want it to be Georgie Bassett!"

"No, no, no!" said the governess, and whispered urgently, whereupon Miss Rennsdale was able to complete her acceptance.

"And I ac-accept wu-with pu-pleasure!" she moaned, and immediately, uttering a loud yell, flung herself face downward upon the sofa, clutching her governess convulsively.

Somewhat disconcerted, Penrod bowed again.

"I thank you for your polite acceptance," he murmured hurriedly; "and I trust—I trust—I forget. Oh, yes—I trust we shall have a most enjoyable occasion. Pray present my compliments to your parents; and I must now wish you a very good afternoon."

Concluding these courtly demonstrations with another bow he withdrew in fair order, though thrown into partial confusion in the hall by a final wail from his crushed hostess:

"Oh! Why couldn't it be anybody but *him!*"

# Monologue in Baker Street

## Vincent Starrett

It was Christmas Eve at 221B Baker Street. Outside the snow was piling up in the streets, but inside the famous living room all was warmth and comfort. Sherlock Holmes and Doctor Watson had been silent together for some time. Suddenly the detective spoke:

"Yes, indeed! Time never runs so slowly as when one is watching a clock."

"How true that is," murmured the doctor, without realizing that his companion had intruded upon his inmost thoughts. Then an expression of bewilderment crossed his face. "My dear Holmes," he cried, "how in the world did you know what I was thinking?"

"Elementary, my dear fellow! You have in front of you a highly polished teapot in which the elongated reflection of your face suggests a portrait of a horse. Obviously you thought so yourself, a few moments ago, for an expression of displeasure crossed your features and you turned your head away.

"Still, for a moment you were thinking of a horse. Naturally this led you to think of Lady Godiva. You visualized her in Coventry, on that historic occasion, and thought how fortunate it was that she was not abroad on such a day as this. You glanced out of the window and shivered.

"The whirling snow suggested the Christmas pantomime we saw the other day, for your face broke into an amused smile; you raised your arms slightly and flapped them in simulation of the Christmas fairies flying about the stage on wires. Wires suggested a telegram, of course, and you remembered that we had not yet received our customary Christmas wire from my brother Mycroft, which in turn reminded you of Mycroft's increasing girth. You looked down at your own waistline and decided that you had better lose a pound or two.

"At this point food was in your mind. You began to think of tomorrow's turkey and sniffed as if already you smelled that savory bird. The turkey naturally reminded you of Henry Baker's Christmas goose, in our adventure of the Blue Carbuncle; you remember how it laid a bonny little egg after it was dead—the Countess of Morcar's blue carbuncle, which in turn reminded you of the charming little blue stones in the ear-rings we purchased for Mrs. Hudson; and this repeated suggestion of Christmas ultimately made you realize the imminence of the holiday. You looked at the clock and saw that it was still twenty minutes to midnight.

"You started to say, Merry Christmas, Holmes! but checked yourself and said something banal instead; but you kept your eye on the clock and I saw that you were impatient to greet me at the stroke of twelve. It was impossible that you could have reached this frame of mind without thinking how slowly time appears to run when one is waiting for something, and at that juncture I ventured to break in on your thoughts and agree with you. Tell me now, have I followed the sequence of images presented to you?"

"You have, indeed," said the doctor. "You are uncanny, Holmes. A few centuries ago you would certainly have been burned as a wizard."

"Perhaps I was," said the great detective idly. "Who knows? But let us hope that the turkey is not burned tomorrow. I see that it is exactly midnight. A merry Christmas to you, my dear Watson!"

# Monster Tales: Return of the Jumbo Shrimp

## Les Daniels

### Return of the Jumbo Shrimp

So a guy goes into a seafood restaurant and orders the jumbo shrimp, deep fried, and while he's waiting for his dinner he starts to think about the jumbo shrimp, and the agony they endure as they're plunged into the boiling oil. He imagines that they might come back to life seeking revenge, and the idea is so horrible that he loses his appetite, so when his order comes he sends it back. And that was The Return of the Jumbo Shrimp.

### Return of the Jumbo Shrimp 2

So a busboy working in the seafood restaurant sees the plate of jumbo shrimp on a counter in the kitchen, and they look okay to him, he's not scared, so he eats one, and it tastes so good that he eats the whole plateful, but it turns out that they're not so good, in fact they're bad, so a few minutes later he runs out into the alley and throws up. And that was The Return of the Jumbo Shrimp, too.

### Return of the Jumbo Shrimp 3

So a stray shaggy dog is walking down the street, he's starving, and he wanders into the alley in back of the seafood restaurant, and there's a puddle of something lying on the ground, and it looks okay to him, so he laps it up, but in fact it's not okay, it's horrible, so he spits it up again. And that was The Return of the Jumbo Shrimp, too, I mean three.

### Return of the Jumbo Shrimp 4

So the shaggy dog is still in the alley and he's still hungry, naturally, and there's a puddle of something on the ground again, so he figures what the hell . . .

# Moti Guj—Mutineer

## Rudyard Kipling

Once upon a time there was a coffee-planter in India who wished to clear some forest land for coffee-planting. When he had cut down all the trees and burned the under-wood the stumps still remained. Dynamite is expensive and slow-fire slow. The happy medium for stump-clearing is the lord of all beasts, who is the elephant. He will either push the stump out of the ground with his tusks, if he has any, or drag it out with ropes. The planter, therefore, hired elephants by ones and twos and threes, and fell to work. The very best of all the elephants belonged to the very worst of all the drivers or mahouts; and the superior beast's name was Moti Guj. He was the absolute property of his mahout, which would never have been the case under native rule, for Moti Guj was a creature to be desired by kings; and his name, being translated, meant the Pearl Elephant. Because the British Government was in the land, Deesa, the mahout, enjoyed his property undisturbed. He was dissipated. When he had made much money through the strength of his elephant, he would get extremely drunk and give Moti Guj a beating with a tent-peg over the tender nails of the forefeet. Moti Guj never trampled the life out of Deesa on these occasions, for he knew that after the beating was over Deesa would embrace his trunk, and weep and call him his love and his life and the liver of his soul, and give him some liquor. Moti Guj was very fond of liquor—arrack for choice, though he would drink palm-tree toddy if nothing better offered. Then Deesa would go to sleep between Moti Guj's forefeet, and as Deesa generally chose the middle of the public road, and as Moti Guj mounted guard over him and would not permit horse, foot, or cart to pass by, traffic was congested till Deesa saw fit to wake up.

There was no sleeping in the daytime on the planter's clearing: the wages were too high to risk. Deesa sat on Moti Guj's neck and gave him orders, while Moti Guj rooted up the stumps—for he owned a magnificent pair of tusks; or pulled at the end of a rope—for he had a magnificent pair of shoulders, while Deesa kicked him behind the ears and said he was the king of elephants. At evening time Moti Guj would wash down his three hundred pounds' weight of green food with a quart of arrack, and Deesa would take a share and sing songs between Moti Guj's legs till it was time to go to bed. Once a week Deesa led Moti Guj down to the river, and Moti Guj lay on his side luxuriously in the shallows, while Deesa went over him with a coir-swab and a brick. Moti Guj never mistook the pounding blow of the latter for the smack of the former that warned him to get up and turn over on the other side. Then Deesa would look at his feet, and examine his eyes, and turn up the fringes of his mighty ears in case of sores or budding ophthalmia. After inspection, the two would 'come up with a song from the sea', Moti Guj all black and shining, waving a torn tree branch twelve feet long in his trunk, and Deesa knotting up his own long wet hair.

It was a peaceful, well-paid life till Deesa felt the return of the desire to drink deep. He wished for an orgy. The little draughts that led nowhere were taking the manhood out of him.

He went to the planter, and 'My mother's dead,' said he, weeping.

'She died on the last plantation two months ago; and she died once before that when you were working for me last year,' said the planter, who knew something of the ways of nativedom.

'Then it's my aunt, and she was just the same as a mother to me,' said Deesa, weeping more than ever. 'She has left eighteen small children entirely without bread, and it is I who must fill their little stomachs,' said Deesa, beating his head on the floor.

'Who brought you the news?' said the planter.

'The post,' said Deesa.

'There hasn't been a post here for the past week. Get back to your lines!'

'A devastating sickness has fallen on my village, and all my wives are dying,' yelled Deesa, really in tears this time.

'Call Chihun, who comes from Deesa's village,' said the planter. 'Chihun, has this man a wife?'

'He!' said Chihun. 'No. Not a woman of our village would look at him. They'd sooner marry the elephant.' Chihun snorted. Deesa wept and bellowed.

'You will get into a difficulty in a minute,' said the planter. 'Go back to your work!'

'Now I will speak Heaven's truth,' gulped Deesa, with an inspiration. 'I haven't been drunk for two months. I desire to depart in order to get properly drunk afar off and distant from this heavenly plantation. Thus I shall cause no trouble.'

A flickering smile crossed the planter's face. 'Deesa,' said he, 'you've spoken the truth, and I'd give you leave on the spot if anything could be done with Moti Guj while you're away. You know that he will only obey your orders.'

'May the Light of the Heavens live forty thousand years. I shall be absent but ten little days. After that, upon my faith and honour and soul, I return. As to the inconsiderable interval, have I the gracious permission of the Heaven-born to call up Moti Guj?'

Permission was granted, and, in answer to Deesa's shrill yell, the lordly tusker swung out of the shade of a clump of trees where he had been squirting dust over himself till his master should return.

'Light of my heart, Protector of the Drunken, Mountain of Might, give ear,' said Deesa, standing in front of him.

Moti Guj gave ear, and saluted with his trunk. 'I am going away,' said Deesa.

Moti Guj's eyes twinkled. He liked jaunts as well as his master. One could snatch all manner of nice things from the roadside then.

'But you, you fubsy old pig, must stay behind and work.'

The twinkle died out as Moti Guj tried to look delighted. He hated stump-hauling on the plantation. It hurt his teeth.

'I shall be gone for ten days, oh Delectable One. Hold up your near forefoot and I'll impress the fact upon it, warty toad of a dried mud-puddle.' Deesa took a tent-peg and banged Moti Guj ten times on the nails. Moti Guj grunted and shuffled from foot to foot.

'Ten days,' said Deesa, 'you must work and haul and root trees as Chihun here shall order you. Take up Chihun and set him on your neck!' Moti Guj curled the tip of his trunk, Chihun put his foot there and was swung on to the neck. Deesa handed Chihun the heavy *ankus*, the iron elephant-goad.

Chihun thumped Moti Guj's bald head as a paviour thumps a kerbstone.

Moti Guj trumpeted.

'Be still, hog of the backwoods. Chihun's your mahout for ten days. And now bid me good-bye, beast after mine own heart. Oh, my lord, my king! Jewel of all created elephants, lily of the herd, preserve your honoured health; be virtuous. Adieu!'

Moti Guj lapped his trunk round Deesa and swung him into the air twice. That was his way of bidding the man good-bye.

'He'll work now,' said Deesa to the planter. 'Have I leave to go?'

The planter nodded, and Deesa dived into the woods. Moti Guj went back to haul stumps.

Chihun was very kind to him, but he felt unhappy and forlorn notwithstanding. Chihun gave him balls of spices, and tickled him under the chin, and Chihun's little baby cooed to him after work was over, and Chihun's wife called him a darling; but Moti Guj was a bachelor by instinct, as Deesa was. He did not understand the domestic emotions. He wanted the light of his universe back again—the drink and the drunken slumber, the savage beatings and the savage caresses.

None the less he worked well, and the planter wondered. Deesa had vagabonded along the roads till he met a marriage procession of his own caste and, drinking, dancing, and tippling, had drifted past all knowledge of the lapse of time.

The morning of the eleventh day dawned, and there returned no Deesa. Moti Guj was loosed from his ropes for the daily stint. He swung clear, looked round, shrugged his shoulders, and began to walk away, as one having business elsewhere.

'Hi! ho! Come back you,' shouted Chihun. 'Come back, and put me on your neck, Misborn Mountain. Return, Splendour of the Hillsides. Adornment of all India, heave to, or I'll bang every toe off your fat forefoot!'

Moti Guj gurgled gently, but did not obey. Chihun ran after him with a rope and caught him up. Moti Guj put his ears forward, and Chihun knew what that meant, though he tried to carry it off with high words.

'None of your nonsense with me,' said he. 'To your pickets, Devilson.'

'Hrrumph!' said Moti Guj, and that was all—that and the forebent ears.

Moti Guj put his hands in his pockets, chewed a branch for a toothpick, and strolled about the clearing, making jest of the other elephants, who had just set to work.

Chihun reported the state of affairs to the planter, who came out with a dog-whip and cracked it furiously. Moti Guj paid the white man the compliment of charging him nearly a quarter of a mile across the clearing and 'Hrrumphing' him into the verandah. Then he stood outside the house chuckling to himself, and shaking all over with the fun of it, as an elephant will.

'We'll thrash him,' said the planter. 'He shall have the finest thrashing that ever elephant received. Give Kala Nag and Nazim twelve foot of chain apiece, and tell them to lay on twenty blows.'

Kala Nag—which means Black Snake—and Nazim were two of the biggest elephants in the lines, and one of their duties was to administer the graver punishments, since no man can beat an elephant properly.

They took the whipping-chains and rattled them in their trunks as they sidled up to Moti Guj, meaning to hustle him between them. Moti Guj had never, in all his life of thirty-nine years, been whipped, and he did not intend to open new experiences. So he waited, weaving his head from right to left, and measuring the precise spot in Kala Nag's fat side where a blunt tusk would sink deepest. Kala Nag had no tusks; the chain was his badge of authority; but he judged it good to swing wide of Moti Guj at the last minute, and seem to appear as if he had brought out the chain for amusement. Nazim turned round and went home early. He did not feel fighting-fit that morning, and so Moti Guj was left standing alone with his ears cocked.

That decided the planter to argue no more, and Moti Guj rolled back to his inspection of the clearing. An elephant who will not work, and is not tied up, is not quite so manageable as an eighty-one ton gun loose in a heavy seaway. He slapped old friends on the back and asked them if the stumps were coming away easily; he talked nonsense concerning labour and the inalienable rights of elephants to a long 'nooning'; and, wandering to and fro, thoroughly demoralized the garden till sundown, when he returned to his pickets for food.

'If you won't work you shan't eat,' said Chihun angrily. 'You're a wild elephant, and no educated animal at all. Go back to your jungle.'

Chihun's little brown baby, rolling on the floor of the hut, stretched its fat arms to the huge shadow in the doorway. Moti Guj knew well that it was the dearest thing on earth to Chihun. He swung out his trunk with a fascinating crook at the end, and the brown baby threw itself shouting upon it. Moti Guj made fast and pulled up till the brown baby was crowing in the air twelve feet above his father's head.

'Great Chief!' said Chihun. 'Flour cakes of the best, twelve in number, two feet across, and soaked in rum shall be yours on the instant, and two hundred pounds' weight of fresh-cut young sugarcane therewith. Deign only to put down safely that insignificant brat who is my heart and my life to me.'

Moti Guj tucked the brown baby comfortably between his forefeet, that could have knocked into toothpicks all Chihun's hut, and waited for his food. He ate it, and the brown baby crawled away. Moti Guj dozed, and thought of Deesa. One of many mysteries connected with the elephant is that his huge body needs less sleep than anything else that lives. Four or five hours in the night suffice—two just before midnight, lying down on one side; two just after one o'clock, lying down on the other. The rest of the silent hours are filled with eating and fidgeting and long grumbling soliloquies.

At midnight, therefore, Moti Guj strode out of his pickets, for a thought had come to him that Deesa might be lying drunk some-where in the dark forest with none to look after him. So all that night he chased through the undergrowth, blowing and trumpeting and shaking his ears. He went down to the river and blared across the shallows where Deesa used to wash him, but there was no an-swer. He could not find Deesa, but he disturbed all the elephants in the lines, and nearly frightened to death some gypsies in the woods.

At dawn Deesa returned to the plantation. He had been very drunk indeed, and he expected to fall into trouble for outstaying his leave. He drew a long breath when he saw that the bungalow and the plantation were still uninjured; for he knew something of Moti Guj's temper; and reported himself with many lies and sa-laams. Moti Guj had gone to his pickets for breakfast. His night exercise had made him hungry.

'Call up your beast,' said the planter, and Deesa shouted in the mysterious elephant-language, that some mahouts believe came from China at the birth of the world, when elephants and not men were masters. Moti Guj heard and came. Elephants do not gallop. They move from spots at varying rates of speed. If an elephant wished to catch an express train he could not gallop, but he could catch the train. Thus Moti Guj was at the planter's door almost before Chihun noticed that he had left his pickets. He fell into Deesa's arms trumpeting with joy, and the man and beast wept and slobbered over each other, and handled each other from head to heel to see that no harm had befallen.

'Now we will get to work,' said Deesa. 'Lift me up, my son and my joy.'

Moti Guj swung him up and the two went to the coffee-clearing to look for irksome stumps.

The planter was too astonished to be very angry.

# Mrs. Joseph Porter

## Charles Dickens

Most extensive were the preparations at Rose Villa, Clapham Rise, in the occupation of Mr. Gattleton (a stock-broker in especially comfortable circumstances), and great was the anxiety of Mr. Gattleton's interesting family, as the day fixed for the representation of the Private Play which had been "many months in preparation," approached. The whole family was infected with the mania for Private Theatricals; the house, usually so clean and tidy, was, to use Mr. Gattleton's expressive description, "regularly turned out o' windows;" the large dining-room, dismantled of its furniture and ornaments, presented a strange jumble of flats, flies, wings, lamps, bridges, clouds, thunder and lightning, festoons and flowers, daggers and foil, and various other messes in theatrical slang included under the comprehensive name of "properties." The bedrooms were crowded with scenery, the kitchen was occupied by carpenters. Rehearsals took place every other night in the drawing-room, and every sofa in the house was more or less damaged by the perseverance and spirit with which Mr. Sempronius Gattleton, and Miss Lucina, rehearsed the smothering scene in "Othello"—it having been determined that that tragedy should form the first portion of the evening's entertainments.

"When we're a *leetle* more perfect, I think it will go admirably," said Mr. Sempronius, addressing his *corps dramatique,* at the conclusion of the hundred and fiftieth rehearsal. In consideration of his sustaining the trifling inconvenience of bearing all the expenses of the play, Mr. Sempronius had been, in the most handsome manner, unanimously elected stage-manager. "Evans," continued Mr. Gattleton the younger, addressing a tall, thin, pale young gentleman, with extensive whiskers—"Evans, you play *Roderigo* beautifully."

"Beautifully," echoed the three Miss Gattletons; for Mr. Evans was pronounced by all his lady friends to be "quite a dear." He looked so interesting, and had such lovely whiskers: to say nothing of his talent for writing verses in albums and playing the flute! *Roderigo* simpered and bowed.

"But I think," added the manager, "you are hardly perfect in the—fall—in the fencing-scene, where you are—you understand?"

"It's very difficult," said Mr. Evans, thoughtfully; "I've fallen about a good deal in our counting-house lately, for practice, only I find it hurts one so. Being obliged to fall backward you see, it bruises one's head a good deal."

"But you must take care you don't knock a wing down," said Mr. Gattleton, the elder, who had been appointed prompter, and who took as much interest in the play as the youngest of the company. "The stage is very narrow, you know."

"Oh! don't be afraid," said Mr. Evans, with a very self-satisfied air: "I shall fall with my head 'off,' and then I can't do any harm."

"But, egad," said the manager, rubbing his hands, "we shall make a decided hit in 'Masaniello.' Harleigh sings that music admirably."

Everybody echoed the sentiment. Mr. Harleigh smiled, and looked foolish—not an unusual thing with him—hummed "Behold how brightly breaks the morning," and blushed as red as the fisherman's nightcap he was trying on.

"Let's see," resumed the manager, telling the number on his fingers, "we shall have three dancing female peasants, besides *Fenella,* and four fishermen. Then, there's our man Tom; he can have a pair of ducks of mine, and a check shirt of Bob's, and a red nightcap, and he'll do for another—that's five. In the choruses, of course, we can sing at the sides; and in the market-scene we can walk about in cloaks and things. When the revolt takes place, Tom must keep rushing in on one side and out on the other, with a pickaxe, as fast as he can. The effect will be electrical; it will look exactly as if there were an immense number of 'em. And in the eruption-scene we must burn the red fire, and upset the tea-trays, and make all sorts of noises—and it's sure to do."

"Sure! sure!" cried all the performers *unâ voce*—and away hurried Mr. Sempronius Gattleton to wash the burnt cork off his face, and superintend the "setting up" of some of the amateur-painted, but never-sufficiently-to-be-admired, scenery.

Mrs. Gattleton was a kind, good-tempered, vulgar soul, exceedingly fond of her husband and children, and entertaining only three dislikes. In the first place, she had a natural antipathy to anybody else's unmarried daughters; in the second, she was in bodily fear of anything in the shape of ridicule; lastly—almost a necessary consequence of this feeling—she regarded, with feelings of the utmost horror, one Mrs. Joseph Porter, over the way. However, the good folks of Clapham and its vicinity stood very much in awe of scandal and sarcasm; and thus Mrs. Joseph Porter was courted, and flattered, and caressed, and invited, for much the same reason that induces a poor author, without a farthing in his pocket, to behave with extraordinary civility to a two-penny postman.

"Never mind, ma," said Miss Emma Porter, in colloquy with her respected relative, and trying to look unconcerned; "if they had invited me, you know that neither you nor pa would have allowed me to take part in such an exhibition."

"Just what I should have thought from your high sense of propriety," returned the mother. "I am glad to see, Emma, you know how to designate the proceeding." Miss P., by-the-bye, had only the week before made "an exhibition" of herself for four days, behind a counter at a fancy fair, to all and every of her Majesty's liege subjects who were disposed to pay a shilling each for the privilege of seeing some four dozen girls flirting with strangers, and playing at shop.

"There!" said Mrs. Porter, looking out of window; "there are two rounds of beef and a ham going in—clearly for sandwiches; and Thomas, the pastry-cook, says, there have been twelve dozen tarts ordered, besides blanc-mange and jellies. Upon my word! think of the Miss Gattletons in fancy dresses, too!"

"Oh, it's too ridiculous!" said Miss Porter, hysterically.

"I'll manage to put them a little out of conceit with the business, however," said Mrs. Porter; and out she went on her charitable errand.

"Well, my dear Mrs. Gattleton," said Mrs. Joseph Porter, after they had been closeted for some time, and when, by dint of indefatigable pumping, she had managed to extract all the news about the play, "well, my dear, people may say what they please; indeed we know they will, for some folks are *so* ill-natured. Ah, my dear Miss Lucina, how d'ye do? I was just telling your mamma that I have heard it said, that—"

"What?"

"Mrs. Porter is alluding to the play, my dear," said Mrs. Gattleton; "she was, I am sorry to say, just informing me that—"

"Oh, now pray don't mention it," interrupted Mrs. Porter; "it's most absurd—quite as absurd as young What's-his-name saying he wondered how Miss Caroline, with such a foot and ankle, could have the vanity to play *Fenella*."

"Highly impertinent, whoever said it," said Mrs. Gattleton, bridling up.

"Certainly, my dear," chimed in the delighted Mrs. Porter; "most undoubtedly! Because, as I said, if Miss Caroline *does* play *Fenella*, it doesn't follow, as a matter of course, that she should think she has a pretty foot;—and then—such puppies as these young men are—he had the impudence to say, that—"

How far the amiable Mrs. Porter might have succeeded in her pleasant purpose, it is impossible to say, had not the entrance of Mr. Thomas Balderstone, Mrs. Gattleton's brother, familiarly called in the family "Uncle Tom," changed the course of conversation, and suggested to her mind an excellent plan of operation on the evening of the play.

Uncle Tom was very rich, and exceedingly fond of his nephews and nieces: as a matter of course, therefore, he was an object of great importance in his own family. He was one of the best-hearted men in existence: always in a good temper, and always talking. It was his boast that he wore top-boots on all occasions, and had never worn a black silk neckerchief; and it was his pride that he remembered all the principal plays of Shakspeare from beginning to end— and so he did. The result of this parrot-like accomplishment was, that he was not only perpetually quoting himself, but that he could never sit by, and hear a misquotation from the "Swan of Avon" without setting the unfortunate delinquent right. He was also something of a wag; never missed an opportunity of saying what he considered a good thing, and invariably laughed until he cried at anything that appeared to him mirth-moving or ridiculous.

"Well, girls!" said Uncle Tom, after the preparatory ceremony of kissing and how-d'ye-do-ing had been gone through—"how d'ye get on? Know your parts, eh?—Lucina, my dear, act ii., scene i— place, left—cue—'Unknown fate,'—What's next, eh?—Go on—'The Heavens—'"

"Oh, yes," said Miss Lucina, "I recollect—

> 'The heavens forbid
> But that our loves and comforts should increase
> Even as our days do grow!'"

"Make a pause here and there," said the old gentleman, who was a great critic. " 'But that our loves and comforts should increase'— emphasis on the last syllable, 'crease,'—loud 'even,'—one, two, three, four; then loud again, 'as our days do grow;' emphasis on *days*. That's the way, my dear; trust to your uncle for emphasis. Ah! Sem, my boy, how are you?"

"Very well, thankee, uncle," returned Mr. Sempronius, who had just appeared, looking something like a ringdove with a small circle round each eye: the result of his constant corking. "Of course we see you on Thursday."

"Of course, of course, my dear boy."

"What a pity it is your nephew didn't think of making you prompter, Mr. Balderstone!" whispered Mrs. Joseph Porter; "you would have been invaluable."

"Well, I flatter myself, I *should* have been tolerably up to the thing," responded Uncle Tom.

"I must bespeak sitting next you on the night," resumed Mrs. Porter; "and then, if our dear young friends here should be at all wrong, you will be able to enlighten me. I shall be so interested."

"I am sure I shall be most happy to give you any assistance in my power."

"Mind, it's a bargain."

"Certainly."

"I don't know how it is," said Mrs. Gattleton to her daughters, as they were sitting round the fire in the evening, looking over their parts, "but I really very much wish Mrs. Joseph Porter wasn't coming on Thursday. I am sure she's scheming something."

"She can't make *us* ridiculous, however," observed Mr. Sempronius Gattleton, haughtily.

The long-looked-for Thursday arrived in due course, and brought with it, as Mr. Gattleton, senior, philosophically observed, "no disappointments, to speak of." True, it was yet a matter of doubt whether *Cassio* would be enabled to get into the dress which had been sent for him from the masquerade warehouse. It was equally uncertain whether the principal female singer would be sufficiently recovered from the influenza to make her appearance; Mr. Harleigh, the *Masaniello* of the night, was hoarse, and rather unwell, in consequence of the great quantity of lemon and sugar-candy he had eaten to improve his voice; and two flutes and a violoncello had pleaded severe colds. What of that? the audience were all coming. Everybody knew his part; the dresses were covered with tinsel and spangles; the white plumes looked beautiful; Mr. Evans had practised falling until he was bruised from head to foot and quite perfect; *Iago* was sure that, in the stabbing-scene, he should make "a decided hit." A self-taught deaf gentleman, who had kindly offered to bring his flute, would be a most valuable addition to the orchestra; Miss Jenkins's talent for the piano was too well known to be doubted for an instant; Mr. Cape had practised the violin accompaniment with her frequently; and Mr. Brown, who had kindly undertaken, at a few hours' notice, to bring his violoncello, would, no doubt, manage extremely well.

Seven o'clock came, and so did the audience; all the rank and fashion of Clapham and its vicinity was fast filling the theatre. There were the Smiths, the Gubbinses, the Nixons, the Dixons, the Hicksons, people with all sorts of names, two aldermen, a sheriff in perspective, Sir Thomas Glumper (who had been knighted in the last reign for carrying up an address on somebody's escaping from nothing); and last, not least, there were Mrs. Joseph Porter and Uncle Tom, seated in the centre of the third row from the stage; Mrs. P. amusing Uncle Tom with all sorts of stories, and Uncle Tom amusing every one else by laughing most immoderately.

Ting, ting, ting! went the prompter's bell at eight o'clock precisely, and dash went the orchestra into the overture to "The Men of Prometheus." The pianoforte player hammered away with laudable perseverance; and the violoncello, which struck in at intervals, "sounded very well, considering." The unfortunate individual, however, who had undertaken to play the flute accompaniment "at sight," found, from fatal experience, the perfect truth of the old adage, "out of sight, out of mind;" for being very near-sighted, and being placed at a considerable distance from his music-book, all he had an opportunity of doing was to play a bar now and then in the wrong place, and put the other performers out. It is, however, but justice to Mr. Brown to say that he did this to admiration. The overture, in fact, was not unlike a race between the different instruments; the piano came in first by several bars, and the violoncello next, quite distancing the poor flute; for the deaf gentleman *too-too'd* away, quite unconscious that he was at all wrong, until apprised, by the applause of the audience, that the overture was concluded. A considerable bustle and shuffling of feet was then heard upon the stage, accompanied by whispers of "Here's a pretty go!—what's to be done?" &c. The audience applauded again, by way of raising the spirits of the performers; and then Mr. Sempronius desired the prompter, in a very audible voice, to "clear the stage, and ring up."

Ting, ting, ting! went the bell again. Everybody sat down; the curtain shook; rose sufficiently high to display several pair of yellow boots paddling about; and there remained.

Ting, ting, ting! went the bell again. The curtain was violently convulsed, but rose no higher; the audience tittered; Mrs. Porter looked at Uncle Tom; Uncle Tom looked at everybody, rubbing his hands, and laughing with perfect rapture. After as much ringing with the little bell as a muffin-boy would make in going down a tolerably long street, and a vast deal of whispering, hammering, and calling for nails and cord, the curtain at length rose, and discovered Mr. Sempronius Gattleton *solus,* and decked for *Othello.* After three distinct rounds of applause, during which Mr. Sempronius applied his right hand to his left breast, and bowed in the most approved manner, the manager advanced and said:

"Ladies and Gentlemen—I assure you it is with sincere regret, that I regret to be compelled to inform you, that *Iago* who was to have played Mr. Wilson—I beg your pardon, Ladies and Gentlemen, but I am naturally somewhat agitated (applause)—I mean, Mr. Wilson, who was to have played *Iago,* is—that is, has been—or, in other words, Ladies and Gentlemen, the fact is, that I have just received a note, in which I am informed that *Iago* is unavoidably detained at the Post Office this evening. Under these circumstances, I trust—a—a—amateur performance—a—another gentleman undertaken to read the part—request indulgence for a short time—courtesy and kindness of a British audience." Overwhelming applause. Exit Mr. Sempronius Gattleton, and curtain falls.

The audience were, of course, exceedingly good-humoured; the whole business was a joke; and accordingly they waited for an hour with the utmost patience, being enlivened by an interlude of rout-cakes and lemonade. It appeared by Mr. Sempronius's subsequent explanation, that the delay would not have been so great, had it not so happened that when the substitute *Iago* had finished dressing, and just as the play was on the point of commencing, the original *Iago* unexpectedly arrived. The former was therefore compelled to undress, and the latter to dress for his part; which, as he found some difficulty in getting into his clothes, occupied no inconsiderable time. At last, the tragedy began in real earnest. It went off well enough, until the third scene of the first act, in which *Othello* addresses the Senate: the only remarkable circumstance being, that as *Iago* could not get on any of the stage boots, in consequence of his feet being violently swelled with the heat and excitement, he was under the necessity of playing the part in a pair of Wellingtons, which contrasted rather oddly with his richly embroidered pantaloons. When *Othello* started with his address to the Senate (whose dignity was represented by the *Duke*, a carpenter, two men engaged on the recommendation of the gardener, and a boy), Mrs. Porter found the opportunity she so anxiously sought.

Mr. Sempronius proceeded:

> " 'Most potent, grave, and reverend signiors,
> My very noble and approv'd good masters,
> That I have ta'en away this old man's daughter,
> It is most true;—rude am I in my speech—' "

"Is that right?" whispered Mrs. Porter to Uncle Tom.

"No."

"Tell him so, then."

"I will. Sem!" called out Uncle Tom, "that's wrong, my boy."

"What's wrong, uncle?" demanded *Othello,* quite forgetting the dignity of his situation.

"You've left out something. 'True I have married—' "

"Oh, ah!" said Mr. Sempronius, endeavouring to hide his confusion as much and as ineffectually as the audience attempted to conceal their half-suppressed tittering, by coughing with extraordinary violence—

> ——" 'true I have married her;—
> The very head and front of my offending
> Hath this extent; no more.'

*(Aside)* "Why don't you prompt, father?"

"Because I've mislaid my spectacles," said poor Mr. Gattleton, almost dead with the heat and bustle.

"There, now it's 'rude am I,' " said Uncle Tom.

"Yes, I know it is," returned the unfortunate manager, proceeding with his part.

It would be useless and tiresome to quote the number of instances in which Uncle Tom, now completely in his element, and instigated by the mischievous Mrs. Porter, corrected the mistakes of the performers; suffice it to say that, having mounted his hobby, nothing could induce him to dismount; so, during the whole remainder of the play, he performed a kind of running accompaniment, by muttering everybody's part as it was being delivered, in an under-tone. The audience were highly amused, Mrs. Porter delighted, the performers embarrassed; Uncle Tom never was better pleased in all his life; and Uncle Tom's nephews and nieces had never, although the declared heirs to his large property, so heartily wished him gathered to his fathers as on that memorable occasion.

Several other minor causes, too, united to damp the ardour of the *dramatis personæ*. None of the performers could walk in their tights, or move their arms in their jackets; the pantaloons were too small, the boots too large, and the swords of all shapes and sizes. Mr. Evans, naturally too tall for the scenery, wore a black velvet hat with immense white plumes, the glory of which was lost in "the flies;" and the only other inconvenience of which was, that when it was off his head he could not put it on, and when it was on he could not take it off. Notwithstanding all his practice, too, he fell with his head and shoulders as neatly through one of the side scenes, as a harlequin would jump through a panel in a Christmas pantomime. The pianoforte player, overpowered by the extreme heat of the room, fainted away at the commencement of the entertainment, leaving the music of "Masaniello" to the flute and violoncello. The orchestra complained that Mr. Harleigh put them out, and Mr. Harleigh declared that the orchestra prevented his singing a note. The fishermen, who were hired for the occasion, revolted to the very life, positively refusing to play without an increased allowance of spirits; and, their demand being complied with, getting drunk in the eruption-scene as naturally as possible. The red fire, which was burnt at the conclusion of the second act, not only nearly suffocated the audience, but nearly set the house on fire into the bargain; and, as it was, the remainder of the piece was acted in a thick fog.

In short, the whole affair was, as Mrs. Joseph Porter triumphantly told everybody, "a complete failure." The audience went home at four o'clock in the morning, exhausted with laughter, suffering from severe headaches, and smelling terribly of brimstone and gunpowder. The Messrs. Gattleton, senior and junior, retired to rest, with the vague idea of emigrating to Swan River early in the ensuing week.

Rose Villa has once again resumed its wonted appearance; the dining-room furniture has been replaced; the tables are as nicely polished as formerly; the horsehair chairs are ranged against the wall, as regularly as ever; Venetian blinds have been fitted to every window in the house to intercept the prying gaze of Mrs. Joseph Porter. The subject of theatricals is never mentioned in the Gattleton family, unless, indeed, by Uncle Tom, who cannot refrain from sometimes expressing his surprise and regret at finding that his nephews and nieces appear to have lost the relish they once possessed for the beauties of Shakspeare, and quotations from the works of that immortal bard.


# Not Just Another Saint Paddy's Day

### Ben P. Indick


L ike all good Irishmen, last week I awoke on March 17th and donned my green finery for the parade down 5th Avenue. Green socks, green trousers, green striped shirt with green paisley tie. I do not have green shoes, but my Reeboks have a green stripe. It has been raining this year and I do not have a green raincoat, but I do have a clear green umbrella. I don't actually go to the parade; I sit in front of my television properly dressed and ready to celebrate and, if truth be told, drink my one glass of stout a year.

Of course I am not really Irish either, but many years ago when I was a timid teenager in high school, I loved vainly and from afar three girls who were Irish and whose names remain forever printed on my mind along with their indisputable and individual qualities. I could name them even now, half a century later, but I shall not. One, with her flashing eyes and bright smile of joy. Another, tall, elegant, aloof, with a squeaky voice which made her all the more painfully beautiful, and of the three the most wonderful simply to be near. The last, sullen, dark, already a sweatered definition of sensuality.

They are old ladies now, my Irish lassies, grandmothers, and their beauty is faded now with the flowers they wore at their graduation. But where their names are stored, their beauty is alive with

310

the memory of a teen-aged awestruck boy. Remembering them and my shyness, today I am Irish and I celebrate it by loving everything Irish. It is no hard chore to admire their literature and their superb stagecraft, poetry even beyond the charms of three girls, but only a worshipful memory affords keen anticipation and pleasure to this parade, foolish by any standard, and the ponderous preparations attendant upon it.

For one who is not born to the Green, special steps must be taken to insure a proper hue beyond that mere clothing may confer. I firmly believe the pigmentation of the skin may be, however temporarily, affected positively. Science has demonstrated that individual skin cells may *lose* pigmentation; my belief is that they may as readily accept new pigmentation. For this, dietary considerations are paramount, and for no less than a week before the Great Event, I assiduously include green vegetables in each meal. Breakfast: asparagus, lettuce (iceberg), green pepper bits in my omelet; lunch: again asparagus, lettuce (romaine), green peppers, peas, celery, cucumber, green squash, spinach, broccoli and green relish for my hamburger followed by a granny apple; dinner: all the foregoing plus Brussels sprouts and green mint jelly for my lamb, and dessert of key lime pie with green tea. At 8 p.m., a bit of creme de menthe, which I do repeat, as, after a few libations, everything within view appears green. A light buffet at midnight consists each night of asparagus with hollandaise sauce, several spears, preferably; one cannot have enough asparagus, I have found. A special snack at 3 a.m. of mint jelly on Irish soda crackers with green tea, and fresh lime quarters, a good accompaniment to the tea at all times. Preceding it, of course, asparagus spears. Without question, after a week's constant diet of asparagus, my complexion will have achieved an appropriate tinge.

Green as a dragon by now, eyes wide with expectant pleasure, I am ready now, and I will not be disappointed! They come! Brave young musicians in colorful band uniforms strut past with baton twirling high school girls, who are, no doubt (and only in the wisdom of my age dare I acknowledge such an irreverent truth) much like my stubborn memories, platoons of dour policemen, politicians whose plastic smiles cannot be dimmed even by rain, kilted bagpipers, helmeted veterans in booted uniforms and belts tight over ample stomachs, and, standing and nodding approvingly, top-hatted, black-suited, white-collared storks, proud Catholic clergy. A jingle by glum, God-haunted Blake twists sinuously through my mind, "Priests in black gowns are walking their rounds and binding with briars my joys and desires." It appears to me that times have really not changed, for a large contingent of young men and women, some more heavily brogued than the marchers, are being forcibly restrained somewhere downtown, shouting and waving placards. Despite this sad knowledge, I joyfully wave a little shamrock flag, wearing my raincoat in sympathetic protection for the brave marchers. I am one with my beloveds, miraculously restored, as am I! This glorious day shyness is gone, as we embrace in our fellowship in Eire, and I call their names, and they mine, one in tremulous squeakiness, but I shall not repeat their names here.

The bands twirl by, the pipers skirl, the Archbishop, an umbrella held above him, my own by proxy, smiles and blesses the participants. The hours pass by along with the marchers, and, finally, the Great Event is over. Now only TV reporters walk the vacant thoroughfare, summarizing and wrapping it up. Far downtown the protesting youths have long since been bundled away in police vans, booked at grimy precinct houses, admonished and released, to sit in subdued rebelliousness with pints of black Guinness, at last to smile and laugh, for, if they have lost a battle, they shout, they have not lost the war. There will be another Great Event another year.

I put my umbrella aside, and turn the TV off. It has been a great day, notwithstanding the inclemency of weather and the politics of controversy. My wife enters. "Okay, Mr. Shamus O'Houlihan, are you through with your parade yet?" she snorts derisively. I nod. "Okay," she continues, "then you can put away that umbrella and raincoat. It's not raining in here." I mumble, "Very funny," but I have to laugh and I put the umbrella in its box and the raincoat in the closet. There is another picture in that hidden recess of my mind, and it is of this woman, long ago; a girl, staring at me from a crowd with cool yet questioning eyes. Not long after that we stood beneath the canopy of a *chupah*, I stepped upon a glass, and held her and her eyes were glistening. She is that same girl today, even if the picture, from long ago, is of a younger person.

I can return to my normal diet now, and immediately my normal sallow complexion is restored. For another year I shall eat broccoli now and then, asparagus very rarely and squash never at all. I shall enjoy Irish literature and theatre for their own beauty, comedy and drama. The album in my mind is closed, but perhaps in an unguarded moment its cover may fall back, pages will slide past and I shall see again my Irish girls, ever young, never forgotten, not their eyes, their voices, certainly not their names, but those I shall not repeat here.

## Nothing but the Best

Brian McNaughton

"You're ugly, you're creepy, you're the filthiest man I ever knew!" Jessica Sexton cried.

"Yes." Ahab Wakefield's head was meekly bowed to hide the fury in his eyes. "But I'm rich."

"And that's the filthiest thing you ever said!"

She flung back his gifts. The emerald necklace bit his cheek. The tiger-skin coat she hurled shrouded him momentarily in the ghost of its original owner's clutch.

"No, please keep them," he said, "they're—"

"Impossible to explain to my husband."

He learned that her laugh could be splendidly scornful. He had possessed only her body, and she had so much more to offer—but it was hopeless.

"*Impossible to explain* . . . like so much else." Having admitted the futility of his love, he allowed his lips to relax into their most comfortable sneer. "How do you propose to explain why you left him? And what you've been doing all this while?"

"Bruce will forgive me. And even if he doesn't, I can go to any hospital for the criminally insane and find a hundred better men than you'll ever be. You don't know . . . *anything*. Did you really think you could impress me with this?" Her toe, perfect to its pallid lunula, nudged the coat with disdain.

"You deserve nothing but the best."

"Do you know how few of these magnificent creatures are left in the world? To kill one of them for a lousy coat—that disgusts me even more than you do."

Ahab sighed, admitting his miscalculation. The greatest burden of his long life, he often thought, was trying to keep up with current fads.

"But there is only one Jessica." The pain of that truth drove him to his knees.

"Very bad." She spoke with critical detachment. "Sometimes I think you learned how people behave from watching silent movies. What I ever could have seen in you, why I should have left the husband I love so much . . ." She paused, as if realizing that these questions had no sane answers. "This hogwash"—her gesture included ancient volumes on swaybacked shelves, dried herbs and fungi hanging from the ceiling-beams, the uniquely malformed skull on his desk—"it doesn't really *work,* does it?"

He rose deliberately to his commanding height and gazed down on her with less warmth than a corpse from a gibbet. "You will see."

Fright was another emotion Jessica had not shown him, and she expressed it fetchingly. As she fled, Ahab vowed to see more.

He had indulged this folly before, and with the same result. To win a love freely given, he had released Chastity Hopkins, of Portsmouth, N.H., from a similar enchantment in 1652. She had called him a pig-swyving pissabed and scurried off to lodge a complaint of witchcraft. Jessica Sexton had no such recourse. In some small ways, the world had changed for the better.

"When will I learn?"

Thester, the malapert creature that nested in the skull, croaked: "Nevermore."

Ignoring his familiar, Ahab took a knife from his desk and cut a strip of tiger-skin long enough to bind his cadaverous waist. He had no qualms about ruining the fabulously expensive coat. Cheating fools was his hobby, and he had paid the furrier with illusory cash. That he had not given Jessica an illusory coat proved the depth of his sincerity. It was fitting that the rejected love-token should be his instrument of vengeance.

"Master!" Thester's agitated claws rattled the skull. "Master, give her the pox, give her the flux, afflict her with some cagastrical distemper beyond the skill of the most learned surgeons—"

"Death by dismemberment and ingestion," Ahab said as he assembled further materials, "is beyond their skill."

"Remember what happened in Avignon in 1329?"

"Avignon? My memory . . ."

"That time you turned into a wolf to assassinate Pope John XXII. And the gamekeeper who sold you the wolfhide belt neglected to inform you that the animal had died after chewing off its trapped leg. Whereupon you learned—"

"Yes, yes, yes!" Ahab snapped, having remembered.

"—whereupon you learned that a three-legged wolf is no match for a pack of hounds. You had to spend the Renaissance in bed."

It was true that Ahab would assume the form of the particular beast whose pelt he used. He gave the strip of fur a covert inspection, but it told him nothing. He would have to translate himself to Malaysia to trace the provenance of the hide, and that might take hours. He dismissed Thester's quibbles.

"My dear abomination, a three-legged tiger—even one that's blind and toothless to boot—will be all that's needed for our loving young couple."

"And their dog?"

He winced. Shape-changing was a young man's game, and Ahab was no longer the sprightly bicentenarian who had disported himself as a crocodile among the wading courtlings of Nitokris. He had feared dogs ever since the Avignon fiasco, but he had forgotten the Sextons' pet, a Doberman pinscher who had in its last life commanded—with notably more audacity than brains—an SS panzer division. Unaware of this background, Jessica had christened it Muffin.

Climbing over the doomed couple's back fence, Ahab was thankful for Thester's reminder. Forewarned, he had rendered himself not just invisible, but inaudible and inodorous. Even so the dog sprang from its doze on the patio and paced the backyard, tunelessly growling the dimly recalled Curse-motif from Wagner's *Ring*. Ahab would never admit to Thester that he'd spared him an embarrassment, but he resolved to find the little horror an especially roly-poly child soon.

He stripped to the furry belt, opened a vein unseen, and made the appropriate symbols in blood on the flagstones of the patio. The dog sprinted and snarled at random shadows as Ahab crouched on all fours and spoke the required words.

Instantly the vigor of a healthy young beast surged through him. The formerly still night echoed with racketing bats and clamorous moths. The neutral smell of the yard was submerged under a canine stench so vivid and frightening that it hurt. It was the memory of Avignon that pained him, of course, potentiated by even the biggest cat's hatred for its old enemy.

As the other enchantments were canceled and Ahab stood revealed in all his fearful symmetry, the stupid dog charged. Ahab's sharper eyes, no doubt, made the puny creature seem like a black and tan locomotive bearing down on him, but he stood his ground and drew back his paw to blast Muffin's bones to gravel.

"What in hell was that?" Bruce Sexton gasped.

"Does it matter?" Jessica tried to draw him down again.

"I guess—" A second piteous cry froze him in the act of being drawn. He tumbled from bed and ran to switch on the patio lights.

"My God! Look—no, *don't* look, Jess. Muffin's got hold of something, a . . ."

"A what?"

Not believing his eyes, he forced them again toward the patio. "It must've been somebody's pet," he said. "But what kind of a nut would dye a rabbit with orange and black stripes?"

# Novelty and Romancement
## A Broken Spell

### Lewis Carroll

I had grave doubts at first whether to call this passage of my life "A Wail," or "A Pæan," so much does it contain that is great and glorious, so much that is somber and stern. Seeking for something which should be a sort of medium between the two, I decided, at last, on the above heading—wrongly, of course; I am always wrong: but let me be calm. It is a characteristic of the true orator never to yield to a burst of passion at the outset; the mildest of commonplaces are all he dare indulge in at first, and thence he mounts gradually;—*"vires acquirit eundo."* Suffice it, then, to say, in the first place, that *I am Leopold Edgar Stubbs.* I state this fact distinctly in commencing, to prevent all chance of the reader's confounding me either with the eminent shoemaker of that name, of Pottle-street, Camberwell, or with my less reputable, but more widely known, namesake, Stubbs, the light comedian, of the Provinces; both which connections I repel with horror and disdain: no offense, however, being intended to either of the individuals named—men whom I have never seen, whom I hope I never shall.

So much for commonplaces.

Tell me now, oh! man, wise in interpretation of dreams and omens, how it chanced that, on a Friday afternoon, turning suddenly out of Great Wattles-street, I should come into sudden and disagreeable collision with an humble individual of unprepossessing exterior, but with an eye that glowed with all the fire of genius? I had dreamed at night that the great idea of my life was to be fulfilled. What was the great idea of my life? I will tell you. With shame and sorrow I will tell you.

My thirst and passion from boyhood (predominating over the love of taws and running neck and neck with my appetite for toffy) has been for poetry—for poetry in its widest and wildest sense—for poetry untrammeled by the laws of sense, rhyme, or rhythm, soaring through the universe, and echoing the music of the spheres! From my youth, nay, from my very cradle, I have yearned for poetry, for beauty, for novelty, for romancement. When I say "yearned," I employ a word mildly expressive of what may be considered as an outline of my feelings in my calmer moments: it is about as capable of picturing the headlong impetuosity of my life-long enthusiasm as those unanatomical paintings which adorn the outside of the Adelphi, representing Flexmore in one of the many conceivable attitudes into which the human frame has never yet been reduced, are of conveying to the speculative pit-goer a true idea of the feats performed by that extraordinary compound of humanity and Indian-rubber.

I have wandered from the point: that is a peculiarity, if I may be permitted to say so, incidental to life; and, as I remarked on an occasion which time will not suffer me more fully to specify, "What, after all, *is* life?" nor did I find any one of the individuals present (we were a party of nine, including the waiter, and it was while the soup was being removed that the above-recorded observation was made) capable of furnishing me with a rational answer to the question.

The verses which I wrote at an early period of life were eminently distinguished by a perfect freedom from conventionalism, and were thus unsuited to the present exactions of literature: in a future age they will be read and admired, "when Milton," as my venerable uncle has frequently exclaimed, "when Milton and such like are forgot!" Had it not been for this sympathetic relative, I firmly believe that the poetry of my nature would never have come out; I can still recall the feelings which thrilled me when he offered me sixpence for a rhyme to "despotism." I never succeeded, it is true, in finding the rhyme, but it was on the very next Wednesday that I penned my well known "Sonnet on a Dead Kitten," and in the course of a fortnight had commenced three epics, the titles of which I have unfortunately now forgotten.

Seven volumes of poetry have I given to an ungrateful world during my life; they have all shared the fate of true genius—obscurity and contempt. Not that any fault could be found with their contents; whatever their deficiencies may have been, *no reviewer has yet dared to criticise them.* This is a great fact.

The only composition of mine which has yet made any noise in the world, was a sonnet I addressed to one of the Corporation of Muggleton-cum-Swillside, on the occasion of his being selected Mayor of that town. It was largely circulated through private hands, and much talked of at the time; and though the subject of it, with characteristic vulgarity of mind, failed to appreciate the delicate compliments it involved, and indeed spoke of it rather disrespectfully than otherwise, I am inclined to think that it possesses all the elements of greatness. The concluding couplet was added at the suggestion of a friend, who assured me it was necessary to complete the sense, and in this point I deferred to his maturer judgment:—

> "When Desolation snatched her tearful prey
> From the lorn empire of despairing day;
> When all the light, by gemless fancy thrown,
> Served but to animate the putrid stone;
> When monarchs, lessening on the wildered sight,
> Crumblingly vanished into utter night;
> When murder stalked with thirstier strides abroad,
> And redly flashed the never-sated sword;
> In such an hour thy greatness had been seen—
> That is, if such an hour had ever been—
> In such an hour thy praises shall be sung,
> If not by mine, by many a worthier tongue;

And thou be gazed upon by wondering men,
When such an hour arrives, but not till then!"

Alfred Tennyson is Poet Laureate, and it is not for me to dispute his claim to that eminent position; still I cannot help thinking, that if the Government had only come forward candidly at the time, and thrown the thing open to general competition, proposing some subject to test the powers of the candidate (say "Frampton's Pill of Health, an Acrostic"), a very different result might have been arrived at.

But let us return to our muttons (as our noble allies do most unromantically express themselves), and to the mechanic of Great Wattles-street. He was coming out of a small shop—rudely built it was, dilapidated exceedingly, and in its general appearance seedy—what did I see in all this to inspire a belief that a great epoch in my existence arrived? Reader, I saw the signboard!

Yes. Upon that rusty signboard, creaking awkwardly on its one hinge against the moldering wall, was an inscription which thrilled me from head to foot with unwonted excitement. "Simon Lubkin. Dealer in Romancement." Those were the very words.

It was Friday, the fourth of June, half-past four p.m.

Three times I read that inscription through, and then took out my pocketbook, and copied it on the spot; the mechanic regarding me during the whole proceeding with a stare of serious and (as I thought at the time) respectful astonishment.

I stopped that mechanic, and entered into conversation with him; years of agony since then have gradually branded that scene upon my writhing heart, and I can repeat all that passed, word for word.

Did the mechanic (this was my first question) possess a kindred soul, or did he not?

Mechanic didn't know as he did.

Was he aware (this with thrilling emphasis) of the meaning of that glorious inscription upon his signboard?

Bless you, mechanic knew all about that 'ere.

Would mechanic (overlooking the suddenness of the invitation) object to adjourn to the neighboring public-house, and there discuss the point more at leisure?

Mechanic would *not* object to a drain. On the contrary.

(Adjournment accordingly: brandy-and-water for two: conversation resumed.)

Did the article sell well, especially with the *"mobile vulgus"*?

Mechanic cast a look of good-natured pity on the questioner; the article sold well, he said, and the vulgars bought it most.

Why not add "Novelty" to the inscription? (This was a critical moment: I trembled as I asked the question.)

Not so bad an idea, mechanic thought: time was, it might have answered; but time flies, you see.

Was mechanic alone in his glory, or was there any one else who dealt as largely in the article?

Mechanic would pound it, there was none.

What was the article employed for? (I brought this question out with a gasp, excitement almost choking my utterance.)

It would piece a'most anything together, mechanic believed, and make it soldier nor stone.

This was a sentence difficult of interpretation. I thought it over a little, and then said, doubtfully, "you mean, I presume, that it serves to connect the broken threads of human destiny? to invest with a—with a sort of vital reality the chimerical products of a fertile imagination?"

Mechanic's answer was short, and anything but encouraging: "mought be—, I's no scollard, bless you."

At this point conversation certainly began to flag; I was seriously debating in my own mind whether this could really be the fulfillment of my life-cherished dream; so ill did the scene harmonise with my ideas of romance, and so painfully did I feel my companion's lack of sympathy in the enthusiasm of my nature—an enthusiasm which has found vent, ere now, in actions which the thoughtless crowd have too often attributed to mere eccentricity.

I have risen with the lark—"day's sweet harbinger"—(once, certainly, if not oftener), with the aid of a patent alarm, and have gone forth at that unseemly hour, much to the astonishment of the housemaid cleaning the door steps, to "brush with hasty steps the dewy lawn," and have witnessed the golden dawn with eyes yet half-closed in sleep. (I have always stated to my friends, in any allusion to the subject, that my raptures at that moment were such that I have never since ventured to expose myself to the influence of excitement so dangerous. In confidence, however, I admit that the reality did not come up to the idea I had formed of it over night, and by no means repaid the struggle of getting out of bed so early.)

I have wandered in the solemn woods at night, and bent me o'er the moss-grown fountain, to lave in its crystal stream my tangled locks and fevered brow. (What though I was laid up with a severe cold in consequence, and that my hair was out of curl for a week? Do paltry considerations such as these, I ask, affect the poetry of the incident?)

I have thrown open my small, but neatly furnished, cottage tenement, in the neighborhood of St. John's Wood, and invited an aged beggar in to "sit by my fire, and talk the night away." (It was immediately after reading Goldsmith's "Deserted Village." True it is that he told me nothing interesting, and that he took the hall-clock with him when he departed in the morning; still my uncle has always said that he wishes he had been there, and that it displayed in me a freshness and greenness of fancy (or "disposition," I forget which) such as he had never expected to see.)

I feel that it is incumbent on me to enter more fully into this latter topic—the personal history of my uncle: the world will one day learn to revere the talents of that wonderful man, though a want of funds prevents, at present, the publication of the great system of philosophy of which he is the inventor. Meanwhile, out of the mass of priceless manuscripts which he has bequeathed to an ungrateful nation, I will venture to select one striking specimen. And when the day arrives that my poetry is appreciated by the world at large (distant though it now appear!) then, I feel assured, shall his genius also receive its meed of fame!

Among the papers of that respected relative, I find what appears to have been a leaf torn from some philosophical work of the day: the following passage is scored. "Is this your rose? It is mine. It is yours. Are these your houses? They are mine. Give to me (of) the bread. She gave him a box on the ear." Against this occurs a marginal note in my uncle's handwriting: "some call this unconnected writing: I have my own opinion." This last was a favorite expression of his, veiling a profundity of ethical acumen on which it would be vain to speculate; indeed, so uniformly simple was the language of this great man, that no one besides myself ever suspected his possessing more than the ordinary share of human intellect.

May I, however, venture to express what I believe would have been my uncle's interpretation of this remarkable passage? It appears that the writer intended to distinguish the provinces of Poetry, Real Property, and Personal Property. The inquirer touches first on flowers, and with what a gush of generous feeling does the answer break upon him! "It is mine. It is yours." That is the beautiful, the true, the good; these are not hampered by petty consideration of "meum" and "tuum"; these are the common property of men. (It was with some such idea as this that I drew up the once celebrated bill, entitled "An Act for exempting Pheasants from the operation of the Game Laws, on the ground of Beauty"—a bill which would, doubtless, have passed both Houses in triumph, but that the member who had undertaken the care of it was unfortunately incarcerated in a Lunatic Asylum before it had reached the second reading.) Encouraged by the success of his first question, our inquirer passes on to "houses" ("Real Property," you will observe); he is here met by the stern, chilling answer, "They are mine"—none of the liberal sentiment which dictated the former reply, but in its place a dignified assertion of the rights of property.

Had this been a genuine Socratic dialogue, and not merely a modern imitation, the inquirer would have probably here interrupted with "To me indeed," or, "I, for my part," or, "But how otherwise?" or some other of those singular expressions, with which Plato makes his characters display at once their blind acquiescence in their instructor's opinions, and their utter inability to express themselves grammatically. But the writer takes another line of thought; the bold inquirer, undeterred by the coldness of the last reply, proceeds from questions to demands, "give me (of) the bread"; and here the conversation abruptly ceases, but the moral of the whole is pointed in the narrative: "she gave him a box on the ear." This is not the philosophy of one individual or nation, the sentiment is, if I may so say, European; and I am borne out in this theory by the fact that the book has evidently been printed in three parallel columns, English, French, and German.

Such a man was my uncle; and with such a man did I resolve to confront the suspected mechanic. I appointed the following morning for an interview, when I would personally inspect "the article" (I could not bring myself to utter the beloved word itself). I passed a restless and feverish night, crushed by a sense of the approaching crisis.

The hour came at last—the hour of misery and despair; it always does so, it cannot be put off forever; even on a visit to a dentist, as my childhood can attest with bitter experience, we are not forever getting there; the fatal door too surely dawns upon us, and our heart, which for the last half hour has been gradually sinking lower and lower, until we almost doubt its existence, vanishes suddenly downwards into depths hitherto undreamed of. And so, I repeat it, the hour came at last.

Standing before that base mechanic's door, with a throbbing and expectant heart, my eye chanced to fall once more upon that signboard, once more I perused its strange inscription. Oh! fatal change! Oh! horror! What do I see? Have I been deluded by a heated imagination? A hideous gap yawns between the N and the C, making it not one word but two!

And the dream was over.

At the corner of the street I turned to take a sad fond look at the specter of a phantom hope, I once had held so dear. "Adieu!" I whispered; this was all the last farewell I took, and I leant upon my walking stick and wiped away a tear. On the following day I entered into commercial relations with the firm of Dumpy and Spagg, wholesale dealers in the wine and spirit department.

The signboard yet creaks upon the moldering wall, but its sound shall make music in these ears nevermore—ah! nevermore.

# Oil of Dog

## Ambrose Bierce

My name is Boffer Bings. I was born of honest parents in one of the humbler walks of life, my father being a manufacturer of dog-oil and my mother having a small studio in the shadow of the village church, where she disposed of unwelcome babes. In my boyhood I was trained to habits of industry; I not only assisted my father in procuring dogs for his vats, but was frequently employed by my mother to carry away the debris of her work in the studio. In performance of this duty I sometimes had need of all my natural intelligence for all the law officers of the vicinity were opposed to my mother's business. They were not elected on an opposition ticket, and the matter had never been made a political issue; it just happened so. My father's business of making dog-oil was, naturally, less unpopular, though the owners of missing dogs sometimes regarded him with suspicion, which was reflected, to some extent, upon me. My father had, as silent partners, all the physicians of the town, who seldom wrote a prescription which did not contain what they were pleased to designate as *ol. can.* It is really the most valuable medicine ever discovered. But most persons are unwilling to make personal sacrifices for the afflicted, and it was evident that many of the fattest dogs in town had been forbidden to play with me—a fact which pained my young sensibilities, and at one time came near driving me to become a pirate.

Looking back upon those days, I cannot but regret, at times, that by indirectly bringing my beloved parents to their death I was the author of misfortunes profoundly affecting my future.

One evening while passing my father's oil factory with the body of a foundling from my mother's studio I saw a constable who seemed to be closely watching my movements. Young as I was, I had learned that a constable's acts, of whatever apparent character, are prompted by the most reprehensible motives, and I avoided him by dodging into the oilery by a side door which happened to stand ajar. I locked it at once and was alone with my dead. My father had retired for the night. The only light in the place came from the furnace, which glowed a deep, rich crimson under one of the vats, casting ruddy reflections on the walls. Within the cauldron the oil still rolled in indolent ebullition, occasionally pushing to the surface a piece of dog. Seating myself to wait for the constable to go away, I held the naked body of the foundling in my lap and tenderly stroked its short, silken hair. Ah, how beautiful it was! Even at that early age I was passionately fond of children, and as I looked upon this cherub I could almost find it in my heart to wish that the small, red wound upon its breast—the work of my dear mother—had not been mortal.

It had been my custom to throw the babes into the river which nature had thoughtfully provided for the purpose, but that night I did not dare to leave the oilery for fear of the constable. "After all," I said to myself, "it cannot greatly matter if I put it into this cauldron. My father will never know the bones from those of a puppy, and the few deaths which may result from administering another kind of oil for the incomparable *ol. can.* are not important in a population which increases so rapidly." In short, I took the first step in crime and brought myself untold sorrow by casting the babe into the cauldron.

The next day, somewhat to my surprise, my father, rubbing his hands with satisfaction, informed me and my mother that he had obtained the finest quality of oil that was ever seen; that the physicians to whom he had shown samples had so pronounced it. He added that he had no knowledge as to how the result was obtained; the dogs had been treated in all respects as usual, and were of an ordinary breed. I deemed it my duty to explain—which I did, though palsied would have been my tongue if I could have foreseen the consequences. Bewailing their previous ignorance of the advantages of combining their industries, my parents at once took measures to repair the error. My mother removed her studio to a wing of the factory building and my duties in connection with the business ceased; I was no longer required to dispose of the bodies of the small superfluous, and there was no need of alluring dogs to their doom, for my father discarded them altogether, though they still had an honorable place in the name of the oil. So suddenly thrown into idleness, I might naturally have been expected to become vicious and dissolute, but I did not. The holy influence of my dear mother was ever about me to protect me from the temptations which beset youth, and my father was a deacon in a church. Alas, that through my fault these estimable persons should have come to so bad an end!

Finding a double profit in her business, my mother now devoted herself to it with a new assiduity. She removed not only superfluous and unwelcome babes to order, but went out into the highways and byways, gathering in children of a larger growth, and even such adults as she could entice to the oilery. My father, too, enamored of the superior quality of oil produced, purveyed for his vats with diligence and zeal. The conversion of their neighbors into dog-oil became, in short, the one passion of their lives—an absorbing and overwhelming greed took possession of their souls and served them in place of a hope in Heaven—by which, also, they were inspired.

So enterprising had they now become that a public meeting was held and resolutions passed severely censuring them. It was intimated by the chairman that any further raids upon the population would be met in a spirit of hostility. My poor parents left the meeting broken-hearted, desperate and, I believe, not altogether sane. Anyhow, I deemed it prudent not to enter the oilery with them that night, but slept outside in a stable.

At about midnight some mysterious impulse caused me to rise and peer through a window into the furnace-room, where I knew my father now slept. The fires were burning as brightly as if the following days' harvest had been expected to be abundant. One of the large cauldrons was slowly "walloping" with a mysterious appearance of self-restraint, as if it bided its time to put forth its full energy. My father was not in bed; he had risen in his nightclothes and was preparing a noose in a strong cord. From the looks which he cast at the door of my mother's bedroom I knew too well the purpose that he had in mind. Speechless and motionless with terror, I could do nothing in prevention or warning. Suddenly the door of my mother's apartment was opened, noiselessly, and the two confronted each other, both apparently surprised. The lady, also, was in her nightclothes, and she held in her right hand the tool of her trade, a long, narrow-bladed dagger.

She, too, had been unable to deny herself the last profit which the unfriendly action of the citizens and my absence had left her. For one instant they looked into each other's blazing eyes and then sprang together with indescribable fury. Round and round the room they struggled, the man cursing, the woman shrieking, both fighting like demons—she to strike him with the dagger, he to strangle her with his great bare hands. I know not how long I had the unhappiness to observe this disagreeable instance of domestic infelicity, but at last, after a more than usually vigorous struggle, the combatants suddenly moved apart.

My father's breast and my mother's weapon showed evidences of contact. For another instant they glared at each other in the most unamiable way; then my poor, wounded father, feeling the hand of death upon him, leaped forward, unmindful of resistance, grasped my dear mother in his arms, dragged her to the side of the boiling cauldron, collected all his failing energies, and sprang in with her! In a moment, both had disappeared and were adding their oil to that of the committee of citizens who had called the day before with an invitation to the public meeting.

Convinced that these unhappy events closed to me every avenue to an honorable career in that town, I removed to the famous city of Otumwee, where these memoirs are written with a heart full of remorse for a heedless act entailing so dismal a commercial disaster.

# The Old, Old Story of How Five Men Went Fishing

## Stephen Leacock

This is a plain account of a fishing party. It is not a story. There is no plot. Nothing happens in it and nobody is hurt. The only point of this narrative is its peculiar truth. It not only tells what happened to us—the five people concerned in it—but what has happened and is happening to all the other fishing parties that at the season of the year, from Halifax to Idaho, go gliding out on the unruffled surface of our Canadian and American lakes in the still cool of early summer morning.

We decided to go in the early morning because there is a popular belief that the early morning is the right time for bass fishing. The bass is said to bite in the early morning. Perhaps it does. In fact the thing is almost capable of scientific proof. The bass does *not* bite between eight and twelve. It does *not* bite between twelve and six in the afternoon. Nor does it bite between six o'clock and midnight. All these things are known facts. The inference is that the bass bites furiously at about daybreak.

At any rate our party were unanimous about starting early. "Better make an early start," said the Colonel when the idea of the party was suggested. "Oh, yes," said George Popley, the Bank Manager, "we want to get right out on the shoal while the fish are biting."

When he said this all our eyes glistened. Everybody's do. There's a thrill in the words. To "get right out on the shoal at daybreak when the fish are biting," is an idea that goes to any man's brain.

If you listen to the men talking in a Pullman car, or a hotel corridor, or better still, at the little tables in a first-class bar, you will not listen long before you hear one say—"Well, we got out early, just after sunrise, right on the shoal." . . . And presently, even if you can't hear him you will see him reach out his two hands and hold them about two feet apart for the other men to admire. He is measuring the fish. No, not the fish they caught; this is the big one that they lost. But they had him right up to the top of the water: oh, yes, he was up to the top of the water all right. The number of huge fish that have been heaved up to the top of the water in our lakes is almost incredible. Or at least it used to be when we still had bar rooms and little tables for serving that vile stuff Scotch whisky and such foul things as gin rickeys and John Collinses. It makes one sick to think of it, doesn't it? But there was good fishing in the bars, all winter.

But, as I say, we decided to go early in the morning. Charlie Jones, the railroad man, said that he remembered how when he was a boy, up in Wisconsin, they used to get out at five in the morning—not get up at five but be on the shoal at five. It appears that there is a shoal somewhere in Wisconsin where the bass lie in thousands. Kernin, the lawyer, said that when he was a boy—this was on Lake Rosseau—they used to get out at four. It seems there is a shoal in Lake Rosseau where you can haul up the bass as fast as you can drop your line. The shoal is hard to find—very hard. Kernin can find it, but it is doubtful—so I gather—if any other living man can. The Wisconsin shoal, too, is very difficult to find. Once you find it, you are all right; but it's hard to find. Charlie Jones can find it. If you were in Wisconsin right now he'd take you straight to it, but probably no other person now alive could reach that shoal. In the same way Colonel Morse knows of a shoal in Lake Simcoe where he used to fish years and years ago and which, I understand, he can still find.

I have mentioned that Kernin is a lawyer, and Jones a railroad man and Popley a banker. But I needn't have. Any reader would take it for granted. In any fishing party there is always a lawyer. You can tell him at sight. He is the one of the party that has a landing net and a steel rod in sections with a wheel that is used to wind the fish to the top of the water.

And there is always a banker. You can tell him by his good clothes. Popley, in the bank, wears his banking suit. When he goes fishing he wears his fishing suit. It is much the better of the two, because his banking suit has ink marks on it, and his fishing suit has no fish marks on it.

As for the Railroad Man—quite so, the reader knows it as well as I do—you can tell him because he carries a pole that he cut in the bush himself, with a ten cent line wrapped round the end of it. Jones says he can catch as many fish with this kind of line as Kernin can with his patent rod and wheel. So he can, too. Just the same number.

But Kernin says that with his patent apparatus if you get a fish on you can *play* him. Jones says to Hades with *playing* him: give him a fish on his line and he'll haul him in all right. Kernin says he'd lose him. But Jones says *he* wouldn't. In fact he *guarantees* to haul the fish in. Kernin says that more than once (in Lake Rosseau) he has played a fish for over half an hour. I forget now why he stopped; I think the fish quit playing.

I have heard Kernin and Jones argue this question of their two rods, as to which rod can best pull in the fish, for half an hour. Others may have heard the same question debated. I know no way by which it could be settled.

Our arrangement to go fishing was made at the little golf club of our summer town on the verandah where we sit in the evening. Oh, it's just a little place, nothing pretentious: the links are not much good for *golf;* in fact we don't play much *golf* there, so far as golf goes, and of course, we don't serve meals at the club, it's not like that—and no, we've nothing to drink there because of prohibition. But we go and *sit* there. It's a good place to *sit,* and, after all, what else can you do in the present state of the law?

So it was there that we arranged the party.

The thing somehow seemed to fall into the mood of each of us. Jones said he had been hoping that some of the boys would get up a fishing party. It was apparently the one kind of pleasure that he really cared for. For myself I was delighted to get in with a crowd of regular fishermen like these four, especially as I hadn't been out fishing for nearly ten years: though fishing is a thing I am passionately fond of. I know no pleasure in life like the sensation of getting a four pound bass on the hook and hauling him up to the top of the water, to weigh him. But, as I say, I hadn't been out for ten years: oh, yes, I live right beside the water every summer, and yes, certainly—I am saying so—I am passionately fond of fishing, but still somehow I hadn't been *out.* Every fisherman knows just how that happens. The years have a way of slipping by. Yet I must say I was surprised to find that so keen a sport as Jones hadn't been out—so it presently appeared—for eight years. I had imagined he practically lived on the water. And Colonel Morse and Kernin—I was amazed to find—hadn't been out for twelve years, not since the day (so it came out in conversation) when they went out together in Lake Rosseau and Kernin landed a perfect monster, a regular corker, five pounds and a half, they said: or no, I don't think he *landed* him. No, I remember he didn't *land* him. He caught him—and he *could* have landed him—he should have landed him—but he *didn't* land him. That was it. Yes, I remember Kernin and Morse had a slight discussion about it—oh, perfectly amicable—as to whether Morse had fumbled with the net—or whether Kernin—the whole argument was perfectly friendly—had made an ass of himself by not "striking" soon enough. Of course the whole thing was so long ago that both of them could look back on it without any bitterness or ill nature. In fact it amused them. Kernin said it was the most laughable thing he ever saw in his life to see poor old Jack (that's Morse's name) shoving away with the landing net wrong side up. And Morse said he'd never forget seeing poor old Kernin yanking his line first this way and then that and not knowing where to try to haul it. It made him laugh to look back at it.

They might have gone on laughing for quite a time but Charlie Jones interrupted by saying that in his opinion a landing net is a piece of darned foolishness. Here Popley agrees with him. Kernin objects that if you don't use a net you'll lose your fish at the side of the boat. Jones says no: give him a hook well through the fish and a stout line in his hand and that fish has *got* to come in. Popley says so too. He says let him have his hook fast through the fish's head with a short stout line, and put him (Popley) at the other end of that line and that fish will come in. It's *got* to. Otherwise Popley will know why. That's the alternative. Either the fish must come in or Popley must know why. There's no escape from the logic of it.

But perhaps some of my readers have heard the thing discussed before.

So as I say we decided to go the next morning and to make an early start. All of the boys were at one about that. When I say "boys," I use the word, as it is used in fishing, to mean people from say forty-five to sixty-five. There is something about fishing that keeps men young. If a fellow gets out for a good morning's fishing, forgetting all business worries, once in a while—say once in ten years—it keeps him fresh.

We agree to go in a launch, a large launch—to be exact, the largest in the town. We could have gone in row boats, but a row boat is a poor thing to fish from. Kernin said that in a row boat it is impossible properly to *"play"* your fish. The side of the boat is so low that the fish is apt to leap over the side into the boat when half "played." Popley said that there is no *comfort* in a row boat. In a launch a man can reach out his feet, and take it easy. Charlie Jones said that in a launch a man could rest his back against something and Morse said that in a launch a man could rest his neck. Young inexperienced boys, in the small sense of the word, never think of these things. So they go out and after a few hours their necks get tired; whereas a group of expert fishers in a launch can rest their backs and necks and even fall asleep during the pauses when the fish stop biting.

Anyway all the "boys" agreed that the great advantage of a launch would be that we could get a *man* to take us. By that means the man could see to getting the worms, and the man would be sure to have spare lines, and the man would come along to our different places—we were all beside the water—and pick us up. In fact the more we thought about the advantage of having a "man" to take us the better we liked it. As a boy gets old he likes to have a man around to do the work.

Anyway Frank Rolls, the man we decided to get, not only has the biggest launch in town, but what is more, Frank *knows* the lake. We called him up at his boat house over the phone and said we'd give him five dollars to take us out first thing in the morning provided that he knew the shoal. He said he knew it.

I don't know, to be quite candid about it, who mentioned whisky first. In these days everybody has to be a little careful. I imagine we had all been *thinking* whisky for some time before anybody said it. But there is a sort of convention that when men go fishing they must have whisky. Each man makes the pretence that the one thing he needs at six o'clock in the morning is cold raw whisky. It is spoken of in terms of affection. One man says the first thing you need if you're going fishing is a good "snort" of whisky: another says that a good "snifter" is the very thing and the others agree, that no man can fish properly without a "horn," or a "bracer" or an "eye-opener." Each man really decides that he himself won't take any. But he feels that in a collective sense, the "boys" need it.

So it was with us. The Colonel said he'd bring along "a bottle of booze." Popley said, no, let *him* bring it; Kernin said let him; and Charlie Jones said no, he'd bring it. It turned out that the Colonel had some very good Scotch at his house that he'd like to bring: oddly enough Popley had some good Scotch in *his* house too; and, queer though it is, each of the boys had Scotch in his house. When the discussion closed we knew that each of the five of us was intending to bring a bottle of whisky. Each of the five of us expected the others to drink one and a quarter bottles in the course of the morning.

I suppose we must have talked on that verandah till long after one in the morning. It was probably nearer two than one when we broke up. But we agreed that that made no difference. Popley said that for him three hours' sleep, the right kind of sleep, was far more refreshing than ten. Kernin said that a lawyer learns to snatch his sleep when he can, and Jones said that in railroad work a man pretty well cuts out sleep.

So we had no alarms whatever about not being ready by five. Our plan was simplicity itself. Men like ourselves in responsible positions learn to organize things easily. In fact Popley says it is that faculty that has put us where we are. So the plan simply was that Frank Rolls should come along at five o'clock and blow his whistle in front of our places, and at that signal each man would come down to his wharf with his rod and kit and so we'd be off to the shoal without a moment's delay.

The weather we ruled out. It was decided that even if it rained that made no difference. Kernin said that fish bite better in the rain. And everybody agreed that a man with a couple of snorts in him need have no fear of a little rain water.

So we parted, all keen on the enterprise. Nor do I think even now that there was anything faulty or imperfect in that party as we planned it.

I heard Frank Rolls blowing his infernal whistle opposite my summer cottage at some ghastly hour in the morning. Even without getting out of bed, I could see from the window that it was no day for fishing. No, not raining exactly. I don't mean that, but one of those peculiar days—I don't mean *wind*—there was no wind, but a sort of feeling in the air that showed anybody who understands bass fishing that it was a perfectly rotten day for going out. The fish, I seemed to know it, wouldn't bite.

When I was still fretting over the annoyance of the disappointment I heard Frank Rolls blowing his whistle in front of the other cottages. I counted thirty whistles altogether. Then I fell into a light doze—not exactly sleep, but a sort of *doze*—I can find no other word for it. It was clear to me that the other "boys" had thrown the thing over. There was no use in my trying to go out alone. I stayed where I was, my doze lasting till ten o'clock.

When I walked up town later in the morning I couldn't help

being struck by the signs in the butchers' shops and the restaurants, FISH, FRESH FISH, FRESH LAKE FISH.

Where in blazes do they get those fish anyway?

# Our New Bedstead

### Frederick Swartout Cozzens

I have bought me a new patent bedstead, to facilitate early rising, called a "wake-up." It is a good thing to rise early in the country. Even in the winter time it is conducive to health to get out of a warm bed by lamplight; to shiver into your drawers and slippers; to wash your face in a basin of ice-flakes; and to comb out your frigid hair with an uncompromising comb, before a frosty looking-glass. The only difficulty about it lies in the impotence of human will. You will deliberate about it and argue the point. You will indulge in specious pretences, and lie still with only the tip end of your nose outside the blankets; you will pretend to yourself that you *do* intend to jump out in a few minutes; you will tamper with the good intention, and yet indulge in the delicious luxury. To all this the "wake-up" is inflexibly and triumphantly antagonistic. It is a bedstead with a clock scientifically inserted in the head-board. When you go to bed you wind up the clock, and point the index-hand to that hour on the dial at which you wish to rise in the morning. Then you place yourself in the hands of the invention and shut your eyes.

You are now, as it were, under the guardianship of King Solomon and Doctor Benjamin Franklin. There is no need to recall those beautiful lines of the poet's—

> "Early to bed and early to rise,
> Will make a man healthy, wealthy, and wise."

Science has forestalled them. The "wake-up" is a combination of hard wood, hinges, springs, and clock-work, against sleeping late o' mornings. It is a bedstead with all the beautiful vitality of a flower—it opens with the dawn. If, for instance, you set the hand against six o'clock in the morning, at six the clock at the bed's head solemnly strikes a demi-twelve on its sonorous bell. If you pay no attention to the monitor, or idly, dreamily endeavour to compass the coherent sequence of sounds, the invention, within the succeeding two minutes, drops its tail-board and lets down your feet upon the floor. While you are pleasantly defeating this attempt upon your privacy by drawing up your legs within the precincts of the blankets, the virtuous head-board and the rest of the bed suddenly rise up in protest; and the next moment, if you do not instantly abdicate, you are launched upon the floor by a blind elbow that connects with the crank of an eccentric, that is turned by a cord that is wound around a drum, that is moved by an endless screw, that revolves within the body of the machinery. So soon as you are turned out, of course, you waive the balance of the nap and proceed to dress.

"Mrs. Sparrowgrass," said I, contemplatively, after the grimy machinists had departed, "this machine is one of the most remarkable evidences of progress the ingenuity of man has yet developed. In this bedstead we see a host of cardinal virtues made practical by science. To rise early one must possess courage, prudence, self-denial, temperance, and fortitude. The cultivation of these virtues, necessarily attended with a great deal of trouble, may now be dispensed with, as this engine can entirely set aside, and render useless, a vast amount of moral discipline. I have no doubt in a short time we shall see the finest attributes of the human mind superseded by machinery. Nay, more; I have very little doubt that, as a preparatory step in this great progress, we shall have physical monitors of cast-iron and wheel-work to regulate the ordinary routine of duty in every family."

Mrs. Sparrowgrass said she did not precisely understand what I meant.

"For instance," said I, in continuation, "we dine every day; as a general thing, I mean. Now sometimes we eat too much, and how easy, how practicable it would be to regulate our appetites by a banquet-dial. The subject, having had the superficial area of his skull and the cubic capacity of his body worked out respectively by a licensed craniologist and by a licensed corporalogist, gets from each a certificate, which certificates are duly registered in the county clerk's office. From the county clerk he receives a permit, marked, we will say, ten."

"Not ten pounds, I hope," said Mrs. S.

"No, my dear," I replied, "ten would be the average of his capacity. We will now suppose the chair, in which the subject is seated at dinner, rests upon a pendulous platform, over a delicate arrangement of levers, connected with an upright rod, that runs through the section of table in front of his plate, and this rod, we will suppose, is toothed into a ratchet-wheel, that moves the index of the banquet-dial. You will see at once that, as he hangs balanced in this scale, any absorption of food would be instantly indicated by the index. All then he is called upon to do is to watch the dial until the hand points to 'ten,' and then stop eating."

"But," said Mrs. Sparrowgrass, "suppose he shouldn't be half through?"

"Oh!" said I, "that would not make any difference. When the dial says he has had enough, he must quit."

"But," said Mrs. Sparrowgrass, "suppose he *would not* stop eating?"

"Then," said I, "the proper way to do would be to inform against him, and have him brought immediately before a justice of the peace, and if he did not at once swear that he had eaten within his limits, fine him, and seize all the victuals on his premises."

"Oh!" said Mrs. S., "you would have a law to regulate it, then?"

"Of course," said I, "a statute—a statutory provision, or provisionary act. Then, the principle once being established, you see how easily and beautifully we could be regulated by the simplest motive powers. All the obligations we now owe to society and to ourselves could be dispensed with, or rather transferred to, or vested in, some superior machine, to which we would be accountable by night and day. Nay, more than that, instead of sending representatives to legislate for us, how easy it would be to construct a legislature of bronze and wheel-work—an incorruptible legislature. I would suggest a hydraulic or pneumatic congress as being less liable to explode, and more easily graduated than one propelled by steam simply. All that would be required of us then would be to elect a state engineer annually, and he, with the assistance of a few underlings, could manage the automata as he pleased."

"I do not see," replied Mrs. Sparrowgrass, "how that would be an improvement upon the present method, from all I hear."

This unexpected remark of Mrs. S. surprised me into silence for a moment, but immediately recovering, I answered, that a hydraulic or pneumatic legislature would at least have this advantage—it would construct enactments for the State at, at least, one-fiftieth part of the present expense, and at the same time do the work better and quicker.

"Now, my dear," said I, as I wound up the ponderous machinery with a huge key, "as you are always an early riser, and as, of course, you will be up before seven o'clock, I will set the indicator at that hour, so that you will not be disturbed by the progress of science. It is getting to be very cold, my dear, but how beautiful the stars are to-night. Look at Orion and the Pleiades! Intensely lustrous in the frosty sky."

The sensations one experiences in lying down upon a complication of mechanical forces are somewhat peculiar if they are not entirely novel. I once had the pleasure, for one week, of sleeping over the boiler of a high-pressure Mississippi steamboat; and, as I knew in case of a blow up I should be the first to hear of it, I composed my mind as well as I could under the circumstances. But this reposing upon a bed of statics and dynamics, with the constant chirping and crawling of wheel-work at the bed's head, with a thought now and then of the inexorable iron elbow below, and an uncertainty as to whether the clock itself might not be too fast, or too slow, caused me to be rather reflective and watchful than composed and drowsy.

Nevertheless, I enjoyed the lucent stars in their blue depths, and the midnight moon, now tipping the Palisades with a fringe of silver fire, and was thinking how many centuries that lovely light had played upon those rugged ridges of trap and basalt, and so finally sinking from the reflective to the imaginative, and from the imaginative to the indistinct, at last reached that happy state of half consciousness, between half asleep and asleep, when the clock in the machine woke up, and suddenly struck eight. Of course I knew it was later, but I could not imagine why it should at all, as I presumed the only time of striking was in the morning by way of signal. As Mrs. S. was sound asleep, I concluded not to say anything to her about it; but I could not help thinking what an annoyance it would be if the clock should keep on striking the hours during the night. In a little while the bedclothes seemed to droop at the foot of the bed, to which I did not pay much attention, as I was just then engaged listening to the drum below, that seemed to be steadily engaged in winding up its rope and preparing for action. Then I felt the upper part of the patent bedstead rising up, and then I concluded to jump out, just as the iron elbow began to utter a cry like unto the cry of a steel Katydid, and did jump, but was accidentally preceded by the mattress, one bolster, two pillows, ditto blankets, a brace of threadbare linen sheets, one coverlid, the baby, one cradle (overturned), and Mrs. Sparrowgrass. To gather up these heterogeneous materials of comfort required some little time, and, in the meanwhile, the bedstead subsided. When we retired again, and were once more safely protected from the nipping cold, although pretty well cooled, I could not help speaking of the perfect operation of the bedstead in high terms of praise, although, by some accident, it had fulfilled its object a little earlier than had been desirable. As I am very fond of dilating upon a pleasant theme, the conversation was prolonged until Mrs. Sparrowgrass got sleepy, and the clock struck nine. Then we had to turn out again. We had to turn out every hour during the long watches of the night for that wonderful epitome of the age of progress.

When the morning came we were sleepy enough, and the next evening we concluded to replace the "wake-up" with a common, old-fashioned bedstead. To be sure I had made a small mistake the first night, in not setting the *"indicator"* as well as the *index* of the dial. But what of that? Who wants his rest, that precious boon, subjected to contingencies? When we go to sleep, and say our prayers, let us wake up according to our natures, and according to our virtues; some require more sleep, some less; we are not mere bits of mechanism after all; who knows what world we may chance to wake up in? For my part, I have determined not to be a humming-top, to be wound up and to run down, just like that very interesting toy one of the young Sparrowgrassii has just now left upon my table, minus a string.

# Papa's Planet

William F. Nolan

Of the late Harrington Hunter Hollister, it must be said that he was very rich, that he had sired a beautiful man-chasing redhead, and that he was a Hemingway fanatic. When he died in 2068,

I ended up with his money, his newly divorced daughter, and his Hemingway collection.

"As my latest and absolutely *last* husband, I want you to have everything," Cecile Hollister told me, wrinkling her attractively freckled nose. "Daddy adored you."

"I adored daddy," I said, trying for sincerity.

She handed me a rolled parchment.

"What's this?" I asked.

"A deed to Papa's Planet. I've never been there, but daddy told me all about it. That's where we're spending our honeymoon."

"We are?"

"You want to see your property, don't you?"

"I guess so."

"We'll leave tomorrow."

Cecile had a way with men.

We left tomorrow.

Five million miles out from Mars, we turned sharp left and there it was: Papa's Planet—a big gray ball of matter floating below us.

"What the devil's *down* there?" I asked.

"You'll find out. Strap in. Here we go."

We made a fine soft-point landing (Cecile could handle a Spacer like a pro) and, when the rocket smoke cleared, I saw a big, wide-chested fellow in khaki hunting clothes approaching us. He was bearded, grizzled, with suspicious eyes. And he carried an elephant gun.

"You critics?" he demanded.

"Nope," said Cecile. "I'm the daughter of Harrington Hollister and this is my new husband, Philip."

"OK, then," said the bearded man, pivoting. "I'm hunting critics. See any, give me a yell."

"Will do," said Cecile. And to me: "C'mon, Pamplona should be right on the other side of the mountain. We can catch the running of the bulls."

"Who was the aggressive bearded guy?"

"Papa, of course. It's his planet."

Running along next to me, just in front of the bulls, a strong-looking guy thumped my shoulder and yelled, "This is swell, isn't it!"

"Yeah, swell!" I yelled back, sprinting to catch Cecile. "Who's the guy back there, yelling?"

"Papa," she told me. "Only he's a lot younger, naturally. This is 1923. Hey, let's cut through this side street. I want to see Paris."

Paris was right next to Pamplona, and Cecile looked radiant walking down the Rue de la Paix. "I'd like to meet Gertrude Stein," she said. "Maybe we can have lunch with her."

A big guy with a mustache pounded past us in a half crouch, feinting at the air with left and right jabs. He was dark-haired, tough-looking. "Hi, daughter," he said to Cecile.

"Hi, Ernie," she called back.

He padded away.

"Wait a damn minute," I said. "Who was *that*?"

She sighed. "Papa, naturally. Only nobody calls him Papa in Paris. Too early. Wrong period."

"Just how many Papas *are* there?"

Cecile stopped and wrinkled her nose. "Well, let's see . . . at least twenty that I know of, and I'm no expert. That was daddy's department."

"And they're *all* here?"

"Sure." She pointed. "Just beyond Paris, across the Seine, is Oak Park, Illinois—which is next to Walloon Lake, Michigan. That's two Papas right there, one for each place. Both are *boy* Papas, of course. One goes to Oak Park High and the other goes trout fishing on the lake."

I nodded. "We've got one here—and another in Pamplona. And there's the one we met near the rocket."

"That was the African one," she said. "Then there's the one in New York with the hairy chest who keeps standing Max Eastman on his head in the corner of Scribner's. And the Papa in the hills of Spain covering the civil war and the one skiing in Switzerland with Hadley and the one on the Gulf Stream in the *Pilar*—daddy dug out a lovely Gulf Stream and I can't wait to see it—and there's the one getting shot in the kneecaps somewhere in Italy."

"Fossalta di Piave," I supplied.

"That's the place," she said, pushing back a strand of delicious red hair. "And there's the Papa in Key West and the one in Venice and the one boxing in the gym in Kansas City. How many is that?"

"I've lost count," I said.

"Anyway, there are *lots* more," said Cecile. "Daddy had his whole factory in Des Moines working overtime for six months, including weekends, just to supply all the Papas."

"Probably one camped out by the Big Two-Hearted River."

"Sure. And another in Toronto, working for the *Star*."

I raised an eyebrow. "Must have cost your daddy plenty."

"It was a tax write-off," she said. "Nonprofit. Besides, he had this big empty planet just going to *waste* up here."

"But—building Paris in the twenties and the streets of Pamplona and the bull rings of Spain and all of Africa—"

"He didn't build *all* of Africa," Cecile corrected me. "Just the important part around Kilimanjaro, where we landed."

"Don't the Papas get mixed up, bump into each other?"

"Never. Each Papa has his assigned place and that's where he stays, doing what he was built for. The Pamplona Papa just keeps running with the bulls, and the African Papa keeps hunting critics."

"Your father sure didn't stint."

"When daddy did a thing, he did it *right*," she agreed. "Now, let's go have lunch with Miss Stein and then visit Venice. Daddy said they did a marvelous job with St. Mark's Square."


Papa was drinking alone at a table near the Grand Canal when our gondola passed by, and he waved us over.

"You smell good, daughter," Papa told Cecile. "You smell the way good leather you find in the little no-nonsense shops in Madrid when you know enough not to get suckered into the big shops that charge too much smells."

"Thanks, Papa," said Cecile, giving him a bright smile.

"I always enjoy the Gritti here in Venice," said Papa, "and ordering a strong lobster who had much heart and who died properly, and having him served to you by a waiter you can trust with a good bottle of Capri near you so you can see the little green ice bubbles form on the cold glass."

He poured us wine. We all saluted one another and drank. The sun went down and the wine made me sleepy.

When I awoke, Cecile was gone.

I said good-bye to Papa and went out to look for her.


She wasn't at Key West, or on the Gulf, or anywhere in Spain, or in Billings, Montana (where Papa was recovering from his auto accident). I finally found her in Paris. On the Left Bank.

"I've fallen in love," she declared. "You can go on back to Earth and forget me."

I shrugged. Cecile was hardly steadfast; as her fourth husband, I realized that. "Who is he?"

"I call him Ougly-poo. That's my special love name for him. He just adores it."

"He isn't human, is he?"

"Of course not!" She looked annoyed. "We're the only *people* on Papa's Planet. But what difference does that make?"

"No difference, I guess."

"He's divine." She smiled dreamily, wrinkling her freckles. "Kind of a classic profile, soft, sensitive lips, exciting eyes . . . He gave me this autographed picture. See?"

I looked at it. "You're sure?"

"I'm sure," she said.

"OK, then," I said. " 'Bye, Cecile."

" 'Bye, Philip." She threw me a kiss.

I walked back to the rocket through a sad, softly falling Hemingway rain. I didn't blame Cecile. The fellow was handsome, witty, brilliant, famous. All the things I wasn't. Girls weren't inspired to call me Ougly-poo.

But then, I wasn't F. Scott Fitzgerald.

# Paranoid Fantasy #1

## Lawrence Watt-Evans

*"Better they should get you, and have it all over with."*

The alarm went off and Nathan woke up.

He glanced out through the bulletproof glass of the window by his bed; seeing no obvious danger, he unstrapped himself, sat up, and turned off the burglar alarm, muttering the charm, "Rabbit, rabbit," as he did so. He took the silver cross from around his neck and dressed for the day, starting with chainmail undershirt and lead-lined jockey shorts.

After replacing the garlic at each window he burned a cone of incense, with the appropriate prayers, to placate the gods. Carefully, his hands protected by rubber gloves, he took his defanged white mouse, Theodosius, from its massive cage, then headed down to the corner restaurant for breakfast, being certain to lock the door behind him, both the three regular locks and the special one the police couldn't open. Always watching for the things that come through the walls, he ate heartily, after feeding a little of everything to Theodosius to check for poison.

Shortly thereafter, Nathan, briefcase in hand, was off to his downtown office. As if from nowhere, his obnoxious neighbor Eddie appeared before him. Nathan had been too busy not stepping on the cracks in the sidewalk to see him coming.

Eddie cried out, "Hi, Nathan! How's business?"

Nathan made a sign to ward off the evil eye, glanced about for other menaces, then muttered something about being late.

"Aw, hell, Nathan, so you'll be a few minutes late! I missed the entire day, yesterday, and nothing's happened to me! You worry too much, you know that? Why are you always . . . hey! What's that? Hey! Help!" This last was said as several large trolls and assorted gargoyles suddenly leaped out of the nearby shrubbery. With nasty giggles and remarks about foolhardiness, they grabbed Eddie, trussed him up tightly, and carried him off.

Nathan watched them go, then continued on his way to the bus stop, unconcerned. *He* was safe from *that* bunch. It was the Others that worried him, and *they* only come out at night.

# Patrons

## Jessica Amanda Salmonson

*for William F. Nolan*

I'm tellin' ya a confidence, understand, so don't let me hear ya breathin' 'bout it to nobody. Okay? Okay. Like I was sayin', this freak walks in just before closin', bar was empty, and he plops down in that very stool you're sittin' in. Didn't act the least bit self-conscious 'bout the way he looked.

Well I ain't no racialist or segregationalist or nothin' like that. And I'm even less inclined to hold a fella's birth defects or accident scars against him. A guy can't help what he is or how he looks, right? Maybe if there'd been customers and someone complained about him, I'd of thrown him out. But I don't give nobody trouble if I don't have to. So I asks him what he wants.

He says he don't know what I got.

I says I got anything regular and at pretty fair prices.

So he orders a chankachooka or some fool thing twice as unheard of. I figure he's being funny so I says coming up. I pour him a Vodka and he takes a sip, looks kind of cockeyed, and takes another sip. "What's this stuff?" he wants to know. So I tell him.

Vodka, eh, he repeats. Yep I says. I thought he didn't like it but he asks for a whole damn bottle, says it's good stuff. Well I get to thinkin' an ugly freak like this maybe he ain't got a job. Maybe he can't pay for a whole bottle. So I tell him it's cheaper if he waits till tomorrow and goes to a liquor store, I charge pretty high for a full bottle consider'n, and I got nothin' smaller than a quart. Any excuse to keep from saying I figures he's a bum with no dough.

Well he had the money all right only it wasn't money. He sets on the bar a chunk of solid gold about a quarter-inch square. Just so happens my old daddy used to be a jeweler until he went bust and fixed watches till he died. I knew it was gold without even scratchin' it. I stare at it awhile, can't think what to say. Finally I says it's illegal to own gold, gotta have a permit or something.

He acts a little surprised and puts it back in his pocket, says most places take gold 'cause it doesn't corrode. He says other places gold's so common they don't want it, though, so he always carries a few of these. He scatters some diamonds on the bar.

Like I said, my old daddy was a jeweler. Maybe I wouldn't know a real diamond from a synthetic, but I knew those rocks weren't glass and even a synthetic is worth a bottle of vodka.

He unscrews the cap and holds the bottle up to the hole in his deformed face and chugs the whole damn bottle without once coming up for air. I once heard of a man dropping dead from doing that. But this freak just looks at me sober as hell and says, "I like the service here. I'm sendin' all my friends to this place."

I says thanks I can use the business. Then I go back to cleaning the rest of the glasses and gettin' ready to close up. He's tellin' me while my back is turned, "I got in a jam on (I think he said) Broscow." (Maybe he said 'in Moscow,' he sounded foreign enough to be from anywhere. Funny he didn't know what Vodka was, though.) "Barely got out of there in my skin. Lost my vocabulary tapes and had to prime myself with your language the old way. I lost my League Planets Dictionary, too, and with my radio on the blink I can't raise the League Local to have them run me through a duplicate. Mind tellin' me where the League Local is located?"

Well I can't make hide nor hair of what he's talkin' about and figure he's puttin' me on again. A bartender gets put on a lot and the only thing to do is ride along with the joke. So I asks, "What league?"

"The only League there is, of course!" He keeps lookin' at me like I'm the freak and he's normal as lamp posts. For a while we stare each other down, me waitin' for the punch line of his joke. He gets to lookin' scared and worried, like he just realized he left the beans on and his whole house might be burning down. Then he just turns around to walk away.

I call to him and say hey you forgot your diamonds. He hesitates a moment then walks back and says, "Keep 'em," generous as all hell, just I shouldn't tell nobody I seen him.

Now a lot of things went through my head right then. I realized he must've stole them diamonds and that gold. I didn't need no hot rocks. But I didn't want to get the poor guy in trouble either. If I had a kisser like his, I'd be breakin' jewelry store windows, too, may my daddy forgive me for sayin' so. So I says I'd keep my mouth shut 'bout him bein' here, but I didn't want to take advantage of nobody and he could keep his rocks. I says if you really want to do me a favor, just do like you promised and send your friends around.

I added that last bit as a piece of psychology, you understand. I figure if I act friendly he won't knock me over the head. He seemed nice enough but if a guy will knock over a jewelry store, why not a bar gettin' ready to close? I didn't think no ugly freak like him had no friends anyhow.

Well that's how it started. He kept his promise and ever since that night they been comin' in, always around closin' time on slack nights when I got no other customers. They order Vodka and they pay with synthetic diamonds; I got a slug of 'em now. Took 'em to a friend of my old daddy's. He says they're valuable enough, best man-made rocks he ever seen, and he doesn't think they're hot. But I ain't takin' no chance cashin' 'em in. Anyway, they drink down their Vodka like it was lemonade and leave before anyone can see them.

Best damn customers I ever had.

But God damn they're ugly.


# The Perfumed Garden

## David H. Keller

Abraham Solomon Jones was still attending the same church to which, as an infant, he had been taken for his baptism. For over twenty years he had regularly helped take up the morning offering. He had been told in no uncertain words that ten years more of such faithful service might result in his being elected an elder. For almost an equal number of years his wife had been in charge of the infant Sunday School class. These facts are given to establish the select social standing of Jones and his wife.

Regularly every week day morning Jones went down the tube and up the tube at night. In the meantime he faithfully sold hot breads and buns in one of the largest downtown groceries. At odd times in the past he had asked for promotion to the canned goods or cereal department, but, these attempts meeting with failure, he had tried to become reconciled to the prospect of selling hot breads and buns during the rest of his life.

To this fate he might have yielded unmurmuring till death did him part from the buns and breads had it not been for an unusual customer who one day bought a dozen hot-cross buns and paused for a few minutes to chatter cheerfully about the antiquity of breads and their symbolism.

"You have a most important position here," he declared.

"Yes?" queried A. S. Jones with a wry smile.

"Indeed, yes! The manufacture and sale of food made of flours has played an important part in the religious life of many nations. For example, take the doughnut, at times called the cruller or fried cake. There is a beautiful illustration of what I mean. Suppose you were living in Rome—"

"Do you mean Rome, New York?"

"No, indeed. Rome, Italy, at the time she was the proud mistress of the world. Imagine yourself a Roman citizen. You worship the Gods popular in the days of Nero. Do you go to a church or a temple? Not at once. First you go to a bakery. There you see various young ladies with baskets of doughnuts, buns, and breads baked in various shapes, and each shape has an especial meaning. You pick out a lady who looks good to you and buy from her a doughnut and a small loaf of bread shaped like a sausage, paying her liberally for them. Then you go into the temple together and worship the Gods and eat the lunch."

"Well, well!" exclaimed Jones. "That was the way they did it in Rome, was it?"

"Yes. You see the antiquity of the ceremony. If you were in Assyria or India you would do the same but with slight variations."

"I don't believe I would. You see I'm a married man and I'm certain my wife wouldn't approve of my buying doughnuts and buns that way and eating them in church."

The man laughed. "I don't believe you know what I'm talking about."

"I'm sure I don't," replied Jones.

But the conversation gave him something to think about. If he was going to spend the rest of his working life in the hot bread and bun department, it would be worth while finding out what the man really meant. He had used the word *symbolism*. Jones looked it up in his pocket dictionary but that did not tell him much. He asked questions in a guarded manner, of various customers without re-

346

sults until one day an old man referred him to the Metropolitan Museum.

Timidly he asked his wife to go there with him some Sunday afternoon and when she found out that many of the pictures were of a religious nature she consented. They joined the throng of bus riders and, in the course of time, arrived at the museum. Jones hired a guide to show his wife all the Biblical art and asked her to excuse him while he looked up some matters regarding the sale of cakes. She thought it odd but felt that she was fortunate to be the wife of a man so interested in his work. With such effort to advance in salesmanship she was sure the day would come when he would be transferred to the canned goods department.

Jones was passed from one man to another until at last he found one who was able to answer his questions. This man, interested in a hot bread and bun salesman who was anxious to know the symbolisms of these foods, spent over two hours talking to Jones and showing him pictures and little clay models of breads and buns, all of which developed a dual meaning under his clever explanations. When Jones finally rejoined his wife he was convinced that he would be arrested a dozen times a day if the police knew what he knew about the reason for the various foodstuffs he sold.

In a way it changed Jones' concept of life. He was never the same afterward. A five cent piece in the collection plate meant more than a twentieth of a dollar towards the church expenses. It meant the price of a bun which might be eaten with a beautiful feminine bun-seller in Rome, in the reign of Nero, in the dark alcoves of one of the smaller temples. He tried to imagine what would happen if he had lived in those days and spent as much as a dollar buying symbolic foods from a lovely lady. From then on he never sold a dozen doughnuts or long hard rolls or ten cents worth of hot-cross buns without wondering whether or not the customer was happier for his or her ignorance of what such shaped foods really meant.

Having started the study of symbols Jones now frequented the public libraries of the city whenever fate gave him the opportunity. His wife, though thrilled that her husband was becoming a student, was not at all pleased with the labored explanations he gave and even went so far as to tell him bluntly that he would be better off preparing his Sunday School lesson in his spare time than spending so much thought on dead heathens.

At last his studies brought him to Burton, that wonderful Englishman who spent a lifetime trying to become an Oriental. As a personality, Burton intrigued Abraham Solomon Jones. He wondered at his bravery in leaving his wife for so many months at a time, and realized that it would be hopeless for him, A. S. Jones, to attempt anything like that. Why, he couldn't spend an evening at Coney Island by himself, let alone years with the ladies of Arabia! It is evident that at this period of his life he was unconsciously dissatisfied with his wife's angularities and longed for contact with softer curves.

He read as much of Burton's writings as he could obtain. At last he learned there was a book called *The Perfumed Garden*. He casually mentioned the title to his wife one evening as she sat busily mending his stockings. She remarked that she thought all gardens had a perfume and asked if it was a book of poems.

"No," he replied. "It isn't poetry but deals with various anthropological subjects."

That word, anthropological, quieted her. For a moment she thought it a sinful word, but it sounded so dignified that she hesitated to make a definite charge against it. Jones had added a very valuable word to his vocabulary and an additional defense for use in his private life. After that he used it in his thinking. It gilded facts that otherwise might be considered somewhat questionable morally.

Jones wanted a copy of *The Perfumed Garden*. He was not at all sure what he would do with it if he bought it. It would be hard to take it home where he had the privacy of a goldfish. But he thought that if it was not too large he could hide it among the hot breads and buns and read it during the noon hour. At least he wanted to buy it.

Its purchase required two things. A place where the book was for sale and the cash to pay for it. Rather timidly he went to the Methodist Publication Society where his Sunday School bought their leaflets, but the best they could offer was *The Garden the Year Around* and *Elizabeth and Her Garden*. Sadly he told them that these were not the books he was seeking. Then he went to several department stores and finally ended in a second-hand bookshop. At last the search became warm. They did not have the book, but told him where he could buy it.

He did not have time to go there that noon; instead he telephoned. A sweet voice at the other end of the wire assured him that they had several copies of *The Perfumed Garden* and that the one they were recommending was illustrated by Malay and sold for twenty-five dollars. That made him hang up the receiver hastily.

Jones received so much a week and he gave exactly that amount to his wife every payday when he arrived home. She gave him his carfare, his Sunday offering, and twenty-five cents for spending money. The rest she spent or saved as she thought best. Jones saved his spending money for one month, then became desperate and instead of putting a silver dollar in the collection every Sunday he shadily dropped in a penny. He just had to have that book, but broke into a cold sweat when the minister preached from the text, "Shall a man rob God?"

At the end of six months he had the necessary twenty-five dollars saved. All he wanted now was an opportunity to spend it. The chance came when his wife announced her intention of spending a week end in the country with her mother. Promptly Jones went to the head of his department, pleaded illness and the necessity of seeing a doctor, and thus got a few hours off the coming Saturday afternoon.

That morning he put on his Sunday suit, put the money in his pocket, and took the tube to the grocery store. The sale of hot breads and buns was active until noon. Then he stopped work, the first time in twenty years, removed his apron, donned his coat, felt in his pocket to assure himself that the money was safe, and gayly started for the bookstore.

It was difficult to find, but find it he did and was much pleased to see that he was the only customer. The lady in charge greeted him most cordially and assured him of her eagerness to assist him in the search for unusual literature. She was a dizzy blonde, who had not yet faded, and her pulchritude from the top of her perfectly coiffured hair to her little red-nailed toes peeking through her wedgies, showed her as expert at exterior decoration as well as at competent book-selling. With a great deal of effort and several blushes Jones was finally able to tell her of his desired book.

"I'm afraid," she replied, "that I can't sell you that book. Its sale is limited to lawyers, physicians, and ministers. Are you a student of sociology?"

"I am an anthropologist," answered Jones.

"Oh! Why didn't you tell me so when you first came in? Of course I'll sell you anything. If you want *The Perfumed Garden* of course you'll want the edition illustrated by Malay. The drawings are so quaint and so thoroughly in sympathy with the text. Here's a mint copy. Do you know *The Dialogues?* Have you seen the new *Casanova?* How about *Fanny Hill?* It must be so interesting to be an anthropologist and study these books. Are you interested in prints? I have a few by Rops. Just make yourself at home. Here's a copy of the book you're interested in, priced at only twenty-five dollars; cheap, too, considering its rarity."

Abraham Solomon Jones sat down and began poring over the book. Then he looked avidly through a book illustrated by Beardsley. The lady showed him a bronze ornament which, she explained, was worn by Roman ladies on certain occasions. Of course it was a reproduction, but perhaps he knew a lady who would appreciate it. He was fascinated but knew that it was something he simply could not give his wife as a Christmas present, even though she was fond of jewelry.

At last Jones realized he must return to the store. As he handed the lady the money for his book he promised her that he would return some day and buy some more books. Very carefully she wrapped his purchase and he left, just as she was trying to explain that she had things other than books to sell. He slipped the book under his vest, just over his heart and longed for Sunday when he could read it between church services.

Back at work he sold hot breads and buns as usual. From nine to ten Saturday night business was dull and he habitually read the evening paper. To his horror, staring at him right on the front page appeared a news-item stating that the Little Bookshop had been raided late that afternoon and that the lady owner had been arrested for selling obscene books and her entire stock confiscated and taken to City Hall in a patrol wagon. The article described the store, the books, prints, and articles of art. It stated that for some months this lady had been flooding the city with evil books, so lewd that the policemen blushed as they carried them to the wagon. The lady protested her innocence and stated that her last sale had been to an anthropologist and was, therefore, perfectly legal. The police were hunting for the anthropologist to ascertain just what kind of a scientific book he had bought.

This news was almost too much for Jones. He expected a visit from a detective at any moment demanding the right to search through the hot breads and buns for a hot book. At last, to his great relief, ten o'clock came and the closing of the store. He left by a side exit, the book carefully concealed under his coat, his heart filled with fear that at any moment he would be touched by the accusatory finger of the law. Almost panting he finally reached the tube. The train was nearly empty. Seated he wiped the sweat from his brow and reached a decision. He could not face the thought of having his house searched and the book found; it would be far better to leave it in the car.

As he rose from his seat to leave the car he dropped the book, but a woman behind him picked it up and, running, handed it to him just as he was passing through the doors. He thanked her and sadly climbed the stairs to the street. Four city blocks away was his home, a three room apartment which had sheltered him and Mrs. Jones for many years. In those four blocks he made two more attempts to rid himself of the book but each time it was returned to him by interested wayfarers who saw it slip from his arms. Desperate, he raced for the entrance to the apartment house. There he paused, conflicting emotions, angels and demons, shades of light and darkness, fought for the possession of his soul. But at last timidity and thoughts of his wife conquered. He raised the book to his lips, kissed it, and sadly threw it into the sewer.

At last he opened the door to the little apartment and turned on the electric light. It was the same poorly furnished place he had left that morning. There was not a single thing in it to recall the voluptuous beauty of his anthropological studies. He recalled the Malay illustrations and a few snatches of poetry interspersed between the prose. Undressing, he fell into bed where he sobbed himself to sleep, with his arms clasped around the bolster. He was nearly fifty years old and he longed for some beauty, some adventure, in his few remaining years.

All night he tossed restlessly. By the first streak of dawn he had arrived at a decision. Dressing hastily he took the long wire used to clean the kitchen drain and went into the street. Boldly he slid aside the iron sewer cover and peered anxiously down. There was his book, securely wrapped, resting on the dry filth of a city sewer. Deftly fishing the package out with the wire he replaced the cover, dusted his pants, and hurried back to his apartment.

Quickly he cooked his breakfast and, between bites of ham, eggs, and rolls, avidly read his precious book. In the meantime rain had begun to fall softly but by nine o'clock it was a veritable downpour. At nine-thirty an elder 'phoned saying there would be no church services because of the cloudburst. Delighted at the prospect of an uninterrupted day he made himself comfortable on the bed and continued reading. There were some parts of the book he couldn't quite understand but he could at least comprehend the general import. At last the book was finished and he closed it with a sigh of contentment. For a few moments he lay lost in the midst of wishful dreams, while he told himself how wonderful it was that he, a poor baker, had become an anthropologist. If only, he thought sadly, if only he had discovered the wonders of anthropology a long time ago, even before he met the prim young lady who became Mrs. Jones!

# Personality Problem

## Joe R. Lansdale

Yeah, I know, Doc. I look terrible and don't smell any better. But you would, too, if you stayed on the go like I do, had a peg sticking out of either side of your neck and this crazy scar across the forehead. You'd think they might have told me to use cocoa butter on the place, after they took the stitches out, but naw, no way. They didn't care if I had a face like a train track. No meat off *their* nose.

And how about this getup? Nice, huh? Early wino or late drug addict. You ought to walk down the street wearing this mess, you really get the stares. Coat's too small, pants too short. And these boots, now they get the blue ribbon. You know, I'm only six-five, but with these on I'm nearly seven feet! That's some heels, Doc.

But listen, how can I do any better? I can't even afford to buy myself a tie at the Goodwill, let alone get myself a new suit of clothes. And have you ever tried to fit someone my size? This shoulder is higher than the other one. The arms don't quite match, and—well, you see the problem. I tell you, Doc, it's no bed of roses.

Worst part of it is how people are always running from me, and throwing things, and trying to set me on fire. Oh, that's the classic one. I mean, I've been frozen for a while, covered in mud, you name it, but the old favorite is the torch. And I *hate* fire . . . Which reminds me, think you could refrain from smoking, Doc? Sort of makes me nervous.

See, I was saying about the fire. They've trapped me in windmills, castles, and labs. All sorts of places. Some guy out there in the crowd always gets the wise idea about the fire, and there we go again—Barbecue City. Let me tell you, Doc, I've been lucky. Spell that L-U-C-K-Y. We're talking a big lucky here. I mean, that's one reason I look as bad as I do. These holes in this already ragged suit . . . Yeah, that's right, bend over. Right there, see? This patch of hide was burned right off my head, Doc—and it didn't feel like no sunburn either. I mean it hurt.

And I've got no childhood. Just a big dumb boy all my life. No dates. No friends. Nothing. Just this personality complex, and this feeling that everybody hates me on sight.

If I ever get my hands on that Victor, or Igor, oh boy, gonna have to snap 'em, Doc. And I can do it, believe me. That's where they crapped in the mess kit, Doc. They made me strong. Real strong.

Give me a dime. Yeah, thanks.

Now watch this. Between thumb and finger . . . *Uhhhh.* How about that? Flat as a pancake.

Yeah, you're right, I'm getting a little excited. I'll lay back and take it easy . . . Say, do you smell smoke? Doc?

*Doc?*

Doc, damn you, put out that fire! Not you, too? Hey, I'm not a bad guy, really. Come back here, Doc! Don't leave me in here. Don't lock that door . . .


# A Piece of Red Calico

## Frank R. Stockton

I was going into town one morning from my suburban residence, when my wife handed me a little piece of red calico, and asked me if I would have time, during the day, to buy her two yards and a half of calico like that. I assured her that it would be no trouble at all; and putting the sample in my pocket, I took the train for the city.

At lunch time I stopped in at a large drygoods store to attend to my wife's commission. I saw a well-dressed man walking the floor between the counters, where long lines of girls were waiting on much longer lines of customers, and asked him where I could see some red calico.

"This way, sir." And he led me up the store. "Miss Stone," said he to a young lady, "show this gentleman some red calico."

"What shade do you want?" asked Miss Stone.

I showed her the little piece of calico that my wife had given me. She looked at it and handed it back to me. Then she took down a great roll of red calico and spread it out on the counter.

"Why, that isn't the shade!" said I.

"No, not exactly," said she; "but it is prettier than your sample."

"That may be," said I; "but, you see, I want to match this piece. There is something already made of this kind of calico which needs to be enlarged or mended or something. I want some calico of the same shade."

The girl made no answer, but took down another roll.

"That's the shade," said she.

"Yes," I replied, "but it's striped."

"Stripes are more worn than anything else in calicoes," said she.

"Yes, but this isn't to be worn. It's for furniture, I think. At any rate, I want perfectly plain stuff, to match something already in use."

"Well, I don't think you can find it perfectly plain unless you get Turkey red."

"What is Turkey red?" I asked.

"Turkey red is perfectly plain in calicoes," she answered.

"Well, let me see some."

"We haven't any Turkey red calico left," she said, "but we have some very nice plain calicoes in other colors."

"I don't want any other color. I want stuff to match this."

"It's hard to match cheap calico like that," she said. And so I left her.

I next went into a store a few doors farther up the street. When I entered I approached the "floor-walker," and handing him my sample, said:

"Have you any calico like this?"

"Yes, sir," said he. "Third counter to the right."

I went to the third counter to the right, and showed my sample to the salesman in attendance there. He looked at it on both sides. Then he said:

"We haven't any of this."

"I was told you had," said I.

"We had it, but we're out of it now. You'll get that goods at an upholsterer's."

I went across the street to an upholsterer's.

"Have you any stuff like this?" I asked.

"No," said the salesman, "we haven't. Is it for furniture?"

"Yes," I replied.

"Then Turkey red is what you want."

"Is Turkey red just like this?" I asked.

"No," said he; "but it's much better."

"That makes no difference to me," I replied. "I want something just like this."

"But they don't use that for furniture," he said.

"I should think people could use anything they wanted for furniture," I remarked, somewhat sharply.

"They can, but they don't," he said, quite calmly. "They don't use red like that. They use Turkey red."

I said no more, but left. The next place I visited was a very large drygoods store. Of the first salesman I saw I inquired if they kept red calico like my sample.

"You'll find that on the second story," said he.

I went upstairs. There I asked a man:

"Where will I find red calico?"

"In the far room to the left. Over there." And he pointed to a distant corner.

I walked through the crowds of purchasers and salespeople, and around the counters and tables filled with goods, to the far room to the left. When I got there I asked for red calico.

"The second counter down this side," said the man.

I went there and produced my sample. "Calicoes downstairs," said the man.

"They told me they were up here," I said.

"Not these plain goods. You'll find 'em downstairs at the back of the store, over on that side."

I went downstairs to the back of the store.

"Where will I find red calico like this?" I asked.

"Next counter but one," said the man addressed, walking with me in the direction pointed out.

"Dunn, show red calicoes."

Mr. Dunn took my sample and looked at it.

"We haven't this shade in that quality of goods," he said.

"Well, have you it in any quality of goods?" I asked.

"Yes; we've got it finer." And he took down a piece of calico, and unrolled a yard or two of it on the counter.

"That's not this shade," I said.

"No," said he. "The goods is finer and the color's better."

"I want it to match this," I said.

"I thought you weren't particular about the match," said the salesman. "You said you didn't care for the quality of the goods, and you know you can't match goods without you take into consideration quality and color both. If you want that quality of goods in red, you ought to get Turkey red."

I did not think it necessary to answer this remark, but said:

"Then you've got nothing to match this?"

"No, sir. But perhaps they may have it in the upholstery department, in the sixth story."

So I got in the elevator and went up to the top of the house.

"Have you any red stuff like this?" I said to a young man.

"Red stuff? Upholstery department—other end of this floor."

I went to the other end of the floor.

"I want some red calico," I said to a man.

"Furniture goods?" he asked.

"Yes," said I.

"Fourth counter to the left."

I went to the fourth counter to the left, and showed my sample to a salesman. He looked at it, and said:

"You'll get this down on the first floor—calico department."

I turned on my heel, descended in the elevator, and went out on the street. I was thoroughly sick of red calico. But I determined to make one more trial. My wife had bought her red calico not long before, and there must be some to be had somewhere. I ought to have asked her where she obtained it, but I thought a simple little thing like that could be bought anywhere.

I went into another large drygoods store. As I entered the door a sudden tremor seized me. I could not bear to take out that piece of red calico. If I had had any other kind of rag about me—a penwiper or anything of the sort—I think I would have asked them if they could match that.

But I stepped up to a young woman and presented my sample, with the usual question.

"Back room, counter on the left," she said.

I went there.

"Have you any red calico like this?" I asked of the saleswoman behind the counter.

"No, sir," she said, "but we have it in Turkey red."

Turkey red again! I surrendered.

"All right," I said, "give me Turkey red."

"How much, sir?" she asked.

"I don't know—say five yards."

She looked at me rather strangely, but measured off five yards of Turkey red calico. Then she rapped on the counter and called out "Cash!" A little girl, with yellow hair in two long plaits, came slowly up. The lady wrote the number of yards, the name of the goods, her own number, the price, the amount of the bank-note I handed her, and some other matters, probably the color of my eyes and the direction and velocity of the wind, on a slip of paper. She then copied all this into a little book which she kept by her. Then she handed the slip of paper, the money, and the Turkey red to the yellow-haired girl. This young person copied the slip into a little book she carried, and then she went away with the calico, the paper slip, and the money.

After a very long time—during which the little girl probably took the goods, the money, and the slip to some central desk, where the note was received, its amount and number entered in a book, change given to the girl, a copy of the slip made and entered, girl's entry examined and approved, goods wrapped up, girl registered, plaits counted and entered on a slip of paper and copied by the girl in her book, girl taken to a hydrant and washed, number of towel entered on a paper slip and copied by the girl in her book, value of my note and amount of change branded somewhere on the child, and said process noted on a slip of paper and copied in her book—the girl came to me, bringing my change and the package of Turkey red calico.

I had time for very little work at the office that afternoon, and when I reached home I handed the package of calico to my wife. She unrolled it and exclaimed:

"Why, this don't match the piece I gave you!"

"Match it!" I cried. "Oh no! it don't match it. You didn't want that matched. You were mistaken. What you wanted was Turkey red—third counter to the left. I mean, Turkey red is what they use."

My wife looked at me in amazement, and then I detailed to her my troubles.

"Well," said she, "this Turkey red is a great deal prettier than what I had, and you've got so much of it that I needn't use the other at all. I wish I had thought of Turkey red before."

"I wish from the bottom of my heart you had," said I.

# Pig

## Rudyard Kipling

Go, stalk the red deer o'er the heather,
   Ride, follow the fox if you can!
But, for pleasure and profit together,
   Allow me the hunting of Man,—
The chase of the Human, the search for the Soul
   To its ruin,—the hunting of Man.

                 —*The Old Shikarri*

I believe the difference began in the matter of a horse, with a twist in his temper, whom Pinecoffin sold to Nafferton and by whom Nafferton was nearly slain. There may have been other causes of offence; the horse was the official stalking-horse. Nafferton was very angry; but Pinecoffin laughed, and said that he had never guaranteed the beast's manners. Nafferton laughed too, though he vowed that he would write off his fall against Pinecoffin if he waited five years. Now, a Dalesman from beyond Skipton will forgive an injury when the Strid lets a man live; but a South Devon man is as soft as a Dartmoor bog. You can see from their names that Nafferton had the race-advantage of Pinecoffin. He was a peculiar man, and his notions of humour were cruel. He taught me a new and fascinating form of *shikar*. He hounded Pinecoffin from Mithankot to Jagadri, and from Gurgaon to Abbottabad—up and across the Punjab, a large Province, and in places remarkably dry. He said that he had no intention of allowing Assistant Commissioners to "sell him pups," in the shape of ramping, screaming countrybreds, without making their lives a burden to them.

Most Assistant Commissioners develop a bent for some special work after their first hot weather in the country. The boys with digestions hope to write their names large on the Frontier, and struggle for dreary places like Bannu and Kohat. The bilious ones climb into the Secretariat. Which is very bad for the liver. Others are bitten with a mania for District work, Ghuznivide coins or Persian poetry; while some, who come of farmers' stock, find that the smell of the Earth after the Rains gets into their blood, and calls them to "develop the resources of the Province." These men are enthusiasts. Pinecoffin belonged to their class. He knew a great many facts bearing on the cost of bullocks, and temporary wells, and opium-scrapers, and what happens if you burn too much rubbish on a field in the hope of enriching used-up soil. All the Pinecoffins come of a landholding breed, and so the land only took back her own again. Unfortunately—most unfortunately for Pinecoffin—he was a Civilian as well as a farmer. Nafferton watched him, and thought about the horse. Nafferton said, "See me chase that boy till he drops!" I said, "You can't get your knife into an Assistant Commissioner." Nafferton told me that I did not understand the administration of the Province.

Our Government is rather peculiar. It gushes on the agricultural and general information side, and will supply a moderately respectable man with all sorts of "economic statistics," if he speaks to it prettily. For instance, you are interested in gold-washing in the sands of the Sutlej. You pull the string, and find that it wakes up half a dozen Departments, and finally communicates, say, with a friend of yours in the Telegraph, who once wrote some notes on the customs of the gold-washers when he was on construction work in their part of the Empire. He may or may not be pleased at being ordered to write out everything he knows for your benefit. This depends on his temperament. The bigger man you are, the more information and the greater trouble can you raise.

Nafferton was not a big man; but he had the reputation of being very "earnest." An "earnest" man can do much with a Government. There was an earnest man once who nearly wrecked . . . but all India knows *that* story. I am not sure what real "earnestness" is. A very fair imitation can be manufactured by neglecting to dress decently, by mooning about in a dreamy, misty sort of way, by taking office-work home after staying in office till seven, and by receiving crowds of native gentlemen on Sundays. That is one sort of "earnestness."

Nafferton cast about for a peg whereon to hang his earnestness, and for a string that would communicate with Pinecoffin. He found both. They were Pig. Nafferton became an earnest inquirer after Pig. He informed the Government that he had a scheme whereby a very large percentage of the British Army in India could be fed, at a very large saving, on Pig. Then he hinted that Pinecoffin might supply him with the "varied information necessary to the proper inception of the scheme." So the Government wrote on the back of the letter, "Instruct Mr. Pinecoffin to furnish Mr. Nafferton with any information in his power." Government is very prone to writing things on the backs of letters which, later, lead to trouble and confusion.

Nafferton had not the faintest interest in Pig, but he knew that Pinecoffin would flounce into the trap. Pinecoffin was delighted at being consulted about Pig. The Indian Pig is not exactly an important factor in agricultural life; but Nafferton explained to Pinecoffin that there was room for improvement, and corresponded direct with that young man.

You may think that there is not much to be evolved from Pig. It all depends how you set to work. Pinecoffin, being a Civilian and wishing to do things thoroughly, began with an essay on the Primitive Pig, the Mythology of the Pig, and the Dravidian Pig. Nafferton filed that information—twenty-seven foolscap sheets—and wanted to know about the distribution of the Pig in the Punjab, and how it stood the Plains in the hot weather. From this point onwards remember that I am giving you only the barest outlines of the affair— the guy-ropes, as it were, of the web that Nafferton spun round Pinecoffin.

Pinecoffin made a coloured Pig-population map, and collected observations on the comparative longevity of Pig (a) in the submontane tracts of the Himalayas, and (b) in the Rechna Doab. Nafferton filed that, and asked what sort of people looked after Pig. This started an ethnological excursus on swineherds, and drew from Pinecoffin long tables showing the proportion per thousand of the caste in the Derajat. Nafferton filed that bundle, and explained that the figures which he wanted referred to the Cis-Sutlej states, where he understood that Pigs were very fine and large, and where he proposed to start a Piggery. By this time, Government had quite forgotten their instructions to Mr. Pinecoffin. They were like the gentlemen, in Keats' poem, who turned well-oiled wheels to skin other people. But Pinecoffin was just entering into the spirit of the

Pig-hunt, as Nafferton well knew he would do. He had a fair amount of work of his own to clear away; but he sat up of nights reducing Pig to five places of decimals for the honour of his Service. He was not going to appear ignorant of so easy a subject as Pig.

Then Government sent him on special duty to Kohat, to "inquire into" the big, seven-foot ironshod spades of that District. People had been killing each other with those peaceful tools; and Government wished to know "whether a modified form of agricultural implement could not, tentatively and as a temporary measure, be introduced among the agricultural population without needlessly or unduly exacerbating the existing religious sentiments of the peasantry."

Between those spades and Nafferton's Pig, Pinecoffin was rather heavily burdened.

Nafferton now began to take up "(a) The food-supply of the indigenous Pig, with a view to the improvement of its capacities as a flesh-former. (b) The acclimatisation of the exotic Pig, maintaining its distinctive peculiarities." Pinecoffin replied exhaustively that the exotic Pig would become merged in the indigenous type; and quoted horse-breeding statistics to prove this. The side-issue was debated, at great length on Pinecoffin's side, till Nafferton owned that he had been in the wrong, and moved the previous question. When Pinecoffin had quite written himself out about flesh-formers, and fibrins, and glucose, and the nitrogenous constituents of maize and lucerne, Nafferton raised the question of expense. By this time Pinecoffin, who had been transferred from Kohat, had developed a Pig theory of his own, which he stated in thirty-three folio pages— all carefully filed by Nafferton. Who asked for more.

These things took ten months, and Pinecoffin's interest in the potential Piggery seemed to die down after he had stated his own views. But Nafferton bombarded him with letters on "the Imperial aspect of the scheme, as tending to officialise the sale of pork, and thereby calculated to give offence to the Mahommedan population of Upper India." He guessed that Pinecoffin would want some broad, free-hand work after his niggling, stippling, decimal details. Pinecoffin handled the latest development of the case in masterly style, and proved that no "popular ebullition of excitement was to be apprehended." Nafferton said that there was nothing like Civilian insight in matters of this kind, and lured him up a by-path— "the possible profits to accrue to the Government from the sale of hog-bristles." There is an extensive literature of hog-bristles, and the shoe, brush, and colour-man's trades recognise more varieties of bristles than you would think possible. After Pinecoffin had wondered a little at Nafferton's rage for information, he sent back a monograph, fifty-one pages, on "Products of the Pig." This led him, under Nafferton's tender handling, straight to the Cawnpore factories, the trade in hog-skin for saddles—and thence to the tanners. Pinecoffin wrote that pomegranate-seed was the best cure for hog-skin, and suggested—for the past fourteen months had wearied him—that Nafferton should "raise his pigs before he tanned them."

Nafferton went back to the second section of his fifth question. How could the exotic Pig be brought to give as much pork as it did in the West and yet "assume the essentially hirsute characteristics of its Oriental congener"? Pinecoffin felt dazed, for he had forgotten what he had written sixteen months before, and fancied that he was about to reopen the entire question. He was too far involved in the hideous tangle to retreat, and, in a weak moment, he wrote, "Consult my first letter." Which related to the Dravidian Pig. As a matter of fact, Pinecoffin had still to reach the acclimatisation stage; having gone off on a side-issue on the merging of types.

*Then* Nafferton really unmasked his batteries! He complained to the Government, in stately language, of "the paucity of help accorded to me in my earnest attempts to start a potentially remunerative industry, and the flippancy with which my requests for information are treated by a gentleman whose pseudo-scholarly attainments should at least have taught him the primary differences between the Dravidian and the Berkshire variety of the genus *Sus*. If I am to understand that the letter to which he refers me contains his serious views on the acclimatisation of a valuable, though possibly uncleanly, animal, I am reluctantly compelled to believe," etc. etc.

There was a new man at the head of the Department of Castigation. The wretched Pinecoffin was told that the Service was made for the Country, and not the Country for the Service, and that he had better begin to supply information about Pigs.

Pinecoffin answered insanely that he had written everything that could be written about Pigs, and that some furlough was due to him.

Nafferton got a copy of that letter, and sent it, with the essay on the Dravidian Pig, to a down-country paper which printed both in full. The essay was rather high-flown; but if the Editor had seen the stacks of paper, in Pinecoffin's handwriting, on Nafferton's table, he would not have been so sarcastic about the "nebulous discursiveness and blatant self-sufficiency of the modern Competition-*wallah*, and his utter inability to grasp the practical issues of a practical question." Many friends cut out these remarks and sent them to Pinecoffin.

I have already stated that Pinecoffin came of a soft stock. This last stroke frightened and shook him. He could not understand it; but he felt that he had been, somehow, shamelessly betrayed by Nafferton. He realised that he had wrapped himself up in the Pig-skin without need, and that he could not well set himself right with his Government. All his acquaintances asked after his "nebulous discursiveness" or his "blatant self-sufficiency," and this made him miserable.

He took a train and went to Nafferton, whom he had not seen since the Pig business began. He also took the cutting from the paper, and blustered feebly and called Nafferton names, and then died down to a watery, weak protest of the "I-say-it's-too-bad-you-know" order.

Nafferton was very sympathetic.

"I'm afraid I've given you a good deal of trouble, haven't I?" said he.

"Trouble!" whimpered Pinecoffin; "I don't mind the trouble so much, though that was bad enough; but what I resent is this showing up in print. It will stick to me like a burr all through my service. And I *did* do my best for your interminable swine. It's too bad of you—on my soul it is!"

"I don't know," said Nafferton. "Have you ever been stuck with a horse? It isn't the money I mind, though that is bad enough; but what I resent is the chaff that follows, especially from the boy who stuck me. But I think we'll cry quits now."

Pinecoffin found nothing to say save bad words; and Nafferton smiled ever so sweetly, and asked him to dinner.

# Project Hush

William Tenn

Secret? We were about as secret as you could be and still exist. Listen, do you know the name of our official listing in Army documents?

Project Hush.

You can imagine. Or, come to think of it, you really can't. Of course, everyone remembers the terrific espionage fever that gripped this country in the late nineteen-sixties, how every official named Tom had another official named Dick checking up on him, how Dick had someone named Harry checking up on *him*—and how Harry didn't have the slightest idea of the work Tom was doing because there was a limit as to how far you could trust even counter-intelligence men . . .

But you had to be in a top-secret Army project to really get it. Where a couple of times a week you reported to Psycho for DD and HA (Dream Detailing and Hypno-Analysis to you carefree civilians). Where even the commanding general of the heavily fortified research post to which you were assigned could not ask what the hell you were doing, under penalty of court-martial—and was supposed to shut his imagination off like a faucet every time he heard an explosion. Where your project didn't even appear in the military budget by name but under the classification *Miscellaneous X Research*—a heading that picked up a bigger appropriation every year like a runaway snowball. Where—

Oh, well, maybe you can still remember it. And, as I said, we were called Project *Hush*.

The goal of our project was not just to reach the moon and set up a permanent station there with an original complement of two men. That we had just done on that slightly historic day of 24 June 1967. More important, in those wild, weapon-seeking times when fear of the H-bomb had churned the nation into a viscid mass of hysteria, was getting to the moon before anybody else and without anybody else knowing about it.

We'd landed at the northern tip of Mare Nubium, just off Regiomontanus, and, after planting a flag with appropriate throat-catching ceremony, had swung into the realities of the tasks we had practiced as so many dry runs back on Earth.

Major Monroe Gridley prepared the big rocket, with its tiny cubicle of living space for the return journey to Earth which he alone would make.

Lieutenant-colonel Thomas Hawthorne painstakingly examined our provisions and portable quarters for any damage that might have been incurred in landing.

And I, Colonel Benjamin Rice, first commanding officer of Army Base No. 1 on the Moon, dragged crate after enormous crate out of the ship on my aching academic back, and piled them in the spot two hundred feet away where the plastic dome would be built.

We all finished at just about the same time, as per schedule, and went into Phase Two.

Monroe and I started work on building the dome. It was a simple pre-fab affair, but big enough to require an awful lot of assembling. Then, after it was built, we faced the real problem—getting all the complex internal machinery in place and in operating order.

Meanwhile, Tom Hawthorne took his plump self off in the single-seater rocket which, up to then, had doubled as a lifeboat.

The schedule called for him to make a rough three-hour scouting survey in an ever-widening spiral from our dome. This had been regarded as a probable waste of time, rocket fuel and man-power—but a necessary precaution. He was supposed to watch for such things as bug-eyed monsters out for a stroll on the Lunar landscape. Basically, however, Tom's survey was intended to supply extra geological and astronomical meat for the report which Monroe was to carry back to Army HQ on earth.

Tom was back in forty minutes. His round face, inside its transparent bubble helmet, was fishbelly white. And so were ours, once he told us what he'd seen.

He had seen another dome.

"The other side of Mare Nubium—in the Riphaen Mountains," he babbled excitedly. "It's a little bigger than ours, and it's a little flatter on top. And it's not translucent, either, with splotches of different colors here and there—it's a dull, dark, heavy gray. But that's all there is to see."

"No markings on the dome?" I asked worriedly. "No signs of anyone—or anything—around it?"

"Neither, Colonel." I noticed he was calling me by my rank for the first time since the trip started, which meant he was saying in effect, "Man, have *you* got a decision to make!"

"Hey, Tom," Monroe put in. "Couldn't be just a regularly shaped bump in the ground, could it?"

"I'm a geologist, Monroe, I can distinguish artificial from natural topography. Besides—" He looked up—"I just remembered something I left out. There's a brand-new tiny crater near the dome— the kind usually left by a rocket exhaust."

"Rocket exhaust?" I seized on that. "*Rockets,* eh?"

Tom grinned a little sympathetically. "Spaceship exhaust, I should have said. You can't tell from the crater what kind of propulsive device these characters are using. It's not the same kind of crater our rear-jets leave, if that helps any."

Of course it didn't. So we went into our ship and had a council of war. And I do mean war. Both Tom and Monroe were calling me Colonel in every other sentence. I used their first names every chance I got.

Still, no one but me could reach a decision. About what to do, I mean.

"Look," I said at last, "here are the possibilities. They know we are here—either from watching us land a couple of hours ago or from observing Tom's scoutship—or they do not know we are here. They are either humans from Earth—in which case they are in all probability enemy nationals—or they are alien creatures from another planet—in which case they may be friends, enemies or what-have-you. I think common sense and standard military procedure demand that we consider them hostile until we have evidence to the contrary. Meanwhile, we proceed with extreme caution, so as not to precipitate an interplanetary war with potentially friendly Martians, or whatever they are.

"All right. It's vitally important that Army Headquarters be informed of this immediately. But since Moon-to-Earth radio is still on the drawing boards, the only way we can get through is to send Monroe back with the ship. If we do, we run the risk of having our garrison force, Tom and me, captured while he's making the return trip. In that case, their side winds up in possession of important information concerning our personnel and equipment, while our side has only the bare knowledge that somebody or something else has a base on the Moon. So our primary need is more information.

"Therefore, I suggest that I sit in the dome on one end of a telephone hookup with Tom, who will sit in the ship, his hand over the firing button, ready to blast off for Earth the moment he gets the order from me. Monroe will take the single-seater down to the Riphaen Mountains, landing as close to the other dome as he thinks safe. He will then proceed the rest of the way on foot, doing the best scouting job he can in a spacesuit.

"He will not use his radio, except for agreed-upon nonsense syllables to designate landing the single-seater, coming upon the dome by foot, and warning me to tell Tom to take off. If he's captured, remembering that the first purpose of a scout is acquiring and transmitting knowledge of the enemy, he will snap his suit radio on full volume and pass on as much data as time and the enemy's reflexes permit. How does that sound to you?"

They both nodded. As far as they were concerned, the command decision had been made. But I was sitting under two inches of sweat.

"One question," Tom said. "Why did you pick Monroe for the scout?"

"I was afraid you'd ask that," I told him. "We're three extremely unathletic Ph.D.s who have been in the Army since we finished our schooling. There isn't too much choice. But I remembered that Monroe is half Indian—Arapahoe, isn't it, Monroe?—and I'm hoping blood will tell."

"Only trouble, Colonel," Monroe said slowly as he rose, "is that I'm one-*fourth* Indian and even that . . . Didn't I ever tell you that my great-grandfather was the only Arapahoe scout who was with Custer at the Little Big Horn? He'd been positive Sitting Bull was miles away. However, I'll do my best. And if I heroically don't come back, would you please persuade the Security Officer of our section to clear my name for use in the history books? Under the circumstances, I think it's the least he could do."

I promised to do my best, of course.

After he took off, I sat in the dome over the telephone connection to Tom and hated myself for picking Monroe to do the job. But I'd have hated myself just as much for picking Tom. And if anything happened and I had to tell Tom to blast off, I'd probably be sitting here in the dome all by myself after that, waiting . . .

"*Broz neggle!*" came over the radio in Monroe's resonant voice. He had landed the single-seater.

I didn't dare use the telephone to chat with Tom in the ship, for fear I might miss an important word or phrase from our scout. So I sat and sat and strained my ears. After a while, I heard *"Mishgashu!"* which told me that Monroe was in the neighborhood of the other dome and was creeping toward it under cover of whatever boulders were around.

And then, abruptly, I heard Monroe yell my name and there was a terrific clattering in my headphones. Radio interference! He'd been caught, and whoever had caught him had simultaneously jammed his suit transmitter with a larger transmitter from the alien dome.

Then there was silence.

After a while, I told Tom what had happened. He just said, "Poor Monroe." I had a good idea of what his expression was like.

"Look, Tom," I said, "if you take off now, you still won't have anything important to tell. After capturing Monroe whatever's in that other dome will come looking for us, I think. I'll let them get close enough for us to learn something of their appearance—at least if they're human or non-human. Any bit of information about them is important. I'll shout it up to you and you'll still be able to take off in plenty of time. All right?"

"You're the boss, Colonel," he said in a mournful voice. "Lots of luck."

And then there was nothing to do but wait. There was no oxygen system in the dome yet, so I had to squeeze up a sandwich from the food compartment in my suit. I sat there, thinking about the expedition. Nine years, and all that careful secrecy, all that expenditure of money and mind-cracking research—and it had come to this. Waiting to be wiped out, in a blast from some unimaginable weapon. I understood Monroe's last request. We often felt we were so secret that our immediate superiors didn't even want *us* to know what we were working on. Scientists are people—they wish for recognition, too. I was hoping the whole expedition would be written up in the history books, but it looked unpromising.

Two hours later, the scout ship landed near the dome. The lock opened and, from where I stood in the open door of our dome, I saw Monroe come out and walk toward me.

I alerted Tom and told him to listen carefully. "It may be a trick—he might be drugged . . ."

He didn't act drugged, though—not exactly. He pushed his way past me and sat down on a box to one side of the dome. He put his booted feet up on another, smaller box.

"How are you, Ben?" he asked. "How's every little thing?"

I grunted. "*Well?*" I know my voice skittered a bit.

He pretended puzzlement. "Well *what?* Oh, I see what you mean. The other dome—you want to know who's in it. You have a right to be curious, Ben. Certainly. The leader of a top-secret expedition like this—Project Hush, they call us, huh, Ben—finds another dome on the Moon. He thinks he's been the first to land on it, so naturally he wants to—"

"Major Monroe Gridley!" I rapped out. "You will come to attention and deliver your report. Now!" Honestly, I felt my neck swelling up inside my helmet.

Monroe just leaned back against the side of the dome. "That's the *Army* way of doing things," he commented admiringly. "Like the recruits say, there's a right way, a wrong way and an Army way. Only there are other ways, too." He chuckled. "Lots of other ways."

"He's off," I heard Tom whisper over the telephone. "Ben, Monroe has gone and blown his stack."

"They aren't extraterrestrials in the other dome, Ben," Monroe volunteered in a sudden burst of sanity. "No, they're humans, all right, and from Earth. Guess *where.*"

"I'll kill you," I warned him. "I swear I'll kill you, Monroe. Where are they from—Russia, China, Argentina?"

He grimaced. "What's so secret about those places? Go on!— guess again."

I stared at him long and hard. "The only place else—"

"Sure," he said. "You got it, Colonel. The other dome is owned and operated by the Navy. The goddamn United States Navy!"

# Rheumatism Movement Cure

## Robert Jones Burdette

One day, not a great while ago, Mr. Middlerib read in his favorite paper a paragraph stating that the sting of a bee was a sure cure for rheumatism, and citing several remarkable instances in which people had been perfectly cured by this abrupt remedy. Mr. Middlerib thought of the rheumatic twinges that grappled his knees once in a while, and made his life a burden to him.

He read the article several times, and pondered over it. He understood that the stinging must be done scientifically and thoroughly. The bee, as he understood the article, was to be gripped by the ears and set down upon the rheumatic joint, and held there until it stung itself stingless. He had some misgivings about the matter. He knew it would hurt. He hardly thought it could hurt any worse than the rheumatism, and it had been so many years since he was stung by a bee that he had almost forgotten what it felt like. He had, however, a general feeling that it would hurt some. But desperate diseases require desperate remedies, and Mr. Middlerib was willing to undergo any amount of suffering if it would cure his rheumatism.

He contracted with Master Middlerib for a limited supply of bees; humming and buzzing about in the summer air, Mr. Middlerib did not know how to get them. He felt, however, that he could safely depend upon the instincts and methods of boyhood. He knew that if there was any way in heaven whereby the shyest bee that ever lifted a two hundred pound man off the clover could be induced to enter a wide-mouthed glass bottle, his son knew that way.

For the small sum of one dime Master Middlerib agreed to procure several, to wit: six bees, sex and age not specified; but, as Mr. Middlerib was left in uncertainty as to the race, it was made obligatory upon the contractor to have three of them honey and three humble, or, in the generally accepted vernacular, bumble-bees. Mr. M. did not tell his son what he wanted those bees for, and the boy went off on his mission with his head so full of astonishment that it fairly whirled. Evening brings all home, and the last rays of the declining sun fell upon Master Middlerib with a short, wide-mouthed bottle comfortably populated with hot, ill-natured bees, and Mr. Middlerib and a dime. The dime and the bottle changed hands. Mr. Middlerib put the bottle in his coat pocket and went into the house, eyeing everybody he met very suspiciously, as though he had made up his mind to sting to death the first person who said "bee" to him. He confided his guilty secret to none of his family. He hid his bees in his bedroom, and as he looked at them just before putting them away, he half wished the experiment was safely over. He wished the imprisoned bees did not look so hot and cross. With exquisite care he submerged the bottle in a basin of water and let a few drops in on the heated inmates to cool them off.

At the tea-table he had a great fright. Miss Middlerib, in the artless simplicity of her romantic nature, said:

"I smell bees. How the odor brings up—"

But her father glared at her and said, with superfluous harshness and execrable grammar:

"Hush up! You don't smell nothing."

Whereupon Mrs. Middlerib asked him if he had eaten any thing that disagreed with him, and Miss Middlerib said:

"Why, pa!" and Master Middlerib smiled as he wondered.

Bedtime at last, and the night was warm and sultry. Under various false pretences, Mr. Middlerib strolled about the house until everybody else was in bed, and then he sought his room. He turned the lamp down until its feeble ray shone dimly as a death-light.

Mr. Middlerib disrobed slowly—very slowly. When at last he was ready to go lumbering into his peaceful couch, he heaved a profound sigh, so full of apprehension and grief that Mrs. Middlerib, who was awakened by it, said if it gave him so much pain to come to bed, perhaps he had better sit up all night. Mr. Middlerib choked another sigh, but said nothing and crept into bed. After lying still a few moments he reached out and got his bottle of bees.

It was not an easy thing to do to pick one bee out of the bottleful with his fingers, and not get into trouble. The first bee Mr. Middlerib got was a little brown honey-bee, that wouldn't weigh half an ounce if you picked him up by the ears, but if you lifted him by the hind leg would weigh as much as the last end of a bay mule. Mr. Middlerib could not repress a groan.

"What's the matter with you?" sleepily asked his wife.

It was very hard for Mr. Middlerib to say he only felt hot, but he did it. He didn't have to lie about it either. He did feel very hot indeed. About eighty-six all over, and one hundred and ninety-seven on the end of his thumb. He reversed the bee, and pressed the warlike terminus of it firmly against the rheumatic knee.

It didn't hurt so badly as he thought it would.

It didn't hurt at all.

Then Mr. Middlerib remembered that when the honey-bee stabs a human foe, it generally leaves its harpoon in the wound, and the invalid knew that the only thing this bee had to sting with was doing its work at the end of his thumb.

He reached his arm out from under the sheets, and dropped this disabled atom of rheumatism liniment on the carpet. Then, after a second of blank wonder, he began to feel round for the bottle, and wished he knew what he did with it.

In the meantime strange things had been going on. When he caught hold of the first bee, Mr. Middlerib, for reasons, drew it out in such haste that for the time he forgot all about the bottle and its remedial contents, and left it lying uncorked in the bed, between himself and his innocent wife. In the darkness there had been a quiet but general emigration from that bottle. The bees, their wings clogged with the water Mr. Middlerib had poured upon them to cool and tranquillize them, were crawling aimlessly about over the sheet. While Mr. Middlerib was feeling around for it, his ears were suddenly thrilled and his heart frozen by a wild, piercing scream from his wife.

"Murder!" she screamed, "murder! Oh! help me! Help! help!"

Mr. Middlerib sat bolt upright in bed. His hair stood on end. The night was warm, but he turned to ice in a minute.

"Where in thunder," he said, with pallid lips, as he felt all over the bed in frenzied haste—"where in thunder are them infernal bees?"

And a large "bumble," with a sting as pitiless as the finger of scorn, just then climbed up the inside of Mr. Middlerib's night-shirt, until it got squarely between his shoulders, and then it felt for his marrow, and he said, calmly:

"Here is one of them."

And Mrs. Middlerib felt ashamed of her feeble screams when Mr. Middlerib threw up both arms, and, with a howl that made the windows rattle, roared:

"Take him off! Oh, land of Scott, somebody take him off!"

And, when a little honey-bee began tickling the sole of Mrs. Middlerib's foot, she so shrieked that the house was bewitched, and immediately went into spasms.

The household was aroused by this time. Miss Middlerib and Master Middlerib and the servants were pouring into the room, adding to the general confusion by howling at random and asking irrelevant questions, while they gazed at the figure of a man a little on in years, arrayed in a long night-shirt, pawing fiercely at the unattainable spot in the middle of his back, while he danced an unnatural, weird, wicked-looking jig by the dim, religious light of the night-lamp. And while he danced and howled, and while they gazed and shouted, a navy-blue wasp, that Master Middlerib had put in the bottle for good measure and variety, and to keep the menagerie stirred up, had dried his legs and wings with a corner of the sheet, and, after a preliminary circle or two around the bed to get up his motion and settle down to a working gait, he fired himself across the room, and to his dying day Mr. Middlerib will always believe that one of the servants mistook him for a burglar and shot him.

No one, not even Mr. Middlerib himself, could doubt that he was at least for the time, most thoroughly cured of rheumatism. His own boy could not have carried himself more lightly or with greater agility. But the cure was not permanent, and Mr. Middlerib does not like to talk about it.

# The Saga of Lizzie Borden

## Jane Rice

I doubt if, today, the Borden Murder Case would cause much commotion. In its era it was a dilly. And, as far as I'm concerned, it still is.

Lizzie Borden, outwardly a stolid, phlegmatic soul, apparently got fed up with a diet consisting mainly of ham and housework and let her parents have it—one at a time—with the business end of an axe. While everyone was certain she was the culprit, there was no conclusive proof. (Fingernail parings and such things had yet to come into their own.) The supposition was that she got in her licks while stark naked and, afterwards, took a bath. From the state in which her parents were found, and from the general condition of the woodwork and wallpaper, she probably needed one. Badly. She stood trial, but, due to lack of evidence, was acquitted. From her parents, she inherited the house and a tidy sum—tidy enough to serve as a secondary motive, anyway—and lived to an autumnal age, puttering unconcernedly around in her garden.

Her notoriety might have faded into the mists of yesteryear had not an unknown wag of the day composed a catchy bit of doggerel. To wit:

> Lizzie Borden took an axe
> And gave her mother forty whacks;
> When she saw what she had done,
> She gave her father forty-one.

It gives us a picture. Erroneous, but skillfully executed: Lizzie so imbued with the spirit of matricide that, in sheer exuberance, she also commits patricide.

However, had it been Gilbert and Sullivan who had immortalized Lizzie in verse, the picture would've been different. No less erroneous, of course, but decidedly different. Like this:

> When I was a lass I shed no tears,
> But ate pork chops 'til they came out my ears,
> Then I hit ma both behind and before,
> And I polished off my papa with a few strokes more.
> I polished off my papa so carefulee,
> That I never, never, never could be proved guiltee!

Jurors' chorus:

> Oh, she polished off her papa so carefulee,
> That she never, never, never could be proved guiltee!

See what I mean? A rather gay lass with uncommonly good legs. I suspect that, when the trial was finished, those jurors all traipsed over to Lizzie's house and got pie-eyed.

James Whitcomb Riley would've given us an industrious sprout of a Lizzie, a teller of tales, beloved of children, the homespun type—and in dire need of immediate psychoanalysis:

> Little Lizzie Borden came to our house tonight,
> To strop the razors, hone the knives, an' make the
> hatchet bright,
> An' grind the scissors nice an' sharp, an' practice with
> the saw,
> An' try the axe out—jest fer size—to s'prise her maw
> and paw.
> An' all us other children, when the supper things uz
> done,
> We set around the kitchen fire an' had the *mostest* fun,
> A listenin' to the murder trials 'at Lizzie told about,
> An' the evidence 'at gits you
> 　　　　　　'Less
> 　　　　　　　　You
> 　　　　　　　　　　Wash
> 　　　　　　　　　　　It
> 　　　　　　　　　　　　Out!

Morris Bishop's Lizzie would've been pushed too far, just pushed too far:

> A maid who got fed up with scrubbin'
> And cookin' and bringin' the grub in,
> 　　Confronted her mom,
> 　　And with artless aplomb,
> She whittled her down to a nubbin.
>
> Her father cried, "Fie!" when he caught her.
> But, keeping her temper, his daughter
> 　　Soon altered his views,
> 　　Then erased all the clues
> With sal soda, soap, and hot water.

Under the tutelage of the Andrews Sisters, Miss Borden emerges as an uninhibited chick with good lungs and, apparently, hiccups:

> L-hizzie met her father at the ki-hitchen door,
> *Beeeeat* me, daddy, with a sol-h-lid four!

The place is jumpin'! When you see what I did
Y' gonna h-hit the ceilin' . . . gonna flip your lid!
A toot . . . a toot . . . a toot le a da . . .

I think Ogden Nash would have given us the most telling portrait of all:

Lizzie
                                    Was busy.


# Santa's Tenth Reindeer

## Gordon Van Gelder

*"Have you ever noticed the anagram?"*

**B**illy Avendil didn't go to sleep on Christmas Eve. He lay awake in bed, watching the minutes tick off his clock. He was nervous, he was excited, he was anxious, he had something up his sleeve.

He waited until he felt that he had waited long enough, then he tiptoed out of his room, taking precautions in case somebody was still half awake. He slid down the banister to avoid the squeaky stairs and because it was fun.

He instantly went to work, setting up his trap, testing it, making sure that everything was right. He considered setting a fire in the fireplace for the twelfth time, and for the twelfth time he decided that Santa would see the fire in time. Especially if his doubts were correct. But that was what he was doing all this for.

Then came the waiting. He sat down behind the tree, chewing his nails. He got up, started pacing, considered taking a cigarette from his mother's pocketbook, decided against it, paced some more, and was getting up for the cigarette when he heard noises on the rooftop.

*Ho ho ho jingle jingle.* The sound of hoofs beat against the roof. Billy raced to his spot behind the tree and gripped the pole nervously. He wondered about the reindeer, for if his theory was right, then the reindeer would be different, but he didn't have time to follow up on the thought.

*Ho ho ho ugh ugh damn oof ugh.* Santa was on his way down. Billy wondered if he should have stuck a knife in the chimney.

*Ah phew ho ho whooooa oof!* Santa emerged from the fireplace, stepped onto the skateboard, and went flying into the tree. Billy pushed the angel off the tree, and it struck Santa on the head with a crash. Then Billy hit Santa on the head with the pole. Santa fell to the floor, unconscious.

Billy tied Santa's hands to the tree, and lashed the feet together. Then he confirmed his theory, and took a picture for proof. He waited for Santa to awaken.

Santa came to with an awful headache. He realized where he was, and he swore, a long string of curses too terrible to repeat. When his "speech" was over, he said, "Why'd you do this, Billy? If it's my presents you want, take them. I don't give a damn. It just means that a lot of kids are going to be disappointed."

"Take your presents and stuff them up your fat rear, one at a time. I don't want your presents. All I wanted was proof of who you are, and I've got it," said Billy.

"All right, son, you've caught me."

"Get lost. My father's upstairs, with enough drugs in him to put an elephant to sleep. I know who you are."

"Damn, I think that you do know."

"That's right, Santa. I know why you always wear red, and it's not because it matches your nose. That was a pretty good joke, with the switch of the names. I liked it."

"I'm thrilled," said Santa unemphatically.

"Aww. Why so sad, Prince? Sad that the cat's out of the bag, along with all the other stuff you've got in there?" asked Billy.

"Do you know what a pain in the, uh, neck you are, Billy? I have stuff to do, and you're keeping me from doing it," said Santa.

"Aww, that's too bad. The Prince of Evil worried that he won't give out enough presents? Tsk tsk."

"You're the snottiest kid I know, and I think that all kids are snotty," said Santa.

Billy made a disgusting noise in response to Santa's statement. "Could you tell me something?" asked Billy. "Why do you do it? Why give out presents, and eggs on Easter, and love on Valentine's Day, why?"

"Take a guess," said Santa dryly. "Are you going to let me loose?"

"Not until I get answers, that's for sure. Why do you do it?" he repeated.

"You're evil, you're clever, figure it out."

"If I could've figured it out, I wouldn't have asked. Tell me."

"More hate comes through love than any other way," said Santa.

"Bull. That ruins the definition of love."

"Really? Think about it. What are half the murders? Husband and wife. How do best friends become best enemies? By chasing after the same person. Don't you see? Love and hate go hand in hand, like life and death. Are you going to release me?"

Billy was considering everything Santa had said. "I see your point, Santa, but there are still things I don't understand. Why give out presents?"

"They go with evil, too. Haven't you ever seen two kids fight over who gets the better present? Just think about the things you ask, and you'll get answers."

"No. True, presents do cause some evil, but they spread a lot of love. So does Valentine's Day, so does Easter, so do all your holidays."

"The world cannot exist without opposites—love and hate, life and death, day and night, and so on. Nobody can do anything without opposites occurring. I try to cause evil, and some good comes of it. Same with you, same with what everyone does. Are you going to let me go?"

"I think I see what you mean. Do I have an opposite?"

"Of course. Everybody does. You'll probably marry her. But I have some bad news for you. Your plan isn't going to work. The picture you took won't convince anybody."

"Yeah, sure, like I'm really going to buy that."

"It's true. They won't accept Santa as something else. It's the opposite theory again. The people think that Santa is good. Believe me. Other people have tried what you're going to."

"You mean, all I've done is going to go to waste?"

"No. I've found out that you're evil, and that's important. You're so evil, in fact, that I have an offer to make to you. How would you like to become a helper of mine, a cupid, or maybe a bunny?"

"No thanks. I couldn't stand it. I'm fine as I am right now."

"You don't want to be an elf, huh? Well, how about a personal assistant? I could make my former one an elf, and let you have the job."

"Very tricky. Then when somebody new comes along, I'm an elf. No thanks. I'm fine as I am."

"I'll level with you. There is a time when certain people have to be removed from the world, or else they would wreak too much havoc. No matter what you say, a good soul is going to change places with you. You may as well get as good a position as you can."

"I don't believe a single word you've said. Take your proposition and shove it."

"That's it." Santa stood up, rearing himself to his towering full height, hands and feet free by some unknown means. His eyes twinkled—with evil and not merriment.

"That's it, Billy. You've had your chance, and you shoved it. No longer shall I ask, I shall *do*. From now on, you will be my helper. One night a year, you will tow me around the world with nine others as evil as you. You will learn what it feels like to be whipped, and what it feels like to freeze on rooftops. For three hundred and sixty-four days, you will live in the Arctic and eat moss. I shall deprive you even of death. Your life will become a living hell, no pun intended." He smiled at the horror in Billy's eyes, and made a motion with his hands . . .

. . . And Billy changed. His smile softened, his eyes filled with awe at the sight of Santa. Santa put out the presents for the Avendil family, winked at the new Billy, and hustled up the chimney, hoping the tenth reindeer would make up for the lost time.

"Ho ho ho! Move, boys! On Donner, on Blitzen, on Vixen! Get your rear in gear, Billy! Merry Christmas to all, and to all a good night!"

# The Second Coming of a First Husband

### Irvin S. Cobb

If only Mrs. Thomas Bain had been content to compare Mr. Thomas Bain with men about him he, for his counter-arguments, would not have been put to a serious disadvantage. Out of her ammunition locker he might have borrowed shells to be fired in his own defense. Did she, for instance, cite the polished beauty of Mr. So-and-So's drawing-room behavior, speaking with that subtle inflection which as good as said that his own society manners left much to be desired, Mr. Bain's rebuttal would have been prompt and ready: He would have spoken right up to point out the fact that So-and-So notoriously neglected his family or that he drank entirely too much for his own good or that he habitually failed to pay his just debts. Mr. Bain was no scandal-monger, understand, still a man must fight back with such weapons as he may command.

But Mrs. Bain's method of attack was entirely too subtle for him; it left him practically weaponless. Out in the world he amply was competent to fend for himself. Beneath the domestic roof-tree, when his wife sat in judgment on him, and his ways, on his small short-comings or his larger faults, he completely was at a loss for proper rebuttal. It gave him such a helpless feeling! It would have given any normal man a helpless feeling. And Mr. Bain was in all essential regards a normal man—a good citizen, a good provider and, as husbands go, an average fair husband.

I would do Mrs. Bain no injustice. She was a normal woman, too. But it is only natural when destiny has fashioned an advantage to fit one's hands that one employs it. Her advantage was a very great one. Her criticisms of Mr. Bain took the form of measuring him off against the mental picture of her first husband.

And her first husband was dead. Now, in common decency, an honorable man—and Mr. Bain was an honorable man—may not speak ill of the dead. What is more, had he, under stress of provocation, been minded to retort that after all Mrs. Bain's first husband was not exactly perfection either, he could have produced no proof in support of the assertion. For he had never seen his predecessor. He knew nobody who had known the deceased. The present Mrs. Bain had been for three years a widow when first he set eyes on her. She had lately returned then from Honolulu; it was in Honolulu that she had been bereft, as the saying is, by the hand of death. And Honolulu is a long distance from Brockway, Mass., where Tom Bain's people, a stay-at-home stock, had lived these five generations past.

So, on those frequently recurring occasions when Mrs. Bain, with a saddened, almost a wistful, air was moved to remind herself of her first husband's marvelous qualities—his temperament, his flawless disposition, his tact, his amiability or what not—there was for her second husband nothing to do except to suffer on in an impotent silence. It is not well that anyone on this earth—and more especially a husband—should be required to suffer discomforts in silence. Suffering calls for vocal expression.

Otherwise, as human beings go, Mr. and Mrs. Bain were well suited, one for the other. It was that dead first husband of hers, who, invoked by her, kept rising up to mar the reasonable happiness which might have been theirs. The thing was getting on his nerves. Indeed, at the time this account begins, it already had got upon his nerves. He had come to the point where frequently he wished there had never been such a thing as a first husband.

There were times when he almost permitted himself the wish that there never had been such things as second husbands, either.

With the acute vividness of a war-scarred veteran remembering the time he was shot, he could recall the occasion when Mrs. Bain's first husband first came into his life. They had been married only a few weeks; the honeymoon was over; he who always had traveled singly was adjusting himself to the feel of double harness. This was an easier job for the lady than for her mate; she had been through the process once before. But while Tom Bain might be a green hand at this business of being married, still subconsciously he already was beginning to adjust himself in his ordained and proper place in the matrimonial scheme as it related to him and this very charming lady. In other words, he had reached the period where he was slipping out of the bridegroom pose into the less studied and more matter-of-fact status of a husband. He was ready to quit acting a part and be his own self again always, though with regard for the limitations and restrictions imposed by the new estate upon which he had entered.

The campaign against him—we may as well call it a campaign—opened on the evening following their return from the trip to White Sulphur. That first day at his desk had been a hard one; so much which seemed to require his personal attention had accumulated while he was away. He left the office pretty well fagged out. On his way home he built up a pleasant vision of a nice quiet little dinner and then a peaceful hour or so in the living-room in slippers and an old smoking jacket.

Mrs. Bain met him at the door with a greeting that put him in thorough good humor. This, he decided, was the best of all possible worlds to live in and his, undoubtedly, was the best of all possible ways of living.

"You're late, dearest," she said. "You've just time to run upstairs and slip on your evening clothes. I've laid them out for you."

"Why, there's nobody coming in for dinner, is there?" he asked. She drew away from him slightly.

"No, there's no one coming," she said. "What difference does that make?"

"Well," he said, "I'm rather tired and so I sort of thought that, seeing there'd be only the two of us, I'd come to the table just as I am."

"Very well, dear," she said, "suit yourself."

But he took note that she had briefened the superlative "dearest" to the shorter word "dear." Also she slipped herself out of the circlet of his encircling arm. Suddenly there was a suggestion—a bare hint—of an autumnal chill in the air.

"Suit yourself," she repeated.

But, as a newly married man, how could he suit himself? He clad himself in the starchy shirt, the high tight collar that nipped his throat, the pinchy patent leathers and all the rest of the funereal regalia in which civilized man encases himself on any supposedly festal occasion. She gave him an approving look when ten minutes later he presented himself before her.

"Tom," she said as they sat down, "I think you always should dress for dinner. Arthur always said that a gentleman should dress for dinner."

He stared at her, puzzled for a moment.

"Arthur?" he echoed.

"My first husband," she explained. "Arthur looked so well in his evening clothes."

"Oh," he said, like that. That was all he said for a minute or so. He was thinking.

She was thinking, too. Practically all women are popularly supposed to have intuition, and certainly this particular woman had her share of it. Probably it was in that very moment of reflection that the lady decided on a future plan of action.

At any rate, this was the beginning. Eventually, Mr. Bain awoke to a realization that he was the victim of a gentle tyranny—that he had fallen captive to an enemy force made up of an affectionate but somewhat masterful lady and the memory of a dead and gone personality. Mrs. Bain's first husband was persistently dogging Mrs. Bain's second husband. Daily, after one fashion or another, he was

382

reminded of Arthur. Arthur, it seemed, had never lost his temper. What made the comparison hurt the more was the indubitable fact that Mr. Bain occasionally did lose his. Arthur had never raised his voice above a well low-pitched key of innate refinement—no matter how irritated he might be. Arthur had been so tidy; Arthur never left his clothes lying about where he dropped them. Arthur had never given her a cross word in all the seven years of their life together. Arthur invariably had been so considerate of her feelings. It was Arthur this and it was Arthur that; she realized her power and she used it. Mrs. Bain's first husband was ever, so to speak, at the elbow of Mrs. Bain's second husband, by proxy chiding him, admonishing him, correcting him, scolding him, even. And for all that he was a naturally sunny-natured and most companionable person, Mrs. Bain's second husband, at the end of the first year of his married life, was in a fair way to become a most unhappy person. Their matrimonial craft was sliding down the rapids toward a thundering Niagara and she didn't realize it and he, thoroughly under the dominion of forces with which he found himself somehow powerless to cope, only dimly and dully appreciated the peril. He wanted above all things to have and to hold his wife until death did them part. But always there was Arthur tagging along, making a crowd of three out of what might have been a congenial company of two.

But, as someone has most aptly said, it's always darkest just before the dawn. In this instance, though, deliverance came to the oppressed, not with the graduations of the spreading dawn but rather with the solid emphasis of a bolt from the blue. There was an evening of bridge with the Tuckers, and Bain, who played well, had for a partner Mrs. Tucker who didn't. It is barely possible that he had betrayed a passing emotion of testiness once or twice. At midnight as they were entering their house Mrs. Bain renewed her remarks on an issue to which reference already had been made on the way home in the cab.

"My dear," she was saying, "I really must repeat again that, to my way of thinking, no amount of exasperation could have justified you in showing your feelings as you did show them at least twice at that cardtable. Now, Arthur would never—"

At this instant Mr. Bain's finger found the push-button just inside the jamb of the living-room door and the lights flashed on. What next ensued—the vocal part of it, I mean—might have suggested to an eavesdropper, had there been one, that the vowel sounds were being repeated by two persons laboring under a strong excitement.

"Ay?" That was his startled ejaculation.

"E-e-e-e!" A shrill outcry, part scream, part squeal, from her.

"I—I—" Mr. Bain again.

"Oh!" Mrs. Bain's turn.

"You!" Her startled gasp of recognition.

"Yes, Evelyn, that's who it is." This, in matter-of-fact tones, was a third voice speaking.

After this for a moment the spell of a terrific stupefaction held both Mr. and Mrs. Bain silent.

Standing in the middle of the floor facing them, was a shadow. I use the language advisedly. With equal propriety I might write down "apparition" or "wraith" or "shape" or "spirit" to describe that which confronted them. I prefer the word "shadow."

It had the outline, somewhat wavery and uncertain, of a man. It had the voice of a man—a voice calm, assured, almost casual. It had the garb of a man or at least it had the nebulous faint suggestion of garbing. But it had no substance to it, none whatsoever. It had no definable color, either. It had rather the aspect of a figure of man done in lines of very thin smoke. You could look right through it and distinguish, as through a patch of haze, the pattern of the wall-paper behind it. And now, as it spoke again, you could in some indefinable sort of way see its voice starting from down in its chest and traveling on up and up and so out at its lips. It was no more than a patch of fog, modeled by some unearthly magic into the semblance of a human form. It was inconceivable, impossible, an incredible figment of the imagination, and yet there it was.

Its second speech was addressed to Mr. Bain, who had frozen where he was, his finger still touching the push-button, his eyes enlarged to twice their size and his lower jaw sagged.

"You are astonished? Permit me to introduce myself. I am Arthur—Mrs. Bain's first husband. I am glad to meet you."

Mr. Bain came to himself all of a sudden. The shackles of twelve months of bottled-in restraint fell from him.

"Are you?" he answered. "Well, I'm damned if I'm glad to meet you."

"I understand." The voice was gentle, almost compassionate. "But you will be glad later on, I think—very glad. Shall we sit down, all of us?"

The Thing took a chair. And the back of the chair cloudily revealed itself as a sub-motif for the half-materialized torso of its occupant. Mechanically, moving jerkily, Mr. Bain followed suit; he also took a chair. Mrs. Bain, uttering whimpering sounds down in her throat, already had fallen upon a couch and was huddled there. It was just as well the couch had been handily near by, for her legs would no longer support her.

Her first husband—we may as well call him that—turned to her.

"Control yourself, Evelyn," he bade her. "There is no occasion for any excitement. Besides, those curious sounds which you are now emitting annoy me. I haven't long to stay and I have much to say."

He cleared his throat—the process might be followed by the eye as well as with the ear—and proceeded:

"I have been endeavoring for months past to bring about this meeting. In fact, ever since shortly after your second marriage to this gentleman. I have sought to return to earth for the one purpose which brings me tonight. But it was difficult—very difficult." He sighed a visible sigh. "It is not permitted that I should explain the nature of the obstacles. I merely say that they were very great. As you will notice, I am not able to even yet attain the seeming solidity—the weight and specific density which I craved to take on. So I just came along in the somewhat sketchy and incomplete guise in which you now see me.

"My reason for coming is simple. I desire to see justice done. Where I was, I could not rest in peace knowing that you, Evelyn, were lying so outrageously and, what was worse, making me an unwitting accomplice, as it were, to your lying.

"Evelyn, you have been a wicked woman. You have done this gentleman here—" including Mr. Bain with a wave of a spectral arm—"a cruel wrong. But what, from my point of view, is even worse, you have done me a grave wrong as well. I may be only a memory—I may say that that precisely is what I am—but even a memory has its feelings, its sense of responsibility, its obligations to itself.

"Very well, having made that point clear, I shall proceed: Sir, for nearly a year past you have been intimidated by the constantly presented image of a paragon. Am I not right? Your peace of mind has been seriously affected. And I resent the slander on my name. It has been an insult which no self-respecting memory should be compelled to stand. Sir, I wish you to know the truth: I was not a paragon, and I thank God for it. I was not the perfect husband this woman would have you believe. I was fussy, faulty, crotchety—and I am proud of it!"

"Oh, Arthur!" Mrs. Bain, under attack, was reviving, rallying to her own defense as powers of coherent speech returned to her.

"Don't 'Oh, Arthur' me—but listen. And you, too, sir, if you will be so good? We quarreled frequently in those years of our married life. She complained of my brusque ways, of my fits of irritability, of my refusal to like many of the people that she persisted in liking, of my tastes and my habits and inclinations. She didn't care for some of my friends; I didn't care for many of hers. I objected to any number of things about her—and rarely refrained from saying so. She has told you that between us there was never a cross word. *Bah!*—there were tens of thousands of cross words. When we got on each other's nerves, which was often, neither of us hesitated to let it be known. When we disagreed over something—or anything—we argued it out—quarreled it out, frequently. We loved each other, it is true, but merely loving did not make either of us angelic. We fell out and made up and fell out again. There were times when we were like a pair of cooing doves and again there were times when the proverbial monkey and parrot had little, if anything, on us. In short, and in fine, sir, we behaved just as the average reasonably well-mated married couple do behave. And for my own sake, and incidentally for yours, sir, I would not have you believe differently.

"That, I believe, is practically all I had to say to you. Having said it, I wish to add a final word to our wife, here. Evelyn, speaking with such authority as is befitting a first husband, I wish to state that, so far as my observations from another sphere have gone, your present husband is a first-rate fellow. I like to think of him as my successor. And I intend to see that he has a fair deal from you. I trust this visit from me has been a lesson to you. Hereafter, in your dealings with him you will please be so good as to stand on your own merits. You will kindly refrain from dragging me into your arguments as an advocate on your side. My stock of patience is no greater than it was before I became a memory—remember that. I sincerely trust it will not be necessary for me to admonish you personally a second time. Because I warn you here and now that next time I shall return under circumstances that may be most embarrassing to you. Next time there will be no privacy about my appearance; I shall appear to you in public. You'll be a talked-about woman, Evelyn. There'll be pieces about you in the paper and spiritualists and trance mediums and delvers into the occult—a meddlesome nosey lot, too, I may add—will make your life a burden for you. So have a care, Evelyn!

"Sir, to you I extend my best wishes. I'm sorry we didn't meet before. Well, some of these days we'll make up for lost time—when you join me on the plane where I am at present residing. Well, I guess that will be about all. . . . Oh, if you don't mind, I'll just dissipate into air and float up the chimney—it's more convenient." Out of a nothingness near the fireplace came a voice growing thinner and fainter: "Good-bye, Bain, old chap; good-bye, Evelyn—and don't forget."

It was at this juncture that Mrs. Bain went off into a swoon. It also should be noted down that even as he sprang to her side to revive her Mr. Bain wore on his face a look of husbandly solicitude and concern, but his feet twittered in a dance measure.

Personally, I do not believe in ghosts. I assume, reader, that you do not believe in ghosts, either. But Mrs. Bain does, and as for Mr. Bain he does, too, firmly—and as a happily married man is each day renewing and strengthening his belief in them.

# The Social Life of the Newt

## Robert Benchley

It is not generally known that the newt, although one of the smallest of our North American animals, has an extremely happy home life. It is just one of those facts which never get bruited about.

I first became interested in the social phenomena of newt life early in the spring of 1913, shortly after I had finished my researches in sexual differentiation among ameba. Since that time I have practically lived among newts, jotting down observations, making lantern-slides, watching them in their work and in their play (and you may rest assured that the little rogues have their play—as who does not?) until, from much lying in a research posture on my stomach, over the inclosure in which they were confined, I found myself developing what I feared might be rudimentary creepers. And so, late this autumn, I stood erect and walked into my house, where I immediately set about the compilation of the notes I had made.

So much for the non-technical introduction. The remainder of this article bids fair to be pretty scientific.

In studying the more intimate phases of newt life, one is chiefly impressed with the methods by means of which the males force their attentions upon the females, with matrimony as an object. For the newt is, after all, only a newt, and has his weaknesses just as any of the rest of us. And I, for one, would not have it different. There is little enough fun in the world as it is.

The peculiar thing about a newt's courtship is its restraint. It is carried on, at all times, with a minimum distance of fifty paces (newt measure) between the male and the female. Some of the bolder males may now and then attempt to overstep the bounds of good sportsmanship and crowd in to forty-five paces, but such tactics are frowned upon by the Rules Committee. To the eye of an uninitiated observer, the pair might be dancing a few of the more open figures of the minuet.

The means employed by the males to draw the attention and win the affection of those of the opposite sex (females) are varied and extremely strategic. Until the valuable researches by Strudlehoff in 1887 (in his *"Entwickelungsmechanik"*) no one had been able to ascertain just what it was that the male newt did to make the female see anything in him worth throwing herself away on. It had been observed that the most personally unattractive newt could advance to within fifty paces of a female of his acquaintance and, by some *coup d'œil*, bring her to a point where she would, in no uncertain terms, indicate her willingness to go through with the marriage ceremony at an early date.

It was Strudlehoff who discovered, after watching several thousand courting newts under a magnifying lens (questionable taste on his part, without doubt, but all is fair in pathological love) that the male, during the courting season (the season opens on the tenth of March and extends through the following February, leaving about ten days for general overhauling and redecorating), gives forth a strange, phosphorescent glow from the center of his highly colored dorsal crest, somewhat similar in effect to the flash of a diamond scarf-pin in a red necktie. This glow, according to Strudlehoff, so fascinates the female with its air of elegance and indication of wealth, that she immediately falls a victim to its lure.

But the little creature, true to her sex-instinct, does not at once give evidence that her morale has been shattered. She affects a coyness and lack of interest, by hitching herself sideways along the bottom of the aquarium, with her head turned over her right shoulder away from the swain. A trained ear might even detect her whistling in an indifferent manner.

The male, in the meantime, is flashing his gleamer frantically two blocks away and is performing all sorts of attractive feats, calculated to bring the lady newt to terms. I have seen a male, in the stress of his handicap courtship, stand on his forefeet, gesticulating in amorous fashion with his hind feet in the air. Franz Ingehalt, in his *Über Weltschmerz des Newt,* recounts having observed a distinct and deliberate undulation of the body, beginning with the shoulders and ending at the filament of the tail, which might well have been the origin of what is known today in scientific circles as "the shimmy." The object seems to be the same, except that in the case of the newt, it is the male who is the active agent.

In order to test the power of observation in the male during these maneuvers, I carefully removed the female, for whose benefit he was undulating, and put in her place, in slow succession, another (but less charming) female, a paper-weight of bronze shaped like a newt, and, finally, a common rubber eraser. From the distance at which the courtship was being carried on, the male (who was, it must be admitted, a bit near-sighted congenitally) was unable to detect the change in personnel, and continued, even in the presence of the rubber eraser, to gyrate and undulate in a most conscientious manner, still under the impression that he was making a conquest.

At last, worn out by his exertions, and disgusted at the meagerness of the reaction on the eraser, he gave a low cry of rage and despair and staggered to a nearby pan containing barley-water, from which he proceeded to drink himself into a gross stupor.

Thus, little creature, did your romance end, and who shall say that its ending was one whit less tragic than that of Camille? Not I, for one. . . . In fact, the two cases are not at all analogous.

And now that we have seen how wonderfully Nature works in the fulfilment of her laws, even among her tiniest creatures, let us study for a minute a cross-section of the community life of the newt. It is a life full of all kinds of exciting adventure, from weaving nests to crawling about in the sun and catching insect larvae and crustaceans. The newt's day is practically never done, largely because the insect larvae multiply three million times as fast as the newt can possibly catch and eat them. And it takes the closest kind of community teamwork in the newt colony to get things anywhere near cleaned up by nightfall.

It is early morning, and the workers are just appearing hurrying to the old log which is to be the scene of their labors. What a scampering! What a bustle! Ah, little scamperers! Ah, little bustlers! How lucky you are, and how wise! You work long hours, without pay, for the sheer love of working. An ideal existence, I'll tell the scientific world.

Over here on the right of the log are the Master Draggers. Of all the newt workers, they are the most futile, which is high praise indeed. Come, let us look closer and see what it is that they are doing.

The one in the lead is dragging a bit of gurry out from the water and up over the edge into the sunlight. Following him in single file, come the rest of the Master Draggers. They are not dragging anything, but are sort of helping the leader by crowding against him and eating little pieces out of the filament of his tail.

And now they have reached the top. The leader, by dint of much leg-work, has succeeded in dragging his prize to the ridge of the log.

The little workers, reaching the goal with their precious freight, are now giving it over to the Master Pushers, who have been waiting for them in the sun all this while. The Master Pushers' work is soon accomplished, for it consists simply in pushing the piece of gurry over the other side of the log until it falls with a splash into the water, where it is lost.

This part of their day's task finished, the tiny toilers rest, clustered together in a group, waving their heads about from side to side, as who should say, "There—that's done!" And so it *is* done, my little Master Draggers and my little Master Pushers, and *well* done, too. Would that my own work were as clean-cut and as satisfying.

And so it goes. Day in and day out, the busy army of newts go on making the world a better place in which to live. They have their little trials and tragedies, it is true, but they also have their fun, as any one can tell by looking at a logful of sleeping newts on a hot summer day.

And, after all, what more has life to offer?

# "Sorry, But We Only Offer That Course in the Fall"

## William Relling, Jr.

The clock on the wall above the classroom door read 7:30. Martin shifted in his seat. *Back to school at last,* he said to himself. *It sure doesn't seem to have changed much . . .*

He looked around at the rest of the dozen or so students in the room with him. There were a few who looked to Martin to be grade school or high school teachers. A pair of insurance salesmen in double-knit suits. Three or four others more slovenly dressed who he guessed were about his own age—maybe they were graduate students. Another one, a pretty blonde girl, sat by herself a few rows behind Martin, near an open window.

Martin looked past the girl through the window behind her. He could see outside that the sun had just barely begun to sink in the late June sky. The days were noticeably longer, Martin told himself, and for the past week the evenings stayed warm for several hours after the sun went down. He could also see a group of elm trees planted just beyond the edge of the school building. The trees were wavering gently in the summer breeze.

A voice from over Martin's shoulder startled him from his reverie: "I haven't seen you around here before."

Martin turned around in his seat and was looking up at a long-haired young man who was standing beside him. The young man unslung a canvas backpack from his shoulders and slid into the desk beside Martin's. "I apologize," the young man said. "I didn't mean to scare you."

Martin smiled. "It's okay. I'm sorry . . . I didn't hear what you said."

"I've never saw you here before. On campus."

"Oh." Martin smiled again. "No. I just started. What I mean is, I dropped out a couple years ago and I just got transferred to the day shift at work and I got my evenings free, so I thought I'd get back into it kinda slow and take some night classes."

The young man nodded. "It's a lot easier," he said. "Summer

school especially. The competition isn't nearly so tough." He gestured over his shoulder toward the two insurance salesmen. "The only ones on campus this time of day are either grad students or geeks."

"Or both," Martin said.

"Yeah," the young man laughed. He reached down and pulled a notebook and a pen from his backpack. "So," he asked, "you a biology major or what?"

Martin shook his head no. "I'm an English major. Or I was. Before."

"This is a biology course, you know."

"Yeah," Martin said. "But my counselor told me I needed another science elective—"

He was interrupted by the appearance of a tall, stocky, dark-haired man who walked into the classroom and set down a briefcase on the instructor's desk in the front of the room. The man looked around at the people in the classroom and smiled. "Good evening, ladies and gentlemen," he said in a quiet voice.

He sat down on a corner of the desk. "As you know," he went on, "this course is *Introduction to Lycanthropy*. Those of you who know me know that I tend to be pretty informal . . ." He nodded to a man and a woman who were seated together in the back of the classroom. "So it's all right with me if you dispense with the 'Mr. Talbot' and just call me Larry."

The instructor opened his briefcase and pulled out a sheaf of papers. "I've got a syllabus here for you with a list of the reading assignments and my office hours and home phone." He slid off the desk and moved around the room, passing out the papers. "We've got a full regular semester's worth of material to cover," he went on, "so I'm afraid that you'll probably have to do more than a little cramming."

Someone in the room groaned.

The instructor returned to the corner of his desk. "I'll be giving you three exams," he said. "The dates are all in the syllabus. I'm not going to be giving you a comprehensive final exam, but I'll still be expecting everybody to be here for every class meeting. Like I said, we have a lot of material to cover."

Martin could feel himself frowning as he listened to the instructor speak, thinking that this was beginning to look like more work than he anticipated. He sighed to himself: *Oh well.*

As Talbot continued to address the class, the evening sky outside grew darker. It wasn't long before a bright full moon was hanging over the horizon. The instructor happened to turn away from the class for a moment to gaze out of an open window, and the room fell into silence as he suddenly paused in mid-sentence. The man was staring with an oddly frightened expression at the rising moon. Then, when the instructor turned back to the class once more, Martin saw that his features had changed.

Talbot's eyes were tinged a jaundiced yellow and rimmed with red. His hairline had grown into a V down the middle of his forehead. His ears were pointed and furry. He wiped a thick line of drool from his lips and climbed on top of his desk. He let out a vicious snarl, then went on with his lecture.

Martin had to steady himself. He turned from the instructor to look around at the rest of the class and was surprised to see that everyone else was oblivious to Talbot's transformation. They were all still scribbling notes.

In the meantime, the instructor had taken off his shoes and socks and was stalking on all fours atop his desk. His nose had become black and moist and shiny, and his face was covered with coarse, dark hair. Talbot's bare feet and hands were hairy as well—more resembling canine paws than human appendages. His teeth had grown into long, sharp fangs, dripping with spittle. He growled and snapped at his class, no longer able to speak intelligibly.

He turned to gaze hungrily at the class. His eyes settled on the blonde girl sitting by the window. For a moment Talbot balanced himself precariously on the edge of his desk.

Then he sprang at the girl.

The wolf-man sailed over Martin's head. The unexpected, fierce attack bowled the girl over in her seat. She screamed as powerful jaws ripped at her throat.

After a time, the girl lay still. The instructor raised himself on his haunches and let out a long, loud howl.

The class took notes while the wolf-man tore the girl apart. All except for Martin, who was glued to his seat in horror, afraid to move, certain that if he broke from his desk and tried to run he, too, would be attacked—

Until he felt a light touch on his shoulder and his heart plummeted.

The young man who was sitting next to Martin had come to his feet and was slipping his backpack onto his shoulder. "Say," the young man asked, keeping his voice low. "Can you do me a favor?"

Shivering with fright, Martin managed to nod weakly.

"I'm supposed to meet my girlfriend at quarter to nine," the young man said. "So would you mind getting the rest of the notes for me?"

# Speak

Henry Slesar

"Hello, Phyllis? This is Manny. I'm at the office."

"Wait a minute—"

"No, please, don't interrupt. I gotta do this my way, Phyllis. This one time you should give me the last word. Ha, that's like a joke, the last word. You know what I'm sitting here with? Dr. Pfeiffer's good-night express, those pills he prescribed me last month for sleeping. I got the whole bottle right here in front of me. Empty."

"Manny—"

"You know why it's empty? On account of they're all inside me, all those nice little white pills pushing against the stomach valves like in the commercial. I wonder if they work fast, fast, fast? I sure hope so—you know me when I make up my mind to do something. This morning, when I got the call from Rodolfo at the Garden, I said to myself, Manny, anybody else in your shoes would kill himself. So why not, I said. Why am I so different from anybody else? I was gonna do it at home, but then I thought, what for? Why should I mess things up for you? Better I should get Pfeiffer's prescription filled at lunch and do it in the office. What could be a more fitting place, this lousy, crummy office?"

"Manny, please listen to me—"

"Maybe you never knew how bad things were with me, maybe I didn't cry enough. You know what I always told you, Phyllis—show business is no business. I would have been better off going into the florist racket with your brother like your family wanted. But kill me, I had to be a circus type. I couldn't be a regular Joe Shnook making paper boxes or wrapping up posies, not me. I had sawdust in my blood. In this day and age, right? They got Cinerama, they got color television, they got World's Fairs, and what does Manny give them? Freaks and novelties, right? Smart, huh? Some genius, your husband, right?"

"Manny, for Pete's sake—"

"But that wasn't bad enough. I couldn't even do *that* right. All I wanted was something unique, something different, and what do I get? One fake after another. One flop after another. That dumb magician from Argentina. That pinheaded cretin. And that bearded lady. Who could forget *him*, that big phony. One after another, phonies, floppolas. Well I'm through. Through with the whole mess—"

"Manny—"

"Yeah, I know, I know. You want to hear what happened to the Siamese twins. That's what finally broke my back, Phyllis, that was the straw. This morning, I get a call from Rodolfo at the Arena. Some wise-guy reporter from the *News* spotted one of the twins in a bar on Third Avenue. Yeah, *one* of the twins. Rodolfo threw me out of the show, of course. He swears I'll never work another circus or carny in the country, and he can do it. No, come to think of it, he can't do nothing to me anymore. Nobody can . . ."

"Manny! Please!"

"It's just no use, Phyllis. All these years I kept saying to myself— *one* act'll do it. One big break. One really great novelty. One blockbuster and I'll be right on top. But you know what I think? I wouldn't know a great act if I saw one. I'm a loser, Phyllis. I'm a wrong-guesser. Nothing good ever comes my way, because I got nothing going for me. That's the truth."

"Manny—"

"So long, Phyllis. You've been a good wife to me and I wish I'd treated you better. But take my word for it—you'll be better off without me . . ."

"Manny, will you please *listen?* This *isn't* Phyllis! Phyllis isn't here, she went out to get some groceries. Manny, this is Rex. Your dog. Your *dog*. I don't know what came over me. When I heard the phone ringing, I just *had* to answer. I knocked it off the table with my paw and I started talking. Manny, can you hear me? It's Rex! Manny, say something. Please! Manny, are you there? Rowf! Manny! Manny!"

# The Stalled Ox

## Saki

Theophil Eshley was an artist by profession, a cattle painter by force of environment. It is not to be supposed that he lived on a ranch or a dairy farm, in an atmosphere pervaded with horn and hoof, milking-stool, and branding-iron. His home was in a park-like, villa-dotted district that only just escaped the reproach of being suburban. On one side of his garden there abutted a small, picturesque meadow, in which an enterprising neighbour pastured some small picturesque cows of the Channel Island persuasion. At noon-day in summertime the cows stood knee-deep in tall meadow-grass under the shade of a group of walnut trees, with the sunlight falling in dappled patches on their mouse-sleek coats. Eshley had conceived and executed a dainty picture of two reposeful milch-cows in a setting of walnut tree and meadow-grass and filtered sunbeam, and the Royal Academy had duly exposed the same on the walls of its Summer Exhibition. The Royal Academy encourages orderly, methodical habits in its children. Eshley had painted a successful and acceptable picture of cattle drowsing picturesquely under walnut trees, and as he had begun, so, of necessity, he went on. His "Noontide Peace," a study of two dun cows under a walnut tree, was followed by "A Mid-day Sanctuary," a study of a walnut tree, with two dun cows under it. In due succession there came "Where the Gad-Flies Cease from Troubling," "The Haven of the Herd," and "A Dream in Dairyland," studies of walnut trees and dun cows. His two attempts to break away from his own tradition were signal failures: "Turtle Doves Alarmed by Sparrow-hawk" and "Wolves on the Roman Campagna" came back to his studio in the guise of abominable heresies, and Eshley climbed back into grace and the public gaze with "A Shaded Nook Where Drowsy Milkers Dream."

On a fine afternoon in late autumn he was putting some finishing touches to a study of meadow weeds when his neighbour, Adela Pingsford, assailed the outer door of his studio with loud peremptory knockings.

"There is an ox in my garden," she announced, in explanation of the tempestuous intrusion.

"An ox," said Eshley blankly, and rather fatuously; "what kind of ox?"

"Oh, I don't know what kind," snapped the lady. "A common or garden ox, to use the slang expression. It is the garden part of it that I object to. My garden has just been put straight for the winter, and an ox roaming about in it won't improve matters. Besides, there are the chrysanthemums just coming into flower."

"How did it get into the garden?" asked Eshley.

"I imagine it came in by the gate," said the lady impatiently; "it couldn't have climbed the walls, and I don't suppose any one dropped it from an aeroplane as a Bovril advertisement. The immediately important question is not how it got in, but how to get it out."

"Won't it go?" said Eshley.

"If it was anxious to go," said Adela Pingsford rather angrily, "I should not have come here to chat with you about it. I'm practically all alone; the housemaid is having her afternoon out and the cook is lying down with an attack of neuralgia. Anything that I may have learned at school or in after life about how to remove a large ox from a small garden seems to have escaped from my memory now. All I could think of was that you were a near neighbour and a cattle painter, presumably more or less familiar with the subjects that you painted, and that you might be of some slight assistance. Possibly I was mistaken."

"I paint dairy cows, certainly," admitted Eshley, "but I cannot claim to have had any experience in rounding up stray oxen. I've seen it done on a cinema film, of course, but there were always horses and lots of other accessories; besides, one never knows how much of those pictures are faked."

Adela Pingsford said nothing, but led the way to her garden. It was normally a fair-sized garden, but it looked small in comparison with the ox, a huge mottled brute, dull red about the head and shoulders, passing to dirty white on the flanks and hind-quarters, with shaggy ears and large blood-shot eyes. It bore about as much resemblance to the dainty paddock heifers that Eshley was accustomed to paint as the chief of a Kurdish nomad clan would to a Japanese tea-shop girl. Eshley stood very near the gate while he studied the animal's appearance and demeanour. Adela Pingsford continued to say nothing.

"It's eating a chrysanthemum," said Eshley at last, when the silence had become unbearable.

"How observant you are," said Adela bitterly. "You seem to notice everything. As a matter of fact, it has got six chrysanthemums in its mouth at the present moment."

The necessity for doing something was becoming imperative. Eshley took a step or two in the direction of the animal, clapped his hands, and made noises of the "Hish" and "Shoo" variety. If the ox heard them it gave no outward indication of the fact.

"If any hens should ever stray into my garden," said Adela, "I should certainly send for you to frighten them out. You 'shoo' beautifully. Meanwhile, do you mind trying to drive that ox away? That is a *Mademoiselle Louise Bichot* that he's begun on now," she added in icy calm, as a glowing orange head was crushed into the huge munching mouth.

"Since you have been so frank about the variety of the chrysanthemum," said Eshley, "I don't mind telling you that this is an Ayrshire ox."

The icy calm broke down; Adela Pingsford used language that sent the artist instinctively a few feet nearer to the ox. He picked up a pea-stick and flung it with some determination against the animal's mottled flanks. The operation of mashing *Mademoiselle Louise Bichot* into a petal salad was suspended for a long moment, while the ox gazed with concentrated inquiry at the stick-thrower. Adela gazed with equal concentration and more obvious hostility at the same focus. As the beast neither lowered its head nor stamped its feet Eshley ventured on another javelin exercise with another pea-stick. The ox seemed to realize at once that it was to go; it gave a hurried final pluck at the bed where the chrysanthemums had been, and strode swiftly up the garden. Eshley ran to head it towards the gate, but only succeeded in quickening its pace from a walk to a lumbering trot. With an air of inquiry, but with no real hesitation, it crossed the tiny strip of turf that the charitable called the croquet lawn, and pushed its way through the open French window into the morning-room. Some chrysanthemums and other autumn herbage stood about the room in vases, and the animal resumed its browsing operations; all the same, Eshley fancied that the beginnings of a hunted look had come into its eyes, a look that counselled respect. He discontinued his attempt to interfere with its choice of surroundings.

"Mr. Eshley," said Adela in a shaking voice, "I asked you to drive that beast out of my garden, but I did not ask you to drive it into my house. If I must have it anywhere on the premises I prefer the garden to the morning-room."

"Cattle drives are not in my line," said Eshley; "if I remember I told you so at the outset."

"I quite agree," retorted the lady, "painting pretty pictures of pretty little cows is what you're suited for. Perhaps you'd like to do a nice sketch of that ox making itself at home in my morning-room?"

This time it seemed as if the worm had turned; Eshley began striding away.

"Where are you going?" screamed Adela.

"To fetch implements," was the answer.

"Implements? I won't have you use a lasso. The room will be wrecked if there's a struggle."

But the artist marched out of the garden. In a couple of minutes he returned, laden with easel, sketching-stool, and painting materials.

"Do you mean to say that you're going to sit quietly down and paint that brute while it's destroying my morning-room?" gasped Adela.

"It was your suggestion," said Eshley, setting his canvas in position.

"I forbid it; I absolutely forbid it!" stormed Adela.

"I don't see what standing you have in the matter," said the artist; "you can hardly pretend that it's your ox, even by adoption."

"You seem to forget that it's in my morning-room, eating my flowers," came the raging retort.

"You seem to forget that the cook has neuralgia," said Eshley; "she may be just dozing off into a merciful sleep and your outcry will waken her. Consideration for others should be the guiding principle of people in our station of life."

"The man is mad!" exclaimed Adela tragically. A moment later it was Adela herself who appeared to go mad. The ox had finished the vase-flowers and the cover of *Israel Kalisch*, and appeared to be thinking of leaving its rather restricted quarters. Eshley noticed its restlessness and promptly flung it some bunches of Virginia creeper leaves as an inducement to continue the sitting.

"I forget how the proverb runs," he observed; "something about 'better a dinner of herbs than a stalled ox where hate is.' We seem to have all the ingredients for the proverb ready to hand."

"I shall go to the Public Library and get them to telephone for the police," announced Adela, and, raging audibly, she departed.

Some minutes later the ox, awakening probably to the suspicion that oil cake and chopped mangold was waiting for it in some appointed byre, stepped with much precaution out of the morning-room, stared with grave inquiry at the no longer obtrusive and pea-stick-throwing human, and then lumbered heavily but swiftly out of the garden. Eshley packed up his tools and followed the animal's example and "Larkdene" was left to neuralgia and the cook.

The episode was the turning-point in Eshley's artistic career. His remarkable picture, "Ox in a Morning-room, Late Autumn," was one of the sensations and successes of the next Paris Salon, and when it was subsequently exhibited at Munich it was bought by the Bavarian Government, in the teeth of the spirited bidding of three meat-extract firms. From that moment his success was continuous and assured, and the Royal Academy was thankful, two years later, to give a conspicuous position on its walls to his large canvas "Barbary Apes Wrecking a Boudoir."

Eshley presented Adela Pingsford with a new copy of *Israel Kalisch,* and a couple of finely flowering plants of *Madame André Blusset,* but nothing in the nature of a real reconciliation has taken place between them.

# The Stampeding of Lady Bastable

Saki

It would be rather nice if you would put Clovis up for another six days while I go up north to the MacGregors'," said Mrs. Sangrail sleepily across the breakfast-table. It was her invariable plan to speak in a sleepy, comfortable voice whenever she was unusually keen about anything; it put people off their guard, and they frequently fell in with her wishes before they had realized that she was really asking for anything. Lady Bastable, however, was not so easily taken unawares; possibly she knew that voice and what it betokened—at any rate, she knew Clovis.

She frowned at a piece of toast and ate it very slowly, as though she wished to convey the impression that the process hurt her more than it hurt the toast; but no extension of hospitality on Clovis's behalf rose to her lips.

"It would be a great convenience to me," pursued Mrs. Sangrail, abandoning the careless tone. "I particularly don't want to take him to the MacGregors', and it will only be for six days."

"It will seem longer," said Lady Bastable dismally. "The last time he stayed here for a week—"

"I know," interrupted the other hastily, "but that was nearly two years ago. He was younger then."

"But he hasn't improved," said her hostess; "it's no use growing older if you only learn new ways of misbehaving yourself."

Mrs. Sangrail was unable to argue the point; since Clovis had reached the age of seventeen she had never ceased to bewail his irrepressible waywardness to all her circle of acquaintances, and a polite scepticism would have greeted the slightest hint at a prospective reformation. She discarded the fruitless effort at cajolery and resorted to undisguised bribery.

"If you'll have him here for these six days I'll cancel that outstanding bridge account."

It was only for forty-nine shillings, but Lady Bastable loved shillings with a great, strong love. To lose money at bridge and not to have to pay it was one of those rare experiences which gave the card-table a glamour in her eyes which it could never otherwise have possessed. Mrs. Sangrail was almost equally devoted to her card winnings, but the prospect of conveniently warehousing her offspring for six days, and incidentally saving his railway fare to the north, reconciled her to the sacrifice; when Clovis made a belated appearance at the breakfast-table the bargain had been struck.

"Just think," said Mrs. Sangrail sleepily; "Lady Bastable has very kindly asked you to stay on here while I go to the MacGregors'."

Clovis said suitable things in a highly unsuitable manner, and proceeded to make punitive expeditions among the breakfast dishes with a scowl on his face that would have driven the purr out of a peace conference. The arrangement that had been concluded behind his back was doubly distasteful to him. In the first place, he particularly wanted to teach the MacGregor boys, who could well afford the knowledge, how to play poker-patience; secondly, the

Bastable catering was of the kind that is classified as a rude plenty, which Clovis translated as a plenty that gives rise to rude remarks. Watching him from behind ostentatiously sleepy lids, his mother realized, in the light of long experience, that any rejoicing over the success of her manœuvre would be distinctly premature. It was one thing to fit Clovis into a convenient niche of the domestic jigsaw puzzle; it was quite another matter to get him to stay there.

Lady Bastable was wont to retire in state to the morning-room immediately after breakfast and spend a quiet hour in skimming through the papers; they were there, so she might as well get their money's worth out of them. Politics did not greatly interest her, but she was obsessed with a favourite foreboding that one of these days there would be a great social upheaval, in which everybody would be killed by everybody else. "It will come sooner than we think," she would observe darkly; a mathematical expert of exceptionally high powers would have been puzzled to work out the approximate date from the slender and confusing groundwork which this assertion afforded.

On this particular morning the sight of Lady Bastable enthroned among her papers gave Clovis the hint towards which his mind had been groping all breakfast time. His mother had gone upstairs to supervise packing operations, and he was alone on the ground-floor with his hostess—and the servants. The latter were the key to the situation. Bursting wildly into the kitchen quarters, Clovis screamed a frantic though strictly non-committal summons: "Poor Lady Bastable! In the morning-room! Oh, quick!" The next moment the butler, cook, page-boy, two or three maids, and a gardener who had happened to be in one of the outer kitchens were following in a hot scurry after Clovis as he headed back for the morning-room. Lady Bastable was roused from the world of newspaper lore by hearing a Japanese screen in the hall go down with a crash. Then the door leading from the hall flew open and her young guest tore madly through the room, shrieked at her in passing, "The jacquerie! They're on us!" and dashed like an escaping hawk out through the French window. The scared mob of servants burst in on his heels, the gardener still clutching the sickle with which he had been trimming hedges, and the impetus of their headlong haste carried them, slipping and sliding, over the smooth parquet flooring towards the chair where their mistress sat in panic-stricken amazement. If she had had a moment granted her for reflection she would have behaved, as she afterwards explained, with considerable dignity. It was probably the sickle which decided her, but anyway she followed the lead that Clovis had given her through the French window, and ran well and far across the lawn before the eyes of her astonished retainers.

Lost dignity is not a possession which can be restored at a moment's notice, and both Lady Bastable and the butler found the process of returning to normal conditions almost as painful as a slow recovery from drowning. A jacquerie, even if carried out with the most respectful of intentions, cannot fail to leave some traces of embarrassment behind it. By lunch-time, however, decorum had reasserted itself with enhanced rigour as a natural rebound from its recent overthrow, and the meal was served in a frigid stateliness that might have been framed on a Byzantine model. Half-way through its duration Mrs. Sangrail was solemnly presented with an envelope lying on a silver salver. It contained a cheque for forty-nine shillings.

The MacGregor boys learned how to play poker-patience; after all, they could afford to.

# The Stout Gentleman
## A Stage Coach Romance

### Washington Irving

"I'll cross it, though it blast me!"
*Hamlet*

It was a rainy Sunday, in the gloomy month of November. I had been detained, in the course of a journey, by a slight indisposition, from which I was recovering; but I was still feverish, and was obliged to keep within doors all day, in an inn of the small town of Derby. A wet Sunday in a country inn! whoever has had the luck to experience one can alone judge of my situation. The rain pattered against the casements; the bells tolled for church with a melancholy sound. I went to the windows in quest of something to amuse the eye; but it seemed as if I had been placed completely out of the reach of all amusement. The windows of my bed-room looked out among tiled roofs and stacks of chimneys, while those of my sitting-room commanded a full view of the stable-yard. I know of nothing more calculated to make a man sick of this world than a stable-yard on a rainy day. The place was littered with wet straw that had been kicked about by travellers and stable-boys. In one corner was a stagnant pool of water, surrounding an island of muck; there were several half-drowned fowls crowded together under a cart, among which was a miserable, crest-fallen cock, drenched out of all life and spirit; his drooping tail matted, as it were, into a single feather, along which the water trickled from his back; near the cart was a half-dozing cow, chewing the cud, and standing patiently to be rained on, with wreaths of vapour rising from her reeking hide; a wall-eyed horse, tired of the loneliness of the stable, was poking his spectral head out of a window, with the rain dripping on it from the eaves; an unhappy cur, chained to a doghouse hard by, uttered something every now and then, between a bark and a yelp; a drab of a kitchen wench tramped backwards and forwards through the yard in patterns, looking as sulky as the weather itself; every thing, in short, was comfortless and forlorn, excepting a crew of hard-drinking ducks, assembled like boon companions round a puddle, and making a riotous noise over their liquor.

I was lonely and listless, and wanted amusement. My room soon became insupportable. I abandoned it, and sought what is techni-cally called the travellers'-room. This is a public room set apart at most inns for the accommodation of a class of wayfarers, called travellers, or riders; a kind of commercial knights errant, who are incessantly scouring the kingdom in gigs, on horseback, or by coach. They are the only successors that I know of at the present day, to the knights errant of yore. They lead the same kind of roving adventurous life, only changing the lance for a driving-whip, the buckler for a pattern-card, and the coat of mail for an upper Benjamin. Instead of vindicating the charms of peerless beauty, they rove about, spreading the fame and standing of some substan-tial tradesman, or manufacturer, and are ready at any time to bar-gain in his name; it being the fashion now-a-days to trade, instead of fight, with one another. As the room of the hostel, in the good old fighting times, would be hung round at night with the armour of way-worn warriors, such as coats of mail, falchions, and yawning helmets; so the travellers'-room is garnished with the harnessing of their successors, with box coats, whips of all kinds, spurs, gaiters, and oil-cloth covered hats.

I was in hopes of finding some of these worthies to talk with, but was disappointed. There were, indeed, two or three in the room; but I could make nothing of them. One was just finishing his break-fast, quarrelling with his bread and butter, and huffing the waiter; another buttoned on a pair of gaiters, with many execrations at Boots for not having cleaned his shoes well; a third sat drumming on the table with his fingers and looking at the rain as it streamed down the window-glass; they all appeared infected by the weather, and disappeared, one after the other, without exchanging a word.

I sauntered to the window and stood gazing at the people, pick-ing their way to church, with petticoats hoisted midleg high, and dripping umbrellas. The bell ceased to toll, and the streets became silent. I then amused myself with watching the daughters of a tradesman opposite; who, being confined to the house for fear of wetting their Sunday finery, played off their charms at the front windows, to fascinate the chance tenants of the inn. They at length were summoned away by a vigilant vinegar-faced mother, and I had nothing further from without to amuse me.

What was I to do to pass away the long-lived day? I was sadly nervous and lonely; and every thing about an inn seems calculated to make a dull day ten times duller. Old newspapers, smelling of beer and tobacco smoke, and which I had already read half a dozen times. Good for nothing books, that were worse than rainy weather. I bored myself to death with an old volume of the Lady's Magazine. I read all the common-placed names of ambitious travellers scrawled on the panes of glass; the eternal families of the Smiths and the Browns, and the Jacksons, and the Johnsons, and all the other sons; and I decyphered several scraps of fatiguing inn-window poetry which I have met with in all parts of the world.

The day continued lowering and gloomy; the slovenly, ragged, spongy clouds drifted heavily along; there was no variety even in the rain; it was one dull, continued, monotonous patter—patter—patter, excepting that now and then I was enlivened by the idea of a brisk shower, from the rattling of the drops upon a passing um-brella.

It was quite *refreshing* (if I may be allowed a hackneyed phrase of the day) when, in the course of the morning, a horn blew, and a stage coach whirled through the street, with outside passengers stuck all over it, cowering under cotton umbrellas, and seethed together, and reeking with the steams of wet box-coats and upper Benjamins.

The sound brought out from their lurking-places a crew of vagabond boys, and vagabond dogs, and the carroty-headed hostler, and that non-descript animal ycleped Boots, and all the other vagabond race that infest the purlieus of an inn; but the bustle was transient; the coach again whirled on its way; and boy and dog, and hostler and Boots, all slunk back again to their holes; the street again became silent, and the rain continued to rain on. In fact, there was no hope of its clearing up; the barometer pointed to rainy weather; mine hostess's tortoise-shell cat sat by the fire washing her face, and rubbing her paws over her ears; and, on referring to the Almanack, I found a direful prediction stretching from the top of the page to the bottom through the whole month, "expect—much—rain—about—this—time!"

I was dreadfully hipped. The hours seemed as if they would never creep by. The very ticking of the clock became irksome. At length the stillness of the house was interrupted by the ringing of a bell. Shortly after I heard the voice of a waiter at the bar: "The stout gentleman in No. 13, wants his breakfast. Tea and bread and butter, with ham and eggs; the eggs not to be too much done."

In such a situation as mine every incident is of importance. Here was a subject of speculation presented to my mind, and ample exercise for my imagination. I am prone to paint pictures to myself, and on this occasion I had some materials to work upon. Had the guest up stairs been mentioned as Mr. Smith, or Mr. Brown, or Mr. Jackson, or Mr. Johnson, or merely as "the gentleman in No. 13," it would have been a perfect blank to me. I should have thought nothing of it; but "The Stout Gentleman!"—the very name had something in it of the picturesque. It at once gave the size; it embodied the personage to my mind's eye; and my fancy did the rest.

He was stout, or, as some term it, lusty; in all probability, therefore, he was advanced in life, some people expanding as they grow old. By his breakfasting rather late, and in his own room, he must be a man accustomed to live at his ease, and above the necessity of early rising; no doubt a round, rosy, lusty old gentleman.

There was another violent ringing. The stout gentleman was impatient for his breakfast. He was evidently a man of importance; "well to do in the world;" accustomed to be promptly waited upon; of a keen appetite, and a little cross when hungry; "perhaps,"

406

thought I, "he may be some London Alderman; or who knows but he may be a Member of Parliament?"

The breakfast was sent up, and there was a short interval of silence; he was, doubtless, making the tea. Presently there was a violent ringing; and before it could be answered, another ringing still more violent. "Bless me! what a choleric old gentleman!" The waiter came down in a huff. The butter was rancid, the eggs were over-done, the ham was too salty—the stout gentleman was evidently nice in his eating; one of those who eat and growl, and keep the waiter on the trot, and live in a state militant with the household.

The hostess got into a fume. I should observe that she was a brisk, coquettish woman; a little of a shrew, and something of a slammerkin, but very pretty withal; with a nincompoop for a husband, as shrews are apt to have. She rated the servants roundly for their negligence in sending up so bad a breakfast, but said not a word against the stout gentleman; by which I clearly perceived that he must be a man of consequence, intitled to make a noise and to give trouble at a country inn. Other eggs, and ham, and bread and butter were sent up. They appeared to be more graciously received; at least there was no further complaint.

I had not made many turns about the travellers'-room, when there was another ringing. Shortly afterwards there was a stir and an inquest about the house. The stout gentleman wanted the Times or the Chronicle newspaper. I set him down, therefore, for a whig; or rather, from his being so absolute and lordly where he had a chance, I suspected him of being a radical. Hunt, I had heard, was a large man; "who knows," thought I, "but it is Hunt himself?"

My curiosity began to be awakened. I inquired of the waiter who was this stout gentleman that was making all this stir; but I could get no information. Nobody seemed to know his name. The landlords of bustling inns seldom trouble their heads about the names or occupations of their transient guests. The colour of a coat, the shape or size of the person, is enough to suggest a travelling name. It is either the tall gentleman, or the short gentleman, or the gentleman in black, or the gentleman in snuff-colour; or, as in the present instance, the stout gentleman. A designation of the kind once hit on answers every purpose, and saves all further inquiry.

Rain—rain—rain! pitiless, ceaseless rain! No such thing as putting a foot out of doors, and no occupation nor amusement within.

By and by I heard some one walking over head. It was in the stout gentleman's room. He evidently was a large man by the heaviness of his tread; and an old man from his wearing such creaking soles. "He is doubtless," thought I, "some rich old square-toes of regular habits, and is now taking exercise after breakfast."

I now read all the advertisements of coaches and hotels that were stuck about the mantel-piece. The Lady's Magazine had become an abomination to me; it was as tedious as the day itself. I wandered out, not knowing what to do, and ascended again to my room. I had not been there long, when there was a squall from a neighbouring bed-room. A door opened and slammed violently; a chambermaid, that I had remarked for having a ruddy, good-humoured face, went down stairs in a violent flurry. The stout gentleman had been rude to her!

This sent a whole host of my deductions to the deuce in a moment. This unknown personage could not be an old gentleman; for old gentlemen are not apt to be so obstreperous to chambermaids. He could not be a young gentleman; for young gentlemen are not apt to inspire such indignation. He must be a middle-aged man, and confounded ugly into the bargain, or the girl would not have taken the matter in such terrible dudgeon. I confess I was sorely puzzled.

In a few minutes I heard the voice of my landlady. I caught a glance of her as she came tramping up stairs; her face glowing, her cap flaring, her tongue wagging the whole way. "She'd have no such doings in her house, she'd warrant! If gentlemen did spend money freely, it was no rule. She'd have no servant maids of hers treated in that way, when they were about their work, that's what she wouldn't!"

As I hate squabbles, particularly with women, and above all with pretty women, I slunk back into my room, and partly closed the door; but my curiosity was too much excited not to listen. The landlady marched intrepidly to the enemy's citadel, and entered it with a storm. The door closed after her. I heard her voice in high, windy clamour for a moment or two. Then it gradually subsided, like a gust of wind in a garret; then there was a laugh; then I heard nothing more.

After a little while my landlady came out with an odd smile on her face, adjusting her cap, which was a little on one side. As she went down stairs I heard the landlord ask her what was the matter; she said, "Nothing at all, only the girl's a fool."—I was more than ever perplexed what to make of this unaccountable personage, who could put a good-natured chambermaid in a passion, and send away a termagant landlady in smiles. He could not be so old, nor cross, nor ugly either.

I had to go to work at his picture again, and to paint him entirely different. I now set him down for one of those stout gentlemen that are frequently met with swaggering about the doors of country inns. Moist, merry fellows, in Belcher handkerchiefs, whose bulk is a little assisted by malt-liquors. Men who have seen the world, and been sworn at Highgate; who are used to tavern life; up to all the tricks of tapsters, and knowing in the ways of sinful publicans. Free-livers on a small scale; who are prodigal within the compass of a guinea; who call all the waiters by name, touzle the maids, gossip with the landlady at the bar, and prose over a pint of port, or a glass of negus, after dinner.

The morning wore away in forming of these and similar surmises. As fast as I wove one system of belief, some movement of the unknown would completely overturn it, and throw all my thoughts again into confusion. Such are the solitary operations of a feverish mind. I was, as I have said, extremely nervous; and the continual meditation on the concerns of this invisible personage began to have its effect:—I was getting a fit of the fidgets.

Dinner-time came. I hoped the stout gentleman might dine in the travellers'-room, and that I might at length get a view of his person; but no—he had dinner served in his own room. What could be the meaning of this solitude and mystery? He could not be a radical; there was something too aristocratical in thus keeping himself apart from the rest of the world, and condemning himself to his own dull company throughout a rainy day. And then, too, he lived too well for a discontented politician. He seemed to expatiate on a variety of dishes, and to sit over his wine like a jolly friend of good-living. Indeed, my doubts on this head were soon at an end; for he could not have finished his first bottle before I could faintly hear him humming a tune; and on listening, I found it to be "God save the King." 'Twas plain, then, he was no radical, but a faithful subject; one that grew loyal over his bottle, and was ready to stand by king and constitution, when he could stand by nothing else. But who could he be! My conjectures began to run wild. Was he not some personage of distinction travelling incog.? "God knows!" said I, at my wit's end; "it may be one of the royal family, for aught I know, for they are all stout gentlemen!"

The weather continued rainy. The mysterious unknown kept his room, and, as far as I could judge, his chair, for I did not hear him move. In the mean time, as the day advanced, the travellers'-room began to be frequented. Some, who had just arrived, came in buttoned up in box-coats; others came home who had been dispersed about the town. Some took their dinners, and some their tea. Had I been in a different mood, I should have found entertainment in studying this peculiar class of men. There were two especially, who were regular wags of the road, and up to all the standing jokes of travellers. They had a thousand sly things to say to the waiting-maid, whom they called Louisa, and Ethelinda, and a dozen other fine names, changing the name every time, and chuckling amazingly at their own waggery. My mind, however, had become completely engrossed by the stout gentleman. He had kept my fancy in chase during a long day, and it was not now to be diverted from the scent.

The evening gradually wore away. The travellers read the papers two or three times over. Some drew round the fire and told long stories about their horses, about their adventures, their overturns, and breakings-down. They discussed the credits of different merchants and different inns; and the two wags told several choice anecdotes of pretty chambermaids, and kind landladies. All this passed as they were quietly taking what they called their night-caps, that is to say, strong glasses of brandy and water and sugar, or some other mixture of the kind; after which they one after another rang for "Boots" and the chambermaid, and walked off to bed in old shoes cut down into marvellously uncomfortable slippers.

There was only one man left; a short-legged, long-bodied, plethoric fellow, with a very large, sandy head. He sat by himself, with a glass of port wine negus, and a spoon; sipping and stirring, and meditating and sipping, until nothing was left but the spoon. He gradually fell asleep bolt upright in his chair, with the empty glass standing before him; and the candle seemed to fall asleep too, for the wick grew long, and black, and cabbaged at the end, and dimmed the little light that remained in the chamber. The gloom that now prevailed was contagious. Around hung the shapeless, and almost spectral, box-coats of departed travellers, long since buried in deep sleep. I only heard the ticking of the clock, with the deep-drawn breathings of the sleeping toper, and the drippings of the rain, drop—drop—drop, from the eaves of the house. The church bells chimed midnight. All at once the stout gentleman began to walk over head, pacing slowly backwards and forwards. There was something extremely awful in all this, especially to one in my state of nerves. These ghastly great coats, these guttural breathings, and the creaking footsteps of this mysterious being. His steps grew fainter and fainter, and at length died away. I could bear it no longer. I was wound up to the desperation of a hero of romance. "Be he who or what he may," said I to myself, "I'll have a sight of him!" I seized a chamber candle, and hurried up to number 13. The door stood ajar. I hesitated—I entered: the room was deserted. There stood a large, broad-bottomed elbow-chair at a table, on which was an empty tumbler, and a "Times" newspaper, and the room smelt powerfully of Stilton cheese.

The mysterious stranger had evidently but just retired. I turned off, sorely disappointed, to my room, which had been changed to the front of the house. As I went along the corridor, I saw a large pair of boots, with dirty, waxed tops, standing at the door of a bed-chamber. They doubtless belonged to the unknown; but it would not do to disturb so redoubtable a personage in his den; he might discharge a pistol, or something worse, at my head. I went to bed, therefore, and lay awake half the night in a terribly nervous state; and even when I fell asleep, I was still haunted in my dreams by the idea of the stout gentleman and his wax-topped boots.

I slept rather late the next morning, and was awakened by some stir and bustle in the house, which I could not at first comprehend; until getting more awake, I found there was a mail-coach starting from the door. Suddenly there was a cry from below, "The gentleman has forgot his umbrella! look for the gentleman's umbrella in No. 13!" I heard an immediate scampering of a chambermaid along the passage, and a shrill reply as she ran, "here it is! here's the gentleman's umbrella!"

The mysterious stranger then was on the point of setting off. This was the only chance I should ever have of knowing him. I sprang out of bed, scrambled to the window, snatched aside the curtains, and just caught a glimpse of the rear of a person getting in at the coach-door. The skirts of a brown coat parted behind, and gave me a full view of the broad disk of a pair of drab breeches. The door closed—"all right!" was the word—the coach whirled off:— and that was all I ever saw of the stout gentleman!

# Sweet Violence

## Morris Hershman

It's true that Anne Wheeler bought a gun and loaded it up with bullets and made plans to kill her husband. But from then on the story goes haywire.

Put Anne Wheeler into anything, though, and it'll go haywire. Anne is one of those fragile looking blondes who dresses well but gets a run in a stocking, who can't ever find her keys and who has no head for figures. What Anne seems to need, of course, is some big strong fellow to take care of the aggravating little things that crop up in a day.

George Wheeler seemed to feel that his mission in life was to help women in distress. His soulmate, of course, would have to be a girl so disorganized as to have made it into a flourishing career.

"George, darling," she'd say, for instance, "I can't find my gloves."

And George darling, who was trying hard to make out the dialogue of some play or movie he had taken her to, would look for that glove till the show was finished and he never did find out if the two lovers got together or if the butler did the murder. When the house lights went on, Anne would find that glove in the pocket of her coat.

She was a dilly—lovable, loose and limp-brained, when it came to anything that really counted.

There was the day she went to the track armed with a pencil, which she stuck blindly into a racing form and came up with a nag that paid $46 on the nose, and she had a ten dollar win ticket on him, to her astonishment, since she didn't know one horse from the other.

Even George was impressed by that one. Impressed, that is, until his little helpmate came out of the powder room with her eyes wide and slightly damp and allowed as how, in the excitement, she'd sort of flushed the win ducat down the point of no return.

Anne became angry at George when he started making com-

412

plaints about her housekeeping, which was perfectly inadequate. Anne worked hard enough at it, but nothing was ever in place. She used to sweep and dust, but the only effect seemed to be that of rearranging the dirt rather than disposing of it.

In the depths of her rage and after a particularly savage set-to, Anne bought a gun, a small revolver. She had to remind herself to buy bullets and then to put the revolver away in a pocketbook which was like a jungle that only a machete could have cleaved a path through. It was her plan only to threaten George if he started to complain once more. She had no plans for any further action.

But she saw red when George started grumbling that night. Certain that she'd finally kill her man, she reached wildly for her pocketbook—

Today, the two of them are living happily ever after. Anne has reluctantly conceded that her housework wasn't up to par and makes strenuous efforts to improve herself. The efforts are paying off, but very slowly. She still makes a point of losing or dropping things when they're out, which George doesn't appear to mind at all.

Nor can anybody deny that Anne's change of heart was abundantly justified, even to her. For the great glaring unmistakable proof of her previous inefficiency is that when she opened up her purse to take out a gun and kill her husband, in all the clutter that made up the contents of her pocketbook, Anne simply couldn't find the gun.


# A Tale of Wet Days

Irvin S. Cobb


In the days before the hydrant-headed specter of Prohibition reared its head in the Sunny South I had this tale from a true Kentucky gentleman. As he gave it to me, so, reader, do I give it to you:

"Yes, suh, to this good day Colonel Bud Crittenden ain't never fergot that time he made the mistake about Stony Buggs and the

Bear Grass County man. It learnt him a lesson, though. It learnt him that the deceivingest pusson on earth, when it comes to seeping up licker, is a little feller with his eyes fur apart and one of these here excitable Adamses' apples.

"Speaking about it afterwards to a passel of boys over in the swopping ring, he said the experience, while dissapinting at the time, was worth a right smart to him subsequent. Previous to that time he said he was in error regarding the amount of licker a little man, with them peculiarities of features I just mentioned, could chamber at one setting.

"Said he knowed some of the derndest, keenest gunfighters in the state was little men and he'd always acknowledged that spare-built, narrer-waisted men made the best hands driving trotting hawses; but he didn't know, not until then, that they was so gifted in the matter of putting away sweet'ning drams.

"It happened the time we all was up at Frankfort nomernating a Clerk of the Court of Appeals. There'd been a deadlock for nigh on to three days. The up-state delegates was all solid for old General Marcellus Brutus Hightower of Limestone County, and our fellers to a man was pledged to Major Zach Taylor Simms, of Pennroyal.

"Ballot after ballot it stood the same way—fifty-three to fifty-three. Then on the mawning of the third day one of their deligates from the mountains was called home suddenly by a message saying a misunderstanding had come up with a neighboring fambly and two of his boys was shot up consid'rable.

"The convention had voted the first day not to recognize no proxies for absentees, and so, having one vote the advantage, we was beginning to feel like winners, when just then Breck Calloway from McCorkin County, he up and taken the cramps the worst way. For a spell it shore looked like he was going to be cholera-morbussed. Breck started in for luxuries in the line of vittles soon as he hit town, and between votes he kept filling hisself up on fried catfeesh and red bananas and pickled pigs' feet and gum drops and cove eyesters and cocoanut out of the shell and ice cream and sardines—greasy minners, Breck called 'em—and aig-kisses and a whole lot of them kind of knick-knacks.

"That mout not a-bothered him so much if he hadn't switched from straight licker and taken on consid'able many drinks of this here new-fangled stuff called creamy de mint—green stuff like what you see in a big bottle in a drug store winder with a light behind it. By the middle of the third day Breck was trying to walk on his hands. He had a figger like one of them Mystic Mazes. 'Course, all kinked up that way, he warn't fitten for a deligate, and Colonel Bud Crittenden had to ship him home.

"I heard tell afterwards that going back on the steam cars the conductor told Breck he didn't care if he was a contortionist, he couldn't practise none of his didoes on that there train.

"So there we was, each side shy one vote and still tied—52 and 52. And at dinner time the convention taken a recess until ha'f past three in the evening with the understanding that we'd vote again at foah o'clock.

"Jest as soon as our fellers had got a drink or two and a snack to eat, Colonel Bud Crittenden, he called a caucus, him being not only manager of Major Zach Taylor Simms' campaign but likewise chairman of the district committee. Colonel Bud rapped for order and made a speech. He said the paramountest issue was how to nominate Major Simms on that there next ballot. Said they'd done trying buying off members of the opposition and other regular methods without no success whatsomever. Said the Chair would now be glad to hear suggestions from any gen'elman present.

"So Morg Holladay he got up and moved the Chair to appoint a committee of one or more to shoot up some deligate or, if desired, deligates, in the other crowd. But the Colonel said no. We wuz in a strange town, fur removed from the time-honored institutions of home, and the police mout be hosstile. Customs differed in different towns. Whil'st shooting up of a man for purely political purposes mout be accepted as necessary and proper in one place; then agin it mout lead to trouble, sich as lawsuits, in another. And so on.

"Morg he got up again and said how he recognized the wisdom of the Chair's remarks. Then he moved to amend his motion by substituting the word 'kidnapping' for 'shooting up.' Said as a general proposition he favored shooting up, not being familiar with kidnapping; in fact not knowing none of the rules, but was willing to try kidnapping as an experiment. But Colonel Bud 'peared to be even more dead set, ef possible, agin kidnapping than agin shooting. He advanced the thought that shooting was recognized as necessary under proper conditions and safeguards, ever'where, but that kidnapping was looked on as bordering on the criminal even in the case of a child. How much more so, then, in the case of a growed-up adult man and Dimocrat?

"Nobody couldn't think of nothing else then, but Colonel Bud 'lowed we was bleeged to do something. There warn't no telling, he said, when another one of our deligates would get to craving dainties and gormandize hisself with a lot of them fancy vittles the same as Breck Calloway had done, and go home all quiled up like a blue racer in a pa'tridge nest. Finally Colonel Bud he said he had a suggestion to advance his ownse'f, and we all set up and taken notice, knowing there wasn't no astuter political leader in the State and maybe none so astuted.

"Colonel Bud he said he was shamed to admit that the scheme hadn't suggested itself to him or ary other gen'elman present before now—it was so plum doggone simple.

" 'We got mighty nigh three hours yet,' says Colonel Bud, 'and enduring of that time all we got to do is to get one of them Hightower deligates deef, dumb and blind drunk—so drunk he won't never git back to answer roll-call; and if he does, won't know his own name if he heered it. We will simply appint a committee of one, composed of some gen'elman from amongst our midst of acknowledged capacity and experience, to accomplish this here undertaking, and likewise also at the same time we will pick out some accessible deligate in the opposition and commission said committee of one to put said opposition deligate out of commission by means of social conversation and licker between the present time and the hour of 4 P.M. By so doing victory will perch on our banners, and there can't be no claim of underhand work or fraud from the other side. It'll all be according to the ethics made and purvided in such emergencies.'

"Right off everybody seen Colonel Bud had the right idee, and he put the suggestion in the form of a motion and it carried unanimous. Colonel Bud stated that it now devolved upon the caucus to name the committee of one. And of course we all said that Colonel Bud was the very man for the place hisse'f; there wasn't none of us qualified like him for sich a job. Everybody was bound to admit that. But Colonel Bud said much as he appreciated the honor and high value his colleagues put on his humble abilities, he must, purforce, sacrifice pussonal ambition in the intrusts of his esteemed friend, Major Zach Taylor Simms. As manager of the campaign he must remain right there on the ground to see which way the cat was going to jump—and be ready to jump with her. So, if the caucus would kindly indulge him for one moment moah he would nominate for the post of honor and responsibility as noble a Dimocrat, as true a Kintuckian and as chivalrous a gen'elman as ever wore hair. And with all the requisited qualifications and gifts, too.

"Needless to state he referred to that sterling leader of Fulman County's faithful cohorts, Captain Stonewall Jackson Bugg, Esquire.

"And so everybody voted for Stony. We knowed of course that while Stony Bugg had both talents and education he warn't no sich genius as Colonel Bud Crittenden when it came to storing away licker; yet so far as the record showed he never had been water-looed by anybody. And we couldn't ask no more than that. Stony was all hoped up and proud at being selected.

"Then there came up the question of picking out the party of the second part, as Colonel Bud said he would call him for short. Colonel Bud said he felt the proper object for treatment, beyond the peradventure of a doubt, was that there Mr. Wash Burnett, of Bear Grass.

"He believed the caucus would ricolect this here Burnett gen'elman referred to by the Chair. And when he described him we all done so, owing to his onusual appearance. He was a little teeny feller, rising of five feet tall, with a cough that unbuttoned his vest about every three minutes. He had eyes 'way round on the side of his head like a grasshopper and the blamest, busiest, biggest, scariest, nervousest Adamses' apple I ever see. It 'peared like it tried to beat his brains out every time he taken a swaller of licker—or even water.

"Right there old Squire Buck Throckmorton objected to the selection of Mr. Wash Burnett. Near as I can recall here's what Squire says:

"'You all air suttenly fixing to make a monstrous big mistake. I've give a heap of study in my time to this question of licker drams. I have observed that when you combine in a gen'elman them two features jest mentioned—a Adamses' apple that's always running up and down like a cat squirrel on a snag, and eyes away 'round yonder so's he can see both ways at once without moving his head—you've got a gen'elman that's specially created to store away licker.

"'I don't care ef your Bear Grass County man is so shortwaisted he can use his hip pockets for year-muffs in the winter time. Concede, if you will, that every time he coughs it shakes the enamel off'n his teeth. The pint remains, I repeat, my feller citizens, that there ain't no licker ever distilled can throw him with them eyes and that there Adamses' apple. You gen'elmen 'd a sight better pick out some big feller which his eyes is bunched up close together like the yallers in a double yolk aig and which his Adamses' apple is comparatively stationary.'

417

"But Colonel Bud, he wouldn't listen. Maybe he was kinder jealous at seeing old Squire Buck Throckmorton setting hisse'f up as a jedge of human nature that-a-way. Even the greatest of us air but mortal, and I reckon Colonel Bud wouldn't admit that anybody could outdo him reading character offhand, and he taken the floor agin. Replying to his venerable friend and neighbor, he would say that the Squire was talking like a plain derned fool. Continuing he would add that it didn't make no difference if both eyes was riding the bridge of the nose side-saddle, or if they was crowding the ears for position.

" 'Now, as to the Adamses' apple, which he would consider next in this brief reply,' he went on to explain, 'Science teached us that the Adamses' apple didn't have no regular functions to speak of, and what few it did have bore no relation to the consumption of licker in the reg'lar and customary manner, viz., to-wit, by swallowing of the same from demijohn, dipper, tumbler or gourd. The Adamses' apple was but a natchel ornament nestled at the base of the chin whiskers. He asked if any gen'elman in the sound of his voice ever see a bowlder on the side of a dreen, enlessen it was covered, in whole or in part, by vines? The same wise provision of Nature was to be observed in the Adamses' apple, it being, ef he mout be pardoned for using such a figger of speech, at sich a time, the bowlder, and the chin whiskers, the vine.

" 'It's the size that counts,' said Colonel Bud Crittenden. 'It natchelly stands to reason that a big scaffolded-up man like Stony Bugg can chamber more licker than a little runt like that Burnett. Why, he could do it if Burnett was spangled all over with Adamses' apples and all of them palpitating like skeered lizards. He could do it if Burnett's eyes were so fur apart he was cross-eyed behind. Besides, this here Burnett is a mountaineering gen'elman, and I mistrust not, he's been educated altogether on white moonshine licker fresh out of the still. When red licker, with some age behind it, takes holt of his abbreviated vitals he's shore going to wilt and wilt sudden and complete.

" 'Red licker, say about fourteen year old, is mighty deceivin' to a mountaineer. It tastes so smooth he forgets that it's strong enough to take off warts.'

"Well, suzz, that argument fetched us and we all coincided; all but Squire Buck Throckmorton, who still looked mighty dubiousome. Anyway, Stony Bugg, he went out and found this here

418

Mister Wash Burnett and invited him to see if there was anything left in the bar; and Burnett, he fell into the trap, not apparently suspicioning nothing, and said he didn't care if he did. So they sashayed off together t'wards the nighest grocery arm in arm.

"Being puffectly easy in our minds, we all went back to the convention hall 'bout half past two. The Forks of Elkhorn William Jinnings Bryan and Silver Cornet Band was there and give a concert, playin 'Dixie' foah times and 'Old Kentucky Home' five. And Senator Joe Blackburn spoke three or foah times. I never before heard Republicans called out of their name like he done it. Senator Joe Blackburn shore proved hisse'f a statesman that day.

"Well, it got on t'wards half past three, and while we warn't noways uneasy we taken to wishing that Stony Bugg would report back. At ten minutes befoah foah there warn't no signs of Stony Bugg. At five minutes befoah foah our fellers was gettin' shore nuff worried, and jest then the doah opened and in comes that there little Wash Burnett—alone! He was coughing fit to kill hisse'f. His Adamses' apple was sticking out like a guinney egg, and making about eighteen reverlutions to the second, and them fur-apart eyes of his'n was the glassiest I ever seen, but it was him all right. He stopped jest inside the hall and turned up his pants at the bottom and stepped high over a shadder on the floor. But he warn't too fur gone to walk. Nor he warn't too fur gone to vote.

"'Fore we could more'n ketch our breaths the chairman called for a ballot and they taken it, and General Hightower was nominated—52 to 51—Captain Stonewall J. Bugg being recorded by the secretary as absent and not voting. And while the up-state fellers was carrying on and swapping cheers with one another, our fellers sat there jest dumfoundered. Colonel Bud Crittenden, he was the first one to speak.

"'Major Simms being beat ain't the wust of it,' he says. 'Our committee on irrigation is deceased. The solemn and sorryful duty devolves upon us, his associates, to go send a dispatch to Mrs. Stony Bugg and fambly informing them that they air widows. Stony, he must have choked hisse'f to death on some free barroom vittles, or else he got run over by a hawse and waggin. Otherwise he'd a'been here as arranged, and that there little human wart of a Wash Burnett would be spraddled out on the floor, face-down, right this very minute, a'trying to swim out of some licker store dog fashion.'

"But jest then we heard a kind of to-do outside, and the doah flew open and something rolled in and flattened out in the main aisle. Would you believe me, it was Stony Bugg, more puffectly disguised in licker than I ever expected to see.

"Two of us grabbed holt of him by the arms and pulled him up on his feet. He opened his eyes kind of dazed-like and looked around. Colonel Bud, he done the talking.

" 'Stony,' he says, not angry but real pitiful, in his tones, 'Stony, why the name of Gawd didn't you git him drunk?'

"Stony, he sort of studied a minute. Then he says, slow and deliberate and thick:

" 'Drunk? Why, boys, I gozzom so drunk I couldn't see him.'

"And as we came on home, we all had to admit you couldn't git a man no drunker than that, and live."

# Tempest in a Tub

### J. M. Bailey

It was all about a wash-tub. Mrs. Villiers had loaned Mrs. Ransom her wash-tub. This was two weeks ago last Monday. When Mrs. Villiers saw it again, which was the next morning, it stood on her backstoop, minus a hoop. Mrs. Villiers sent over to Mrs. Ransom's a request for the hoop, couched in language calculated to impugn Mrs. Ransom's reputation for carefulness. Mrs. Ransom lost no time in sending back word that the tub was all right when it was sent back; and delicately intimated that Mrs. Villiers had better sweep before her own door first, whatever that might mean. Each having discharged a Christian duty to each other, further communication was immediately cut off; and the affair was briskly discussed by the neighbours, who entered into the merits and demerits of the affair with unselfish zeal. Heaven bless them! Mrs. Ransom clearly explained her connection with the tub by charging Mr. Villiers with coming home drunk as a fiddler the night before Christmas. This bold statement threatened to carry the neighbours over in a body to Mrs. Ransom's view, until Mrs. Villiers remembered, and promptly chronicled the fact, that the Ransoms were obliged to move away from their last place because of non-payment of rent. Here the matter rested among the neighbours, leaving them as undecided as before. But between the two families immediately concerned the fire burned as luridly as when first kindled. It was a constant skirmish between the two women, from early morning until late at night. Mrs. Ransom would glare through her blinds when Mrs. Villiers was in the yard, and murmur between her clenched teeth—

"Oh, you hussy!"

And, with that wonderful instinct which characterises the human above the brute animal, Mrs. Villiers understood that Mrs. Ransom was thus engaged, and, lifting her nose at the highest angle compatible with the safety of her spinal cord, would sail around the yard as triumphantly as if escorted by a brigade of genuine princes.

And then would come Mrs. Villiers's turn at the window with Mrs. Ransom in the yard, with a like satisfactory and edifying result.

When company called on Mrs. Villiers, Mrs. Ransom would peer from behind her curtains and audibly exclaim—

"Who's that fright, I wonder?"

And when Mrs. Ransom was favoured with a call, it was Mrs. Villiers's blessed privilege to be at the window and audibly observe—

"Where was that clod dug up from?"

Mrs. Ransom has a little boy named Tommy, and Mrs. Villiers has a similar sized son, who struggles under the cognomen of Wickliffe Morgan; and it will happen, because these two children are too young to grasp fully the grave responsibilities of life—it will happen, I repeat, that they will come together in various respects. If Mrs. Ransom is so fortunate as to first observe one of these cohesions, she promptly steps to the door, and, covertly waiting until Mrs. Villiers's door opens, she shrilly observes—"Thomas Jefferson, come right into this house this minute! How many times have I told you to keep away from that Villiers brat?"

"*Villiers brat!*" What a stab that is! What subtle poison it is saturated with! Poor Mrs. Villiers's breath comes thick and hard; her face burns like fire, and her eyes almost snap out of her head. She has to press her hand to her heart as if to keep that organ from bursting; there is no relief from the dreadful throbbing and the dreadful pain. The slamming of Mrs. Ransom's door shuts out all hope of succour. But it quickens Mrs. Villiers's faculties, and makes her so alert, that when the two children come together again, which they very soon do, she is first at the door. Now is the opportunity to heap burning coals on the head of Mrs. Ransom. She heaps them.

"Wickliffe Morgan! what are you doing out there with that Ransom imp? Do you want to catch some disease? Come in here before I skin you." And the door slams shut, and poor Mrs. Ransom, with trembling form and bated breath and flashing eyes, clinches her fingers, and glares with tremendous wrath over the landscape.

And in the absence of any real, tangible information as to the loss of that hoop, this is perhaps the very best that can be done on either side.

# Truman Capote's Trilby
## The Facts

### Garry Kilworth

I have never been a great lover of hats. For one thing they tend to crush one's hair and leave it looking like sweaty straw. For another, individual hats are never thoroughly in fashion these days and wearers are considered faintly eccentric. Even in the city they draw the occasional amused smile or nudge, unless seen on the head of someone stepping out of a Rolls Royce. Of course, there are places where a hat is completely acceptable, such as at sporting events—Ascot, or the boat race—but for people like me, on a modest income, buying a hat for a single occasion is an extravagance. Finally, I think my head is the wrong shape for most hats. It supports headgear which moulds itself to the skull, like a ski hat, but tends to reshape less obsequious millinery into something almost grotesque in outward appearance.

It was, therefore, with some surprise that I found myself staring at the trilby in the window of Donne's of Oxford Street.

Purchasing a trilby requires special nerve and should really only be undertaken by a person with a charisma impossible to influence, like Bogart or the Orson Welles of *The Third Man*. The trilby has a personality, an ego, all of its own. If the wearer is not strong enough to resist alteration, it is better to steer clear of such forceful dominant items, the demi-gods and despots of hatlands and the high country.

In any case, the trilby has a dubious history, which is difficult to deny. It flaunts an ancestry which most of us would prefer to keep locked in a cupboard with all the other skeletons: forefathers that witnessed—let's not mince words—*took part in* such infamous deeds as the St Valentine's Day Massacre, and later attended the funerals without so much as a droop of the brim. The Roaring Twenties and the trilby are inseparable. A gangster's hat. Phillip Marlowe gave it back some fictional respectability, but the taint remains. Of course, women too have worn the trilby, but since women tend to be promiscuous in the use of headwear we can assume that any honor regained from that quarter is open to question. In the forties, again, its reputation sank to a very dark level when the Gestapo adopted it (along with its constant companion, the trench coat) as part of their uniform, not to mention its sinister association with Papa Doc's Haitian secret police, the terrible *Tontons Macoute*. So, the trilby is not exactly a gentleman's hat, its motives are questionable to say the least, and it often ends its days perched on the back of an Australian head in some sweltering outback creek, keeping off the flies.

It is a hat given to swaggering gestures and sloping cuteness, famed for its slouch.

Consequently, when I saw this particular trilby in the shop window, and felt a strong urge to buy it, I tried to allow my intellect to govern my emotions. I was shocked by the strength of those emotions. They produced fantasies of the kind I used to have in my youth. I saw myself travelling on the Paris metro, men staring at me in envy and women attempting to attract my attention. These pretty pictures used to precede a lot of purchases as a young man. Apparently they were still powerful enough to rule my head, because I found myself in the shop, self-consciously trying on the trilby. I left the place wearing it.

The effect on the city's populace was not startling, but I felt rather good just the same. The hat seemed a natural part of me, and I wondered, even after those first few paces along the pavement, how I had ever managed without it. Confidence entered my bones: my step was light. I passed a group of Italians, sitting outside the Café München drinking beer. One of them pointed with his chin, the way Latins do, and the others looked and nodded gravely. They approved. Italians are known to have good dress sense, so this increased my feeling of well-being.

Once on the tube, if the women did not exactly jostle each other for a better view of my new hat, they certainly gave it second glances. My self-consciousness evaporated almost completely. In the shop the sales assistant had placed the hat on my head in a conventional position. I now tipped it at a rakish angle, emphasizing, I was sure, my angular jaw. The world grew lighter.

Back at my two-roomed flat, I took the trilby and placed it where I could see it, on the dresser which also served as a desk. This piece of furniture stood exactly opposite the doorway between my kitchen-diner and the bedroom, and I made a meal, then sat and studied the article from my position at the table. It was grey with a dark grey band. Not immediately exciting in its aspect, but there was a certain charm which gave me a possessive glow of satisfaction. This was my hat, no one else's. Also, there was an independence about this trilby which enhanced my feeling of ownership. This self-possessed hat had chosen *me*.

That evening I took the hat to see Harrison Ford's rugged-looking trilby in *Raiders of the Lost Ark*. We both admired the way it managed to remain on Ford's head, even during the most frantic stunts. Towards the end of the performance we were asked to leave because a woman sitting behind us could not see the screen, but by that time most of the best scenes were over.

The next morning I wore it to work. The journey was delightful, but on reaching the office in Theobald's Road, I arrived at the same time as Jason Rachman, one of the company's high-fliers.

"Nice lid," he said with a smirk, as we went through the double-doors together.

"It's a trilby," I said, "not a *lid*."

He stopped, looking taken aback. I had never spoken to him as firmly as that before, and I think he was shocked at my assertiveness. He looked slightly confused for a moment, then said, "No, no—I'm serious. It suits you. I've often thought of buying a trilby myself—never had the nerve. Perhaps now that you've got one, I'll have a go so long as you don't mind me copying . . ."

I was feeling magnanimous.

"Not at all," and I gave him the address of the shop. No one had ever asked me such things before.

At first I placed the hat on my desk, within reach, but one of the managers passed by and told me to put it on the hat rack at the entrance to the office. I had no choice.

The following Saturday I made a terrible mistake. I don't know what made me do it. I suppose, after one has taken a tremendous new step, a giant stride, the temptation to go much further is very strong. I remember as a younger man I went on a youth hostel tour of the Scottish Highlands, and it was so successful I considered a trip to Tibet. Of course, the latter would have been a disaster. I'm not equipped, mentally or physically, for scaling the Himalayas, but the bug had got me and I felt that I could take on anything that mountain ranges had to offer. Fortunately finances prevented me from making a complete idiot of myself.

Not so on Saturday. On Saturday I went the whole hog. I bought a fresh band for the crown of my trilby, a Big White Hunter thing that screamed at people from fifty yards away. A leopardskin band. How crass. How stupid! How *kitsch*. Who did I think I was? Hemingway?

The hat hated it of course. I wore the band for one morning only and then replaced it with the old grey ribbon. The leopardskin attracted the wrong sort of attention and made me feel vulnerable once more. After that experience, I never tried changing the hat again, and accepted it for what it was.

We settled into certain behavior patterns, the trilby and I. One thing I learned was that it needed to be treated with respect and care. It was not a hat to be skimmed, James Stewart style, across the room, aimed at a peg or chair. Such undignified methods of removal were not to its liking, and I had not the lean grace of Mr. Stewart to enable me to bring the action off with the same aplomb. Also, contrary to Gene Kelly's doctrine, it did not improve for being danced through the streets in a downpour. Nor did it enjoy being crushed in a Cagney grip, or being battered into a shape reminiscent of Bogart's face. It was best placed, not tossed or jammed. I liked light, airy spaces, not dark corners. It enjoyed attention, but only for itself, not because of the angle at which it was worn, or how much of my brow showed beneath the brim.

We got on fine together, for several months. So well, in fact, that I began to take it for granted.

We made lots of new friends, who would call at the flat, or telephone to arrange an evening out: friends of both sexes. Although no really special relationship developed, these newcomers in my life became important to me.

There was Tag, a West Indian with a stylish beret; and Jake, a young Lancastrian who sported one of those colorful knitted caps. Then of course there was Beatrice, who always wore nice curled-brim bowlers: the kind of hat you often see on Cheltenham young ladies. Finally, there was Mona. Mona had seen *Annie Hall* six times and had consequently purchased a hat the twin of that cute, lopsided affair worn in the film by Diane Keaton.

Mona was my favorite. We once spent the night together and she put her Annie Hall hat under my trilby, so that they fitted snugly, one in the other.

"For company," she said.

Following in my footsteps, so to speak, Jason Rachman bought a trilby too, which he wore to the office, but I felt it was inferior to my own hat. It lacked refinement. Oh, it had a little panache and a certain sardonic humor, but its charm could not make up for its lack of sophistication, and it really was a rather shallow piece of head-gear. Jason knew this, but he defended his trilby with a shrug and a smile, which was only right and proper.

As I said before, I began to take my trilby for granted, and that's when things started to go wrong between us.

Looking back on it, I suppose it was my fault. Things began to get pretty hectic at the office, especially after my promotion. I hardly had a minute to myself. My social life too, was a whirl of activity. Everything was done at a run, and, to my eternal shame, I forgot my trilby one evening, leaving it behind at the office.

The following morning I remembered it at about ten o'clock, but it was gone from its usual place on the rack. It eventually turned up behind someone's desk, dusty and covered in fluff. Anyway it was in a sorry state. I sent it to the cleaners and what with one thing and another was unable to retrieve it for two weeks.

Then I left it at home, several days running, simply forgetting to wear it. Unforgivable, but there it is: you don't realize the impor-tance of these things at the time. Finally, the last straw was when I took Jason's trilby in mistake for my own. The next day, when we exchanged, correcting the error, I could see the experience had clearly upset my trilby quite badly. Jason had gone downhill a little since he had been passed over on the promotion ladder and tended to frequent bars and dives until the early hours of the morning. There were small stains on the brim and crown of my trilby and it had lost its shape in some steamy atmosphere.

That same evening, as I stepped out of the tube station at Tottenham Court Road, the hat blew off my head, sailed along Charing Cross Road, and got taken by a side-draught down Denmark Street. I ran after it, past the music shops and a rather sinister looking bookshop, but it had disappeared from the scene. I stood there for a while, by the small church on the corner, searching crannies and railings, but my hat had gone.

At first I tried to shrug it off. After all, it was only a hat, and there were plenty more of those to be had. Not that I actually wanted another hat (I told myself) since I seemed to have outgrown the need. I was more mature, more self-assured, and no longer concerned by the world and its ways. There were plenty of friends to visit and go out with, to the cinema or theater. In fact a hat was rather an encumbrance. One had to find places to put it, or carry it in one's hand. Being without it was a kind of freedom. It had done me a favour, blowing away like that. I was free to go where I wished, with whom I wished, whether they were bare headed or not. Liberty is a heady tranquilizer, after a loss.

Unfortunately, my new friends did not turn out to be the kind of people I had previously thought. There were excuses and evasions, and they fell away from me with mumbled apologies. Even Mona. She told me one evening that we had better not see one another again, since she did not (after all) feel we were suited.

"It was fun," she said, "but our worlds are too far apart."

I think she felt embarrassed, walking along The Strand with a hatless man, because she remained a good two feet away and kept glancing down at the pavement, as if afraid of being recognized by someone she knew. She refused the offer to take her for a drink, saying she was on the wagon, and later that week I saw her in the company of a flat-capped fellow with a Plebeian brow. She cut me dead, in the street.

Anyway, all of my so-called new friends went the same way— towards the exit. I can't say it didn't upset me, because it did. I was terribly depressed. It was all so unfair.

There were problems at work, too. Some Japanese businessmen visited the firm and they were left in my hands. I was so distracted by the decline of my social life however, I unwittingly neglected them and the result was a reprimand from one of our directors.

"And do something about your appearance," said my boss afterwards. "You seem to have gone to seed lately. This company depends upon smart executives to give it a good image. A haircut would make a difference . . ."

After a week of sleepless nights, I reluctantly went looking for my lost trilby. I suppose I had hoped that it would turn up on its own, without effort on my part. Although I hadn't marked the leather headband, I had written my name and address on a piece of paper and tucked it inside. I scoured the found ads and rang various lost property offices, without success. Finally, I took to wandering the streets after work, searching the alleys. Once, I snatched the head-gear off an old tramp, thinking it was my trilby, but I had made a mistake and had to apologize while the old fellow remonstrated with me, using the most obnoxious language. It took five pounds to get rid of him.

There was a period when I saw the trilby everywhere: on the tube, outside a cinema, going to work. But always, on closer inspection, it turned out to be a stranger which just happened to resemble my trilby superficially. Having once made an error in recognition, I was most careful not to handle these look-alikes, but the wearers often resented my staring, even from a distance, hurrying away into the crowd, or turning to glare at me.

Shortly after this period I lost my job through non-attendance at work. I didn't care any more. I began to hit the bottle.

Miserably, as the weeks went by, I toured the London streets, extending my area of search, and growing more despondent, and, yes, more resentful towards my erstwhile headwear. There were several million hats in London. What chance did I stand of finding one particular hat? The weeks crept into months, and gradually my frustration turned to anger, my anger to hatred. I convinced myself that my trilby was deliberately avoiding me. There were still times when I got morose and maudlin—where I missed it dreadfully—but many hours were spent over a glass bitterly regretting wasted dreams and shattered hopes. It seemed so silly—one breeze, one single breeze, and we had parted forever. My hatred bred a rage within me which was beyond my control. I told myself I would not be responsible for my actions should I ever lay hands on that hat again. I bought myself another, a Sherlock Holmes deerstalker, and though we were not entirely compatible we were tolerant with one another, hoping to grow closer together as the relationship matured.

One day in October, when I was least expecting an encounter, I finally saw my old trilby plastered against a fence by the wind. I knew it instantly, though it had aged dramatically since I had last seen it. I went to it, picked it up, dusted if off—and rammed it into the nearest waste bin amongst some discarded Coke cans and cigarette packets! Remembering I had the trilby's replacement on my head I tipped my new deerstalker contemptuously at my ex, and hoped the humiliation was complete. I went home, determined to forget our association.

Six nights later the police came to my flat.

They questioned me concerning my whereabouts on an evening two nights previously. Eventually, they took me away, and in the presence of a lawyer, charged me with the murder of a woman whose corpse had been found near the Thames, close to Waterloo Bridge. A trilby—my hat, with name and address still inside the band—had been found pinned beneath her body. They later produced this item of clothing in court. Since it was associated with me it had gained the same sort of notoriety and attention from the gutter press as myself. However, it was its role as principal witness for the prosecution that seemed to suit it best. Like I said earlier, the trilby has a bad track record: you can't trust a trilby. When the prosecuting counsel pushed it in front of me, his accusations tying me in knots, it didn't help my case any when I threw lighter fuel on the brim and tried to set light to it.

However, at the last hour my own counsel called a witness to the stand who had seen the woman earlier the same evening that she died, and he stated that she "had the face of a suicide." (This remark was subsequently stricken from the record, but not from the minds of the jury.) Coupled with this was a statement from a medical consultant who had independently examined the body. In his professional opinion the police doctor was mistaken. He himself was convinced that the dead woman could have sustained such injuries as a result of a fall, say from a bridge parapet onto concrete.

Despite the controversy which raged in the press, I was acquitted and walked from the courts 'a sadder but wiser man', though not without a stain on my character. There were those who were still convinced of my guilt, not least among them the police.

I never saw my hat again. The last I heard, it went on the stage. Someone had written a play around my court case, and the exhibit used in the actual court room where the trial took place was considered the main crowd puller at the theater. My ex was a box office success, right from the opening night.

Since then a certain tabloid has fostered the tale that the hat was privately purchased by Truman Capote, shortly before his death: that it attended wild New York parties and was passed around superstars and celebrities. This is an extravagant claim, to which I give little credence. To my knowledge Mr. Capote preferred a more flamboyant form of headwear, such as a panama—certainly not second-hand grey trilbies, no matter how colorful their histories. Nevertheless, to most people my hat has become 'Truman Capote's trilby', for which unlikely title I should be grateful. My connection with the item has almost been forgotten: overshadowed by the charismatic influence of the famous author's name.

Good luck to it. I know one thing. I shall never trust a trilby again, as long as I live. They're not worth it. They use you up and then they blow away. And when they've had enough of the street life, they have the audacity to expect to be taken back again, no questions asked. They want the magic to last forever, and as everyone knows, things don't work out like that. Magical relationships grow into ordinary lives, sooner or later.

# Two Dead Guys Walkin' Around Eatin' People

## John R. Platt

It was the best of Thai, it was the worst of Thai.

"Whatsamatter, Joe Bob," asked Remo between bites from the young Thai woman's shoulder. "You don't look much like you're enjoyin' your meal there."

Joe Bob picked at the dead man on the table in front of him and sighed. "Sorry Remo," he said, a piece of kidney dangling lazily between his fingers. "This . . . this just don't taste much the way I expected."

"Yer welcome to have some of mine, if you want," Remo offered.

"Oh, no," Joe Bob protested. "I 'preciate the offer, really I do, but I couldn't."

"Now don't you go gettin' all self-sacrificin' on my part, Joe Bob," Remo said. "You know I'll never be able to finish this sweet young thing by myself. She'll just go to waste." He tore off an arm, shook some of the blood off with a noisy splat so it wouldn't drip, and offered it to his friend. "Go on, I insist."

Joe Bob hesitated, then graciously took the proffered meat from Remo's grey-tinged hand. "Yer a good man, Remo. I thank you." He bit into the arm, and closed his eyes as the juices ran down his throat. "Ah, now this is more like it," he said, smiling as he drew the arm closer for a second bite.

Remo laughed gently. "Glad you like it, Joe Bob. Hey, why don't you pass me a bit of that guy. Maybe it'll be more to my likin'." Joe Bob tossed him a foot, and Remo nibbled at it, rolling the meat around on his tongue, trying to discern the odd flavor. "Well I'll be damned," he said when it finally dawned upon him.

"What's that, Remo," asked the other dead man.

"Well, Joe Bob, I can see why this feller didn't satisfy your cravin' for Thai. There's definitely a taste of MSG here."

"You mean . . ."

"Yup. This here's Chinese food."

"Well I'll be."

"Makes you wonder—what's the world comin' to when you walk into a Thai restaurant and get served Chinese?"

"Hell in a handbasket. That's what my daddy used to say."

"I'd be more'n inclined to agree with you, my friend. More'n inclined."

Remo and Joe Bob had been together for the better part of two years now, ever since the fateful day at the east Texas chemical plant. After the accident, the two co-workers had been shocked to find themselves ostracized by their friends and family. With no one to turn to but themselves, they took to the road. Just like a Hope and Crosby movie, only without the singing. And with more cannibalism.

"People can be so mean," Joe Bob said one day last April, several months into their cross-country trip.

"They fear what they don't understand, my brother," said Remo, munching on a hitchhiker they'd picked up in Williamsville, New York.

"Ain't it the truth," Joe Bob replied.

The Thai restaurant in Camden, New Jersey, had been closing down for the evening when Joe Bob and Remo stumbled across it that night. It wouldn't be opening again the next day.

Remo sat back and belched, then loosened his belt. "Oh man," he said, rubbing his distended belly. "Don't know when I last had a meal like that."

"Know what'cha mean," replied Joe Bob, rooting around near the cash register.

"What'cha lookin' for over there," asked Remo.

"Toothpick. Got a little piece of somethin' stuck right here." He made a sucking sound and poked at his teeth with his tongue.

"I told you to watch that gristle, man."

Joe Bob just grunted in return.

When Joe Bob got back to the table, toothpick in hand, Remo was lethargically spinning a tabletop display of business card-sized advertisements. The plastic block held three or four cards on each side, promoting services ranging from aluminum siding to religion.

"Hey Joe Bob, are we seekin' God?"

Joe Bob picked at his teeth. "Can't say as I want to meet him. Not after we ate those nuns last year."

"Oh yeah . . . Hey, how about piano lessons? I always wanted me some culture." Remo said, tapping at another card under the scratched plastic.

Joe Bob held up a rotted hand, the finger bones poking through more places than not. "Don't think we'd be the best students. 'Sides, we'd prob'ly eat the teacher."

"Point taken." Remo continued to twirl the spinner, a far-away look in his eyes. The other zombie sat quietly across from him. He knew how Remo got sometimes after eating. The man missed his family something fierce. Joe Bob couldn't say as he blamed him, but he still felt twinges of jealousy. At least Remo had a family to maybe go back to. Joe Bob's wife would never have taken him back, even if he hadn't already eaten her.

Suddenly Remo stopped spinning the box and grabbed it between both hands. He stared at it for a few seconds, then started clawing at the edges, pulling it apart. The cards scattered around the table. "Remo," asked Joe Bob. "Remo, you alright?"

No reply. Remo tore through the cards, flipping them over to read them, then tossing them aside. "Remo, stop, yer scarin' me." Again, no reply.

Finally, Remo picked up one of the last cards, and he sat still again for a few moments, staring at it. Then he looked up at Joe Bob and slowly turned the card to face him.

"Dr. Marvin Kasselbaum," Joe Bob read. "Specialist in eating disorders." He looked past the card and into Remo's decaying, but suddenly hopeful face.

"Do you suppose that's what we have, Joe Bob? An eating disorder?"

Joe Bob sat back and sucked at his toothpick. He looked over at the corpses of the restaurant waiters, then sighed as he noticed the fork still sticking out of the young woman's shoulder. "Ain't much point disputin' that," he said.

Dr. Marvin Kasselbaum stroked his neat, graying beard and stared at his two newest patients. Remo and Joe Bob sat across from him, fidgeting in the visitors' chairs in front of the doctor's huge oak desk. A clock ticked in the back of the room, the sound echoing through the air as the three men sat quietly.

At last, Dr. Kasselbaum coughed and ran his fingers through his hair. "Of course you realize, this would have been a lot harder for me to accept if you hadn't just taken a bite out of my nurse."

Remo bowed his head and shuffled his feet on the thick shag carpet, creating sharp crackles of static electricity. "We did apologize for that, Doc."

"You said she'd be alright," Joe Bob piped in. "I only took a small bite."

"Yes . . . well . . . ." Dr. Kasselbaum hesitated and glanced from one zombie to the other. "You . . . you realize that this isn't exactly something I have much experience with, don't you? I normally deal with anorexia, bulimia, obesity, that sort of thing. Not . . . zombies."

Remo and Joe Bob looked at each other, then back to Dr. Kasselbaum. "Anorexia?"

"Ah, yes, anorexia nervosa, actually. It's basically a self-imposed starvation, brought on by an extreme lack of self-esteem. And, well, not only do you two look fairly confident of yourselves, you also look pretty well fed."

Joe Bob patted his stomach, still swollen from last night's meal. "That much is true, Doc."

"As for bulimia nervosa, that involves eating in binges—"

Remo sat up quickly, causing Dr. Kasselbaum to jump back in his chair. "But Doc," he said. "That's what we do!"

Kasselbaum swallowed loudly, wiped some sweat from his forehead. Had Remo just licked his lips? "Um . . . yes . . . well, bulimia is also accompanied by an obsession with one's weight, again, a product of poor self-esteem. The victim vomits up his or her meals rather than digest them."

Joe Bob gave a disgusted sneer and settled back into his chair. "A sin to waste good food like that," he mumbled.

Remo stumbled out of his chair on stiff legs and started pacing around the room. "Look Doc," he said, "I can't keep on livin' like this. Can you help us or not?"

Kasselbaum's eyes followed the zombie as he circled the tiny office, back and forth, back and forth, leaving small oily stains on the carpet every few feet. He looked at Joe Bob, who was still staring at him. This time he was sure that Joe Bob had just licked his lips. "Uh . . . well . . ." He turned back to Remo, who had stopped his pacing and stood at the window, peering out at a group of children playing noisily in the schoolyard next door. A tiny tear ran down Remo's cheek.

Kasselbaum let his gaze fall to his desk. He rubbed his hands together. He looked up. "Gentlemen, I honestly don't know if I can help you. But I'll do my best."

Remo's face lit up and he stumbled to his chair. "Thank you, Doc. You don't know how happy this makes me."

"Yes, well, just sit down Mr. . . . Remo, I need to ask you both a few questions." Kasselbaum pulled a pad and pencil out of his desk while Remo angled his stiff body so that it fell into the chair. "Now," he continued, "tell me about this insatiable appetite of yours."

"Uh . . . we see people, and we eat them," said Remo.

"Yeah, that's pretty much it," echoed Joe Bob.

Dr. Kasselbaum sighed. "I had to ask," he mumbled to himself. "Okay," he said, louder this time. "Is it just people? How about other animals? Cats? Dogs? Mice?"

Joe Bob's white face drained of what little color it had left. "My God, Doc, we're zombies, not fuckin' savages."

"Geez, Doc, if that's the kind of opinion you have of us, we're not gonna get very far," said Remo.

"Okay, okay," said Kasselbaum. "Help me understand this. You're zombies. So you're dead, right?"

"Yes."

"S'far as we can tell."

"So your eating people—does it serve a physical need? Do you get hungry? Do you digest your food? How often do you defecate?"

Remo's eyes widened, then he turned his head away from Kas-

434

selbaum. "Actually, I don't think I've . . . ah . . . gone . . . ever since . . ."

"Since the accident you mentioned."

"Yeah."

"And that was . . . ?"

"Two years ago."

Kasselbaum raised his eyes towards the ceiling and tapped his pencil on the desk. "I see, I see." He stuck his tongue out of the corner of his mouth as he rubbed his beard with his other hand.

"What do you see, Doc?" Joe Bob asked.

Kasselbaum turned back to the two dead men. For the first time since they had entered, there was a look of excitement in Kasselbaum's eyes. "Well, I'd have to do some testing to be sure," he said, "but I've got a few ideas." He waved his pencil like a professor's pointer as he spoke. "Cannibalism goes way back in human history. There have been a few cases where it was a question of hunger, but those were really aberrations.

"You see, cannibalism tends to be less about physical need than a mental need. Primitive cultures often ate members of their own tribe or a warring tribe to bring certain qualities of the person they were eating into themselves. Knowledge, power, that sort of thing."

"Um . . . Doc, I hate to burst your bubble, but I don't think I'm any smarter'n when I started out here," said Remo.

"No, that's not quite it. You see, you could be eating people out of a physical need, and that's where we'd need tests to be sure. You could be driven to eat human beings out of a need to replace the parts of your body that you've lost. You are dead, after all, and you've been rotting for two years now."

"D'ya think that's it?" Joe Bob asked.

Kasselbaum stopped for a moment. "Actually, no. I don't. If human . . . meat . . . were keeping you from falling apart, I think you'd be in a lot better shape than you are now. The thing is . . . well, you guys look like shit."

"Gee, thanks."

"That your medical opinion there, Doc?" Remo mumbled.

Kasselbaum ignored the zombies' comments. "That brings us to my second theory. Your need to consume human flesh could be a psychological one. Like I said, you could be trying to bring something into yourself from the people you're eating."

"What would that be," Remo asked, one eyebrow raised, the other dangling loosely on a piece of half-connected skin.

"That's simple," Kasselbaum replied. "Life."

The answer hung in the air for a few moments. Finally, Joe Bob spoke up. "So if this is all in our heads, what do we do about it?"

"Well, basically, if what I suspect is true, the treatment will be much the same as many of my other clients. People with eating disorders often have a preconceived notion of who they are supposed to be, and what they are supposed to look like. Their nervosas are based on that need to be thin. I try to teach them to be happy with themselves. To recognize and accept who they are and to be happy with that."

"So what comes next?" Remo asked.

"Well, it will probably take months of therapy," Kasselbaum began, looking not at the zombies but at his datebook, moistening his fingers as he flipped pages through the next month. "Three, maybe four sessions a week. Careful monitoring, a controlled diet. The local medical school will surely be interested in my results." Kasselbaum licked his own lips. "There might be a grant in this somewhere."

Remo and Joe Bob looked at each other, then turned back to the fantasizing doctor. "So, what yer sayin' is that . . . we need to accept that we're dead," Joe Bob said.

"Exactly," Kasselbaum smiled.

"And to be happy with what we are," said Remo.

"True, true! You understand."

Remo and Joe Bob stood stiffly from their chairs and reached out their hands to the beaming doctor behind the desk. "Thank you, Doc. You have no idea how much we needed this," Remo said.

Dr. Kasselbaum stood and took Remo's cold hand, shaking it vigorously. "My pleasure, my boy. I'm sure that together we can work wonder—

"Uh, Remo, you're . . . hurting my hand there."

Remo and Joe Bob smiled.

"Oh shit," said Dr. Kasselbaum.

"Mmmm, good ribs," said Joe Bob, picking one of Dr. Kasselbaum's gray chest hairs out of his teeth. "How's your meal over there, my brother?"

Remo swallowed a juicy morsel from the young blonde nurse. "Mmmm. Scandinavian."

436

# Upon My Soul

## Jack Ritchie

L ife is hell," Merton said. Not quite, I thought, but I nodded. "She's absolutely the most beautiful girl in the world," Merton said. "Perfect in every detail."

I hadn't been too well briefed when I took the assignment to negotiate for his soul. "How old are you?"

Merton sipped his martini. "Twenty-one."

"And her name is Diana?"

Merton peered at me. "How did you know?"

"You must have mentioned it," I said.

"How come I'm telling you all this?"

"Every man needs to talk sometime," I said. "Now your problem seems to be that you are infat . . . in love with this Diana and she apparently doesn't know that you exist?"

"A goddess," Merton said. "A divine goddess."

"Yes," I said. "But you have a keen desire to bring her down to earth, so to speak. Perhaps I can help you."

Merton had consumed three martinis, and I thought that he was sufficiently insulated to withstand any shock.

"Merton," I said. "I'll come directly to the point. I am here to purchase your soul. And in exchange for this, I will grant you 20 years of supreme bliss with Diana."

His eyes were a bit bleary as he stared at me. Then he chuckled. "You're kidding."

"No," I said. "I'm not kidding."

He leaned closer. "I don't see any horns."

"Very well," I said, "if you insist." I waited until the bartender looked the other way and then produced a pair. I withdrew them after a moment. Merton paled.

"I'll be damned," he said. Naturally, I hoped so. He seemed considerably more sober. Then he said, "I'm five-feet-three and 130 pounds. What can you do about that?"

"How does six-feet-two strike you? And about 190?"

"I'm nearsighted and have a touch of astigmatism."

"That will be corrected." I took some papers out of my briefcase. "You may read the fine print. I have nothing to hide." Merton ordered another martini. I waited until he finished reading and then said, "Sign here where I've marked an X in pencil. The original and three carbons, please."

"Now hold it," Merton said. "You're giving me 20 years of happiness on earth and in exchange for this, I go to hell? For eons and eons? Forever?"

"It doesn't seem so long," I said, "if you keep busy."

He shook his head. "Twenty years is but an instant of time. It is so infinitesimally small that it cannot be measured as a proportion of eternity."

"How about 30 years?" I asked.

"No. The same principle holds whether it's 30 or a billion. Eventually it'll pass and leave not even a dimple on the cheek of time." No question about it, people are getting more sophisticated every day. Merton sipped his drink. "I prefer to sweat it out on earth and meet Diana in Heaven."

I smiled. "In the first place, what assurance do you have that you will reach Heaven under any circumstances? Not to mention Diana's chances. According to our projection at headquarters, Diana appears headed straight for . . ."

Merton interrupted me. "How long have you been in this business?"

"Longer than I care to think."

"And you've made a success of it?"

"My batting average is rather high," I admitted modestly.

"When the time comes to pick up a person's soul, does he ever welsh?"

"We do not accept welshing," I said. "A bargain is a bargain. But you would be surprised the lengths people go to. Some of them even hire lawyers."

"But do they ever beat you out of the deal?"

"Well," I said, "there have been a few cases."

"On what grounds?"

"Repentance and remorse. However, if you'll look at paragraph 16c in the contract, you'll notice that repentance and remorse are no longer considered valid excuses."

He was thoughtful. "I once heard Diana say she was on a diet. You don't suppose as the years go by she'll . . ."

"I guarantee that she will not gain an ounce."

"She comes from the Bronx," Merton said.

"I will see that she acquires a Virginia accent. It's quite popular these days." I pushed my pen closer to him.

He stared at it. "If I'm going to be six-foot-two and 190, it seems to me that spending 20 years with the same woman is one hell of a long time. Even if it is Diana."

"Ah," I said. "You are a shrewd bargainer, a man of the world. It is a pleasure to do business with you. Suppose I arrange that a new woman enters your intimate life every year? Do you prefer blondes? Brunettes? Redheads?"

"Mix 'em up," Merton said. His fingers touched the pen. "Did you ever notice that women talk too much? I mean *all* women?"

"Sorry," I said, "some things even *I* can't change."

He picked up the pen. "If I sign this, I see it binds me completely. And what about you? Does it bind you?"

"Naturally," I said. "Once I have your four signatures, the agreement becomes ironclad. There is nothing I can do to change it. My hands are tied."

He smiled and swiftly signed.

I retrieved and put the contracts in my briefcase. "Now to keep my part of the bargain." I waved my hand and gave Merton 60 pounds and an additional 11 inches in height. I also saw to it that his clothes and shoes fit properly.

He stood up and looked at the bar mirror. Merton was pleased. Quite pleased. He looked down at me and grinned. "Of course, you realize that when I signed that contract, I was under the influence of alcohol?"

I blinked. "Now see here, we both entered into this agreement in good faith."

He picked up the martini glass. "The bartender really shouldn't be serving me these. I won't be 21 until next month. That makes me a minor."

He downed the martini and walked toward the door. "See you in 20 years. At the trial."

I watched him go. He probably would get Daniel Webster to defend him, too.

Gerald, my district supervisor, appeared beside me. He frowned. "Henry, it looks like you've failed again."

"People keep outsmarting me," I said. "I never claimed I was a brain. Besides, I hit a run of bad luck."

He smiled significantly. "Really? Is that all it is?"

"Of course."

"We've been keeping an eye on you lately, Henry," he said. "We feel that—perhaps subconsciously—you aren't doing the best you can."

"But that's not true," I said. "I've signed up 21 clients since I joined the firm."

He nodded. "But every one of them managed to weasel out somehow when his time came."

"That's not my fault," I said defensively. "You simply ought to write tighter contracts."

He studied me. "Henry, we try to run an unhappy ship. You don't fit in. I'm afraid we'll have to let you go."

I stared at him. "Go? But what about my seniority?"

"I'm sorry," Gerald said. "You'll get your official pink slip in the mail."

When he was gone, I tried to raise my horns. I didn't have any. I was an ordinary human being again. I grinned. Yes, Gerald, there are more ways than one to skin a cat.

# The Vigil

## W. W. Jacobs

I'm the happiest man in the world," said Mr Farrer, in accents of dreamy tenderness.

Miss Ward sighed. "Wait till father comes in," she said.

Mr Farrer peered through the plants which formed a welcome screen to the window and listened with some uneasiness. He was waiting for the firm, springy step that should herald the approach of ex-Sergeant-Major Ward. A squeeze of Miss Ward's hand renewed his courage.

"Perhaps I had better light the lamp," said the girl, after a long pause. "I wonder where mother's got to?"

"She's on my side, at any rate," said Mr Farrer.

"Poor mother!" said the girl. "She daren't call her soul her own.

I expect she's sitting in her bedroom with the door shut. She hates unpleasantness. And there's sure to be some."

"So do I," said the young man, with a slight shiver. "But why should there be any? He doesn't want you to keep single all your life, does he?"

"He'd like me to marry a soldier," said Miss Ward. "He says that the young men of the present day are too soft. The only thing he thinks about is courage and strength."

She rose and, placing the lamp on the table, removed the chimney, and then sought round the room for the matches. Mr Farrer, who had two boxes in his pocket, helped her.

They found a box at last on the mantelpiece, and Mr Farrer steadied her by placing one arm round her waist while she lit the lamp. A sudden exclamation from outside reminded them that the blind was not yet drawn, and they sprang apart in dismay as a grizzled and upright old warrior burst into the room and confronted them.

"Pull that blind down!" he roared. "Not you," he continued, as Mr Farrer hastened to help. "What do you mean by touching my blind? What do you mean by embracing my daughter? Eh? Why don't you answer?"

"We—we are going to be married," said Mr Farrer, trying to speak boldly.

The sergeant-major drew himself up, and the young man gazed in dismay at a chest which seemed as though it would never cease expanding.

"Married!" exclaimed the sergeant-major, with a grim laugh. "Married to a little tame bunny-rabbit! Not if I know it. Where's your mother?" he demanded, turning to the girl.

"Upstairs," was the reply.

Her father raised his voice, and a nervous reply came from above. A minute later Mrs Ward, pale of cheek, entered the room.

"Here's fine goings-on!" said the sergeant-major, sharply. "I go for a little walk, and when I come back this—this infernal cockroach has got its arm round my daughter's waist. Why don't you look after her? Do you know anything about it?"

His wife shook her head.

"Five feet four and about thirty round the chest, and wants to marry my daughter!" said the sergeant-major, with a sneer. "Eh? What's that? What did you say? What?"

"I said that's a pretty good size for a cockroach," murmured Mr

Farrer, defiantly. "Besides, size isn't everything. If it was, you'd be a general instead of only a sergeant-major."

"You get out of my house," said the other, as soon as he could get his breath. "Go on! Sharp with it."

"I'm going," said the mortified Mr Farrer. "I'm sorry if I was rude. I came on purpose to see you to-night. Bertha—Miss Ward, I mean—told me your ideas, but I couldn't believe her. I said you'd got more common sense than to object to a man just because he wasn't a soldier."

"I want a *man* for a son-in-law," said the other. "I don't say he's got to be a soldier."

"Just so," said Mr Farrer. "You're a man, ain't you? Well, I'll do anything that you'll do."

"*Phh!*" said the sergeant-major. "I've done my little lot. I've been in action four times, and wounded in three places. That's my tally."

"The colonel said once that my husband doesn't know what fear is," said Mrs Ward, timidly. "He's afraid of nothing."

"Except ghosts," remarked her daughter, softly.

"Hold your tongue, miss," said her father, twisting his moustache. "No sensible man is afraid of what doesn't exist."

"A lot of people believe they do, though," said Mr Farrer, breaking in. "I heard the other night that old Smith's ghost has been seen again swinging from the apple tree. Three people have seen it."

"Rubbish!" said the sergeant-major.

"Maybe," said the young man; "but I'll bet you, Mr Ward, for all your courage, that you won't go up there alone at twelve o'clock one night to see."

"I thought I ordered you out of my house just now," said the sergeant-major, glaring at him.

"Going into action," said Mr Farrer, pausing at the door, "is one thing—you have to obey orders and you can't help yourself; but going to a lonely cottage two miles off to see the ghost of a man that hanged himself is another."

"Do you mean to say I'm afraid?" blustered the other.

Mr Farrer shook his head. "I don't say anything," he remarked; "but even a cockroach does a bit of thinking sometimes."

"Perhaps *you'd* like to go," said the sergeant-major.

"I don't mind," said the young man; "and perhaps you'll think a little better of me, Mr Ward. If I do what you're afraid to do—"

Mrs Ward and her daughter flung themselves hastily between

the sergeant-major and his intended sacrifice. Mr Farrer, pale but determined, stood his ground.

"I'll dare you to go up and spend a night there alone," he said.

"I'll dare you," said the incensed warrior, weakly.

"All right; I'll spend Wednesday night there," said Mr Farrer, "and I'll come round on Thursday and let you know how I got on."

"I dare say," said the other; "but I don't want you here, and, what's more, I won't have you. You can go to Smith's cottage on Wednesday at twelve o'clock if you like, and I'll go up any time between twelve and three and make sure you're there. D'ye understand? I'll show you whether I'm afraid or not."

"There's no reason for you to be afraid," said Mr Farrer. "I shall be there to protect you. That's very different to being there alone, as I shall be. But, of course, you can go up the next night by yourself, and wait for me, if you like. If you like to prove *your* courage, I mean."

"When I want to be ordered about," said the sergeant-major, in a magnificent voice, "I'll let you know. Now go, before I do anything I might be sorry for afterwards."

He stood at the door, erect as a ramrod, and watched the young man up the road. His conversation at the supper table that night related almost entirely to puppy-dogs and the best way of training them.

He kept a close eye upon his daughter for the next day or two, but human nature has its limits. He tried to sleep one afternoon in his easy-chair with one eye open, but the exquisite silence maintained by Miss Ward was too much for it. A hum of perfect content arose from the feature below, and five minutes later Miss Ward was speeding in search of Mr Farrer.

"I had to come, Ted," she said, breathlessly, "because tomorrow's Wednesday. I've got something to tell you, but I don't know whether I ought to."

"Tell me and let me decide," said Mr Farrer, tenderly.

"I—I'm so afraid you might be frightened," said the girl. "I won't tell you, but I'll give you a hint. If you see anything awful, don't be frightened."

Mr Farrer stroked her hand. "The only thing I'm afraid of is your father," he said, softly.

"Oh!" said the girl clasping her hands together. "You have guessed it."

"Guessed it?" said Mr Farrer.

Miss Ward nodded. "I happened to pass his door this morning," she said, in a low voice. "It was open a little way, and he was standing up and measuring one of mother's nightgowns against his chest. I couldn't think what he was doing it for at first."

Mr Farrer whistled and his face hardened.

"That's not fair play," he said at last. "All right; I'll be ready for him."

"He doesn't like to be put in the wrong," said Miss Ward. "He wants to prove that you haven't got any courage. He'd be disappointed if he found you had."

"All right," said Mr Farrer again. "You're an angel for coming to tell me."

"Father would call me something else, I expect," said Miss Ward, with a smile. "Good-bye. I want to get back before he wakes up."

She was back in her chair, listening to her father's slumbers, half an hour before he awoke.

"I'm making up for tomorrow night," he said, opening his eyes suddenly.

His daughter nodded.

"Shows strength of will," continued the sergeant-major, amiably. "Wellington could go to sleep at any time by just willing it. I'm the same way; I can go to sleep at five minutes' notice."

"It's a very useful gift," said Miss Ward, piously, "very."

Mr Ward had two naps the next day. He awoke from the second at twelve-thirty a.m., and in a somewhat disagreeable frame of mind rose and stretched himself. The house was very still. He took a small brown-paper parcel from behind the sofa and, extinguishing the lamp, put on his cap and opened the front door.

If the house was quiet, the little street seemed dead. He closed the door softly and stepped into the darkness. In terms which would have been understood by "our army in Flanders" he execrated the forefathers, the name, and the upbringing of Mr Edward Farrer.

Not a soul in the streets; not a light in a window. He left the little town behind, passed the last isolated house on the road, and walked into the greater blackness of a road between tall hedges. He had put on canvas shoes with rubber soles, for the better surprise of Mr Farrer, and his own progress seemed to partake of a ghostly nature. Every ghost story he had ever heard or read crowded into his memory. For the first time in his experience even the idea of the company of Mr Farrer seemed better than no company at all.

The night was so dark that he nearly missed the turning that led to the cottage. For the first few yards he had almost to feel his way; then, with a greater yearning than ever for the society of Mr Farrer, he straightened his back and marched swiftly and noiselessly towards the cottage.

It was a small, tumbledown place, set well back in an overgrown garden. The sergeant-major came to a halt just before reaching the gate, and, hidden by the hedge, unfastened his parcel and shook out his wife's best nightgown.

He got it over his head with some difficulty, and, with his arms in the sleeves, tried in vain to get his big hands through the small, lace-trimmed wristbands. Despite his utmost efforts he could only get two or three fingers through, and after a vain search for his cap, which had fallen off in the struggle, he made his way to the gate and stood there waiting. It was at this moment that the thought occurred to him that Mr Farrer might have failed to keep the appointment.

His knees trembled slightly and he listened anxiously for any sound from the house. He rattled the gate and, standing with white arms outstretched, waited. Nothing happened. He shook it again, and then, pulling himself together, opened it and slipped into the garden. As he did so a large bough which lay in the centre of the footpath thoughtfully drew on one side to let him pass.

Mr Ward stopped suddenly and, with his gaze fixed on the bough, watched it glide over the grass until it was swallowed up in the darkness. His own ideas of frightening Mr Farrer were forgotten, and in a dry, choking voice he called loudly upon the name of that gentleman.

He called two or three times, with no response, and then, in a state of panic, backed slowly towards the gate with his eyes fixed on the house. A loud crash sounded from somewhere inside, the door was flung violently open, and a gruesome figure in white hopped out and squatted on the step.

It was evident to Sergeant-Major Ward that Mr Farrer was not there, and that no useful purpose could be served by remaining. It was clear that the young man's courage had failed him, and, with grey head erect, elbows working like the sails of a windmill, and the ends of the nightgown streaming behind him, the sergeant-major bent his steps towards home.

He dropped into a walk after a time and looked carefully over his shoulder. So far as he could see he was alone, but the silence and loneliness were oppressive. He looked again, and, without stopping to inquire whether his eyes had deceived him, broke into a run again. Alternately walking and running, he got back to the town, and walked swiftly along the streets to his house. Police-Constable Burgess, who was approaching from the other direction, reached it at almost the same moment, and, turning on his lantern, stood gaping with astonishment. "Anything wrong?" he demanded.

"Wrong?" panted the sergeant-major, trying to put a little surprise and dignity into his voice. "No."

"I thought it was a lady walking in her sleep at first," said the constable. "A tall lady."

The sergeant-major suddenly became conscious of the night-gown. "I've been—for a little walk," he said, still breathing hard. "I felt a bit chilly—so I—put this on."

"Suits you, too," said the constable, stiffly. "But you Army men always was a bit dressy. Now if *I* put that on I should look ridikerlous."

The door opened before Mr Ward could reply, and revealed, in the light of a bedroom candle, the astonished countenances of his wife and daughter.

*"George!"* exclaimed Mrs Ward.

*"Father!"* said Miss Ward.

The sergeant-major tottered in and, gaining the front room, flung himself into his armchair. A stiff glass of whisky and water, handed him by his daughter, was swallowed at a gulp.

"Did you go?" inquired Mrs Ward, clasping her hands.

The sergeant-major, fully conscious of the suspicions aroused by his disordered appearance, rallied his faculties. "Not likely," he said, with a short laugh. "After I got outside I knew it was no good going there to look for that young snippet. He'd no more think of going there than he would of flying. I walked a little way down the road—for exercise—and then strolled back."

"But—my nightgown?" said the wondering Mrs Ward.

"Put it on to frighten the constable," said her husband.

He stood up and allowed her to help him pull it off. His face was flushed and his hair tousled, but the bright fierceness of his eye was unquenched. In submissive silence she followed him to bed.

He was up late next morning, and made but a poor breakfast.

His after-dinner nap was disturbed, and tea was over before he had regained his wonted calm. An hour later the arrival of a dignified and reproachful Mr Farrer set him blazing again.

"I have come to see you about last night," said Mr Farrer, before the other could speak. "A joke's a joke, but when you said you would come I naturally expected you would keep your word."

"Keep my word?" repeated the sergeant-major, almost choking with wrath.

"I stayed there in that lonely cottage from twelve to three, as per agreement, waiting for you," said Mr Farrer.

"You were not there," shouted the sergeant-major.

"How do you know?" inquired the other.

The sergeant-major looked round helplessly at his wife and daughter.

"Prove it," said Mr Farrer, pushing his advantage. "You questioned my courage, and I stayed there three hours. Where were you?"

"You were not there," said the sergeant-major. "I *know*. You can't bluff me. You were afraid."

"I was there, and I'll swear it," said Mr Farrer. "Still, there's no harm done. I'll go there again tonight, and I'll dare you to come for me."

"Dare?" said the sergeant-major, choking. "Dare?"

"Dare," repeated the other; "and if you don't come this time I'll spread it all over Marcham. Tomorrow night you can go there and wait for me. If you see what I saw—"

"Oh, Ted!" said Miss Ward, with a shiver.

"Saw?" said the sergeant-major, starting.

"Nothing harmful," said Mr Farrer, calmly. "As a matter of fact, it was very interesting."

"What was?" demanded the sergeant-major.

"It sounds rather silly, as a matter of fact," said Mr Farrer, slowly. "Still, I did see a broken bough moving about the garden."

Mr Ward regarded him open-mouthed.

"Anything else?" he inquired, in a husky voice.

"A figure in white," said Mr Farrer, "with long waving arms, hopping about like a frog. I don't suppose you believe me, but if you come tonight perhaps you'll see it yourself. It's very interesting."

"Wer—weren't you frightened?" inquired the staring Mrs Ward.

Mr Farrer shook his head. "It would take more than that to frighten me," he said, simply. "I should be ashamed of myself to be afraid of a poor thing like that. It couldn't do me any harm."

"Did you see its face?" inquired Mrs Ward, nervously.

Mr Farrer shook his head.

"What sort of a body had it got?" said her daughter.

"So far as I could see, very good," said Mr Farrer. "Very good figure—not tall, but well made."

An incredible suspicion that had been forming in the sergeant-major's mind began to take shape. "Did you see anything else?" he asked, sharply.

"One more," said Mr Farrer, regarding him pleasantly. "One I call the Running Ghost."

"Run—" began the sergeant-major, and stopped suddenly.

"It came in at the front gate," pursued Mr Farrer. "A tall, well-knit figure of martial bearing—much about your height, Mr Ward—with a beautiful filmy white robe down to its knees—"

He broke off in mild surprise, and stood gazing at Miss Ward, who, with her handkerchief to her mouth, was rocking helplessly in her chair.

"Knees," he repeated, quietly. "It came slowly down the path, and halfway to the house it stopped, and in a frightened sort of voice called out my name. I was surprised, naturally, but before I could get to it—to reassure it—"

"That'll do," said the sergeant-major, rising hastily and drawing himself up to his full height.

"You asked me," said Mr Farrer, in an aggrieved voice.

"I know I did," said the sergeant-major, breathing heavily. "I know I did; but if I sit here listening to any more of your lies I shall be ill. The best thing you can do is to take that giggling girl out and give her a breath of fresh air. I have done with her."

# When a Felon Needs a Friend

## Morris Hershman

If Irving Shiner hadn't been such a bug for poetry he would have been an average prisoner along with all the rest of us, except for being a little smaller and a lot more polite.

The first time I ever saw him, he was walking sadly into my cell. His big brown eyes were watery and his lips were puckered. A runty guy, like I said, about three foot one in socks.

He bowed a little when I gave him my name and said he was sure we'd get along. But he did it out of habit, I saw. Most "fish," new men, are sad at the start.

"Cheer up," I told him. "The worst is yet to come."

"Not for me it isn't. My collection's been sold."

"What did you collect? If it's dirty pictures, there's some floating around the exercise yard that'll knock your eyes out."

"Books."

"Dirty books?"

"I kept them spotless. Poetry."

Well, I shrugged and told him what the cell procedure was. I explained to him that with seniority on my side, I had first call on the lower bed and the sink and the toilet. He listened very sadly, looking down at what was in his hands. I guessed it was a theater program.

"If you've got tickets for a show in a few weeks," I said, "you're not going to make it."

He hesitated. "Do you suppose that after a month or so I could get a night off?"

"Night off what?" I asked, telling myself he'd picked a helluva time for a wisecrack.

"Away from here." I must have looked bug-eyed because he said, "Even if a man hates his wife, he can still get a night away once in a while."

"Look, chum," I said. "This here prison ain't like a wife. You're supposed to be re-hab-il-it-ated. Why else do you think they got one psychologist for all six hundred prisoners if not to rehabilitate you? Answer me that one, chum."

But Irving kept pacing the cell, like a lot of new men do. He was holding this program in one hand, actually a schedule of future events of some kind, and muttering to himself, "I never miss him when he comes to town. Three times I've heard him."

"You gotta get used to it," I said. "One bad thing about prison is that they don't let you go anyplace. Who is this 'him' you never miss?"

"A man named W. H. Auden. He's a poet and once in a while he comes to town and reads aloud from his poetry."

"You're kidding!" I said, and if he hadn't looked so serious, would have burst out laughing. "Brother, if you turn out to be one of those spies the warden sends around sometimes, will I be surprised!"

Irving didn't hear that, he was too busy wringing his hands. "And Auden's not alone this time, either! Imagine W. H. Auden together with the *Pro Musica Antiqua!*"

I'm not making up any of this. It seems that the Pro boys, Irving tells me, are an orchestra, and when they get wound up, they play old-time music. In fact, some of the stuff goes back centuries.

And on account of this combo and a poet, Irving Shiner was having conniptions. I told him anything could happen till the night of the big show, in a month, and he went to sleep.

Well, time marches on, like the fellow said. Irving got himself transferred out of the machine shop and into the prison hospital. He was such a nice guy that he managed to get along with everybody.

I never asked him why he got sent up. But he did mention once that he was in for at least five years, so I suppose the judge had felt that he had an antisocial streak in him somewhere.

In his free time Irving used to read books of poetry from the library.

After a couple of weeks he got restless and muttered things like, "Two weeks to go," or "Not much time left." You'd have thought he was getting out any day.

At City Prison, they line us all up in front of our cells after dinner and a guard comes along to make sure you haven't checked out. In front of my cell one night, who should be missing but Irving! At first I figured that maybe he'd lost his way or stopped off at the library to give back a book. But no, there wasn't a trace of him.

450

The guards took it pretty seriously, of course, and in no time at all, sirens were going full blast. We prisoners stood around in our cells and scratched our heads and muttered. The natives were restless that night. I'll tell *you!*

You see, the whole setup was crazy. An escape is usually planned for months and months by a dozen shifty-looking guys who'd sell their grandmothers for a gun. This time *one* guy—and a poetry-loving jerk at that—had gone like a puff of smoke. I think it was the poetry angle that bothered a lot of us.

Restless or not, I must have slept like a rock that night. When I woke up to the gong at half past seven, the first thing I saw was that the center of the mattress above me was saggy, as if somebody was resting on it. That was hard to figure; new prisoners aren't usually admitted late at night.

But I saw the small feet climb down the ladder and the small body and that stupid look of you-know-who!

"When did they find you? Why weren't you put in solitary?"

"I came straight back here." Irving stretched out his hands half an inch for morning exercises, and looked happy. "I had a wonderful time last night. Auden was just wonderf——"

I was grabbing my hair in chunks before I calmed down. "Let's see if I've got this right, Irving," I said. "You left us for one night and went to hear poetry and some third-century Dixieland, is that it?"

"Of course. I'd never want to be a fugitive, and I had given my word of honor to somebody that I'd come back."

"Your word of honor," I said a little weakly. "That changes everything."

He gave a heavy sigh; off somewhere in dreamland, as it turned out. "Next month at Auditorium Hall, they're going to have a poetry reading by Stephen Spender."

"Well," I said, to bring his mind back to practical things, "the warden may not like any of this. Not unless something has changed him overnight."

It was true. Irving, the little screwball, wouldn't spill a word about how he got out and that upset the warden so much as to land Irving in solitary for seven big days. Count 'em, seven.

But the men couldn't stop talking about it. Once in the exercise yard, when I was watching a couple of them pitching pennies, Clyde Redland came over to me. He was one of the hard guys.

"Is it true about that weasel, Shiner?" Clyde asked. "I heard he left to hear somebody reading poetry and came back by himself? Is it true?"

"Yep. He says he gave his word of honor to come back to us."

"In that case, he might want to try to dodge again." Clyde rubbed his chin with a noise like dynamite blasting down the side of a mountain. "Just when you think you've seen it all, somebody comes along with a brand-new gimmick."

I suppose this is as good a place as any to tell you about Clyde Redland, if you don't happen to remember. In the early fifties, Clyde was a big man in retailing circles. All the big companies knew him standing behind a gun.

A couple of days later in the exercise yard, when most guys were making bets on the sly or talking big talk, I saw Clyde sitting in a corner and frowning over a book.

"Something about horses?" I asked, coming over to him. Clyde was a big bettor, not too long ago.

He stopped making faces over some of the words he was reading, and wiped his lips. "Just something I wanted to read."

His hammy hands weren't able to hide the whole title and I saw one word.

*"Poetry?"* I gaped. "You?"

"It's a hobby." He glowered at me, dropping a hand from the two guys named Robert Penn Warren and Cleanth Brooks. "Any objections?"

"No, I think it's great," I said real quick, looking down at his clenched fist. "Everybody ought to have a hobby."

It was none of my business. Clyde had realized that Irving was one of those stubborn guys who couldn't be worried by threats, so he'd hit on the notion of making a friend out of him, I'd guess, and doing a double sneak one fine night.

Later on, when little Irving was out of solitary, I used to see him and Clyde walking together around the exercise yard.

Once I found an excuse to edge a little closer to them, and there was Clyde Redland scratching his cheek and saying, "If y'ask me, Irving, that's a lotta crap, because one a these here impressionist poets like Rimbaud . . ."

I won't forget it to my dying day! Longer.

Well, the word of Clyde's gimmick was getting around fast. One of the men, Muscles Gargan, a minor-league hard guy, started borrowing books from the library.

Over dinner one night, though, I heard Clyde telling Muscles very quietly, "I hear you're going in heavy for Ezra Pound, huh, Gargan?"

"Yeh, kinda. I like that stuff."

"Don't. Lay off poetry, you get me? Don't ever let me catch you reading again, not even the jokes."

Muscles laid off.

Rumors were that the warden was pretty much upset by signs of spreading culture, so I guess there was a little good in it after all. Even a guard like Lucifer Addison, a bug on poetry himself, couldn't figure it out and used to stand by the gate making faces and shaking his head like he expected moths to come zooming out.

From his point of view and the warden's, things got worse. Clyde started a poetry column in the inmates' monthly newspaper. He had become editor years ago, because he knew that copies of the paper were sent to members of the parole board. His editorial policy, by the way, was in favor of automatic parole and outlawing the death penalty. Also he wanted to see ex-cons as wardens of prisons.

Then Clyde himself started writing poems for the paper. One of them was about his sweetheart and his gray-haired mother standing at the gate and crying buckets because Clyde had beaten up another prisoner and lost his crack at parole.

But with all Clyde's buildup it was Irving alone who ducked out on us one night to go to a poetry reading, and came back next morning to a sentence of two weeks in solitary.

Clyde was sore because he hadn't been asked along. He had been hoping to duck out of the place with Irving and then forget to come back.

But when Irving finally came back to the land of the living, by which I meant he left solitary, Clyde was all buddy-buddy with him again, listening for days to him talking over what gave at the poetry reading.

"What rhythm!" Clyde broke in once, only he said it "riddim." "I always liked Stephen Spender."

That was in the exercise yard one late afternoon close to the end of summer. I was nearby, walking around to keep warmer.

Clyde said, hesitating, "I guess it's not nice to ask a friend . . ."

"What's a friend for," Irving said proudly, "if he doesn't help out when you need him."

"Well, I'd kinda like to go along with you to the next big reading at A.H." That was Auditorium Hall. "Or any other place. When you decide which one."

"Sure, glad to have you," Irving said affably, the damn fool! "But you have to give me your word of honor that you'll be back, or my contact, Addison, gets into trouble."

That would be Lucifer Addison, the other legitimate poetry nut in the place, the guard at the front gate.

"I've got a set of keys that bring me down to the gate and back." Irving grinned. "Nothing to it, as long as I use them before Addison leaves for the night."

"I give you my word of honor I'll be back," Clyde said. "Why, hell, we'll be together the whole time."

So Irving pulled out sets of programs for poetry readings and they tried to decide. Clyde said he wanted to see Ogden Nash, but Irving held out for six nights later to see e. e. cummings—all small letters to the name. Irving won out, of course. They were his marbles, if you know what I mean.

Not till the movie next night did I get a chance to talk to Clyde. "It's none of my business, Clyde, but you'll get that little goon into a god-awful mess."

Clyde nodded. "You don't expect me to go hear poetry and come back, do you?"

"You'll get Addison, the guard, in a mess, too, if you can get past him in the first place. Maybe he's not as stupid as Irving, but I guess he is."

"Well"—Clyde was thoughtful—"like I was saying to Irving just the other night, 'Suffering for Truth's sake is fortitude to highest victory.' "

"What?"

"That's a quotation from *Paradise Lost,*" Clyde explained, very snooty, "by John Milton. It's poetry."

I was a little jumpy myself on the day that E.—no, I'm sorry, it's e.—e. e. cummings was supposed to give a poetry reading. I happened to know the day on account of a listing published in the inmates' paper on what used to be the sports page.

During dinner, I happened to look across the table at Irving, and he was eating that mess we had as if he was at the Ritz, with little pinkie out, so help me.

Well, for part of the way later on, it was the same old story, starting with Irving missing after dinner. The warden was just short of calling cops to raid every poetry reading in town—about five or six of them that night, according to the prison paper—but decided against it because the damn things would likely be finished by the time the raids could be organized.

Another angle that stopped him was finding out that Clyde Redland wasn't around, either. That made it a legitimate escape, the big brass felt, and probably the two of them had gone off hand in hand and weren't coming back. Irving Shiner, that archfiend, had finally stopped playing games with the law and broken out for real, taking Clyde Redland along as muscle man.

The one point that genuinely bothered me, aside from what Irving Shiner must have been going through, was why Addison, a guard, had helped Clyde get away. But I figured it as a combination of Irving's pleas and the good impression Clyde had been making in the last few months.

In the morning I woke up to see, as usual, the upper mattress sagging again. I was glad Irving had gotten back in one piece, I admit, and I figured he must have spent a restless night telling himself what an awful mess he was in.

But no, he came bouncing off the bed like a young boxer, ready for any trouble.

"A wonderful night," he said to me. "Great poet, I don't suppose you've ever seen e. e. cummings." He shrugged. "Clyde was a little restless, I'm afraid."

I gaped at him. But it was time for lineup, so we couldn't talk. In the morning, they line us regularly in fives. I looked around to see the hole in the line that Clyde's absence must be causing, but it had been filled in, somehow. I looked to see who was in his place and it was—yep, Clyde Redland himself, in person.

Of course the guards called him and Irving out of line and marched them off to the warden's office, where I guess there was what newspapers call an exchange of ideas.

All the boys knew that Clyde hadn't suddenly been converted to the poetry lover's way of life; something had gone wrong. What it was, I didn't get to find out till a month later, when the boys were let out of solitary. Clyde wouldn't talk to Irving, but he snarled it out to the rest of us.

"That little weasel fixed my wagon," he gritted. "Addison, the guard, wasn't willing to let me out at first, but Irving said I'm his friend and he'd appreciate it. No dice. Irving said, 'I tell you what. Why don't you come along, too, and keep watch on him?' I got annoyed, and Addison still wasn't buying, so Irving said, 'To make sure my friend behaves, bring a gun.'

"I'd still have had a chance but Irving said, 'You can put handcuffs on him, if you want to.'"

"Oh, no" one of the cons said, closing his eyes in pain.

"That's not all," Clyde grunted. "Irving put in the clincher. 'And to make absolutely sure,' he said, 'bring leg irons for him.'"

Clyde took a deep breath. "And there I sat, shackled and handcuffed, with a gun on me if I made a move, for two solid hours listening to . . ."

But he cursed steadily for weeks after that, and there's no point in repeating all those words.

# With Nott in the Terrible Targa

William F. Nolan

In May of 1999 motoring history was made on the still-primitive isle of Sicily as surely as my name is Withersby Price-Bracketts.

It all began in the early winter with a fairy-soft rap-a-tap at the door of my lodgings at Lower Herringbone Lane in Upper Sussex. I opened the door to a smiling Lord Smedley, who playfully tweaked my famous red moustache, quickly swigged down a snifter of his hopelessly-sweet Bitter Lemon tonic and, casually seating himself on my rare Louis IV, proceeded to declare with bold aplomb that we, as a team, could win the "Terrible Targa" come May.

The last such open-road contest in Sicily had been run in 1931, and devil take the fact that some of the roads dated back to the Punic Wars and had not been repaired for nearly 2,000 years. The '99 race would be 1,656 miles long—or 18 brisk laps around the delightfully-rugged Big Madonie mountains. A healthy 35 hours of all-out dicing!

I protested to Nott that I was no racing driver and couldn't be expected to hold my own against the likes of "Lucky Piero" Baluggi, Count Razzpopalo (pronounced "Razz-pop-a-lo"), the incredible

Jimmy Snit, or the wild-haired Marquis de Fuzze. But Nott threw back his lionlike head and laughed away my fears.

"I'll do all the driving, old top," he said. "Your job will be childishly simple. By deft, pre-arranged hand signals, you shall warn me as to the nature of each of the 2,200 curves en route—as to whether the onrushing corner is dicey, dodgey, saucy, naughty, semi-saucy, non-dicey, semi-dodgey, non-naughty, dicey-naughty, dodgey-saucy, saucy-dicey, or dicey-saucy-naughty."

Indeed, this sounded simple enough and I immediately agreed, dizzily overwhelmed at the prospect of 35 hours of unparalleled intimacy with Lapland's fabled gift to Motor Sport. (Smedley Nottingham was educated in England, and bears a British name, but is—as we all know—a Laplander by birth who proudly drives under his distinctive family colors: a band of mottled chocolate mounted on a field of puce.) As I would have an opportunity afforded no other journalist, I was quick to organise our preparations.

Pre-race practice in Sicily is something of a bother, since one's route is often blocked by torpid sheep, confused chickens, ill-tempered dogs, wild pigs, near-sighted donkeys, sullen mules, wine-sodden cyclists, massive haywagons, smelly hordes of mud-streaked, half-clad *bambini*, and herb-crazed goats. Not to mention the normal road traffic. Therefore, the idea of setting out over these clogged by-ways in a 5.7-litre supercharged open-cockpit Black Snapper with old Nott at the wheel was, at the least, stimulating.

My job, during practice, was to log each nasty corner on the complex mountain circuit; no small task this, since we eventually discovered that all but two (the first and the last) of the 2,200 corners were nasty. In fact, my jottings became something of a problem, and when Nott found that he could no longer see the road ahead over my mounded notepaper (having driven entirely through a peasant's wattle shack) he voiced an obscene complaint. I was quick to assure him that I would be able to transcribe it all onto a handy map-roll. (This I later did, but since the finished roll weighed in excess of two hundred pounds, and measured over six miles in length, I realized I would have to trust to my all-too-fallible memory.)

The Snapper chaps were quick to restore our 5.7 to racing trim (after having removed the unfortunate shack owner's feathered hat from our manifold) and we set out for another practice go, exchanging pleased sniggers at the crudely-painted graffiti which urged: AVANTI NOTTINGHAM! VIVA PRICE-BRACKETTS! CIAO!

This time, Nott let me take the wheel for a short run to demonstrate the absurd simplicity of the new Snapper gear unit. First was left-forward; second, center-rear; third, center-forward; fourth, right-rear; fifth, right-forward; sixth, forward-rear; seventh, center-left; eighth, right-backward; ninth, backward-forward; tenth, right-left. The only real trick was in keeping the car moving in a single direction, since reverse could be engaged in any other gear, as desired—and Nott derisively poked his tongue out as we shot smartly into reverse at 100 kph. I sheeplishly paid the price of a ploughman's crude haywagon which put Nott in high good humour!

At the Snapper garage we had the 5.7 put back into tip-top shape and merrily set off for a third practice go at the circuit.

The run was undistinguished, save for a prankish teammate's loosing of a giant 12-ton boulder which tumbled colorfully down the mountain directly into our path. Nott, chuckling good-naturedly, informed me that this was the work of the young, puckish American, Billy Broadway, who was bumped out of a ride by Nott's having accepted Snapper's offer of a factory 5.7 for the Targa.

"The Yanks possess an odd sense of fun," I muttered, brushing rock shards from my famous red moustache while Nott threw back his lionlike head and roared out his delight.

The start of the fabled contest was set for the morning of May 10. We would be flagged off the line promptly at 6 A.M., just 60 seconds behind our great rival, Count Enrico Razzpopalo, who was mounted on a potent 6.7-litre Macaroni. However, as Nott was wont to remark: "In the Targa, cubic inches do not the winner make!" To which I would jokingly reply, in the rough patois of Marseilles: *"C'est bien ma poisse."* (Roughly translated as, "In life, anything is possible.")

May 10 dawned sweet and golden over Sicily. As the starting flag dropped, I realized that we were well and truly under way on the great adventure, and that I sat next to a driver more god than man, who would provide me with a most memorable ride in this historic running of the legendary Targa. Away!

Nott coolly threw the Snapper into the first easy corner, only to face one of our many setbacks: the steering wheel came off in his hands. "Gad! Gad! Gaaaaad!" he screamed shrilly, wrestling the big Snapper into a ditch.

I watched him vault, sylphlike, from the cockpit and enter a beanfield. He was back in a trice with a long stalk, which he had speedily braided for strength, and with which he cunningly secured the wheel. Then we were off once more, with Nott casually selecting seventh gear through the narrow village streets of Cerda at a perky 200 kph, whilst the coarse peasantry drove to right and left in our path. (It appeared that we had taken a wrong turning upon entering the town, but we were soon smartly back en route.)

Ahead of us: a bright patch of moving red. "Razzpopalo!" screamed Nott, jamming his pink jumpboot against the firewall. I watched the rev needle seek 7,800 rpms as we closed on Nott's famed rival. We had drawn abreast when an enraged gorilla leaped from an olive tree to land directly in front of our Snapper. Since gorillas are not indigenous to Sicily I can only assume it was an escaped zoo animal. Of whatever origin, the beast so annoyed my friend from Lapland that he decided to drive through a stone wall into a shallow ravine in order to avoid bodily contact.

Nott sipped a sweetened Bitter Lemon tonic and tweaked the cheeks of a brazen-eyed, bare-shouldered hoyden whilst I pounded away at the cruelly-twisted coachwork to free our wheels. When I was finally able to announce our roadability once again I looked about to find the great Laplander missing. Then the flimsy door of an uncouth shack opened and a slightly-rumpled Nott emerged with a smirk, adjusting his jumpboots. "Smashing, these peasant crumpets!" he declared, vaulting back into the cockpit. "All right, Withers, be about it! Push, man, *push!*"

Sweating, but wryly amused, I managed to manhandle our Snapper back onto the road.

"Razzpopalo!" screamed Nott, accelerating briskly away.

Our fine Italian Count was no match for a freshly-determined Lord Smedley, and I sat back, prepared for some supremely swift motoring.

I was not to relax for long, as the corners on the long climb to Caltavuturo occupied my full attention. I signaled each turn: two right fingers raised with a recessed left index finger; or three fingers each hand, in a Dracula claw shape; or thumbs up in an always-silly wiggle-waggle-wiffle . . . Whatever signal the corner required, I faithfully provided.

Nott was an absolute marvel (as I knew he would be) on this winding stretch of road (aptly described by a fellow-journalist as "writhing like a demented serpent"), elbows a blur as he spun the wheel hither and yon, pinkly-booted feet playing the pedals, eyes flashing merrily under his moss-green goggles. As we missed one corner entirely and plunged over a tumbled nest of boulders and spiny cacti, regaining the road in a seemingly-endless series of agonizing, death-defying slides, I realized that fear did not exist in this imperturbable Laplander. I hastily unwrapped a sucking sweet and fed it to him whilst he drove, and was rewarded with a rude gesture indicating his comradely acquiescence.

On we swept, overtaking car after car—which was not that difficult since these machines were off the road, upside down, often with their drivers pinned beneath. We saw several gloved hands protruding from crushed bonnets, waving frantically to us as we passed—and Nott never failed to wave back sportingly with rousing good cheer.

A red daub ahead: Razzpopalo!

"Razzpopalo!" screamed Nott.

This time we had no problem in passing the mad Italian with the pierced earlobe. His Macaroni had no rubber left on the rims (how the Count loved to corner!) and this had slowed him. No sooner had Nott flashed past with a cool grin than we heard a jarring *thump* against our rear deck. The laughing-eyed Italian had thrown a makeshift hand-bomb at our departing Snapper, but luckily it had failed to detonate.

"Cheeky sod!" exclaimed Nott.

More hazards to contend with on the dizzying 3,000-foot descent from Polizzi. Our brakes failed utterly at the halfway point—but Nott had a brilliant idea: he told me to hang myself over the rear deck and drag our spare wheel on the road to slow us down. This worked splendidly, although I was something of a grotty mess when we reached bottom. As Nott hastily relined the brakes I tried, with but limited success, to remove several dozen nettlesome cactus brambles from my famous red moustache.

Soon we were briskly away—with old Nott really intent on some eleven-tenths motoring. I sat transfixed as he threw our Black Snapper over the ribboning road at apparently suicidal speeds. I was *so* transfixed, in fact, that I forgot to signal for a dicey-naughty corner, and over we went, *carump!* into a field of ripe asparagus.

"Drat you, Withers! Heads up! Bit of a fluke we're still alive."

I looked properly chastened as we climbed out to access the damage. It seemed we had sustained a partial seizure of the swivels, and I said so.

"Snapper swivels do *not* seize," Nott churlishly informed me, running his keen eyes over the machine.

460

"Then what the deuce?"

Nott smiled in triumph and held up a bit of crumpled black fur. "Your seized swivel is no more than a fallen gorilla which now lies deceased beneath our wheels."

"*Another* gorilla?" My jaw hung slack.

"Quite so, Withers. Now, shall we essay the circuit again, or do you intend standing there for the duration of the race with your jaw hanging slack?"

Nott was absolutely correct in chiding me and I sheepishly wrestled the Snapper back onto the road just as the Marquis de Fuzze bellowed past us in his modified three-stage Cutlet.

"De Fuzze!" screamed Nott, and blasted off to overtake. The Cutlet was not as fast as Razzpopalo's Macaroni—and we caught the Marquis in the square at Collesano, forcing him directly into the central fountain. His machine exploded in a rout of colorful rainbow mist as Nott and I exchanged roguish grins at our good fortune.

Now, as we whipped along, the country was all vivid yellow gorse and wildflowers in the meadows, the distant layer-cake majesty of Mount Etna rising above us to the east, gray-green vineyards and silvered-green olive groves under the warm-butter sun. Ah, Sicily!

I was shaken from my reverie by a warning sign ahead: SCOLTA PERICOLOSO!—and by a sharp poke in the ribs from Nott.

"Signal?" he yelled.

I tried to recall the finger sign for dicey-saucy-dodgey, but threw up both hands in disgust—which, unfortunately, was the signal for flat-out. Old Nott, trusting me implicitly, floored the pedal. We shot smartly off the lip of a blind cliff.

I felt the utter fool as we arrowed down—and Nott turned to give me a rather severe frown, which I most surely deserved.

Luck, however, had not deserted us. Our gallant Snapper buried itself, harmlessly, in a deep-piled haywagon, center-on in the field. The rude peasant who owned the wagon began to complain stridently, but I silenced his cries by offering him our sack of sucking sweets. In Sicily, it seems, sucking sweets are a rarity, and we were soon back on the road with the odoriferous assistance of his cross-eyed team of haggard mules.

Out of Campofelice we entered the fast, three-mile straight along the sea-front. At this juncture, I might mention that Nott's penchant for personal cleanliness was carried to an extreme, it appeared to me. Whenever we entered a long straight he would promptly turn the wheel over to me and proceed to take a brisk sponge bath of bottled mineral water in the close confines of our cockpit. It was during the first of these ablutions that we had our close call with the cannon ball.

It has long been a quaint Targa custom to fire a shot from the high watchtower fronting the Mediterranean in order to warn those ahead that a competitor has entered the final stretch leading to Start-Finish. In this case, the custom all but proved our undoing, since the hurtling cannon ball, with a demoniac shriek, passed cleanly across our bonnet whilst I steered and Nott sponged. Another few inches to the rear and it would have taken both our heads with it.

(We later learned that the puckish Yank, Billy Broadway, had asked to operate the cannon. To this day—though Nott laughingly discounts the idea—I feel that the all-too-close cannon shot was a deliberate attempt on our persons.)

The next 16-and-three-quarter laps were equally crowded with incident, but in the spirit of a perky narrative I shall proceed apace to the climax of the great event to recount the thrilling finish, rather than dwell at unnecessary length over such trivia as our rescue, by gas-balloon, from a 70-foot crevice during an out-of-season cyclone, however exciting such a description might be to the non-purist reader who seeks gaudy thrills in lurid periodicals in place of solid motor racing facts more appropriate to a true account of this nature.

That final quarter-lap was nothing short of remarkable—and had I not fortified myself with an intake of crude peasant wine during a gas-up (as the Americans say!), I might well have bolted the machine out of sheer panic. The cause of my near-dereliction was a rustic band of unshaven brigands armed with snaggy-snouted pistols who waylaid us near the splendidly-scenic village of Castelbueno.

"Steecka theem up!" they demanded.

I instantly threw up both hands and Nott (again mistaking my gesture for a flat-out command) slammed down the throttle and we roared away. A few stray shots rattled into our battered Snapper as we put the group behind us, and Nott and I shared a grim smirk at our fortunate escape. Lady Luck had again served as our loyal handmaiden.

With but a few miles remaining we were naturally in the lead.

(One must keep in mind that Smedley Nottingham has won every race he has entered since the age of nine, which weighs in his favor.)

However, the supercharged 7.7 twin-hinged Bloater of "Lucky Piero" Baluggi was pressing us rather cheekily, and Nott chanced moving into tenth gear in the apex of a hairpin—a feat which only he could bring off with any degree of success. As it happened, a fat boar was blocking the roadway and we barely edged past him. The hog, I am happy to report, was unscathed. However, a ruddy-faced peasant woman accompanying the beast cursed violently as Baluggi's Bloater caught her hard in the bum, propelling her into a handsome stand of ancient olive trees.

This abrupt contact adversely affected Baluggi's machine. He pulled to the side of the circuit, understandably miffed at having stripped his concentric crown gears. Ho! Ho!

Nott, his lionlike head thrown back in wild laughter, failed to see that the next bridge was out. We sailed into clean blue space once again, landing with such force that I lost my crash hat, glasses, custom dentures and matching red hairpiece.

Still, despite all wounds, the dauntless Snapper was able to limp onward to the checker—and we crossed the line first after 35 hours, 12 minutes, 2.4 seconds—sans petrol, brakes, windscreen, transmission, exhaust system, body paneling, and the drop seat from my racing coveralls. We were also without a steering wheel, as Nott's braided beanstalk had snapped.

Yet we had won! We had beaten the incredible Jimmy Snit, whose 9-litre Schrab finished a full hour to our rear.

Caked with mud, sans drop seat, my famous red moustache in outrageous posture, I was naturally loath to exit the machine, but Nott insisted that I be lifted out on the shoulders of scrofulous, foul-breathed peasants—but no matter. Pride in one's station was out of place at a moment such as this.

I embraced Lord Smedley, knowing that we had well and truly spoilt all records—and how vividly I recall those final crisp words from the famed Laplander's lips.

"Drat you, Withers! Stand back! You're messing me about with those clumsy, mud-caked hands of yours."

Which was how that ungrateful clot thanked me for helping him win the immortal Targa! Next year, let me assure you all, I shall be in Snit's Schrab. *Then* we'll see who wins the bloody motor race!

# Witch Hunt

### Lawrence Schimel

Greg and Pete were playing ball in Pete's backyard. Greg made a low throw and Pete dove to catch it. Pete threw the ball back and Greg had to run almost all the way to the fence to catch it. Greg was just about to throw the ball back to Pete when a black cat crossed his path.

"Don't throw it!" Pete shouted.

But it was too late.

Greg hadn't seen the cat, since it was behind him, so he didn't know he now had bad luck.

They watched the ball fly through the air and crash through the window of Pete's house.

"I'm sorry," Greg said. He knew they'd be in trouble now. Pete's mother would take away the ball and they wouldn't be allowed to play catch in the backyard anymore.

"That's okay," Pete said. "It wasn't your fault. A black cat crossed your path just before you threw it. That's why I tried to tell you to stop."

"A black cat crossed my path! Oh no! I'm going to have bad luck until we find the witch the cat belongs to."

"How will we recognize her?" Pete asked his best friend.

"Simple," Greg said. "A witch wears a black hat and all black clothes, has a black cat, and flies on a broom. Besides, I'll feel it in my bones when we find the right one."

"Sounds simple enough," Pete agreed, and they set off about town, looking for witches.

"There's the witch!" Pete cried. He was pointing at a young woman who was coming out of the coffee shop. She was wearing a black beret, and was dressed all in black.

"That's not a witch," Greg said, "that's Mrs. Wimberly's oldest daughter. She works at the record store."

"How do you know she's not a witch?" Pete asked. "She's got a black hat."

"But it's not a witch's hat. Besides, I can't feel it in my bones."

They continued down the street.

"There's the witch!" Pete cried. He was pointing at a woman sweeping her front porch. The dust rose off the porch in small white clouds.

"That's not a witch," Greg said, "that's Helena's mother. Helena's the red-haired girl who was in our art class last year."

"But she's got a witch's broom!" Pete insisted. "She's only using it to sweep with now, but at night she uses it to fly across the moon. She's a witch in disguise!"

"Maybe, but I can't feel it in my bones," Greg said, so they wandered on.

"Look! That must be the witch's house," Pete said. He was pointing up Mr. Donaldson's driveway. A black cat was sitting in front of the garage.

"That's not the witch's house," Greg said, "Mr. Donaldson lives there all by himself and his cat has one white paw. Besides, I can't feel it in my bones."

"Well," said Pete, and they walked on, looking for witches.

Suddenly Greg stopped short. "There she is," Greg whispered.

"Where?" Pete looked around, but all he saw was a woman at the bus stop. She was wearing a blue coat and a red-and-white checkered scarf, and was reading a book while she waited. "I don't see a witch," Pete said.

"Right there," Greg whispered, pointing at the woman at the bus stop. "I feel it in my bones."

"Her?" Pete's voice rose in volume as he pointed at the woman as well. "She can't be a witch. She hasn't got a black hat. She hasn't got any hat at all! She's not dressed all in black, she hasn't got a black cat, and if she was a witch she'd fly home on her broom, not wait for the silly old bus to come. She can't be a witch."

The woman looked up and saw the two of them pointing at her and whispering. She suddenly stood up and walked toward them.

"It's very rude to walk about pointing at people, young men," she said.

She pointed her finger back at them, and turned them both into toads.

# The Worst Fog of the Year

## Ramsey Campbell

Thick fog had been drawn over the fields. Since the encircling horizon was invisible, the boundaries of the pale landscape were defined only by a dull silence. The moon was a dab of grey paint on the sky. Ahead, above the surface of the fog, Gaunt saw parallel lines of hedge marking the road which led to the house. With its gables piled askew against the sky the house resembled a waterlogged box soaking out of shape.

Almost before he was ready Gaunt was inside the house and passing along the dark hall, glimpsing a stretched grin on the face which adorned the post at the foot of the banister, a heavy curtain weighted with dust and gradually sagging across a mirror, oak panels displaying framed portraits which appeared to have grown beards of dust. At the end of the hall a fan of electric light lay half closed on the carpet. Gaunt inched past the heavy oak door and its brass meringue of a doorknob, into the room.

Two women sat on couches with rolled arms of thick black leather. Around them the room was piled with silence. The tea in the porcelain cups abandoned on a black table was clouding over like two miniature ponds, and beside the cups and their silver tray an orchid was crushed within a paperweight. Heavy velvet curtains twice Gaunt's height almost curtained a long window.

The older woman reached beside her for a poker, which she thrust into the fire beyond the marble proscenium of the fireplace. Her gaze never left her companion's face, and the pistol in her hand never wavered. "What time is it now?" she demanded.

The young woman shook back her black hair from its band and threw out her wrist to consult her watch. "One o'clock."

The gun rose a fraction. "Don't lie to me."

"Twenty to twelve," the young woman said, shivering. "For God's sake, won't you see what you're doing? We can still leave. There's time."

"Almost midnight," the other said happily, and then her voice sharpened. "Don't bring God into it. It's God's will that we're here. Whatever happens will be meant to happen."

"Rubbish," Gaunt snorted.

The woman patted her greying hair into place with her free hand while the girl shrank back into the crook of the couch. "Even if you can't cover your knees, pull your skirt down. Your father won't want to see you looking like that, whatever your boyfriends like."

"You," the girl said wearily, "are mad."

"If you knew that," Gaunt demanded, "why did you let her lure you here?"

The woman raised the gun until the eye of the barrel was level with the right eye of her victim, then she threw the weapon on the hearth. "Go on, and take your atheism with you. God couldn't be so cruel to your father. God will let him come to me."

The young woman made to reach for her, but drew back. "He's dead, mother. He's been dead for months."

"Don't you know I still love him, whoever he married? Do you think I could be frightened of him?" All at once the mother's eyes looked as dangerous as the barrel of the gun. "You're afraid of how he may punish your sins, when you should be weeping for the pain you caused him."

The girl sprang up and kicked the gun, which skidded away beneath the table while the cups chattered like teeth. "That's right, you run," her mother jeered. "He's out there waiting for you. You know you're meant to stay until he comes. Why else do you think tonight is the worst fog of the year?" And behind her the music crept up—for that, of course, was the title of the film.

Outside, over the fields which surrounded the house, patches of fog were wearing thin. A threadbare strip like the ghost of a path, perforated by brittle grass-blades, led towards the house. At the end farthest from the house, blades bent suddenly and sprang up; then others stirred closer to the building. Although the fog hung close to the ground, what troubled the grass was crawling beneath the fog.

For the second time Gaunt wanted to leave. The first had been in London, in a cinema off Tottenham Court Road. Surrounded by snoring men, he'd realised that the young woman was trapped. Her own stupidity and inconsistency had trapped her, or those qualities of the script had, and his feeling compelled to will her to escape had infuriated him. Now, having seen it once, he knew her fate, yet more than ever he was urging the film to let her go. He would have left the cinema, except that he was the entire audience for the press show. At least nobody would know he wasn't watching, and so he closed his eyes. With luck he might nod off, just like one of the Londoners who had nowhere but the cinema to sleep; he'd been lying awake for nights trying to think what to make of his life.

In front of him was dimness not unlike midnight fog, and the sounds of stealthy crawling in the grass. Why was he here? He mightn't even be allowed to review the film. His editor had hinted that his reviews were too analytical for a small-town newspaper and in particular for the cinema manager, a friend of the editor's. If the editor gave way to persuasion then Gaunt would have to, like a minor character required to behave as the script demanded. He heard movement dragging through the grass, and thought he could hear the squeak of soil clenched in a groping fist, though last time he hadn't. He felt as if he was dreaming the film, in which case he had to accept some blame for its absurdity, for that of his own situation, for the absurdity of talking to the film in the dark as though it was as real as himself and as though his feelings could make any difference. "Pointless," he muttered. "Meaningless, you and me both." He drew a breath to groan as though the film could hear his impatience with it. For a moment he was enclosed in a humming silence; his head swam unpleasantly, and the fog in his eyes seemed to surge at him. Then he heard grass rustling around him.

Had the projectionist turned on the stereophonic sound? He needn't have bothered; it wouldn't improve Gaunt's view of the film. Perhaps the speakers had momentarily gone wrong, because the sound had ceased. Gaunt's eyes lay shut, and his mind lay inert, until behind him he heard the young woman run to draw the curtains.

"He won't come through the window. He'll use the front door as he has every right to," her mother said, and Gaunt opened his eyes. He wasn't in the cinema, he was in the room.

For a moment he thought he was experiencing some new visual gimmick. The room seemed unreal; it seemed somehow to have crammed itself into his eyes. He was nearest the table, and he made himself dip one shaky finger into a cup of tea. The skin of the stagnant brew gave way, and the chill of the liquid shivered up his arm.

He couldn't cry out. The chill had seized his throat, and he couldn't even swallow. His mind was struggling to deny what he was experiencing, but was this really more absurd than his everyday life? As soon as he had the thought, it seized him, and the room opened out around him. "Did he come through the front door for my sister?" the girl cried behind him.

Gaunt lurched aside and stared at her. She was gazing at her mother, who lay in an attitude of regal indifference on the couch. Gaunt shoved one hand almost into the daughter's face, but she didn't flinch. Neither woman could see him. It was he who was unreal.

"No doubt," the mother said.

"And for my brother? Did you lure them both here?"

"They came when they were called," the mother said, and with a hint of bitterness, "He let them see him, but he didn't show himself to me."

"But you saw what he did to them. You saw how they were stuffed with earth."

"Don't you say that! Don't you dare suggest he could do that to anyone!"

We're all mad, Gaunt thought wildly. Everything is. He almost touched the girl to convince himself that she was real, but what would that or its opposite prove? He stood in the room, unable to stir, and then he heard a scratching at the front door.

"He's your father!" the woman shouted as her daughter flinched towards Gaunt. "Don't you let him see that you're frightened of him!" She flung herself at the young woman and grabbing her wrist, dragged her along the hall to the front door. Gaunt felt as if the wake of her violence was carrying him along, past a mirror in which he might or might not be glimpsing himself. There was silence except for the panting of the women; even the front door appeared to be holding itself still. Then something scratched at the foot of the door.

The daughter fought. Gaunt wanted to help her, but the idea felt like a pit into which he would never stop falling. Suddenly several objects like blackened splintered knife-blades were thrust under the door. They were fingernails.

The daughter screamed and wrenching herself free, fled along the hall. Gaunt thought her flight had released him until he felt himself being rushed after her. As he ended up in the middle of the room, the mother came in and locked the door. "He won't mind if I open the window for him," she said. "It'll be like an assignation."

The daughter caught up the silver tea-tray as if it was the only weapon she could bring to mind, sending the cups trundling across the carpet. "After I cleaned up for him," her mother shouted, "and you didn't even wash up!" She captured her daughter's wrists, and the women wrestled for possession of the tea-tray. Flashes of light from it blinded Gaunt, who closed his eyes as if that might help him escape. Then they sprang open. At the window, muffled by the curtains, he'd heard a feeble thud of stone on glass.

The woman released her daughter and ran to the curtains. She dragged them open, and the fog bellied forwards to soak up the light from the room. At the bottom of the right-hand pane Gaunt saw a stone rear up slowly, strike the pane and spatter it with mud, fall back to hang suspended for a moment and then thump the grass. Around the stone were five discoloured things like blades.

The blows were growing stronger. From outside the window came a choking cough, and a shower of mud obscured the glass. The mother pulled the upper bolt free of its socket and stooped to the bolt at the foot of the window. Her daughter ran at her, lifting the tray to batter her down. Then the pane gave way, and the stone thudded on the carpet.

Gaunt staggered back, closing his eyes. The gun! He fell to his knees and groped under the table. Nothing. The women screamed, and what sounded like a mound of earth fell through the window into the room.

As Gaunt scrabbled under the table he heard sounds of padding and scraping, like the progress of an injured dog that was causing the floor to quiver. He forced his eyes open, and saw the gun ahead of him, just out of reach. He hitched himself forwards, and the mother bent to pick up the gun as the young woman stumbled to the door. A shadow fell across Gaunt's path. He peered wildly along it and confronted something like a face.

It was crushed and discoloured. It might almost have been a mask shaped of mud and insufficiently baked. Parts of it were moist, other parts were crumbling. The sight of it paralysed him while a frayed hand wavered up from the carpet and reached towards him with its askew nails.

When Gaunt didn't move, the hand faltered to the ragged lips. Deliberately, and with some effort, the mouth produced a handful of glistening mud, and then the hand came swaying towards Gaunt's face. He felt his lips twitching uncontrollably. It was waiting for him to open his mouth.

He couldn't keep it shut now that an outraged scream was building up inside him. The prospect of his fate made not just his mouth but his whole body squirm. The convulsion released him, and he squirmed aside, seizing the wrist, which was mostly bones, and twisting it. Its flimsiness took him unawares. The arm tore loose from the shoulder, and Gaunt went sprawling. Instead of bones and tendons, the arm ended in a bunch of wires and metal rods.

Gaunt staggered to his feet and gave the mutilated dummy a kick to convince himself it had stopped moving. The mother stood frozen, gun in hand, in the act of turning to shoot her daughter in the leg. The daughter was almost at the door, her hand outstretched to grasp the key. How long before the shot revived the action of the scene? Gaunt sprinted to the door and turned the key, then clutched at the young woman's hand.

He didn't know where he meant to lead her, but in any case the knowledge would clearly not have helped. As soon as he tugged at her cold hand, her arm came away at the shoulder.

He felt the walls and floor and his sense of himself begin to give way to the dark. Absurdity was everything. Everything he touched betrayed it. He lurched away from the standing remains of the young woman, towards the husk of her father. Which of them might come lopsidedly for him?

Neither, by the look of it, and the gun would never go off. None of them would ever move again, and there was no point in his moving when there was nowhere for him to go. They were nothing. In destroying them, he'd destroyed nothing. But if he were capable of destroying no more than a symbol of the threat of nothingness then surely he, if nothing else—

He cried out wordlessly, shocked by the pain: the cinema seat had sprung up at last and smacked his arse.

# X-ing a Paragrab

As it is well known that the "wise men" came "from the East,"
and as Mr. Touch-and-go Bullet-head came from the East, it
follows that Mr. Bullet-head was a wise man; and if collateral proof
of the matter be needed, here we have it—Mr. B. was an editor.
Irascibility was his sole foible; for in fact the obstinacy of which men
accused him was any thing but his *foible,* since he justly considered it
his *forte.* It was his strong-point—his virtue; and it would have required all the logic of a Brownson to convince him that it was "any
thing else."

I have shown that Touch-and-go Bullet-head was a wise man;
and the only occasion on which he did not prove infallible was
when, abandoning that legitimate home for all wise men, the East,
he migrated to the city of Alexander-the-Great-o-nopolis, or some
place of a similar title, out West.

I must do him the justice to say, however, that when he made up
his mind finally to settle in that town, it was under the impression
that no newspaper, and consequently no editor, existed in that particular section of the country. In establishing the *Tea-Pot* he expected to have the field all to himself. I feel confident he never
would have dreamed of taking up his residence in Alexander-
the-Great-o-nopolis had he been aware that, in Alexander-the-
Great-o-nopolis, there lived a gentleman named John Smith
(if I rightly remember), who for many years had there quietly
grown fat in editing and publishing the *Alexander-the-Great-o-nopolis
Gazette.* It was solely, therefore, on account of having been mis-
informed, that Mr. Bullet-head found himself in Alex——suppose
we call it Nopolis, "for short"—but, as he *did* find himself there,
he determined to keep up his character for obst——for firmness,
and remain. So remain he did; and he did more; he unpacked
his press, type, etc., etc., rented an office exactly opposite to that
of the *Gazette,* and, on the third morning after his arrival, issued
the first number of the *Alexan*——that is to say, of the *Nopolis Tea-*

*Pot:*—as nearly as I can recollect, this was the name of the new paper.

The leading article, I must admit, was brilliant—not to say severe. It was especially bitter about things in general—and as for the editor of the *Gazette,* he was torn all to pieces in particular. Some of Bullet-head's remarks were really so fiery that I have always, since that time, been forced to look upon John Smith, who is still alive, in the light of a salamander. I cannot pretend to give *all* the *Tea-Pot's* paragraphs *verbatim,* but one of them runs thus:

"Oh, yes!—Oh, we perceive! Oh, no doubt! The editor over the way is a genius—Oh, my! Oh, goodness, gracious!—what *is* this world coming to? *Oh, tempora! Oh, Moses!*"

A philippic at once so caustic and so classical, alighted like a bombshell among the hitherto peaceful citizens of Nopolis. Groups of excited individuals gathered at the corners of the streets. Every one awaited, with heartfelt anxiety, the reply of the dignified Smith. Next morning it appeared as follows:

"We quote from the *Tea-Pot* of yesterday the subjoined paragraph: '*Oh,* yes! *Oh,* we perceive! *Oh,* no doubt! *Oh,* my! *Oh,* goodness! *Oh,* tempora! *Oh,* Moses!' Why, the fellow is all O! That accounts for his reasoning in a circle, and explains why there is neither beginning nor end to him, nor to any thing he says. We really do not believe the vagabond can write a word that hasn't an O in it. Wonder if this O-ing is a habit of his? By-the-by, he came away from Down-East in a great hurry. Wonder if he *O's* as much there as he does here? '*O!* it is pitiful.'"

The indignation of Mr. Bullet-head at these scandalous insinuations, I shall not attempt to describe. On the eel-skinning principle, however, he did not seem to be so much incensed at the attack upon his integrity as one might have imagined. It was the sneer at his *style* that drove him to desperation. What!—*he,* Touch-and-go Bullet-head!—not able to write a word without an O in it! He would soon let the jackanapes see that he was mistaken. Yes! he would let him see how *much* he was mistaken, the puppy! He, Touch-and-go Bullet-head, of Frogpondium, would let Mr. John Smith perceive that he, Bullet-head, could indite, if it so pleased him, a whole paragraph—ay! a whole article—in which that contemptible vowel should not *once*—not even *once*—make its appearance. But no;— that would be yielding a point to the said John Smith. He, Bullet-head, would make *no* alteration in his style, to suit the caprices of any Mr. Smith in Christendom. Perish so vile a thought! The O

473

forever! He would persist in the O. He would be as O-wy as O-wy could be.

Burning with the chivalry of this determination, the great Touch-and-go, in the next *Tea-Pot*, came out merely with this simple but resolute paragraph, in reference to this unhappy affair:

"The editor of the *Tea-Pot* has the *honor* of advising the editor of the *Gazette* that he (the *Tea-Pot*) will take an opportunity in to-morrow morning's paper, of convincing him (the *Gazette*) that he (the *Tea-Pot*) both can and will be *his own master*, as regards style;—he (the *Tea-Pot*) intending to show him (the *Gazette*) the supreme, and indeed the withering contempt with which the criticism of him (the *Gazette*) inspires the independent bosom of him (the *Tea-Pot*) by composing for the especial gratification (?) of him (the *Gazette*) a leading article, of some extent, in which the beautiful vowel—the emblem of Eternity—yet so offensive to the hyper-exquisite delicacy of him (the *Gazette*) shall most certainly *not be avoided* by his (the *Gazette*'s) most obedient, humble servant, the *Tea-Pot*. 'So much for Buckingham!' "

In fulfillment of the awful threat, thus darkly intimated rather than decidedly enunciated, the great Bullet-head turning a deaf ear to all entreaties for "copy," and simply requesting his foreman to "go to the d——l," when he (the foreman) assured him (the *Tea-Pot!*) that it was high time to "go to press": turning a deaf ear to every thing, I say, the great Bullet-head sat up until day-break, consuming the midnight oil, and absorbed in the composition of the really unparalleled paragraph, which follows:—

"So ho, John! how now? Told you so, you know. Don't crow, another time, before you're out of the woods! Does your mother *know* you're out? Oh, no, no!—so go home at once, now, John, to your odious old woods of Concord! Go home to your woods, old owl,—go! You won't? Oh, poh, poh, John, don't do so! You've *got* to go, you know! So go at once, and don't go slow; for nobody owns you here, you know. Oh! John, John, if you *don't* go you're no *homo*—no! You're only a fowl, an owl; a cow, a sow; a doll, a poll; a poor, old, good-for-nothing-to-nobody, log, dog, hog, or frog, come out of a Concord bog. Cool, now—cool! *Do* be cool, you fool! None of your crowing, old cock! Don't frown so—don't! Don't hollo, nor howl, nor growl, nor bow-wow-wow! Good Lord, John, how you *do* look! Told you so, you know—but stop rolling your goose of an old poll about so, and go and drown your sorrows in a bowl!"

Exhausted, very naturally, by so stupendous an effort, the great

Touch-and-go could attend to nothing farther that night. Firmly, composedly, yet with an air of conscious power, he handed his MS. to the devil in waiting, and then, walking leisurely home, retired, with ineffable dignity to bed.

Meantime the devil, to whom the copy was entrusted, ran up stairs to his "case," in an unutterable hurry, and forthwith made a commencement at "setting" the MS. "up."

In the first place, of course,—as the opening word was "So"—he made a plunge into the capital-S hole and came out in triumph with a capital S. Elated by this success, he immediately threw himself upon the little-*o* box with a blindfold impetuosity—but who shall describe his horror when his fingers came up without the anticipated letter in their clutch? who shall paint his astonishment and rage at perceiving, as he rubbed his knuckles, that he had been only thumping them to no purpose, against the bottom of an *empty* box. Not a single little-*o* was in the little-*o* hole; and, glancing fearfully at the capital-O partition, he found *that,* to his extreme terror, in a precisely similar predicament. Awe-stricken, his first impulse was to rush to the foreman.

"Sir!" said he gasping for breath, "I can't never set up nothing without no o's."

"*What* do you mean by that?" growled the foreman, who was in a very ill humor at being kept up so late.

"Why, sir, there beant an *o* in the office, neither a big un nor a little un!"

"What—what the d——l has become of all that were in the case?"

"*I* don't know, sir," said the boy, "but one of them ere *G'zette* devils is bin prowling 'bout here all night, and I spect *he's* gone and cabbaged em every one."

"Dod rot him! I haven't a doubt of it," replied the foreman, getting purple with rage—"but I tell you what you do, Bob, that's a good boy—you go over the first chance you get and hook every one of their i's and (d——n them!) their izzards."

"Jist so," replied Bob, with a wink and a frown—"*I'll* be into em, *I'll* let em know a thing or two; but in de meantime, that ere paragraph? *Mus* go in to-night, you know—else there'll be the d——l to pay, and—"

"And not a *bit* of pitch hot," interrupted the foreman, with a deep sigh, and an emphasis on the "bit." "Is it a *very* long paragraph, Bob?"

"Shouldn't call it a *wery* long paragrab," said Bob.

"Ah, well, then! do the best you can with it! we *must* get to press," said the foreman, who was over head and ears in work, "just stick in some other letter for *o*, nobody's going to read the fellow's trash anyhow."

"*Wery* well," replied Bob, "here goes it!" and off he hurried to his case; muttering as he went: "Considdeble vell, them ere expressions, perticcler for a man as doesn't swar. So I's to gouge out all their eyes, eh? and d——n all their gizzards! Vell! this here's the chap as is just able *for* to do it." The fact is that although Bob was but twelve years old and four feet high, he was equal to any amount of fight, in a small way.

The exigency here described is by no means of rare occurrence in printing-offices; and I cannot tell how to account for it but the fact is indisputable, that when the exigency *does* occur, it almost always happens that *x* is adopted as a substitute for the letter deficient. The true reason, perhaps, is that *x* is rather the most super-abundant letter in the cases, or at least *was* so in the old times long enough to render the substitution in question an habitual thing with printers. As for Bob, he would have considered it heretical to employ any other character, in a case of this kind, than the *x* to which he had been accustomed.

"I *shell* have to *x* this ere paragrab," said he to himself, as he read it over in astonishment, "but it's jest about the awfulest *o*-wy paragrab I ever *did* see:" so *x* it he did, unflinchingly, and to press it went *x*-ed.

Next morning the population of Nopolis were taken all aback by reading in *The Tea-Pot*, the following extraordinary leader:

"Sx hx, Jxhn! hxw nxw? Txld yxu sx, yxu knxw. Dxn't crxw, anxther time, befxre yxu're xut xf the wxxds! Dxes yxur mxther *knxw* yxu're xut? Xh, nx, nx!—sx gx hxme at xnce, nxw, Jxhn, tx yxur xdixus xld wxxds xf Cxncxrd! Gx hxme tx yxur wxxds, xld xwl,—gx! Yxu wxn't? Xh, pxh, pxh, Jxhn, dxn't dx sx! Yxu've *gxt* tx gx, yxu knxw! Sx gx at xnce, and dxn't gx slxw; fxr nxbxdy xwns yxu here, yxu knxw. Xh! Jxhn, Jxhn, if yxu *dxn't* gx yxu're nx *hxmx*—nx! Yxu're xnly a fxwl, an xwl; a cxw, a sxw; a dxll, a pxll; a pxxr xld gxxd-fxr-nxth-ing-tx-nxbxdy, lxg, dxg, hxg, xr frxg, cxme xut xf a Cxncxrd bxg. Cxxl, nxw—cxxl! Dx be cxxl, yxu fxxl! Nxne xf yxur crxwing, xld cxck! Dxn't frxwn sx—dxn't! Dxn't hxllx, nxr

476

hxwl, nxr grxwl, nxr bxw-wxw-wxw! Gxxd Lxrd, Jxhn, hxw yxu *dx* lxxk! Txld yxu sx, yxu knxw—but stxp rxlling yxur gxxse xf an xld pxll abxut sx, and gx and drxwn yxur sxrrxws in a bxwl!"

The uproar occasioned by this mystical and cabalistical article, is not to be conceived. The first definite idea entertained by the populace was, that some diabolical treason lay concealed in the hieroglyphics; and there was a general rush to Bullet-head's residence, for the purpose of riding him on a rail; but that gentleman was nowhere to be found. He had vanished, no one could tell how; and not even the ghost of him has ever been seen since.

Unable to discover its legitimate object, the popular fury at length subsided; leaving behind it, by way of sediment, quite a medley of opinion about this unhappy affair.

One gentleman thought the whole an X-ellent joke.

Another said that, indeed, Bullet-head had shown much X-uberance of fancy.

A third admitted him X-entric, but no more.

A fourth could not suppose it the Yankee's design to X-press, in a general way, his X-asperation.

"Say, rather, to set an X-ample to posterity," suggested a fifth.

That Bullet-head had been driven to an extremity, was clear to all; and in fact, since *that* editor could not be found, there was some talk about lynching the other one.

The more common conclusion, however, was that the affair was, simply, X-traordinary and in-X-plicable. Even the town mathematician confessed that he could make nothing of so dark a problem. X, everybody knew, was an unknown quantity; but in this case (as he properly observed), there was an unknown quantity of X.

The opinion of Bob, the devil (who kept dark about his having "X-ed the paragrab"), did not meet with so much attention as I think it deserved, although it was very openly and very fearlessly expressed. He said that, for his part, he had no doubt about the matter at all, that it was a clear case, that Mr. Bullet-head "never *could* be persvaded fur to drink like other folks, but vas *con*tinually a-svigging o' that ere blessed XXX ale, and, as a naiteral consekvence, it just puffed him up savage, and made him X (cross) in the X-treme."

# ACKNOWLEDGMENTS

Grateful acknowledgment is made to the following for permission to reprint their copyrighted materials:

"**The Advent on Channel Twelve**" by C. M. Kornbluth, copyright © 1958 by C. M. Kornbluth. Reprinted by permission of the agent for the author's Estate, Richard Curtis Associates, Inc.

"**After You, Montagu**" by Howard Wandrei, copyright © 1971 by August Derleth. Reprinted by permission of Harold Hughesdon.

"**All Moon-Beasts Amorphous and Mephitic**" by Peter Cannon, copyright © 1994 by Peter Cannon. Reprinted by permission of the author.

"**Believing in the Twentieth Century**" by Darrell Schweitzer, copyright © 1996 by Terra Incognita. Reprinted by arrangement with the author.

"**Broker's Loan**" by Donald Wandrei, copyright © 1930 by the Board in Control of Student Publications, University of Minnesota. Reprinted by arrangement with Harold Hughesdown.

"**The Case of Jack the Clipper, or a Fimbulwinter's Tale**" by David Langford, copyright © 1997 by David Langford. Reprinted by permission of the author.

"**Chalk Talk**" by Edward Wellen, copyright © 1973 by Mercury Press, Inc. Reprinted by permission of the author.

"**A Change of Lifestyle**" by Joe and Karen Lansdale, copyright © 1984 by Joe R. Lansdale. Reprinted by permission of the author.

"**Chasing the Ugly Dog**" by Tom Piccirilli, copyright © 1993 by Tom Piccirilli. Reprinted by permission of the author.